the demon's spell

COLLEGE OF WITCHCRAFT BOOK FOUR

ALICIA RADES

Lucas

ONE

Summoning a demon was a recipe for disaster, but disaster had already struck—and it was time to raise some hell.

My pulse quickened as I snuck into Miriam College of Witchcraft. A dark hall loomed ahead, and a shiver traveled down my spine. I listened closely, but I didn't hear anything.

Over a week had passed since the Burning. The priestesses had burned Amy alive on school grounds, along with two of our other classmates and one of our professors. Riots had broken out, and at least a dozen people had died. The school was supposed to be closed for winter break, but the magic surrounding it had been weak since the night of the fire. It wasn't hard to get through the wards and sneak inside.

I created a light orb and shone it down the hall. "Clear," I whispered, gesturing my friends forward.

The snow crunched under Nadine's feet as she tiptoed through the darkness. Talia and Grant crept closely behind her. Our three cats—Isa, Oliver, and Gus—slunk along at our feet, moving so quietly that I couldn't hear them.

"I'm not sure about this, Lucas," Grant hissed. "This isn't a good idea."

"We don't have any choice," I replied.

Nadine stepped into the deserted hallway. "We need answers, Grant. The school's library is the only place we're getting them."

"There has to be another way," he insisted.

"There's no time," I said. "The priestesses summoned a demon a week ago. Doesn't it bother you that nothing has happened since then?"

I shivered just thinking about it. I'd only witnessed the demon for a mere second, but the sight of his hollow eye sockets still shook me to my core.

"Isn't that a good thing?" Grant asked. "I mean, we don't *want* anything bad to happen."

I shook my head. "It means the priestesses have bigger plans. They didn't summon that demon on impulse; otherwise, chaos would've broken out by now. We know they're using this demon to find the Oaken Wands, and once they have all five, they're going to control the coven's magic. But there's gotta be more to it. Demons don't do favors. The priestesses have already proven that they'll kill innocent people for their cause. We need to find out what else they're willing to sacrifice. Whatever deal they made with this demon can't be good."

"But summoning a *demon* for answers?" Grant sighed. "What if we're not strong enough to talk to this guy? What are we going to do—persuade him to our side? Demons can't be reasoned with."

Nadine bit her lower lip. "It's risky, but Lucas is right. Another demon will know what kind of deal the priestesses made. They could have answers about the priestesses' plans. We need to figure out what we're up against. Talia, what do you think?"

Talia took a deep breath, and her gaze roamed over Grant. "If we have any chance against the priestesses, we need to be a step ahead of them. I'm willing to go through with this ritual… if you are."

Grant reached for Talia. Her hand had been broken by a rogue spell the night of the Burning, but Helena's herbs had sped up the healing. "This could be really dangerous," he said. "People keep getting hurt."

"That's why we *have* to do this," Talia responded. "We need to know what the priestesses are up to so we can stop these witch hunts. My broken hand is nothing compared to what they did to Amy."

The hallway went dead silent when Talia mentioned Amy. My stomach churned. The sight of our friend's burning body was seared into my mind. Images from that night flashed behind my lids, and I thought I was going to hurl. We'd held a private memorial, but it wasn't anywhere close to the closure we needed.

I couldn't save her… but maybe I could stop future burnings. It was the only way to make up for my failure that night.

"Okay," Grant said, looking defeated. "Let's keep moving. For Amy."

We crept down the hall. Floorboards creaked beneath our feet, and the cats sniffed the air, as if they might be able to detect incoming threats. I looked around corners, but I never saw another soul. We made it to the library undetected.

The library was filled with two levels of bookcases. Tall, arching windows filtered in light from the quarter moon, and wind whistled from outside.

"What are we looking for, exactly?" Grant asked.

"A ritual to summon demons," Nadine said casually, like we did this every day.

"Our professors don't teach demon summoning," Grant pointed out. "It's forbidden, because of how dangerous demon deals can be. Are you sure they'd keep those kinds of books here?"

"The college library is open to the public," I reminded him. "There has to be something here. The coven summoned demons for centuries. There's no way it's been erased from our history."

"If there's anything, it's a restricted-access book." Talia stepped up to the nearest bookcase and ran her fingers across the spines. "They're marked with black dots. I remember when I found a book on hauntings for one of my classes, and the librarian wouldn't let me check it out. She said it was for professors and alumni only."

"Then we're looking for any restricted demonology book," I said. "Let's hope this doesn't take us all night."

I stepped down one of the aisles to begin my search, but before my hands landed on a book, a *crash* sounded from the upper level of the library. I froze.

"What was that?" Grant hissed.

I listened closely, and though it was faint, I caught the sound of footsteps upstairs.

"Someone's here," Nadine whispered.

"Do you think someone followed us?" Talia asked, sounding worried.

I glanced toward the doors. There was only one way in and out of the library. "No. They were here before us."

Nadine sighed, and she stepped out into the center of the room. "Okay!" she called up the stairs. "You can come out now."

"Nad," I hissed. For all we knew, it was one of the priestesses. But Nadine was fearless.

When no response came, Nadine raised her voice further. "I am a high priestess of the Miriamic Coven. I demand that you show yourself at once, or suffer the consequences."

Someone huffed, and footsteps sounded as they emerged from the shadows. A tall, thin female stood at the top of the balcony, and the shadow of a cat prowled beside her. She held a thick book in her arms. I couldn't tell who it was in the darkness, until she spoke.

"There's no need to be so dramatic, Nadine," Chloe said. "It's just me."

Grant conjured a battle orb in his hand within a second, and my fingers sparked with magic. I moved to Nadine's side in an instant.

"What are you doing here, Chloe?" I demanded.

She strolled along the balcony casually, like she didn't find Grant's magic to be a threat in the slightest. "The same as you—looking for answers."

"Answers about what?" Nadine asked curiously.

"The Waning," Chloe stated as she descended the stairs. "Our magic is disappearing more frequently, and for longer periods of time. Things have been worse since the Burning. It's too weird that all our magic went out at the same time that night. I thought if there was a way to end it, perhaps everything else could be solved, too. But now you have me curious about demons. What exactly do you know?"

The four of us hesitated, and Nadine shot me a nervous glance.

"Like we'd tell you," Grant sneered. "You'll run off and tell your priestess grandmother."

Chloe stepped into the moonlight, and I caught the scowl on her face. "Did I not prove myself to you during the Burning? I'm on your side."

"We were all desperate that night," Grant pointed out. "You've been nothing but mean to us otherwise. Hell, you tried to *hang* Nadine!"

"When I was *cursed*," Chloe reminded him.

"But it was still your choice," he shot back. "You called me Hispanic scum."

"And you have every right to be mad at me about that," Chloe said. "Look, I know I can't make up for the past. I can't say sorry and hope that it will magically fix everything. Come on, Lucas. I was at your Evoking Ceremony."

"Because you wanted to make Ryan jealous," I reminded her.

"Ryan and I are *long* over," she assured me. "I know what kind of bitch I was, but I've changed. Please let me show you that. All I ever wanted was to protect the coven, and I know that's what you want, too. I'm here doing research just like you, so let me help."

I'd never heard Chloe beg the way she was pleading with us now. I was skeptical, but I heard the truth in Chloe's words.

"Well, you can't help us," Grant insisted. "Tell her, Lucas."

I hesitated. She *had* helped us escape arrest the night of the Burning. "It might be useful to have a Mentalist on our side."

"Lucas!" Grant balked.

"I'm serious," I said. "Chloe's passionate, driven, and manipulative—"

"Which is why we can't tell her anything!" Grant cried. "She already knows too much."

"Or it's why we need her," I countered. "But we can't work with her unless it's unanimous. Nad?"

Nadine hadn't taken her eyes off Chloe. She studied her, as if searching for the lie behind her words. Isa stepped forward and sniffed Chloe's cat. The cat sniffed her back, and the two began purring and licking each other.

Chloe gazed down at them. "Marley agrees. He likes you guys."

Talia frowned. "We're not taking opinions from your cat."

Nadine turned to me. "I think Lucas is right. We need a Mentalist. The Oaken Wands will work best if we have all five Casts working together."

"But *Chloe*?" Grant whined.

"Chloe's as headstrong as I am," Nadine said. "If we're going to butt heads, we might as well do it on the same side. Once this is all over, the coven will have to make amends with each other. If we can't do that with Chloe, the coven has no hope. We have to be the start of that. I vote to work with her. What's your vote, Tal?"

Talia eyed Chloe curiously. "She does seem… different. And she did help us during the Burning. She wouldn't have done that if she wasn't on our side. I don't like the idea, but Nadine's right. We need to start forming alliances, or we don't stand a chance."

Grant scowled. I didn't blame him. Chloe had been awful to all of us, but a grudge wasn't going to win us this war.

His eyes darted toward the cats, who were purring. That must've persuaded him, because he said, "It's obvious you care deeply about the coven... and we could use your help."

Chloe opened her mouth to say something, but Grant cut her off.

"But if it even *looks* like you're about to betray us, so help me, you'll be standing at the gallows next," he threatened.

Chloe crossed her heart. "I wouldn't dream of it."

The strange thing was, I believed her. Chloe honestly wanted to work with us.

"So what's this about demons?" Chloe asked.

"Oh, boy," Nadine sighed. "There's a lot to catch you up on."

Chloe shrugged. "Then let's get started."

We sat around one of the study tables, and I told her how I'd witnessed the Imperium Council summon a demon at their headquarters. They were looking for answers about where to find the Oaken Wands, and the demon wanted to make a deal. I hadn't learned what deal they'd made, but we came here tonight to figure it out.

Chloe blew a breath when I finished, like she couldn't quite believe it. "I never thought my grandma would resort to demon deals, but this... ooh, this is bad."

"In what way, exactly?" Talia asked curiously.

"Demons can make all sorts of contracts," Chloe pointed out. "One of the things they often trade for is souls, but you can't just give them the right to anyone's soul. It has to be yours... or your kin."

Nadine's jaw dropped. "So you could be at risk? You don't think your grandma would make that kind of trade, do you?"

Chloe looked worried. "After the Burning, I don't think I know my grandmother at all. I honestly don't know what lengths she'll go to anymore. We need to figure that out."

Chloe dropped the book she'd been holding onto the table. "Luckily, I ran across this just before you showed up."

My eyes scanned the thick tome. *Advanced Demonology.*

"You were looking into demons before we arrived?" I asked.

Chloe nodded. "I'm exploring all angles. The Waning could definitely be caused by demon magic."

"It is demon magic, actually," Nadine said. "The Imperium made me do a spell with them to figure it out. They confirmed it's demon magic, but there's no way to know if it's a deal, an artifact, or if a demon is working independently."

Chloe's lips curled back. "We need to find out. Problem is, this damn book won't open!"

She tugged on the front cover, but it didn't move, as if it'd been glued shut.

"Let me see…" Nadine slid the book across the table and splayed her palm over it. She pressed her lips together, like she was concentrating hard. "This ward is a joke. I can break it no problem."

Nadine closed her eyes, and black magic billowed out of the pages, swirling up her arm. As a Curse Breaker, Nadine had the unique ability to move magic from one place to another. It was what allowed her to break curses, but it had other perks, too, like breaking wards. Most wards were too strong for a single Curse Breaker to break, but Nadine was getting better. I was confident she could break this simple ward with ease.

She transformed the ward magic into a battle orb. It crackled in her palm for a second, then shot out of her hand and whizzed across the library. It slammed into a nearby shelf and knocked a bunch of books to the floor. I winced as the sound filled the room.

"Whoops," Nadine said. "I really need to work on that."

"You don't think anyone heard that, do you?" Grant asked.

"Relax," Chloe said. "No one's here."

Nadine opened the book to the table of contents, and Talia leaned forward, her eyes bright with interest. "Let's see…" Nadine mused. "Demon summonings…"

"This looks promising," Talia said, pointing.

Isa peeked over the edge of the table and hissed, as if warning us not to go through with this. Nadine stroked her fur. "It's okay, girl. We'll be careful."

Isa let out a low growl, but Nadine ignored her and turned to the spell Talia had pointed out. She studied the page for a moment before saying, "This looks simple. All we need to do is draw a sigil and speak an incantation—oh, wait. This spell uses blood magic."

"So?" Chloe asked.

Talia gaped at her. "Blood magic is *bad*."

"Why?" Chloe challenged. "If I cut my hand open, I'm not hurting anyone but myself. I don't see the problem."

"Because it's tricky and can backfire on you," Nadine pointed out.

Chloe shrugged. "Same with summoning a demon. You know the real reason the coven doesn't sanction blood magic, right?"

I eyed her curiously. "What are you getting at?"

"Blood magic is powerful," Chloe pointed out. "We're like magical reservoirs—batteries that can be recharged. That's why your magic returns every time you're affected by the Waning. Our magic comes from Alora, but once we're recharged, we hold our magic in our blood. The coven doesn't want us using blood magic because they don't want us to know how powerful we really are. They're afraid of it, plain and simple."

Talia narrowed her eyes. "That has to be a conspiracy theory. The coven banned blood magic to protect us."

Chloe shrugged. "Believe what you want, but I'm convinced. You already know the priestesses aren't above lying. Is it so hard to believe they would lie about this? *Of course* blood magic is going to backfire the first few times you use it—just like *any* magic. They tell you it's dangerous so you won't ever use it and realize how strong you really are."

Chloe made a good point, one I had never considered before. I used to trust the priestesses. I didn't anymore.

"I think it's worth a shot," I said.

Grant crossed his arms and leaned back in his chair. "Perhaps we should let Chloe do the honors."

He was testing her, trying to see if she was bluffing. Chloe was more than up for the challenge. "I don't mind," she said.

Nadine nodded. "Then let's begin."

She conjured a marker and began drawing the sigil on the tabletop, glancing at the book every now and then to make sure she got it right. It was a circle, with a five-pointed star inside and all sorts of runes surrounding it.

The moment Nadine finished drawing the sigil, an icy chill filled the room. I shivered and wrapped my arms around myself. "Does anyone else feel that?"

Talia shot a glance around the room. "Definitely weird."

"Well, we *are* summoning a demon," Grant said. "It *should* be weird, shouldn't it?"

"Grant's right," Nadine said. "Let's keep going."

Chloe conjured a pocketknife. As she lifted her hand above the sigil, her cat hissed and ducked under her chair. Chloe pressed the blade to her palm—

Wind swept through the library so fast that the demonology book slammed shut. Chloe squealed and leapt backward. Her blade thudded to the ground. The cats all hissed and huddled together under the table. Grant grabbed Talia. She buried her face into his chest, while Nadine and I leapt to our feet.

I pulled her closer to me, but my gaze darted around the room. "It can't be a demon," I said breathlessly. "We didn't finish the summoning."

"*Something* is here," Nadine emphasized in a wavered breath.

"What, like a ghost?" Talia squeaked.

An ominous scratching filled the room. My pulse quickened when I looked down at the table. I grabbed Nadine tighter and pulled her close to me. Lines appeared on the tabletop, as if someone was carving them into the wood right in front of me, but no one was touching the table. Letters formed in front of my eyes, breaking the sigil and spelling out words.

My mouth went dry as I read the words aloud. *"History will repeat itself. He has come to kill. Return to the past to vanquish the demon for good."*

I barely finished reading the words before a white, ghostly figure appeared. All I saw was the outline of a woman before a high-pitched shriek filled the library. My friends and I slapped our hands over our ears. The ghost swooped across the table, air billowing out from the hem of her dress. The gust was so strong that it nearly knocked me over.

The ghost slammed straight into Talia, and she was blasted backward. Talia screamed as her chair flew across the library. Her chair toppled over near the entrance, and she rolled across the ground. The ghost vanished, but Talia lay on the floor, unmoving. I raced toward her. Grant and I reached her at the same time, and we gently rolled her over.

"Tal!" Grant cried. "Talia!"

She groaned, but she looked up at the ceiling with an empty gaze, like she was slipping in and out of consciousness.

Nadine stood over us, her hands slapped over her mouth. "Dear Goddess."

Life returned to Talia's gaze, but she gritted her teeth, like she was in pain.

"What hurts?" I asked.

"Ugh, everything," she complained. "I'll be fine, though. Just one hell of a bruise."

Grant helped her sit up.

Talia pressed her hand to her forehead. "What the hell was that?"

"A warning," Chloe stated.

My blood chilled. I knew Chloe was right. "Whoever that ghost was, she didn't want us summoning a demon. She came to deliver an answer herself."

"But what does it mean?" Nadine asked. *"Return to the past?* I thought witches didn't have time travel magic."

"We don't," Chloe said. "You'd have to be a demigod, at least, to perform that kind of magic."

"We don't need that kind of magic anyway," I said, rising to my feet. *"History will repeat itself.* It's obvious, isn't it? This demon has been here before. We just have to figure out when and why, and we'll find the answer to getting rid of him."

The library fell silent. None of us wanted to acknowledge the last part of the warning. My heart hammered as the words repeated in my mind. *He has come to kill.*

This demon had been set loose on the coven by the priestesses. There was only a matter of time before he claimed his first victim.

nadine

TWO

Returning to classes felt like walking to the gallows. The pyre had been removed from school grounds after the Burning, but the grief and horror from that night remained. Dark clouds swirled above the school, like our Goddess ached for our losses.

Lucas and I sat in the parking lot our first day back. I didn't move to get out of the car. I'd asked him to drive me to school, because I wasn't sure I'd have the courage to return on my own. Lucas and I had been through a lot, but he was my rock—my person. If I ever needed anything, I knew that he'd be there for me. My hands knotted in my lap as I stared up at the towering spires of Miriam Mansion.

Lucas noticed my hesitation. "Take as long as you need."

I tore my gaze away from the school. "I'm nervous to go back."

"I understand completely. After what happened here, I think we all are."

People were angry about the Burning, and they needed someone to blame. The priestesses had made sure that blame would fall on us. Lucas and I had spoken out against the priestesses that night, and the coven blamed us for inciting the riots. I wasn't sure how safe it was to go back to school, but we had to. It was the only place we were getting answers to stop the priestesses and bring an end to the Waning.

We sat in silence for a few moments before Lucas asked, "Do you want to talk about it?"

I shook my head. It wasn't his job to fix me. Mother Miriam wanted me to be strong. "I can handle it."

He placed his hand on mine in a kind gesture. "We'll do this together."

My shoulders dropped, and some of my anxiety washed away in his presence. Lucas seemed to move slowly as we got out of the car, like he worried what lay in store for us, too. I squeezed his hand as we crossed the parking lot. Just having him near me was enough to calm my racing heart.

A group of students from the campus band had gathered around the main entrance and played music on various stringed instruments. I thought it was meant to lift our spirits, but the music sounded more melancholy than anything. Professor Warbright used his wand to conduct the tune, but he looked a bit uncomfortable. He was a short, plump man who wore round spectacles and carried a pocket watch in his suit vest. He taught music classes, along with Mortana magic, and was often cheerful. Usually, this man could lift anyone's spirits. Today was a different story, though. Even his kind smile couldn't make us feel better.

"Lucas, Nadine," Professor Warbright greeted. "Nice to have you back."

"Thank you, Professor," I said, though my tone felt stilted.

Isa and Oliver followed along at our feet as we entered the Main Foyer. The cats shot glances around the room, like they were on edge. The lively chatter that usually filled the room had been replaced by hissing whispers and harsh glares. People moved through the foyer in small groups composed entirely of their own Casts. No one wanted to walk these halls alone. The Alchemists who usually brewed potions in the fireplace on the first day back were nowhere to be seen.

A group of Mentalists glanced our way, and one girl twisted her nose at us when she saw we were holding hands. The message was clear. Lucas and I were from different Casts. We didn't *belong* together.

"I can't believe they had the nerve to show their faces," I heard someone say. I glanced over to see it was Stacey—an Alchemist in some of my classes. She stood next to Gwen and Valerie, talking loudly.

I expected to see Lena and Camille with them, but they weren't around. I instantly knew why. Lena was Mortana, and Camille was a Mentalist. Friendship meant nothing to these girls—not after the Cast lines had been drawn so harshly following the Burning. I didn't like any of them, but it was sad to see. The priestesses thought they were saving the coven with their harsh punishments and scare tactics. They were only tearing it apart.

"They should be in jail," Gwen sneered, loud enough for us to hear. "They're the ones who started the riots."

"Smearing Priestess Stella's name should've earned them the noose," Valerie added.

I halted in my tracks. My blood boiled at the accusations. Lucas and I had told the truth the night of the Burning—how Priestess Stella had been behind the production of nightshade, and how she'd framed Professor Daniels for murder. But the coven didn't believe the truth. We'd been forced to release a statement claiming it was all a lie and that Stella had died an admirable death. It was part of the deal to exonerate my friends, along with handing over the Alchemy Wand and Crock of Death to the Imperium Council.

Valerie conjured a copy of the *Miriamic Messenger* and deliberately opened it. My eyes caught the headline on the front page: *Curse Breaker Priestess Confirms Corruption Among Council.*

My teeth gritted. I'd scanned the article this morning, but I didn't have the stomach to finish the whole thing. It'd been about the statement the priestesses forced us to make. The paper called me corrupt and claimed the coven couldn't trust me. I had half a mind to tell these bitches the truth, but Lucas tugged on my hand. He must've read the intent in my eyes.

"Nad," he said gently. "We can't let it get to us. There's no going back on our deal with the priestesses, but we can move forward and find a way to fight back."

I hesitated. Gwen noticed me glaring and threw her head back in laughter. There was nothing I could do, and it pissed me the fuck off. Isa hissed at her, but she only cackled louder.

"How can we fight back when no one trusts us?" I asked lowly. "The priestesses have made sure of that."

"I'm working on it," Lucas assured me. He tugged my arm again, and I had no choice but to follow him.

"Ugh, her cat probably has fleas," Gwen said. "I can't believe the Head-mistress let them back into the school."

Gwen was dangerously close to getting a battle orb to the face. I glanced back just in time to see a shimmering ball of magic form beneath her feet. It swelled upward, and she screamed as she lost her balance and went crashing to the floor. Stacey and Valerie squealed and rushed to help Gwen stand, but she looked frazzled. She shot glances around the room, as if looking for the culprit. The magic had been nearly invisible, and I didn't know where it'd come from.

Lucas draped an arm around my shoulder and pulled me close. He chuckled under his breath as we started up the grand staircase.

"Was that you?" I asked.

He smirked. "It might've been."

"How'd you do that?"

"Shield magic," he stated simply.

"I didn't know you could do that. You're getting better. It's hard to project shields from a distance," I remarked. "Thanks for standing up for me."

Lucas smiled, then placed a kiss on the top of my head. "Always."

We reached the top of the stairs, and my heart stalled when we turned down the hall. Lucas dropped his arm.

Every door was propped wide open, and men in black uniforms moved in and out of the rooms, barking at the students. They all had the same buzzcut, along with wands attached to their hips. Nearby, Gregory and Brayden huddled together, looking like they were trying to stay out of their way.

"Prank potions are banned on school property." One of the men snatched a potion out of Onyx's hands.

"That's for my Alchemy class," Onyx snapped. "You wouldn't know a prank potion from poison."

"Whatever it is, I'm keeping it," he sneered. "Move along."

It wasn't until the guy turned that I realized I recognized him. Frederick James wore a cunning smirk. I glanced around the hall, and more of the faces clicked. I spotted Ryan leaving one of the rooms with a collection of crystals in his hands, and Nolan—one of the Tarantulas—held a pile of wands. All the Tarantulas were here, along with a jerk named Leroy who'd bullied Lucas more than once. Avery Mitchel strolled down the hall with her head held high, her hair twisted into a tight bun. There were several others, but I didn't know their names.

Hell, these weren't *soldiers*. They were *students*.

I couldn't sit idly by, not like I had with Gwen downstairs. I let go of Lucas and marched straight up to James.

"Hey, asshole," I growled. "Since when are prank potions banned? What gives you the right?"

James laughed and looked down at me with a smug expression on his face. "Well, well, well, look who it is. The *Curse Maker*."

Lucas stepped in front of me. I didn't need him to come to my rescue, but I was kind of glad he did. James wasn't intimidated by me—priestess or not. But Lucas was the same height and build as he was, and it made him shrink back half a step.

"Touch Nadine, and you'll regret it," Lucas threatened.

James smirked. "What, you think the priestesses will come after me? Nah, the threats they made to me last semester are no good anymore. In fact, they've *hired* me to keep your ass in line. Upset me, and *you'll* regret it."

"Yeah, I'm sure," Lucas said sarcastically. "I saw what you did during the riots. You murdered Sadie. You should be in jail. Why would the priestesses hire you?"

James's smile grew wider. "Haven't you heard? Miriam's Executors get all sorts of perks, including all charges wiped. Besides, I didn't touch Sadie. Her heart gave out."

"Because you used your fucked-up Mentalist powers on her!" Lucas raged.

I grabbed his hand to calm him down. We didn't need a fight breaking out here in the middle of the hall. What we needed was answers.

"What are you talking about?" I demanded. "What exactly is Miriam's Executioners?"

"We're not *executioners*," James sneered. He drew himself up, like he was proud. "We're *Executors*, as in, executors of Miriam's will. We carry out the law. We've been hired to keep the peace among the student body."

Peace, my ass. They'd been hired to incite fear and create chaos.

"In return, we get free tuition and guaranteed jobs on the police force once we graduate," James stated proudly. "Oh, and if anyone—and I mean *anyone*—does something to defy the priestesses' orders, I have every right to drag them to the gallows myself. It'll be fun putting that noose around your neck, *Curse Maker*."

"Fuck you, James," I snapped.

"Ooh," he practically sang. "You wanna go right now? I was expecting to have at least a few weeks to prepare for your hanging."

"What exactly do you have against Nadine?" Lucas demanded.

"She's not my only problem, buddy," James said. "I still haven't forgotten that punch you threw last summer."

"Then you know I'm not scared to fight back," Lucas replied coolly.

"You can try," James taunted. "But I see only one priestess on your side. I've got four. Let's see who wins *that* fight."

"I suppose we'll see eventually," Lucas stated in a clear challenge.

James stared him down a moment longer, before he scoffed. "I can't wait to see it go down."

He walked off, looking proud of himself.

"I wish I knew a spell that would suffocate him," I said. James was already taunting another student for bringing a frog onto campus.

"It's best we don't cast curses," Lucas whispered lowly. "Look who else is here."

I glanced down the hall. Fury rose in my bones when I saw Officer Baker step out of one of the dorm rooms. He was the asshole who'd arrested Professor Daniels before she'd been hanged. I noticed a shiny new sheriff's badge attached to his uniform. Apparently, he'd been promoted. I spotted a dart gun on his hip, and it chilled me to think what kind of magical serum might be inside.

"This is your one and only warning," Sheriff Baker told a girl.

She followed him out of the room, and I recognized Lydia from my Miriamic Law class. She wore a horrified look behind her purple glasses. Sheriff Baker lifted a piece of paper and tore it in half. Lydia threw her hand over her mouth as the sound ripped through the hall.

"You can't do this!" she cried.

"All depictions of gods and goddesses apart from Mother Miriam are banned," Sheriff Baker snapped.

A guy stood beside Lydia—another student from my Miriam Law class named Quentin Martin. He was much taller than Lydia, with straight black hair that fell into his eyes. His hands curled into fists. "That's for her Supernatural Religions class!"

Sheriff Baker smirked. "Not anymore. Check your schedule. That class no longer exists."

What the hell were the priestesses up to? We had to do *something*. I grabbed Lucas and started dragging him into my dorm room. We couldn't talk out in the open like this.

A girl stepped in front of me before I got to the door. She was shorter than me, but she looked ruthless as she placed her hands on her hips and glared at me. She had no visible tattoos, and she looked younger than me. I wondered if she even had her powers yet. She had to be a freshman.

"Empty your pockets," the girl demanded in a firm tone.

"Excuse me?" I shot back.

"All students are to be searched before entering their dorms," she stated. "Empty. Your. Pockets."

"I don't know who you think you are—"

"I'm Mira Benson," she cut me off, like that name was supposed to mean something to me. "And I'm an Executor. You will obey me or—"

"*I'm* a high priestess," I told her. "What you're doing is unjust. Do yourself a favor and quit while you still can."

She tilted her chin up. "You may be a high priestess, but you're still a student. And students have to answer to the Executors."

Leroy overheard her and started laughing. "Stop acting so tough, Mira. You're not as important as you think you are."

"Shut up," she snapped. "Just because you have your powers doesn't mean you're stronger than me."

"I don't know what you're trying to prove, little sis, but *strong* is the last word I'd use to describe you," Leroy said. "Come back when your powers awaken. Then we'll see who's stronger."

"You're an ass!" she shouted.

I wasn't interested in this sibling drama. I went to push past her, but Mira planted herself in front of my door. "You're not getting through until you—"

A loud *crash* sounded from a dorm room nearby, followed by the sound of shouting. "You can't take my wand!"

"I need a little help in here!" an Executor shouted over the sound of a scuffle.

"Don't move," Mira demanded before running off to help.

We didn't listen. We entered my dorm, and we found Grant and Talia sitting on her bed. Tears streamed from Talia's eyes, and Grant held her close to his chest. I knew instantly that the officers had already been here.

"What'd they do?" I asked softly.

Talia sniffled and sat up straighter. "They took my sheet music. They thought it was incantations for battle magic."

Lucas's nostrils flared. "They did the same thing to me last semester with my poems."

Talia wiped her eyes. "It's fine. I can rewrite the songs—"

"It's *not* fine," I interrupted. "They're taking your songs today, but what will they take tomorrow? Yeah, wands and crystals can be replaced, but they've already taken more than that. They can't replace our friends… they can't replace Amy."

"I know, but what are we going to do?" Talia asked. "The last time we fought back, riots broke out and people died."

"Then we try something else. This is just the beginning of whatever the priestesses have planned," I said.

"We have to come up with a plan of our own," Lucas agreed. "I already have some ideas."

I shot a glance toward the open door. If we shut it, we'd attract Sheriff Baker's attention, and I did *not* want to deal with him. I lowered my voice. "We need somewhere to talk—somewhere we can meet up all semester. It'll raise suspicion if other Casts are coming and going from our room all the time. We're already taking a risk by remaining roommates."

"The abandoned mansion?" Grant suggested.

"That's a safe spot, but do we want to go there every time we have to talk?" I asked. "I'd like something closer, if possible."

"I might know a place on campus," Lucas said thoughtfully. "There's an abandoned classroom near the pool. The newspaper club used to use it to print *The Epitaph*, but no one's been there in a while. No one ever goes down there."

"That's perfect," I said. "Let's split up, and we'll meet there in fifteen minutes. I'll tell Chloe. Lucas, see if you can find Mandy. Talia and Grant, find Miles. We need everyone."

"Sounds good," Talia agreed.

I left the room first, with Isa at my heels. I kept my head down as I passed the student officers, but they were preoccupied searching rooms, so no one bothered me. Isa and I headed downstairs, and I spotted Chloe leaving the cafeteria. Her eyes met mine. We fell into step beside each other, though we kept our distance so it didn't look like we were talking. Our cats gave each other friendly nods.

"You saw what's going on upstairs?" Chloe asked quietly.

"Yes. Meet us in the old *Epitaph* room in fifteen minutes," I said.

Chloe went in the opposite direction. I circled back, until I found a dark hall beyond the locker room entrances. This had to be the place Lucas was talking about. There weren't any doors, except the one at the end of the hall. The whole corridor smelled dusty, like no one had been down here in over a year.

I entered a small room with no windows. It had certainly been an old storage closet at one time, but had been converted into a meeting room for the newspaper club. Old shelves still stood along one wall, with piles of articles stacked haphazardly upon them. A counter stretched across the other side of the room, with an ancient computer and big printer on it. A single alchemy station with a burner and cauldron was set up on the opposite end of the counter. It was perfect.

Chloe was already there, seated at the large meeting table in the center of the room. Her cat prowled along the tabletop. The door opened. Talia and Grant slipped inside, followed closely by Miles. He glanced around the room.

"Where's your sister, Talia?" Miles asked. "I thought she'd be here."

Talia shook her head. "Tate's in no condition to join us. She's in rehab."

"Is she doing better?" Miles asked.

Talia hesitated. "A little, but it's going to take some time until she's back on her feet."

"Tell her I wish her well," Miles said.

Talia nodded. "I will."

Lucas and Mandy arrived shortly after. Everyone remained quiet as they took a seat at the meeting table. Miles sat on the counter. Lucas and I were the only ones left standing.

"Thank you all for coming," I said. "We called this meeting because we're asking you guys to join us in… a revolution, I suppose. What happened the night of the Burning *cannot* happen again. I'm not willing to lose more innocent lives. It's clear that the priestesses are willing to risk anything to get our magic back and to control it themselves."

"That's not a risk that we believe is necessary," Lucas added. "We're here to develop a plan to end the Waning, the burnings, the hangings… all of it. We need to make sure that at the end of all this, everyone has access to their powers, not just the people the priestesses choose. The priestesses have started a war on their own people, and we need to find a way to bring all the Casts back together so we can solve this peacefully."

"First, we need to know that we can trust everyone in this room," I said. "If you're not willing to go up against the priestesses, it's best that you leave now, before you learn anything that could get you killed."

Chloe gave me a confident nod.

"You know I'm in after what they did to Amy," Mandy stated.

"Same," Miles agreed.

"Before we tell you what we know, I suggest we take a witch's vow," Lucas said.

I furrowed my brow. I'd never heard of it. "How does that work?"

"It's a potion that seals promises," Grant explained. "We each present a strand of hair and drink the potion. If you break the promise… you die."

"That actually seems very useful to the priestesses," I pointed out. "Why don't they use it, especially at priestess induction ceremonies? They could've used a witch's vow to make sure I wouldn't betray them."

"The coven doesn't like to use them," Chloe said. "They're a lot like demon contracts and fae deals. Specific wording can be used to trick and manipulate people. But in this case, I think Lucas is right. This is serious, and we need to know we can trust each other."

"I'm in," Miles agreed. "We just have to make sure we word it right."

Grant conjured a pile of Alchemy supplies so large that items began spilling onto the floor. "I can get started on the brew. It should only take a few minutes."

He went to the alchemy station and lit the burner.

Lucas took out a sheet of paper. "How do we word this promise?"

"It should be as simple as possible," I suggested. "We agree to keep this room and everything we talk about in it a secret."

"That's too rigid," Mandy said. "It's why a witch's vow can be just as dangerous as a demon deal. Are you sure about this? We don't accidentally want to kill anyone by getting the wording wrong."

"I'm sure I don't want the priestesses getting their hands on information," I said.

Mandy pressed her lips together. "All right. How about this? *By my life or death, I vow to protect the coven and do what I believe will be for the good of all.*"

"That's exactly what we're going for," Lucas said, scribbling it down.

"I'm almost done," Grant announced, tossing in a few more herbs that made the cauldron bubble. "All that's left is a strand of hair from each of us to seal the deal."

We all gathered around the alchemy station, and one by one, we plucked a hair off our heads and tossed it into the brew. It bubbled each time.

Grant conjured several potion vials and ladled the potion into each one, then handed one to each of us. "Together, we'll recite the promise, then drink the potion at the same time. We will be bound by the vow to protect the coven together."

"Here it is," Lucas said, setting his piece of paper on the counter so we could all see. "Ready?"

We spoke the vow in unison. *"By my life or death, I vow to protect the coven and do what I believe will be for the good of all."*

We drank our potion, and it went down easily. When we finished, we gathered around the meeting table again.

"Thank you everyone for agreeing to be a part of this," I said. "As we've all taken the vow, you deserve to know what we're up against. The priestesses have tasked me with finding the Oaken Wands. They exist. A single Wand can attract the magic of its Cast, but we need all five Wands to redistribute it. The Wands are stronger together, and they're the only way to end the Waning. The priestesses plan to use them to control the coven's magic. They've summoned a demon to find the Wands. When we went searching for answers, we were given a message from beyond. This demon has been to Octavia Falls before. Our goal is to gather enough information to banish him from the coven before he can raise hell. Meanwhile, we need to find the Oaken Wands before the priestesses get their hands on them."

"And we need to protect as many people as we can in the process," Lucas added.

Chloe crossed her arms. "You know my grandmother will kill anyone she has to in order to get her hands on those Wands."

"Yes, and we have to do all this without being caught by the Executors," I said.

"What do we do about the fact that the *Miriamic Messenger* is calling to have Nadine removed from the Imperium Council?" Grant asked.

Thank the Goddess I didn't read the whole article. I'd have lost my shit. "They can't do that," I said. "There's no one to replace me. The law requires that I stand on the council."

"The priestesses make the laws," Grant pointed out. "They can change them."

"We also don't know how long you'll be the only Curse Breaker," Talia added. "People turn nineteen and get their magic every day. You may not be the only Curse Breaker for long."

"Then we have to move fast," Lucas stated.

"Once we have more information, how do we plan to fight back?" Grant wondered.

"It's obvious, isn't it?" Miles said with a slight smirk. "We overthrow the council."

Talia's eyebrows shot up. "What, *kill* the priestesses?"

Miles shrugged. "If they were gone, maybe someone we trust could take their place. Then we can overpower them. The priestesses aren't innocent. You've killed people already. You can do it again."

"No," Chloe said firmly. "Every move we make has to be calculated. If we kill the priestesses, we lose all favor with the coven, and everything we're trying to do falls apart. We'd need support in order to put someone we trust on the council. Otherwise, we're hanged for treason and the new priestesses could be worse than the last. It's not going to work."

"Even if killing the priestesses is the wrong move, Miles brings up a good point." My stomach clenched as I carefully prepared my next words. "We *have* killed people. I'm not proud of it, but I have to own up to it. I killed the witches at Pinewood Manor. Lucas killed Stella. Grant killed two officers the night of the Burning. And yes, I stand by the belief that those choices were necessary in order to save each other, but I'm not willing to continue sacrificing lives to win this war. That's what the priestesses are doing, and it's what we stand against."

I drew a deep breath. "We all need to be on the same page about what our values are, and what we're willing to endure. The choices we will face are *going* to be difficult. I know, because we've already faced many impossible decisions. But it takes just one of us to make the wrong decision for this entire thing to fall apart. So... what exactly are we willing to risk?"

Silence filled the room, and no one met my gaze.

Finally, Chloe cleared her throat. "The difference between you and the priestesses is that you did what you had to in order to survive. They've taken innocent lives and twisted their stories to suit their own agenda. We're here to fight the injustice of wrongful persecution and the persecution of innocents."

Grant sat up straighter. "You're right. This is a war. I can't take back what I did to those officers, but some of you wouldn't be standing here if I hadn't. We have to decide what happens when innocent lives are in immediate danger. What happens when our only choice is to eliminate their oppressors or let the innocents burn at the stake? If something like the Burning happened again… what choice do we have?"

I stared at a spot on the table, thinking hard. Death and destruction was the last thing I wanted. I just wished we could all get along, without hurting each other. But the priestesses had made it clear they weren't willing to do that.

"We protect innocent lives," I answered simply.

Lucas squeezed my hand to show he agreed with me. "We'll do everything we can to keep the peace, but if innocent lives are in danger, we have to save them. This coven is nothing if we don't protect our most vulnerable people."

"So, what's our plan?" Miles questioned.

"Our first step is to rally people to our side," Lucas answered. "We can't go up against the priestesses alone. We have to show them that the coven won't stand for their methods. They're trying to scare us, but if we show them that the coven is prepared to retaliate, they may be willing to negotiate."

"The priestesses will never work with us," Mandy sneered.

"We have to believe there's a chance," I argued. "We all want the same thing. We want to end the Waning and restore our magic. But we can't sacrifice innocent lives to do that."

"How do we get people to work with us?" Talia asked. "The priestesses were ready to kill Felicia, Samantha, and Darcy. The priestesses wanted to burn them simply for helping people escape the riots, yet none of those girls wanted anything to do with a revolution. We tried talking to them over break. They're terrified."

Lucas pressed his lips together thoughtfully. "If the priestesses can turn people against us using the *Miriamic Messenger*, then maybe we can do the same thing."

I eyed the big printer in the corner. "*The Epitaph.*"

"That's risky," Talia argued.

"Everything we do for this movement is going to be risky," I pointed out. "We have to be willing to take those risks."

"We can't confront the priestesses head-on," Talia insisted. "It will put a target on our backs."

"I'm already a target," I argued.

"Which means we have to be careful, or they'll take aim." Talia sounded really worried. "We need to do this with as little conflict as possible, or things will get out of hand very quickly."

"What are you suggesting?" I asked.

Talia thought about it for a moment. "We can write the article, but it should be under a pseudonym. And it shouldn't be *The Epitaph*. It should be something new, because the priestesses already know Lucas was working on an article for *The Epitaph* last semester. We can print a hidden message, so even if the priestesses get their hands on it, they won't know what we're up to."

"I can do that," Lucas offered.

"You should write two papers," Grant suggested. "Keep writing for *The Epitaph*. Write boring stuff no one cares about, and then change your writing style for this new paper. That way, the priestesses think you've been scared into compliance and won't suspect you."

"Good idea," Lucas agreed.

"To keep our operation secret, I can find a spell that will ward off this whole hallway," Mandy offered. "We've got something the priestesses don't have. We have all five Casts on our side, which makes us stronger."

"Mandy is right," I said. "She'll find a spell that will work. Lucas can print an article to get people on our side. Does anyone else have things they'd like to help with?"

"I'd like to work on finding ways to grow our powers," Chloe offered. "Most of us lost our magic the night of the Burning, and we didn't get it back for a few days. If the Waning hits us that way again, in a critical moment like that, it could make all the difference. This war would literally come down to chance."

"What are your ideas?" I wondered.

"Crystals, for starters," Chloe said. "I know magically-infused crystals are banned on school grounds, but if this room is warded, we can store them here."

"We'd have to learn transference," Lucas said. "It's advanced magic."

"If we hope to have any chance against the priestesses, we need to get on their level," Chloe said. "Advanced magic or not, we need to learn transference, so we have magic available to us if the Waning hits."

Transference was the power to transfer magic into crystals. Those crystals could then be used as reservoirs, like batteries for our magic. I could perform transference with ease, because of my Cast abilities, but only the most talented witches from other Casts could accomplish it. Even other races had difficulty with it.

"I can help," I offered. "I should be able to transfer your magic into a crystal."

Chloe nodded firmly. "That's the best place to start. And… I want to start learning blood magic."

"Blood magic?" Mandy asked warily.

"It's powerful," Chloe said. "You can use magic in blood to boost your powers and perform spells you've never dreamed of."

"I know what blood magic is," Mandy said. "I also know it's dangerous."

"We need to take risks," Chloe insisted.

"And how exactly are you going to source blood ethically?" Mandy asked. "How do we use it without hurting anyone? Besides, if the coven finds out we're using blood magic, it's over. No one will convert to our side. We'll be burned at the stake without question."

"Mandy's right," I said. "No matter how powerful it is, it's going to hurt us."

Chloe frowned. She didn't have to like it, but Mandy made a valid point. There were lines we couldn't cross, and this was one of them.

Miles swung his feet, bouncing his heels off the cabinet below the counter. "In the meantime, I can go undercover with Miriam's Executors. I'll join and see what information I can get from the inside."

Grant shook his head. "You're my brother. They're not going to take you."

"We could stage a public fight," Miles suggested. "It shouldn't be hard to convince people I've disowned you. Remember that time I convinced Mom you broke my arm?"

"It was pretty convincing," Grant admitted. "All right. We can stage a fight."

"Grant and I can work on finding information about the next Wand," Talia said. "We know there's one in the school. Internship applications are open with Professor Richards, and he maintains the school's history records. We might be able to get some information in the school's archives that could point to its location."

I knew it was my turn to make an offer. My throat closed up, but I forced myself to speak. "I want to contribute in every way I can, but I also want to be very honest about what I can handle. I have dialysis three times per week, and that's extremely time consuming. My life literally depends on it, unless I manage to get a kidney transplant. Lucas is a match, but the priestesses have blocked the surgery from happening. It'd be a miracle if I made it to the top of the transplant list anytime soon. Working around my dialysis is going to be a little difficult, but I'm going to do my best."

"Then how about you focus on something you can do during dialysis?" Lucas suggested. "You're a priestess, which means your intuition should be growing stronger. You can work on honing that power, and maybe we'll learn something about where to go next."

I nodded. "I can do that. There's one more thing. Who can dig into coven history and learn about demons who have visited the coven before? We need to get more information about the warning we received."

"I can," Mandy offered.

"I can help," Chloe added.

Mandy crossed her arms and scoffed. "I'm not working with *her*."

"Bitch, you did not just say that," Chloe snapped.

"See what I mean?" Mandy demanded.

Chloe drew a deep breath to calm down. "Sorry. I'm trying to do better."

Mandy shot her daggers. "You called Amy a squinty-eyed dyke and said I was her fat Spanish sidekick. I'm not even Spanish! You can't just walk in here like everything has changed just because you broke your curse."

"But everything *has* changed!" Chloe snapped. "I may not be able to change what I said in the past, but I'll damn well make an effort to change the future."

Lucas quickly stepped in. "If we can't get along, the priestesses have already won."

"You don't have to do anything if it's too overwhelming," I promised Mandy.

"No, I want to," Mandy assured me.

"I'll work with Mandy on the demon research," Grant cut in. "Talia and Chloe can research the Wands. Does that work for everyone?"

I nodded firmly, and others quickly agreed. I held my head high as I announced, "Then it's time to get started. The priestesses have created an army with Miriam's Executors, but we'll defend our people. We'll be the coven's shield."

"That's a cool name, actually," Miles remarked.

Lucas nodded in agreement. "The Coven's Shield, it is."

Hope surged through my chest. With all of us together, I felt like we actually had a chance of defeating the priestesses.

An uprising had begun. The priestesses wanted a witch hunt, but they would face a revolution.

lucas

THREE

Classes started the next day, and my head still buzzed with all the information we covered in our meeting. The talk of killing people shook me, even though I didn't regret killing Stella. She was responsible for Amy's death. But I feared it wasn't the last time I'd make a choice like that.

The coven didn't know the truth about what happened that night, and it drove me mad. If only they knew what they were truly up against, we could protect them better. But the priestesses had made sure Nadine and I couldn't tell *anyone* what really happened to Stella. Hell, I couldn't even tell my therapist. I was still seeing Dr. Mack, even though she'd denied my psych eval for the kidney transplant. Despite her evaluation, she was still a good therapist. I figured if I stuck with her long enough, I could show her how much I'd changed. She didn't think I was ready for the transplant now, but I would change her mind.

I was still trying to sort out my thoughts when I entered my Advanced Mortana Magic class. Chatter filled the classroom, but I kept my head down as I headed to an empty chair at the back of the room. Oliver followed beside me and plopped down at my feet, licking his paws.

I wasn't really paying attention until I heard Lena from a few rows up. She spoke so loudly, the whole class could hear her. "Have you seen our professor yet? He's *so* hot."

Samantha shifted uncomfortably in her chair. Lena didn't usually talk to Samantha, but she was the only girl nearby. Lena had to tell *someone* the latest gossip, I was sure.

"Uh, I guess Professor Warren's kind of… cute?" Samantha said.

Lena laughed loudly. "I'm not talking about Professor Warren. He's not teaching this class this semester."

My brow furrowed. Professor Warren was my advisor and easily one of my favorite professors. He'd *definitely* been listed on my schedule as the professor for this class.

"What happened?" Samantha asked, sounding worried.

Lena waved her hand. "He picked up a senior lecture or something. I don't know."

A group of girls entered the room. They spoke over one another, and I couldn't make out what they were saying. Lena sat up straight in her chair as the girls gathered around her. "You saw him?" she asked brightly.

"He is *so* cute," one of them gushed. She tried to keep her voice down, but I could hear every word.

Lena bounced in her chair. "Right? I mean, I might have to schedule some *private tutoring*, if you get what I mean."

Leroy leaned over the desk next to her. "I'm available for private tutoring sessions."

Lena wrinkled her nose. "Ew. Get lost."

Leroy straightened himself and pointed to the badge on his black uniform. "In case you forgot, sweetheart, I'm an Executor now. You can't talk to me like that."

Gregory snorted and mumbled something under his breath. I didn't catch what he said.

"What'd you just say to me?" Leroy snapped. A few sparks shot from his fingers in warning.

I threw my hands up and formed a shield between them. "Leave him alone."

Gregory shrank down in his seat. "I said nothing. Absolutely nothing."

"That's what I thought," Leroy growled. "It best not happen again. And drop your fucking shield, Lucas. You're not impressing anyone. What a loser."

Leroy spun toward the front of the room. I kept my shield up a few moments longer and studied him. He wasn't the kind of person to let this go.

Then I realized why he had. It was because of the Waning. Those small sparks of magic were all he had. He couldn't form a battle orb right now to save his life.

Good. Maybe he'd leave the rest of us alone.

A man strolled into the room then, and all chatter died instantly. He didn't have to say a thing to get the class to quiet. It was like his mere presence commanded his attention. I didn't know who the guy was, but he had to be our new professor. Oliver bristled at my feet and growled lowly.

Our professor looked like he'd just walked off a movie set where he played a stockbroker. The guy was over six feet tall, with a strong jaw and dark hair that he wore slicked back. He wore a nice suit and walked with unrivaled confidence in his stride.

Something about him seemed very familiar, but I couldn't place my finger on it. I'd certainly never met him before, but perhaps I'd seen him around Octavia Falls.

"Hello," he said in a deep, smooth voice.

An arrogant smirk crossed his face, and Lena gave a loud sigh. A few of the other girls snickered, like they couldn't control themselves. Hell, he'd only said one word, and he was already charming the entire female student population.

"Now *that's* a guy I'd like to be mentored by," Leroy said in a low tone. He didn't mean it in a sexual way, but it sure sounded like it.

Our professor's dark eyes scanned the room. A shiver traveled down my spine when his gaze moved over me. I guess I could see where the girls found him attractive, in a conventional sense, but his arrogance left me feeling uneasy. Whatever he was doing to charm everyone else, I was unaffected by it.

He straightened his suit jacket at the front of the room. "Welcome to Advanced Mortana Magic. I'm Professor Leto, and I'll be teaching this class this semester. You may not recognize me, but rest assured I am well versed in death magic. I've just returned to Octavia Falls after a long... sabbatical. Let's get started."

He moved toward the back of the room as he spoke. "It's come to my attention that your professors prefer to explore your necromancy magic through the use of cat skeletons. Is that correct?"

"Yes," Lena answered eagerly.

"Do you ever wonder why they don't teach you using *real* human remains?" Professor Leto asked, placing his hand on the doorknob of the storage closet.

"Ethics," Gregory said.

"Nonsense," Professor Leto argued. "Many witches and warlocks donate their bodies to the coven after death. Ethics are not a factor."

"Then what is?" Gregory asked.

"Fear, I suspect," Professor Leto answered. "If you fear the human body, perhaps you will fear death itself. Imagine what a witch or warlock might do if they feel comfortable around a corpse."

I didn't know what he was getting at, but I kept my gaze on him. He definitely gave me the chills, and I was determined to figure out why.

Professor Leto opened the storage closet, and he wheeled a table out of it. It wasn't until he shut the door that I got a good look at what lay on the table.

My insides twisted at the sight of a pale corpse. An old man lay naked on a metal table. A thin white sheet covered his middle, but that was it.

I have lived a full life. I am ready to go.

The words echoed in my mind as if I was hearing them now for the first time, but I wasn't. This last thought had come to me last night. It'd *definitely* come from this guy. I didn't even have to question it; my magic just *knew.*

I didn't know the old man's name, but knowing his last thought while he lay cold in front of me felt too weird—too personal.

All eyes remained on the corpse as Professor Leto wheeled the man to the front of the room. I wanted to hurl. We'd never used human corpses in class before, and my unease grew. This man should be laid to rest properly, not used for necromancy playtime.

"This is Mr. Derek Livingston," Professor Leto said casually, as if introducing us to a guest lecturer. "Thanks to his generous donation, you'll be practicing your magic on him today. You're quite fortunate he died when he did. What a wonderful way to kick off the semester."

We weren't *fortunate.* This was a man's corpse, for Alora's sake. Mr. Livingston deserved more respect.

But what was I supposed to say? That we couldn't do this? Necromancy was common throughout the coven, and Mr. Livingston *had* agreed to this before he died.

So why did I feel so on edge?

"There are so many necromancers in the Miriamic Coven," Professor Leto said. "It's a shame that you've only been taught to use your magic for fun, rather than exploring the practical uses. Imagine, for instance, if the fae launched a strike on the witches. It's safe to assume that many people would die in battle. With so many necromancers, you could reanimate the dead and multiply your army. You'd never lose numbers in a battle. Perhaps that's why there are so many necromancers... so that in times of war, you may defend yourselves."

He had a point, but I didn't like the way he spoke of the dead like that. Like they had no value other than body count.

"Animal skeletons are *one way* to practice your necromancy powers, but the true magic occurs when manipulating real human corpses," Professor Leto lectured. "If you are willing to get uncomfortable for just a few moments, you will see that you're capable of so much more than you imagined. Who would like to volunteer first?"

Hands shot up all throughout the room. Lena practically leapt out of her seat.

Professor Leto nodded toward her. "Yes, Miss..."

"Hahn," Lena said eagerly. "Lena Hahn."

"Miss Hahn, if you will." He gestured her forward, and she practically raced to the front of the room. He placed a hand on her shoulder to guide her in front of the corpse, and she snickered.

I watched curiously. I didn't want to blink, for fear of missing something. There was something very wrong about this lesson—about this *professor*—but I couldn't quite figure it out. It was more than just the way he spoke about the dead.

"Let's see where you're at," Professor Leto told Lena. "Try to reanimate this corpse."

Lena nodded, then hovered her hands over the body. She stood rigid with her shoulders back, like she was trying too hard to impress our professor. Dark red magic swirled out of Lena's hands and twisted around Mr. Livingston's arms. She lifted her hands, and the corpse's hands followed like a puppet. After a moment, she lost control, and Mr. Livingston's hands slammed back onto the table.

Lena bit her lip. "I'm sorry. I thought I had it."

"Try again," Professor Leto said in a smooth tone.

Lena's magic swirled out of her hands again. This time, the corpse sat all the way up before Lena lost control. A loud *thwack* sounded throughout the room as he slumped against the morgue table.

Professor Leto tapped his foot, like he was thinking hard. "I see we have a long way to go. Who'd like to try next?"

More students raised their hands, and Professor Leto called them up in turn. Most students couldn't do more than make his fingers wiggle, but Samantha got his eyes to open and made his head swivel, like he was really looking at us. There was no life in his eyes, though, and it was really eerie.

Professor Leto pushed Samantha to try something else. She shifted her weight between her feet, looking uncomfortable, but she must've wanted to impress him. She reanimated Mr. Livingston's vocal chords and made him sing a rendition of *Stayin' Alive* while he blinked lifelessly.

Everyone laughed, except for me and Samantha. All the color had drained from her face, and she looked like she was about to puke.

"Thank you, Miss Stone," Professor Leto said, excusing her back to her seat. She hurried back to her chair as fast as she could. "Would anyone else like to try?"

By now, all the necromancers in class had taken a turn, and we were nearing the end of the hour.

Professor Leto cocked an eyebrow. "Anyone?"

"I can try again!" Lena offered.

He pressed his lips together and didn't even look at her. "Perhaps someone who hasn't gone... you in the back?"

He pointed directly at me, and my guts twisted involuntarily. Oliver jumped to his feet, alert. It wasn't that I had a problem standing in front of class. There was something about *him* and his eerily familiar dark eyes that shook me to my core.

"I'm, uh, not a necromancer, sir," I said. "This class is for all Mortana, not just those who can reanimate the dead."

"Well, you have death magic, do you not?" he asked snidely.

"Yes, but—"

"Then come on forward," he insisted. "Let's see what you can do."

Leroy laughed under his breath as I reluctantly stood from my chair. He wasn't a necromancer, either. His Mortana magic was much more sinister. He was the worst kind of Death Warlock—the kind that could kill on sight. I'd like to see *him* give this a shot.

I headed to the front of the room, my knees shaking the whole way. Oliver kept his eyes on me, watching closely. The closer I came to the front, the more I wanted to rush back to my seat. Hell, I wanted to race out of the room and just keep running, until I was as far away from this guy as I could get. I couldn't explain it, but an innate *knowing* told me something was amiss.

"I'm really not—" I started.

"It's ungraded, I assure you," Professor Leto interrupted. He gestured for me to stand in front of the corpse. "Show us what your death magic can do."

I stood there for a second, not really sure what he was asking. "I don't work with corpses."

"You're Mortana. Of course you do," he said, like what I'd said was ludicrous. "You must have some influence over death. You might be surprised by what you can do. Give it a go."

He wanted me to show him my powers? All right.

"I have lived a full life," I said. "I am ready to go."

Leroy laughed. "So dramatic."

Leto, on the other hand, eyed me curiously. "What does that mean, exactly?"

I shrugged and gestured to Mr. Livingston's corpse. "Ask *him*. It's what I heard when he died."

I thought I read intrigue in Leto's features, but it was hard to tell. "What is your name?" he asked.

"Lucas Taylor," I told him. There was no recognition in his features, and I was surprised he hadn't heard of me. I was the only one of my kind in all the coven. "I'm the Reaper's Apprentice."

His face fell for a moment, before lighting up. "Ah, yes, of course. Mister Taylor… I've been looking forward to having someone like you in my class. Reapers can read energy signatures, correct?"

He winked at me, like we shared a secret, but I had no idea what he meant. Whatever energy signatures he was talking about, I'd never sensed them…

"You may return to your seat." He placed a hand on my shoulder, but I stopped dead.

The whole room seemed to vanish, and an ominous sensation swept through me. I couldn't explain the feeling that hit me, because I'd never felt anything like it before. An image of a ram's head might as well have flashed in front of my eyes and replaced Professor Leto's human features; that's how eerie the feeling was. It was there one second and gone the next. I just *knew* the truth. Whoever this guy was, he didn't belong in this realm.

The rush I'd felt vanished, but that uneasy feeling in my gut remained. He seemed unaware of what I'd just experienced. I glanced around the room, wondering how no one else had noticed. They all just sat there, waiting for me to return to my seat. How did they not see what I did?

My magic twisted in my belly, confirming the truth over and over again. I realized that Professor Leto had been right. Reapers *could* read the energy signature of a soul. We were responsible for moving souls from one realm to the next, and so we had to know where a soul belonged. I was the only one who knew the truth.

Professor Leto was a demon.

The demon.

The one the priestesses had summoned. The one they'd made a deal with. He must've had magic to conceal his true features, but I knew without a doubt it was him. That's why he looked so familiar to me—because I'd seen him in the Imperium headquarters, stepping out of a portal to the Abyss.

Every instinct in my body told me to slay this demon right here and now. He belonged in the Abyss, not roaming the halls of Miriam College of Witchcraft.

But I couldn't kill him. Demons weren't alive… not really. Everything I'd learned about vanquishing demons involved spellwork, but this was no ordinary demon. He'd made a deal, which had tethered him here. He had business here on Earth. Banishing him to the Abyss wasn't going to be easy.

"Mister Taylor," Professor Leto prodded. He cocked his head toward my desk. "I said you may return to your seat."

I cleared my throat. "Yeah, it's just… our hour's up."

He stared me down for a second, before his lips curled into a smile. "I suppose it is. Class dismissed."

Everyone shuffled out of their seats. I went to leave, but Leto's hand tightened on my shoulder. My body went rigid as he leaned into me.

"Let's keep this our little secret, shall we?" he whispered.

My stomach plummeted to the floor. He *knew* that I knew.

"I have an arrangement with the priestesses," he added.

It was a threat. If I did anything, I'd have to answer to the priestesses. Surely, they'd find a reason to hang me.

I forced down the lump in my throat and spoke dryly. "What secret?"

He smirked. "Exactly."

Fuck, this was bad, but I knew immediately what I had to do. I had to study him, to find out why he was here at the school of all places. It was one thing to come here looking for the Oaken Wands. It was another to pose as a professor, to settle in like he was planning on staying here for a while. His plans with the priestesses were bigger than we could ever imagine, and I was determined to find out what he was up to.

I had to tell Nadine and the others as soon as possible. I wasn't risking them running into him before they knew what he was. They should all be leaving class right about now.

Leto finally released his hold on me. I didn't get a chance to turn and flee before a scream came from down the hall.

"Somebody help!" a man yelled. "He's not breathing!"

I felt the blood drain from my face. Leto just looked at me with an indifferent expression. He didn't give one flying fuck that someone was in danger. Fuck him.

I ran out of the classroom and sprinted down the hall toward the sound of the voice. Oliver raced after me. When I turned the corner to the hall that led to the cafeteria, I skidded to a halt. A group of people stood in front of me, and I couldn't get a clear view of what was going on, but I couldn't mistake the pool of blood soaking into the carpet. Nobody did anything. They just stood there, dumbstruck.

"Out of the way!" I shouted. I grabbed someone and shoved them aside.

"Watch it!" Gregory sneered. I hadn't even realized it was him. I was too overcome with horror to take in anything but the crime scene.

Professor Perez lay in a pool of his own blood. His breath wavered as he stared up at the ceiling. He was barely holding on.

Professor Warbright knelt over him, pressing his shaking hands to a wound in the center of his chest. His wand lay next to him, like he'd already tried casting a spell to stop the bleeding, but it hadn't worked. Blood seeped through Warbright's fingers and trailed down Perez's suit coat.

"Call the infirmary!" Professor Warbright barked at a nearby student. "Quickly!"

A few students took off running down the hall. Oliver yowled loudly as I rushed to Perez's side and dropped to my knees. Blood seeped through my jeans, but I didn't pay attention to it. I conjured a first-aid kit I kept with me and tore open a roll of gauze.

"Here, Professor. Use this," I told Warbright as I wadded the gauze over the wound. He placed his bloody hands atop mine and pressed down with me. It wasn't enough. Not even close. Blood coated my hands.

"Hang in there, Professor Perez," I pleaded.

Perez's eyes glossed over, and his hand shook as he reached up to grab my arm. "I... I..."

He couldn't speak, and a lump formed in my throat. Professor Perez was too young to die.

I forced the lump downward. "We're getting you help."

"Too... late..." he rasped. Perez fumbled for me, and I took his hand in mine, squeezing tightly.

"No, it's not," I insisted.

"You're going to be all right, Zachary," Professor Warbright promised, though he sounded entirely uncertain.

Perez opened his mouth again to say something, but nothing came out. His eyes rolled back in his skull, and his hand went limp in mine.

"No!" I shouted, but his voice cut through my thoughts a moment later, confirming the truth that couldn't be undone.

It wasn't him.

A pile of bricks seemed to tumble over me as Perez's last thought played through my mind. I didn't know what he meant, but one thing was for certain.

This had been a very violent death. Those thoughts always hit harder.

My Mortana magic sensed death permeating the hall, and I could feel the void where his lifeforce was meant to be. But it was gone now—severed far too early. Professor Perez was only in his forties, and he was already gone...

Several of my Mortana classmates must've felt his death as well, because someone gagged, and another began to sob loudly. Even Leroy cursed under his breath.

"Out of the way!" someone barked.

I looked up to see my advisor, Professor Warren. He forced the crowd of onlookers apart, and several nurses from the infirmary followed behind him. He stopped dead when he saw the sight in front of him. The nurses gasped.

I spotted my friends in the back of the crowd. They must've come from the cafeteria. Nadine's eyes watered as she took in the scene. My heart slowed slightly at the sight of her. She had a way of calming me down when no one else could. But there was nothing she could do that could take away the true horror of this moment.

I sat back. I couldn't bring myself to stand, because I was still shaking. "It's too late," I told Professor Warren in a hoarse tone. "He's already gone."

"What happened here?" he demanded.

"I—I don't know," I stammered.

"Everyone is to return to their classes," Professor Warren instructed. "This hallway is off-limits for the rest of the day."

He was firm, and people respected him. The crowd began to disperse slowly. A few people didn't move right away, because they were too shocked by what happened. Gregory stared for a few moments longer, before turning and nearly ramming into Professor Leto. I didn't know he'd followed me.

Leto barely noticed him. He was too engrossed in the scene, gazing down at Perez's lifeless body with a hungry look in his eyes. It was more like he was looking at a fresh, juicy steak than a corpse.

Leto looked far too pleased about this—almost like he was admiring his own handiwork. The warning we'd received in the library crossed my mind.

He has come to kill.

It *couldn't* have been him. I'd been in class with him for the last hour, and he hadn't left my sight before the screams started. He had a rock-solid alibi.

Could that be what Perez meant by his last words... *It wasn't him?*

Perhaps he knew something was amiss within the school, and he knew I'd suspect the demon… only Professor Leto wasn't responsible.

I didn't know what to make of any of this. It had all happened too fast.

The crowd dispersed until there were only a few people remaining, including the professors and nurses.

I got to my feet, but Professor Warren stepped in front of me. "Stay, Lucas. You're going to have to answer a few questions."

"Uh… okay," I said. I glanced down the hall, where Nadine stood. She pointed to herself, then to the cafeteria, to tell me she'd be waiting for me there. I nodded to her, and she turned toward Talia and Grant to leave.

Two figures rushed down the hall, and the students parted to let them through. Headmistress Verla and Sheriff Baker slowed when they spotted the body. All the color drained from Verla's features.

Sheriff Baker threw his shoulders back. I wasn't surprised to see him here. He'd been hanging around the school lately, managing Miriam's Executors. "Everyone stand back," he ordered. "This is an active crime scene."

Warbright shook as he got to his feet and backed up so far that his back pressed against the wall. He was a necromancer, but he was still pretty young, in his mid-thirties at most. Necromancer or not, it was pretty clear he'd never dealt with a human corpse before.

Professor Leto had been right about one thing. Even warlocks with death magic weren't comfortable with human death.

Verla slowly approached Professor Warren. She grabbed his arm, but she never took her eyes off Perez. When Professor Warren caught the surprise in her features, he put an arm around her and gave her a squeeze before releasing her. It was meant to be a kind gesture, and she snapped back to attention.

"Someone better start talking," Verla stated firmly.

"I heard Professor Warbright scream…." I started.

Warbright cleared his throat, but his voice shook. "I was headed to the cafeteria when I found him. We had planned to meet for lunch to discuss our teaching plans for next week, as we teach the same freshman-level Mortana class. I tried to stop the bleeding, but it was too much. I yelled for help, but the injuries appear to be caused by a complicated battle spell. There was nothing I could do."

"You have blood on your hands," Sheriff Baker snapped. It wasn't a question, but an accusation.

"I—I was trying to stop the bleeding," Warbright stammered. He looked back at Perez's lifeless body and choked up. He threw his hand over his mouth, before realizing he had blood all over his hands. He doubled over and tried not to gag.

"You were first at the scene," Sheriff Baker accused.

Warbright shook from head to toe and tried to hide his sniffles. He could hardly stomach a corpse, let alone explain himself. More than that, this man had lost a teaching partner—a *friend.*

"Sheriff, can't you see this man is innocent?" I demanded. "He can't handle the sight of blood. Do you really think he's capable of hurting someone like this?"

Sheriff Baker narrowed his eyes on me. "What exactly are *you* doing here? Seems awfully strange you would just *stumble* across a crime scene like this."

"I heard the screams, just like twenty other students leaving class," I stated.

Professor Leto stepped forward. I didn't know what he was still doing here.

"Sheriff, might I suggest you gather your evidence before interrogating the witnesses?" Leto said. "This body is at a very critical stage postmortem. We may have a chance to preserve it for use in our classes."

So *that's* what that hungry look had been about. Did he see us all as nothing more than walking corpses? No wonder he belonged in the Abyss.

"Are you *serious* right now?" I snapped. Demon or not, I wouldn't let this slide.

Leto smirked. "The priestesses asked me to teach Mortana magic. I only have the best interest of my students at heart."

Verla frowned. The way she glared at Professor Leto indicated she had a less than pleasant relationship with him. I wasn't sure she'd wanted him to teach here, but if the priestesses demanded it, she didn't have a choice.

"With all due respect, Professor Leto, this man just died," Verla said, trying to keep her cool. "Let's take a moment to process this. If this is truly what it looks like, the school is unsafe. It's imperative we respond to this in an effective manner that ensures the safety of our students and faculty. Sheriff, what are your thoughts?"

Sheriff Baker conjured a rubber glove and snapped it on his hand. He carefully bent and lifted the gauze off Professor Perez's chest. A sickly expression crossed his features, before he composed himself.

He stood up straight and cleared his throat. "It definitely looks like foul play involving magic. We will be conducting a thorough investigation."

Professor Warren turned to me. "Lucas, do you have any idea who could've done this?"

My gaze darted to Professor Leto for a moment, but he didn't notice. "Why would I?"

"You heard his last thought, didn't you?" Professor Warren asked. He was trying to be helpful.

I nodded. "Yeah, but he didn't say who killed him."

"What exactly *did* he say?" Sheriff Baker demanded.

I hesitated. I didn't like to share people's last thoughts. If they were meant for the coven to hear, then they'd be available to everyone, but they weren't. *I* was the one tasked with holding on to them.

But this was a murder. If I could contribute to catching the killer, then perhaps I could save a life.

"He said, '*It wasn't him*,'" I told the sheriff. He looked annoyed that that's all there was, so I added, "I don't know what it means. It could be about his death, or something else entirely."

Sheriff Baker looked less than pleased. He turned to Verla. "Headmistress, can you think of anyone who would have a reason to target one of your staff members?"

She shook her head. "People loved Professor Perez. He's been teaching intercast magic for years, and we've never received a complaint—"

She cut off, and something in her features changed.

"Perhaps his position made him a target," she said thoughtfully. "The Casts are dividing, yet his role is to teach how the Casts are stronger together. Perhaps someone didn't take kindly to those values."

Baker smirked, like he thought Perez got what he deserved. He didn't voice his opinions, though. Instead, he said, "It's an angle we'll consider."

He asked a bunch of other questions, but I didn't know the answers to them. Eventually, he let me go.

I rushed to the nearest bathroom as quickly as I could. Oliver followed and meowed softly once we were alone. He seemed concerned, but I didn't know what to tell him. I leaned over the sink and began scrubbing my hands vigorously. By now, the blood had dried onto my skin. My stomach hollowed as the bloody water swirled down the drain. I could still feel the pressure of Professor Perez's hand in mine, and the way it went limp when his spirit departed his body.

The door opened, and I jumped when Professor Warren entered the bathroom. I straightened at the sink, but continued washing, even though the water had run clear already.

"Professor," I rasped.

"I came to check if you were all right," he said gently.

I kept my gaze on the water as I answered. "I'm the Reaper's Apprentice. I hear people die every day. This is normal for me."

The words felt ingenuine, like I was speaking off a script.

Professor Warren frowned. He knew me well enough to know when I was lying. "This was far from ordinary, Lucas. A man was murdered, and he died right in front of you."

I shuddered. He was right. This was fucked up.

I turned off the water and shook my hands out. "His thought was... heavy. Someone definitely targeted him."

"Any idea who?" Professor Warren asked.

"No!" I snapped. What exactly was he accusing me of? "You already asked me that. If I knew, don't you think I would've said something?"

"You told the truth about his last thought?" he asked curiously.

"Yes, of course."

Professor Warren sighed. "I'm only trying to help, Lucas. We've gotten to know each other well, and I thought... well, I thought it seemed like you were hiding something back there."

I leaned against the sink. "If I was, you won't believe what I have to say."

"Try me," he offered. It was obvious he really cared and wanted to be here for me.

I drew a deep breath. The priestesses could hang me for this, but it didn't matter. Innocent people were dying, and I'd gladly hang if it meant saving them.

I spat it out. "Professor Leto is a demon summoned by the Imperium

Council to help them end the Waning, and despite the fact that I—along with twenty other students—saw him in class right before Professor Perez was attacked, I know he's somehow involved."

Professor Warren didn't react to my accusation right away. Instead, he looked thoughtful.

I frowned. "I told you that you wouldn't believe me."

"No, no, I believe you," he assured me. "I believe that's your version of events. You've just gone through something very traumatic, and you're trying to rationalize it in any way you can. You need answers. We all do."

I scoffed.

"I want to believe you, Lucas," he promised. "But do you really think the priestesses would summon a demon and let him into the school?"

"Yes!" I cried. "The priestesses burned people at the stake on the school grounds not even a month ago. You think they wouldn't resort to this? Ask yourself why you've never met this guy before."

"He's been on sabbatical," Professor Warren said. "Many members of the coven, professors particularly, travel often, especially between supernatural races. They study their magic and trade with them."

I nearly snorted. "Or they're summoned straight from the Abyss and bring a wave of destruction with them."

"He's a good guy," Professor Warren said. "He volunteers at the hospital."

"Because he wants you to believe he's a saint!" I insisted. "This isn't over, Professor. He's planning something with the priestesses."

"You said it yourself that he was with you when the attack happened," Professor Warren pointed out. He thought he was helping, but he was doing the exact opposite.

"Maybe he teleported, or cast a curse. I don't know how he did it, okay? I'm not crazy!"

"Of course you're not. But these things can be misinterpreted when you're not thinking straight."

I couldn't help myself. I went off on him. "You think I'm this troubled, depressed kid who can't handle his powers, but you don't even know me anymore. You're just going to stick your head in the sand when I really need you. Be scared all you want, Professor, but be brave enough to face it! I know what my magic told me. And I know without a doubt that this coven will be destroyed if I don't do something to stop it."

I stomped past Professor Warren and out of the room with Oliver at my heels.

"Lucas," Professor Warren called after me, but I didn't turn back.

Professor Warren had been there for me for the last two years. I could always go to him when I needed to talk. He was the father figure that my own dad wasn't. I really needed him to believe me right now…

But he didn't.

It was too much to even think about, so I pushed it aside. I couldn't handle it on top of Professor Perez's death.

My friends would believe me, and I needed to tell them everything right away.

Blood had dried into my jeans, but I didn't care. I hurried to the cafeteria and found Nadine, Grant, and Talia huddled around a small table in the corner. Nadine scribbled something down in a notebook. I didn't mean to look, but I caught a glimpse of her notes. It was a list of everything she'd witnessed at the scene. She thought she could solve this.

Nadine turned when she heard me. She subconjured her book. "Are you going to be all right?"

"What *happened?*" Grant asked.

I glanced around the crowded cafeteria. Several people looked my way. I was certain *everyone* was talking about what happened to Perez.

"I have a lot to tell you, but we need to go somewhere private," I said.

No one needed to ask where. There was only one place we could—the old *Epitaph* room, where The Coven's Shield had met before.

Our cats rushed into the room ahead of us. As soon as the door clicked shut, the confession spilled out. Nadine tried to comfort me, but I was too worked up to sit down. I paced around the room as I told them everything that happened, from when I entered my Advanced Mortana Magic class to when I met up with them in the cafeteria.

Nadine's jaw dropped as she listened. "The priestesses let the demon on campus? Are they insane?"

"Yes," Grant said dryly.

"It's too much of a coincidence that someone was murdered the day he showed up," I said. "But he was with me when it happened… and with Perez's last thought… I just don't know what to make of it all. Professor Warren didn't believe me. I don't know who else to go to."

Nadine got a thoughtful look on her face. "We can trust Headmistress Verla, but… this is dangerous, and she'll try to stop us for our own safety."

"Then where do we start?" Grant wondered.

"Can we figure out what kind of demon we're dealing with?" Nadine suggested. "That at least should tell us something. Maybe there's a spell that will get rid of him."

I pushed my fingers through my hair. "Maybe, but he's already made a deal, so getting rid of him won't be easy."

"Good thing we're the ones he's up against," Nadine said proudly. "We can do this."

"This might help," Grant offered.

He had conjured a thick book. I recognized the black leather binding. It was the same restricted demonology textbook we'd found in the library when we snuck in over break. Grant had taken it to help with his demonology research.

"Mandy and I have been researching demons, and we've narrowed it down a bit," Grant said. "Most demons with ram features, like those Lucas described, are lesser demons. They're more powerful than monsters, but they're not as dangerous as demonic gods. They like to wreak havoc on small areas at a time, and they enjoy sticking around to take it all in, rather than sweeping across the globe quickly and destroying everything in their path. But there are different types, all with various appetites for chaos."

"Like what?" I questioned.

"Some feed off of betrayal," Grant explained as he flipped through the book. "They'll create gossip and turn friends against one another. Others are energized… sexually. They manipulate affairs. And some feed off murder."

My stomach clenched. "Which ones are those?"

Grant stopped as he came to the page he was looking for. He turned the book toward me, and the drawing of the demon sent a shiver down my spine. He looked exactly like the demon I'd seen in the Imperium headquarters, with the body of a man and the head of a ram.

"If he's involved in the murder, I think we can say with certainty that he's a Nex demon," Grant said.

"Nex… meaning… death?" Talia asked.

"In Latin, it's loosely translated as *violent death*," Grant confirmed.

"These demons literally get energy from murders and violent deaths. They feed off the events like we eat food."

Talia drew a sharp breath. "*Leto*! That's Latin for something, too, isn't it?"

Talia conjured her incantations textbook and flipped to the glossary. "Yes, oh my Goddess. It's literally in his name. *Leto* is to slay, kill, murder."

I furrowed my brow. "So he chose his name as... what? Some dig against the coven because we use Latin in our spellwork?"

"It seems fitting for a smug asshole like him," Talia said. "Leto's taunting us. The coven uses Latin because when the first necromancer was born, Miriam went to study necromancy. That's when she learned of the fae, who believed necromancy was a form of dark magic. Miriam didn't want to associate with the fae, because they would've killed her family for practicing dark magic. Through her research, she found that necromancy had been practiced in ancient societies, and the texts she found were all written in Latin, originating from the Roman Empire. But the fae couldn't read Latin, because it was already a dead language by that time. To hide the coven's magic from the fae, Miriam studied the language and wrote all her grimoires in Latin. Even if the fae got their hands on a spellbook, they couldn't translate them, and they wouldn't know what kind of magic Miriam was using. They couldn't steal her spells, either."

"Thanks for the history lesson," Nadine said. "But what does this mean?"

"If Leto wanted to hide what he was, he'd choose another name in a different language," Talia pointed out. "But it's Latin, which we're familiar with. He's putting it right in front of our faces, to show he's better than us when the coven doesn't figure it out. He's definitely behind this."

"But Lucas said he wasn't there when it happened," Nadine mused. "So how'd he orchestrate it?"

"I don't know," Grant said, sounding worried. He flipped from one page to another. "I don't see that in here."

"Could he have bribed someone to do it for him?" Nadine theorized. "Maybe he's making other deals."

"It's possible," I said thoughtfully. "But whoever did this was long gone before anyone found Perez."

"How long will this satiate the demon?" Nadine asked. "How much time do we have before he strikes again?"

Grant shook his head. "I don't know. He could go weeks, or even months between killings. Demons are very unpredictable. The more violent the murder, the more power he'll get, so that can change the timeline."

"We have to get rid of him," Nadine stated.

"How?" Talia asked. "He's on the priestesses' side, so we can't turn him in. This isn't a typical exorcism or banishment. The priestesses are coven representatives, which means when he made that deal, he made a deal with the entire coven. He'd have to fulfill his end of the bargain before we could get rid of him for good."

I crossed my arms. "There has to be another way. We must find a way to vanquish him ourselves, by any means necessary."

I knew it sounded impossible, but we had no other choice.

"What if we went public?" Talia asked. "The coven might force him out of town."

Nadine shook her head. "The priestesses will deny it. No one will believe us, and it'll give them more reason to burn us at the stake."

"Everyone in class seemed to love him," I added. "I don't know if he can compel people or what that was about, but I wouldn't be surprised if the coven took his side."

Grant frowned. "Then we have to find a powerful spell to stop him."

He flipped another page, and Talia grabbed his hand to stop him. "Wait. What's this?"

Grant eyed the page. "It looks like a spell for Seers, used to identify demon magic."

"Can it tell us how he killed Perez?" I asked.

"It might. I can try it," Talia offered.

"Then let's do it," I agreed.

Talia conjured a crystal ball and placed it on the center of the table. Our cats sat nearby, watching the ritual. Nadine conjured a bundle of sage, and she handed each of us a clear quartz crystal to amplify the spell's energy.

I took the crystal and gripped it tightly. Goddess, I hoped this worked.

Grant conjured a few candles, and I lit them with my lighter, then lit

Nadine's herbs. She walked around the room, cleansing the area with the smoke.

"It will take a few minutes for me to get into a trance," Talia said. "You guys can help with the spell by sharing positive intentions with me, okay?"

Nadine nodded. "Sounds easy enough."

Talia reached for me on one side and Grant on the other. Nadine set her sage bundle aside, and we all joined hands. Silence fell over the room as Talia concentrated on her crystal ball. I closed my eyes and sent positive, encouraging vibes her way. It was hard, because I was still shaken by everything that happened. I took deep breaths to try to calm myself.

After a few minutes where nothing happened, Talia shifted.

"Is it working?" Grant asked.

She shook her head. "Not yet. I need to focus better... I need music. Do you guys mind if I sing?"

"Not at all," I said. "Do whatever you need to."

Talia closed her eyes again, and her melodic voice filled the room. I'd never heard the lyrics before, and I realized it was because she was making them up on the spot.

"Goddess of the coven
Be with us now
We must stop what's coming
We don't know how

Danger lurks these halls
Death is all around
What magic has caused this?
The answers must be found."

I felt Talia stiffen, and I opened my eyes to see her staring deep into the crystal ball. Something in her features had shifted, like she wasn't in the room with us anymore. The ball began to glow a bright white. I wasn't a Seer, so I couldn't make out whatever Talia saw—but hell, I felt the spell working.

A strange wind began to swirl around us. Nadine and I shot nervous glances around the room, as if expecting a ghost to appear. Talia was so deep in her trance that she didn't seem to notice.

"Should we stop?" Grant asked, sounding worried.

"No, let her keep going," I said. "She's getting something—"

A gust swept through the room and whipped our hair in all directions. The candles blew out, and Talia gasped.

She dropped my hand and shrank into Grant. He placed an arm around her shoulder, and she cuddled into him, squeezing her eyes shut tightly.

"Tal!" He shook her a bit. "What'd you see?"

She winced. "It was confusing."

Grant stroked her hair. "Take all the time you need."

Nadine quickly conjured a water bottle. "Here."

Talia opened her eyes and sipped the water. "Thank you."

After a few deep breaths, she finally relaxed. "I can't really explain what I saw. It was more like a feeling. Lucas was right. The demon is definitely involved, but I can't decipher the details. All I know for certain is that this wasn't another demon deal. He used some sort of spell to kill Professor Perez."

"What kind of spell?" I asked.

She took another sip of water. "I'm not sure, but it felt like something that could be broken—like a curse, but not a curse. Once a curse is cast, it's out there for good. You can't undo it. This is different. He has more control over the spell, like he chooses how and when to use it."

"A curse that's not a curse..." Nadine mused. "What if he's marking people for death and controlling their fate?"

"That would fit with what I saw," Talia confirmed.

"If it's anything like a curse, I could break it," Nadine said. "But I'd have to know who he's targeting... and break the spell before someone else gets hurt."

A hopeless feeling settled over the room.

"Mandy and I will keep researching Nex demons," Grant said, but it was the only thing any of us could offer. The alternative seemed impossible. "We'll do our best to figure out how his spell works."

We had no idea when Professor Leto might strike again. We had to break the demon's spell...

Before another innocent person died and Professor Leto became even stronger.

nadine

FOUR

The atmosphere around school seemed to grow even darker over the following days. By now, everyone knew there was a murderer roaming campus, and no one knew who they could trust. Headmistress Verla was shoulders-deep in parental complaints, and she'd canceled my mentorships indefinitely until things got sorted out.

I didn't mind, because I already had a paper to write for my Criminal Justice class. Professor Clarke assigned us an essay where we had to detail how the coven's judicial system differed from that of the United States' government. He spoke highly of the priestesses, and I had to be careful about what I put into my essay, because I knew he was looking for specific answers. The more I studied Miriamic law, the more I found that the coven could really get away with anything. It made me sick to think about what the priestesses might do with their power.

I finished the essay during my dialysis on Friday. The nurse didn't say anything as she unhooked me from the machine, though she kept throwing glances at the cauldron tattoo on my arm—the one I'd gotten to fool everyone into thinking I was an Alchemist. Everyone knew it wasn't my real Cast mark, and she looked pretty bitter about it. I noticed the same cauldron tattoo on the back of her neck. She was obviously really offended that I'd tried to cross Cast lines.

Bitch, I'd just been trying to *survive*.

Isa growled lowly at the nurse, sensing her hostility. I nudged my cat with my foot, and she quieted.

The nurse turned away from me as I started gathering my things. I stood, and an intense wave of dizziness passed over me. I immediately sat back down, because I thought I might pass out. My vision went black for a moment, then settled. Isa meowed loudly, sensing something was very wrong.

"Excuse me," I called to the nurse. She barely looked my way and obviously didn't care.

"You're all done. You can go now," she said harshly. She clearly didn't want me here a moment longer.

"I'm really dizzy," I told her.

She frowned, but she didn't say anything as she brought over a blood pressure cuff and placed it around my arm. "Low blood pressure," she announced. "It's a common side effect caused by a drop in fluids during dialysis. Drink some water, and you'll be fine."

That's all she said before turning away from me. She didn't even *offer me* water. If it wasn't obvious before, it was clear that the coven wouldn't hesitate to take sides. This woman couldn't care less if I dropped dead on the dialysis floor. It was ironic that the very people who were supposed to keep me alive were the same ones who'd be cheering for the noose the second the priestesses sanctioned it.

I left the dialysis room, because I didn't want to be around this nurse longer than I had to. I found some water near the registration desk and sipped on it in the waiting room. It helped.

"Come on, Isa," I told my cat as I stood. "We better go, or we're going to be late."

The sun had set by the time I left the hospital. I drove to Octavia Hall, where the priestesses had ordered a meeting. I had no idea what they wanted to discuss, but I pulled my cloak tighter around my shoulders and walked inside.

When I entered the Imperium headquarters, the priestesses were already there, but they weren't the only ones. At the fireplace, a man with an Alchemy tattoo stirred something inside of a cauldron. He was short and plump, and his hands shook as he added ingredients. He wore a white coat and a chef's hat. The man shot a nervous glance at me before returning to his potion. He picked up a wand nearby and waved it over the cauldron. Magic swirled into his brew. When he set the wand aside, I realized with horror that I recognized it.

It was the Alchemy Wand. The priestesses were using one of the Oaken Wands… for what?

Another woman sat at the meeting table, laughing with Margaret like they were old friends. The woman had to be in her late fifties, with long black hair and sharp features. She sat straight with her shoulders back, commanding everyone's attention. She wore a black dress and dark eye makeup.

She poured wine into four glasses while she laughed casually, then distributed them around the table. I noticed there wasn't a glass for me. I didn't drink alcohol and would've refused anyway, but it was a clear way of excluding me.

The woman stopped laughing as soon as I entered the room. Her features fell into a frown, and she eyed me up and down. She shot a quick glance at Isa, before looking me over once more.

"This is her?" she asked the other priestesses. Her tone was full of judgment.

Tingles spread across my arms. Hell, that look was worse than the one Lilian gave me. Put them both together, and I was ready to crawl out of my skin.

"Yes, this is Priestess Nadine," Charlotte answered.

The woman pursed her lips. "Well, don't keep us waiting, *priestess*."

The way she spoke my title sounded like poison on her tongue.

"I believe I'm on time," I stated confidently as I strolled over and took my seat. Isa jumped onto my lap.

The woman checked the clock on the wall and lifted her chin higher. "Yes, well, a minute longer and you'd have kept us waiting. Let's get started."

The way she took control of the meeting caught me off guard. "Excuse me, but who exactly *are* you?" I asked.

"Nadine!" Lilian scolded.

"It's okay, priestess," the woman assured her kindly. "Everyone else in the coven may know who I am, but Miss Evers didn't grow up here, did she?"

I didn't miss the way she used my last name instead of my official title. She spoke in a way that strongly implied I was an outsider, like I should be ashamed I grew up outside the coven. She was obviously trying to belittle me.

"This is Claudia Sinclair," Priestess Margaret introduced, taking control. It was my understanding that Priestess Lilian had been on the council the longest, inducted around the same time as my grandfather. But Margaret was the oldest, and she was often the one to lead our meetings. "Claudia is the owner of Miriam's Magical Goods. Her company is the main importer and exporter of magical goods within the coven."

So she was rich and powerful. Got it.

"Is that what this meeting is about?" I asked. "Supernatural trade?"

Claudia threw her head back in laughter, like my question was ridiculous. "Miriam's Magical Goods operates to the utmost standards. I assure you that my company has it handled. The priestesses don't need to worry about trade. We're here because you need a fifth priestess."

She flipped her hand over, and that's when I noticed the eye tattoo on the inside of her arm.

"You're here to replace Stella," I stated bluntly. The three other priestesses looked eager to have her on board already. It was obvious she'd already charmed them into a decision. She was here to get *my* vote.

"Well, someone must." Claudia laughed.

"We'll have to vote you onto the council before the induction ceremony next Halloween. Why should we consider you?" I asked.

Her eyebrow twitched, like she was shocked I'd be so bold as to ask the question. If she thought I was just going to sit back and watch this meeting take place, she was wrong. We needed good people on the council, and something about her superior attitude and utter disrespect for my position already left a bad taste in my mouth. However, I was willing to keep an open mind and give her a chance to convince me.

"For one, I have many resources, which I am willing to make available to the coven as needed," Claudia offered.

Money. She had money.

"I have *many* connections," she continued. "If anyone within the coven dares to step out of line, the priestesses will have every magical resource at their disposal to ensure that person's magic is kept in check."

I already saw where she was going with this, and I didn't like it one bit.

"These resources would be donated to the coven, then?" I asked, already knowing the answer.

Claudia laughed. "Magical resources are not free, my dear. We would of course use taxpayer dollars. That's what the money's there for, after all."

Yeah, and it'd go straight into her bank account. She didn't want to be on the council for noble purposes. All she saw was dollar signs.

"What's your gift?" I asked. "What makes you the strongest Seer, and the best fit?"

Claudia narrowed her eyes. "It is not a woman's *magic* that makes her fit for the council."

"Traditionally, the strongest woman in her Cast serves on the council, correct?" I challenged. "It ensures the coven is protected by the most powerful government. We perform many spells together, and there will be more spells to come as this conflict continues. Right now, there's someone dangerous inside Miriam College, and whatever differences the priestesses may have with one another, I think we all want to catch him."

I shot a glance around the meeting table. Charlotte stared down at her hands, and Lilian stiffened. Margaret held her breath.

They *knew*. These bitches *knew* what that demon had done, and they'd just let him get away with it! Ooh, this was not going to end well for them.

But they didn't know that I knew, and perhaps I could use that to my advantage. I couldn't accuse them of anything just yet. I had to let them keep believing I was ignorant to the demon roaming Octavia Falls.

"So my question is, will your power help us protect the coven?" I asked Claudia.

She opened her mouth to say something, but Lilian stepped in. "Claudia Sinclair is powerful in many ways. I hardly think an interrogation regarding her magic is necessary. She has intense knowledge of magical artifacts and connections with other races that could earn us allies if we encountered an international dispute."

"What about what's happening in our own coven?" I asked calmly. "Shouldn't we start there? Someone killed Professor Perez. Perhaps Mrs. Sinclair can demonstrate how she can help us by joining us in a spell. There must be *something* we can do to identify the killer."

It was a challenge, but the priestesses refused.

"Nadine, please," Margaret said. "We're not here to discuss that at the moment. We're here to vote Claudia onto the council."

I kept my gaze on Claudia as I spoke, watching for her reaction. "And I'm willing to offer my vote if you can show me she's the best choice."

Claudia opened her mouth, but she snapped it shut a second later. "I have nothing to prove to *you*."

I folded my hands in front of myself. I was sick of everyone treating me like I was only here out of convenience. Mother Miriam had accepted me as a priestess. She'd told me I belonged here. And I wasn't going to let anyone tell me differently.

I was a fucking priestess, for Alora's sake. And that meant something to me. I made a promise to protect this coven when I joined the Imperium Council. I would do everything in my power to fulfill that promise.

"With all due respect, Mrs. Sinclair, you *are* here to get my vote," I stated firmly. "So yes, I do believe I'll need more information before committing. What are your qualifications?"

Claudia scoffed. "The council has no requirements for this job position."

"A job position?" I cocked an eyebrow. "This isn't a *job*. This is a life-long commitment to the goddess and the coven."

Hell, we weren't even paid. The other priestesses came from family money or owned businesses in town. I'd had the thought that they'd refused pay because they didn't need the money and it looked noble, but I knew better than to ask.

Claudia drew her chin up. "And what qualifications did you have when you joined the council, Miss Evers?"

She was challenging me, but I wouldn't back down so quickly.

"In a few years, I'll have my degree in Criminal Justice," I told her. "I'm studying Miriamic law. Many priestesses train their whole lives before taking on this position. Do you have a background in coven law and supernatural history, and if not, will you be studying it during your time on the council?"

Claudia shifted in her chair. She was obviously getting really fed up with me. I thought my questions were completely justified.

She pursed her lips. "I have an extensive background in supernatural trade, which I believe will serve you well on the council."

"The other priestesses have been forming diplomatic alliances for years," I pointed out.

Claudia frowned. "It would be a tragedy if you made an enemy out of someone who has so many supernatural allies."

It was a threat if I ever heard one.

"Things around here need to change," Claudia continued.

"Yes. That we can agree on," I said.

"I have many ideas for where to make these changes, in order to ensure a strong and compliant coven," she said confidently, like she'd put a lot of thought into this. "For starters, we must restructure the way the coven spends its tax dollars, so they can be used in the most effective manner. We must eliminate any unnecessary expenses that divert money from important investments. We'll begin at the school, which has proven to be a large expense on taxpayers. I believe the priestesses have already advised the school board to cut unnecessary classes."

I thought of Lydia's Supernatural Religions poster, which the Executors had torn up. They couldn't fool me. They weren't cutting classes to save money. They were getting rid of any classes that taught us to think for ourselves.

"Next, we'll cut the park fund completely and gather volunteers to maintain our park system," Claudia continued, sipping on her wine like she was merely talking about the weather. "And we'll eliminate government-funded health insurance for students—"

"Hold on," I interrupted.

The mere mention of eliminating student health insurance terrified me to the core. Grammy helped pay for one of my health plans, but the insurance I got through the school supplemented it. Without my insurance, I'd never be able to cover my medical bills. We had a health center on campus, and all care was covered for students. If a student needed emergency medical attention at the town's hospital, most of that was covered, too. It was all part of our tuition plan. If the priestesses took away our insurance, most of us couldn't afford to seek medical attention —not for emergencies, or birth control, or anything.

"You can't leave students without health insurance," I insisted.

Claudia lifted her chin. "If students want health care, they should pay for it themselves privately. Surely, the students' parents will cover it. And the scholarship kids can go without. All they really need is an education, anyway."

I couldn't believe she was suggesting this. Lucas's parents would never contribute a penny. Students like him would be helpless. Lucas would no longer be able to afford therapy. His mental health could spiral, and that could put him in real danger. If things got really bad, I couldn't stomach the thought of Lucas going to the emergency room only to be turned away.

"The coven doesn't even cover student insurance," I pointed out. I tried to hide my anger, but my tone turned harsh. "The cost is included in tuition."

"Yes, but the coven owns the college," Claudia reminded me. "We can take that money currently spent on school-sponsored insurance premiums and put it toward more useful things."

"What's useful about letting your people die because they can't afford healthcare?" I growled.

"I think it's a great idea," Lilian cut in. "Claudia is right. People don't appreciate the things they get for free. We should make them work for it. No more handouts."

"But it's not free," I argued. "They're already paying for these things through taxes and tuition—"

"The alternative is to raise taxes, and I daresay the coven will not be pleased with that," Margaret cut in. "We must start thinking about putting more money into our military, to protect the coven in times of war. The young couple that now sits on the throne of the fae monarchy is aggressive. King Elijah and Queen Gabriella are already making threats, and Malovia's military is growing. We need to be prepared if the fae decide to take their fight overseas."

"I agree," Priestess Charlotte said. "We must start this restructuring right away."

They were really going to do this, with or without my say.

"Yes, this is a problem," I said. "But we have to give our coven resources to fight with! We can't fight the fae if our people are sick and we're cutting the classes that are supposed to strengthen their magic."

"I got a full-time job to pay for my tuition and healthcare when I went to Miriam College," Margaret said. "It's not fair that these kids are getting free rides when I had to pay for the same thing out of pocket."

"That was back when you could afford tuition on a full-time job," I pointed out. "Witches and warlocks are *required* to attend Miriam College and learn their magic, yet a full-time job can't cover it—and that's *if* you can get a full-time job between classes, which is impossible scheduling. Instead, we're expected to take out tens of thousands of dollars of loans *from the coven* so the Imperium Council can profit off the interest! Make it make sense. Communities need to take care of their people. If our people's needs aren't met, they can't contribute to the community. You can't just take from people without giving back."

Claudia frowned. "The community doesn't need people who can't contribute."

"But they *can* contribute, if you provide them the resources," I insisted. "If you want your people to learn how to control their magic, give them free public education and make sure their health is taken care of—"

"Nadine, can we stop this already?" Lilian huffed. "You're being unrealistic. Claudia is clearly the best choice to place on the council. She has wonderful ideas. She's well respected, and we need to be thinking long-term. Forget what's happening in the coven right now. What happens five years from now if the fae attack? We will need Claudia on our side."

"Not if the coven tears itself apart first!" I snapped.

"And I'm perfectly well equipped to deal with that matter," Claudia insisted. "How hard can it be to get a few witches and warlocks to obey us?"

I was getting pissed. It was obvious the other priestesses chose her because they knew she'd take their side on whatever issue they wanted to press.

I tried to keep my voice even. "We don't need people to obey us. We need them to trust us and respect us. We need to be there for them. Otherwise, when war *does* break out, you'll have no army."

"We must *command* respect!" Claudia sneered. "What are a few lives in comparison to the masses? Place me on the council, and together, we will develop firm plans to end the Waning and restore our magic in the quickest way possible."

"By sacrificing people at the stake," I growled. She was no different from the other priestesses.

"If it forces people to obey us, then yes!" Claudia cried.

"How do you not realize that the coven's problems are created out of not taking care of our people?" I demanded. "Professor Carlisle turned to crime because he needed better healthcare. Professor Daymond only dealt drugs because he wasn't secure in his retirement. What about the innocents—children and the elderly and the disabled getting caught in the crosshairs? Your method ensures that innocent people will die."

"What does that matter?" Claudia asked. "A few innocent lives are required to end this. If people see that their safety isn't the only thing at stake—but that their family and friends could die as well—who is going to stand up to us? The coven will be at peace again."

"What is peace without freedom?" I demanded. "You're planning to imprison your own people!"

Claudia straightened her shoulders. "It's for their own good."

My teeth ground together. She was repeating the same thing the other priestesses had said. Their methods were sick and twisted… wicked, even. And yet they couldn't see it. They thought *I* was the evil one because I dared to question them.

"Besides, who cares if a few old people die?" Claudia added. "We need healthy, able-bodied people to fight for us. Disabled people don't contribute to society anyway."

My jaw dropped. The *audacity*.

"*I'm* disabled," I told her.

Claudia looked me up and down. "You look perfectly fine to me."

Oh, this bitch did not just go there.

"I think Claudia makes some good points," Charlotte said. "I'd love to have her on the council and hear more of her ideas."

"Agreed," Margaret said.

"Claudia has my vote as well," Lilian added. "Which leaves Nadine. Hector, a drink, please."

The Alchemist at the fireplace nodded. He hadn't said anything this whole time, and I still didn't know what he was doing there. He placed a ladle into the cauldron and scooped the brew into a cup, then brought it over to me. His hands shook, and a few drops spilled onto the table. He didn't say anything before scurrying back to the cauldron.

I eyed the clear liquid curiously. A slight mist billowed out of the cup and hissed. Isa ducked her head under the table. Instinct told me to run far, far away.

"What's this?" I asked.

"This is Hector's own brew," Margaret said. "I wonder if you've met Hector. He works at the school."

Hector wrung his hands together. "At the Cat-fé, priestess," he said kindly, nodding to me.

"He's the head cook at the cat café on campus," Margaret explained. "He's kindly volunteered to help the council with our brews when necessary."

Hector's features paled, and rage flared through my gut. He was scared shitless. There's no way he volunteered for this. They were threatening him with something, though I didn't know what. I knew one thing for certain, though. The priestesses wouldn't have hired him to use the Alchemy Wand unless they couldn't use it themselves. The Wand had rejected Margaret—the Alchemy priestess—so they'd found someone who *could* use it and forced him to work for them.

This was exactly the kind of thing I stood against. My heart broke for Hector. I had to do something to help him.

Margaret gestured to the brew in front of me, which I still hadn't touched. "This is a dangerous potion, Nadine. Slow acting, but effective. We looked the other way the night of your crimes, but any new crimes will get you hurt."

I noticed how she didn't refer to that night as the Burning, like the rest of the coven did. She shifted the blame onto me, never once acknowledging that the other priestesses were responsible for the unthinkable.

"Should you continue to defy us, Hector will place this potion into every item on the café menu," Margaret continued. "Your classmates will die, and it will be *your* fault."

My knees shook under the table, but I wouldn't fall for her fear tactics.

"You're not going to poison them," I stated. "We made a deal when I handed over the Alchemy Wand. I've done nothing wrong, and voting *no* breaks no laws."

"Claudia *will* be on this council!" Margaret snapped, slamming her palm onto the table. Her patience with me had worn thin.

I crossed my arms. "You're right, so what are we even doing here? The council works on a majority-rules system, and I know the three of you have already made your decision. So what do you need my vote for anyway?"

"It's best if we have a unanimous vote," Charlotte said. "We must show the coven that we're united."

"If you don't vote Claudia onto the council, the coven will be notified,"

Lilian added. "Do you really want them to see you as the odd-man-out, Nadine? You want the coven to trust you, yes?"

"I do, which is why I have to choose my integrity," I said. "I want the coven to know that I will not be manipulated, and that I will always make the choice that I believe is best for them."

I shot a glance toward Hector, and I saw the smallest bit of a smile touch his lips before he looked away.

"I vote no," I stated confidently.

Lilian pursed her lips. "Very well. We'll inform the *Miriamic Messenger* of what has happened at tonight's meeting. By next week, everyone will know you voted against us. Meeting adjourned."

She was trying to scare me, but I wasn't frightened. I left the room feeling confident in my decision.

Isa followed me downstairs. My car keys jingled as I pulled them out of my cloak. I kept important things in the pockets, like my keys, medication, and wand, just in case the Waning hit and I couldn't access my magical stash for a few days.

Darkness blanketed the corner of the lot where my car was parked. I was still reeling in anger after what the priestesses had said. I started the car and pulled onto the street...

And my heart immediately stopped.

"Priestess Nadine," someone hissed.

I nearly jumped out of my skin. I slammed on the brakes and instantly formed a battle orb in my hand. But when I looked over at the passenger seat, a woman with kind eyes stared back. She had a mess of curls piled atop her head, and Isa hopped across the middle console to jump onto her lap.

My first reaction was to fight, but a sense of calm washed over me when I looked into her eyes. Instinct told me I was safe, so I closed my fist, and the battle orb disappeared.

"I know you," I said, trying to place her. "You own a shop downtown."

She nodded. "I'm Everly Hall, a Seer with automatic writing powers. I wrote the prophecy you and Lucas share."

The wording of the prophecy played in my mind.

> *By fire and noose*
> *The coven will fall*

Division and suffering
Destruction to all

Great power of the chosen
The coven be made whole
By the only witch of her kind
And a reaper bound to her soul

"Right, but… what are you doing in my car?" I asked.

Isa purred in her lap. Even though it was weird to find her in my car, I was certain she had good intentions.

"I'm sorry to intrude like this, but I had to talk to you in private," she said. "The priestesses don't know I'm here. You must act as if everything is normal."

"Okay. You have my attention." I placed my hands on the wheel and slowly drove down the street.

"I believe what you said about Stella at the Burning is true," she said. "The priestesses made you lie about it in that interview with the paper, didn't they?"

I pressed my lips together. "I'm not allowed to confirm or deny that. What makes you believe me?"

"I was supposed to be on the council next, if I lived long enough to see the Seer position open," she said. "The priestesses called me in for a secret meeting, and we discussed what measures must be taken to facilitate peace among the coven. They wanted to force people to comply, but I disagreed. They rescinded their support for my nomination."

My jaw tightened. "And I suppose if I nominated you, it wouldn't matter, because they'd vote for Claudia anyway."

"Yes," Everly said. "I'm not here to get your nomination, Nadine. I'm here to tell you that I'm on your side. I know what your prophecy says, and I know you are meant to bring the coven together again."

A silence stretched through the car. "Prophecies aren't for certain, though," I said. "Mother Miriam told me you only saw the path I was on, because it was the path I chose. The end result could change. You could get hurt by getting involved. Are you sure you're okay with that?"

Everly held her head high. "I'm the one who relayed the prophecy. I became involved the second the spirits contacted me. Regardless of how things end, I'll be damned if I'm on the wrong side of history. I'm not afraid of what the priestesses might do to me, but I am afraid of what they might do to *you*. The coven needs you to stay alive. You can't fight this alone, Nadine. Let me help. Allow me to be the voice that goes up against them."

"I can't put you in danger like that," I argued.

"We're already in danger. All of us," she said. "The less they target you, the better chance you have of fulfilling your prophecy. I want to do this."

I glanced toward her once more. "How do I know I can trust you?"

"Use your intuition," she encouraged.

I pressed my lips together as I turned down another street. "I'm still trying to figure out my intuition."

"It's simple, though not easy. It takes practice," Everly said kindly.

"You have experience with intuition?" I asked.

"We all have it. It's not unique to the Miriamic Coven."

"Mine is supposed to be quite strong, so I can receive messages from Mother Miriam," I stated. "But I don't think I quite get how to listen to it."

"Intuition always speaks calmly," Everly said. "If you feel fear behind your ideas, that's your ego talking—the human part of your brain that's trying to keep you safe. Intuition speaks from your spirit. It sees no threats, because it knows that your decision to follow it will lead you in the right direction."

"So I just follow whatever feels safe?" I asked.

"No, because sometimes we're afraid of perfectly safe things, due to our limiting beliefs. And sometimes the things inside our comfort zone are not serving us as well as we believe. If you can clear your fears, you will be able to hear your intuition more clearly."

"That's why the priestesses are acting the way they are," I said thoughtfully. "They're afraid of the Waning, and so they can't hear their intuition that might tell them how to fix it."

"Most likely."

"What if your intuition is telling you to do something that *is* unsafe?" I wondered. "Like going up against the priestesses, even if it could get people hurt? Do I still do it, even though my fear is justified?"

"Consider then if the potential outcome is greater than the short-term danger," Everly said. "Not everything your intuition tells you to do will be a safe, sound decision. It won't always be easy. But even when a threat is present, your intuition knows that going through that journey will lead to greater things, and you will come out safe on the other side. Allowing yourself to explore short-term struggles may help you see that the outcome *is* the safer long-term option. Your intuition will always lead you to the places you are meant to be."

I came to a stop sign and looked over at Everly. I felt so at ease in her presence, and I knew with every fiber of my being that I could trust her. I hated the thought of putting anyone else in danger, but Everly was sincerely offering her support. I couldn't turn her down, because without her, we may not win.

"My intuition trusts you," I told her. "I just don't want anyone getting hurt."

"That's a choice I'll make for myself," she said. "You should be proud of what you're doing. I understand it's not easy to be part of a prophecy like this, but I know you have what it takes. You have something the priestesses don't. You have a desire to learn and to do better."

Her words struck me. It seemed natural to want to do better... but maybe it wasn't.

"Thank you, Everly," I said. "And welcome to The Coven's Shield."

I dropped Everly off at her shop, then drove to Grammy's. I had so much information to process. Right now, I just needed a big hug from my grandma.

When I arrived, she sat in the living room, crocheting a blanket. She looked surprised to see me. Cornelius perked up when he spotted Isa at my feet.

"Nadine," Grammy said kindly. "I'm so glad to see you! I was going to wait to show you this, but I guess the cat's out of the bag. What do you think?"

She lifted the afghan she was working on. It was half done and beautiful, with an intricate swirl of purple and teal colors.

"It's lovely, Grammy," I said.

She smiled. "You inspired me with all those tie blankets you make for the nursing home. I wanted to donate one myself."

"They'll love it, Grammy. We... uh, need to talk."

She looked really confused as she set her afghan aside. "Is everything all right?"

I shook my head and sank into the cushion beside her. "Not really. I just had a meeting with the priestesses. They're talking about cutting student health insurance. I know I have a supplemental plan, but that only covers a portion. I don't know how I'm going to pay for dialysis."

"It's okay," Grammy insisted, but she sounded a bit distressed. She hurried over to a stack of bills and found my most recent medical bill. "Let's see. It looks like your private insurance pays for half… this doesn't seem so bad. Three treatments a week… oh, dear."

Her features fell, and my stomach twisted. I knew what dialysis cost, and it was more than the average family made in a year. No way was Grammy making that kind of money.

She must've noticed the hopeless look on my face, because she sat down and wrapped me into a hug. "I'll pay for it, Nadine. Don't worry."

I leaned into her hug, but it didn't ease the pit forming in my stomach. The priestesses were messing with so many people's lives. "Where are you getting the money? I know you don't brew enough potions to cover everything—my tuition, my insurance, my bills. It's too much!"

"We'll figure it out," she promised.

"How? You're not selling the house for me."

She stroked my hair. "We have *some* to get us by for a while. Grampy had a small life insurance policy I invested, and I got some money from selling your parents' house."

"You helped them buy that house. It's your money."

"It's money I always intended to go toward your tuition."

"That's great we can pay for my tuition, but add the dialysis treatments on top of that, and we'll be bankrupt in less than two years. I shouldn't be buying two years of my life with my inheritance."

"There are other government assistance programs outside the coven," Grammy offered.

I shook my head. "Mom and Dad looked into those when I was first diagnosed. They're designed to screw you over, Grammy. And what about all the other people who can't afford their tuition or healthcare? I might have two years left, but other people won't even have *months*."

I gasped as I realized something. "Goddess, the priestesses are hurting people to get to *me*. If I can't afford my healthcare, I can't stand up to them. They're literally going to let my disease kill me. The average wait-time for a kidney is three to five years. Even if I leave the coven, I could be dead before I reach the top of the transplant list!"

The implications of what this meant shook me to my very core. This policy change would affect so many people.

Grammy forced me to look at her. "Listen to me. You must remain well, Nadine, at whatever cost. Right now, you have to focus on saving yourself, because you're not responsible for the world."

"But *I'm* the one the prophecy speaks of. My destiny is to protect the other witches and warlocks out there who aren't as lucky as I am."

"You can't worry about everyone else, not when you're falling apart yourself. What's important is that you *stay alive*, for the coven's sake. If you really want to help them, you'll have to help yourself first. Do you understand?"

Grammy hugged me tightly to her chest, and I closed my eyes as I embraced her. I knew with all my heart that she was right.

That didn't mean I wasn't responsible for everything that was happening out there. I was a priestess. It was my job to stop this.

But I felt I had less power than I ever had before. I might be a priestess, but that didn't mean the rest of the Imperium Council was going to listen to me.

So the only option was to go above their heads, and find something more powerful than they were. Uniting the Oaken Wands was the only way out of this mess.

I prayed the task wouldn't be as hopeless as it felt now.

☾

I HAD to tell my friends what was happening. We planned to meet up at the old *Epitaph* room the following day. I invited Everly to join us.

When I arrived, Talia was alone, singing a beautiful song. The room had completely transformed. All the stacks of old papers had been organized neatly on the shelves, and the dust had been cleaned up. Talia stood on the counter, draping purple and teal curtains around the room. The drapes framed a huge map of Octavia Falls that she'd tacked to the wall. Above the meeting table hung a pretty black chandelier. It looked like Talia had made it from craft supplies by herself. Small witch lights hovered like flames around the chandelier and lit up the room. It was gorgeous.

Talia stopped singing when I entered. "Oh, shoot. I've run out of time."

"No, it's okay," I assured her. "I'm a bit early anyway. I love what you've done with the place."

Isa jumped onto the table, where Gus was lounging. She walked over and started licking his ears.

Talia shrugged and hopped off the counter. "I thought the Gravestone could use some sprucing up, if we're going to spend a lot of time here."

"The Gravestone?" I asked.

"Grant and I came up with it," she said. "We thought our meeting place should have a code name, and this is where we write *The Epitaph*, so…"

"So you write it on a gravestone." I chuckled. "Clever. I like it."

Talia reached into a box she'd brought along and fiddled with a few items before setting them back inside. "I just… wish we were meeting under better circumstances."

"I agree." I picked up a small round music box and flipped the top open, but no music came out. It was really pretty, with a gorgeous rose design carved into the metal. "What's all this?"

"It's just some of my antiques. I thought I'd decorate the room with them, but I don't know where to put them."

"Is this new?" I asked, handing her the music box. "I don't recognize it."

"No, I just haven't found a place for it. I've had it since last Halloween. Grant bought it for me."

"That's sweet," I said. "You guys make a great couple. I'm glad you're together."

She blushed. "Thanks. I'm glad you and Lucas worked things out, too."

The door opened, and Lucas stepped inside. "Did I just hear my name?"

"We were just gossiping," I teased. I wrapped an arm around his waist and placed a kiss on his lips. My heart fluttered.

"Don't let me interrupt," he joked. "But everyone else is on their way."

"Including Everly," I said. I'd already told them about what happened last night. They agreed that we could trust her, and that we needed her on our side.

"Do you think anyone else will show up?" Talia asked.

Lucas sighed. "I hope so."

Lucas had written an article for his new publication containing a secret message. We'd dropped stacks of the printing all around school, and I'd seen people with copies all week. The secret message told anyone who was willing to fight with us to meet us here today. I really hoped a few people had deciphered it. We needed more people on our side.

It wasn't long before our friends arrived. Chloe and Mandy sat across from each other, and Miles lounged on the counter. All the cats had gathered on the table, licking their paws and grooming each other. Grant arrived last.

I checked the time. A light knock came at the door then, and I opened it. Everly stood there, wearing a kind smile on her face.

"It looks like I found the right place," she said.

I opened the door wider. "Yes, it's a bit crowded, but come on in."

Everly entered the room, and her gaze traveled over our group. She nodded to each person in turn. "Hello, how are you?"

Chloe sat up straighter in her chair. "Look, we agreed to have you here, but before we get into any details, I'd like to know something first."

"Anything," Everly offered. "I have nothing to hide."

"Why do you want to help us?" Chloe asked.

Everly took a deep breath, carefully considering her answer. "Because the priestesses intend to break the coven. I wish to heal it."

Chloe eyed her longer. "She should take the witch's vow. The same one we did."

"If that will make you trust me, then I'll do it," Everly agreed.

Grant got to work on the brew, and Everly took the same vow we had.

Mandy glanced around the room. "I don't know if anyone else is coming. Should we cast our ward now?"

"Let's give it a few minutes," Grant suggested. "*Someone* must've deciphered Lucas's clues."

Lucas frowned. "I don't know, guys. It was a good idea, but maybe we were too subtle about it."

Grant sighed. "It looks like this is all we have, then. Let's cast the ward and get to work."

The ward Mandy had found was pretty straight-forward, but with all five Casts together, we were certain it would hold. We all joined hands and spoke an incantation. Magic shimmered throughout the room, before settling into the walls.

Once we cast the ward, I cleared my throat and stepped forward. "As you all know by now, Everly has offered to be the face of The Coven's Shield. No one decoded our secret message, so we need to be more aggressive about getting our message out there. We need people to see that we can challenge the priestesses and change what they're doing. The system is made by people, and it can be changed by people. Everly can help with that."

"What are your ideas?" Chloe asked.

"We have to be loud enough that people hear our voice, but not so loud that the priestesses strike us down right away," Everly said. "I host weekly Seer classes at my shop. I teach crafting to help Seers hone their powers through art. I know most of my students will join us. The *Miriamic Messenger* is writing a feature about the classes this month. I can use that platform to voice opinions that oppose the priestesses."

"But the *Miriamic Messenger* only prints Imperium propaganda," Grant complained. "They've already branded the coven's divide as the Miriamic Conflict."

"Then we'll be subtle, until it's time to make noise," Everly said. "My classes teach that improving your own magic makes the community stronger. When it comes to magic, one plus one does not equal two. Put two witches together, and their magic is more powerful than two witches on their own. I can speak on this concept all day. My students will side with us."

Lucas nodded. "This is a good place to start. Has anyone else made progress?"

Talia shook her head. "Chloe and I were both denied internships with Professor Richards. We might be able to get into the archives room ourselves, but there's a wait list."

Mandy raised her hand. "Grant and I found a few mentions of demons in old newspapers. The most recent one that involved killings was eighty years ago, during the Great Supernatural War. A group of college students summoned a demon thinking he might be able to help the coven during the war, but he slaughtered them all. He killed a few others before the priestesses vanquished him."

"Do you think it's the same guy?" I asked.

Mandy looked uncertain. "Based on the news reports, this demon killed people himself. It's different from what Lucas said happened to Professor Perez. But maybe he learned from the past and changed up his tactics."

"Keep looking into it," I suggested. "See if you can find out how the priestesses got rid of him."

Mandy nodded firmly.

"How's it going with the Executors, Miles?" Lucas asked.

"Grant and I staged a fight, like we talked about," he said.

Grant rubbed his neck. "Yeah, one hell of a fight. You didn't have to go that hard, you know."

Miles shrugged. "I had to sell it. The recruiters bought it. I'm in, but I haven't started my training yet. I'll let you know if I get anything—"

He cut off when a high-pitched squeal filled the room. Magic began flashing across the walls, pulsing red.

I shot out of my chair. "What is that?"

Mandy shot a nervous glance around the room. "Someone's trying to get through our ward!"

"How's that possible?" Lucas demanded.

"I don't know," Mandy said. "The spell was iron-clad."

Lucas formed a battle orb in his hand and swung the door open. I rushed behind him. We were prepared to defend ourselves. I reached the end of the hall and turned the corner. When we stepped outside of the ward, the alarm stopped. In fact, the whole hallway seemed to vanish. Behind us appeared a solid wall. I'd never guess there was something hidden there at all. Isa batted at the wall, and her paw went through it.

Our friends followed us, and it looked like they were ghosts walking through the wall. We looked up and down the hall but saw no one.

"This ward is strong," Mandy insisted. "It only lets our allies through. If anyone else finds our entrance, it should feel like a solid wall. I don't know why the alarm is going off."

"We should figure it out before we continue," I stated. "We don't want to take any unnecessary risks."

Lucas nodded in agreement. "In the meantime, we should go back to our dorm rooms."

"I need to check a few books in the library," Mandy said. "It might just be a flaw in the spell."

"Let me know if you need anything," Everly offered.

Everyone quickly dispersed, but Lucas and I turned back toward the ward.

"Mandy did a good job," I said. "I don't get it."

"I can't even tell the ward's there," Lucas agreed.

"But I can," a woman said. She stepped around a corner, and a fat black cat waddled beside her. I went rigid as Headmistress Verla approached us. "Your ward is good, but mine is stronger. I was notified the moment you cast your ward, and I overheard everything."

"Headmistress…" I started.

She held her hand up to stop me. "I understand what you're doing here, Nadine… and I want to help. The priestesses have taken more from me than you'll ever know."

She kept an even tone, but I saw the pain behind her eyes. "They hung my sister, and they provided me with no support when my son died. I'd sooner die than let this injustice continue. No one deserves a death like Nicole's."

Her sister's name sent chills down my spine. I quickly gathered my composure. "This means a lot, Headmistress, and we'd love to have your help. There's a lot to catch you up on."

"Then by all means, let's get started," she suggested.

"We should talk in private," Lucas said, gesturing her through our ward.

The three of us stepped into the hall with our cats, where we couldn't be overheard. Isa huddled next to Oliver. Verla passed through the ward easily, accepting her as a member of The Coven's Shield. The alarm had stopped going off, now that Verla wasn't trying to break through it.

"There's a demon inside the school," I started, and the confessions spilled out from there. Lucas and I told Verla everything. By the time we finished, she had her finger to her chin.

"I knew something was off about Professor Leto when we hired him, though I didn't know how to prove it," she said. "Why didn't you tell me any of this before?"

"I thought you'd stop us," I admitted. "This is all so dangerous, and I thought you'd want me to stay out of danger because you care too much."

"I do care about you, Nadine," she insisted. "Far more than any headmistress has the right to care about her students. But doing nothing would be dangerous, too. You're a priestess, and you're doing the right thing."

"I want to do right by the coven," I said. "Do you know anything about demon spells and how to stop him?"

"There are so many ways demons manipulate contracts," Verla said. "Without knowing the terms of his contracts, we can't know how the spell works or how to break it. There may be a way I can help against the priestesses, though. If I can brew a potion to take away their magic, they'd lose their power and be forced to step down. If they're left vulnerable, they could be persuaded to break their contract with the demon."

"I've never heard of a potion like that," Lucas said. "Is it even possible?"

"We never thought the Waning was possible until now," Verla pointed out. "If the Waning is possible, so is this. I believe Nadine and I could brew such a potion if we combine our powers. Her Curse Breaker powers could take theirs away."

I didn't like this.

"Whether it's possible isn't the question," I argued. "We could be caught, and by Miriamic law, we'd suffer far greater than a hanging."

"I'm well versed in Miriamic law," Verla said. "I have a law degree myself. However, we're in the perfect position to blame it on the Waning."

"And still, we're stooping to the priestesses' level," I replied. "If we're controlling who has magic and who doesn't, we're no better than them."

"This is war, Nadine," Verla pressed. "I hope you're prepared to have your morals challenged, or you will not win."

I shook my head. That couldn't be the only answer. "I believe we can win in our own way. I won't become like the other priestesses."

Verla sighed. "If that's the way you want to do it, I can't force you to brew this potion. But think about your decision carefully. I know you don't wish for people to die, and we may have to make tough decisions to prevent that."

"We'll find another way." I had to believe that.

"I will be on your side for all of it, but choose wisely," Verla said. "Because if this demon is allowed to run rampant, there's no telling who will be alive by the end of it."

FIVE

Verla could prove useful to The Coven's Shield, but not until we all got on the same page. Nadine didn't want to become like the priestesses. I didn't, either. Verla seemed to think we had to in order to defeat them. We'd talked about making tough decisions, and this was going to be one of the hardest of all. Stick to our morals, or defy them for the greater good? Those couldn't be our only two options.

My stomach churned as I sat in the back of my Advanced Mortana Magic class on Monday, trying not to hurl. Professor Leto projected gruesome pictures onto a screen at the front of the room and lectured on how necromancers could use various body parts as weapons. He described using intestines as ropes to strangle enemies, as well as other gruesome descriptions. He believed that the more death you saw on the battlefield, the stronger you were. He had a real fascination with reanimating the dead. I didn't think he could do it himself, but he sure found joy in necromancy.

It wasn't the photos that bothered me, though. It was *him*. It made me sick knowing there was a murderous demon roaming these halls, and there wasn't a damn thing I could do to stop him.

Even with Verla on our side, he was untouchable. She couldn't fire him, not when the rest of the school board had a say. And most of them had their heads so far up the priestesses' asses that they couldn't see daylight. He wasn't going anywhere.

We hadn't figured out how he'd been vanquished in the past, either, so that wasn't helpful.

I studied him carefully as he paced in front of the room. He was arrogant, but he moved in a calculated manner. He chose his words carefully, though he sometimes slipped up and said things like *your coven*. No one else seemed to notice he didn't belong here, though.

Professor Leto excused the class. I hurried toward the door, but I was one of the last to leave.

"Lucas," Professor Leto called before I could make a break for it.

My blood ran cold, but I composed myself before turning to him. "Yes, Professor?"

He folded his hands and waited patiently before the other students left the room. Oliver's fur stood on end, and the door remained open. At least I had a quick escape if I needed it.

"What did you think of my lecture?" he asked. "Interesting, yes?"

"Sure, if you're a necromancer," I said. I didn't know why he cared about my opinion. It wasn't like he needed validation from me. His ego was bigger than Octavia Falls.

"Ah, but you're no necromancer," he said calmly. "I saw the way you watched me during class. You seemed… engrossed in the lecture."

He was goading me, like he wanted me to admit to something, though I didn't know what.

"Perhaps you could lecture on reaper powers in the future," I suggested coolly. "Seeing as you seem to know more about my magic than I do."

He'd known I could read energy signatures before I did. I wondered what else he knew.

Professor Leto took a step forward. He wore a cunning smirk and eyed me up and down. "What a pleasure that would be. There's *so* much you don't know. But perhaps I'll keep these things to myself. After all, what use would my secrets be if my enemies knew them as well?"

"Enemies?" I cocked an eyebrow, and sarcasm dripped from my tone. "I thought we were just becoming friends."

Leto scoffed. "We could be, but I know what you think of me."

He began to circle me. He was so close now; we were nearly touching. But I didn't flinch. I was more pissed than anything.

"I see your hesitation each time you enter my class," he taunted. "I smell your fear whenever I approach. I sense your longing to scream."

"You killed Professor Perez," I snapped.

Most people would act shocked by such an accusation, but Professor Leto stopped in front of me and chuckled. "Prove it."

I narrowed my eyes. "I don't know how you did it, but I know you've done it before, and you'll do it again. Why are you here?"

"Isn't it obvious?"

"I meant at the school," I growled. "Whatever the priestesses promised you is nothing more than empty promises."

He laughed. "You have no idea what you're talking about. Are you suggesting I change my loyalty and make a deal with *you*?"

I almost snorted. "Like I'd ever be so stupid. I'm warning you to leave. You won't kill anyone else before I'm done with you."

He smiled, like this was nothing more than a friendly chat. "I like your confidence."

I shrugged. "Confidence is easy when you know you're going to win."

I couldn't say that for sure, but it sure as hell felt good to say out loud.

Leto eyed me up and down. "Then tell me, Lucas. How will you win? How exactly are you going to stop me?"

"What use would my secrets be if my enemies knew them as well?" I repeated his words back to him.

He was practically grinning now, clearly amused. "As far as enemies go, I like you, Lucas. Perhaps under different circumstances, we could be allies. You say you're not stupid enough to make a deal with me, but you're clearly stupid enough to make an enemy out of me."

The smile quickly fell from his face. His expressionless features gave me the chills.

"I'd watch my back if I were you," he said, before returning to his desk.

I knew it was my cue to leave, and I backed out of the room slowly. Oliver followed, never taking his eyes off Professor Leto. It wasn't until I was out of the room that I finally turned and bolted down the hall. I glanced behind myself when I turned the corner, but the hall was empty. I relaxed and slowed my step.

I found Nadine waiting for me in the Main Foyer. Her eyes lit up when she saw me.

"Ready for lunch?" I asked as I took her hand. Her touch helped me forget about Leto. Goddess knew I didn't need to be worrying about him, not unless there was something I could do about it.

Nadine glanced toward the cafeteria. "Actually, I had a better idea. Want to go to the Cat-fé?"

"Always," I told her.

Nadine kept her voice low as we headed across campus. When we arrived at the Cat-fé, it was almost empty, which was odd for this time of day. Darcy and Onyx sat at a table near the window. It sounded like they were discussing their Alchemy classes, but they were the only people here.

Even the cats seemed to notice the tense atmosphere. Most of the cats lounged, rather than playing with the toys in the corner. Isa and Oliver kept close to our side.

Nadine and I approached the counter. Kenna Farlane—a Seer from my Intercast Magic class—stood behind the counter, arranging fresh cupcakes in one of the displays. She stopped when we approached, and she wiped her hands on her apron.

"Lucas, Nadine," she greeted kindly. "How can I help you?"

Nadine looked around the café. "Is everything... all right here?"

Kenna dropped her gaze. "People hardly come in anymore. It's too small and gets easily crowded. They don't want to be by the other Casts."

Nadine's jaw dropped. "That's ridiculous! I'd face the other Casts any day for your famous cupcakes."

Kenna giggled. "In that case, have one on the house."

She pulled two cupcakes from the display and slid them across the counter. One had multi-colored frosting with star sprinkles, and the other was made to look like a cat. They looked too beautiful to eat.

"Thanks, Kenna," I said. "But at least let us tip you."

"It's fine, really," she insisted. "I just want to know what you think."

Nadine picked up the one with the stars. She took a bite, and her shoulders sagged in delight. "Oh, my goddess! They're amazing."

"You think?" Kenna sounded excited. "I'm trying to get better by April."

"That's right! You have that baking competition in Paris coming up." I remembered she'd mentioned it in my Intercast Magic class last semester.

She nodded. "I know it's months away, but I'm really excited."

Nadine swallowed another bite of cupcake. "You'll win for sure."

Kenna pushed her hair behind her ear. "Thanks. Is there anything else I can get you?"

"Actually, we're looking for Hector," Nadine said.

"He's in the middle of a batch of croissants, but you can go to the kitchen. I'm sure he wouldn't mind," Kenna offered.

I finished off my cupcake, then headed to the kitchen with Nadine. Hector looked up from his dough when we entered, and he instantly stiffened.

"Priestess," he said, his hands trembling.

"It's okay," Nadine assured him kindly. "I'm not here for the Imperium Council. I'm here to help you."

Hector's bottom lip quivered, and he broke down into sobs. "I don't know what to do anymore, Priestess."

I hurried to his side and placed a comforting hand on his back. "We're going to get you the help you need. Why don't you tell us what's going on?"

Hector shook, and I guided him over to a stool. He sat and drew a deep breath. "I can't say. I'm sworn to secrecy."

"It's okay," Nadine encouraged. "You can tell us."

"No, you don't understand," he pressed. "I'm *sworn* to secrecy."

"Magically?" I asked.

He nodded.

Nadine looked thoughtful. "You're sworn to keep this secret with the priestesses, right?"

He nodded again.

"Well, I'm a priestess," Nadine pointed out. "Maybe the spell will allow you to talk to me."

Hector's eyebrows furrowed, like he hadn't thought of that. He spoke slowly, as if testing out the theory. "They're... threatening my wife."

His shoulders relaxed when he managed to get the words out. Relief flooded his features, and the confession spilled out of him. "The priestesses came to me, claiming to have a job they wanted me to apply for. I thought it was something at one of the restaurants in town. They gave me that wand, and it worked for me, but I don't think it worked for others."

"What makes you say that?" I asked. It sounded like there was more to the story.

"I heard them mention Magnus Knight," he said. "He was their first choice for this job, but for some reason, it didn't work out."

Magnus had been working with Stella on nightshade production. It made sense the priestesses had gone to him first. They already knew how morally corrupt he was and that he'd help for the right price. But if the Wand didn't choose him, they couldn't use him.

Nadine pressed her lips together. "They haven't convicted him, which means they're still using him. If not for the Alchemy Wand, then they're keeping him around because they think he'll be useful in some other way. Hector, do you know anything about the wand they're making you use?"

He shook his head, and I saw the honesty in his eyes. "It's special, that much I can tell. The magic I feel when I use it is… unmatched."

"Have you ever heard of the Oaken Wands?" I asked him.

"They're real, aren't they?"

I nodded. "The priestesses need you to use the Wand, because they can't use it themselves."

"I don't want to use it," he pleaded. "Please, help me."

"We intend to," Nadine stated. "What are the priestesses making you do?"

"Brewing poison," Hector admitted. "But it's different than anything I've ever encountered. The poison can kill, but it's more than that. I haven't figured out the details. The priestesses give me instructions, and I follow them. If I don't, they'll hang my wife. And I know I shouldn't do it… but I just love her so much."

Hector began to sob again.

"It's not your fault," I assured him.

"Th-they haven't used the poisons yet, but I'm afraid they will," Hector said. "And when that happens, the blood will be on my hands."

"You're innocent," Nadine stated. "We won't let the priestesses get away with this."

"But how are you going to get me out of this? I can't run. They'll find me." Hector gasped, like he'd come up with a great idea. "I know! I can be a spy. I can alert you if the priestesses order me to use the poison."

"That puts you in grave danger," Nadine said.

Hector stood and curled his hands into fists, like he'd already made up his mind. "They've already threatened my family. I may be bound to secrecy, but I will not let them use me as a puppet."

"Are you sure about this?" I asked him.

He nodded firmly. "If I flee now, they will find another person to use their Wand. The least I can do is help. I'll figure out what the poison does and how they plan to use it, and I'll report back to you."

"It looks like we just found another member of The Coven's Shield," Nadine said. "We'll get you out as soon as we can."

Hector reached out to shake Nadine's hand. "It is your courage that inspired me, Priestess. The way you stood up to the others was honorable. You were right, and the Casts must work together. If anyone can save the coven, it's you, Priestess Nadine."

☾

I FELT ACCOMPLISHED once we'd left the Cat-fé after talking to Hector. I wouldn't admit it, but I was skeptical when we'd formed The Coven's Shield. I hadn't been sure how we would get people on our side. Part of me wished to take the easy way out—to slay the priestesses and bring an end to this conflict.

But I knew that would only break the coven further. Our efforts meant nothing without the coven's support.

The priestesses deserved to pay for what they'd done… but we had to be patient. The coven was in a fragile position right now, and one wrong move could tear us apart.

But we were making progress. Already, three new people had joined our cause. That gave me hope.

Nadine had class later that day, so we parted ways. I was on my way back to my room when someone called my name. I turned to see Professor Warren flagging me down.

Great. I was still a bit sour about our last meeting.

Oliver eyed him skeptically, and I cleared my throat. "Professor?"

"Lucas, I'm glad I found you. I have some… advising topics to go over. Do you have some time?"

"Not really," I lied. I didn't want to talk about my classes right now. I had other things to work on.

"It will only be a minute," Professor Warren pressed. "I'd like to talk about the… essay you wrote."

He shot a glance up and down the hall, but no one paid us any attention. While he was looking around, he conjured a paper and curled it in his hands. I caught sight of big letters spelling out *The Shield* scrawled on the front. It was the fake newspaper I'd created, the one with our coded message.

I forced my pulse to settle, as to not give anything away. "I, uh, suppose I have time."

Professor Warren subconjured the paper. "Come with me."

He led me to his office and closed the door behind me, then slapped his copy of *The Shield* onto his desk.

"You could've told me," he stated. He wasn't really *upset*, but he didn't sound happy, either.

I sank into the chair beside me. "Told you what, exactly? You didn't believe me last time. Why should you believe me now?"

Professor Warren dropped his gaze. He kept his eyes on Oliver, but I could see the regret in his features. After a few moments, he straightened his suit coat and sat behind his desk.

"I'm very sorry about that," he admitted. "I should've listened closer. I'm willing to keep an open mind. Do you care to explain what's going on?"

I eyed the newspaper on his desk. "Why don't you tell me first?"

Professor Warren picked up the paper and turned it toward me. He'd scribbled all over it, and various words had been circled and connected together. "I deciphered your clues. You're forming a secret society to go up against the priestesses, aren't you?"

I chewed the inside of my cheek. He'd really broken my trust that day in the bathroom, after Professor Perez's murder. I wasn't sure how much to reveal to him.

"What makes you think I wrote that?" I asked.

Professor Warren frowned. "I've read enough of your essays to know your writing style. You're a very good writer."

"Well, I am a journalism major," I stated bluntly.

"And I'm glad you've decided to keep writing. Don't worry. Your secret's safe with me. I meant it when I said I was sorry."

He waited for my response, but I wasn't sure what to say.

He drew a deep breath. "I may not know for certain that Professor Leto is a demon, as you mentioned in the bathroom, but I'm willing to accept the idea… and I want to join you."

It took me a moment to digest his words. "Really?"

He nodded. "Yes. You were right. I was scared, and I was unwilling to accept the truth. I don't believe a thing they've written about you in the *Miriamic Messenger*. We have to fight this."

Professor Warren would never know how relieving it was to hear him say that. He'd been like a father to me since my Freshman year of college, and Verla had been a bit like a mother to Nadine after her own mom died. Having both of them on our side felt crucial. It was like The Coven's Shield wasn't complete without them.

"That means a lot to hear, Professor," I said. "I accept your apology."

"I'm here to help in any way I can," he offered.

"Then perhaps you can help us understand what we're up against," I suggested. "Do you know anything about demons?"

"A bit, though Professor Daniels was the expert on demons."

And she was dead. Stella had framed her for murder, and the priestesses had hanged her.

"I know there are many different types, and that their powers differ," Professor Warren said.

"We know Professor Leto is a Nex demon," I told him. "How strong does that make him?"

"From my understanding, that would make him a lower form of demon," Warren explained. "Unless he came across some other power source, he wouldn't be able to access the full extent of demon abilities. He wouldn't possess the ability to control spirits or compel a person like more powerful demons could, for example. He *might* have some level of torture magic and teleportation, but his powers would still be limited by his classification."

"What do you know about demon contracts?" I questioned.

"Demon contracts are tricky, and that's why the coven no longer works with them," Professor Warren explained. "To enter a demon contract, you must be a willing participant, but that doesn't always mean what we think it means. To a demon, it may simply mean taking an action that *he* interprets as consent."

"With the right wording, you can be tricked into a contract?" I asked.

"Yes. They use similar tricks as the fae."

"So all he'd have to do is ask someone if they ever thought of death, and if they said yes, he'd interpret that to mean they want to die? Contract made. You're marked for death."

"That's my understanding," Warren said.

"How would he handle that with the priestesses? They summoned him, so they had every intent of singing a contract."

"When a witch summons a demon, they're the one in control for the time being," Warren explained. "They have the power to send the demon back to the Abyss until a contract is signed. I'm certain the priestesses did whatever they could to word the contract in their favor. The demon would be willing to sign it in order to bind himself on Earth. It makes banishment next to impossible, unless the contract is broken. Even then, banishing him would require a strong enough spell."

"How do you break a demon contract?" I asked.

"Demon contracts are all about consent," Warren said. "To break a contract that the priestesses made, one of them would have to withdraw their consent. That *must* be followed up with spellwork to banish him. Otherwise, he will enact revenge. The spellwork becomes more complicated the stronger a demon becomes. Most witches die before they're able to complete the banishment spell, because they've broken the contract that was protecting them from the demon in the first place."

I sighed. "The priestesses won't break the contract."

"Remember that demons have twisted ways of establishing consent, though," Warren said.

"So we could trick the priestesses into breaking it?" I wondered. "Or we could trick the *demon*."

"It's possible, but you'd need to know the original terms of the contract."

"There's no way to get our hands on that, though." I contemplated it all for a moment. "What about his victims? Can they withdraw their consent to die?"

"That *should* be the case, but they may not entirely know what they're consenting to."

"Could you look into this deeper, Professor?" I asked. "There's got to be a way to banish him."

"I'll see what I can find," Warren said. "In the meantime, there's something else I wanted to discuss."

He drew a stack of papers out of a drawer and handed them to me. I furrowed my brow as I scanned the front page. It was an application of some sort.

"What's this?" I asked.

"It's a paid internship," he explained. "I'm looking for a student teacher to help with my Freshman-level Mortana classes. The position usually goes to seniors, but the student I hired this year quit already."

I set the papers back on his desk. "I'm not really qualified… am I?"

"You've taken the Freshman-level classes," he pointed out. "I simply need help with grading and occasional tutoring. I know your journalism professor is prejudiced toward our Cast, and he won't approve you for a journalism internship. You deserve this opportunity. Besides, it will give us a chance to work closer together."

I was touched that he wanted me to work with him.

"Thank you, Professor."

Despite the tension between Professor Warren and me, I was excited to have him on our side, and I was ready to get started on my internship right away. I told Nadine about his offer on our way to class the next day. Oliver and Isa had stayed behind in our rooms.

"That's great!" Nadine said. "I'm really happy for you."

"Thanks," I replied. "I think it'll be good. I'll be out there interacting with other students. Maybe I can use this position to recruit people."

"That would be really helpful," Nadine agreed.

"Plus, I qualify for a car loan now," I said proudly. I'd never owned a car before. "It's not much, but I found an old beater at the used lot downtown. I'm picking her up after class."

"Lucas, that's great! I'm really happy for you," Nadine said as we entered the classroom.

Our Astral Travel class took place in one of the meditation rooms. We sat on yoga mats while we listened to Professor Poppy's lecture. She was an older Seer, and it sounded like she had a lot of experience on the astral plane.

We were a week into school, and Professor Poppy had mostly covered astral travel theory. The astral plane was a level of existence that all witches could access through their spirit, but it was difficult to master. It involved separating your spirit from your body and entering a plane of existence populated by ghosts and other spiritual beings.

It could be dangerous, too. You never quite knew what types of spirits you might encounter there, or what might happen to your body while your spirit was away. It left you vulnerable, and enemies could attack your body while your spirit was away. Such an attack could trap you on the astral plane, because your spirit was still living without the ability to return to its body. An astral traveling soul was different than a ghost—a visitor to the astral plane, rather than a resident. A living person had to return to their own body eventually. Professor Poppy cautioned us greatly, but also encouraged us to not be afraid.

"We can use astral projection in many positive ways," Professor Poppy had said. "Seers often use it to communicate more clearly with ghosts. When witches are separated, they can connect on the astral plane and communicate across distances. Through meditation, you can travel the world and escape to places that your spirit finds healing. It is truly a spiritual journey unique to each of us."

I personally wanted to use it to spy on Leto. We couldn't use it on the priestess, not with the wards around their headquarters. And they couldn't come here, either. Professor Poppy said you can only astral travel onto school grounds if you're already inside the school. It's to keep students safe while we practice our powers.

"Today, you will be attempting astral traveling for the first time," Professor Poppy announced. "Most of you will not get it on your first try, and that's okay. Though there are many ghosts around the school, it's unlikely that you'll encounter any on the astral plane, unless you are a Seer yourself. Ghosts will only show up if they want to communicate with you, and most are too confused to know the difference. However, should you encounter another spirit on the astral plane, you need not be afraid. Simply let them be, set the intent to return to your own plane, and your spirit will be reunited with your body. Let's begin with a meditation to cast our protection spell, in order to protect our mind, body, and spirit while on the astral plane."

Nadine and I adjusted our pillows and lay down on our yoga mats. She looked over at me and winked.

"Last one to the astral plane owes the other dinner," she teased.

I smirked. "Only if you're the one on the menu."

She giggled, then glanced around to make sure no one heard. "You're on."

She took my hand, and I relaxed deeper into the mat. At the front of the room, Professor Poppy guided us into meditation. I imagined my magic like a ball of light, and I sent it out around myself, cocooning my body in a protective shield. It was unlike the shields I'd made before, meant to project defensive magic. This one permeated inward, protecting my spirit from malevolent beings.

The meditation continued, until I hovered on the edge of sleep. I let myself fall deep into the meditation, until I was unaware of how much time had passed. I felt something tugging at the corners of my mind, and a weightless sensation suddenly overcame me. My whole body buzzed with a new sensation, like I could feel the energy of the room around me. My eyes shot open, and I glanced around the room... only to see two versions of Nadine next to me.

They weren't the same, though. One version looked solid as she lay beside me with her eyes closed. Her chest rose and fell slowly. The other sat cross-legged beside her body and appeared as an ethereal being floating several inches off the ground. She had all Nadine's familiar features, but her skin glowed with a rainbow of colors. As I sat up, the world seemed to move around me differently, like the colors didn't quite move as quickly as the shapes. I waved my hand in front of me—my spirit hand, because my real hand was still holding Nadine's from where I lay on the mat. I could see straight through my hand. It was so surreal.

"I guess that means I owe you... dinner?" I teased.

Nadine beamed. "I was wondering when you'd show up."

"That was easier than I thought it'd be," I remarked.

"I was trying to pull you onto the astral plane with me," Nadine said. "I guess it must've worked."

I recalled the tugging at the corners of my mind. "I think I felt that. But why was it so easy for you?"

She shrugged. "I'm a priestess, and my intuition is supposed to be growing. Maybe astral travel comes along with that."

I looked around the room, but I didn't see any other spirits. At the front of the room, Professor Poppy continued her guided meditation, but she didn't look at Nadine or me. It was like we weren't even there.

"Let's see what we can do." I took Nadine's hand in mine. Her spirit felt solid, even though we couldn't touch anything else. Professor Poppy had encouraged us to explore the school if we managed to astral travel. Our feet floated off the ground, and we didn't have to move our legs as we hovered across the room. The sensations in my body shifted as we moved. It was a little disorienting, like I was drunk or high.

"Everything feels weird here," I remarked.

"I feel it, too," Nadine said. "It's like a buzzing inside of me, a lot like my Curse Breaker powers. Every time we pass someone, it gets stronger. I think we're feeling their energy."

That made sense. Professor Poppy said things would feel different on the astral plane.

I led Nadine to the closed door and paused. "You ready?"

She looked eager to test it out. "I'm ready."

I floated forward, but the solid wall felt like nothing but air. We entered the hallway, and it was like stepping into a brand-new world. The school we saw wasn't quite our own. All the furniture and artwork on the walls were in the right spots, but there were things that weren't there before. Translucent vines grew up the walls, like the plants themselves were made of spirit. Cats made of rainbow colors chased each other down the hall. Witch lights hovered everywhere, twinkling above us. I reached upward to touch one, and it buzzed away from me. I realized it wasn't a witch light at all, but a spiritual being. They were like Fortune Fairies that existed only on the spiritual plane. It was like a whole world stacked on top of our own.

Nadine spun around, taking in all the magical colors. She stopped, and I followed her gaze to see a ghost hovering nearby. It was an old man, probably a professor who had died ages ago. "We should talk to him," Nadine suggested. "He might've overheard something about the demon or the Wands."

"Excuse me, sir?" I asked.

The man didn't even look at us. I took Nadine's hand, and we floated toward him.

"Sir? We'd like to talk to you," Nadine said gently.

The man noticed us, but he got a terrified look on his face and spat, "You shouldn't be here!" A cat at his feet hissed and went pouncing behind him, until they both disappeared through the wall.

Nadine frowned. "Ghosts don't want to talk to us, I guess. We're live spirits invading their space."

"They're probably more comfortable with Seers," I agreed. "I'm sure it's not often they see astral travelers."

"Where did I put it?" someone mumbled. Nadine and I turned to see Professor Wykoff walking down the hall. She carried a big stack of papers and flipped through them. "Ah, there it is. Can't lose my article. I spent all night on it."

She kept walking and didn't see us standing there. I didn't move, because I wanted to see what would happen. Professor Wykoff walked straight through me, and she didn't notice a thing. She didn't feel solid, but I felt a strange energy when we touched. My form glowed brighter.

I flipped my hands around, watching the colors sparkle. "I think I just stole some of her energy."

"That makes sense," Nadine said. "If ghosts can harness energy, then so can our spirits."

I eyed the light switch nearby thoughtfully. "Ghosts can also manipulate electricity and make lights flicker. Maybe…"

I put my hand to the wall, and it went straight through. I couldn't feel the wires, but I felt a tingle of energy ripple up and down my form. The lights overhead dimmed, then flickered a few times.

Professor Wykoff squealed, nearly dropping all her papers. "I welcome only friendly spirits into my space. If you wish me harm, be gone!"

She took a deep breath, then continued on her way.

"We can scare people. That's a perk," I teased.

"Yes, but the real question is, how fast can we fly? Race you!" Nadine's spirit went flying down the hall so fast she was practically a blur.

I set the intention to chase after her, and my spirit took off in flight. A thrill traveled through me as I flew down the hall after her.

"Not fair!" I called.

Nadine's laughter rang down the hall with an ethereal echo. "Come catch me!"

No one even glanced our way as I chased Nadine through the hall, laughing loudly. We reached the Main Foyer, and she flew upward to the second level. I caught up to her and grabbed her around the middle. It was so good to hear her laugh. We couldn't have fun like this out in the open anymore—not with the conflict going on in the coven right now. It was sad, really.

Nadine swatted at me playfully. "Fine, you win."

"What's my prize?" I asked, drawing her body close to me as we floated toward the ceiling.

Her gaze flickered toward my lips, and I leaned toward her. She closed the distance between us, and our spiritual lips connected. Kissing her was different on the astral plane. On the physical plane, every sensation existed only in your own body. When I kissed Nadine in spirit form, it was like I felt what *she* felt, too. The thrill and excitement pulsed through each of our spirits like we were one.

We floated downward, until we were a few inches off the ground again. We weren't far from Nadine's dorm, and we could hear the distant sound of Talia's piano from inside her room.

"Do you think Talia can feel us?" I wondered. "If we play around with it, maybe we can learn what it feels like when someone's astral traveling into your space."

"We can try it, as long as she's decent and she and Grant aren't… you know."

That was the last thing I wanted to walk in on. "Grant's in class," I said.

I floated over to the door, but my spirit slammed into something solid. "That's weird. We walked through Professor Poppy's classroom just fine."

I pressed my hands to the door. Even though I was in spirit form, it felt solid.

"The dorm rooms are warded, aren't they?" Nadine asked. "I don't think it's going to work."

Just to double check, Nadine reached for the door handle. To my surprise, her spirit curled around the handle like it was solid, and the door opened. Except what we found behind it wasn't Nadine's dorm. It was a small closet, so small the door could barely open all the way. Items hovered in mid-air, but none of it looked special. I didn't understand, until I saw a piece of paper I recognized with words scribbled down in my handwriting.

"That's a poem I wrote you," I realized.

Nadine peered into the closet curiously. "This is my stash!"

I furrowed my brow. "I don't get it. How are we accessing your stash like this?"

"Our stash is a pocket universe we create to hold our belongings. It makes sense that it exists on the astral plane," Nadine said. She reached out and plucked the poem from the air. "It's solid here."

I took the piece of paper from her and turned it over in my hands. "I didn't know this was possible. It makes you wonder…"

I reached for a key floating mid-air, but the second my hand passed through the doorway, my spirit was blasted backward. An intense pain shot through my entire form, and I smashed against the wards on the other side of the hall.

"Lucas!" Nadine cried.

I winced. It was a different kind of pain than I'd felt before, though. It was like my energy had been drained.

"That answers that question," I said. "You can't access each other's stashes from the astral plane. They're protected. Only you can open the door to your own stash."

"That's good, because otherwise people could steal things and lose them on the astral plane," Nadine said. "I see why trying to access someone else's stash can be dangerous. Professor Carlisle said that in Conjuring Basics. Do you want to find your stash?"

"Sure, we can see if mine's here."

Nadine closed her door, and we floated down the hall. I tried to open my dorm room, but my hand went right through the handle.

"Mine should be here, like yours," I said.

"Maybe it's not about where you live," Nadine theorized. "My dorm room is my only real home right now, so it makes sense that this is where I would metaphorically keep my stuff. Yours could be anywhere."

"I wonder why we aren't taught how to access them on the astral plane," I said.

"Maybe it's not something everyone can do," Nadine wondered. "If I have more powers as a priestess, maybe it's something only talented witches and warlocks have ever accessed."

"That's possible—" I stopped dead when I saw a woman float across the hall. She went down the grand staircase, and I lost sight of her. "I thought I saw... Professor Ward."

That couldn't be right, because she'd died the night of the Burning. But I was on the astral plane, which meant it was entirely possible I'd just seen her ghost.

Nadine's jaw dropped. "Lucas, we have to follow her! What if she learned something after she died? Ghosts see things and talk to each other, don't they?"

Nadine grabbed my hand, and we flew down the hall and over the railing. We stopped beneath the grand staircase and looked down both hallways. My heart leapt when I saw her. The hall began to blur, and a sensation tingled throughout my body.

"Shit, I think I'm about to wake up," I told Nadine.

She grabbed my shoulders. "Deep breath. Fall deeper into the meditation."

She drew deep breaths, and I copied her. The hall seemed to stabilize around me, but when I looked up, Professor Ward was gone.

"Come on." I led Nadine down the hall. We raced so fast that we ran through a couple of students, but they didn't notice.

We turned down a nearby hall, and I stopped in my tracks when I saw Professor Ward standing there. She looked as solid as the day she died, but there was definitely life missing from her eyes. She wore the same clothes she had died in, but the burns were gone.

She stood in front of her abandoned classroom, just staring. It was like she wanted to walk inside, but she didn't know how. I wasn't sure she had any idea what she was doing.

I slowly approached her. "Professor Ward?"

Her gaze snapped in my direction. She wore a shocked expression, like I'd just awoken her from a long nap.

"Lucas," she said with a frown. I'd never quite been her favorite student. "If you're here about your semester final, it will have to wait."

I furrowed my brow. Did Professor Ward know she was dead?

"I'm actually here about something else," I said slowly. "Do you... remember what happened to you?"

She tilted her chin upward. "I have an impeccable memory. Of course I remember—"

She cut off abruptly. Her eyes darted up and down the hall, like she was searching for something important.

"How did I…? Where are my keys?" She shoved her hands into her pockets, but they were empty. "You took them! I need to get into my classroom."

"Professor, please," Nadine pleaded. "We want to help."

Professor Ward was frantic, and she started pacing up and down the hall. "No, I need to get inside! I need… I need…"

"She must have unfinished business," I whispered to Nadine.

"We helped Daymond cross over," Nadine said lowly. "Maybe we can help her."

"Professor, what is it that you need?" I asked. "Perhaps we can get it for you."

She stopped pacing, and she slowly withdrew her hands from her pockets. "I… I can't remember."

"It's okay," I told her calmly. "It's perfectly common to be confused."

"I'm not confused!" she shouted. "I know perfectly well that I just need to get inside—"

She reached for the door handle, but her hand went straight through it. Her eyes bulged, and she stared down at her fingers in horror.

"I—I'm dead… aren't I?" Her voice shook as realization dawned. Slowly, she lifted her gaze to mine. "And you?"

"Astral traveling," I told her.

"Thank the Goddess the priestesses didn't get to you," she said, sounding relieved. She may not have liked me personally, but she didn't wish death upon me. "What did they do to me? I remember…"

She trailed off, and she wore a calculating look. It was common for ghosts to forget their deaths, especially if they were violent. It kept them from reliving the trauma over and over again.

"Do you remember the pyre?" Nadine asked softly.

Professor Ward closed her eyes and winced slightly, like it was all coming back to her. "I remember the flames…"

Red welts formed across her skin. They morphed into black, charred remains as her memories returned. It was gruesome to see.

"*We didn't deserve this,*" I said quickly, to distract her. The burn marks faded, and her skin became smooth, like it'd been when she was alive. "That's what your last thought was."

Professor Ward looked a bit sick. "We *didn't* deserve any of it... the accusations, the flames... Why am I still here when the young girls moved on?"

"You mean Amy, Christine, and Ashley?" Nadine asked.

Professor Ward nodded, but she had a confused expression on her face, like she didn't quite recognize the names.

"Professor, you said there's something you need to get inside your classroom," I reminded her. "Perhaps we can help... and maybe in return, you can help us."

"How?" she asked.

"We were wondering if you knew anything about a demon in Octavia Falls, or if you've spoken with anyone about the Oaken Wands," Nadine said. "There are ghosts inside the school who know about both, but we don't know who. Have you heard anything?"

Professor Ward shook her head. "I haven't approached the others. The astral plane is... an odd place. I wish I could be of more help."

"It's okay, Professor," I assured her. "You've suffered enough, and I think it's time you move on. Let's see what we can do for you."

I gestured her forward, then stepped through the doorway to her classroom. They both followed behind me. Professor Ward shot a curious glance back at the door, like she didn't know she could do that.

The room was dark, except for a bit of light filtering in through the curtains. No one had been in here since the Burning, that much was obvious. A stack of our final papers still sat on the desk at the front of the room, and the display full of Professor Ward's collection of magical artifacts hadn't been touched at the back of the room.

Professor Ward looked around. "I came here for something, but I don't recall..."

"Is there a message that you want us to give to your family?" Nadine asked.

Professor Ward shook her head. "No, I don't think that's it... There was something I was supposed to keep safe."

"You taught Protection Magic," I said. "Could you be talking about your students?"

She wore a calculating look. "It was more like..."

Her eyes connected with the display of artifacts at the back of the room. She'd spoken about them in class before, when we'd discussed enchantments. Most of these objects were enchanted with protection spells.

Nadine and I watched curiously as Professor Ward crossed the room. She walked over to the cabinet like she was magnetized to it. She stopped in front of a beaded bracelet and stared.

"That's a black obsidian bracelet," I said. "You talked about the crystal in class, how we could use it to shield against negative energies."

Professor Ward furrowed her brow. "I'm afraid I wasn't totally honest about this bracelet. It's enchanted. I need it for… The Coven's Shield."

Her features softened. "I remember now. I witnessed your first meeting, and I know you plan to go up against the priestesses. I worried for you, because if I could see your meeting, others could spy on you. This bracelet is made to protect the wearer from astral spies. The Coven's Shield must take it. Split the beads up amongst your friends, so that astral travelers and ghostly spies cannot enter your space."

"Professor… I don't know what to say," I told her.

"A *thank you* shall suffice," she said.

"Is there any other way we can help?" Nadine asked.

Professor Ward drew a deep breath, then relaxed her shoulders. "I may not have deserved my death, but I deserve a good afterlife. I'm ready to go."

I reached out a hand toward her. "Let's get you to Alora, Professor."

I didn't know why I said it like that. It just felt *right*. The moment her hand connected with mine, the energy in the room shifted. Tingles spread throughout my spirit as a beautiful bright light filled the room. I turned to see a portal opening, shining light on us as bright as the sun. I had to shield my eyes.

An innate knowing told me the portal led to Alora. The doorway to our afterlife had appeared for Professor Ward the same as it had done for Professor Daymond when he was ready to cross over.

Nadine's jaw dropped as she took in the beautiful energy. It wasn't just a light source. Love from our afterlife flooded through the portal, warming my soul to the very core. Professor Ward's eyes watered, but she didn't move.

"Are you ready?" I asked.

She nodded, and a tear streaked her cheek. She couldn't take her eyes off the portal as I led her forward. I stopped at the edge of it, because I couldn't go through with her.

"Goodbye, Professor," I said. "And thank you."

Professor Ward finally tore her gaze from the portal to look at me. "I'm sorry for being so hard on you, Lucas. I could've been a better teacher."

"You'll be a great teacher in the afterlife," I said.

She smiled. "I hope to be. If there's one last bit of wisdom I can give before I leave, it's this. Never give up, Lucas. Your protection magic is strong, and the coven needs protectors like you."

"I'll do my best," I promised.

"I know you will," she said, before turning back to the portal.

She dropped my hand and stepped through, until the beautiful bright light enveloped her. In the blink of an eye, the portal closed shut. Warmth permeated my spirit.

Nadine gaped, like she couldn't believe what she just saw. "She was your assignment—just like with Professor Daymond. But how come I could see the portal this time?"

"It must be because you're on the astral plane," I said. "Things are different here."

Tingles spread through my form, and the room began to fade around me. Nadine's gaze darted around the room, like she felt the same thing.

"The meditation must be coming to an end—" I started to say, but I didn't finish before the room disappeared around me completely. I felt my spirit whip back into my body, and I gasped as I jolted awake.

Nadine's fingers moved against mine. We were back in the meditation classroom, and Professor Poppy stood at the front of the room. Students started to sit up, but no one had seemed to notice that Nadine and I had been gone.

"I hope you have all enjoyed that experience, even if you did not manage to astral travel," Professor Poppy said. "Did anyone happen to get it?"

Nadine and I exchanged a glance, but neither of us said anything. It was no secret that witches and warlocks could astral travel, but the priestesses didn't know we could do it yet. This was a tool we could use to our advantage, and we didn't want this getting back to them.

Professor Poppy excused the class, and I took Nadine's hand as I left the room.

"Astral traveling could be useful to us," Nadine whispered as we headed toward Professor Ward's old classroom. "We could use it to get in contact with ghosts who can help us."

"We have to be careful," I replied. "The only reason we saw Professor Ward is because she wanted to contact us specifically. If there are spirits who want to help us, there are others who will want to help the priestesses."

Nadine nodded and said, "If they're not already."

SIX

The first time I astral traveled was incredible. There were no words for an out-of-body experience, because the purely spiritual encounter couldn't be communicated through language. I tried to astral travel each night following our meeting with Professor Ward, but I'd only achieved it once. I tried finding the priestesses in my astral form, but they must've had their own protection spells. The Imperium headquarters were warded tightly, as were their homes. In class, astral travel had been simple, but I had a lot to learn before it came naturally. In the meantime, we had to find some other way to fight against the priestesses.

During my dialysis session on Friday, I focused on honing my intuition. It was hard, because I wanted to be out there fighting and taking action; instead, I was attached to this machine. Figuring out how to listen to my intuition was all I *could* do right now. I prayed to the Goddess it helped us.

I put in earbuds and listened to a soft piano tune Talia had recorded for me. I closed my eyes and counted my breath, focusing on relaxing each muscle in my body from my head down to my toes. I couldn't get comfortable, because my skin was really itchy. It was a side effect of dialysis.

I scratched my arms, then resituated myself and tried to get comfy again. Isa curled in my lap, and I stroked her head to distract me from my discomfort. She purred heavily, which really helped.

All right, intuition. What do you have to say? I wondered.

Nothing.

Okay, my intuition wasn't going to be loud. Let's try something else.

I played a game with myself. Every time I heard someone pass in the hall, I'd try to guess if it was a nurse, a doctor, or a patient. Then I'd open my eyes before they were gone to see if I was right.

I only got one right. That was something… right?

I definitely needed more practice.

After dialysis, I met up with Chloe at the Gravestone. We'd agreed to start learning transference together. By charging crystals with our magic, we'd have magical reservoirs to draw from when we were affected by the Waning. Chloe had arranged all kinds of crystals on the meeting table, and she clutched a red stone.

It was strange being alone with her. We hadn't been alone since the night in Pinewood Manor, when we'd broken our family curse.

Marley was on the table, batting at a crystal that teetered on the edge. Isa jumped onto the table and pounced on the crystal, knocking it onto the floor. The two cats went chasing after it, pawing at it under the table.

I glanced at Chloe's pile of crystals. "How's it going?"

She sighed. "I haven't mastered transference, if that's what you're asking."

I set my water bottle on the table and sat down beside her. I sipped on my water to help with my dry mouth, which was another side effect of dialysis. "Maybe I can help."

Chloe hesitated, like she too felt the tension between us. "We might as well try."

I held one hand out to her and took a crystal in the other. "I should be able to act as a conduit and move your magic into this crystal."

Chloe placed her hand in mine, and though I wanted to yank away from her, I held on. I reached out my magic and searched for hers, but I couldn't find it. It was like it was secured behind a brick wall.

"This is different from the magic I've worked with before," I said thoughtfully.

"How?" Chloe asked, sounding intrigued.

"I've transformed the magic of curses, and I've pulled magic out of crystals, but yours is resisting me."

"That makes sense," Chloe said. "If the Curse Breaker Cast could take magic from anyone at any time, they'd have taken over the coven ages ago."

"I'd have to overpower you," I theorized. "And I'd have to be exceptionally talented to overpower another witch, let alone any other supernatural."

"So this won't work?" Chloe asked.

"I think it will," I said. "But we have to work together. You have to willingly give me your power."

"I can try."

I tilted my head. "Just like that? You really trust me?"

"I have to," she stated simply. "My only other choice is to trust the priestesses. I may not like it, but you're a better choice than them any day."

I offered a kind smile. "Okay, let's see what happens."

I drew a deep breath and relaxed my shoulders. I reached out with my magic again, and something powerful brushed up against it. I felt a surge of energy, then tingles like pinpricks all over my skin. I tugged on Chloe's Mentalist powers, and I was shocked by how smoothly the magic moved through me. Energy flowed up one arm and down the other, pooling into the crystal in my hand. The crystal began to glow a slight red, and Chloe gasped.

"I can feel it!" she said. "It's like casting a spell. I feel my energy leaving me. But it's calm, too—flowing peacefully."

I continued funneling magic into the crystal, until I couldn't push any longer. When the crystal was charged, I severed the connection between Chloe and me. I dropped her hand and lifted the crystal proudly.

Chloe smiled. "Wow! That was so easy. I can't believe... well, I honestly can't believe we work together so well."

I smirked. "We *did* break our family curse together. This should be a piece of cake."

"Yeah, but we were so desperate then." Chloe took the crystal from me and placed it in a black bag.

I eyed her curiously. She seemed so different from the girl I'd met when I first came to Octavia Falls. "Chloe, can I ask you something?"

"Sure, but I can't promise I'll have an answer," she said, without meeting my gaze.

"What happened that night?" I asked. "It's like once you got rid of the curse, you became a different person. I don't get it because I'm still… basically the same."

"I guess you didn't have as much to change as I did."

I furrowed my brow. "What do you mean?"

Chloe grabbed another crystal and spun it around in her hands. "I didn't change because we broke the curse. I mean, I guess that was part of it. I don't feel so *angry* anymore. My emotions aren't as intense, you know? But…"

She sighed. "I'm changing because of you, Nadine."

"Me?" She couldn't be serious.

Chloe shrugged. "You showed me that things could be different, that you and I could work together, even if we were enemies. I realized I'd gotten so wrapped up in my pride that I forgot what was important. I've had to shift an entire identity. I'm *still* working on it. Sometimes I don't know who I am anymore."

This seemed really hard for her to admit, and I actually felt for her.

"I believe people can change, and you're proof of that," I told her.

She offered a kind smile. "Thanks. I'm really trying. All I ever wanted was to protect the coven, but I saw what I'd become if I kept going down the path I was headed."

"You'd become your grandmother?" I joked.

Chloe laughed. "Yes, and that's the *last* thing I ever want to do. It's hard figuring out who I really am, but I think it'll be worth it in the end."

"You should be proud of yourself. You've come a long way."

She drew a deep breath. "And I have a long way to go. But thank you."

"I think it gets easier with time," I added.

Chloe nodded. "In some ways."

"I'm glad we're figuring things out," I told her honestly. "It gives me hope for the rest of the coven."

Chloe nudged me playfully. "Look at us, agreeing on shit."

I laughed. "Strange, isn't it?"

"Ah, but we're witches," Chloe said. "Strange is kind of our thing."

I held up another crystal. "Want to try some more strange shit?"

She beamed. "Absolutely."

We continued charging up crystals, until Chloe felt her magic draining. I didn't want to siphon everything at once, so I suggested we stop for the day and continue once her magic had recharged.

By the time we left the Gravestone, I felt really relaxed around Chloe. Hell, maybe we *were* becoming friends.

I went to the Lounge, where Lucas and I had planned to meet for dinner. He took my hand, and my gaze traveled down to his enchanted bracelet. Each student had one, as they were keys to our dorms.

We had retrieved Professor Ward's bracelet like she instructed. We'd shared the beads amongst our friends and added them to our school bracelets. I couldn't even tell which one was the protection bead, which would protect The Coven's Shield from ethereal spies. No one would ever guess we had them.

"I need a Calming Cappuccino," Lucas said, gesturing toward the Lounge's restaurant. "It's been a busy week. I didn't realize how much time Professor Warren's internship would take up. Do you want anything?"

"Absolutely. I've been craving Barry's Enchanted Muffins," I said.

We headed to the counter. Isa and Oliver both meowed loudly, until we ordered them treats. When we turned to find a table, we spotted Grant and Talia near the doors, waving us over. They shared a worried look, and my guts twisted. I instantly knew something was wrong. I subconjured my box of muffins, and we slipped out into the hall to follow them.

"Are you guys all right?" I asked.

Grant glanced around, but no one was close enough to hear. "I assume you haven't read the paper today?"

I shook my head. "We haven't had a chance."

Grant conjured a copy of the *Miriamic Messenger*. It was already folded to the article he was looking for. He handed it to me.

Talia chewed her lower lip. "Professor Wykoff wrote a letter to the editor. We're worried about her."

I scanned the article. It was a protest against the Burning and a call to have the Imperium Council audited by an impartial party. Professor Wykoff was kind with her words, but her message was loud and clear. She opposed the priestesses.

Lucas read over my shoulder. "How'd this even get printed? The *Miriamic Messenger* has been printing nothing but propaganda for a month."

"That's why we're worried," Talia said. "It must serve their purpose somehow. They'll paint her to be crazy, or invalidate her in some way to devalue everything she's said. They must intend to use this to increase support of their own message. The Coven's Shield has to do something to protect her."

"We will—" Lucas started to say, but a scream tore down the hall, cutting him off.

"You're hurting me!" a woman cried.

Fuck. We were already too late.

My friends and I took off down the hall, our cats following. A crowd had formed in the Main Foyer, and I could barely see what was going on. Chloe and Miles stood at the back of the crowd, and I stopped beside them.

My stomach dropped when I saw Sheriff Baker dragging Professor Wykoff toward the main doors. It was all too reminiscent of the time he'd hauled Professor Daniels off campus. She had been hanged later that night. I hoped to the Goddess Professor Wykoff wouldn't suffer the same fate.

A group of Executors stood nearby, cheering Sheriff Baker on.

"We can do this the easy way or the hard way," Sheriff Baker threatened.

"I'm trying—" Professor Wykoff started, but she cut off when she tripped on her skirt and went sprawling forward. Onlookers all around the room gasped.

"We have to stop this," I insisted, trying to push through the crowd.

Talia grabbed my arm to stop me. "What are you going to do, Nadine? We can stand in front of the doors and protest, but the Executors will stop us."

Chloe heard us and whirled in our direction. "We *have* to protest. And we have to be loud about it. Nadine, stall for us. I have an idea."

Miles hesitated. "I'm going with her," he decided. He abandoned the Main Foyer and followed Chloe. Their cats raced after them.

I shoved my way through the crowd, until I reached the front. Sheriff Baker had yanked Professor Wykoff to her feet, and he slapped a pair of handcuffs onto her wrists.

"I said I'd go peacefully!" she cried. "Why are you—ow!"

"I demand you stop this at once!" I shouted.

One of the Executors stepped in front of me. Avery crossed her arms and glared at me. "Take one more step, and you'll be arrested next."

Bitch, I'm not afraid of you!

"The priestesses hired you, and as a high priestess of the Miriamic Coven, you work for *me*," I snapped. "I suggest you get out of the way, before you lose your job."

I pushed past her before she could respond.

Sheriff Baker had stopped, and he looked less than amused. "Not *you* again."

I kept my head held high. "What exactly is going on here?"

"This woman no longer works here, yet she refuses to remove herself from the premises," Sheriff Baker said through clenched teeth. He knew he was required to answer me, though he wouldn't do so happily.

"I was only packing my things—" Professor Wykoff started, but she cried out when Sheriff Baker yanked on her handcuffs.

A few students began whispering, and I turned to see Headmistress Verla and Professor Warren pushing their way through the crowd.

"Sheriff, what is this?" Verla asked.

He relaxed a little, like he expected her to deal with me so he could leave and get this over with.

"I believe Professor Wykoff is perfectly capable of escorting herself off school property," Verla said. She looked sad, like she hadn't wanted this to happen, but didn't have any other choice. The school board must've voted against her.

"This public display is unnecessary," Professor Warren added.

"The priestesses have requested I remove her before charging her for trespassing," Sheriff Baker sneered. "If you have a problem with it, bring it up with the other priestesses."

"I *will*," I said simply. I pulled out my phone and brought up Priestess Margaret's number.

"Drop the phone!" Sheriff Baker demanded.

Verla's eyebrows shot up. "I believe she's well within her rights. She is a priestess, after all."

Sheriff Baker wasn't interested in listening to me—priestess or not—

but he respected Verla. He muttered under his breath. "Going against the priestesses' orders proves you're corrupt."

I ignored him while I spoke with Priestess Margaret on the phone.

"Nadine," she sighed. "Do we really have to do this?"

"Yes," I stated. "I demand an explanation."

Priestess Margaret didn't sound pleased. "We'll be right there."

The priestesses must've been close by, because they arrived minutes later. The main doors burst open as the three priestesses strode into the school. Claudia followed behind them. Though she didn't wear a cloak like the priestesses, she had a confidence about her that made her seem like she belonged. My stomach instantly twisted at the sight of her. I didn't like Claudia any more than I liked any of the other priestesses.

"What is the meaning of this?" Lilian demanded.

"I could ask you the same thing," I said.

No one had moved. The crowd of students watched on quietly.

"What exactly has Professor Wykoff done to justify this?" I asked.

Priestess Margaret turned her nose up at me. "Perhaps you can take that up with the school board and stop wasting our time. The board is the one to decide who works here."

"Yet the Imperium Council has influence over them," I pointed out. "The coven owns the college. You can hire and fire whoever you want. Professor Wykoff was already packing her things when she was arrested. Why persecute her for going peacefully?"

"She is spreading lies!" Claudia burst.

"If that's the way you feel, then the *Miriamic Messenger* never should've published her piece in the first place," I shot back.

"Headmistress, please," Priestess Charlotte said. "You must control your students."

"I'm perfectly capable of managing my students," Verla stated confidently. "But Nadine is a priestess, and like all priestesses, she governs over me."

Verla spoke innocently, like she wasn't taking one side or the other. The priestesses still liked her, and we weren't prepared to give them a reason otherwise.

"Nadine is a single priestess," Margaret said. "She does not speak for the entire Imperium Council. Professor Wykoff has proven herself unfit in a teaching position for reasons I daresay she may not want to be made public."

She was lying. Professor Wykoff was nothing more than an example—a display of what would happen if anyone dared to speak up.

"Sheriff Baker is well within his rights to escort her off campus," Margaret added, before turning to me with a heavy sigh. "Nadine, why do you insist on being so difficult? You know you'll be outvoted."

She spoke loud enough for everyone to hear. She was purposely trying to discredit me publicly, as she'd done many times in the past.

"I want the coven to know that every innocent person you persecute will have someone behind them who will stand up to you—so that they can stand up to you, too," I said.

"Or we can just arrest you for obstruction of justice," Priestess Lilian suggested.

"How does that work on a priestess?" I asked.

Margaret narrowed her eyes. She stepped so close to me so only I could hear her. "You better tread carefully, Nadine. We can turn the coven so far against you that they'll administer the noose themselves."

"Go ahead and give them the courage to hang a priestess," I hissed. "And watch them march the entire Imperium Council to the gallows."

Margaret's features faltered. She opened her mouth to say something, but a collective gasp traveled around the room, cutting her off. Margaret's gaze snapped upward. I turned to see two figures stepping up to the balcony—Chloe and Miles. They wore dark robes with hoods over their faces. All that could be seen under the hoods was tape covering their mouths. Nooses hung limply around their necks.

They climbed over the banister and steadied themselves on the other side.

"What is this?" Lilian barked. "I demand you get down at once!"

They ignored her. Chloe grabbed Miles's hand, and then… they jumped.

People screamed, and gasps traveled around the room as they fell through the air. All at once, they came to a halt mid-air. Their ropes stretched above them, as if attached to an invisible wire, and their heads hung limply. Their bodies spun around, their toes hovering off the ground. It looked so real that my stomach twisted into horrible knots.

Chloe had used her telekinesis to create the illusion. When she said we had to be loud, she meant it. Though they hadn't said a word, this protest was louder than any words would ever be.

If they can take your voice, they can take your life.

"This is ridiculous!" Charlotte cried.

"For heaven's sake, Lilian!" Margaret snapped. "Get them down from there!"

Lilian's nostrils flared. She lifted her hands, and my friends began to float through the air toward her. Chloe must've been resisting her with her power, because the crease between Lilian's eyebrows grew deeper. She looked like she was struggling. Lilian was stronger than Chloe, though. The moment Lilian overpowered her, my friends crashed to the ground. It happened so fast that they caught themselves with their hands.

Chloe let out a pained cry. "Run!" she told Miles.

He didn't listen, though. He rushed to her side and tried to help her up, but she pushed him away.

"Go," she insisted.

He peeked toward the priestesses from under his hood. Lilian was already marching toward him. Chloe used her Mentalist powers to force Miles away from her, and he took off running down the hall.

Lilian grabbed Chloe by the hood of her cloak and yanked her upright. Chloe stumbled to her feet, but she favored one of her hands, like it'd been injured when she fell.

"I bet you think you're so funny," Lilian sneered. "Let's see how comical you feel when you're truly hanging from the gallows—"

Lilian yanked Chloe's hood down, and she gasped when she locked eyes with her granddaughter. All the blood drained from her face. It was clear to everyone in the room that Chloe was the last person she expected to be underneath that cloak.

Chloe yanked the tape off her mouth. "Hello, grandmother."

"Chloe Jane Olson," Lilian sneered. The conversation was meant just for them, but everyone in the room heard. "Just wait until your father hears about this!"

"Yeah, that should be fun," Chloe said dryly.

"Maybe you'd like to think about it while spending the night in a jail cell," Lilian threatened.

"That seems like an awfully fair punishment," Chloe stated. "You've hanged women for far less."

A muscle popped in Lilian's jaw. "Sheriff, handcuff this student and take her away."

Sheriff Baker conjured another set of handcuffs.

"Priestess, is this really necessary?" I asked. "She's your granddaughter."

"And she will receive proper punishment for this gross display," Lilian said. "The priestesses are simply trying to keep the coven safe. Chloe has interfered, and dare I say, you are dangerously close to being arrested yourself."

Sheriff Baker grabbed Chloe's wrist and yanked it behind her back.

"Watch it," Chloe snapped. "This bitch sprained my wrist."

Lilian glared at her. If it was anyone else, she'd have their tongue cut out. But it was her granddaughter, and no matter what they thought of each other in this moment, they were still family.

Lilian turned to the crowd and spoke loudly. "Let it be known that violent displays of protest like the one you just witnessed are hereby outlawed. Anyone who interferes with the process of justice will be sentenced accordingly. The Imperium Council is working night and day to bring an end to the Waning and restore the coven's magic. We ask for your full cooperation until this matter can be resolved."

Murmurs of agreement traveled around the room, but my stomach clenched. Lilian was trying to sound kind, like she was doing them all a favor. The truth was, she wasn't asking a damn thing. She was *demanding* it. And she would demand compliance until she stripped these people of their magic altogether… and of their very humanity.

"We thank you for your cooperation," Lilian said, before turning toward the doors. Her cloak billowed around her as she ordered Sheriff Baker to escort Chloe and Professor Wykoff off campus.

Marley, Chloe's cat, stood at the top of the stairs and yowled loudly as the priestesses marched the women outside. Professor Wykoff hung her head, but Chloe shot me a proud smile as she passed. She didn't seem bothered at all by her arrest. She'd *intended* to get arrested.

The room burst into conversation once the priestesses left.

"She deserved it," Avery told the other Executors. They loudly agreed with her.

Verla stepped to the middle of the room and raised her voice. "Everyone, back to your dormitories."

The crowd began to disperse. Lucas rushed up to me and took me in his arms.

"Are you all right?" he asked.

I sighed. "I'm fine. I'm more worried about Chloe."

"You did all you could," Lucas assured me.

"There must be more we can do," I insisted.

"Go back to your dormitories and get some rest," Verla suggested. "Jonathan and I will discuss what we can do to keep the priestesses happy while also protecting the students."

I didn't know who she was talking about until Professor Warren nodded in agreement. I never knew his first name before now.

"I want to help," I offered.

"You may be a priestess, but I'm the headmistress of this school," Verla said. "I'm responsible for keeping the students safe, and I intend to do just that. We all have our roles in this, and this is mine. Please, Nadine. Let *me* worry about the students."

"Okay," I agreed, though I didn't like it.

Professor Warren and Headmistress Verla left the Main Foyer together. By now, everyone else was gone. I took Lucas's hand, and we started up the stairs. I stopped halfway, and he paused with a concerned look on his face.

"It's fine," I told him. "Just out of energy today. Damn, this place needs an elevator. I know the school was built ages ago, but accessibility for the disabled is seriously lacking."

"I thought you were doing better since dialysis started," Lucas said. He was genuinely trying to understand.

I took a deep breath and forced myself to walk the last few steps. "I *am* doing better. Magic doesn't flare my symptoms as badly anymore, but my body is still trying to heal from the shit it's gone through in the last two years. I'm still fatigued most of the time. I'm just really good at hiding it."

"We'll fix this," Lucas said, sounding so confident. He didn't understand what a losing battle advocating for yourself could be sometimes. "You can't be the only one in school who needs accommodations."

I practically snorted. "Maybe if the priestesses let me have a say, I could do something about it. I'm not holding my breath until this conflict is over."

His room was empty when we arrived. Our friends must've gone to my room with our cats, and a piece of me felt slightly relieved. I didn't want them to see me break down.

And that's exactly what I did. I sank onto Lucas's bed and buried my face in his pillow. I just wanted to scream or cry... or *fight*. And I felt powerless.

Lucas sat on the bed beside me and placed a hand on my back. "Talk to me, Nad."

I rolled over. The moment Lucas saw the worried look on my face, he kicked his shoes off and lay on the bed next to me. He took me in his arms, until my head rested on his chest. He drew me close and pressed a kiss to the top of my head.

"I'm here for you," he whispered.

"That means a lot," I said. "Because we really need each other right now. We all do. And that's the problem. The coven is so divided, and there seems to be nothing I can do about it. I couldn't protect Professor Wykoff. Who knows what they'll do to her? All for... what? Questioning authority? That shouldn't be a crime."

"I know," Lucas agreed. "And we'll change it."

"How can you know that?" I asked. "I think that's what scares me most. That we *don't know*. Our efforts could be all for nothing."

"They won't be," he promised. "We have the prophecy."

"Which can change," I reminded him. "Lucas, I'm so scared about the future. If I knew with certainty that everything would be okay, then maybe I could deal with it. But who could predict what was going to happen today? How much more uncertainty will the coven have to endure?"

"I know it's scary, Nad, but that doesn't mean it's not worth trying. Yes, there are so many *what ifs*, but what about all the good things that could happen, too?"

"Is it still worth it if it doesn't work out, though?" I asked in a small voice.

"I think it is," Lucas said. "Our magic is stronger together, but the more you grow your individual magic, the stronger the group is as a whole. I think it's like that with our other strengths, too... empathy, love, passion, talents, and values. The good we do has an impact. We can choose to sit back and do nothing, or we can choose to fight it, and find joy and happiness in the midst of all of it."

I sniffled and offered a small smile. "How do we stay positive in all this?"

"I don't think it's about being happy and positive all the time," Lucas said. "We're still allowed to feel something, but we have the choice to let those feelings take over or not. Bad things happen, and we don't necessarily have control over that reality. The reality we control is inside of ourselves. At least, that's what Dr. Mack says. Our internal reality reflects in our outside world, because it impacts our actions. That's why we need to keep fighting, because if we don't, we don't even stand a chance."

"What if taking action is what damns us all?" I wondered.

Lucas shook his head. "We can only damn ourselves if we abandon what we believe in. We're not going to do that."

"You're right," I agreed. "I could never."

"That's why the prophecy talks about *us*," Lucas pointed out. "Whatever happens, we'll make a lasting impact. That, I know for certain."

I sighed. "As hard as it is, I wish I could find the good in all of this."

"There's plenty," Lucas said. "We're making change, Nad. Long-lasting change. Burnings and hangings have been taking place in the coven for centuries. When we're finished, the coven will be done with witch hunts. That's a positive, for sure."

"It doesn't feel like anything is changing," I whispered. I laid my head on his shoulder again and melted into him. I really needed this right now. "What other good do you see in the coven?"

I loved to hear him talk so positively. Lucas hadn't always been like this. When I met him, he focused more on the bad than on the good. It was so nice to see this shift in him. His therapy had really been helping.

"I love the sound of cats purring, and the way they jump sideways at each other when they play," he said. "I love the sound of rain on the window, and the way it drips down the glass. I love when the clouds part just so slightly that a ray of sunshine shines down on you and warms your skin. I love when we get our grades back in class, and you see someone smile because they did better than they thought they would. And the smile was only meant for them, but you catch it anyway, and you get to share in that tiny little celebration."

His smile grew the longer he talked, and all I could do was stare at him in admiration. He looked up at the ceiling, like he forgot I was even there. My heart warmed.

"I love when someone's laughing so hard that they snort," he continued. "You just know they're having a really good time. I love when you're writing poetry and it just flows out of you, and it's so perfect that you can't even believe you wrote it. I love when—what?"

Lucas caught me staring. "What's wrong?"

I shook my head. "Nothing. You're so incredible. I love you."

"I love you, too. More than you'll ever know." He pushed a strand of hair behind my ear, and butterflies danced around in my stomach. "I could talk about every little thing I love about you all day."

Heat rose to my cheeks. "Go on," I encouraged.

Lucas smiled, like he was more than happy to oblige. "I love the way you lift your chin when you face conflict. Your confidence is fucking hot. I love the way your shoulders drop when Isa jumps into your lap, because you always look so happy and relaxed when she's around. I love the way you bite your lower lip when you're trying to solve a puzzle, and the way your ass looks when you're doing yoga."

I smirked.

"I like the way your ass feels in my hands..." He placed his hand on my hip, then slowly moved downward. He watched me the whole time, to make sure he had my permission. I couldn't help but bite my lower lip as heat pooled between my thighs. Lucas grabbed my ass, and I inhaled a sharp breath.

"Keep talking," I begged. I hadn't had much of a sex drive lately; it was a side effect of dialysis. But talking to Lucas like this really turned me on. Emotional talk was like foreplay for us.

"I like the way your breasts feel against me," he teased, before dipping his head and running his nose along my collar bone.

My heart began to beat faster as his breath ran over me. "Maybe we should do something about that."

"Maybe..." he teased. Lucas yanked my shirt off, and I climbed on top of him, straddling him. Lucas got a hungry look in his eyes as he took me in.

I unclasped my bra and let it fall away. Lucas shivered beneath me, and his hands trembled in anticipation as he ran them up my body. My breath came in shallow heaves, and my heart hammered as he took my breasts in his hands and squeezed. I could feel his erection through his jeans.

An idea came to mind. Lucas watched me curiously as I drew away and conjured the box of Barry's Enchanted Muffins I'd bought earlier. I opened it and carefully picked out a special one. It was chocolate, one of the first ones I'd ever tried. I popped it in my mouth, and the magic washed over me. I felt a tingling in my chest… and my boobs were suddenly three cups bigger.

If I thought his dick couldn't get any harder, I was wrong. I shimmied my giant boobs at him. "The magic only lasts a minute."

Lucas grabbed my breasts and pushed his face into them. I threw my head back and laughed as he made silly noises. Fuck, I loved when he was playful like this.

"I think I need to keep a few of these on hand. This is fun!" I shimmied my boobs at him and accidentally smacked him in the face. "Dear Goddess! I'm so sorry."

He grinned. "Watch it. Those things are dangerous weapons."

I snorted as my boobs shrank back to normal. "Like you don't have a weapon of your own in your pants."

"Is it a weapon you're willing to handle?" he joked.

"Are you challenging me?" I asked. "I told you the first time we met, I run straight into danger."

He grabbed me around the waist and flipped me over, until I was lying flat on my back. "Then let me show you just how dangerous I can be."

Lucas undid his pants, and I let out a wavered breath as I watched him undress. Fuck, he could take me through every inch of danger, and I'd still feel safe in his presence. My gaze traveled down his muscled torso, to his generous length. My panties were *so* wet.

Lucas finished undressing, then undid my pants and pulled them down my legs slowly, seductively. He smiled when he saw the lace panties I wore. Lucas pulled my panties off, then ran his fingers over my most sensitive areas. He slid a finger inside of me, and I tilted my head back in pleasure.

"What do you want?" he asked.

I leaned over and opened the top drawer of his nightstand, where he kept his condoms. I pulled one out and ripped it open.

"I want you inside of me," I said breathlessly. I rolled the condom over his length. He gently slid inside of me, and I gasped.

He buried his face into my hair and whispered, "I love it when you make those noises. And the way you smell. And the way you… taste."

He pressed his lips to mine, and I rolled my tongue over his. My heart boomed in my chest, and I had to run my fingers through his hair to keep them from trembling. Each time he thrust into me, a wave of pleasure spread through my body. I wrapped my legs tightly around him, and hugged him close to me. Involuntary gasps escaped my lips each time he moved. We fit together so perfectly, and I wanted to enjoy every drop of desire and passion we shared with one another.

When Lucas moaned, I couldn't take the passion building up inside of me any longer. I had to take control. I thrust my hips upward and made him roll over, until I was on top. Lucas closed his eyes, and his blissful features made me want to ride him harder—to pleasure him in every way possible, because he deserved every beautiful moment we could possibly share together.

I reached down to begin pleasuring myself, but Lucas felt it. He joined me, moving his thumb over my clit. My stomach fluttered.

"You shouldn't have to put in all the work," he told me. "Let me help. I want to learn."

I let him take over, and I kept my hands busy by running them over his arms and chest. "A little lower," I suggested. He moved his fingers, and I gasped when he found the right spot.

"Like that?" he asked.

"Just like that," I begged. I rolled my hips, but I was forced to slow down. "Sorry, I'm too exhausted."

"Don't apologize," he said reassuringly. "Do you want to stop?"

I shook my head. "No."

"Then allow me," he offered. Lucas curled his arms around me and gently rolled me over, until I was on my back. It made me feel so safe with him.

Lucas moved inside of me, and I melted into the mattress as I took in every incredible sensation. I loved the feel of his skin against mine, and the way his cock rubbed against me. He moved above me so gently, like he knew exactly what I needed from him.

Pleasure began to build up inside my body.

"Lucas," I breathed.

He squeezed my nipple lightly, because he knew how much I liked it. A glorious sensation burst through me, sending tingles out through my extremities. I contracted around him as I moaned in pleasure. Lucas reached his peak, and his moans drove me wild.

When we finally came down from the high of orgasm, I opened my eyes to see him totally relaxed. A smile spread across his face.

When we finished cleaning up, I pulled the blanket over both of us. We both breathed heavily, but we seemed to melt into the bed together as he wrapped his arms around me. I sank so deep into him, that it felt like our souls had converged into one. It was such a beautiful moment.

"That was amazing," I whispered.

"And to think, we can do that anytime we want," Lucas said.

"I want to," I agreed. "But I worry about my health. That's the first time my libido has returned in weeks, and I couldn't keep up."

Lucas propped himself above me and pushed a strand of hair out of my face. "Don't worry, my dear. We'll take it at whatever pace you want."

"But it's not fair that you have to do all the work."

"I don't mind being the main performer. We can still have fun sex, because sex comes in all forms, and can be adjusted based on what your body needs at the time."

I curled into him. "I have accommodations for every area of my life. I don't want them for sex as well."

"I need adjusting, too. Sometimes I'm so depressed, it's hard to be in the moment. But you usually make that up for me. So I can support you in this area, too. It's only a big deal if we make it one. We get to write the rules about our relationship, nobody else does."

He was being so understanding and sincere, which made me feel confident that we would get through anything together. Some people didn't understand why Lucas and I had gotten back together, but I knew I'd made the right choice. No matter what happened, I always wanted to be with him.

I hoped one day, we'd be able to make this permanent.

Nadine and I stayed curled up beneath my sheets all night. I hadn't slept so well in… forever. Being with her felt more magical than my actual magic. She was incredible in every way, and I wanted to fall asleep every night holding her.

Even my outlook on life was better when I was around her. Maybe I didn't believe every word that came out of my mouth, but I believed it enough to count. It was a hell of a lot better believing in *something* than nothing at all.

Grant had never returned to our room, so I assumed he'd stayed the night with Talia. The school was quiet the following morning. A few people moved through the halls to get breakfast, but almost nobody spoke. The whispers that filled the halls were so hushed that I could hardly hear them.

Grant and Talia were leaving the cafeteria when we arrived. They wore matching shirts with a cartoon drawing of a cat on them.

"Fun night?" Nadine teased when we approached. She bent down to pet Isa, who was following beside our friends

Talia ducked her head, and Nadine's features immediately paled. She'd clearly said something wrong.

"We *were* having fun, but Ryan ruined it," Talia said bitterly. "We're trying to avoid him."

My hands curled into fists. "What'd the asshole do?"

Grant frowned. "Last night, we were... getting intimate, and he showed up demanding he had a right to search the room. I threw on some pants and answered the door, but he shoved past me. Talia was under the covers. He humiliated her!"

Talia gritted her teeth. "He did it on purpose, because he doesn't think people of different Casts should be together. He was *trying* to humiliate us."

"I could strangle him!" Grant growled. I knew he would if he could get away with it.

"He's an Executor," Talia reminded Grant. "It's best we don't make things worse."

Nadine formed a battle orb in her hand. "I'll fry his ass for you. Where is he? In the cafeteria?"

"If anyone's frying his ass, it'll be me," Grant insisted.

"Guys, stop," Talia begged. "I don't want Ryan hurting anyone, and he *will*. You know it. Let's just go into town and get breakfast."

Isa and Oliver meowed loudly, and Gus sat down, planting himself firmly in the hall.

"I don't think the cats want to come," Grant said. "I bet they want to go hunting."

I got an idea. "Maybe we can send them on a hunt of our own. They can keep an eye on Professor Leto."

"That's a good idea," Nadine agreed. "He's not going to notice a few random cats roaming around. They're all over the school."

I knelt to scratch Oliver behind the ears. "Follow Professor Leto. Let us know if you find anything."

The cats shared a meow, like they agreed to the task, then went running off in the other direction.

I stood. "We'll see if we can get an update on Chloe and Professor Wykoff in town. We can take my car."

I'd picked up the old beater earlier this week. My internship paid well enough that I could afford the monthly payments. Nadine offered to let me drive her car whenever I wanted, but I really wanted my own. I'd never had my own car, and there was a sense of freedom that came with it. Yeah, the wheel wells were rusted, and the car shook when it drove down the road, but it was *my* rusted old piece of shit. I was proud.

Talia looked a little hesitant when she saw the sedan.

"Don't give her that look," I teased.

Talia plastered on an innocent expression. "What look?"

"Like you expect a wheel to fall off." I smacked the hood. "She's reliable… I think."

Grant walked around the car, inspecting it from all angles. "Bro, I think you got scammed."

I shoved him. "Relax. She's not going to break down."

"I like it," Nadine said proudly, sliding into the passenger seat. I beamed.

Once we got on the road, though, Nadine didn't seem as enthusiastic about the car as before. She held on to the dash.

"This thing is *really* shaky, Lucas," she said. "My dad and I worked on old cars together. I might be able to get it running smoothly."

My dad and I had never had a relationship like that. He didn't teach me anything—let alone anything about cars.

"That'd be great, Nad," I said. "It'd be fun to get under the hood with you."

"I can think of a few things he'd like to *get under*," Talia snickered from the backseat.

I pulled into a parking spot on Main Street. I was surprised to see there were hardly any cars around. Usually, this part of town was packed. But it was still January and quite chilly out, with thick cloud cover overhead. Perhaps no one wanted to brave the cold.

I didn't notice until I stepped out of the car that I'd parked in front of a jewelry shop. My gaze roamed over the window, and I caught sight of an engagement ring, with beautiful teal stones swirling around a shimmering diamond. I couldn't help but think how beautiful the ring would look on Nadine's finger.

My heart lifted at the thought. Could I really be thinking about proposing? No, it was too soon. Yet, I knew with all my heart that I wanted to marry Nadine some day. I didn't even have to question it. Nadine took my hand, and I snapped my attention back to her. I didn't think she'd noticed what I was looking at. Good, because when the time came, I wanted it to be a surprise.

"Ooh, Crystal's Psychic Café! I love this place," Talia said as we headed toward a nearby restaurant for breakfast.

"What's a psychic café?" Nadine asked.

"There's no menu," Talia explained. "The servers can read your mind—not all your thoughts, just enough to know what you want to eat—and they'll bring your food out without you even asking!"

"That's cool, but what if you don't know what you want?" Nadine asked. "Or what if they don't have it on the menu?"

"Trust me, they get it right every time," Talia promised.

I opened the door, and my friends stepped inside. The host stopped us near the front counter.

"I'm going to have to see your Cast marks," he said.

I furrowed my brow. "Excuse me?"

He pointed to a sign on the window I hadn't seen before, which read *No Mortana*. "We verify each customer to ensure your safety."

"Mortana aren't dangerous!" Nadine protested. "This is unlawful."

The host must've thought we'd be a problem, because he drew himself up. "We reserve the right to refuse service to anyone at any time. No shoes, no *mark*, no service."

I was so shocked that I didn't know what to say. I hadn't expected this.

"We just want some breakfast," Grant said. "You're really going to turn away paying customers?"

"If you bring death into this establishment, then yes," the host sneered. "This guy's the Reaper's Apprentice, isn't he? You three can stay, but I'll have to ask the reaper to leave."

My hands curled into fists. Who did he think he was, banning my Cast like this?

"Look, buddy," I snapped. "Death isn't always a bad thing. The Mortana exist for a reason. We protect the coven during war, and we help people cross over after death. If you can't see the Mortana for what they are, then you don't deserve their business."

He shrugged, like he was totally indifferent to it. "You're right. I guess I don't. You can walk out yourself, or I'll throw you out."

"You can't deny us service like this—!" Nadine started, but the host grabbed her arm. He really wasn't kidding about throwing us out.

"Don't fucking touch her!" I yelled. I threw up a shield between them, so strong that the host was blasted backward. He crashed into a nearby table.

Patrons screamed as they leapt out of their chairs. "Call the police!" a woman yelled.

Grant grabbed me. "Time to go."

"They can't get away with it," Nadine protested as our friends dragged us down the sidewalk.

"Believe me, we don't want to eat there anyway," Talia said.

"This is unfair!" Nadine burst, planting herself on the sidewalk several stores down from the café. "This isn't about one meal. I know it sounds silly to fight about breakfast, but this is bigger than that. We can't walk away from injustice like this. If we let them get away with this, what else will they get away with?"

"The priestesses are brewing poisons," Grant hissed. "Who knows who else could be?"

Talia nodded in agreement. "We have to be careful."

Nadine frowned. "If anyone can get away with this, things are only going to get worse."

Talia sighed. "The only way to stop it is to go to the priestesses, but they probably sanctioned it in the first place."

Grant's stomach rumbled. "In the meantime, can we find someplace to eat? We can talk about this over breakfast."

I nodded. "Let's see what's open."

We walked down the street, and my guts twisted into knots as we passed shops with signs that read things like *Alchemists Only* and *Must Present Cast Mark*. Grant might be hungry, but I'd quickly lost my appetite. No wonder there were so few people shopping today. There were only so many places that would let a person in. Trying to find somewhere open to all Casts was next to impossible.

The more we walked, the more I noticed *Closed* signs over the doors and going-out-of-business sales advertised in the windows. It seemed half the shops were closing down. We slowed, until we came to a complete stop to take it all in.

Talia gaped. "I had no idea things were this bad."

Nadine spun around. "Looks like our economy is going to shit."

"It happened so fast." Grant wore a puzzled look.

"People are afraid," I pointed out. "They're cutting their customer base by limiting Casts, and their customers are already going to limit spending because they're uncertain what's going to happen next. If businesses aren't sure they can make next month's rent or cover payroll, what do they do?"

"The priestesses are going to have to choose between the economy or their own power," Nadine said thoughtfully. "We have to support our people."

Something crashed in an alleyway nearby. I thought it sounded like broken glass. Nadine went rigid, and we exchanged a glance. A groan came, and it sounded like someone was in trouble. We took off running toward the sound.

I slowed when we reached the alleyway. A bearded man sat slumped against the side of a building, next to a dumpster. Glass lay shattered at his feet, and the strong scent of alcohol filled the air.

"Aw, fuck," the man slurred. He reached for the broken glass, but he swayed so hard he couldn't find it. We rushed over to him.

"Sir, the glass is broken," I told him. "Don't touch it."

I placed a hand on his chest to help him sit upright, but he shoved me. "Geh off eh me," he said drunkenly.

My jaw dropped when he looked my way. His hair was longer than I remembered, and he'd grown a short beard, but it was definitely Magnus Knight. I didn't know whether to help him or let him stay in this alleyway. He'd killed Professor Daymond and run drugs through the coven. He was the reason Professor Daniels was hanged. He'd wronged the coven in so many ways. It looked like he'd completely given up on life.

Nadine didn't have the same reservations. She saw a sad, sick man in front of us and rushed to help him. She knelt to his level.

"Magnus?" she said softly.

"Who's askin'?" he demanded, lolling his head from one side to the other. "Oh… you're that Curse Breaker, aren't ya?"

"You're not well," Nadine pressed. "Let us get you some help."

Grant conjured a few potions ingredients and fumbled with them. A vial fell out of his hand and clattered to the pavement. "I might be able to brew something to help."

"You can't help me," Magnus slurred. "I'm done. Ruined! The priestesses have blamed me for nightshade."

"Well, you *were* responsible," Talia muttered, but Magnus didn't hear her.

"My businesses are shutting down," he continued. "The priestesses are going to kill me."

"If they wanted to kill you, they would've already," Nadine said. "Perhaps with cooperation, they'll lower your sentence."

"They've already sen'enced me to this hell. You think they'll put me in jail when they can enjoy the sa'isfaction of watching my world crumble around me? They'd rather watch me waste away. I'm done. If the priestesses don't kill me, I'll be dead sooner than later." Magnus stumbled to his feet and slurred, "You're a priestess. You can go to hell with the rest of them."

He shoved Nadine, and I caught her. He didn't seem to care as he stumbled down the alleyway. My nostrils flared. *Nobody* touched my girl like that. I went to step forward, but Magnus stopped behind a dumpster and started retching.

I had the thought that leaving him there was worse than anything else I could do to him. "Whatever trouble he gets himself into is his own damn fault."

"We have to at least tell the police, so he doesn't hurt anyone," Nadine said. "We should get him someplace safe, for everyone's sake."

A man emerged from a doorway nearby, carrying a garbage bag. He stopped dead in his tracks when he heard the sound of Magnus puking. The man's shoulders slumped. "Not again."

He tossed his garbage bag into the dumpster, then went over to Magnus. "Come on. Let's get you inside, sober you up."

Magnus muttered something, but I wasn't sure what it was.

The man caught sight of us down the alleyway, and his features darkened. "Come to see the show, kids? Get out of here!"

"Let's go," Talia said, sounding disgusted. "Magnus is *his* problem now."

I kept an eye on Magnus, until he had disappeared inside the building with the man. At least he was off the streets.

As we emerged from the alleyway, we heard shouting down the street. A group of people had gathered around a shop, and they sounded angry—though I couldn't make out their words. There had to be a dozen of them or more. Someone threw their coffee at the window, and it splattered everywhere. At least, I thought it'd been coffee. As the liquid seeped down the glass, it appeared that the glass itself was melting. The window remained intact, but it looked like goop in so many places that we could no longer see through it. The coffee must've been a potion of some sort.

"You're what's wrong with this coven!" someone shouted. "You shouldn't be allowed to stay in business!"

"That's Everly's shop," I realized.

Nadine grabbed my wrist, and I followed her gaze. A police car drove down the street in the direction of the protesters. I thought the police would stop this… but they didn't. The squad car kept driving straight past the angry mob.

"They're not going to do anything!" Talia squeaked.

"They probably organized it in the first place," Grant sneered.

Nadine's lips tightened. "Screw them. Someone has to do something."

We started racing down the sidewalk, and we threw ourselves in front of the protesters.

"Stand back!" Nadine demanded.

"You can't tell us what to do," someone growled.

"I am a high priestess of the Miriamic Coven," Nadine reminded them. "You reserve the right to protest, but violent acts and vandalism will not be tolerated."

"This *business owner* should be charged with violent acts against the coven!" a woman in the crowd demanded. She shook an angry fist at the shop, and I spotted a Seer tattoo on her hand. "She's letting all Casts inside and refuses to keep Seers safe in their own space!"

"We're being oppressed!" a guy shouted. He couldn't have been more than a few years older than me. I thought I recognized him, but I wasn't sure where I'd seen him before.

"This woman is imposing on our rights to shop peacefully by allowing other Casts inside. This is a *Seer* shop," his friend added.

Everly had refused to ban anyone from her shop, and these people thought she was *oppressing* them? Since when did preserving someone else's rights become oppression?

"Seriously, Clay? And Carl, come on," Talia said. "She's hurting no one."

"Your brother's getting into your head," Clay shot back. "Think for yourself."

That's when I realized where I'd seen them before. They were in the Wicked Warlocks, the band Talia's brother sang in.

I realized then why all the other shops had put signs in their windows.

People were demanding spaces for their Cast *only*, and business owners feared losing money if they didn't meet consumer demands.

"My brother hasn't said anything to me," Talia told the two Wicked Warlock musicians.

"Then you're a traitor to your Cast!" Carl yelled. "Get 'em!"

The mob started forward, but a door creaked open behind us. Everly stuck her head out of the shop and hissed, "In here!"

I threw up a shield to block the mob as we scrambled inside. The door clicked shut behind us, and heavy fists pounded against the glass. Whatever potion they'd used to vandalize Everly's shop had made it so I couldn't see through the windows, but I could still make out their shadows coming for us. My heart hammered as I backed away, pushing Nadine behind me. The door shook. I expected it to burst apart at any moment and for the protesters to force their way inside.

"My shop is protected," Everly said calmly. "They can't get inside."

Nadine breathed a heavy sigh, sounding relieved. "What is *wrong* with them?"

"They're angry," a girl said.

I'd been so focused on the door that I hadn't realized there were other people in the shop with us. I turned to see Chloe sitting on the counter, casually shuffling a deck of tarot cards like the mob outside didn't bother her. She wore a brace on her wrist but otherwise looked fine. Verla stood nearby, and another man sat in a chair, though I didn't recognize him. He had to be in his late sixties. He wore a nice suit and a kind smile. He seemed at ease.

"Chloe, you're all right!" Nadine said brightly.

She set the tarot deck aside and hopped off the counter. "Of course I am. I knew I would be. That's why I got arrested on purpose. I had to show that the priestesses will silence anyone."

Chloe gestured to the protesters outside. "I guess people didn't get the message, though. Thank the Goddess Headmistress Verla was there to negotiate for me."

Verla stepped forward. "The priestesses assigned me as Chloe's lawyer, since she's still a student and therefore my responsibility. They think I'm on their side, and I was able to convince them that convicting her would do more harm than good."

"My grandmother may be awful, but she's still family. She let me off easy. I didn't even get a charge, just a night in jail," Chloe said.

"Is there any way you can convince her to change what she's doing?" Nadine asked. "These people are angry about the wrong thing."

"They don't even realize the priestesses are the ones oppressing them," Grant added. "They don't know where to assign blame."

Chloe frowned. "I'm not on those kinds of terms with my grandmother anymore. More or less, she didn't want something on my record that would look bad for the Olsons. She's not going to change something that's serving her, and clearly, this is. These people will take the priestesses' side, because they think *we're* the enemy."

"We're trying to help them!" Talia insisted.

"We can't help people who don't want to be helped," Chloe said.

"But we *can* still help those who need us," Everly said. "I've been in touch with your professor, Angela Wykoff. She was released from custody this morning, but she's quite shaken up about what happened."

Thank the Goddess. I thought for sure they would hang her. Either Chloe's protest had scared them or Verla had been quite persuasive.

"I've cast a protection spell on her home, and I've offered her a job here," Everly said. "She'll be all right. In the meantime, I'd like you to meet a friend of mine. This is Mister Connor."

"Please," the man said as he stood. "Call me William."

He reached out a hand, and we all shook it in turn.

"William Connor," Grant mused. "You own the Gingerbread House, don't you?"

"Yes, along with Connor's Funeral Home and several other businesses. I bought the candy shop after…" He trailed off. "Well, after the unfortunate incidents with the previous owners. I just couldn't bear to see it shut down. The kids love it so much. What's happening outside these doors isn't right, and Everly says I may be able to help."

"I know exactly what we need," Verla suggested. "A safe house. Is that something you can put together?"

William nodded, looking happy to help. "Yes, absolutely. I already have a property outside town that would serve well as a safe house."

"Outside town?" Nadine asked. "No, we're not leaving. If anything, we need a safe house here, where we can continue our work."

"It's merely a precaution," Verla said.

"It's giving ourselves the option to give up," Nadine insisted. "I don't care how hard things get. We can't leave."

"Nadine's right," I agreed. "A safe house is a good idea, but it's got to be easily accessible in case we need it in a pinch. We can use the abandoned mansion behind the school. It's already enchanted with protection spells."

Verla shook her head firmly. "Too many people know about that place. The priestesses could easily find us there. I say we take William's offer. We don't have to use it, but at least the option will be there."

"All right," Nadine reluctantly agreed. "But I'm not leaving the coven unless I have to."

Verla turned to William. "Can you stock the safe house with supplies and ensure the wards are undetectable?"

He nodded. "I can. There's one other way I can help, too. Claudia Sinclair has offered me an investment opportunity, and if I take it, I may learn more about the priestesses' intentions."

"You should take it and let us know what you learn," Nadine said. "Thank you for your help."

"I just want to see the coven heal," he replied.

The banging on the door grew louder, and Talia jumped from beside me. She shot a nervous glance at the door. "We should probably get going."

"There's a back door you can use," Everly offered. "Get back to school safely, okay?"

"We will," Nadine said. "Thank you for all your help."

Everly smiled. "Of course."

The four of us left out the back door, and we circled around the block. We were passing by a liquor store when a man rushed out, head down so that he didn't see us. It was like he expected everyone to just move out of his way. I didn't see him in time, and he rammed straight into me.

"Watch it!" he growled.

I felt the blood drain from my face. I knew that voice all too well. I felt like I was eight years old again, being screamed at for Goddess knew what. I wanted to hide away in a corner and become invisible.

The man stopped in his tracks when he noticed me. "Lucas?"

My jaw tightened as I forced myself to respond. "Dad."

Fuck, I hadn't seen him in… I didn't know how long. The only way we communicated these days was through my mother, and neither of us ever had much to say. Dad looked like he'd aged ten years since I'd seen him last. His gut was bigger than ever, and his hair had grayed.

His lips curled into a sneer. He obviously wasn't happy to see me, either. "You should be ashamed of yourself after the way you treated your mother when the house burnt down! She deserves more respect."

Goddess, here we went. I hadn't even said two words, and he was already yelling at me.

"You're one to talk about respect," I mumbled.

"How *dare* talk to me like that?" he growled.

My heart seemed to shrink inside my chest, becoming smaller and smaller. Retreating inside myself was the only way I'd ever learned to protect myself from him. Wasn't he embarrassed, yelling at me in front of all my friends? I didn't get how he could do it. Hell, *I* was embarrassed for him.

Nadine pushed her way in front of me. "You call yourself a father, but you never—"

"Nad, stop," I insisted. She was going to get herself hurt.

My father chuckled. "You need your girlfriend to stand up for you? Is that what it means to be Mortana? Perhaps if you'd been a Mentalist like your old man, you could fight your own battles."

I grabbed Nadine's arm and pushed her behind me. If Dad was going to go off on me, I didn't want my friends getting caught in the crosshairs.

"It must be great, sitting in your cushy dorm with all your expenses paid on your fancy scholarship while your mom and I are struggling to get back on our feet," Dad ranted. "You could've helped us move into our new apartment."

"If you think of your son as nothing but free labor, then you're not a father," Nadine snapped.

My hand tightened around her wrist. Sticking up for me was only going to make it worse.

"You're gonna question my worth as a father? No, no, no. Ask *him* why he chose to be such a shitty son," Dad sneered. "Now he's moved on to ruin your life, huh?"

"Maybe I was a shitty son because I got tired of being beat." I shouldn't have said it, but I needed to distract him from Nadine. I wasn't going to let him talk to her the way he spoke to me.

"The only reason I turned to the bottle was because you and your brother were such huge disappointments," he said. "I had dreams, but I never got to pursue them after you came along. I could've been a big wig executive at a fancy law firm. I would've had money."

I would've snorted if I thought he wouldn't hit me for it. Dad had no interests outside of alcohol and gambling. To think he'd ever make it as a lawyer was laughable.

"You should call your mother once in a while," my dad added. "She's been real sad lately. A good son would at least check up on her."

Of course he was using my mother as a weapon against me. He always did. Despite that, I couldn't respond. I took whatever blows he delivered, because I knew if I hit back, he'd hit back harder.

"Eric would've called," my dad taunted as he shook his bag of liquor at me. "But he's gone. Maybe if you weren't sneaking around breaking into cemeteries that night, you could've been there to stop him."

Something inside my chest broke at the mention of my brother. It took me back to times when Eric and I would hide in the closet to escape my father's wrath—when his Mentalist powers would get out of control, and things would start spinning around the room. There was no talking my father down. The only way to save yourself was to let him run out of steam, until he eventually got tired of torturing you.

I feared the bottles of liquor would come flying out of his hands and hurt someone. All I wanted to do was run as far away from my father as possible, to never see him again… to disappear.

And that's exactly what I did. I didn't know how it happened. One second I was standing on the sidewalk in the middle of Octavia Falls, and the next, my stomach felt like it was spiraling outside my body. Flashes of color passed by my vision, then everything stopped.

My feet hit solid ground, and I regained my bearings. I looked around to see that I was standing on the lawn in front of Miriam Mansion.

How had I gotten there?

I spotted a couple headed toward their vehicle at the other end of the parking lot, but otherwise the yard was empty. No one had seen me suddenly appear.

What the hell had happened?

My phone buzzed, and I rushed to answer it.

"Lucas, thank the Goddess," Nadine's worried tone came over the line. "You disappeared into thin air! But… how?"

"I… I don't know." This kind of thing didn't happen in the Miriamic Coven.

"Your dad thinks we've hexed him with some sort of illusion magic," Nadine said.

"Get out of there," I demanded. "I don't want you anywhere near my father. There's an extra set of keys in my glove compartment. I'm back at school. I don't know how I got here."

"We'll be there right away," Nadine promised.

I was still shaken by the whole experience. I could hardly bring myself to move. I managed to make it to the front steps, but once I was there, I collapsed and just sat there. My head spun, and I kept running over what my father had said in my mind. I didn't want to believe any of it, but I'd been conditioned to believe every word that came out of my father's mouth. Even years apart from him hadn't changed that.

He was right. I couldn't fight my own battles. I was a shit son. If my mom was to lose any son, it should've been me… not Eric.

Perhaps my brother was on to something. He'd disappeared. Like I wanted to right now.

I found myself conjuring my wand and spinning it around in my hands. It'd be so easy to just end it all. Just one battle spell to the side of my head, and I'd be gone. All of this would be over.

I didn't want to do it. I had things to live for—*people* to live for. My life had never been better. But the coven was suffering, and maybe Nadine would be better off fulfilling the prophecy without me getting in the way.

I couldn't help the intrusive thoughts. I didn't *want* to feel this way. But there was something appealing about just ending it all.

I placed the tip of my wand below my chin. I wasn't going to do it. I just wanted to see what it'd feel like to get close… to see how far I'd really take it.

To scare myself out of it.

"Lucas!" Grant's voice made my whole body go rigid, and I subconjured my wand like it'd never been there in the first place. Nadine had pulled up in front of the school, and my friends piled out of the car. I stood, but I didn't say anything.

Nadine rushed toward me, and she threw her arms around me. Her hug soothed me unlike anything else. I felt like I could breathe again.

"I'm all right," I told her. At least, I would be.

"You were there one second and gone the next," Grant started.

"I know," I said. "There was definitely something magical about what happened. But who has the magic to do something like that—to *teleport* me somewhere? Could the Waning not just be taking our magic, but messing with it somehow? The only other explanation is—"

It hit me like a hearse going a hundred miles an hour.

"Goddess, I think I know what happened." I glanced toward the front doors to the school. Someone could walk out at any moment.

"Maybe we should talk inside," Grant suggested.

I nodded, then led everyone toward the Gravestone, where we wouldn't be heard. We passed Miles in the hall, and he caught the serious look on my face. He followed closely behind us, his cat at his heels. Grant quickly filled his brother in. My friends all took a seat, but I remained standing.

"It was portal magic," I stated. "I'm sure of it. We keep saying the coven's portal magic is shit, but we know it exists. In limited capacities, at least."

"What are the chances of a portal showing up on Main Street and teleport you back to the school?" Talia asked.

"Professor Leto said he knew more about my magic than he'd ever let on. He was talking about portal magic," I said. "It wasn't a random portal, Tal. I created it myself."

"Of course," Nadine said. "Reapers use portal magic to cross realms. Leto didn't tell you because if you can open portals to other realms, he's in trouble."

Miles tapped his chin. "This isn't the first time you've made a portal. A portal appeared in the forest when you helped Professor Daymond cross over."

"And with Professor Ward," Nadine pointed out. "They were your assignment before the portals ever opened. You must've opened them yourself, without realizing it."

"Exactly," I said. "Problem is, I don't know how to control it yet."

"*Yet*," Nadine emphasized. "But you're going to get better."

Nadine's unwavering faith in me was humbling. I had an important job in all this, a reason why the prophecy spoke of me. I just needed to be reminded of it.

"Yet," I agreed with a firm nod. "I'm going to practice my portal magic.

And when I can finally control it, I'm opening a portal to the Abyss, and we're sending Professor Leto back to hell."

My friends seemed energized by my certainty.

"The library must have resources on portal magic, right?" Nadine asked.

"It's rare in the coven, so I wouldn't hold my breath," Talia said. "But we can look."

"You girls go," Grant offered.

I didn't understand why he sent them off, until the door closed behind them and Grant and Miles both turned to me. Grant sighed. "We need to talk."

"If it's about my dad, I've already done a forgiveness ceremony," I stated. "I just want to move on."

"It's not about that, exactly," Grant said slowly. "I think it's time you talk to Dr. Mack about medication."

That wasn't happening. "I appreciate the help, but I'm not taking meds."

"Why not?" Miles asked, sounding genuinely curious.

"I don't know… it's just…" I stumbled over my words. "I don't want to put a band-aid over my depression. I want to figure it out myself."

Miles frowned. "I'm not going to say I understand your particular diagnosis, whatever it may be."

"Officially, I've got major depressive disorder," I said flatly. "I also *exhibit symptoms of childhood trauma.*"

"Right," Miles said. "And depression presents itself differently in everybody. I won't pretend I know everything you're going through, but meds really helped me when I was struggling."

"I can handle it on my own," I insisted.

"Sometimes depression isn't something you can just *cure* on your own," Miles said. "Your brain doesn't function the way other people's do, but that doesn't make it wrong or mean you're anything less than normal. Your normal is different, and there are tools available to help you manage, if you're willing to accept them."

I was getting angry the more he talked. "I said I didn't want them," I snapped. "I know you're worried about what happened with my dad, but medication isn't going to fix what he did."

"No, but they can help you manage," Miles said gently. "I'll tell you what a friend told me once. You're in the driver's seat, Lucas. People can throw trash into your car, but you can toss it right back out. Anything outside your vehicle is out of your control and not your problem."

"Then why does it feel like it is!?" I yelled.

Why couldn't they take no for an answer?

"We're only trying to help," Grant assured me.

"Well, you can stop trying," I snapped. "I'll handle it!"

I stormed out of the room before either of them could say more. I hurried toward my car. Grant wanted me to talk to Dr. Mack? Fine, I would. But I wasn't going on meds.

Hell, I really needed Dr. Mack's advice right now, because I was spiraling.

I got to the clinic and rushed to the reception desk. "I need to see Dr. Mack right now."

My heart raced, and it seemed like the receptionist looked at the computer for a whole minute before saying, "I'm not seeing an appointment for you. It's Lucas, right?"

"I don't have an appointment," I said. "It's an emergency."

"I'm afraid she's working right now," the receptionist said. She thought she was being helpful.

"I don't care if she's busy. I *have* to talk to her."

The woman hesitated. "Give me one moment."

She picked up her phone, and I swear it was the longest phone call in history. "Yes, um, I have Lucas Taylor here for you... I tried to tell him, but he says it's an emergency... All right."

She hung up the phone and gestured to the waiting area. "Dr. Mack will be right out."

As if I could sit down right now. I paced around the waiting room until Dr. Mack arrived.

"Lucas," she said kindly. "Let's talk."

I practically sprinted into her office. The second I sat down, it all came spilling out of me. Dr. Mack wore a nervous expression as she sat there listening. "I saw my Dad, Dr. Mack. I wasn't prepared for it, and I didn't think it'd be this bad, but the things he said to me were awful. I used to think it was normal, and now I just can't help but feel—"

"I can't see you anymore," Dr. Mack blurted.

My stomach dropped, and for a moment, it felt like time itself had come to a halt. I couldn't have heard her right. "I—I know I came unannounced…"

She pressed her fingers to her eyes, like this was too stressful. Was I that annoying?

"I want to help you, Lucas," she said slowly, as if choosing her words carefully. "I really do, but I can't. You shouldn't be here."

"What do you mean? I was just here earlier this week. What changed?"

"Your health insurance was denied," she stated bluntly.

I felt the blood drain from my face. For a second, I thought we could fix this. A few phone calls to the health insurance company, and we'd be golden. Until I realized… she wasn't saying there was a problem with my insurance. She was saying I didn't *have* insurance anymore. Fuck the priestesses and their fucking war on healthcare. Without school insurance, I lost all my mental health resources, and they didn't even bother notifying me!

"This is bullshit!" I cried. "There must be something we can do. Put me on a payment plan. I have a job now."

"A part-time job?" she asked with a sigh. "Lucas, it's not enough. I'm afraid clinic policy states that once you reach a certain threshold, those bills must be paid before I can see you again. You do understand you've already attended several sessions that must be paid out of pocket?"

"Then let me pick up a job here to pay for it," I begged. "I'll do part-time janitorial services. *Something*. You can't drop me, Dr. Mack. I need you."

"I've helped you all I can," she said gently, as if the world wasn't crumbling down. Couldn't she feel it? The whole ground seemed to shake… or was that me?

"This can't be it. If I don't have you, I don't… I don't… Goddess, it's not just my therapy. It's… it's Nadine. Without you, I'll never get the psych approval. Her kidney…" I couldn't get the words out.

"Let's take some deep breaths," Dr. Mack encouraged.

"Why should I listen to you!?" I shot out of my chair. "You don't want to help me. You just want my money."

"Lucas. I. *Do*. Want. To. Help. You." She was so firm. Her tone softened when she said, "But I *can't*."

I realized there was more to the story, something she couldn't tell me.

I didn't know if she was magically bound, or if someone was holding a threat over her head. It had to be the priestesses.

Dr. Mack spoke carefully, deliberately. "There are oaths I took as a therapist when I began my practice, something we call doctor-patient confidentiality. I would sooner quit my practice than break my oaths."

Her message came across clearly. The priestesses had tried to get her to divulge information from our sessions so they could use it against Nadine and me. The health insurance situation was merely convenient timing. Dr. Mack wasn't dropping me because she didn't care. She was doing it to protect me.

I didn't want to be protected. This didn't just come down to my therapy. It affected Nadine's transplant, too.

"What about the psych eval?" I asked. "Have I destroyed my chances?"

"I may have the power to see the future, but this time, I truly don't know what the future holds." It was very clear there was nothing more she would say—for both our sakes.

I swallowed the lump rising in my throat. "I guess this is it, then."

"For us? Yes," she said. "For you? No. There are many people in your life who are willing to help you."

She gave me a sharp look. There was so much she was trying to tell me without saying it out loud. Hell, for all I knew, the priestesses could be watching. The best I could tell, she knew I needed to talk to someone right now, and she was encouraging me to speak to a trusted source.

All right. I could do that…

Maybe.

I returned to the school and found Isa and Oliver lounging in front of the fireplace in the Main Foyer. I went over to stroke Oliver's fur. "Find anything, buddy?"

Oliver looked up at me with a sad expression on his face. That's when I noticed the scratch on his chin.

My stomach dropped as I pulled him into my arms. "What happened to you?"

Oliver couldn't respond, but he purred as I inspected the wound. It wasn't deep enough to need stitches, but it'd get infected if I didn't keep a close eye on it.

I couldn't tell if someone had done this to him, or if he'd gotten into an altercation with another cat. If Professor Leto had caught him following him, I didn't think he'd hesitate to hurt him. It was stupid of me to send him to spy on Leto in the first place. He'd learned nothing, and he got hurt for it.

"You two go back to the dorms," I instructed. "I don't want you getting hurt. I'll be back soon."

The cats ran off, and I continued down the hall. I paced nervously in front of Professor Warren's classroom. He'd given me advice before. Surely he'd be able to help.

Warren's office was located at the back of his classroom, but I remained in the hallway. All I had to do was open the freaking door, but I couldn't.

Maybe I didn't need his advice. I'd bottle it up, like I used to… until it all came spilling out. Fuck, what was I supposed to do?

Before I could make a decision, the classroom door opened. "Ah, Lucas," Professor Warren said brightly. "You caught me just in time. I was on my way out."

I couldn't mask the emotions on my face. Professor Warren noticed, and the corners of his lips turned down. "Let's talk."

I followed him through his classroom, and he shut his office door behind us. I plopped into the red chair across from his desk. Professor Warren sat behind his desk and waited for me to speak. I couldn't spit the words out.

Finally, he broke the silence. "What can I do to help?"

He didn't pry, and I appreciated that. He wasn't asking me what was wrong, or trying to get a story out of me. All he wanted to do was help. I tried to steady my breath.

"I know I've been hard on you in the past—" he started.

I scoffed. "Not even close."

Had this man ever *met* my father?

"I'm just having a hard time putting my thoughts into words," I admitted. "I lost my therapist."

His shoulders fell, and he looked genuinely sorry for me. "Perhaps I can help you find someone to replace your doctor."

"It's no use. No one's going to take me without insurance, and my internship doesn't pay *that* well. It's just… Professor, I don't think I can do this without my therapist."

A weight came off my shoulders when I admitted that. It wasn't easy to be vulnerable around anyone but Nadine, but part of me wanted to just put it all out in the open.

"The last thing I want is to see you out of therapy before you're ready, but perhaps you're stronger than you believe," Professor Warren said.

"I don't know about that."

"Look at all the progress you've made," he reminded me. "Of course your therapist has been there to support you, but it was *you* who did the work."

"Without her guidance, how will I know what to do? Professor, it's not just about me. I'm getting better, and I was *so close* to convincing Dr. Mack of that. Just a few more weeks, and she would approve my psych eval for Nadine's kidney transplant. I just know it."

Fuck, I was a wreck. This was all my fault.

"You can't blame yourself," Professor Warren insisted.

"Why not?" I demanded. "Nadine's going to suffer because of me."

It was the last thing I wanted to admit to myself. It's why I'd come to Professor Warren and not her. I just couldn't watch Nadine's hopes crumble all over again. I had to bring myself to a better place before I told her, because I had to be there for her fully when I broke the news.

"I'm sure Nadine will understand," Professor Warren said. "She won't blame you."

"*I* will, though," I growled.

I was *not* in a good place right now, and it really worried me. I couldn't return to my old habits. In some ways, depression was like an addiction—comfortable and familiar. If I went back there, I didn't know how I'd pull myself out this time.

"Let's just take a moment to process this, and we'll come up with a solution," Professor Warren suggested.

His tone gave me pause, and I eyed him curiously. "You say that like you know what it's like. Do you?"

He always seemed so sure of himself. It never occurred to me that maybe he understood more than I gave him credit for.

Professor Warren shifted, and he twisted a pen around in his hands. He didn't look at me, which was odd. He was always so attentive and serious. "I know what it's like to lose a therapist when you need them the most."

The room fell dead silent. I never knew Professor Warren had been in therapy. Learning that made me feel slightly more at ease, because maybe he really *did* understand. Maybe that's why he tried to help me for so long… because he knew what it was like to be in my position.

"What happened after you lost your therapist?"

"Things got better eventually," he said. "But it took time."

I wanted to learn more, but I didn't want to prod. Still, I found myself asking, "What happened?"

Warren drew a deep breath, as if contemplating how much to tell me. "My therapist and I talked about many things. You understand how things build up over the years."

He stared down at his pen, as if almost forgetting I was there. "We talked of my childhood and my absent father, and we discussed the failed fertility treatments Roberta and I went through, then the pain of losing her to cancer… I should've sought out therapy when I lost my wife, but I didn't reach my breaking point until years later. I thought I was finally finding happiness again. I was dating. Things were going well. And when my girlfriend got pregnant… well, it was one of the happiest moments of my life… until it wasn't. Turns out, the baby wasn't mine. I still love her in many ways, but…"

Professor Warren must've realized he'd said too much, because he cleared his throat and sat up straighter. "But that wasn't your question, I suppose. Therapy shouldn't be reserved for those who have reached their breaking point. We should embrace therapy at all stages. And I think that's what helped me get better, even after my therapist retired— accepting that I was worthy of help, even at times when I wasn't completely falling apart. You don't have to be at the end of your rope to get help, and help can appear in your life in many ways."

"I'm not sure I understand what you're trying to tell me, Professor," I said.

He leaned forward in his chair. "Just because you've lost Dr. Mack doesn't mean you've lost everything. You have friends and teachers and people who will be by you every step of the way if you allow them in. We'll find you another therapist, but in the meantime, you must trust yourself and your friends to help you through this."

"I don't want my friends to feel like they have to fix me," I admitted.

"They don't see it that way. I promise you. They want to help, as do I."

"You've actually been a big help already," I admitted. I didn't want to keep talking about my feelings, though. I just wanted to stop thinking about it, so I asked, "Do you know anything about portal magic?"

He knew I was trying to change the subject, and he played along. "The coven has some resources on it, but it's not covered in your classes. It'd take a special set of gifted witches to cast a portal, and they're generally considered unsafe to pass through anyway. Portals are more of a fae power. Why do you ask?"

"I want to open a portal to the Abyss," I stated simply. "We need to banish this demon somehow."

"I'm afraid we'll have to find another way. To even find someone with the ability to cast a portal—"

"I can do it," I blurted.

Professor Warren didn't move for a second.

I shrugged. "I'm a reaper, and reapers have the power to travel between worlds."

"Yes, but you're telling me that you used a portal, and you're still alive…? That kind of power…" Professor Warren's eyebrows pinched together.

"How much do you *really* know about reapers?" I asked. "There's only one per generation, so how much information can really be out there? Maybe all this power you think I'll obtain once I die is inside me already. I've already created portals. I just need to learn how to control them."

"Do you have any idea what kind of power you have? This is a very unique gift."

"That's why I intend to figure it out, so I don't fuck up," I said.

Professor Warren looked thoughtful. "You do realize this could be very dangerous."

"It's even more dangerous if I ignore what I'm capable of," I pointed out.

Professor Warren stood from his desk and pulled a book off the shelf. "This book has a section on portal magic. I suggest you use it carefully."

I reached for it, but he pulled it away at the last second.

"Don't let anyone find out you have this," he stated in a grave tone, before placing it into my hands. "This book is dangerous, Lucas. And if people discover you have this kind of power at your disposal… they will kill you for it."

EIGHT

Meeting Lucas's dad shocked me more than it should have. I'd heard stories. I knew what his dad was like. I should have been prepared. And I still couldn't believe a parent could talk to their child like that. There may be a demon roaming the coven, but Jay Taylor was the true monster.

I brought breakfast to Lucas's room the following morning, because I knew he'd forget to eat otherwise. We sat beside each other on the couch, and he managed to eat a few bites of fruit while he told me what happened yesterday.

"This is unfair!" I cried. "The priestesses can't take away your healthcare."

Lucas frowned. "They can, and they did."

"Then I'll pay for it," I decided, like it was already settled.

"Therapy costs over a hundred dollars per session," he said gently. "Where are you going to get that kind of money?"

"Grammy and I have *some*."

"Which needs to go toward your dialysis," he insisted. "You literally need your healthcare to survive. I don't."

It wasn't necessarily true, but I didn't say that out loud. Instead, I said, "That doesn't make your therapy any less important."

"I'll take a break from therapy for now." He wasn't going to let me pay

138

for his sessions, no matter how much I pressed. "Professor Warren has been helpful before. He can help me again. He gave me a book on portals."

I could tell he was trying to change the subject. I didn't want to press and make this harder on him, so I said, "That's good, because Talia and I didn't find anything in the library."

"See? He's already helping," he said.

I thought he was only saying that so I'd drop the topic, but over the following week, I noticed huge improvements in his mood. His internship gave him a lot of one-on-one time with Professor Warren, and whatever they talked about really seemed to help Lucas.

"Did you know that Professor Warren used to snowboard?" Lucas asked me as we headed to my dorm after lunch Friday. "He was on a team and everything."

"No, I had no idea. That sounds fun, though."

"He says he wants to take me snowboarding sometime."

"Ooh, a ski resort weekend?" I asked. "Count me in. A weekend with a good mystery novel and hot cocoa in front of a cozy fireplace sounds great."

"That's not really what you're supposed to do at a ski resort," he teased. "The slopes are there for a reason."

"Yeah, for *you*." I laughed. I knew it wouldn't happen anytime soon, not with everything going on right now, but it felt good to imagine a future where we *could* plan a weekend away.

We reached my dorm room, and I stopped in my tracks when I entered. I flung my hand over my eyes. All I saw was a flash of Grant's skin under the blanket and Talia's brown hair spilling over the pillow.

I whirled on my heel and accidentally slammed into Lucas. "Sorry! We'll leave."

Talia burst into laughter. "Relax. We're decent."

Slowly, I turned around. Grant tossed the blanket off of them, and I was relieved to see he was fully dressed from the waist down. Talia wore jeans and a t-shirt, but I'm pretty sure I saw her adjust her bra. They'd *definitely* been fooling around.

"How's it… um, going?" I asked. I went over to sit on my bed, where Isa was taking a nap. I sat beside her and stroked her head.

"We weren't doing anything bad, if that's what you're asking," Grant said as he pulled a t-shirt over his head.

"Sure you weren't," I teased.

"We're all adults here. But you know, just in case..." Lucas conjured a condom and tossed it at Grant.

He caught it, and his face fell when he realized what it was. "We weren't—I wasn't—"

"You guys can fool around whenever you want. Just maybe give us some warning," I suggested.

"The last thing I want to see is your naked ass," Lucas cracked.

"You mean you don't want to see *this*?" Grant shook his butt in Lucas's direction, and Lucas shoved him away. He fell onto the bed.

"Jokes aside, you two have nothing to be ashamed of," I said. "And no pressure, either. Just use protection, okay?"

"Believe me, the condom box will see its fair share of use before we graduate." Talia gestured to the jewelry box on her dresser. We'd been keeping condoms in there since our first semester.

"They don't need to know how often we use it," Grant hissed, but it was more a joke than anything. Either way, he seemed eager to change the subject. "You guys wouldn't happen to have dinner plans, would you?"

Lucas shook his head. "No, why?"

"Talia and I are planning a date tonight. We were going to get dinner on The Hearse, then see a show at Starlight, but the show would start before we finished dinner. I don't want the tickets to go to waste. Do you want them?"

Grant held out two tickets for The Hearse, the traveling diner set inside a limousine.

I shrugged. "It sounds like fun. I have dialysis tonight, but I should be finished in time for dinner."

"If you call them, you can schedule a pickup time," Talia said.

Lucas took the tickets from Grant. "Thanks, guys. This sounds great. How much do I owe you?"

Grant waved his hand. "Don't worry about it. Just have fun."

That night, Lucas met up with me outside the hospital after dialysis. He was alone, as we'd left Oliver and Isa back at school. He was dressed in a button-down shirt and nice slacks, and he'd combed his hair back in this really sexy way. He eyed me up and down when he saw me. The desire in his eyes made me blush under his gaze. I wore a modest black dress with warm tights, nice boots, and a leather jacket over top.

"You look hot," he told me, holding his elbow out to me.

I hooked my arm through his. "Thank you. You're looking pretty fine yourself."

His gaze darted down to my lips. He lowered his voice and whispered, "Maybe later I can get that dress off you."

"I'll be disappointed if you don't," I teased, before leaning over to kiss him.

As I drew away, I heard the sound of a vehicle approaching. The Hearse pulled up in front of us, and a man emerged from the limo to hold the door for us. Lucas handed him our reservation tickets, and we climbed inside.

The Hearse was the size of a train on the inside, big enough to fit at least a hundred people. It was Friday night, so the restaurant was packed. Soft, warm lighting illuminated the red tablecloths. Water trickled down the windows, like a beautiful waterfall. Overhead, we could look out through the moonroof at the twinkling stars. It all felt very romantic.

We passed by a group of students crowded around a large table. I didn't know most of them, but I recognized Mira. She was Leroy's younger sister, the girl who'd confronted me outside my dorm on our first day back. She caught sight of me passing by and whispered something to her friend. They both burst out laughing.

My mood soured, but I ignored them and followed the host to a small table near the back. He seated us near a platform, where a woman sat playing piano. I recognized her as Monica, a woman who ran a music shop downtown. Talia had brought me to Hallowed Harmonica a few times to shop the collection of antiques.

Monica's beautiful tune filled the car, and I instantly relaxed at the calm music. I remembered Talia had told me Monica's Mentalist powers could influence a person's emotion through music. She was really good at it, because I hadn't felt this relaxed in a long time.

"How was your day?" Lucas asked once we'd ordered our drinks.

"It was good." I could see the town passing by as a blur of color behind the waterfall windows, but the ride was so smooth it barely felt like we were moving. "I visited the nursing home before dialysis. Rose and I finished our puzzle."

"That's great. You've been working on it for weeks," Lucas said.

The waiter arrived with our drink order, along with a basket of bread.

I sipped my raspberry lemonade. "Rose is doing better this week. The doctors have her on new meds, and I think they're really helping."

"How was dialysis?" he asked.

I shrugged. "Same as always. I'm still doing my intuition work during my sessions. I'm getting better at it. How about you?"

He broke apart a piece of bread. "I ordered the parts for my car. We should be able to start working on her soon."

"I can't wait. You'll be surprised how she runs once we fix her up."

"Speaking of surprises…" Lucas reached into his pocket and pulled out a small box wrapped in shimmering black paper. He slid it across the table toward me.

I furrowed my brow as I lifted it. It barely weighed a thing. "You didn't have to get me a present. This isn't a special occasion."

Hold on. Could it be a ring… already? Had Grant been in on it by offering the tickets to throw me off? A thrilling shiver traveled up and down my body when I thought of Lucas proposing.

Lucas shrugged. "I wanted you to have this back."

I didn't know what he meant, until I unwrapped the box and found my grandmother's key tucked inside. It was an old antique she'd received from my grandfather, rumored to be enchanted with a protection spell. It hung off a chain, so you could wear it like a necklace.

I was a little disappointed it wasn't a ring, but I was happy to see he'd kept this.

"Lucas, no." I handed the box back to him, but he wouldn't take it. "I gave it to you. It's yours."

"But your grandma gave it to *you*," he argued. "Don't you think she'd still want you to have it?"

"It's not hers anymore. It was mine, and I gave it to you," I said. "It was a gift."

"When we broke up, I should've given it back."

"It's yours," I insisted.

"Then I'm giving it to you."

"You already gave me a key, remember?" I reminded him. "The one you found in the abandoned mansion."

"Then you can have two," he offered with a smile.

I sighed. Neither of us was going to cave. He wanted me to have this because it was a family heirloom, and I wanted him to have it so that it'd protect him—in whatever limited capacity it could.

I glanced toward the windows. We must've been outside of town now, because I saw no lights, just the blur of trees passing by.

"How about we share?" I suggested. "Whoever needs it most at the time will wear it."

Lucas smiled and reached for the key. "That sounds perfect. Tonight, it's yours."

He unclasped the chain and leaned across the table to secure it around my neck. "It looks great on you—"

Lucas cut off as the entire limo jerked, like the driver had slammed on the brakes. Everything happened all at once. Piano notes clashed together the same time a collective scream filled the air. My heart lurched as I went flying out of my chair, and Lucas and I landed on the ground next to each other. Tires squealed, and a loud *thud* sounded from overhead. I barely caught a glimpse of something moving above us through the moonroof, but it was gone a moment later.

I didn't have a moment to process it, because The Hearse continued spinning, like the driver had yanked on the wheel. We went over a bump, and people screamed as they were tossed upward.

Lucas threw himself on top of me, and I felt a warm sensation cradle me to his chest. It was more than just his arms around me. Something magical wrapped around my entire form, cocooning me close to him.

One second we were on the ground, and the next we were flying upward, toward the ceiling. I screamed as we went tumbling around and around. Glass shattered, and screams seemed to fade away into the night.

It all happened so fast that I could barely process any of it. Within moments, everything came to an abrupt halt. I was so disoriented, I didn't quite know where I was.

Slowly, I began to make sense of my surroundings. I lay flat on my back, and the full moon shone through the trees. Ice-cold snow seeped through my dress, making me shiver. Screams of agony filled the air, and people called out names I didn't recognize. For a moment, all I could do was stare at the stars above me. I wasn't sure how I'd gotten on the ground.

My body ached, but I pushed myself upright. My heart raced as I glanced around frantically for Lucas. We'd been thrown from the limo, but somehow, I hadn't been hurt. It must've been that magic I felt cocooning me before the car went off the road. Whatever it was had saved me.

"Nad!" Lucas screamed, his cry tearing through the darkness. I spotted him scrambling toward me. He grabbed me and pulled me close to him, cradling me to his chest. "You're all right. I protected you."

I realized then that the magic I'd felt around us had come from him. He'd created a shield that formed to our bodies to keep us from getting hurt.

"I'm fine. Are you?" I pushed against him. I had to see his face. "Lucas, talk to me! Are you hurt?"

He clutched me so tightly that I couldn't move. He pressed his head against mine and whispered in a ragged breath, "There are so many voices."

Slowly, I dared to look around, and horror rocked my body. The Hearse sat mangled not far away, lying upside down and smashed against a line of trees, wheels spinning toward the sky. The headlights flashed before going out completely. A man hung upside down from the driver's seat, and blood pooled out of a large wound on his head. He blinked several times, and his gaze turned in my direction. The guilt in his features felt like a dagger to my gut. He looked utterly devastated by the realization of what he'd caused. Mira and her friends crawled out of The Hearse's broken windows, evacuating the broken vehicle.

We were outside of town, on one of the forested roads that led toward a scenic lookout. Glass shards scattered across the snow, and bodies lay across the road and in the ditch. Pools of blood stained the ground. There were so many unmoving bodies...

Lucas pulled me tighter to his chest. I could only imagine the thoughts flittering through his mind at that moment. He always said the traumatic deaths hit harder. This had to be horrible for him, worse than anything I could possibly witness.

Screams continued to fill the night, and Lucas dropped his arms. "Help them," he said.

"What about you?" I couldn't leave him.

"I'll be fine." He winced, like another dying thought had entered his mind. Lucas conjured a first-aid kit and shoved it into my arms. He clutched his stomach and pushed at me. "Go!"

Someone screamed from nearby, pulling my attention off Lucas. People raced in so many directions, and I couldn't tell who was hurt and who was dead. I heard Lucas gag, and my stomach twisted into knots. The best way to help him was to help the others. I had to prevent as many deaths as possible.

My gaze landed upon a man nearby. He lay on his back, his arm twisted at an odd angle. Blood coated his body in so many places that I didn't know where it was coming from. He stared upward, but his eyes seemed to gloss over. He opened his mouth, like he wanted to scream, but nothing came out.

I raced over to him. "Hold on. We're going to get you help."

He turned his gaze toward me, but he looked straight through me. His mouth bobbed open, but only a gurgling sound escaped. My stomach clenched as blood sputtered from his mouth and trickled down the side of his face.

A moment later, his entire form went limp, and his head sagged to the side. My whole body began to tremble as I witnessed the life leave his eyes. From behind me, I heard Lucas gasp, and I knew this man's last thought had entered his mind.

A gut-wrenching wail pierced the night. A woman covered in bruises stumbled through the snow toward me.

"Ian! Ian!" she cried. The woman shoved me aside and threw herself on top of the man, sobbing. After a moment, she turned her bitter gaze on me and growled, "What have you done!? Get away from him, you wicked wench."

There was nothing I could do. He was already gone.

Nearby, a woman clutched her stomach and cried in agony. In the moonlight, I could make out her dark hair, which contrasted against the white snow. It was Monica, the piano player.

I abandoned the dead man and ran over to her. "I'm here to help."

She drew ragged breaths. "I wasn't supposed to be here tonight. It was a last-minute job…"

"Shh…" I told her. "Let me take a look—"

I stopped abruptly when I guided her hands away from her stomach. A thin, curved piece of glass stuck out of her skin, and blood poured from the wound. It looked like it was a broken wine glass.

"Goddess, it hurts," Monica cried. "Take it out."

She reached for the jagged piece of glass, but I stopped her. "No! You have to keep it in until paramedics arrive. If you take it out, you could bleed out."

Monica hesitated. She was panicked and really out of it. I quickly opened the first-aid kit and unwrapped a huge wad of gauze. I carefully pressed it against the wound, making sure not to press the glass in any further.

"Hold this firmly," I told her. "The EMTs will be here soon."

"Please… if I don't make it…" Monica's voice shook.

"You will," I promised, but my stomach clenched, because there was no way I could know that for certain.

I heard the sirens off in the distance. It gave me hope, but only so little. I wasn't sure they would make it in time. Even if they could save Monica, there were so many others who wouldn't make it.

A guy from school stumbled past me, blood oozing from a gash on his head. He would certainly need stitches. He wore a confused expression and blinked a few times, like he couldn't see clearly. "Lydia! Lydia!" he screamed. I recognized him from my Miriamic Law class.

"Quentin!" I called. I rushed to my feet and caught him before he collapsed onto the ground. He was really heavy, though, and I had to guide him to lie in the snow.

"Wh—where's Lydia?" he rasped.

I glanced around frantically, but I didn't spot her. He tried to sit up, but I pushed at his chest. "Quentin, you're hurt. You have to lie down."

He furrowed his brow and winced, then reached up to touch the gash on his head. The second he saw the blood, his eyes rolled back into his skull, and he passed out.

Shit.

Color drained from his face, until his lips were paler than his skin. I scrambled for more gauze and tried to stop the bleeding.

"Stay with me, Quentin!" I demanded, though I didn't think he could hear me.

Time seemed to speed up and slow down all at once. I couldn't make sense of how much time had passed before the paramedics arrived. Sirens wailed, and red and blue lights shone off the trees as several ambulances pulled up. EMTs rushed onto the scene, administering first aid as quickly as possible.

"Miss, you have to move!" I was vaguely aware of someone guiding me away from Quentin and Monica. I didn't know what to do but step back and let them take over. My blood-covered hands shook. There had to be *something* I could do.

I heard Lucas gasp from behind me, and I snapped back to attention. I whirled toward him to see him hunched over on his knees. He clutched his stomach with one hand and pressed the other palm to his forehead.

Fuck, people were still dying.

I rushed over to him and wrapped my arms around him. His whole body shook, and he was covered in a thick sheen of sweat. "I'm here," I told him. Lucas seemed to appreciate my proximity, because he reached out and squeezed my hand.

"There are dozens," he said in a strained whisper. He lifted his head. "Dozens of people are dead. How did this happen?"

I didn't think he expected me to have an answer, but I wanted so desperately to reassure him. There was nothing I could say to make this tragedy better.

Still, I tried. "It was an accident," I said, but I could taste the lie on my tongue.

Lucas knew it was a lie, too, and he clutched me tighter. "It was *him*, Nad. It had to be."

My blood ran cold. We knew the demon fed off traumatic deaths. A mass tragedy like this could satiate him for months. Horror twisted in my belly, because I knew that Lucas was right.

He drew a deep breath, and I could tell that the dying thoughts had stopped—or slowed down, at least. "I don't know how he did it, but we have to find out, so we can prevent him from doing this again."

His eyes locked on something in the distance. I followed his gaze to see Sheriff Baker and several other officers climbing out of their squad cars. Sheriff Baker began barking orders.

A pair of EMTs passed by him, carrying the driver on a stretcher. As other officers rushed away to follow the sheriff's orders, Baker stepped in front of them. "I have a few questions," he told the paramedics. It wasn't a request, but a demand.

"It'll have to wait, Sheriff," one of the paramedics said. "This man needs medical attention. He has internal bleeding—"

"It will only take a minute," the sheriff said.

This man needed time to recover, for Alora's sake! The driver looked to be in his early sixties, with a cauldron tattoo on the back of his hand. Blood matted his gray hair, and bruises covered his body. Though the EMTs had wrapped gauze around his head, the blood was starting to seep through.

Lucas nudged me. "Go."

I didn't have to be told twice. I snuck toward the edge of the road and slid behind one of the ambulances. Sheriff Baker couldn't see me, but I could hear him clearly.

"Clyde Walsh, you're the driver, correct?" Sheriff Baker asked.

"Yes." The man on the stretcher groaned, like speaking was difficult for him. He sounded barely conscious.

"Can you tell me what happened here?" Baker asked.

"I don't know," Clyde said. "I can't explain it."

"Give it a try," Baker encouraged.

I crept a little closer, listening intently.

"I saw a… a *thing* in the middle of the road." Clyde's voice shook. "It scared the hell out of me."

"Can you describe this *thing*?" Baker pressed.

Clyde drew a deep breath, but it sounded pained. "It looked like a man, but he… he was nothing but bone. He wore a black cloak and was just… standing there."

Clyde gagged. "I think I hit him."

I recalled the thump I heard and the flash of movement outside the moonroof. He'd definitely hit *something*. But what Clyde was describing sounded like…

"Sir, are you saying you saw a *reaper*?" Baker asked.

"I don't know! I've killed all these people. It's my fault. I must be going crazy. I—I…" Clyde broke out into sobs, and he spoke so incomprehensibly that Sheriff Baker ordered the paramedics to take him away. They loaded him into another ambulance, along with several other seriously injured individuals, and drove away. There weren't enough stretchers or ambulances for everyone.

I was about to head back to Lucas when I heard a familiar voice. "What a *tragic* accident. You made the right call by cutting our meeting short, Priestess."

I peeked around the side of the ambulance. I wanted to hurl when I saw Professor Leto appear with the priestesses. He walked right alongside them, like he belonged in their ranks. His gaze roamed over the scene, and though he tried looking sad, he wasn't selling it. Hunger blazed in his eyes, like he was eating this up.

"Sheriff, what have you learned?" Priestess Margaret demanded.

"We're still working on gathering accurate numbers," he said. "I interviewed the driver, but he doesn't seem to remember anything. He claims he saw a *reaper*, but that's not possible."

"Let's see what the other witnesses know," Margaret said. A shiver traveled down my spine. I wasn't sure if she wanted to learn something from them… or make sure certain secrets stayed buried.

The priestesses went in different directions. Margaret walked straight up to the nearest girl, who had a blanket around her shoulders and was watching the paramedics. She turned, and I realized it was Mira. She had scratches and bruises on her face, but her injuries were minimal compared to others.

"Excuse me, miss," Margaret said.

Mira's features changed when she realized she was in the presence of one of the priestesses. She bowed her head. "Mira Benson, Priestess."

"Ah, Mira. Yes, I recall. You're an Executor, correct?"

Mira nodded. "Yes, Priestess."

"Can you tell me what you saw?"

Mira shook her head. "I saw nothing, Priestess. One second we were dining, and the next… we were upside down. It all happened so fast."

Margaret wore a calculating look. "There's nothing else? Nothing… suspicious?"

"Nothing but the atrocious music they were playing," Mira said snidely.

I was offended for Monica. Her songs were beautiful.

"If there's *anything* I can do to help, please, let me know," Mira said, like she'd sell her soul to the priestesses if they asked.

"We will," Margaret promised. "Take care of yourself, Miss Benson."

Priestess Margaret started walking in my direction, and I hurried back toward Lucas before she could spot me. Monica was being ushered into an ambulance now, and an EMT was wrapping Quentin's wound.

Lucas got to his feet, and some of the color returned to his cheeks. The worst of the deaths were over. "Did you learn anything?"

"Some, but I'm not sure what to make of it." I glanced around, but there were so many people nearby. I didn't want to be overheard. I grabbed Lucas's arm and led him around the front of The Hearse and into the trees. I lowered my voice. "The driver said he saw a reaper standing in the middle of the road. That's why he slammed on the brakes. He swerved to avoid it."

Lucas's eyebrows shot up. "Yeah, that'd scare the hell out of me, too."

"Do you think Leto could've summoned one? Maybe that's the spell he's using. He could be controlling a reaper, and that's why no one saw what happened to Professor Perez."

Lucas furrowed his brow, looking thoughtful. "I doubt it. The reaper's power would rival a demon's. They're too strong to be controlled. Plus, even Seers typically can't see reapers. They exist on a different plane than we do, on a higher level than even the astral plane. Only ghosts can see reapers."

"Could he see one if he was marked for death?" I wondered.

"There's been accounts of seeing reapers moments before you die, but the driver's still alive. It doesn't make sense. Even if a reaper knew what was about to happen and was hanging around to collect souls, he wouldn't cause it. Reapers don't mess with fate like that." Lucas sounded certain.

"Maybe it wasn't a reaper at all," I said. "I heard something hit The Hearse. The driver swore it was a skeleton dressed in a black cloak, but it must've been… solid." My voice trailed off as I caught sight of something fluttering in the wind. A black piece of fabric hung from The Hearse's grill.

Lucas followed my gaze. "Solid, indeed."

We crept toward The Hearse. No one was watching us, as they were too busy attending to the injured. Curiously, I reached out to touch the piece of fabric. I half expected my fingers to go straight through it, like I was imagining things, but I touched solid fabric and plucked it from where it was embedded in the grill. I ran my fingers over the frayed edges, then handed the swatch to Lucas. He inspected it closely.

"This was no reaper," he said with certainty.

I pressed my lips together. "Clyde sounded *sure* it was a skeleton. Could Leto be using necromancy magic?"

Lucas shook his head. "There's no way. The way he teaches necromancy is weird. It's like he's obsessed with it but can't do it himself."

"So he's using a necromancer—manipulating them somehow."

"He must be," Lucas agreed. "Do you think the priestesses know?"

I looked toward the priestesses, who were still questioning witnesses. "They know something. The last thing we want is for them to find out how much *we* know. It's better if they continue to believe we're ignorant."

Lucas subconjured the fabric swatch. "Agreed. Let's go before anyone sees us poking around."

We trudged through the snow and returned to the road. Our feet barely touched the pavement before someone shouted, "Sheriff, arrest him!"

The priestesses pushed through the crowd, and Lilian pointed an ugly finger at Lucas.

I planted myself in front of my boyfriend. "He didn't do anything!"

"Eyewitness testimony states there was a reaper on the road," Sheriff Baker said as he conjured a pair of handcuffs. "He's the Reaper's Apprentice. He's coming down to the station for questioning."

Sheriff Baker hadn't believed the story about the reaper a minute ago. Now he was arresting Lucas for it? It seemed awfully convenient.

"I can't control reapers!" Lucas protested.

"Where's your evidence?" I demanded.

"Where's *yours*?" Lilian sneered.

"Lucas is innocent until proven guilty, so I believe *you're* the one who must supply evidence," I stated. "We were in The Hearse the whole time. He couldn't have cast a spell outside the vehicle."

"Nadine's right," a voice came from nearby. We turned to see Quentin leaning against one of the squad cars. He had a blanket wrapped around his shoulders, but he was still shivering. He was hurt, but not in bad enough shape to be taken by ambulance. "I saw the two of them just before it happened. They were dining, like the rest of us. It couldn't have been him. Whatever we hit, it wasn't a reaper."

Margaret narrowed her gaze on us. She couldn't arrest Lucas without probable cause, not with all these people watching. "Rest assured, we *will* get to the bottom of this. Come, Sheriff. We have more witnesses to question."

The priestesses turned away, and I breathed a sigh of relief. "I'm calling Talia and Grant to come and get us."

"Can I come?" Quentin asked. "I need to get to the hospital as soon as possible. They took Lydia on a stretcher, but the ambulance drove off before I could get to her. They won't let me in any of the ambulances. They're taking the worst cases first."

"We'll drop you off at the hospital," Lucas said. "Let's get out of here before they accuse us of anything else."

NINE

Seventeen.

That's how many people had died. I counted. Fifteen people had died at the scene, and another two at the hospital.

I barely remembered how we got back to the school that night. My head swam with all the thoughts I'd picked up from the crash. There'd been so many, yet I could remember each one, as if their words were playing over and over in my mind like a recording.

This can't be the end.

I hope my wife makes it.

I have lived.

That last one was sad and finite, the way he spoke it in past tense. His life was over.

The worst ones were the loudest, as trauma always produced the most regrettable thoughts. I listened to each with reverence, and did my best to accept each one in turn. That didn't make the blow any easier to handle, though.

The atmosphere was tense the following day. The halls were oddly quiet, and even the cats seemed to move at a slower pace, like they too could sense the melancholy of it all. I met up with Nadine for breakfast, but neither of us said much of anything.

Nadine finally spoke as we left the cafeteria. "How are you doing? Be honest."

"I'm… processing it," I said simply, though it was anything but simple. I truthfully didn't know how to answer the question.

Nadine gazed up at me as we headed toward the grand staircase. "We're going to get through this together—"

Nadine stopped in her tracks when someone stumbled on the stairs in front of us. The person she'd nearly ran into tripped down the last two stairs and clutched the railing to keep from falling flat on his face.

It was Quentin. He had a line of stitches across his forehead and bruises all over his face. He looked past me, but his eyes didn't seem to focus on anything. He tried to pull himself upright, but Nadine and I rushed over to him.

I pressed on his shoulder. "Sit down."

He collapsed onto the bottom stair and looked up at me, confused. "Lucas?"

"Fuck, Quentin, you probably have a concussion. What are you doing here?" I asked.

He shook his head. "No, no, I'm fine."

"Didn't the doctors give you pain killers?" I demanded. "We have potions for this kind of thing!"

"I refused them," he said, without explaining further.

Nadine sat on the stair next to him and conjured a bottle of water. "You look really pale. Here, drink something."

He hesitated, but he uncapped the water bottle and began sipping it.

"What's going on?" Nadine asked. "Weren't you admitted to the hospital?"

"They discharged me," he said. Color started returning to his cheeks now that he was sitting down. "There aren't enough beds. They had to send some of the injured to the school's infirmary as it is. The doctors can hardly keep up."

Seventeen people may have died last night, but there were dozens more that needed serious medical treatment.

"Not like I can afford it anymore, anyway." Quentin conjured a piece of paper, which he handed to Nadine. "The doctors discharged me with *this*."

Nadine gaped, and I glanced down to see a long string of numbers. It was a medical bill, and a hefty one at that.

"But you need medicine!" Nadine cried.

Quentin scowled. "Not according to the doctors. They said something about a coven-wide healthcare reform."

"We'll find a way to pay for this," Nadine promised.

Quentin sniffled. "It doesn't matter. Nothing matters anymore."

My brow furrowed. "What are you talking about?"

Tears filled his eyes. "It's Lydia. I just got the call. Her diagnosis… it's…"

He broke down into sobs. I could barely make out what he was saying. "Even if I find a way to pay my bill, there won't be enough to pay hers. Her parents were both laid off a week ago. Her insurance is gone. I'm on my way… t—to see her…"

"We'll go with you," Nadine offered.

Quentin sniffled and wiped his nose. "That's really kind of you, but I—"

He tried standing up, but he swayed on his feet. I rushed to catch him, and he sagged against me. "Woah," I said. "You're still recovering."

"I need to see her," he snapped. I knew he would, whether we were with him or not.

"Then let us help you," I said. "We'll make sure you get there safely."

Quentin hesitated. "Fair enough."

He seemed a little more confident in his footing, but I stayed close to him, in case he passed out. We made it to the school's infirmary without incident.

I'd been to the infirmary more than once, and it was always quiet and slow. Today, though, it was like stepping into an entirely different hospital. Doctors rushed down the halls, and nurses shouted orders at each other.

"I'll be with you in a minute," the receptionist told us.

Quentin glanced up and down the halls, fidgeting with a small velvet box he'd conjured.

"What's that?" Nadine asked. It sounded like she was trying to make conversation, to calm Quentin down.

He glanced down at the box, like he forgot he'd been holding it. "Oh, I um…"

He sighed. "I guess you've already figured it out, huh? It's a ring, for Lydia. I was going to propose last night before… well, before the accident."

He opened the box and showed us the ring. A shimmering diamond sat upon a twisted gold band.

Nadine smiled. "She's going to love it."

Quentin placed the box in his pocket, but he looked heartbroken. "I hope so."

The receptionist caught our attention, and Quentin rushed to give her information. She pointed us down the hall toward Lydia's room. My stomach twisted as we passed by rooms with patients connected to IVs, and others with tubes down their throats. There were people of all ages here, not just students. I'd never been more grateful for my protection magic, because it was the only reason Nadine and I weren't in the same situation.

We stepped into Lydia's room. She lay flat on her back with her neck in a brace. She tried to turn her head to look at Quentin, but she couldn't move. Bruises covered her skin, and she had an IV in her arm. She was conscious, so that was reassuring.

Quentin dropped to his knees beside her bed and took her hand in his. He began kissing her hand, all the way up her arm, until he pressed his lips to hers.

He pushed the hair out of her eyes. "I'm so sorry, Lyd. The doctors say—"

He choked up before he could finish.

"It's okay, Quen," she told him, but her voice was barely audible. She was in rough shape.

"But you… you'll never walk again." Quentin's voice broke, and my heart crumbled into a million pieces along with it. I had no idea her diagnosis was this serious.

Tears welled in Lydia's eyes. "I'm alive. That's all that matters."

Quentin drew a deep breath. He was trying to stay strong for her. "We'll figure this out together. I'm here for you, babe."

Nadine pulled me aside and whispered lowly. "I have to meet with the priestesses and convince them to change their minds about our healthcare. They have to at least cover the accident. These people don't deserve this. They weren't given enough notice."

"Where is she!?" someone barked from down the hall.

Nadine's features paled, and the two of us rushed into the hall to see the three priestesses marching toward us, Sheriff Baker leading the way.

Nadine's features contorted into rage, and she threw herself in front of the priestesses, stopping them in their tracks.

"You can't do this to these students!" she snarled. "Stripping them of their insurance was one thing, but giving them no notice, no time to come up with an alternative? It's beyond cruel!"

Priestess Lilian frowned. "We don't have time for your dramatics."

"Well, *make* time!" Nadine demanded. "These people deserve to know they're going to be taken care of."

Margaret waved her hand, like a few students were the least of her worries. "We have dozens of people to take care of right now. As far as medical treatment goes, there is little supply and huge demand. We'll save the ones who can pay."

Priestess Charlotte stepped forward and got so close to Nadine that their noses almost touched. Nadine didn't back down, though. "If you'll excuse us, we have business to attend to," Charlotte sneered. I'd never heard her speak in such a hostile way. It was like the other priestesses were rubbing off on her. "You can either join us in sentencing the person behind this, or get the hell out of our way."

The priestesses stepped around Nadine and marched down the hall urgently.

"I'm coming with," Nadine stated.

The priestesses were in too much of a hurry to care that I followed. They barely noticed me racing behind them. Sheriff Baker opened a door at the end of the hall and led the priestesses into a patient room. I stepped in behind them, and my stomach churned.

Monica sat propped up on her bed, and a cat lay curled next to her. She had her shirt lifted slightly and looked to be inspecting a huge bandage around her middle. I spotted a small line of blood that had leaked through. Her eyes widened as the priestesses marched into the room, and she dropped the fabric.

"Priestesses," she said kindly. "How may I help you?"

Sheriff Baker stepped in front of everyone, his heavy boots pounding on the floor. "Monica Torres, you're under arrest for the mass murder hereby known as The Hearse Tragedy."

Monica gasped, and her cat leapt to its feet and hissed at Baker. "What do you mean? I didn't do anything! What are you—ow!?"

Baker grabbed her wrist and slapped handcuffs on it, yanking on her

IV. He secured the other side of the handcuffs to the bed. Monica broke out into sobs. It all happened so fast.

"Monica didn't do this!" Nadine shouted. "She was next to us the entire time. What evidence do you have?"

Priestess Margaret pointed an ugly finger at Monica. "This woman is a Mentalist capable of manipulating emotions through music. She was playing piano moments before The Hearse crashed. She hypnotized the driver!"

"We have witness testimony," Charlotte added. "Passengers say they were hypnotized by her music."

"But I—I didn't—" Monica started, but Lilian cut her off.

"Save your prayers for Mother Miriam," she growled.

"Monica deserves a fair trial!" Nadine demanded. "Have the driver testify! What does he have to say about this?"

"Nothing, seeing as he's dead," Lilian said coldly. "And *she* killed him."

Clyde must've been one of the people who'd died in the hospital. I couldn't help but think he'd have survived if the sheriff hadn't stopped him for questioning.

Priestess Margaret held her head high. "We have all the evidence we need. The judge has already met with our witness and sided with us."

The priestesses created the laws, but the judge carried out sentencing. It was rare for a judge to defy the priestesses, as their job was to simply enforce the laws—much like the sheriff. Even without enough evidence, I was sure they could persuade the judge.

"Who are your witnesses?" Nadine demanded. "I'm a priestess. I have a right to know."

"It doesn't matter," Lilian said. "Monica's execution is set to take place tonight."

Nadine gritted her teeth. "The coven is already mourning the death of seventeen people, and you plan to host another hanging?"

Lilian smirked. "Who said anything about a hanging?"

She turned toward Monica, looking proud of herself. "I suggest you put some thought into your dinner request tonight. It will be the last meal you'll ever eat."

With that, the priestesses swept out of the room. Monica's sobs grew louder. "I didn't do it!" she cried, the chains of her handcuffs rattling.

I wanted to go to her, but Sheriff Baker planted himself in front of

Monica's bed. He crossed his arms in a hostile manner. "This woman is the property of the Miriamic Police Department. It's time you leave."

Sheriff Baker whistled, and two Executors entered the room. I didn't recognize them. They had to be a few years older than us. They were both taller than me, with bulging muscles.

"Escort them out of the infirmary," Baker ordered.

Hands landed on Nadine and me.

"We won't let them do this to you, Monica!" I shouted as they dragged us out of the room.

"We know you're innocent!" Nadine yelled.

Monica's sobs echoed down the hall. My stomach felt like it had fallen out of my abdomen and was dragging along the floor behind me. I couldn't imagine what terrors Monica felt, knowing she had only hours to live.

The Executors escorted us down the hall and past the reception desk. Fury ignited in my bones when I spotted Professor Leto seated in the waiting room. He had one ankle propped up on his knee and was reading a magazine, like this was nothing more than an average day at the dentist. He seemed wholly unbothered by what was happening here. I'm sure he was *pleased*, sitting around waiting for death—waiting to *feed*. Wasn't this fucker satisfied by now?

Rage overcame me. I barely felt in control of my body as I yanked my arm out of the Executor's grasp. I marched straight up to Professor Leto and ripped the magazine out of his hands. Pages went flying as I flung it across the room. I grabbed Leto by the collar with one hand and punched him so hard with the other fist that his head hit the wall. It might've knocked the average person out, but Leto just smirked at me.

"You did this!" I raged.

Leto kept his cool, like I hadn't just sucker punched him in the jaw. "How could I have anything to do with this when I was nowhere near the site of the crash? I was in a meeting with the priestesses when this *tragic* accident occurred."

Of fucking course he had a rock-solid alibi. The priestesses would vouch for him even if he didn't.

"You did this, and now another innocent person is going to die," I growled. "How dare you come here and claim you have a place in this coven—"

Executors yanked my arms back. I didn't know where they'd all come from, but there were suddenly half a dozen soldiers pulling me backward.

"Lucas!" Nadine cried.

Someone slapped handcuffs onto my wrists, and I suddenly felt all my energy drain. They had to be made of noxite, a magical metal that could inhibit supernatural power.

"I'm terribly sorry, sir," one of the Executors told Professor Leto. "We'll escort him away immediately."

"No," Leto said, holding a hand up to stop them. He stood and wiped at a cut on his lip, though I didn't see any blood. His gaze moved over me, and a shiver traveled down my spine. He leaned forward, so close I could feel his hot breath against my cheek.

He spoke so only I could hear, sounding amused. "You're bold, Lucas, attacking me when you know what I am."

He leaned away, just far enough for me to catch his eyes flash red. "No point in ruining the fun I'm having just yet. I haven't been entertained like this in centuries."

He winked. "Don't worry. I won't tell the priestesses that you know what I am. It'll be our little secret."

His features hardened as he whispered coolly, "But make no mistake, once I get tired of you, you'll meet the same fate as the others."

My blood ran ice-cold as he drew away, laughing.

"Let him go," Leto told the Executors nonchalantly. "I won't be pressing charges."

The Executors released my cuffs, and Nadine and I hurried out of the infirmary as fast as we could. A group of Executors stood at the end of the hall, laughing like The Hearse Tragedy had never happened. I spotted Mira among them.

Nadine leaned over to me to whisper, "I bet Mira's the witness. She offered to help the priestesses. She's lying for them so they have someone to blame."

"Let's see what she knows," I suggested.

"Mira," Nadine stated firmly. "The priestesses would like to have a word."

"I'll catch up with you guys later," she told her friends. She waved them off, leaving us alone in the hall.

Mira approached us, looking Nadine up and down. "Why would they send *you?*"

"Because I'm a priestess," Nadine said coolly. "Tell me why you lied."

She scoffed. "I don't *lie.*"

"So the priestesses lied to *me* when they told me you talked to the judge?" Nadine was manipulating Mira, and she was pretty damn convincing at it.

Mira frowned. "I *did* talk to the judge."

"And you told her Monica Torres hypnotized you?" Nadine pressed.

Mira crossed her arms but didn't answer.

"You realize an innocent woman is going to *die* because of *your* testimony," I growled.

Mira scowled. "Who are *you* to question me? I'll tell the priestesses you guys are harassing me. I don't believe they actually sent you."

"Go ahead and ask them," Nadine bluffed. "But be quick about it. They don't like people who waste their time."

Mira hesitated. She obviously didn't want to upset the priestesses. She narrowed her eyes at Nadine and spat, "Just stay away from me."

My hands curled into fists as she turned on her heel and walked away. "Mira's so desperate to get on the priestesses' good side. She doesn't care that she killed an innocent woman."

Nadine shook her head, like she refused to believe this was happening. Slowly, determination entered her features. "We're not going to take this lying down. The priestesses haven't won yet."

☾

MONICA WAS PRONOUNCED dead at 6:28 p.m. that night. She had been poisoned by the priestesses, and by the following morning, the entire coven believed she was responsible for The Hearse Tragedy.

The setting sun peeked through the clouds on Sunday evening, as if sending rays of hope down on an otherwise melancholy day. An anonymous donor had arranged the funeral funds, and the service was scheduled the evening following her death.

Talia sniffled from the back seat as we drove to the funeral home to pay our respects. "At least we know someone's on our side," she said softly. "Clearly, someone cared enough to pull this together so quickly."

"We don't know that," Grant said harshly. "It could be a ploy pulled by the priestesses to parade Monica's dead body through the streets."

"Grant's right," Chloe agreed. "Something about this doesn't feel right."

Nadine and I exchanged a sad glance, but neither of us spoke.

We pulled up outside the funeral home and climbed out of the vehicle, our cats following. There were only a few other cars here. My stomach sank. Monica deserved a bigger funeral than this. So many people who had loved her hadn't shown up, simply because they took the priestesses' word. They had ruined Monica's reputation, and they didn't seem to care at all.

The priestesses stood near the front doors, speaking lowly to one another. Claudia Sinclair stood beside them, wearing a black dress that looked nearly identical to the priestesses' robes.

"What are they doing here?" Talia sneered.

Chloe scoffed. "They've come to see who would dare come to mourn a *traitor*. They want to see who opposes them. Why do you think I tagged along? I want my grandmother to see just what I think of her."

We climbed the steps. The priestesses kept their sharp gazes on us the whole time, and my skin crawled. Inside, a few people milled around, but they were mostly funeral home workers. The room that held the casket was practically empty. People spoke in such low whispers that it was almost too quiet.

Talia gestured to a woman who stood near the casket. "That's Monica's sister."

A cat prowled at her feet. I thought it must be hers, until the cat pawed at her for attention. She kicked it away rather harshly.

"Get off of me, you diseased rat," she growled, and the cat slunk away, letting out a mournful mew.

Talia gasped. "That's Binx, Monica's cat!"

"We should talk to her sister," I suggested. Nadine and I walked to the front of the room, while Talia, Grant, and Chloe went to coax Binx out of the corner.

Nadine cleared her throat as we approached. "Excuse me, Meredith?"

The woman turned. I expected to see tears in her eyes, but she wore a stoic expression.

"Priestess." Meredith nodded to Nadine, before her eyes traveled over me. "I expected to see you here, but who is *this*?"

Clearly, I wasn't welcome.

"He's come to pay his respects," Nadine said. "We're terribly sorry for your loss."

"Don't be," Meredith snapped. "My sister deserves no respect. What she's done is deplorable."

My stomach twisted into knots. I wished I could tell her the truth.

"Meredith, please," Nadine pleaded. "She was your sister."

"That means nothing after what she's done," Meredith said. "My sister was always so wrapped up in her career. She never had time for dating or kids. Now look what she's left with. Nothing, just as a traitor deserves. Don't bother with your condolences. I'm only here to ensure she's buried, along with her memory."

I opened my mouth to say something, but Nadine placed a hand on mine. She shook her head, and I had to remind myself what we'd agreed upon. Trying to change the coven's mind was futile. There was nothing I could do to convince this woman of her sister's innocence. Meredith took our silence as the end of the conversation, and she breezed past us without another word.

"That was intense," Talia said as she approached us, alongside Chloe and Grant. Talia held Binx tightly in her arms, stroking his head while he purred.

Nadine frowned. "One day she'll know the truth. Once we have all the Oaken Wands and this conflict is over, I'll make sure we clear Monica's name."

Chloe stepped toward the casket and gazed down at Monica's lifeless features. "I wish we didn't have to lose any more lives to get there."

Monica's body was still, and her black hair stood out against her pale skin and the white sheets. She reminded me of Snow White, though there was no handsome prince who would come to save her in this twisted fairy tale.

Talia stepped closer to the casket. Binx jumped out of her arms and onto Monica's chest. He batted at his owner's chin, like he expected her to move, but nothing happened. Binx turned a sad gaze up at Talia, and she sniffled as she shook her head. Binx meowed softly, and our cats echoed his cry. He curled up on Monica's chest and closed his eyes. I could practically feel his heartbreak as my own.

"I'm gonna miss her, too, buddy," Talia said. She reached into her pocket and pulled out something that I thought was a wand at first, but had silver buttons all over it. I realized it was piccolo, a tiny flute just barely over a foot long.

Talia's voice cracked when she spoke. "I bought this the first time I met Monica. It was years ago, back when Hallowed Harmonica had just opened. I was still a kid. I came into her shop and saw the baby grand piano sitting there. I couldn't help but sit down and start playing. I didn't know she was listening. She just stood there until I was done, and when I finished, she... she told me she thought I was really good, and that I should try composing music. She saw something in me that I couldn't see myself. I kept coming in, just to play that beautiful piano and talk to her about music. She was always so welcoming."

Talia closed her eyes and ran her fingers over the piccolo. Her lids flickered, and I realized she was replaying a memory in a vision. "She asked once if I'd ever played anything but piano, and I told her I hadn't. Then she asked if I could pick one other instrument to learn, what would it be. And I said flute, but not a regular flute. I wanted a tiny one—a piccolo. She brought this down from a shelf and gave it to me and said, *You can start now.* I told her I couldn't take it, but she insisted I should *borrow* it. I never got to give it back. I never got to thank her for all she did for me."

Talia choked up, and she placed the piccolo inside the casket beside Monica's body. "I'm going to miss her."

Grant wrapped an arm around Talia. "I didn't know her well, but I know one thing. Monica was one of the kindest people in all the coven. She will be missed."

"Her death will not be in vain," Chloe growled. "*That* I can promise."

A man cleared his throat, and we were ushered to our seats. Most of the seats were empty, except for my friends and I seated in the front, the priestesses in the back, and a few other people who knew Monica.

The service was short, and one of the funeral workers delivered the eulogy. I didn't think he'd known Monica, judging by how generic his speech was. I supposed Meredith had been slated to give the eulogy, but she'd most certainly refused.

The workers closed the casket, and we watched as they loaded Monica's body into the hearse. Talia held Binx tight in her arms, but he tried to struggle free. He yowled loudly, and the other cats joined in, as if singing a song of mourning.

We climbed into the car and followed the hearse through town. The sun had dipped low in the sky, and people lining the streets appeared as ominous shadows as dusk fell. They had come to watch. They screamed obscenities and threw rotten vegetables as the hearse passed through town.

Soon, the crowd disappeared behind us, and the cemetery gates loomed ahead. The graveyard was empty when we arrived, apart from a few chairs set around a fresh grave. We shivered as we stepped out of the car, and snow crunched beneath our feet as we passed by gravestones. We were in a far corner of the cemetery, where most of the graves were still covered in snow. Monica's grave was one of the cheapest lots, in an area of the cemetery used only by those everyone had forgotten about.

We took our seats, and I kept my eyes on the hearse parked nearby. The funeral workers opened the back, and the priestesses gathered around. They opened the casket and peered inside at Monica's body once more, like they wanted to be certain she was dead.

"Very well," I heard priestess Margaret say. "Let's get this over with."

The workers carried the casket to the grave and arranged it onto the casket-lowering device. A funeral worker said a few more words before they lowered the casket into the frigid ground.

Talia's sobs seemed to echo off the trees as we headed back to the car following the service. Binx scratched at her, but she held him firmly to her chest so he wouldn't jump into the grave.

We were the last to start our car, except for the workers and the priestesses. I drove through the cemetery slowly, letting the other cars go ahead, until they'd disappeared ahead of us. Instead of following the other cars, I pulled into Headmistress Verla's driveway. Her property neighbored the cemetery and was concealed by a thick forest of trees.

"What are we doing here?" Talia asked, wiping her eyes.

I pulled around the side of the house, where we couldn't possibly be seen from the road, and cut the engine. Nadine and I jumped out of the car.

"Come on," I told the others. "Leave the cats here. We don't have much time."

The urgency in my tone made them move quicker than I thought possible.

"Time for what?" Chloe demanded.

"Shh…" Nadine hissed. "Follow us."

We barely made it a few steps before four shadows stepped out from the dark—two men and two women. I could barely make them out in the fading light. "This way," a woman hissed, waving us toward them. Nadine and I locked hands as we tiptoed through the forest, following behind a woman with a cane. I could feel Nadine's rushing pulse.

"Guys," Talia protested. "What's going on?"

"We have to be quiet," Nadine whispered.

"I don't like this…" Chloe muttered, but she followed us anyway.

We reached the iron gate surrounding the cemetery, but we stayed back in the trees, where we couldn't be seen. Everyone remained silent as we watched the funeral workers bury Monica's casket. The priestesses, along with Claudia, watched intently, and they didn't appear satisfied until every last granule of dirt covered Monica's casket.

"The coven got their revenge," Priestess Margaret said, sounding satisfied. Her voice carried over the cemetery. "We can finally put this issue to rest. Come along, ladies."

The four women turned on their heels and climbed into a black sedan nearby. We waited silently as the funeral workers picked everything up and left the cemetery behind them. The cold wind whistled as the *clang* of locking gates filled the air. The sound of tires faded down the road.

"Come quickly," the woman said. "There's no time to waste."

She rushed along the fence line and stopped a few yards down. She grabbed two of the fence's iron rods and moved them aside. It looked like they'd been damaged long ago, and it gave us just enough room to crawl through. She ushered her three accomplices through the fence first, then my friends and I followed. We raced across the cemetery.

"Slow down," Grant protested. "Are you going to tell us what's going on?"

"They're here to help," I said as we came to a halt beside Monica's grave.

"Here to help with what—?" Talia demanded, but her words stopped dead when one of the women lifted her hands. The dirt covering Monica's casket moved at her command. Out in the open and in the light of the stars, we could finally make out the strangers' features.

Hattie gave a slight smile as she moved aside the grave dirt using her magic. She was the half-witch who owned The Jolly Pumpkin downtown, the witch who'd told Nadine and me about the Crock of Death while we were investigating nightshade. She was part-Nivita, a race of elementals who could control the earth.

Beside her stood Headmistress Verla, William Connor, and Hector Lawson. Talia gaped as she took in each of their faces. Slowly, the casket rose from the grave, controlled by Hattie's Earth magic.

"What are you doing!?" Grant shouted. "You're defiling her grave!"

Grant went to take a step forward, but I placed a hand on his chest. "We have to get her out."

"But she's dead!" Grant cried.

Beside him, Chloe's face was calculating. I saw the moment she figured it out. The second Hattie pulled the casket from the ground, Hector rushed forward and threw the top open. He pulled a potion vial from his coat pocket and dripped the liquid past Monica's lips.

Nadine wore a look of regret. "I'm sorry, Grant. We had to let you believe she was dead."

Talia's voice shook. "But she *is* dead… she—"

A huge gasp cut her off, and Monica shot upright in her casket. She clutched Hector. Relief flooded my veins.

"It's okay, it's okay," Hector said over and over. Monica seemed to calm down as his kind voice filled the night.

"Come, my dear," William said, helping Monica out of her casket.

Monica's knees shook. "I'm okay? W-what happened?"

"The poison wasn't real," Hector said.

Talia and Grant shared a collective gasp.

"I'm sorry we couldn't tell you," Nadine said. "We needed the priestesses to believe your grief was authentic."

"Monica!" Talia raced forward and flung her arms around Monica's neck.

"She's weak," Hector said.

Grant scratched his head, still trying to process it. "How did you pull this off?"

"We called in as many favors as we could," Nadine explained. "The priestesses planned to poison Monica, and we knew they'd get Hector to do it, so we went to him and warned him. With Lucas's death magic and my Curse Breaker powers, Hector was able to brew a potion that would *mimic* death. We worked together to make the brew—and the antidote—and Hector swapped the potions. We had to make the priestesses believe she was really dead."

"Hattie agreed to help us retrieve the casket," I told them. "And Verla offered to give us a place to hide our car, so we could return unseen. And William—"

"You were the anonymous donor," Chloe realized.

William nodded kindly. "It is my funeral home, after all."

"You held the funeral so the priestesses would come," Chloe said. "If we'd have broken Monica out before she was poisoned, they'd come after us—all of us."

"They will never know she lives," William said.

"There's a safe haven in California that welcomes refugees of all races," Hattie explained. "I lived there for some time. Though tension is high among the Elementai, the town of *Hok'evale* is a safer place for Monica now than Octavia Falls."

"Thank you!" Monica cried. "Thank you. I don't know what to say."

"Say you'll go to *Hok'evale*," Verla requested. "Promise you'll stay safe."

"Yes, of course," Monica said. "But Binx—"

"He's in the car," Talia told her, sounding elated. She was so happy to have Monica back. "You'll take him with you."

Monica began sobbing. "You have all been so kind, but how will I get to *Hok'evale*?"

William gestured toward Verla's house. "I have a car waiting for you."

"And take this," Hattie offered, pressing a piece of paper into Monica's hands. "These are your directions, and your instructions for when you arrive. Find Jakob Weatherby and tell him I sent you."

Monica wiped the tears from her eyes. "Thank you. All of you."

"Come," William encouraged, helping Monica through the snow.

Behind her, Hattie waved her hands. The casket returned to the earth, buried once more. If I hadn't been here to see it, I'd never believe the grave had been disturbed. She turned to follow William and Monica, and we all trailed behind her.

Grant didn't let us get far. He placed his hands on his hips and stepped in front of Nadine and me. "You sons of bitches. You actually did it. And you managed to hide it from us, too." At first, I thought he was upset, but then he clapped me on the shoulder and said, "Well done."

I beamed as Grant went to follow the others. Nadine smiled up at me, and I slung an arm around her shoulder.

"He's right, I suppose," Nadine said. "Despite everything we've endured the last few days, we saved one innocent life, and that's something to celebrate."

"I suppose," I said. "We can't save every innocent soul, but we saved Monica. And I guess if the coven destroys itself, people like Monica will still be safe."

Nadine squeezed me close. "The Miriamic Coven will live on in those we save… so let's save as many as we can."

TEN

It snowed that night, covering our tracks to Monica's grave. The priestesses would never know she was still alive. It gave me hope that we could save others like we saved her.

Lucas and I walked down the hall the following day, our steps appearing lighter than they had in weeks. Even Isa and Oliver seemed more at ease. I skimmed the latest article in *The Shield*, which had been printed and distributed this morning.

"This is really good," I told Lucas. "I think it could really spark change around here."

"Thanks," he replied. "I mean, not that I have anything to thank you *for*."

I read a passage under my breath. *"We must be intentional in our approach to protect the coven, and consider the implications of reacting radically. There comes a point when boycotts morph into witch hunts, and innocents become ostracized, censored, discriminated against, and even executed without a fair trial. If we seek to censor those who oppose our own viewpoints, we destroy the structure that free speech is built upon, and we replace it with the foundation to censor ourselves, until we are all left speechless, and only a single voice remains."*

I held up the paper. "It sounds like the coven could really learn a thing or two from this Caesar Peppertrine guy."

Lucas smirked when I mentioned his pseudonym. "Oh, yeah. That guy's quite wise. More people should listen to him."

I started laughing, but a voice inside the Lounge cut me off. "Caesar Peppertrine is a menace!"

Lucas and I stepped toward the doors and peered inside the Lounge. Onyx sat on one of the couches, holding a copy of *The Shield*. Gwen, Stacey, and Valerie loomed over her.

"Who does this guy think he is?" Gwen sneered. She yanked the paper out of Onyx's hands and tore it in half. "He talks as if dangerous criminals should just be set free. Criminals *should* be silenced so the rest of us can live in peace. This whole article is anti-Miriamic. Don't tell me you agree with him, Onyx. People like him are what's wrong with the coven."

"So you've read the article?" Onyx asked coldly. "Same as I was doing. There's nothing wrong with staying informed."

"Go read your garbage somewhere else," Gwen snapped. She tossed the torn bits of paper into the air, and they fluttered to the ground.

"I'd rather read it anywhere but here anyway." Onyx scoffed as she scooped up her cat and shoved her way past Gwen. She ducked out of the Lounge so fast, she didn't notice us standing there. Her purple hair concealed her features, and I wasn't sure she was all right.

"Come on," I said, gesturing to Lucas.

We rushed down the hall behind Onyx, and our cats followed swiftly behind us. We turned the corner and found her standing near an ornate window. She gazed out over the yard, stroking her cat's head.

"Onyx?" I took a step toward her.

She jumped, like she hadn't heard us approach. She turned and bowed her head. "Priestess."

"Are you okay?" I asked.

"Fine," she said. "I just wish I'd stop running into Gwen."

"There must be something I can do to help," I offered.

"You *are* helping," Onyx said. "The coven needs people like you. I saw the way you stood up to the priestesses the day they arrested Professor Wykoff. Despite all their threats, you're not afraid to stand up for what you believe in." She looked toward Lucas. "Same goes for you, Caesar Peppertrine."

Lucas hesitated. "I—I'm not—"

"Don't worry, I won't tell anyone," Onyx promised. "I figured it out myself. It's an anagram for Reaper's Apprentice. It's one of your clues, isn't it?"

She conjured a sheet of paper and unfurled it. It was tattered on the edges, and there were marks all over it, like she'd spent a lot of time studying it. She showed it to Lucas, and I saw it was the first article he wrote, the one with the code about our meeting that no one had deciphered. "I haven't quite decoded the whole thing, but I figured out your pen name. It wasn't difficult. You guys aren't exactly quiet about what you think of the priestesses. I want to help. Where do I sign up?"

Onyx had been my lab partner when I'd been posing as an Alchemist my second semester. She'd helped us the night of the Burning. She'd set off a distraction so we could rescue the students who'd been captured. I trusted her and knew she'd be a great addition to the team.

"We were just on our way to get to work," I told her. "Follow us."

We led Onyx down a maze of hallways. We stepped through our ward, and she couldn't take her eyes off the magic shimmering down the hallway.

"Wow, this is amazing," Onyx said as we led her inside. "I'd never guess this was here."

Our friends were already there, gathered around the meeting table. Chatter died down when we entered the room. Talia and Grant were organizing crystals, while Miles helped Chloe make photocopies at the printer. Mandy had her nose buried in a book, and the cats were keeping themselves entertained with a ball of yarn. A box of cookies sat in the middle of the table, and everyone was nibbling on them.

"Onyx!" Grant cried, swallowing a mouthful of cookie. They were both Alchemists and must've had some classes together. "You're joining The Coven's Shield?"

Onyx smiled. "I am. What is it you guys do here?"

"Drugs, sex, and rock and roll," Miles sang.

Chloe elbowed him in the side. "Don't listen to him. He just finished a Silly Slushie from the Lounge."

Miles snickered. "Someone has to keep the vibe lively."

Chloe grabbed a stack of papers and straightened them out. "We're making plans, learning magic, and building an arsenal to give us something to draw from during the Waning."

Onyx reached for one of the crystals on the table and flipped it over in her hands. "That's a really good idea. Too bad magical crystals are banned on campus."

"That's why it's called a secret society, my dear." Miles snickered.

"Anyone want a cookie?" Grant offered. "Talia and I made them."

"Yes, please." Miles came up behind Grant and grabbed one from the box.

"Good, because if I eat any more, I'm going to get diabetes," Grant joked.

"Anyone else want one?" Miles asked with a full mouth. He picked up the box and held them out toward Talia and Chloe. "Murphy? Olson?"

Talia took one, but Chloe scrunched up her nose. "Ew, don't call me that."

"Why not?" Miles asked. "It's your name."

Chloe frowned. "Not for long. I'm changing it."

"Really?" Miles looked interested and plopped down on an empty chair beside Grant. "What are you changing it to?"

"I'm not sure yet," Chloe said. "I haven't come up with anything that suits me."

Miles shrugged. "Bryant's a good last name."

She frowned. "Chloe Bryant? No, thanks. I'm not using *your* last name."

"What about something witchy and powerful?" I suggested. "Chloe… Bloodhex?"

Chloe laughed. "Yeah, *that'll* scare my enemies."

"Chloe Da Beast," Onyx suggested with a laugh.

"That sounds like a rapper name," Grant said. "She needs a villain name, like Chloe DeVil."

"I'm not stealing puppies for coats!" Chloe protested. "I'll figure something out. Just… call me Chloe for now, okay?"

Talia could see Chloe was getting uncomfortable, and she quickly changed the subject. "Speaking of new names, my brother is looking for a new band name. He keeps hounding me for suggestions. Any ideas?"

"What's wrong with Wicked Warlocks?" Lucas asked. "I like that name."

Talia frowned while she separated large crystals from small ones. "He can't exactly use that name for a new band. The Wicked Warlocks broke up."

"What'd Tyler do?" Grant asked, setting one of his crystals aside.

Talia sighed. "Tyler didn't *do* anything. It was all Clay and Carl. Tyler said he didn't think it was right that the priestesses cut our insurance, and his friends disagreed. They argued, and Tyler thought it was best if he stepped away. I don't blame him. He chose his integrity, so he's trying to get a *new* band together."

Grant frowned. "I can't believe Carl agrees with the priestesses. He's got allergies he's always going to the doctor for."

"Yeah, but he's out of school, so he's got private insurance," Talia pointed out. "Apparently, he doesn't care as long as it doesn't affect him."

Grant snorted. "I'd like to see him say that to my face. I can't afford my insulin without insurance! I'm on my last refill. I'm going to have to brew synthetic shit to get by."

Horror crossed Onyx's face. "Grant, you can't. That brew has never been perfected."

Grant drew himself up. "Then I'll be the one to perfect it. The only reason no one's pursued it is because there's no money in it if diabetics can produce it themselves."

"It's dangerous," Onyx pressed. "You'd have to have a doctorate in Alchemy to be anywhere close to perfecting that serum. It's not a simple one-time potion. You have to take it multiple times a day, every day. You don't know how that will affect you."

Grant frowned and mumbled, "Yeah, I guess."

"You must be able to get on your parents' insurance," I insisted.

Grant shook his head. "With all these businesses shutting down, Dad's been laid off. He lost his insurance with his paycheck. His savings are barely enough to keep him afloat. And the provider doesn't take my mom's insurance."

"Our healthcare is too expensive," Onyx complained. "I found a lump last week, and I called to have it checked out, but without insurance, the check-up alone is a whole month's pay. I mean, I only work part-time as a nursing assistant at the hospital, but it's all I can do between classes."

My jaw dropped. "That's ridiculous!"

Onyx waved her hand. "I'm sure it's nothing."

"But it *could* be something," I said. It made me ill thinking about any of us going without healthcare. "We have to do something."

"What can we do?" Grant sounded hopeless. "You can advocate for us with the priestesses, but unless something changes fucking tomorrow, some of us are shit out of luck."

"We'll set up a fund," I offered. "We'll gather donations to cover immediate care, until we can get this sorted out. The funds will go to students involved in The Hearse Tragedy, and people like you, who can't go without their medication."

Chloe crossed her arms. "I wish it were that simple. The priestesses will figure that if we can crowdfund our own healthcare, we don't need our insurance back. Besides, who's going to donate? With all the layoffs, no one's got extra cash."

I sighed. "What else can we do? Grant needs insulin now. Lydia needs physical therapy—and probably surgery. The least we can do is try."

"We should see what kind of money we can raise," Lucas suggested. "How's everyone else doing with their research?"

Mandy looked up from the book she'd been reading. "The Coven's Shield is growing, and so should our meeting room."

She was right about that. We were packed in here like sardines.

"I found a space-bending spell," Mandy said. "It should be pretty simple to cast."

"Isn't that dangerous?" Miles asked. "I mean, can't it clash with the spell on the school? I heard a few students tried the spell on their dorm room ages ago, and it backfired and spread to the east stairwell. It's the reason the Vanishing Stairwell blinks in and out of existence."

"Yes, but that's only because they didn't perform the spell right," Mandy said. "Space-bending spells require a member from all five Casts. They're not particularly difficult; it's just that we haven't had a Curse Breaker in the coven for over forty years."

"I've done a few space-bending spells with the priestesses," I said. "I know I can do it, and I've been feeling a lot better since I started dialysis, so I should be able to handle it."

"Perfect," Mandy said. "Who else wants to volunteer?"

Grant, Talia, Lucas, and Chloe raised their hands, and Mandy handed us the spellbook.

The five of us joined hands, and magic began to swell between us as we spoke the incantation. I felt their power grow within me as I gathered it together, forming it into a ball in the center of our circle. The magic glowed and shimmered, like a rainbow-colored bubble. My friends continued the incantation, while I focused on funneling their power into the magical ball. It grew around us, until it completely encompassed us and expanded to the corners of the room. As it grew even further, the room grew with it, stretching the walls and carpet and elongating the counter. The room expanded to four times its original size.

"Wow! This is great!" Miles raved as we finished the spell. He began racing around the room, leaping and spinning like a ballet dancer.

Chloe frowned. "You really need to lay off the slushies."

"But why would I do that when I'm having so much fun?" Miles teased. He spun by her and grabbed her hands, yanking her into the middle of the room and spinning her around. Our cats raced to follow, and they frolicked around the room, tackling each other. Miles tripped over his cat, Kiki, and Chloe fell on top of him. She paused for a moment, staring down at him.

The door opened, and Chloe quickly scrambled to her feet and cleared her throat. "Headmistress."

Headmistress Verla walked into the room. Professor Warren and Everly followed behind her. Verla took in the size of the room, before her eyes fell on me. "You did this?"

"I had some help." I gestured to my friends. "I hope everyone's a little more comfortable now. Let's have a seat and discuss what we've learned."

We all sat around the meeting table. The furniture was unaffected by our spell, but it was nice to have the extra room to move around.

"Let's start with Everly," I suggested. "How's it going converting new members?"

"I've convinced a handful of witches to join our side," she said. "However, the priestesses are keeping a close eye on me. They find it suspicious that I won't ban certain Casts from my shop. I've been careful with my message, but I believe it's effective. Our numbers are growing."

"Miles, have you gotten anything from the Executors?" Lucas asked.

Miles leaned back in his chair. His Silly Slushie must've started wearing off, because his tone became serious. "I haven't heard anything. The Executors are nothing but a bunch of idiots doing the priestesses' bidding. The most interesting thing that's happened is a fistfight between

Ryan and James when they blamed each other for the Waning. It's more or less a *whose-dick-is-bigger* contest."

Chloe scoffed. "Ryan's not winning that one."

"Amen, sister," Mandy laughed.

At least they could agree on something.

"Though the fight between Gregory and Leroy was pretty interesting, too," Miles said. "Last night, Leroy tried to confiscate Dungeon tickets off Gregory, and Gregory cursed him."

My jaw dropped. "Cursed?"

Miles waved his hand. "It was a short-lived hex. He made these boils break out on Leroy's face. It was pretty grotesque. But once they popped, they were gone."

Verla's brow furrowed. "I wasn't made aware of this."

Professor Warren tapped his chin. "The Executors aren't answering to authority. That's not good."

"Was Gregory arrested?" Talia asked.

Miles shook his head. "Nah, he made a break for it, and the other Executors let him go. We've all been itchy for Leroy to get what's coming to him."

"That means the Executors can turn against their own," I said. "They're not loyal to one another, just the priestesses."

"This also means things are escalating," Lucas pointed out. "Gregory never would've gotten away with cursing someone before."

"No one else wanted to get cursed, either," Miles added. "The Waning's been hitting the Executors hard."

I furrowed my brow. "What could that mean?"

"I don't know that it *means* anything," Miles said. "I mean, the Waning's always kind of centered around the school, hasn't it? It's random."

"Maybe it's not," I realized for the first time. "I mean, we know it's more prevalent on campus. What if there are other patterns we haven't noticed? What if there's a way to predict when the Waning will affect someone?"

"I don't think something as complicated as the Waning is predictable," Verla said. "There's simply more people living at the school than anywhere else in the coven."

Lucas pressed his lips together. "Nadine, you've been working on your intuition. What does that tell you?"

"I'm not sure," I admitted. "Intuition is difficult. It's hard to tell if the thoughts coming through my head are my own, or if they're a message from Mother Miriam. I'm still trying to learn how to tell the difference. But… I feel that if there's a pattern, we have to track it down, right? It's like a puzzle, and maybe we can solve it if we had all the pieces."

"I know someone very good at puzzles," Lucas pointed out.

I nodded. "I'll look into it and see if I can find any patterns."

"I'll join you in that research," Verla offered. "Uncovering clues could certainly give us an advantage over the priestesses."

I nodded in agreement. "Talia, Chloe, any clues about the Wands?"

Talia shook her head. "We're working on it. We've gotten into the archives room a few times, but there are a lot of records to look through. So far, we haven't found anything."

"Mandy? Grant? Anything on the demon?" Lucas asked.

Grant frowned. "I've been searching records for traumatic deaths, but it's a lot, man. Any one of them could've been connected to a demon. We've been trying to narrow it down, but no mention of demons in the coven's records yet."

Mandy bit her lip and straightened a pile of papers in front of her. "I *may* have found something last night, but I can't be sure that it's legit. It's just a rumor."

"There may be some truth to the rumor," I said. "What's the story?"

"This is a photocopy of an old article in *The Epitaph*," Mandy said, handing out copies. "About fifteen years ago, a student did a series on coven legends. One of the stories he wrote about was the Mystic Wands Suicide."

Chloe wore a calculating expression. "Mystic Wands… that's the shop downtown where the owner hanged himself in the back, isn't it? That place is supposed to be spooky haunted."

Grant scoffed. "You're telling me. That ghost is holding one hell of a grudge."

Onyx tilted her head. "What do you mean?"

"He means we saw it," Talia said ominously.

Miles snorted. "Yeah, right."

"Look, I know you never believed us, but we saw what we saw," Grant snapped.

Miles's features paled. "It was Halloween when I dared you to go into that shop. I thought you were trying to scare us. I didn't think you'd actually seen anything!"

"What's the legend?" I asked, eyeing the article Mandy handed me.

"Decades ago, a man by the name of Adrik Harvey was found dead in the back of his wand shop, hanging in the back room," Mandy explained. "At the time, it seemed like a pretty straight-forward suicide case. His body was buried, the noose was removed, case closed… or so the coven thought. When they went to clean out the shop, Adrik's ghost got violent. Anyone who went inside the shop got hurt, so the shop was left abandoned. Many rumors have sprung up throughout the years, suggesting he didn't kill himself at all, but that he was murdered. Some say his wife did it. Others claim it was his competitor. No one quite knows what happened in the back room that day, but one thing about his haunting remains consistent."

My blood turned ice cold as I scanned the article. *"Leave, demon scum... or die,"* I read out loud.

Mandy nodded. "That's what he says to anyone who enters the shop, right before he attacks."

Talia's face had turned paper white. "Th—that's what he said to me…"

All eyes turned to her, but Lucas was the first to speak. "What happened in that shop?"

Talia cleared her throat. "Last Halloween, Miles dared Grant to go inside Mystic Wands. Legend says that the noose is still hanging in the back, and Grant was going to get a picture of it. But I heard him scream, so I ran inside… and the ghost was there. He called me *demon scum*, and I thought he must just be confused, right? We're descended from a demonic god, so we have demon blood. I thought that's all he meant. But what if he was talking about *the* demon?"

"Of course," I said in realization. "The demon feeds off traumatic deaths. If he cast a spell on Adrik that made him hang himself, it would certainly look like a suicide, and it's a recipe for a vengeful spirit."

Grant tapped his chin. "He must think anyone who enters the shop is the demon returning."

"Then we have to go back to Mystic Wands and help him move on," Lucas insisted. "He might not even know he's dead. If we can talk to him, maybe he'll remember some things. He might know how to get rid of the demon."

Grant bit his lip. "It's not that simple. He's not there anymore."

Lucas furrowed his brow. "He's been there for decades. Where could he possibly be now?"

"Um… we kind of trapped him," Talia admitted.

"*Trapped* him? How?" Lucas asked.

Talia stood and walked over to one of the shelves she'd decorated. She picked up the pretty music box she'd brought with her other antiques. "We're not totally sure how it happened. Grant threw my music box at him, and it… sucked him in. It's like it was protecting us."

"So we release him," Lucas said, like it was simple. "We get answers, and he gets closure."

"We don't know how to release him," Talia admitted. "The music box worked when I bought it at Hallowed Harmonica, but after it sucked him in, the box broke. It hasn't worked since."

"Can you get any visions from it? I asked.

"I've tried," Talia said. "There was something strange about the visions. I heard screaming, but I also saw… happy memories. I thought I could clear the bad memories, but now I get nothing when I touch it."

"What if we fix it?" Chloe asked. "Maybe it will release the ghost and we can talk to him. Or maybe your visions will restart."

"Can I see it?" Grant held his hand out to Talia, and she handed him the music box. He looked deep in concentration as he inspected it. "I can *try* to fix it, but it'll be tricky."

"Hopefully we'll find something," I said.

"There's something else," Mandy added. "Look at the dates."

I scanned the article, and my stomach dropped. "Adrik died the same year as my grandfather. So, the demon was here with him. My grandfather was *murdered*. That's pretty damn traumatic. You think the demon marked him for death?"

"I think it's worth considering a connection," Mandy said.

Chloe looked uncertain. "But my grandfather confessed to the murder. He spent his life in jail. He was responsible, not a demon."

"Perhaps he was working with the demon," Mandy theorized. "We still don't know who summoned him in the past. If this is the timeframe the ghostly warning talked about, maybe your grandpa's the one who summoned him before."

"How does this help us, though?" Chloe asked. "Nadine and I both researched our family curse. I'm not sure there's anything else to learn about it."

"Chloe's right," I said. "But something about this… it must be connected. We're going to have to fix the music box before we figure it out. Good work, Mandy. This might actually give us some answers."

Mandy smiled proudly and took a seat again.

Lucas turned to Professor Warren. "Have you learned anything more about how to break a demon contract?"

Professor Warren sat straighter in his chair. "I'm afraid the Miriamic Police Department confiscated most of Professor Daniels's notes on her demonology research. The headmistress and I have dug up what we can, but there's not much more to learn than what we already know. In order to break the contract and banish the demon, the priestesses would have to withdraw their consent. I think we all know that's not going to happen unless something drastically changes—and quickly."

The room went silent as we all considered this. Verla was the first to speak, though her tone was ominous. "I think we all know what needs to happen."

My stomach sank, because I knew she was right, even if I didn't want to do it.

"I thought we agreed we wouldn't," Lucas said, though he too seemed to be considering it.

"Do what, exactly?" Chloe asked.

Verla explained. "I believe with enough power and the right ingredients, we can artificially manufacture the Waning through a potion. If the priestesses lose their power, we'd gain the advantage. They won't let a demon roam the coven if they're left powerless."

"That's a fantastic idea!" Chloe exclaimed. "Why haven't we done it yet?"

"Because it goes against what we stand for," Lucas said. "This is the kind of thing I wrote about in *The Shield*. Taking away each other's power leaves us all vulnerable. But…"

He looked over to me, and I already knew what he was going to say.

"But perhaps we have to bend our morals this one time, for the greater good," I finished for him.

"Let's think about this," Mandy said carefully.

Professor Warren's brow knitted deep in thought. "It may be our only option to breaking the demon contract."

Everly nodded along. "Then we have to do it before something like The Hearse Tragedy happens again."

Images from that night flashed through my mind. I saw the crimson color of blood seeping into the snow, along with the lifeless stares of the recently deceased. The image of flashing emergency lights in my mind morphed into flicker flames, taking me back to the night of the Burning. I could still hear the crackle of the fire and the shrill cry of Amy's dying screams. My stomach twisted, because I knew if the priestesses had their way, it'd happen all over again. The priestesses would sanction far worse than the Burning or The Hearse Tragedy during their search for the Oaken Wands.

"Lucas and I watched innocent people die at the hands of the demon," I said. "We all saw what happened the night of the Burning. The longer the priestesses are in power, the more people will die. We said when we formed The Coven's Shield that innocent lives would come first. I don't think we have a choice anymore."

"No," Mandy insisted. "We always have a choice. The priestesses won't hesitate to react to an attack like this. We don't know how many people will die as a result. This could be a mistake."

"It could be our only chance," Verla pressed. "We could get rid of the demon *and* gain power over the Imperium Council. I'm afraid Nadine is right. We no longer have a choice."

"I think we all know this is a morally gray decision," I added. "But the world isn't black and white. We can't pretend that it is. All we can do is our best to save as many innocent lives as possible."

Nobody protested, because we all knew what needed to happen. The world *wasn't* black and white… and it looked like we didn't have any other option but to immerse ourselves in shades of gray.

☾

Everything was in place by the time the priestesses called a meeting that Friday. Verla and I had created the brew, which we handed off to William. He met with Claudia that week about her investment offer, and he'd slipped the potion into the wine she served at every meeting. I entered

Octavia Hall that night feeling like this could save us all. Finally, it could all be over.

I started up the stairs, but when I reached the second floor, my heart leapt. A hand came out from the shadows and grabbed me. "Let go of me—"

"Priestess," a voice came in a hushed whisper.

I realized it was Hector. I quickly followed him into a small, dark office next to the stairwell.

He trembled. "I figured it out, Priestess. I know what they're making me brew. The poison not only kills, but *controls* its victims. The priestesses will have control over people in the afterlife. It will trap their souls here, so the priestesses can use their spirits in time of war. They intend to test it on their own people, then use it as a weapon against the fae. They want to build a dead army."

My stomach dropped out of my abdomen. I didn't know such a thing was possible, and it was far worse than I imagined. Killing their own people was one thing, but making them into slaves in the afterlife? This went beyond wicked.

I placed my hand over my mouth. "If they control the spirits of those who take this poison, it won't be long before they realize Monica is alive —if they haven't already."

"Th—they'll blame me for getting the potion wrong," Hector stammered. "If they find me unfit for the job, they'll find someone else to use their Wand."

"We have to get you out of town," I decided immediately.

"Right now?" he asked in a trembling voice. "I have a wife. I—I…"

I swallowed the terror rising in my chest. "We have a plan that's already set in motion. The wine they're drinking tonight will take away their powers. The priestesses won't get a chance to use their poison. If you leave before it's done, they'll suspect you. We must play along as if everything is normal. Can you do that, Hector?"

His hands continued to tremble, but he drew a deep breath. "I will do my best, Priestess."

"Go upstairs now," I instructed him. "We can't be seen together. I'll be there soon."

Hector nodded and hurried out of the room. I waited a few minutes before making my way upstairs. When I entered the Imperium headquarters, Hector was at the fireplace, brewing the poison the priestesses were forcing him to make. The priestesses laughed and chatted like he wasn't even there. I didn't understand how they could be laughing in the midst of everything they were planning. Their laughter quickly died when I entered the room.

Claudia glanced at the clock. "You're late."

"I got here as quickly as I could after my dialysis appointment," I stated coolly. I wasn't going to let her forget that she was playing with people's lives with her health insurance reform. "Skipping my treatment for organ failure wasn't an option."

"There's no need to be dramatic, Nadine," Lilian said.

"I'm simply stating the truth," I replied. "You called a meeting to discuss the changes being made in the coven. This is a pressing matter I believe we should discuss."

"The matter of student health insurance is already settled," Margaret said. "We're here to discuss other matters."

"What is more important than saving the lives of your people?" I asked. "Students are losing access to therapy and life-saving medications because they can't obtain health insurance to pay for it. I take life-saving treatment three times per week, and the Imperium Council has voted it unnecessary. Explain that to me."

"Suffering is a simple fact of life," Claudia said. "Sometimes, certain people must suffer so that others don't have to."

Her statement was like a punch to the gut. I couldn't believe she'd said that.

"We're the Imperium Council," I stated. "We have the power to help our people. No one has to suffer."

"I disagree," Claudia said firmly. "Sacrifices must be made for the greater good. That said, I believe we can move on."

Claudia stood and pulled a bottle of wine, along with five wine glasses, off the shelf behind her. She began pouring the wine as she spoke. "I have ideas for a new community center. A fresh design will give us new opportunities for hosting events, which can prove profitable to the coven."

Community centers weren't supposed to be profitable. They were meant to bring the community together, and we had the means to provide free resources and events for free. I forced myself to bite my tongue this time as I watched Claudia pour the wine. She passed the wine glasses to each priestess, before placing a glass in front of me.

This was it. Within moments, the priestesses would be stripped of their powers and blame it on the Waning. I held my breath as Priestess Margaret lifted the wine glass to her lips. She tilted the glass… and paused. Her eyes landed on me, and the other priestesses hesitated.

"Aren't you going to drink some, Nadine?" Margaret asked. "Claudia has been kind enough to provide this fine wine. It's rude to refuse it."

"I'm afraid I'll have to decline," I said. "I don't drink alcohol."

"I'm sure one or two glasses are fine," Margaret said.

"I have lupus and kidney disease, and I take several medications," I reminded her. "It's something I've chosen to stay away from for my health."

Margaret set her glass down. She didn't take her eyes off me as she said, "Hector, come over here."

I felt all the blood drain from my face.

Margaret shoved her wine glass into his hands. "Drink this."

Hector hesitated, and his eyes darted in my direction. He knew what would happen if he drank it.

"Priestess," I protested. "Is it necessary to embarrass him like this? I simply have health issues that prevent me from consuming alcohol."

"It's all right," Hector said. "I'm sure the wine is lovely."

Hector shot me a glance, and I read the intent in his eyes. He was willing to make a sacrifice, to strip his magic and trick the priestesses into drinking the brew themselves. I didn't get a chance to protest further before he put the glass to his lips. I watched in horror as the red liquid slid into his mouth.

He smiled kindly as he set the glass in front of Margaret. "Lovely, indeed. The priestesses have wonderful taste—"

The words halted on his tongue. He gasped, then threw his hand over his throat. His face turned red as he tried and failed to find air, and he dropped to his knees.

"Hector!" I screamed. I shot out of my chair and rounded the table toward him. I tried to catch him, but he fell through my arms and landed on his back on the floor.

"I could smell it!" Margaret snarled. "Someone has poisoned our wine!"

Hector began convulsing.

"No!" I cried. I placed my hand on his chest, searching for the magic that caused this. I had to be able to stop it, like I could stop a curse.

But it was too late. Hector's body went limp, and saliva dripped down the side of his face as the life left his eyes. It had happened in seconds. I stared down at his corpse, unable to believe what I'd just seen.

That wasn't how the potion was supposed to work. Something had gone horribly wrong.

The priestesses didn't seem to care that a man had just died in front of them. Lilian shot out of her chair and pointed a finger at me. "She tried to poison us!"

"I didn't!" I cried, scrambling backward. If there ever was a time I thought I might face the noose, it was now. I certainly *looked* guilty.

Hell, I *was* guilty. I never intended something like this to happen, though.

"You refused to drink the wine," Lilian accused. "You knew this would happen."

"I didn't! I swear." That was the truth. I never in a million years thought someone would die from this. I trembled as I got to my feet, steadying myself against the bookcase behind me. "Honest to the Goddess, I don't drink alcohol. I didn't know."

"You're lying!" Margaret accused. She lunged forward and grabbed me by the arm. "One way or another, we'll get the truth out of you."

Margaret yanked me so hard that I stumbled forward and caught myself on a chair. She forced me into it, then conjured a vial and held it above my head. It had to be poison. She was done with me. She wanted me gone for good.

I created a shield around myself and tried to make a break for it, but my feet swept out from under me. Lilian flicked her fingers, and an invisible force shoved me back into the chair. She was using her telekinesis on me. Pressure curled around my hands, and I realized she'd created a shield to keep my hands contained. If I tried to fight back with magic, it would backfire on me. The priestesses surrounded me, and I trembled.

"Margaret, are you sure you want to use that on her?" Charlotte asked. "The ingredients are rare. We have a limited supply."

Dear Goddess, they were going to make me die a horrible, painful death.

"If there ever was a time to use a truth serum, it is now," Margaret said, before grabbing me by the hair and yanking my head back.

I couldn't move. My whole body was rendered immobile by Lilian's magic. Claudia grabbed my jaw and forced my mouth open, and Margaret poured the potion past my lips. I tried not to swallow it, and the liquid gurgled in my throat.

"Swallow!" Claudia snapped. She put her hand over my mouth and nose, forcing me to swallow.

The potion burned my nose, and my eyes watered. I felt my whole body sag as the magic took hold of me.

Margaret smirked proudly. "Now tell us, Nadine. Did you poison the wine and try to kill us?"

My throat felt like fire was rising inside of it as the magic forced an answer out of me. "No," I said honestly.

I didn't realize I'd said it until I heard my own voice. The potion would make me tell the truth, whether I wanted to or not. Technically, I *hadn't* tried to kill them, and I barely squeaked by with a half-truth.

Margaret's nostrils flared. She had fully intended on catching me in a lie and executing me for it. "If it wasn't her, then who? No one but *her* had access to the wine."

Claudia gasped. "The wine came from my house. I had a glass earlier this week with a business partner, William Connor."

"We must question him at once!" Lilian barked. "Nadine is free to go… for the time being."

She released her hold on me, and I ran out of the room as fast as I could, my throat still burning.

I was still trembling when I got back to the school. I marched straight to Headmistress Verla's office and entered without knocking. She sat at her desk, reading a large textbook under the light of her lamp.

Her features paled when she saw me, and she leapt to her feet. "Nadine, what happened? Did it work?"

"No, it didn't work!" I snapped. "Hector's *dead*! The priestesses got suspicious, and they made him drink the wine. You told me the potion would take their powers, not kill them! Was it true? Is it even possible? Do we even have the power to mimic the Waning, and if we did, how long would it last? Tell me the truth!"

I had to believe Verla had good intentions, but I feared the worst. Had she lied to me because she knew I wouldn't be part of an assassination attempt? Or had it all been an accident?

Verla placed her hand over her heart and staggered back into her chair, collapsing against the frame. She looked as shocked as I was to hear that the potion didn't work the way we intended. "It should've worked. We put your power to siphon magic inside the potion. It should've stripped them of their powers!"

"What if I'm not that powerful?" I wasn't sure the potion was even possible. "Tell me, Headmistress. Did we screw up, or was this your plan all along?"

Verla's hands trembled. "I had no intention of brewing a poison. If I wanted to brew a poison, I wouldn't have needed your help. I truthfully didn't know how potent the potion would be, but I don't see how we could've ruined it to this degree—"

"Did William have something to do with it? His name came up as a suspect at the meeting," I demanded.

She gasped and threw her hand over her mouth. "He slipped the potion into the wine bottle at his meeting earlier this week, as was our plan. He must've seen an opportunity and switched it out."

"We can't let this happen," I insisted. "This is a betrayal of our trust. We agreed on a plan, and he went against it! We can't trust him to be part of The Coven's Shield anymore."

"I agree," Verla said as she grabbed her coat. Odin jumped out of his cat tower to follow her. "I will go speak to him."

"I'm coming with you."

She held up her hand to stop me. "Not until I speak with him first. It may not be safe for you. We don't know how deep this betrayal runs. What if he intended to poison *all* the priestesses, including you, Nadine? Go back to your dorm and wait until I get back."

"But Headmistress—"

"You need to stay safe," she pressed, and she grabbed my arm tightly. "Don't make me ward my office and lock you in here, because I swear to the Goddess, I will do *whatever* it takes to protect you."

Verla wasn't giving me a choice. She was genuinely scared I was in grave danger, and she forced me to return to my dorm room.

I didn't sleep that night. I lay awake, staring at the ceiling and wondering if Verla would manage to speak with William in time.

At dawn, I heard the sound of a cat scratching at my door. I opened it, and saw Odin. I followed him down to Verla's office. She had returned and appeared thoroughly exhausted…

And defeated.

"No," I gasped, though I already knew the truth. I could see it in her eyes.

"I'm sorry, Nadine. But the priestesses got to him first," Verla informed me grimly. "We will never know the truth of why he betrayed us, because William Connor is dead."

By all official accounts, William died from a fall down the stairs. He'd broken his neck and was dead instantly. The priestesses had staged an accident, but we all knew what happened. They had laid judgment upon and killed William all in one night. If they were that determined to stay in power at any cost, then all of us in the Coven's Shield needed to be very careful.

I was still pondering it long after I heard the news. I wasn't paying attention to where I was going as I walked down the hall. Someone rushed out of a dorm room, knocking into me so hard we both fell on our asses. Oliver jumped out of the way before I could land on him. The guy had been carrying a box, and all the contents scattered. He lay flat on his back, and it wasn't until I stood to help him up that I saw it was Quentin. He groaned as I helped him sit.

"You all right?" I asked.

He frowned, looking totally defeated. "As good I can be, considering."

He started putting things back into the box, and I hurried to help him. I picked up a comb, a tube of toothpaste, and a small potted plant that had spilled dirt everywhere.

I scooped the dirt back into the pot. "Where are you going with all this?"

"Home. I'm moving back in with my parents."

"You're moving?" I balked.

He sighed as we finished packing the box. "I have to. I'm dropping out, and I can't afford my own place."

"You can't drop out!" I protested. It was unheard of to drop out of Miriam College of Witchcraft. Our magical training was imperative to learning our powers. "If you can't afford it, we'll get you a scholarship."

Quentin snorted as he lifted the box and stood. "They've already taken our healthcare. How long until they cut our scholarships, too?"

His question was like a punch to the gut, because I knew all too well how possible it was. I wouldn't be here without my scholarship, and the last thing I wanted was to drop out of school. I couldn't imagine what Quentin was going through.

He sighed. "It's not about tuition. It's Lydia's medical bills. The doctors are hopeful she'll walk again, but only with ongoing care. If I don't get a full-time job to pay for it, they won't treat her."

"Nadine set up a fund online—"

"That's already been taken down."

I gaped. She'd only organized the fundraiser a few days ago. "How's that possible?"

Quentin shrugged. "Someone reported it to the site she set it up on. I guess they think she's scamming people or something."

My hands curled into fists. The priestesses had to be behind this.

"This is what I have to do," Quentin said. "I have no other choice. Goodbye, Lucas."

Quentin stepped around me and hurried down the hall. All I could do was watch him leave, because I didn't know what else *to* do. I couldn't tell him he was making a mistake. He was doing everything in his power to help Lydia. I couldn't tell him we'd find another way to pay for it, because we'd already tried, and we'd failed.

"Damn it," I growled under my breath. There was only one way I *could* help, and that was finding the Wands, banishing the demon, and fixing the coven.

I headed to the library and found a secluded area behind stacks of books. The study area had a single couch that looked out a window toward the forest. I liked it here, because it was quiet and the view was nice. It helped me concentrate.

I sat with my legs propped up on the couch and the textbook Professor Warren had given me spread across my lap. The book detailed all sorts of rare magic, and sifting through it for details on portals was tedious and time-consuming work.

Everything I read talked about fae portals. The fae were said to be able to access different realms easier than other races. It's how they came to Earth from their home realm, Edinmyre, centuries ago. According to the book, portals were merely holes punched through the fabric of reality.

In theory, all I had to do was imagine the place I wanted to go, focus my magic, and connect two points in space. Maybe it was that simple for the fae, but their entire magical system was based on manipulating their reality. Hell, they could make illusions solid just by *believing* in them. That magic didn't come so naturally to a warlock.

Hours must've passed as I flipped through the book. It was past dark, and I had to be the last person here.

I lifted my hands and pictured a portal blooming in front of me. A few sparks came out of my fingertips, but no portal. If we couldn't get the priestesses to break the contract, and we couldn't open a portal to hell to send this demon through, then I didn't know what options we had left.

I heard footsteps, and I quickly subconjured my book. Nadine emerged from behind the bookcases, and I relaxed. Oliver lounged on the windowsill, licking his paws. Isa jumped onto the sill beside him and stared out the window.

Nadine had dark circles under her eyes, and she yawned as she untied her cloak. She draped it over the back of the couch, before falling into the cushion beside me. "I thought I might find you here. Mind if I join you?"

"Not at all," I told her. "How are you feeling today?"

Nadine frowned. "Honestly? Tired. I haven't been able to sleep."

"How can I help?"

She shook her head. "You can't. Insomnia's a side effect of dialysis. Even if it wasn't, I don't know if I'd be able to sleep with everything going on. What are you researching?"

I didn't miss how quickly she changed the subject. "Portals. You?"

Nadine pulled a thick tome out from under her arm and opened it. "I've been researching demons. I'm supposed to be looking for patterns in the Waning. Since we know demon magic is behind it, I thought I could start there."

I wrapped an arm around her. "Have you learned anything?"

She sagged in my arms. "So far, nothing. Literally, *nothing* like this has ever happened in the coven before. I think it's why the priestesses are so intent on finding the Wands. Even *they* don't know what they're up against, so having the Wands gives them the best chance at obtaining power."

"Maybe *nothing* is a clue itself," I suggested.

"That's a good point, but I don't really know what it means… I just know what we're doing now isn't working. I'm sick of watching people die. We need answers."

"It does you no good if you can't read straight," I said. "You need energy to help other people, and that starts with taking care of yourself. You need to rest."

Nadine eyed me. "That's unlike you to say."

I shrugged. "I've picked up a thing or two from my therapist. If you push yourself too hard, you could end up in the hospital again. So please, tell me how I can help, because I want to."

Nadine rested her head on my shoulder, her body warm and soft against mine. "All I can do is keep up my treatment. I'm doing better on dialysis. I really am. We're both in a better spot with our health right now."

I furrowed my brow. "What do you mean? I was never sick."

She pulled away, eyebrows pinched together. "Yes, you were. You may not have been physically ill the way I am, but mental illness is just as serious."

I chuckled. "It's not like I was lying in a hospital bed."

"But you *could've* been… or worse."

My stomach sank at the reminder. I knew what she was saying. My depression had pushed me to limits I didn't even know I had—made me think in ways I never wanted to. I'd be damned if I hadn't thought how easy it would be to make it all go away.

My stomach hollowed just thinking about it. There were times when I thought I *was* better, and times when it felt like I was faking it—like one little trigger would break me and send me right back down the dark pit I'd dug so long ago.

"Have I really changed that much?" I wondered.

She nodded. "You have, but it's all for the better."

"If you like me for who I am now, then why'd you fall for me back then? I don't get it."

"Your depression never scared me," she said gently. "It's not who you are. Ever since you started therapy, I can see that you're discovering more of your true self every day. And I love watching it, because every time I learn something about you, I fall deeper and deeper in love with you."

"My depression *is* a part of me, though—probably always will be," I pointed out. A dark pit opened in my stomach, and I couldn't stop it. My thoughts flickered to all the bad I tried so desperately to ignore. "I can go to therapy and take meds, but I don't know that I'll ever be *cured* of my depression, just like your symptoms can go into remission but you'll always have lupus. Every time I think I'm doing better, a wave comes back and knocks me off my feet. Even if I'm happy sometimes, I'll still always have to use tools to manage. It won't always be easy for us. That seems unfair to you. I don't know why you would want to stick around."

Nadine's eyebrows pinched together, and she looked really hurt by what I said. "How could you ever think I wouldn't want to be here?"

I didn't look her in the eye. "You're amazing. How could *I* be worthy of your love?"

"Depression or not, you have always been worthy of love," Nadine insisted. "Worth isn't something you earn. It's inherent. In good times or in bad, I will always love you. My love for you doesn't change with how you're feeling, just like your love for me remains consistent regardless of how ill I am."

I squeezed her hand. "I can believe that on good days, but why can't I believe it now?"

Nadine took my face in her hands, forcing my gaze back to hers. "Deep down in your heart, you know it's true. This is just a story you're telling yourself in the moment. Let's bring you back to reality. Take a deep breath, and tell me five things you can see."

Nadine was using the coping technique Dr. Mack had taught me. It was supposed to help with anxiety. I guess I could play along.

"I see you, books, the window, the cats, and… the trees outside."

"Four things you can touch?" she asked.

"You, the couch, the floor, and my clothes."

"Three things you can hear?"

I hesitated. There wasn't much sound in the library. Nadine waited patiently for me. "Um, I hear the air conditioner, Oliver licking his paws, and your breath."

She nodded encouragingly. "Two things you can smell?"

I inhaled deeply. "The library has a distinct smell… maybe it's books? And your perfume. You smell like roses."

"And one thing you can taste," she said.

I ran my tongue along my teeth. This was always the hardest one. "I guess I still taste some mint from the gum I was chewing earlier."

"Good," Nadine said, squeezing my hands again. "Three more deep breaths. How do you feel?"

I finished my breaths, and I felt much lighter. "Better than before. I just get so worried. Aren't you scared my depression will never truly go away?"

She shook her head. "No, because there's more to you than that. If I'm going to love you, I'm going to love all parts of you. When I say you're improving for the better, I don't mean to reject those parts of you. Rather, I want to welcome the other parts."

"Like what?" I wondered. "What exactly is it that you love about me?"

Nadine gaped, like she couldn't believe I didn't see it. "I *admire* you, Lucas. You're incredibly kind, and always looking for ways to help people. You stand up for your friends, and you stand by your values. You're willing to take risks, and when people tell you that you can't do something, you do it anyway. You're strong, loyal, and smart."

My heart swelled in my chest. "That sounds more like you than me."

"Maybe I love you because we're similar in those ways," she said. "All I know is that you're selfless and caring, and when I'm around you, I feel safe. You were the first person to accept me when I came here, and you've never asked me to be something that I'm not. I can be myself around you, and you love me for me. I met you when I was at a vulnerable point in my life, and you listened and tried to understand. You've always been there for me even when I'm being headstrong and stubborn. You take care of me when I'm out of spoons."

"Spoons?" I asked.

"Spoon theory is a story for people with chronic illnesses," she explained. "Each spoon represents the energy needed for a task. People with chronic illnesses have to manage their spoons more than others, because we only have so many spoons available to us every day. Once you're out of spoons, that's it. You don't have any more energy for the day. If you borrow from your spoon supply for the next day, you're in a deficit, so you have fewer spoons to use for tomorrow. Walking up stairs might be a spoon for me, and for someone with depression like you, getting out of bed might be a spoon."

I had never thought of myself as chronically ill before. It didn't physically ache to get out of bed and shower like Nadine or Miles experienced. But some days… I just couldn't do it.

"That makes a lot of sense, actually," I said.

"Another reason why I love you. You're open minded and willing to learn and grow." She paused before adding, "Other people would tell me to comply with the priestesses and be quiet—don't make a sound—but you're here at my side fighting this with me. You support me in every way I could ever ask."

A smile broke across my face, and it felt *so good*. "Of course I support you. You're amazing."

I leaned down and brushed my lips across hers. My heart leapt, and my pants tightened. Nadine knew how to lift my spirits. When she said good things, I actually believed her.

Nadine smirked as we drew away. "You look excited."

"I've got the best girl in the world in my arms. You're the reason I've changed, and you should take credit for it. You make me see the good in the world. You give me hope. Hell, you're here to calm me down when I need it, and you're always so kind. If it weren't for you, I'd never believe we stood a chance against the priestesses. But I have to believe we do, because I believe in *you*."

Nadine blushed. "That means a lot. Thank you, Lucas."

She lifted her chin, and I kissed her again. Only this time, it wasn't soft and sweet. She parted her lips, and my tongue slid inside her mouth. My heart hammered as my hand came up to cradle the back of her neck. She slid her hand downward, and my dick became rock hard. Damn, all I wanted was to take her right here in this library.

"I want you," she begged.

I was starting to notice a pattern with Nadine. Every time we talked about our feelings, she got really horny. Maybe because when we talked, we were already vulnerable to one another, so it was easier to strip away the rest and connect in a full experience—emotionally and physically. It hadn't always been easy for me to talk about my feelings, but with

Nadine, I felt like I could be vulnerable in any capacity, and she would still love me. It was the best feeling in the world.

I guess we both had some sort of emotional kink or something.

I pulled her on top of me. Nadine kissed me harder, and I lay on my back. The weight of her body on top of me was enthralling. My hands roamed over her, then dipped beneath her waist band. I squeezed her ass, and she giggled. She must've really liked it, because she straddled me and kissed me harder. She rolled her hips, and my heart pounded harder.

Nadine drew away, breathing hard. I could tell she was exhausted, so I wrapped an arm around her back and laid her gently on the couch. She smiled as I knelt beside her and pushed the fabric of her shirt upward. She eyed me curiously as I placed gentle kisses all over her skin. I reached for the button on her jeans.

"May I?" I asked.

She let out a wavered breath. "Hell, yes."

Something about fooling around in a public space must've really turned Nadine on, because she was already wet when I slid my fingers down her pants. She tilted her head back and let out little gasps as I played with her.

I silenced her with a kiss, then whispered, "Keep quiet. We're in a library."

Nadine bit her lower lip in wanting. "We're alone, aren't we?"

I chuckled. "I'd hope so. If you want privacy—"

"No," she begged. "I think it's hot. I want you to make me come right here, Lucas."

Her desire for me drove me wild, and I had no choice but to comply with her every demand. I wanted to please her in every way possible. Nadine kicked off her shoes, and I helped her strip off her pants. I grabbed her cloak and tossed it over her legs for privacy, then ducked my head beneath it.

Nadine gasped as my tongue grazed over her clit. Her soft, warm legs wrapped around my neck. My head spun as I inhaled the sweet scent of sex. I wanted to fuck her right here, but I wanted to make it last. I knew if I entered her, I'd be done for in moments.

So I pleasured her in the best ways I knew how. My tongue roamed over her body the way I knew she liked it. She tangled her fingers in my hair, begging for more. I slipped my fingers inside of her as I came up for air. Nadine's features appeared blissful as she took in each sensation. Her hands curled around the fabric of the couch.

"Harder," she begged.

I pulled three fingers out of her, then pressed them into her again, over and over as deep as I could go while my thumb massaged her clit. With each movement, the whole couch shook ever so slightly that the books on the shelf beside us rattled. I liked the sound.

Nadine couldn't control herself. She let out heavy breaths and said, "I'm so close."

I ducked my head again and circled her clit with my tongue three more times before she gasped. She contracted around my fingers, and her legs tightened around me. I hadn't even come, and I felt like I could fly. Pleasuring her *really* turned me on.

Nadine went limp as she came down from the high. I made sure the cloak was covering her legs before I came to kneel beside her. She kept her eyes closed, like she was still soaking it all in.

I pressed a kiss to her forehead. "That was hot."

Her eyes peaked open, and she smiled. "So fucking hot," she agreed. "I want to pleasure you now."

I pushed the hair out of her face. "You're exhausted."

She frowned, which made me feel awful, because this was supposed to be a happy moment. "It's not fair if I get off and you don't."

"I don't want to make you do anything that could compromise your health."

She pressed her lips together. "Maybe there's something else we can try… Have you heard of astral sex?"

I tilted my head, intrigued. "Sex on the astral plane? Sure, I've heard of it."

"When we astral travel, I feel different. Maybe I'll have more energy there," she suggested. "I want to try it."

Hell, I wasn't about to say no. Nadine slipped her pants back on, and we left the library, our cats following. My dorm room was dark and empty when we arrived. Grant had placed a note next to my bed that read: *At Talia's. Might be gone all night.*

I waved the note at Nadine. "I guess you're staying here tonight."

"I have no problems with that." She removed her shirt and dropped it beside her. As she reached for her bra clasp, I stopped her.

"Let me," I whispered.

Nadine dropped her arms and let me take the lead. My dick was practically struggling out of my pants before her bra fell away. I carried her to the bed and set her down gently, then I stripped off my own clothes and crawled into bed beside her. Her skin was so warm against mine, and my dick was rock-hard.

I curled her in my arms and pressed a kiss to the top of her head. "Sleep well."

She relaxed against me, and I buried my nose into her rose-scented hair. Goddess, she smelled so sweet. I closed my eyes as blissfulness overcame me…

An odd sensation came over my body. When my eyes opened, Nadine was standing above me. I shivered at the sight of rainbow colors dancing off her naked form. I sat up straight, taking in the strange sensations of the astral plane.

"We did it!" Nadine said happily. She bounced a bit in celebration, and I couldn't take my eyes off her breasts. Goddess, she was a work of art.

She noticed and took a step back, showing off her raw ethereal form. "You like this?"

Even in spirit, I could hardly catch my breath. "You're sexy as fuck."

"You are, too," she said, coming forward to run her hands over my spirit. It was different when she touched me on the astral plane. It was more than just skin on skin. Our connection ran deeper here.

"I wasn't sure we'd be able to do it. I've been practicing, though. When I'm with you, I get really relaxed, and it was easy." She beamed. "We can go anywhere, and no one will see us."

"Unless they're astral traveling, too," I reminded her with a laugh. "I already know you're fantasizing about fucking in the Main Foyer."

"I'll go wherever you want me to," she said. "We can take our spirits anywhere as long as it's not warded. Professor Ward said we just have to imagine it, and our spirits can go anywhere, right?"

I pressed my lips together. Nadine wanted me to choose… I took her hand. "I have an idea."

I closed my eyes, and when I opened them, I was enveloped by darkness. It took a few moments for my spiritual eyes to adjust. Under the light of the stars, gravestones began to take shape. Snow dusted the cemetery grounds, but the air felt warm to my spirit form. It should have felt strange to be out in the open completely naked, but the image of laying Nadine naked over one of these graves turned me on more than I thought it would. Maybe it was the Mortana in me, but damn it, I never wanted her more.

Nadine beamed, then grabbed me around the waist and pulled me close.

"Fuck," I growled, taking her face in my hands.

I kissed her passionately, and her hands roamed over my body. I grabbed her ass and hoisted her upward, and she wrapped her legs around my middle. I didn't have to hold her there; she floated weightlessly. I trailed kisses down her neck as she took in heavy breaths. My dick hardened as we floated upward, making out over the graves. We didn't have to say a word, as our hands did all the talking.

Her fingers tangled in my hair. "Lay down, Lucas."

We floated downward, and I set her gently on the ground, still kissing her all over. Nadine guided me onto my back, then climbed on top of me. Slowly, she eased down onto my cock.

We didn't need a condom here on the astral plane, and I'd never felt her like this before. Goddess, it was like heaven inside of her—warm and silky. I didn't know whose grave we were on top of, but it didn't matter. I'd fuck her on each one of these graves if I could last all night.

Nadine rolled her hips over me like she never had before. She moved with passion and desire, pleasuring me in ways that made my head spin.

"Oh, my—" Nadine didn't get a chance to finish her plea, because she peaked at that moment. Passion surged through me as she contracted around me, and in that instant, I was done for. My passion erupted, and I came with her.

We fell to the ground, panting. Nadine curled into me. It felt so good when I held her to my chest. It was oddly tranquil in the graveyard. I was so at peace.

It wasn't lost on me that this peace existed only inside our dreams. I knew what horrors existed in the real world. I knew what dangers we'd face when we woke. But maybe it didn't have to be that way. For a fleeting moment, I knew what peace felt like.

And I was going to hang on to it… for as long as I possibly could.

nadine

TWELVE

I didn't remember how I'd gotten back into my body, but at some point, I had drifted off to sleep. I awoke to the sound of heavy fist pounding at the door. I was curled in Lucas's arms, still lying in his bed. Lucas and I exchanged a quick glance, then rushed to put clothes on. He opened the door. At first I thought it was Grant, but instead, we found three Executors I didn't recognize standing in the hall.

"There she is!" one of the men growled, pointing a finger at me.

I kept my voice steady. "What is the meaning of this?"

"You were out past curfew!" one of them accused. "You've just earned yourself one hefty fine, lady."

"You can't prove that," Lucas protested. People passed by in the hallway, and several stopped to watch.

The Executor scoffed. "Our men are stationed all over campus. No one saw the Curse Breaker return to her room last night. If you want to contest it, you can take it up with the priestesses."

One of the Executors shoved a paper at us, and I took it without thinking. I glanced down to see three numbers scrawled across the bottom of the page. Shit, he wasn't lying about the hefty fine.

"You can't do that!" Lucas snarled. One of the Executors cracked his knuckles, and another curled his hands into fists. They looked about ready to start a fight.

I placed a hand on Lucas's shoulder. "It's all right. Clearly, I've learned my lesson. I won't violate curfew again."

The Executors seemed pleased, and I took that as our cue to slam the door in their face.

Lucas turned to me, disbelief written across his features. "This curfew is ridiculous! It's just another means to control us. We can't just stand here and let it happen."

"It's just a fine," I said. "I'll find a way to pay for it. They clearly came here looking for a fight, and I wasn't going to satisfy them. If I got away with it because I'm a priestess, it shows people I'm above them, and I don't want to be. Let's show them that I'm their equal and build some trust."

"At least let me pay the fine," he offered.

I pulled the ticket behind my back when he reached for it. "You need money for your car repairs. I'll get a loan from Grammy. Don't you have to get to your internship anyway?"

"Shit," Lucas groaned. "I'll see you later."

I headed back to my dorm room. I was almost to the grand staircase when I spotted Talia, Grant, and Chloe near the big window that looked out over the forest. Grant was holding Talia, and I could see tears brimming in her eyes. Chloe looked to be comforting them, though I couldn't hear what she was saying. Gus circled Talia's feet, looking distressed, while Marley rubbed against her leg.

I rushed toward them, Isa following close behind. "What's wrong?"

Talia wiped her nose. "Grant and I—we..."

Was it their magic? The Waning? It'd only been getting worse—affecting more people at once and lasting longer.

Chloe gave me a clueless look, like she had no idea what was going on and had just found them this way. "You can tell us what happened."

Grant kept his voice low, but it shook. "We don't know what to do. Last night... it was our first *real* time and..."

"The condom broke," Talia blurted.

All the blood in my body drained to my toes. Thoughts raced through my mind a million miles an hour. This could be a good thing... or not. "We'll figure it out," I promised.

Talia sniffled. "We can't have a baby right now. We have to finish school first. This wasn't part of our plan."

"There's stuff we can do to prevent this," Chloe said. "You're not pregnant yet. It takes a few days for the egg to implant."

Talia sighed. "I know, but we just went to the health center. They won't help."

Talia broke into sobs, and Grant wrapped her tighter in his arms. I rubbed her back. A few people passing through the hall looked our way. Chloe shot them harsh glares, and they hurried past us.

"They've got to give you something," Chloe insisted. "There has to be some emergency contraceptive program for people without insurance."

"Not in this coven," Grant sneered. He sounded angry now. "If you can't afford healthcare, you're screwed."

Chloe's hands curled into fists. "I'll get it for you."

Talia blinked away the tears. "You'll what?"

Chloe lifted her head, confident in her decision. "I'm on my parents' insurance. I'll tell them it's for me, and I'll get you the pill."

Talia looked skeptical. "You'd really do that for me?"

"Yes," Chloe said firmly. "I protect my people. Believe me, these priestesses don't want to cross me."

Grant hesitated. "That's really generous of you."

"It's the right thing to do," Chloe replied.

"Come on," I told Grant and Talia. "Let's go somewhere private."

I led Talia and Grant back to our dorm, while Chloe headed to the health center on campus. I did my best to reassure them both, but I truthfully didn't know what to say in this situation. All I could do was be there for them, no matter what happened.

I must've been helping, though, because they both seemed to calm down by the time Chloe returned with a pill and a bottle of water. Talia seemed much more relaxed after she took the pill, but she asked Grant to stay with her. They curled up in bed together. I didn't think either of them would make it to class today.

I got ready for the day, then left as fast as I could to give them space. I swung by the campus post office to get my mail before heading to class. Professor Clarke handed back our essay results in Criminal Justice, and I was disappointed to see the grade I got. I had worked really hard on that essay, and I knew I deserved an A. Professor Clarke had nearly failed me, all because I was a Curse Breaker.

Verla was passing through the hall when I left class. She noticed the paper in my hand and asked, "Research?"

I shook my head. "It's my Criminal Justice essay. I almost failed."

She knitted her eyebrows. "Can I see?"

We stopped in the hall while she skimmed my paper. "You definitely deserve a better score. I'll speak with your professor."

"What good is it going to do?" I asked. "We have more important things to worry about anyway."

"This *is* important," Verla insisted. "Discrimination is a weapon the priestesses are using to divide the coven. Jonathan and I are proposing new policies for this kind of thing within the school, but the school board is dragging their feet implementing them."

"While you're advocating for your students, can we *please* update the school to ADA standards?" I asked. "Lydia's in a wheelchair. She can't even get to her dorm room anymore."

"We had an elevator installed years ago, but it broke down," Verla said. "Updating it could interfere with our space-bending spells. We have dorm rooms on the first floor for students who need them. We've done our best to accommodate."

She was trying to help, but she didn't get it. The school could do better. They just didn't want to.

I gritted my teeth. "How's the school handling the Waning? Half of the students in my Enchanting class are failing because they haven't had enough magic all semester to complete the assignments."

"We're instructing professors to change their grading structure, at least for the time being." She glanced up and down the hall, then lowered her voice. "Have the priestesses found any more Wands?"

"They only have the Alchemy Wand, and we've hit a dead-end with the others. At this point, I'm not sure the Wands are our best option."

"Stay hopeful, Nadine," Verla encouraged. "I'm keeping a close watch on Professor Leto, so if he happens to find a Wand, we'll know. We can't let the priestesses get their hands on them."

I agreed wholeheartedly, but if we didn't find the other Wands at all, none of it mattered. Eventually, our magic would disappear completely.

I wasn't going to let that happen.

At dialysis that evening, I decided to go over my notes I kept in my journal. But when I lifted my palm to conjure it, nothing happened.

"The Waning?" someone asked. I turned to see Onyx wearing scrubs, prepping a dialysis machine.

"Yes, unfortunately," I said. "I'm getting sick of it."

"I thought so. I know that look."

I tiled my head. "I didn't know you worked at the dialysis center."

I remembered she'd said she worked part-time as a nursing assistant, but I'd never seen her here before.

"I'm not usually in this department," she said. "They send me wherever they need help for the day. I've been in the ER a few times, at the dialysis center once or twice, but my favorite is the maternity ward."

"You're majoring in medical studies, then?" I asked.

She nodded as she continued arranging medical supplies. "I have my CNA certificate, then I'll get my nursing license, but I'll be going for my doctorate eventually. If I pass my exams, I'll have my nursing license by the end of the semester. I want to specialize in women's health."

"That's really cool," I told her. "I'm majoring in Criminal Justice."

"That makes sense, since you're a priestess." Onyx kept her gaze on another nurse as she walked a patient out, leaving us alone in the room. "Can I ask you something about being a Curse Breaker?"

"Sure, ask me anything," I offered.

Onyx sat on the chair beside me. "How does your magic work? You can use Alchemy crystals. I've seen you."

I remembered the first day of my Alchemy 101 lab, when I was still posing as an Alchemist. Onyx had been my lab partner, and our cauldron exploded. I'd dropped my Alchemy crystal, and she'd handed it back. I always wondered if she suspected something.

"When did you figure out what I was?" I asked.

"I wasn't sure, actually," she said. "I knew the crystal held magic as soon as I touched it, but I still believed you were an Alchemist. I didn't say anything, because I thought you needed the crystal for your disability."

"It *would* help, but that's not why I was using it."

Onyx frowned. "It's lame they don't allow these crystals in class anyway. Some people need accommodations like that."

I eyed her curiously. "You say that like you know."

She shook her head. "I'll never fully understand your chronic illness. But I think working with crystals would help with my powers. Sometimes, it feels like my magic is trapped inside of me, and if I could just *feel* what that power felt like, maybe I'd be comfortable working with it."

She dropped her gaze. "I don't think it was your fault our cauldron exploded that day."

I couldn't believe she thought so little of herself. "Onyx, you're a talented witch. You made that exploding potion during the Burning to distract the guards. It seemed really advanced."

"I guess I'm good at *some* potions. Not so much at others."

"Don't discount your strengths," I encouraged.

Onyx chuckled, though it sounded forced. "That's easy to say when you're good at something *other* than destruction. I destroy everything I touch."

"That's not true," I argued.

"It is. Our cauldron isn't the only thing I've destroyed..." She trailed off, like she'd said too much.

My heart broke for her. "What do you mean?"

"It's nothing. I didn't mean that—"

"Then why'd you say it? A part of you must believe it."

"I don't know. Maybe because that's what I've heard my whole life." She sighed. "My parents got divorced after I was born. My mom says my dad never would've left if it wasn't for me. I guess he didn't want me, and I ruined their marriage."

"That has nothing to do with you," I promised. "Your parents couldn't handle having a kid, and that's on them."

Onyx wiped her nose, and her sleeve rolled up. I spotted a purple bruise on her upper arm. She caught me staring and quickly dropped her arm, like it might erase what I'd seen.

"What happened?"

She rubbed her arm. "I exploded another cauldron."

I didn't know if it was my intuition, or if I caught something in her tone, but I didn't believe her. "I'm good at keeping secrets. I made everyone believe I was an Alchemist for months."

Onyx chuckled, but it sounded like she was more uncomfortable than anything. "I guess you're right. But I've never told anyone this before, so you can't tell anyone—even Lucas."

I made an X across my heart. "Your secret's safe with me."

Onyx drew a long breath. "It was my mother."

My jaw dropped. "Your *mom* did that to you?"

"She didn't mean it," Onyx insisted. "Mom's never hurt me before."

"That doesn't make it okay," I said.

"I know that. I'll never be okay with the way she treats me, but I can't stop it, either."

"You can just leave, stop seeing her, right?"

Onyx shook her head. "It's not that simple. My mother's a narcissist. If I ignore her calls, she'll just show up on campus. If I moved across the country, she'd follow. One second I can be her perfect little daughter, and the next I'm her mortal enemy. If I show any sort of independence, she goes off on me. Suddenly, everything's *my* fault. She'll claim I don't love her, or I don't care. To her, I'm an extension of her. I'm not my own person. Goddess, it's exhausting."

"That's unfair. There must be something we can do."

Onyx sighed. "All I can do is placate her."

"I'm a priestess. I'll put your mother in her place," I offered. I would, too.

"Trust me, there's no reasoning with my mother," Onyx said. "As it is, she flipped when I mentioned it was unfair the priestesses cut our insurance. That's literally all I said, and she went on a tangent about how entitled I was. Entitled! For something I already pay for! It was worse than when I came out as asexual."

My jaw dropped. "Why would she have a problem with that?"

Onyx rolled her eyes. "Because I'm not giving her grandbabies."

I was so angry for Onyx. I wanted to believe there was a solution, but I didn't know her mother. I didn't know what extremes she'd go to, and I certainly would never understand what Onyx was feeling. I realized I didn't know much about Onyx at all, and that made me sad. She seemed like a really wonderful, interesting person.

"If there's ever anything I can do to help, let me know," I said.

"Thanks," she replied. "For now, I'm just doing my best to ignore my mother and focus on getting my nursing license. Speaking of which, I should probably get back to work."

"Thanks for chatting with me," I told her. "It gets lonely during dialysis sometimes."

She glanced around the empty room. "I can stay, if you'd like."

"I don't know if I'll be much fun," I teased. "My only plans were to go through my mail."

Onyx shrugged. "It's that, or you can watch me work."

I dug inside my bag and pulled out my mail. I opened a greeting card from Talia that had a picture of a stone that said, *"You Rock!"*

I showed Onyx, and she laughed. I tossed aside a few pieces of junk mail, then opened an envelope that was marked from the hospital.

My stomach sank the moment I saw the numbers. It was a bill for my dialysis treatments, but I didn't see the insurance coverage anywhere. The bill was over $500 for just one treatment! My heart hammered as I mentally calculated how much that would cost per year. I realized it was over seventy-eight thousand dollars annually. Holy shit. How could anyone possibly expect me to pay that?

Onyx must've noticed the fallen look on my face, because she asked, "Is everything all right?"

I shook my head. Complete hopelessness sank in my gut, and I wanted to burst into tears. I literally didn't know how I was going to survive on dialysis. What if they took my treatment away because I couldn't pay?

Isa could tell I was distressed, and she pressed her head against my leg. It was at that moment that a tight, sharp pain shot up my leg.

"Ow!" I grabbed my leg, and it felt like holding a rock. My muscle was cramping, and it hurt like I'd been stabbed.

Onyx shot to her feet. "Muscle cramps?"

I winced. "Yeah, I guess."

"It's a common side effect. It just means your fluid levels are out of balance. Let me get a doctor."

The doctor came over and checked my machine. He adjusted a few settings, then gave me some meds that were supposed to help. I just wanted to rip the tubes out and never come back here. The doctor kept a close eye on me, which made me really uncomfortable, because I just wanted some fucking privacy.

Onyx wanted to stay to keep me company, but the doctor made her leave when her shift was over. I was left all alone for the rest of the session.

I fled the hospital as soon as I could. I sat in my car, but I didn't go anywhere. I was afraid my leg was going to cramp up while I was driving and I'd crash or something. It was a terrifying thought. Instead, I called Lucas.

"Can you come pick me up?" I asked him.

"I'm on my way."

Lucas didn't even ask questions. He was just there for me when I needed him. He pulled up next to me in the parking lot a few minutes later. I got out of my car and fell into his arms. A sob broke from my chest, and for the first time in a long time, I let myself break down.

Lucas held me close and rubbed my back. He didn't have to say anything. Just having him here with me helped. Finally, when I stopped shaking so badly, he drew away and said, "Let's sit down."

We sat in my car—me in the passenger seat, and him in the driver's seat. Our cats meowed from the back seat. I handed him my dialysis bill.

"I don't know what to do," I sobbed.

His eyes widened. "I thought you had private insurance."

"I did! I wouldn't put it past the priestesses to go after that, too. They want my own body to poison me."

"That's not going to happen. Put your seatbelt on." Lucas turned on the ignition.

I furrowed my brow. "Where are we going?"

"We're going to talk to your grandmother. We're going to figure this out. I promise."

Lucas left his car in the parking lot and drove us to Grammy's. Our cats followed us up the sidewalk.

Grammy was in the kitchen when we entered the house. "Nadine, is that you—?"

She cut off when she met us in the hallway and saw my red, puffy eyes. She wiped her hands on her apron. "What happened?"

I handed Grammy my bill, along with the fine I'd received earlier. Together, they were over a thousand dollars. It made me physically ill to show them to her. "I need help, Grammy. I don't know how I'm going to pay for this."

Her features fell as she looked them over. "We can handle this. We can —oh, dear. They don't seriously think they can charge this per treatment!"

"Apparently, they can," I said bitterly.

"Have you heard anything from Nadine's insurance?" Lucas asked.

"This is the first I've heard anything!" she cried, obviously pissed. "I don't pay those premiums for nothing. I'm going to have a word with this so-called *medical insurance company*. Take a seat in the living room."

Lucas and I sat on the couch, while Grammy paced back and forth with the phone to her ear. Lucas held me close, but I couldn't help but feel hopeless as the minutes passed.

The moment Grammy connected with a representative, she started barking into the phone. "Yes, you can help by telling me how you dare to call yourselves an insurance company when you can't even pay a simple medical bill... You want to talk to the insured? Talk to me. I pay her insurance premiums... I'm her grandmother. That's who I am! Screw you and your bureaucracy."

After talking circles with the representative for at least ten minutes, she put the man on speaker phone. Dear Goddess, I didn't want to talk to them. I just wanted this to be over. I gave them my details, and Grammy went off on them. "What's the meaning of this bill? You're supposed to cover my granddaughter's health insurance... No, I don't want excuses. I want answers!"

Grammy was ruthless. At one point, I thought the representative was going to hang up on her. Somehow, Grammy managed to make them escalate our call to a supervisor, who told us there was a processing error when my school insurance was canceled. We had to convince them they were my primary insurance company, then told us to call the hospital to send them the bill again.

It must've been hours before we got everything sorted, and I wasn't even sure it *was* sorted by the end of it. By the time Grammy hung up, I had a massive headache.

"If you have any more problems with them, you come to me," Grammy insisted. "I won't sleep until my granddaughter gets her treatments. Are you hungry?"

I shook my head. "I'd just like some tea. I have a massive headache."

"I have a ginger blend you'll love," she said. "And matus tea for Lucas?"

He nodded. "You know me well."

Grammy returned from the kitchen a few minutes later with a tray. She set it on the coffee table, then handed us each a hot teacup. She took one for herself, then sat in the chair across from us. "Have you found any more clues about the Wands?"

I shook my head. I thought Grammy was trying to make small talk, but the question felt heavy. "All we know is there's a Wand somewhere inside the school, but we haven't figured out where."

Grammy sipped her tea. "I wish I knew where Nicholas had hidden the Wands. I've gone through every box, every journal. If he recorded anything more like had about the Alchemy Wand, I'm afraid it's gone."

"It's not your fault," I assured her. "I'm sure he never told you to protect you."

She shook her head, looking thoughtful. "There's got to be another way, some sort of magic we can use. Even if the Wands can't be tracked, we have to be able to get close… an intuitive nudge, perhaps."

"I've been practicing my intuition," I remarked. "I have so much down-time during dialysis. But so far, I've mostly just been meditating. Nothing has really jumped out at me."

"Intuition isn't loud," Grammy said. "In fact, it's the quiet nudges you need to listen to the most."

"I've been more or less waiting for this big message to hit me out of the blue," I admitted. "Perhaps I need to take my intuition in steps."

Grammy nodded. "I'm here to help you every step of the way. You'll figure it out. I know you will."

"Is that your intuition talking?" I teased.

Grammy smiled. "I know my granddaughter, and I know you'll stop at nothing to achieve your goals."

She was right. Death would have to claim me first before I stopped fighting for this coven.

Problem was, a part of me feared it just might.

Grammy shifted in her chair. "Close your eyes. I'm going to say a few things, and you'll tell me your initial reaction. Don't question it; just notice if the sentence feels light or heavy."

"I don't have any magic right now, though," I told her. "Does intuition work with the Waning?"

"I believe it should, as even non-magical races have some form of intu-ition," Grammy said.

"Okay, I'll try it." I closed my eyes and took a deep, calming breath.

"The first thing you must do is trust in your higher self—the part of you that exists spiritually. In some instances, it may even span lifetimes," Grammy said. "What does it feel like when I say that you and Lucas are meant to be together?"

Of course we were. I couldn't imagine being with anyone else. "It feels light. Deep down in my soul, it feels true."

"Good, now how does it feel when I say that you will save the coven?"

My chest tightened, and my breath hitched. "*Very* heavy."

"That's your fear—your ego," Grammy explained. "You cannot see the truth of the situation until you are able to uncover that fear. It's like your ego is shouting above the whisper of your intuition."

"How do I stop being afraid?" It sounded impossible.

"We must dig deep and examine your beliefs. What is it that's truly scaring you, and what evidence do you have that the belief is untrue? Replace that with evidence of the truth you want to believe."

I pondered it for several moments. "I guess I'm afraid because I can't know for certain. There are so many different outcomes, different variables. How can I claim I know the future before it gets here? Even Seers can't be sure their visions will come to pass."

"If I understand correctly, you fear what the coven will become if you fail," Grammy said. "But isn't there a chance you'll win?"

"Sure there is."

"Therefore, you already have evidence that failure is not the ultimate truth. I wonder what would happen if you embraced the uncertainty."

I pondered her words. "I don't see how that would help. If I just accept the future is uncertain, I haven't fixed the problem. I still don't know what's to come. How can we be sure we're making the right choices?"

"We don't," Grammy said simply. "But maybe that's okay."

I shook my head. "I don't think I could ever be okay with that."

"That's simply a story you're telling yourself," Grammy said. "We can change those stories."

"How?" I asked.

She sat straighter in her chair. "What I'm about to say may feel uncomfortable, but I want you to sit with it for a while. Would you still like to hear it?"

I nodded. "Yes."

"When we fear the uncertain, it's our ego's way of trying to protect us," Grammy explained. "The fear center of our brain is trying to experience the outcome before it happens, so that we can prepare for the worst. But this actually increases the perceived threat. Our worry is not rooted in the actual outcome, but in the way we expect to feel about the given outcome.

If you can convince your ego that those stories aren't necessarily true, you may quiet it enough to hear your intuition come through."

"I can't just stop being afraid," I countered. "I can't just force myself to be happy if the coven is destroyed."

"It's not about eliminating your fear, but seeing through it," Grammy said. "You still get to grieve. You get to feel sad and angry, and that's perfectly *healthy* to process those emotions in the wake of a tragedy. But there may be a part of you that fears you won't be able to handle it."

"I can handle grief," I told her bluntly. "Uncertainty is scary because I've *been* in dangerous and traumatic situations where I wasn't okay. People say trauma makes you stronger, but just because I survived it doesn't mean I ever want to be in that place again."

Grammy nodded, like she understood. "There may be other emotions you are trying to avoid, such as disappointment."

I wanted to tell her she was wrong, but I felt a twinge of truth to her words. "I don't want to see people suffer. I have a hard time forgiving myself when people get hurt."

I thought of Amy, of all the women who died upon the pyre, and the others in the riots the night of the Burning. I couldn't allow something like that to happen again.

"Being at peace with uncertainty does not mean you're indifferent to all outcomes," Grammy said gently. "It doesn't mean that you won't feel grief or disappointment. It simply means that you can go forward knowing you can choose to forgive yourself, no matter what happens. If you accept the future is uncertain, the only certainty you'll ever need is the knowledge that whatever *does* come, certain or not, is something that you will be able to handle. *That* is truth, because it comes from inside of you."

"I think I like being in control and in charge because if I can predict how things will play out, I can manage my energy better," I admitted. "If I don't know what's going to happen, I can't predict how much energy I'll have, or if my body can manage. I need to know how to prepare."

Grammy looked contemplative. "I'm sensing something even deeper."

I hesitated. I knew the truth, even if I didn't want to consciously admit it to myself. My voice became small as I said, "Even if I do *my best*, I'm scared it won't be good enough to save everyone."

"And why must you save everyone, Nadine?" Grammy asked.

"I want everyone to live!" I cried. "Not just survive, but to live full lives."

It was only after I reacted that I realized she wasn't accusing me of anything. She was asking me to reflect on it.

Grammy remained calm. "I understand that, and it's truly great that you want to help people. But sometimes, it is out of our hands. It makes you no less of a witch or a priestess or a good person if you can't save everyone. All you can do is stay true to yourself, knowing you've done the best you can. Then you can face anything."

My shoulders fell. "I want to believe you. But it just doesn't seem that easy."

"Just because it's simple doesn't make it easy," Grammy told me. "Changing your mindset is not a switch that can be flicked on and off. It takes time, and perhaps some growing pains, but I believe in you, Nadine."

I frowned. "I'll never be comfortable seeing people get hurt."

"I'm not asking you to get comfortable with it," Grammy said gently. "Only that you can trust yourself to handle it."

Lucas rubbed my leg. "I'm with Nadine. Sometimes it feels like we're running a marathon and not getting anywhere."

Grammy nodded thoughtfully. "Lucas, you're very good at carrying other people's burdens. That's why you're the Reaper's Apprentice. But carrying other people's burdens is not always a good thing. They can weigh you down."

He ran his fingers through his hair. "I know."

"But do you know that you can let them go?" she asked.

"I can. The thoughts I collect aren't as heavy as they used to be. I can let them go now."

"What about other burdens?" Grammy questioned.

Lucas sipped his tea, but he didn't say anything.

"Letting go doesn't mean ignoring it, or eliminating it from your conscious awareness," Grammy said. "It doesn't even mean you don't want to help."

"A burden is a burden," Lucas stated. "You don't just get to set it aside like setting a book on the table."

Grammy cocked an eyebrow. "Why not? Perhaps it will give you the perspective to examine these things from other angles. Redefining burdens and how to manage them may help you both fulfill your prophecy. I've seen the way you two interact. You're both very firm in your independence. You downplay what you're going through so the other doesn't worry. You're so afraid of asking for help, because you don't want to burden each other."

I was offended. How could Grammy think there was anything wrong with trying to protect each other?

"I fail to see the problem," Lucas said flatly.

"Yeah, we're doing just fine, thanks," I agreed.

Grammy sighed. "You're failing to see the point. Independence is not the goal. You're a team, which means you must learn *interdependence*."

I narrowed my eyes. "And what exactly does that mean?"

"When you're born, you're dependent on your caretakers," Grammy explained. "As a child, you need someone else to feed you, clothe you, care for you. You need your caretaker's approval to survive. As you grow older, you learn how to care for yourself. You learn how to feed yourself, bathe yourself, and you even discover that you no longer need to depend on others' approval, because you can find that love within yourself. What many people forget is that there is a third stage, called interdependence—where you become dependent on each other once more."

"How is that a good thing?" I asked. "If we give up our independence to rely on each other, how can we ever function on our own?"

"It's a different sort of dependence in which we know ourselves, our truth, and our own worth independently. We don't rely on others to give us self-worth. Then we use our strengths to contribute to the community. *Independence* allows you to become authentic to your role, instead of fighting against it. *Interdependence* is about working together to create a harmonious relationship *through* your independence. You maintain your independence as you work to lift each other up."

Grammy leaned back in her chair. "Think of the relationship between bees and flowers. The bees feed on nectar from the flowers, and as they fly from flower to flower, they pollinate the plants. The flowers support the bees, as the bees support the flowers. Each has their own independent job, but they work together harmoniously. It is the same in the coven, and how our magic works. Our strengths come together to make us stronger. I see you both struggling with this."

"That's not true," I protested.

"Not true?" Grammy questioned. "Nadine, how often do you ask Lucas for help? And Lucas, I know you care deeply about Nadine, and the last thing you want is to see her hurt. But for Alora's sake, stop acting like she's fragile. You know her better than that!"

The room went silent. Grammy's words had hit hard, and Lucas and I both knew she was right. I'd asked for Lucas's help tonight, but that was only because I'd reached a breaking point. I usually offered my help but never asked for it.

I stared down into my tea leaves. "I guess I *do* try to handle things by myself."

Lucas swept my hair over my shoulder. "And I suppose I don't always fully open up to you, because I don't want to make it your job to fix me. That's not fair to ask."

I frowned. "It's hard to watch you suffer. I just want to help."

"Maybe all I need from you sometimes is a hug," he admitted.

"I don't want to cross your boundaries," I said.

Lucas took my hands in his. "I have no boundaries when it comes to your affection. I'll try to ask for it more when I need it, all right?"

I nodded. "And I'll try to be more open, too."

Grammy smiled. "I'm glad to see you two working together."

"We're a team," I said. "We *do* have some stuff to work on, but for now we should probably get going. It's late. Thank you for everything, Grammy."

"Anytime," she said kindly. "You two take care."

Lucas and I left the house. He stopped at the end of the walkway and shoved his hands in his pockets. "Nad, do you really think we have that much to work on?"

"I'm not sure," I said quietly. I really thought we were in a good spot, but what Grammy said really made me think about it. Lucas and I *were* both strong people, and I think sometimes that made us hold back from each other.

He sighed. "Help me out here. You can be honest with me."

I sighed. "All right. The honest answer is yes and no. We've made so much progress in the last year, and I love that we're both growing. But maybe we have more blind spots than we thought. And maybe they're not all bad, and there's no one to blame. But if there's problems between us, I want to solve them."

He nodded. "I do, too."

"How can I help you?" I asked.

He shook his head. "I don't need anything right now."

"It may not be about what you *need*," I pressed. "What do you *want*?"

He dropped his gaze and sighed heavily. "I want you to ask *me* for help. Sometimes, it feels like you don't need me the way I need you."

"Of course I need you, Lucas," I argued. I couldn't believe he didn't see that.

"Then let me be there for you," he begged. "I'm not asking for validation or anything like that. It's not that I want to feel wanted. I know you want me here. But I want to help *before* you reach the end of your rope."

I curled my arms around him, and he held me close. I rested my head on his shoulder, taking in his warm embrace. It felt so good. "Right now, this is what I need. Thank you for being there for me tonight, Lucas."

He pressed a kiss to the top of my head. "I'll be there for you, Nad. Always."

THIRTEEN

Nadine and I were in a better place than we'd ever been, and we were still learning new things about our relationship every day. I liked that we were growing together. It made me feel close to her.

I didn't leave her side until my Astrology class the next day. I entered the big circular room with a glass ceiling, a fireplace, and bookcases lining the walls. I took a spot at my usual desk, and Oliver jumped onto my lap.

Professor Loren stepped to the front of the room, her long black dress flowing around her ankles. She was a Mentalist who taught Incantations and Moonology, and she was one of the few professors who I still liked. Most professors had taken an intense disliking to anyone who wasn't in their Cast, and it made our coursework this semester challenging.

"We've spent the last few weeks discussing the power of the planets in your spellwork," Professor Loren began. "However, I'd like to take a short detour today to discuss an astrological feature specific to Miriamic Lore."

Professor Loren turned on the projector, and a display of the night sky shone on the walls. "You all know the story of Mother Miriam—how her prayers to the gods were ignored, and so to escape her abuser, she summoned a demon, a rejected god with unimaginable power. Santos, the father of all Miriamic people, fell in love with her. They lived a life together on Earth, and together birthed five children—half-mortals who were known as demigods. We know that each of these children was born with a different power, and each of them became the first of their Cast. What you may not know is that on the night of each child's birth, Santos gave them a gift. As a god, he possessed the power to place stars in the sky. Each child received their own star."

Professor Loren pointed her wand at the wall. Light shone out the end of it, drawing attention to a specific star in the night sky. "The stars, in order: Maud, Percival, Cecilia, Mortimer, and Alora."

"Alora?" Lena asked. "We can see our afterlife from here?"

"Our afterlife exists in another realm," Professor Loren explained. "The name Alora is used in many places within our lore, because it is not simply our afterlife. Alora was one of the five children. Each of these stars was named for the child it appeared for."

She pointed to each star in turn. "Maud was the firstborn daughter, and she had the power of Alchemy—one of the best potion-makers there ever was. Percival was the second eldest, and he possessed the power of telekinesis and the ability to manipulate people's thoughts. He was the first Mentalist. Next came Cecilia, a Seer who could predict the future and see into the past. Miriam and Santos's son, Mortimer, held power over death. He could predict when people would die, and was said to have influence over death itself. He was the first Mortana, as well as the first member of the Reaper Order."

A shiver traveled down my spine when she spoke of Mortimer. I felt an instant connection to him. He was the first reaper in the coven. I wondered if I could summon his spirit and learn more about my powers.

"Finally, their last daughter was born, Alora." Professor Loren pointed to a fifth star. "She was a powerful witch capable of many things, including breaking curses—hence the name Curse Breaker. However, her power was very versatile, with the ability to siphon and even absorb others' powers, and move magic from one place to another. Although Curse Breakers today can only manipulate witch magic, Alora was a demigod, and she was powerful enough to manipulate even the fae. It is one of the many reasons the fae despise us."

Professor Loren paced at the front of the room and continued. "With Alora's powers of magic manipulation, the children learned how to combine their magic together, creating powerful spells unlike anything we see today. Our afterlife was named after Alora because of what she and her Cast represented—unity."

She turned back to the constellations projected around us. "As the children grew up, they married and had children of their own. The coven grew, and each child left a legacy behind—not just their magic, which we are each marked for, but their stars. Just as you can use the planets to assist in your spellwork, you can use Miriam's stars. Each star presents its own energy, and attuning to the star of your Cast can help you perform spells with great precision."

Lena's hand shot up. "How do we attune to the star?"

"When your Cast star is visible in the night sky, sit outside under the stars and meditate," Professor Loren said. "Focus on the star's location above you, and you should feel a connection, like a rope pulling you toward the star. That's its energy shining down upon you. Draw upon it to cast your spell. Alchemists use this technique often by waiting to brew difficult potions at night, when they can focus their magic using their star, Maud. Don't worry if you don't feel a connection the first try. It can be a difficult task to master. I suggest you begin working with your star on clear nights, when its power is easiest to access."

I digested the lesson with interest. I'd heard of Miriam's stars before, but I'd never given them much thought. Now I felt excited to learn more about them. I raised my hand and asked, "Is this a source of energy we can pull from to combat the Waning?"

Professor Loren frowned. "I'm afraid not. These stars are not themselves energy sources. They're tools to focus your power, much like a wand."

She began walking around the room, passing out papers. I looked down at mine to see it was an essay rubric. "Each of you will be required to write an essay on your Cast star, detailing its history, and three spells you can cast using your star. Be sure to detail *why* the star is important in these spells, and how it can enhance the spellwork."

She continued the lesson, teaching us how the stars appeared in the sky at different times of the year. I left class with my head buzzing. I wanted to use my star right away.

I waited until nightfall before gathering my things and pulling my coat on. Oliver meowed at my feet. He really wanted to come; he loved the outdoors.

"Where are you going?" Grant sat at his desk, tinkering with Talia's music box. The whole thing was in pieces, though it was laid out neatly for Grant to examine it.

"I'm going to try portal casting under the stars," I told him. "You should stay and work on fixing the music box."

Grant ran his fingers through his hair, looking frustrated. "There's not much more I can do at this point. I took it to Professor Warbright to see if he could help, and he said there were parts missing. They're on backorder. I thought I could still get it working, but until those parts come, I can't fix it."

"You're welcome to come along," I offered. "Just… don't laugh. I'm still learning."

"I can't make promises, but I'll do my best," he teased.

Grant and I snuck outside. Dusk had fallen, and the cold night air bit at my face. Oliver kept close to my side as we crossed the school grounds and entered the forest. We walked for a while, until we came to a clearing near the river. It was secluded here, but there was enough break in the trees to see the stars.

I gazed upward through the bare canopy. My eyes landed on the Big Dipper, and I followed the stars to locate Mortimer in the sky. "See that star right there?" I asked, pointing.

Grant nodded. "That bright one?"

"Yeah, that's my Cast star," I said. "We learned about it in Astrology. Did you know it was named after the first reaper?"

"I suppose that makes sense. He was one of Miriam's kids, right?"

"Yes. I'm supposed to be able to use the star to focus my spellwork. If I can use it to open a portal to hell, we can send Professor Leto through it."

"Sounds like fun!" Grant sat on a dry log, and Oliver began pacing along the log beside him. "Let's see what you can do."

I drew a deep breath and turned my gaze toward my Cast star. Several long minutes passed, and I didn't feel any different. I dropped my shoulders and shook off the nerves. I had to ground myself in the moment.

I ran through five things I could see, four things I could feel, three things I could hear, two things I could smell, and one thing I could taste. When I finished the exercise, I turned back toward the star and focused. I felt a slight tugging at the center of my chest, like the star and I were connected.

"I've got it," I told Grant. "I just have to take that focus and put it into the spell."

I closed my eyes and pictured the cemetery across town, because it was secluded, yet familiar. I'd already astral traveled there once, so I figured I could portal there, too. I placed all my intention on the cemetery, feeling my magic well up inside of me as I pictured it clearly in my mind. I opened my eyes, but nothing had happened.

I tried again. And again.

I didn't understand why I couldn't do it. My powers felt strong. I wasn't affected by the Waning, and I could feel my Cast star helping.

"What does your book say about casting portals?" Grant asked.

"It's pretty straight-forward, but for some reason, I don't understand it." I conjured the book Professor Warren had given me, along with a small witch light, and started reading. *"Portal magic is cast through the intent of uniquely gifted supernaturals. To cast a portal, one must simply visualize the place they want to go, and their intention will reshape reality."*

Grant pressed his lips together. "That seems too easy. You must be missing something."

"I've read the book cover-to-cover," I said. "This is how the fae do it. I should be able to do it, too."

"You're not a faerie. It's gotta be different for you," Grant encouraged. "You've created portals before. What did it feel like?"

"I didn't really know what I was doing," I admitted. "When I portaled away from my dad, I just wanted to disappear. I set an intention, and it just… manifested. Maybe it's because I was desperate."

Grant tilted his head. "I don't know that desperation is the answer. If your magic is anything like the fae, they have to believe in their power to make it happen. You must've believed in your power to disappear from your dad. Tonight, you're desperate to prove something to yourself, to make it work so we can banish Professor Leto. But the more desperate you are, the more you're affirming that you don't believe in yourself."

"I don't exactly have the luxury of letting this happen on its own," I said. "We're running out of time to figure this out before Leto kills again."

"That's what's tripping you up," Grant theorized. "You don't trust yourself to get it *now*. We need a different approach. Can I see the book?"

I handed it to him. I'd been through the sections on portals so many times, I didn't know what he could possibly find that I hadn't.

Grant began reading under my witch light. *"Portal magic is a manipulation of reality. This is why the Arcanean fae and the Elves—rest their souls—are the primary portal casters in supernatural society. Both races are talented illusionists, and one must be skilled at manipulating reality in order to cast a portal.* Goddess, how old is this book? They're talking about the Elves as if they're still alive."

I shrugged. "Pretty old, I guess. But I know all this. The book goes on and on about reality manipulation, but it doesn't say *how* to do it."

"What are you *trying* to do?" Grant asked. "What's your thought process?"

"I'm doing what the book says. I'm imagining where I want to go, then focusing my magic on that."

"So you're more or less trying to teleport?"

"Well, yeah. That's basically what a portal is."

"No, a portal is a means of transport," Grant said. "If you want to travel across the country, you've got to get on a plane. The reality manipulation isn't connecting points A and B. It's creating a step between them. A portal itself is a different reality, and you must step into that reality in order to come out somewhere else inside our own reality. You're trying to step through a door on the other side of a room without walking into that room *first*."

"That doesn't sound any easier than what I was doing before."

"Just try it," he encouraged.

I faced away from him and held my palms up. This time, I focused on what it felt like when I'd slipped through the portal that day with my father. I thought of the flash of colors and the disoriented feeling I'd gotten. *That* was the reality I was trying to access.

Grant gasped, and my eyes shot open to see sparks of magic filling the air in front of me. "Keep it up!" Grant cried.

I imagined sliding through this other realm, to the cemetery on the other side. The portal expanded just enough that I spotted a gravestone… then it slammed shut. All I saw was the empty forest beyond us.

"Hey, you did it!" Grant cried. "Great job."

It hadn't been a large portal—only big enough to reach a hand through—but I'd *done* it. That in itself was a victory. "That *was* easier than I thought. I was imagining it all wrong this whole time. Let me try again."

I closed my eyes and lifted my hands. I pictured what the portal realm felt like, then imagined the cemetery in my mind. I thought of a pathway forming between the clearing we stood in and the cemetery on the other side of town—a wormhole that would connect the two points in space. When I opened my eyes, the portal had returned. The edges flickered, but I took a deep breath to calm myself, and the portal stabilized.

"That's it!" Grant encouraged. "Keep going."

I set a simple intention, and the portal expanded to my command. It bloomed as tall as I was. Through the portal, we saw shadows of gravestones, and I spotted a leaf tumbling across the top of the snow.

Grant's jaw dropped as the entire cemetery came into view. "Whoa, Lucas. You did it!"

I smiled proudly. "Pretty damn impressive, huh?"

Grant approached the portal slowly, inspecting it from every angle. He walked behind it, like he was double checking to see if the cemetery was there. I noticed the longer I held the portal open, the more tired I became.

"Wow," Grant breathed as he came back to the front. "So... can I touch it?"

He reached toward the portal. The moment he touched it, he was blasted backward and landed flat on his back in the snow. I heard a *thwack*, and Grant cursed as his head smashed into a rock. My heart leapt, and the portal slammed shut. Oliver nearly toppled off his log at the suddenness of it all.

"Grant!" I rushed to his side and helped him sit up. His whole body shook. "Where are you hurt?"

He pressed a hand to his head, and his fingers came away bloody. "Ugh, everywhere. It feels like I was electrocuted. Your portals aren't stable."

"Yeah, I can see that," I said sarcastically. "We've got a start, but no one's going through my portals until I figure this magic out."

"Fair enough." He groaned as he got to his feet.

"Goddess, Grant. Sit down. Your head is bleeding." I forced him to sit on the log, then I conjured a first-aid kit.

He took the gauze from me and pressed it firmly to his wound. "On the bright side, we don't care if Professor Leto gets hurt, so we can just toss him through to the Abyss."

"A valid point," I said. "Let's see if I can buy him a one-way ticket. Don't touch it this time."

He held one hand up in surrender. "I promise I won't!"

I lifted my hands, and sparks appeared in the air in front of me. I imagined the darkness of the Abyss. I'd seen it before—once when I'd fought a reaper trying to take Nadine's spirit to the Abyss, and once when I witnessed the priestesses summon the demon. This should be easy.

But it wasn't. I willed the portal to widen as I funneled my magic into it. I pictured the Abyss in my mind with such clarity, I almost believed it was right in front of me.

I got nothing but sparks.

My arms grew heavy, until it felt like they weighed a ton. My knees shook, and I nearly toppled over. Grant had to help me sit down on the log. I had no idea portal magic would tire me out this much.

"What's going on?" he demanded.

"It feels like I've just benched a thousand pounds," I told him.

"Maybe you should take a break," Grant suggested.

"I *need* to figure this out," I protested. "I've opened portals to Alora before. Those are effortless. I didn't even know I was doing it. This shouldn't be any different."

"But it *is* different when you have a soul to guide through," Grant said. "You're in the middle of reaping when you're doing it. It's a different sort of magic."

"But it's close enough that I can still create portals," I argued. I lifted my hands. Creating a portal to Alora should be simple.

Again, nothing but sparks.

My whole body swayed, and I had to stop before I passed out. I steadied myself on the log, my head spinning. "You're right. Opening portals to other realms is definitely harder. I can't even stabilize a portal to a place a mile away."

"You'll get it," Grant encouraged.

I scoffed. "Yeah, but when?"

The longer Leto remained in Octavia Falls, the more people would die.

I wasn't going to master portals tonight. That much was obvious. If I couldn't use Mortimer's star to open a portal to the Abyss, then I'd find another use for it.

Grant and I returned to our dorm room, and I got into bed early. I left the curtains open, so I could see Mortimer's star from my bed. I focused on the star and fell into a deep meditation.

I'd only astral traveled twice, and Nadine had helped pull my spirit onto the astral plane both times. I wasn't sure it would work.

A feeling of weightlessness overcame me, and I opened my eyes to see that even in the dark, the astral plane shimmered beautiful rainbow hues. I got out of bed and stood. My body remained motionless on the bed, but Oliver perked up his ears.

I closed my eyes and imagined myself in Leto's classroom. When I opened them, I was standing beside my desk. The room was dark, but I heard the rustling of papers and followed the sound. Professor Leto sat in an office at the back of the room, marking papers with a red pen.

I crossed my arms. "So this is what you do during your free time? You grade papers? How positively... normal."

Of course, he couldn't hear me. Didn't make it any less fun to taunt him.

To be honest, I was surprised he was doing it at all. I'd have thought he'd think he was too good to carry out menial human tasks.

Unless that was the point... He was playing the part, playing *human*. I bet he got off on it. I didn't think Leto would do anything that didn't please him in some way.

Leto checked the time on the wall, then placed his papers in a neat stack, straightened his tie, and left the room. I followed behind in my spirit form. He went to his car and slipped into the driver's seat. I imagined myself in the back seat, then appeared there.

Leto turned on the music, and a classical tune played through the speakers.

"Huh, I would've taken you for a heavy metal guy," I said. "This is weird. Actually, it's almost painful."

Then Leto started *singing*—like full on belting like a Broadway performer. He wasn't using words, just belting to the tune.

"Dear Goddess," I sighed. What a strange man.

Leto turned up the music even *louder*. You'd think he was a teenager on spring break, blasting their music on a road trip.

Maybe that's what this was to him. He was running around the coven murdering people and playing professor, having the time of his life because he'd never been set free before. It was like he was some high-school kid that had snuck out of his parents' house for a night of pranks. How fucking pathetic.

Leto pulled up to a fast-food drive-through.

I leaned forward to check the menu. "Huh, let's see. What would a demon order? Flaming hot wings?"

Leto leaned out the window. "I'd like a hamburger, no toppings, and a water."

"Boring!" I cried. "At least order some French fries."

"Make that two waters," Leto added.

I eyed him curiously as he got his food at the window. He was being way too fucking normal, but strange at the same time. What sort of psychopath ordered nothing on his burger and no freaking French fries? Was this how he thought humans behaved? Was this some sort of fantasy of his—living life as a human? Where were bloody knives hiding in his glove compartment and posters of his victims all over his office? I was definitely expecting serial killer vibes, but this was… dull. Perhaps I'd uncover his secrets at his home.

But Leto didn't go home. Instead, he pulled into the hospital parking lot.

Okay, this was getting a little weird. What could he possibly be doing here?

Leto got out of the car, and I followed him inside, where he greeted the receptionist by first name. He winked at her, and she giggled before handing him a volunteer badge.

"Ah, yes. Charming people into thinking you're a good guy," I said sarcastically. "What kind of hospital volunteer could murder dozens of people?"

Leto continued waltzing down the hall like he owned the place. I heard crying coming from a room nearby. Leto stopped and peered inside. A woman sobbed at the bedside of an old man, who lay motionless on the bed. My best guess is it had been her husband. The machines he was hooked up to were already shut off, and I didn't see his spirit anywhere. He must've already gone with his reaper.

"Ma'am, the doctor would like to speak with you." The nurse was trying to get her out of the room so they could take the body to the morgue.

"No—no!" the woman shouted when the nurse touched her. The pain of her sobs seemed to permeate the hospital walls.

Leto chuckled lightly. The sick fuck was enjoying this!

"So it's not just traumatic deaths you get off on?" I spat, even though he couldn't hear me. "You've got to sit here and watch the family grieve!"

Leto kept his eyes on the sobbing woman, but he smirked. "The human experience is oddly complex. Grief is a trauma all its own, don't you think?"

His gaze landed on my spirit, and if I'd been in my body, my heart would've stopped dead. He could see me!

"You asshole," I growled. "This whole time, you've just been fucking with me!"

Leto smirked and turned away, not acknowledging me one bit. It was like I wasn't even there. Demons were supernatural creatures. It made sense that he could see and hear things that a normal person couldn't.

"What exactly are you doing here?" I snapped. "Just observing, or playing with fate?"

Leto ignored me. I grabbed for his arm to stop him, but my hand went straight through him. Leto turned the corner, and I followed… but he had vanished.

What the hell? Where had he gone?

Of fucking course demons could teleport.

I was about to tear the hospital down to look for this creep, before a child's voice carried down the hall.

I'm not scared.

It was an ethereal whisper, but it wasn't someone's last thought. It was more distorted and quiet—distant in a way. It was like I was hearing the voice of a child on the brink of death. She hadn't quite passed yet, but death was imminent. Normally, I'd never hear a voice like this, but it must've had something to do with being a reaper in my spirit form.

An energy I'd never felt before seemed to draw me forward, pulling me toward this dying soul. It was another reaper power; I was sure of it. It had to be how reapers found their assignments. My bones seemed to buzz with the intuitive *need* to get to this child. I had to be there for her when she passed, to help her to the other side.

I let the ethereal tether lead me down the hall, until I floated through a doorway and into a hospital room. A young girl around eight years old lay on the bed, surrounded by doctors. A man and a woman, who I assumed were her parents, stood at her bedside. The little girl had no hair, and her skin had paled so much that I could barely make out her lips. Leto completely fell from my mind as I took in the sick girl. My heart broke for her.

"It's too soon," the woman pleaded with the doctors.

"Leukemia operates on its own timeline," one of the doctors replied kindly.

"It's okay, Mama," the little girl said weakly.

She turned slightly when she spoke, and her gaze fell upon me. No one should've been able to see me, but she looked *right at me*.

Something shimmered around her form. It took me a moment to realize it was her spirit. It was as if she was trying to leave her body, but didn't know how to let go.

Of course she could see me. She was dying. She already had one foot on the astral plane.

Her mother knelt beside her bed, squeezing her hand. "Oh, Nora. Mommy loves you so, so much."

I barely heard what else her mother said, because I was so entranced by Nora. It seemed I was seeing double—her physical, ill features beneath her brave spiritual face. Nora was ready to go. She just needed someone to help her cross over.

I stepped closer to her bedside. "Nora, my name is Lucas."

I know who you are, she said in my mind. Her spirit was speaking to me, though her lips didn't move. She looked so weak, I wasn't sure she could say anything more, even if she tried. *I don't want to go.*

I knelt beside her and placed my hand in her palm. She didn't quite feel solid, but I could feel her spirit struggling to reach the astral plane. "It's okay to be scared."

I don't want Mama to be sad.

"Sometimes it's okay for people to be sad, and that's not your fault," I told her. "Sadness is how we remember the people we love. Your parents can take care of themselves, and they'll always remember you. But you've had a long hard fight, and it's time for you to rest now."

How can you know that for sure? she asked.

Even though I was in spirit, my chest twisted, and my voice cracked. "My brother died a few years ago. I was sad for a long time—still am. But he needed to go his own way, and I needed to go mine. I promise you, Nora, all your parents want is a chance to say goodbye."

Tears brimmed her eyes, and she turned back to her parents one last time. Weakly, she whispered. "I love you, Mama and Papa."

Her father ran his fingers over the side of her face. "We love you, too, pumpkin."

"We will *always* love you," her mother said.

"I'll be waiting for you. Goodbye," Nora whispered.

Then her spiritual fingers curled around mine, and she became completely solid to me. I pulled her upright, straight out of her body. The broken corpse she'd left behind sagged into the bed, and her parents broke out into heavy sobs. But their cries seemed distant, because Nora's last thought stole my attention as it played in my mind.

I'm glad Lucas was here.

My heart swelled, and it took everything I had not to break down into sobs in front of this child.

Nora floated over to her mother. She touched her spiritual fingers to her mother's heart. Her mom gasped, like she could feel the coolness of her daughter's touch.

"It's going to be all right, Mama," Nora said. "I feel much better now."

Nora turned toward me. "She'll get better, too, won't she?"

I nodded. "Yeah. She will."

A portal bloomed in the corner of the room, filling the hospital room with blinding light. No one noticed, and they didn't see us cross the room toward it.

"All you have to do is step through," I told her, guiding her forward.

Nora hesitated and looked back at her parents.

"It's all right," I told her. "There's a wonderful world on the other side where nobody's sad anymore. Everyone works together, and there's always time to play."

I didn't truly know what Alora was like, but it didn't feel like I was lying. Somehow, I just knew that's what it would be like.

"Mother Miriam and all your ancestors are waiting for you," I told her. "Your parents will be there soon. They won't forget you."

Nora took a deep, calming breath before looking up to me one last time. "Thank you, Lucas. I'll never forget what my reaper did for me."

She took a step forward, and the light consumed her, until she had vanished completely.

The moment she was gone, I let the tears fall from my eyes. Nora's parents sobbed across the room, but I was alone in this corner. Nothing mattered right now but the profound moment I shared with Nora.

I'd used my experience with depression for *good*. It allowed me to see the grief that others felt, and know there was hope on the other side of it. All this time I thought I'd been dealt a shit hand at life, when actually, it made me a better reaper.

For the first time, I wasn't just grateful for all the awesome things in my life. I was thankful for the bad, too. Because my darkest days enabled me to help people like Nora. Eric's death… and what I thought was my darkest ending… had been someone else's brightest beginning.

I'd helped souls cross over. But I was just beginning to understand what being a reaper meant. Not just for me.

But for my coven, too.

I spent the rest of the week tuning in to my intuition. I meditated during my Wednesday dialysis appointment, and I repeated Grammy's exercise during class. What felt heavy, what felt light? What kind of stories was I telling myself that weren't necessarily true? My mind raced, and I had to stop by the campus store to pick up a new journal so I could jot it all down. I missed most of what Professor Hernandez said in Enchanting, because I kept coming up with new ideas.

Talia found me in the cafeteria Thursday evening, jotting in my notebook while I nibbled on grapes. Gus bounded up to Isa's side, and I dropped them both cat treats.

"What's that?" Talia asked as she set her tray across from me.

"Grammy taught me some things about intuition, and I'm journaling about it," I told her, flipping through the notebook. "I've filled twenty pages."

Talia's eyebrows shot up. "Wow, you got all that from your intuition?"

"It's not all intuitive hits. I'm more or less learning what my intuition *isn't* saying. I think if I can break down some of my thought patterns, I can open myself more to these messages."

Talia leaned across the table, looking interested in my process. "Can you give me an example?"

I turned back a few pages and scanned my notes. "Okay, here's a story I've been telling myself... We've hit a dead end with the Wands. So I ask myself if that's the ultimate truth or not. I said no, that it's not. We have all kinds of clues, and perhaps the location of the Wands is staring us in the face. We just need a new perspective."

"Could your intuition guide you to this new perspective?" Talia asked, poking her alfredo with her fork.

"I think so."

"Where does your intuition say to look?"

I thought about it for a moment. "My initial reaction says there's nowhere else *to* look, but that feels heavy. It's clearly not true, because we would've found the Wands if it was."

Talia swallowed her food. "Okay, try this. True for false… the rumors are true. There's a Wand inside the school."

"True," I answered. "That feels light. I'm pretty sure it's here."

"How about this? True or false. There's a *clue* inside the school that will lead us to the Wand."

That statement was harder to discern, but after a few moments, I realized it felt light. "Yeah, I think there is."

"Why don't we use your intuition to find this clue?" Talia asked.

My chest still felt light, and I knew she was on to something. "That's a great idea! The Wands are protected by magic, so intuition may not be enough to track them. But if we can track down a clue, we might find it!"

Talia shoved a few noodles in her mouth. "Then what are we waiting for?"

We quickly finished eating and headed out of the cafeteria. I stopped in the middle of the hall, wondering whether to go right or left.

Talia eyed me curiously, noticing my hesitation. "Truth? The clue lies to the right."

I closed my eyes and furrowed my brow, but my body didn't react to the statement. "Can you reword the question?"

"Truth? Turn left to find your answers."

Something in my chest lifted, and I got excited. "I feel like we should go left."

Talia smiled and skipped alongside me. "Ooh, this is fun! It's like a treasure hunt."

She was absolutely right. Hunting down the Wands had never been *fun*, but this was like a game. My intuition seemed to play along when I felt at ease.

We reached the end of the hall. "Truth? The clue is this way," Talia said, gesturing to our right.

I shot a quick glance to the left, but something about that side of the hall churned my gut. "Yes, it's to the right."

We kept going until we hit a crossroads, and Talia repeated her questions, taking each hall in turn.

"Straight feels right," I told her.

We passed by classrooms and study areas until we made it all the way across campus and stopped outside the library. Talia eyed the big double doors. "Do you think there's a clue in the library?"

I tried to focus on how my body felt in response to her question, but I couldn't tell what my intuition was trying to say.

"Maybe we missed something," she suggested. "We could turn back—"

"No," I said. "Turning back doesn't feel right. We've been combing through the library for clues about the demon, but maybe we missed something about the Wands. Let's check it out."

We walked slowly through the library. I assessed the energy of each aisle as we passed, trying to get a feel of where to find this clue.

"It's here," I told Talia softly. "I'm just not sure where."

She glanced around, until her gaze turned upward. "Truth? The clue is on the main level."

My chest got heavy. "Not true. It must be upstairs."

The upper level of the library wasn't laid out as well as the main level. We walked through mazes of rooms, all piled to the ceiling with bookcases. The books here were all covered with dust and hadn't been touched in a long time.

Talia gestured to an open doorway. "Truth? The clue is in here."

I shook my head. "I've been in that room looking for demonology textbooks. I sense whatever we're meant to find is somewhere we haven't looked yet."

"Mm…" Talia mused, before stopping in her tracks. She gazed down a row of bookcases. "How about in there?" She gestured to a room I'd never been in before, and I felt a slight nudge to go in that direction.

"It's worth checking out." I started forward, and Isa crept along at my heels. No one made a sound as we entered a small room no bigger than our dorm, lined with short aisles of bookcases. The room was dark, with nothing but a tiny window in the corner to let in the light. The sky was overcast today, and I could barely make out the words on the spines of the books. We'd entered some sort of records room.

"Maybe—" Talia started, but she cut off when a moan came from the corner behind one of the bookcases.

Talia shot me a confused look and mouthed, *Ghost?*

I had no idea what it could be. I lifted my finger to my lips to tell her to be quiet, then gestured her forward. Isa and Gus inched forward slowly, like they did when they went hunting mice. We snuck to the back of the room and peeked around the bookcase.

I gasped when I realized what we'd walked in on. Gregory had Brayden pinned against the wall, their lips connected in a passionate make-out session. Gregory's hand was down Brayden's pants, and Brayden moaned in pleasure. Talia took a step back, and a *thud* sounded as she knocked a book off the shelf.

Gregory spun around when he heard us. I instantly fled. I felt awful for interrupting their private moment, and the last thing I wanted to do was make it awkward for them.

"Wait!" Gregory cried, stopping us before we reached the door.

"It's not what it looks like," Brayden insisted, the sound of his zipper filling the room.

"It's fine," I said, turning toward them as they emerged from the shadows. "We didn't mean to interrupt."

"We—we were just studying," Gregory stammered. "A—and…"

"Please don't tell anyone!" Brayden burst.

"There's nothing wrong with what you were doing," Talia said. "I think love of any kind is beautiful."

Gregory sighed. "We're not hiding our relationship because we're gay. It's because we're different Casts."

"Why's that a problem?" I asked. "Talia and I are both in intercast relationships."

Gregory crossed his arms. "Yeah, and that's exactly why we're keeping ours a secret. Have you not heard the way people talk about you?"

Talia huffed. "It's not like we're the first intercast couples. People marry outside their Cast all the time."

"Not as often as you think," Gregory said. "We've done the math. Only twelve percent of marriages in the last fifty years have been intercast."

"That's not a good reason to hide who you love," I argued.

"Sure it is, when the coven starts calling for your head," Gregory stated.

He sounded really worried, and it broke my heart. Gregory wasn't exactly my favorite person on the planet. His intentions were morally questionable at best, but I didn't believe he deserved a target on his back.

"We won't tell anyone," I promised.

Gregory's shoulders slumped. He looked utterly defeated, and I didn't think I'd ever seen him like that before. "Come on, babe. Let's go."

He grabbed Brayden's hand, and they left the room.

Talia crossed her arms and turned toward me. "This is bullshit. Twelve percent or not, the priestesses are breaking up families."

I gritted my teeth. "I know."

Talia sighed. "Any intuitive hits?"

I glanced around the room, but all feelings I had when we entered were gone. I was too bothered by what Brayden and Gregory had said. I didn't particularly *care* what people were saying behind my back, but I *did* care what kind of precedent it set for the rest of the coven.

"I think we're going to have to come back another day," I admitted. "Let's go."

I started to take a step, but Isa jumped in front of me, blocking my way to the door. She meowed loudly, like she didn't want me to go. I stopped in my tracks.

"Okay… I guess we're not going." A chill spread over my skin, and my breath turned to vapor in the air. "Do you feel that?"

Talia shot a wary glance around the room. "This time it's *definitely* a ghost."

Thud!

Talia and I both jumped, and Gus hissed loudly. A book had fallen off a nearby bookcase. I eyed it curiously from where it lay on the ground. It was spread open to a page of old photographs.

"Malicious spirit, or helpful?" I wondered.

Talia's voice shook. "You tell me."

I inched closer to the book and picked it up. As my eyes roamed over the page, I realized it was an old Miriam College yearbook. It showed a full-page spread of the Astrology Club. Judging by the hairstyles and fashion in the photographs, these photos were taken around forty years ago.

"Does this mean anything to you?" I asked Talia.

"I've been through the yearbooks, but those records are in a different room." Talia ran her fingers over the spines of the books on the shelf, eyeing the years. "These ones must've been moved. They're in the wrong spot."

"Well, *someone* wanted us to find them. What do you think it means?" I started flipping to the next page, but Talia stopped me.

"Wait!" she cried, grabbing my wrist. I turned back to the Astrology Club page, and Talia pointed to a woman in one of the photographs. She was older than the students in the photo. She must've been their professor. "This is our clue! We found it!"

I looked closer at the woman she'd pointed to. I thought she looked familiar, but I couldn't place her. The caption contained her name. *Professor Angelica Stratton.*

"That's her! It's the ghost who attacked me in the library over break," Talia said, sounding excited. "Nadine, it's the woman who warned us about the demon."

I gasped when she pointed it out. I *had* seen her before, but merely for a second. "She must know more. I'll bet you anything she's the one who knocked this book over. She wants us to go find her. We need to grab Miles, because we're talking to this woman. Tonight."

We found Miles in his room. The second he heard we wanted to talk to a ghost, he was all-in.

"Hell yeah, I'll help you hunt this ghost," he'd said. "Tell me everything you know."

I showed him the yearbook we'd taken from the library. "That's her."

Recognition crossed his features. "Hey, I know her!"

"You've spoken to her before?" Talia questioned.

"A few times, yeah. She's a sweet lady. You're sure she knows something about the Wands? She's never mentioned them."

"Maybe she didn't know you were helping us," I theorized. "You know where to find her?"

"Sure," Miles said. "They don't call her the Lady of the Tower for nothing."

I'd heard of the Lady of the Tower. She was once an astrology professor at the school, and she haunted her old classroom.

"I'll call Lucas and Grant and tell them to meet us there," I said while pulling up Lucas's number.

We hurried to the astrology tower as quickly as we could. Lucas and Grant arrived the same time we did.

"What'd you find?" Lucas asked, sounding a bit winded.

"A ghost!" Talia said chipperly. "Well, not yet, technically. But we know who the ghost is."

I showed them the yearbook and explained how we'd found it. "She warned us about the demon, and now she wants to tell us more."

"Why haven't we looked into her before?" Lucas asked.

"Wait… Mandy and I *did* look into an Astrology professor," Grant said. "We were researching traumatic deaths that happened around the same time as the wand shop owner died. But this one was a heart attack. She died of natural causes."

"Or that's what the demon wanted people to think," Miles pointed out.

"Let's find out what really happened," I said.

We started up the twisted staircase that led to the highest turret in the mansion. Miles opened the door at the top, and we entered into the expansive astrology classroom. It was cold up here, and I shivered a bit. Lucas noticed and wrapped me in his arms.

Miles took a cautious step forward. "She's here. I can feel her. Angelica? Professor Stratton? It's me, Miles. We've spoken before."

A slight breeze swept through the room, rustling my hair. Miles spun around, searching for the ghost. "I get the sense she wants to talk, but I can't see her."

"Maybe we need to help draw her out," Lucas suggested.

"A séance, yeah," Miles replied thoughtfully. "That might help us connect to her. Let's set it up right here."

We gathered around the fireplace in the corner and sat in a circle. Grant conjured a few candles, and we all joined hands.

"Calm your minds," Miles encouraged. "We must expel all dissonance and tune ourselves to her spirit."

I drew a deep breath and relaxed my shoulders. From beside me, I felt Lucas and Talia do the same.

"Professor?" Miles called out. "I think there's something you want to tell my friends—"

Miles stopped dead in his tracks, and he stared at something I couldn't see. I knew it had to be the Lady of the Tower.

A few beats passed before he said, "Is that so…? Let me help you speak with my friends."

Miles reached his hand out to thin air, and within moments, an ethereal form appeared before our eyes. The woman had to be around fifty years old when she died. She wore a long, flowing dress, and she hovered several inches above the ground. She had kind eyes, unlike the first time I'd seen her in the library. We all got to our feet.

"I'm so glad you found me," Angelica said, her soft, ghostly tone filling the room. "I deeply apologize. I struggle to make my presence known at times. Since the Waning began, it takes a great deal of energy. Even *my* magic is drained as a result."

"That means we may not have much time," I said. "Professor, you've been trying to contact us."

"Yes," she confirmed. "I appeared to you in the library. What you were about to do was very dangerous, and I had to stop you."

"What can you tell us?" Lucas asked.

"I know many things," Angelica said. "The first of which is that you must do everything in your power to banish Professor Leto. I have stuck around this tower year after year to ensure that he *never* returns."

"You've met him, then?" Grant asked. "Before or after you died?"

Angelica frowned. "Both, I'm afraid. It was the demon himself who killed me."

A shiver traveled down my spine, and I held up her yearbook. "This is from forty years ago, just before you died. That's when the demon was here before, wasn't it? It's the same time Adrik Harvey died in his wand shop. The demon killed you both."

"Yes. He used a spell to poison me."

"You told us that *History will repeat itself. He has come to kill. Return to the past to vanquish the demon for good*," I reminded her. "What did you mean by that? How do we vanquish him?"

Angelica's eyebrows pinched together, like she couldn't quite remember.

"Ghosts are often confused," Miles reminded us. "Time can seem jumbled to them—"

"No," Angelica protested. "I remember. One of Professor Leto's victims sent him back to hell. But that… that was after my death. The details are… fuzzy. You must find out how they did it. Then you can do the same."

Grant pressed his lips together. "This person could still be alive. If we figure out who it was, we can talk to them and learn how they did it."

"Unless the victim didn't make it," Talia mused. "Adrik was one of his victims, and his ghost threatened to kill demons. What if he was the one who banished him?"

"Then we need to fix that music box and get answers," Lucas insisted. Grant was still working on that.

"Professor," I said. "We found your yearbook while searching for clues about the Oaken Wands. We've heard there may be a Wand inside the school. Do you know anything about it?"

"Yes," she said, sounding more confident. "One of my former students, a man named Nicholas Tucker, brought the Seer Wand to the school many years ago."

"That's my grandfather," I remarked.

"He came to me just before I died," she said. "We spoke of the space-bending spell inside the school. He wanted to know if he could bend reality to hide a specific object, though he didn't say what it was at the time. I got the sense that whatever it was, he wanted no one to ever find it. I said, *Why bother with new spells, Nicholas? There's already one place inside the school not a soul will dare set foot.* It was only after I died that I witnessed him hide the Wand."

"And he went to that place?" Lucas asked. "Where not a soul would dare set foot?"

"The Vanishing Stairwell!" I realized.

"Yes, the Seer Wand is there. You must find it before Professor Leto does. Find the Wand, and find the person who banished him previously… before it's too late." Angelica's form flickered, and she disappeared before our eyes.

Talia was the first to speak. "How do we get through the Vanishing Stairwell safely?"

"I don't know if we *can*," Miles said.

Grant frowned. "The best we can do is hope we get lucky and that it doesn't disappear while we're inside."

"It's too risky!" Miles protested. "Is this Wand really worth dying for?"

"Yes," I answered automatically. "These Wands are the key to ending the Waning and the entire Miriamic Conflict. If we don't find them, the coven will destroy itself. I'm willing to chance the Vanishing Stairwell for a Wand."

Lucas squeezed my hand. "I'm in."

"I'd feel better if we were prepared," Talia said.

"Agreed," Grant added. "We might want some food and water in case the entrance vanishes and we're stuck for a few days. Everyone needs to understand the risk."

"I'm talking more sure than that," Talia said. "What if we can stabilize the staircase, so it doesn't vanish anymore?"

Miles looked skeptical. "And how exactly do you suggest we do that?"

"Space-bending spells are complicated and require a lot of power, so you need a member from each Cast to complete the spell," Talia said. "The Vanishing Stairwell exists in the first place because some students screwed up their spell. They didn't have enough people. But we have witches and warlocks from all the Casts now. We can shift the power of that old, glitchy spell that causes the stairwell to vanish. We could *fix* the Vanishing Stairwell and ensure our safe return."

My heart surged in excitement. "Talia's right. All we have to do is iron out the spell the students screwed up, and we'll be safe."

Miles looked uncertain. "How do we know the spell will hold?"

"I've done space-bending spells before," I pointed out. "And I've transformed curses into other spells. Changing this spell should be simple."

"We need one person from each Cast," Lucas said. "I say we find Chloe and get ourselves a Wand."

Grant nodded firmly, indicating he was in. "Let's go."

We left the astrology tower and found Chloe sitting near the big window at the top of the grand staircase, working on a paper for her Mentalist class. Marley sat in her lap, purring. She must've noticed the urgency in our expressions, because she slammed her textbook closed and immediately subconjured it.

"Something's wrong," she said. It wasn't a question.

"We need to talk," I told her in a low whisper. I glanced around the hall, but no one passed by. I explained everything we'd learned from Angelica, along with our plan to get in and out of the Vanishing Stairwell safely.

"Will you help us?" I asked once I'd finished.

"For a Wand? Hell yeah," Chloe said.

We started down the hall, our cats following. I buzzed with energy, knowing the next Wand was so close. To my relief, I could see the gray stone walls and the twisted iron railing beyond the arched doorway. The stairwell was unpredictable—we never knew when it'd appear—but as luck would have it, it was open for us. I steeled my nerves and stepped through the doorway. My friends followed close behind.

Miles curled his hands around the railing and looked down the winding staircase. "Not gonna lie. This place gives me the creeps—"

He turned around, and all the blood drained from his face. A scream tore from his lungs, echoing down the stairwell. Miles stumbled, like an invisible force had shoved him. The cats spooked, and they all went racing back into the hall. He landed against Chloe, and she tripped through the doorway, screaming as she stumbled forward. Miles toppled over, but he didn't reach the doorway before Chloe's screams stopped abruptly. My guts sank as Miles slammed into a solid wall.

He frantically ran his hands over the flush wall. "No, no!"

Panic rippled through me as I stepped forward and pressed my palms to the wall. I had to see for myself that it wasn't some kind of illusion.

The wall was solid. We were trapped.

"It was a ghost," Miles said, his tone shaking. "He pushed me!"

Talia conjured her phone, and her features paled. "No service."

"This is bad," Lucas said. "We *needed* Chloe to stabilize the spell. We don't know how long we'll be in here."

"I—I have snacks," Grant stammered, conjuring granola bars and a water bottle from his stash.

"Thanks, Grant," Lucas said tensely. "But that's unhelpful with the spell."

"I just meant, if we're stuck in here…" Grant's features fell.

"We'll figure something out," I promised, though my tone gave away my panic. "My grandpa got in and out of this stairwell safely. The doorway could reappear at any moment."

"If we're *lucky*," Grant emphasized. "People have died down here."

"Lucas has portal powers," Miles said frantically. "We can just portal out."

Lucas frowned. "Not unless you plan on dying. I haven't mastered my powers yet. People will get hurt."

Talia stepped forward. "Everybody calm down. We'll find a way out. There's enough of us here, maybe we can still stabilize the spell."

I shook my head. "Not without all five Casts. We need Chloe, or something powerful enough to replace her. Two Seers aren't enough to replace a Mentalist in a group spell."

Silence fell over the stairwell for a moment as the horror sunk in. Finally, Talia spoke. "What about… a hundred Seers or more? An Oaken Wand can produce that kind of magic."

"Yes," Lucas agreed, sounding relieved. My racing heart calmed. There was a chance of getting out of here.

"The Seer Wand should be powerful enough to perform the spell accurately," I said. "At least enough to get us out."

"I'm sorry, I'm sorry," Miles muttered. He was crouched on the ground, his back against the wall where the doorway should be.

Grant knelt beside him, trying to calm him down. "Talk to me, bro."

Miles shook. "I've never seen a ghost like that before. He was… grotesque. His features were hollow, haunting. The sound of his voice was… horrifying. He wanted us to leave."

"Do you think he's protecting the Wand?" I wondered.

"Probably," Lucas said. "He obviously wanted to scare us for a reason."

"This was different," Miles explained. "It was like I could *feel* his fear, like he transferred some of it to me."

"Perhaps he was an Empath before he died," Talia theorized.

"Maybe we can talk to him," I suggested. "We can reassure him we're here to use the Wand for good. Maybe he can help us."

"Hey, ghost," Talia said kindly. "Hi, um, we're trying to protect the Wand, too. If you could *not* attack us, that'd be great."

Miles curled his arms around his knees and shivered.

"Do you see him?" Grant asked.

Miles squeezed his eyes shut tightly. "He says he doesn't know what you're talking about."

"Then why'd he try to scare us?" Lucas asked. "Miles, can you bring him out so we can talk?"

"I can try." Miles lifted his head and stared at something I couldn't see. "Will you talk with them?"

Miles appeared to be listening to the ghost's response. After a few moments, he got to his feet. He reached his hand out, and a ghost materialized in front of us.

My blood ran cold at the sight of the man. He was young, around our age, but he didn't quite look human. His eyes were sunken in, and his pale, sickly skin stretched tightly across his cheekbones. He looked like he hadn't eaten in weeks. When Miles said he could feel the man's fear, he wasn't lying. Terror ignited in my chest just looking at him.

"You shouldn't have come here," the ghost growled, his voice echoing in an ethereal way that shook me to the core.

I swallowed the lump in my throat. "We wouldn't have come if we had any other choice. Please, we mean you no harm."

"I'm a ghost," the man sneered. "I cannot be harmed. My fear is for *you*."

"You're… trying to protect us?" Lucas asked.

"Of course!" the ghost yelled. "I haunt this stairwell, scaring students away so that no one will meet the same fate as me."

Talia stepped forward. "You're Cooper Gates, aren't you? I've heard of you. You died down here twenty years ago."

Cooper glanced between us all, looking uncertain. "It seems much longer to me."

"I'm Talia, and these are my friends Lucas, Nadine, Grant, and Miles. You don't have to scare us anymore. The stairwell vanished, and we're trapped. We have nowhere to go. Frightening us accomplishes nothing at this point. We may have a way out, but we need you to stop terrifying us."

Cooper paused for a few beats, but he must've agreed with Talia, because the hollowness in his features seemed to fill in, and his skin grew more vibrant. Though he was still transparent, he appeared more human. The fear coursing through my veins settled.

"I'm sorry I had to frighten you." Cooper's voice became even, sounding like it would've when he was alive. "It's the only thing that keeps people away. I wish someone had scared me away when I entered."

"What happened to you?" Talia asked curiously.

Cooper dropped his gaze. "The stairwell was supposed to be a shortcut to class, you know? But I was a freshman and naive. The entrance closed while I was inside. I was trapped, and I starved to death. A month passed before the entrance appeared again, and by then… no one dared to come looking for me, fearing the same would happen to them. Now, I do my best to keep people away. My empathic powers aren't what they were when I was alive, but it's usually enough. You five were not so lucky."

"We'll get out of here," Talia assured him. "There's a special wand somewhere in the stairwell we can use."

Cooper furrowed his brow. "I've never seen a wand down here."

"Are you certain?" I asked. "A witness told us my grandfather hid it down here."

"Then perhaps it was before my time," Cooper said. "You're welcome to look around."

"It shouldn't be that hard," Lucas said. "The stairwell isn't very big."

Cooper gave a harrowed, bitter laugh, though I didn't understand why.

"Let's start at the lower level," I suggested. I started down the stairs, and my friends followed. I kept my eyes on the stone bricks along the wall, watching for one that might be out of place and could fit a wand behind it. Grant stomped on the stairs, checking to see if any of them might be hollow underneath. Lucas inspected the railing, looking for anything that might jiggle out of place.

We were all so preoccupied in searching for the Wand on the staircase that we didn't notice the shift in the air until we reached the bottom of the stairs. A warm breeze passed by my skin, and I gasped when I lifted my gaze. Lucas stiffened beside me, and I realized why Cooper had been laughing.

"These stairs seem pretty solid—" Grant started, but Talia cut him off by grabbing his sleeve. Grant looked up and cried, "Hallelujah! A way out!"

My guts twisted. "I wouldn't be too sure about that."

Ahead of us stood an arched doorway, similar to the one we'd entered. But instead of the school hallway that should've been there, a dark forest stretched in front of us.

"This isn't right." I took a cautious step toward the door. "There should be snow on the ground."

I peered into the forest. The air brushing across my skin was warm like on a summer night. It felt nothing like February.

"The moon cycle's wrong, too," Lucas observed. A full moon loomed over the trees, but it should've been a new moon.

"What is this?" I wondered. "A fae illusion?"

"It's real," Cooper said, appearing before me. I jumped, but my heart quickly settled. "I'm sure you've heard the story of how the Vanishing Stairwell came to be."

Lucas nodded. "Some students tried creating a space-bending spell in their room, but it spread to the stairwell and clashed with the school's space-bending spell."

"The stairwell wasn't the only part of campus it affected, though," Cooper explained. "The students *collapsed* space. A piece of the forest just outside these walls was more or less… *sucked* into the stairwell."

Grant stepped into the forest, gazing around in wonder. "It's a pocket universe! Like our stash, but bigger!"

"Exactly," Cooper said, following Grant through the doorway.

The rest of us paused, but Cooper turned back. "It's all right. The doorway won't vanish. The stairwell and this forest are connected."

Lucas grabbed my hand, and together, we entered the dark forest. Talia and Miles followed close behind. Talia's jaw dropped as she took it all in. A stick crunched beneath my feet, and a pine scent filled my nose. I glanced back the way we came, and the stone archway stood in the middle of the forest like a portal. In the center of it, I could still see the stairwell, but on either side was nothing but forest for as far as the eye could see.

At first glance, it looked just like the forest outside the school, but when my arm brushed the needles of a spruce tree, they lit up with a cool blue color. A bug fluttered onto the luminescent needles, and it glowed the same beautiful hue.

"Looks like you found yourself a Fortune Fairy," Cooper said. "These insects are said to bring good luck."

"Good, because we're going to need it." Grant crept forward and knelt down to inspect a nearby plant. It looked like a tulip, but when he brushed its purple petals, the flower opened and whipped vines out of the center. Grant jumped back. "Ow, that hurt!"

"Watch the plants around here," Cooper warned. "Back at school, your teachers harvest these magical plants, but here, they grow freely. Most of them are harmless, but some of them are touchy."

I couldn't take my eyes off it all. Black mushrooms grew up the sides of an old stump. They had purple dots that looked like amethyst crystals embedded into the fungus, which shimmered in the moonlight. Vines as thick as my leg twisted up the trunk of a large tree, and they seemed to pulse as if they were breathing. As we kept walking, I passed under an old, twisted apple tree with the most delicious-looking red apples hanging from their branches. When I reached up to grab one, I noticed they felt smooth and hard like glass.

"They're inedible," Cooper told me. "But they're pretty to look at, aren't they?"

"Gorgeous. I wish we could eat them." I was eager to see what curious plants we'd find next. It was like stepping into a witchy Wonderland.

"How does all this grow here?" Talia asked.

"It's a closed ecosystem—a bit like a terrarium," Cooper explained. "It exists outside your reality, sort of *beside* it, so close that sometimes the realities touch. Sunlight bleeds through, as do the moon and stars."

"It's warm," Grant remarked. "Does winter not happen here?"

"It does," Cooper said. "But time moves differently here. In this tiny universe, it's summer."

Miles stared far out into the forest. "How big is this place?"

Cooper shrugged. "A few acres. It's hard to tell where the forest begins and ends. If you walk far enough in one direction, you'll end up right back where you started. Believe me, I've been here long enough to explore every inch of this place."

"But you've never seen a Wand?" Talia questioned.

Cooper shook his head. "If it's here, it must be buried."

"This place is too big to go digging just anywhere," Lucas said. "We need to narrow it down."

"Maybe my grandpa marked it somehow," I theorized. "Cooper, are there any strange rocks or trees around here?"

"There's a boulder that way," he said, pointing.

"That's as good a place as any to start," I said. "Lead the way."

Cooper guided us through the forest, and Lucas conjured a witch light so we could see through the trees. It wasn't a long walk before we came upon a large boulder as tall as my waist.

I walked around it, inspecting it from every angle. "There are no markings, but perhaps my grandfather didn't need any if it's the only rock in the forest."

"It's the only large one I know of," Cooper stated.

"Then let's start digging." Lucas got to his hands and knees and began ripping apart the underbrush. Within moments, his hands were covered in a thick layer of dirt.

I knelt beside him and started digging. The ground was wet, and the dirt was heavy, but I continued digging deeper. When the ground became so hard that I couldn't dig any deeper with my hands, I started moving outward, moving further and further from the rock. The Wand had to be here *somewhere*.

I didn't know how much time had passed. At some point, Talia stopped digging and asked Cooper to show her around the forest. She didn't go far, but I kept my head down and continued digging to uncover the Seer Wand.

Hours must've passed, because the sun was already starting to peek over the horizon when Grant plopped down on the boulder and gave a heavy sigh. "We need a break. We've been at this all night."

He wiped the sweat from his brow and conjured his water bottle. He took a sip through the straw, then passed it to me. He looked exhausted, and I suddenly realized how tired I felt.

"I'm not ready to give up." I took a drink, then handed the water to Lucas. "I'll tear apart this whole forest to find that Wand."

"We all will," Lucas agreed. "But Grant's right. We need to get some food and rest. The Wand isn't going anywhere."

"We can't stay here forever," I protested. The idea of starving to death like Cooper had chilled me to the bone. I felt awful for him.

"We have time," Grant said, conjuring a handful of granola bars. "I'm diabetic, so I always have snacks on me. I have enough to last for days."

"Which you have to ration between the five of us," I reminded him.

Miles drank the rest of the water. "Speaking of your diabetes, you should eat something."

Grant didn't protest. He knew he was well overdue for a meal. He tossed each of us a granola bar, then conjured his insulin supplies and got to work checking his blood sugar levels. He pricked his finger and analyzed his blood on a small device. I didn't pay much attention, because I was so used to it by now, until I witnessed Grant conjure a potion vial and take a sip. He turned away from us slightly, like he didn't want us to see.

"What's that?" I asked.

"My insulin," Grant said innocently, subconjuring the vial before I could get a good look.

I narrowed my eyes. "You have to inject insulin, not drink it."

"Not this," he said. "Magic doesn't play by the same rules. I don't really understand the mechanics, but so far this potion hasn't failed me. I feel great."

Lucas frowned. "I thought you agreed you wouldn't be making your own potions for this."

Grant sighed. "What else do you expect me to do? This stuff is great. I don't have to refrigerate it, and I'm basically done with needles. Plus, I don't have to wait to eat. It kicks in immediately. Really, I feel good."

"But you don't know the long-term effects," Lucas pointed out.

"Someone has to be a guinea pig for this stuff," Grant said. "I could help a lot of people."

"How much do you have left?" I asked warily.

Grant looked away from me. "Enough."

"Enough for what, exactly?" I pressed. "Be honest, Grant."

"It's enough, okay?" he insisted. "We'll find the Wand before I run out."

Lucas and I shared a skeptical glance. "What does your intuition tell you?" he asked me in a low whisper.

I took a deep breath. My whole body seemed to buzz, even though I was tired as hell. I couldn't tap into my intuition when I felt this desperate.

"I'm not sure," I admitted.

Lucas sighed, but his eyes locked on something in the distance. "Here comes Talia. Hopefully she found something."

I turned to find Talia pushing her way through the trees. Cooper followed her, but he paid no mind to the trees and simply floated through them.

"Anything?" I asked.

She sighed and plopped down on the rock beside Grant. He handed her a granola bar. "I've got nothing. I've been trying to get visions of your grandpa to see where he hid the Wand, but there's *nothing* from forty years ago. It's just decades of season changes."

"Maybe Nicolas never came down here after all," Miles theorized. "Angelica said she saw him *after* she died. Ghosts get confused."

"Wait…" Cooper said. "Your grandpa came down here forty years ago *your* time?"

I nodded. I barely had the energy to answer.

"Then Talia's been looking in the wrong place," Cooper said. "Remember that time moves differently here. Forty years ago your time could've been over a century here."

Talia's jaw dropped. "Of course! I'm so stupid."

"No, you're not," Grant protested.

"It was a dumb mistake. Let me try again." Talia splayed her hand over the boulder and closed her eyes. Nobody moved for several minutes, so she could concentrate. When Talia's eyes began to shake beneath her lids, I knew she was having a vision. She must've found something.

Her eyes shot open, startling me a bit. "It's not here."

Miles's shoulders slumped. "We came down here for nothing?"

"No, I mean, not *here* at this rock," Talia said. "I can see your grandpa in my mind, but he walked straight past this rock. He didn't stop here. He went that way."

Talia pointed, and we all got to our feet to hurry in that direction, though none of us moved quickly. We'd been up all night and were all exhausted. Grant shoved down the last of his granola bar and followed behind us, stepping over the deep holes we'd dug.

Talia stopped at a huge tree and ran her fingers over the bark. She furrowed her brow as the vision passed, like she couldn't quite make sense of it. "The visions are hazy," she told us. "It was so long ago, only the oldest trees remember. I see a shadow… going that way."

Talia pointed forward, and we continued through the forest. She kept stopping at big trees and small rocks, following the path my grandfather had taken so many years ago. Finally, she stopped at one of the largest trees in the forest. Above us, thick branches twisted in a way that reminded me of the Protection Tree. Talia leaned against it, splaying her palm wide. Several silent moments passed as she contemplated the vision.

"This is it," she finally said, opening her eyes. "The tree was much smaller back then, but it remembers. Your grandfather placed the Wand in the tree. He said he was giving it back to the earth, where it had come from."

"Of course." I joined her to run my hand over the trunk. "The Wands came from a branch of the Protection Tree. It seems fitting to graft it back into an oak."

"Is the Wand part of the tree now?" Grant asked.

I shook my head. "The Wands can't be destroyed. The magic is faint, but there's definitely a supernatural energy pulsing through this tree. The Wand is in there, but the tree grew around it."

"Let's blast this tree apart and get that Wand, then." Grant drew his arm back and tossed a battle orb at the tree. It bounced off, and the five of us ducked as it came back in our direction. The orb went flying into the forest and exploded against the ground. Grant winced.

Lucas walked around the tree, inspecting it from every angle. He aimed a few battle spells at it, but they just bounced right off. He tried wrapping a shield around the middle of the tree, trying to reverse-engineer the spell to slice through it. He gritted his teeth, and the spell backfired, knocking him off his feet.

"Looks like we're going to have to use brute force." Lucas conjured his scythe, but he frowned. "That's not going to work. We need an ax."

"Or a chainsaw would be nice." Grant forced a chuckle.

"Yes, let me just conjure my *chainsaw*," I said sarcastically.

"I have an idea," Talia said. She began walking around, picking up sticks and tossing aside the ones she didn't like. After a few minutes, she'd gathered a thick stick and a flat rock that was sharp on one end.

"Can I use that?" she asked Lucas, gesturing to the scythe he was still holding. She used the blade to slice her stick down the middle, splitting it less than a quarter of the way down. She wedged one end of her rock into the slice, then secured the top ends of the stick together with the hair tie around her wrist. She held up her makeshift ax triumphantly, and I was impressed with the quality.

"Let's see what it can do," Lucas said. Talia handed him her ax, and he stepped up to the tree. "Where's the Wand at?"

I ran my hands up and down the bark, until I noticed an area that seemed to buzz at a higher frequency than the rest. It was higher than my head, about as tall as Lucas. "Here," I said, smacking the tree.

Lucas took my arm and guided me far behind him. "Stand back."

He swung the ax at the tree as hard as he could, but it merely bounced off. A piece of bark flew off, but that was it. Lucas tried a few more times, but it became clear fairly quickly that this wasn't going to work.

Talia frowned. "It was worth a shot."

"It was creative," I encouraged. "We'll just have to think of something else."

"What if we burn our way through?" Talia wondered.

"A green tree this big isn't going to burn down," Miles pointed out. "Plus, we could end up burning down the whole forest before we get out of here."

"We don't have to burn the whole thing down," Talia said. "We can contain the fire, burn a hole to the center. It might take some time with it being so big and green, but it may be the best chance we've got."

"That could work," Lucas agreed. "Let's get started."

Lucas conjured a pocketknife and started carving out a small hole in the tree. Meanwhile, the rest of us gathered dry leaves and small twigs. Once the hole was large enough to hold a few leaves, Lucas carefully laid tinder inside and conjured a lighter. The fire went out almost immediately, and we tried again.

"Hey, Grant, can I see your water bottle?" Lucas asked. He pulled the cap off and took the straw out of the inside. He lit the tinder again and used the straw to gently blow air at the fire. The fire glowed a bright orange, and he continued adding tinder until the fire finally grew hot enough to light the edges of the hole.

"It's working!" Talia cried.

"I'll need to keep tending it," Lucas said. "You four should rest. We'll take turns."

I *was* really tired, and only one of us needed to work the fire at a time. "All right, but it's my turn once I wake up."

"Fair enough," Lucas said.

"I'll stay here, keep you company," Cooper offered.

Talia took my arm. "There's a moss bed over there, and it's nice and shaded. It'll be a good place to lie down."

Talia led me over to the moss bed, and Grant and Miles followed. We weren't far from Lucas. My stomach sank a little, because I hated leaving him there to do all the work while we slept. It would take us forever to burn the center out of that tree, but we had to.

Miles lay down first and was already snoring before the rest of us got settled in. Grant and Talia snuggled tightly against one another, her head on his shoulder. I lay on my side, wanting nothing more than to cuddle up to Lucas—or at the very least, pull Isa close in my arms. I wondered how she was handling us disappearing the way we did. I hoped she wasn't worried.

We'd get out of here… we *would.*

I couldn't quite get comfortable on the ground, so I rolled over—and shrieked. A mere inch from my nose lay a human skull. I scurried backward, nearly squashing Talia and Grant behind me. They startled and grabbed me, trying to calm me down.

"Goddess, Nadine," Miles said, sounding a bit annoyed that I'd roused him from his sleep. "It's like you've never seen a human skeleton before."

"Not right in my face!" I forced my breathing to slow as I took in the full skeleton. The human remains were nothing but bones, which were covered in dirt and looked quite old.

Lucas came tearing through the forest. Cooper floated along behind him, looking worried. "What happened?" Lucas demanded breathlessly.

"I'm fine," I assured him. "Really. I just didn't expect to see…" I gestured to the skeleton.

"Oh, yeah." Cooper sounded guilty. "That'd be mine. I should've warned you."

"Yours—?" I practically choked. "That's your body?"

Cooper shrugged, like he was used to it by now. "That's what happens when no one comes to rescue you."

I gaped. "You should be laid to rest!"

"Don't bother," he said. "You've spent all night digging. You don't have to waste your energy on my grave."

"You deserve a funeral!" I protested. "Lucas is a reaper. He can help you cross over—"

"I don't want to," Cooper interrupted. "I'm serving my purpose here by scaring people away from this place. I'm not leaving."

He said it so firmly that there was no arguing with him.

Lucas took my hand and guided me away from Cooper's remains. He laid me gently on a bed of moss and kissed my forehead. "We'll help him cross over once we get out of here. Sleep well, my miracle."

"I'll try," I told him, and that's all I remember before exhaustion overcame me and I drifted off.

When I woke hours later, the sun was already in the western sky. It had to be early afternoon, and I was parched and hungry. I looked over to see Miles and Grant still sleep. I could hear Talia's and Lucas's voices off in the distance.

I was achy this morning from sleeping on the ground, and it took me a while to actually get to my feet and walk over to them. As I got closer, I saw the glowing embers of our fire inside the tree. There weren't flames; rather, the fire burned in a circle, eating away at the wood from the inside out. The hole was bigger than before, but there was still a long way to go until we reached the center. It wasn't exactly a quick solution, but it was the best tool we had.

Talia tended to the fire, blowing through the straw to feed it oxygen. Every now and then, she added leaves or twigs to make it burn hotter. Cooper stood by watching, and Lucas sat on a log, sipping water from Grant's water bottle. I didn't know where he'd gotten it, because I thought we'd finished off the water last night. His eyes drooped, and bits of dirt stuck to his sweaty skin. He looked absolutely exhausted.

"I want to see Tyler do a punk rock cover," Lucas said with a laugh. "I think he'd be really good at it."

"I know, right?" Talia agreed. "That, or a ballad. I've been trying to get him to sing one forever, but as soon as I start the first few chords, he won't even go *near* the song. Says it's *not him*."

"But he has a great voice. Put it together with your lyrics, and I'm sure it'd be great." Lucas turned around, noticing me for the first time. A smile spread across his face when he saw me. "Nad, it's good to see you up. Here, drink something."

Lucas shoved the water bottle in my direction, and I took a small sip.

"It's okay," he encouraged. "There's a spring nearby. There's enough for everyone."

I was relieved to hear that, so I didn't hold back. I chugged the rest of the water. I was really hungry, but I didn't say anything and hoped the water would help fill me up.

"We found some berries, too," Talia said, gesturing to a big leaf with a pile of blueberries atop it.

"Don't eat too many," Cooper warned. "I lived off those for a few days when I came here, but that might've been the thing that killed me. Too many blueberries are *not* nice to the gut."

"I'll start with just a few," I said, popping a couple in my mouth. Sweet juice burst across my tongue, but I ate slowly, trying to make them last.

Lucas grabbed for a few, and I noticed his hands shaking. "You need to sleep," I told him.

"I'm fine—" he started.

"You haven't slept in over twenty-four hours," I said. "Talia and I have this covered. I love you too much to watch you pass out from exhaustion."

Lucas sighed. "All right, but wake me up if you find the Wand."

"We will," I promised, though at the rate this was going, I figured we had another day or two before we retrieved it.

Lucas went to lie down on the moss bed, while I ate up the rest of the berries and offered to pick more. Talia continued tending the fire, and I went off on my own. I found the spring on my way to the berry patch and used the water to clean up, then gathered a fresh batch of blueberries. When I returned, Grant and Miles were awake, and Miles was feeding more dead leaves into our tiny fire. He winced slightly every time he moved, and I worried his arthritis was flaring.

"You all right, Miles?" I asked.

"Great," he said. I was certain he was lying, but he was insistent.

"Berries?" I asked.

"Oh, those look fantastic!" Grant sat down to get to work on his insulin. As he started munching on berries, he conjured the rest of his food. There were a few granola bars, some candy, a long beef stick, and a large bag of trail mix.

He spread them out and spoke with a full mouth. "This is all I've got."

"At least it's something," I said. "You really came prepared."

Grant shrugged. "I have to be."

As the day wore on into evening, I became more and more hopeful that the Wand was within reach. We each took turns tending the fire. Miles and Cooper cracked jokes to pass the time, and for a few hours, I felt like I could forget we were trapped at all. By the time the full moon began to rise, I could sense the magic of the Wand growing stronger. We were getting close, though it still seemed so far away. We were only halfway through to the center.

Lucas woke shortly after sunset and joined us at the site of the tree. Grant forced him to eat berries and a few handfuls of trail mix. We were already running low on food, and I worried how much would be left before we made it out of here.

"I'll take the night shift," Lucas offered.

I gave him a kiss, then returned to the moss bed to get some sleep. The day had been long, and though we were making progress burning through the tree, it seemed to be taking forever. I tossed and turned all night, not able to get comfortable. I kept hoping Lucas would come and wake us to tell us he'd found the Wand.

But I woke up the next morning with no such news.

The hole had burned wider, but not by much. I spent the day helping tend the fire and gathering the last of the berries I could find. My stomach dropped when I realized we'd picked the bushes clean. It wouldn't be long until we ran out of food completely.

Night fell once again, marking our third night inside the stairwell. We'd entered Thursday evening, which made this Saturday night. I was acutely aware that I'd missed my Friday dialysis session, but I didn't say anything. I didn't want anyone worrying about me.

My last dialysis session was Wednesday evening. I always went two days without dialysis over the weekend, so I could handle it this long, but I'd be on my next treatment by now. I didn't know how much longer my body could take it. I was really tired, and it didn't help that we weren't getting enough food or sleep.

Talia tended the fire, while we listened to Cooper and Miles tell stories. Lucas whittled at a stick with his pocketknife to keep his hands busy. Grant conjured Talia's music box and fiddled with it. I was starting to think the thing was beyond repair, but Grant looked like he needed something to do. Above us, Fortune Fairies glowed different colors, performing a beautiful lights display against the dark sky.

Grant picked up one of the last two granola bars and held it out to me. "Hungry?"

I hesitated. We only had a few berries left, and my stomach ached in hunger, but Grant needed to eat every five to six hours. I could wait until we made it out of here. We were *so* close.

"No, I'm good," I lied.

"Tal?" Grant asked, holding it up to her as she tended the fire. The hole was much bigger now, and we could easily reach inside. I knew we had to be getting close, but we hadn't spotted the Wand yet.

"I'm full on berries," she said, though I was certain she was lying. "You can have it."

Talia winced and clutched her stomach when she turned around. It looked like she was trying to hide her discomfort.

On second thought, she didn't look too well. Maybe she *had* eaten too many berries.

Grant insisted that Miles and Lucas eat, but they both declined as well. It was like we'd all collectively agreed to let Grant take the rest of the rations. We knew how much he needed them. If Grant didn't eat regularly, his blood sugar would drop to dangerous levels. He'd slip into a diabetic coma. He'd pass out, and by that time, he'd need immediate medical intervention, or he could die.

"Have I ever told the story of when Grant accidentally drank a hair-growth potion when we were kids?" Miles asked, trying to distract Grant from the topic of food.

"Nooo," Talia said, sounding intrigued.

Grant groaned. "Aw, man. Don't!"

"I *have* to," Miles argued, already laughing. "You were, what? Eight? This was right when Dad was starting to bald, so naturally, he got some hair-growth potion to slow it down. He liked to add it to his coffee in the morning. Just as Dad finishes making his coffee, our baby brother Trenton starts crying. Dad sets his coffee down and goes to console him."

"Oh, no," Talia said. "I can already see where this is going."

Miles started laughing so hard he could hardly catch his breath. "Grant thought it was chocolate milk! The look on his face when he realized it was coffee! I'll never forget it!"

Grant groaned. Lucas smirked without taking his eyes off the stick he was whittling away at.

"The amount of hair this kid grew..." Miles clapped Grant on the back. "I'm talking down to his shoulders, with a full creeper 'stash. He runs to the bathroom and—"

"Don't you dare," Grant warned.

"Aw, come on," Cooper protested. "We've got to hear this part."

Miles couldn't stop laughing. "I just remember... hearing from the bathroom... *There's not supposed to be hair down there!*"

My jaw dropped, and I started laughing.

"Did you learn something about puberty that day?" Lucas cracked.

Grant frowned. "It wasn't like that."

"It was *exactly* like that," Miles insisted. "Dad had to sit us down and tell us about *all* the places men grew hair. I don't think Grant's touched coffee since."

Grant crossed his arms. "I drink it every now and then—"

"Fuck!" Lucas cried.

My heart lurched. I didn't see what happened, but the laughter in our group died instantly. Lucas shot to his feet, dropping his stick and pocketknife. Blood dripped into the dirt.

Lucas sucked a breath. "My knife slipped."

I reached for his hand, which he clutched tightly with the other. "Let me look."

He pulled away from me, and I knew it had to be bad. I quickly conjured a first-aid kit I kept with me. I uncapped a bottle of hydrogen peroxide and poured it over his hand.

"Fuuuck." Lucas sucked a breath between his teeth and turned away from me.

"Babe, you're going to have to let me help!" I insisted. "If we don't take care of it now, it's going to get infected."

"Fine," he conceded.

Lucas held out his hand, and I saw that he'd sliced the side of his pointer finger. Blood poured from a huge gash. I didn't think he needed stitches, but it was going to get *bad* if the cut got infected. I grabbed a few pieces of gauze and soaked up the blood, then slathered antibiotic ointment over it. I unwrapped more gauze and pressed it tight to the bloody wound.

"Press on this firmly," I told him, before frantically turning back to my first-aid kit to search for supplies.

"Is there anything I can do—?" Grant started to ask, but Talia cut him off.

"I see it!" she screamed.

I glanced over to her to see she was gazing into the hole we'd burned. She had a look of wonder on her face, and my already racing heart jumped. Lucas grabbed the bandage I was holding and said, "I've got this. You worry about the Wand."

I didn't want to leave Lucas alone, but I couldn't take my eyes off Talia. Miles, Grant, and Cooper quickly gathered around her.

In the middle of the hole we'd burned away, I could see the swirling designs of a wand embedded into the tree. Like the spiral handle of the

Alchemy Wand, which had a cauldron symbol carved into it, the Seer Wand contained the carving of an eye. Everything else about it was different, though. Where the Alchemy Wand had a bulb on the end and a smooth blade, the Seer Wand had delicate swirls expertly carved into it. The handle of the Seer Wand twisted in a more intricate way than the Alchemy Wand. The embers didn't touch the Wand, because it was indestructible and impervious to fire.

"We found it!" Grant cried.

"Hallelujah!" Miles shouted.

Talia picked up the scythe Lucas had left resting against the tree. Using the tip of the weapon, she chipped away at the last bit of embers surrounding the Wand. She wedged the tip of the scythe between the Wand and the tree, prying it free. It fell into the bed of embers, but didn't burn. Carefully, Talia reached for the Wand.

The tree began to sway above our heads, and a heavy wind swept through the air. Leaves swirled around us, and embers scattered across the forest. Talia screamed as her hair whipped around her face.

"What's happening!?" she shouted.

The tree groaned, and before our very eyes, the glowing embers faded. The hole we'd burnt through the tree shrank.

"No!" I screamed. I lunged for the Seer Wand inside, but the hole slammed shut, and my knuckles slammed into solid wood.

"We were *so close*!" Grant cried.

"How is this possible?" Miles demanded. He clawed at the bark, as if he could get through, but it was no use. The tree had sealed the Seer Wand inside.

Talia shivered as the wind died down. "The tree must be magical."

"I can break a protection spell." I stepped up to the tree and splayed my palm over the bark. I tried connecting with the magic inside of it. If I could twist the magic to my will, we could retrieve the Wand. But the magic didn't respond to me.

I stepped back. "Something about this magic is different. The spell must be sustained by the Seer Wand."

"There has to be a way to get it," Talia insisted. "If the tree is magic, then we have to fight it with magic."

Talia slammed a battle orb into the trunk, but it fizzled out. She hammered her fists against the tree, smashing magic into it over and over again. The tree didn't respond.

Talia fell to her knees in defeat. "Please," she begged the tree. "We are good people. The coven is losing magic, and we intend to restore it. We will use the Seer Wand for good."

Silence filled the forest.

Grant knelt beside Talia and wrapped his arms around her. "It's not going to work, Tal. We've tried everything."

"So that's it?" Miles asked. "We give up?"

"If you have any other suggestions, I'm open to ideas," Grant bit at him. "I see only one option left, and that's to return to the top of the stairwell and pray for a miracle. We're not getting out of here with the Seer Wand, but we still have a chance the stairwell will open up again."

I didn't want to admit it, but Grant was right. We'd spent days trying to get to the center of that tree. We'd tried to get through via magic. If we stayed any longer, we'd be out of food, and Grant could fall severely ill. I needed my dialysis treatment. Being upstairs when the doorway opened was our only option.

"Grant's right," I said. "We should gather our things. Let's fill up our water and go."

I grabbed the water bottle and took Lucas's hand. "Come with me?"

We walked off, but instead of heading toward the spring, I started toward the moss bed.

"The spring's that way," Lucas said.

I lowered my voice. "I know Cooper didn't want us to bother, but I think we should bury his bones before we go. It's the respectful thing to do. I know if we don't make it, I'd want someone to come bury us. I just want to do one last thing right."

Lucas shivered. "Isn't it best that we respect his wishes?"

"He's requesting we leave him alone so he doesn't burden us." I stopped when we reached Cooper's bones, and I got sad looking at them. "Though, I suppose we shouldn't touch his bones without his permission. But maybe we could say a few words. No one else has ever done it for him, and I think he deserves at least that much."

Lucas nodded. "He does."

I cleared my throat. "Cooper, I admire you. You've stuck around in this stairwell for so long, trying to protect people when you didn't have to. You've followed Mother Miriam's teachings in an incredible way, by protecting the coven even after death. She'd be proud of you, and I hope that one day you get to meet her."

Lucas drew a deep breath. "What can I say? Coop, I haven't known you long, but I like to think that we'd be friends if we'd gone to school together. You've really helped keep our spirits up these last few days. I wish you the very best."

"Thank you both."

Lucas and I spun around to see Cooper standing there. Neither of us had realized he'd followed.

"No one has ever thanked me for what I'm doing down here," Cooper said. "Hell, I'm not sure anyone really knows I exist. To know that what I'm doing is appreciated... well, it means the world."

"Of course it's appreciated," I told him. "I don't know what we would've done down here without you."

"That means a lot." His voice cracked. "You can bury my bones if you'd like."

"You deserve to be laid to rest," Lucas said. "We'll be gentle with them."

Lucas and I gathered Cooper's bones and took them over to the boulder where we'd already upturned the earth. We reverently arranged the bones and covered them with dirt. It was a shallow grave, but a grave nonetheless.

Lucas stared down at the grave once we'd finished. "I hope this helps, Coop. We're going to miss you once we get out of here."

If we got out of here.

"You'll visit us, won't you?" Lucas asked.

Cooper chuckled. "If I ever leave my post, I'll give you a call."

"I'm counting on it," Lucas said.

It felt like a sad moment, but it was strange that Cooper was still there with us. He refused to move on, and though I knew our effort was appreciated, I didn't feel that we'd truly laid him to rest.

"You should clean up," Cooper suggested.

I got the sense that Cooper wanted to be alone at his grave. Lucas and I headed off toward the spring to wash the dirt off our hands, and Cooper hung back. By the time Lucas and I returned to the oak, Cooper was already back, though he was much quieter than before. Our friends had cleaned up our stuff.

"You were gone a while," Talia remarked. "Is everything okay?"

I nodded. "We just had to say goodbye."

The tree groaned, and the leaves above us rustled. We all turned to look, and my heart stalled in my chest. I couldn't believe what I was seeing.

A tree branch twisted, until the end of the branch touched the trunk of the tree. A hole formed before our eyes, and the tree reached inside of itself to retrieve the Wand. The branch stretched toward me, offering us the Wand.

I hesitated. How was this possible?

Lucas nudged me. "Take it, Nad."

Relief flooded my body as I took the Wand in my hand. "Thank you," I told the tree.

The leaves above us shook, as if the tree was responding.

"We did it!" Talia cried. "How did we do it?"

"Nadine and I buried Cooper's bones," Lucas said. "We must've somehow proven ourselves to the tree. It must trust us to take care of the Wand."

I held it out to Talia. "Here. It belongs to your Cast."

"This means we can get out of here!" Grant cried. He picked Talia up and spun her around in celebration, and she laughed as she held the Seer Wand over her head.

Lucas and I hugged, and Cooper gave Miles a high-five that never quite touched him. I could hardly believe we'd done it. Everyone laughed in relief.

"Awesome," Miles said once the celebrations settled. "Can we do the spell now?"

"Yes!" Talia held up the Wand, and we all watched on curiously, waiting for something to happen. When Grant had used the Alchemy Wand, magic had twisted up his arm and glowed green.

But when Talia tried it… nothing happened.

She furrowed her brow. "It's not working!"

"It's a fake?" Cooper asked.

Talia shook her head, and I could see the heartbreak in her eyes. "The Wand has to *choose* you. We banked our whole plan on it choosing us. We proved ourselves to the tree, but not to the Wand."

My stomach sank, because I couldn't imagine why the Seer Wand wouldn't choose her. Talia was one of the most honest, caring people I knew. She was brave and had a kind heart. Why wouldn't the Wand want to work with her?

The silence within the forest was deafening.

Talia turned to Miles. "You're a Seer, too. You should try it."

He looked skeptical. "If it didn't choose you…"

"It's worth a shot," I said, though I still couldn't wrap my head around the Wand rejecting Talia.

Miles took the Wand from her. I held my breath, expecting something to happen. I could feel Lucas stiffen beside me. But several long moments passed, and nothing happened.

"I don't feel anything," Miles said, sounding defeated. He handed the Wand back to Talia.

"It's hopeless?" Talia's voice cracked.

"No," Lucas protested. "It's not. We're getting out of here."

"But how?" Grant asked. "Without a Mentalist or the power from the Seer Wand, we don't have enough power to stabilize the spell. The only thing we can do is sit around and wait for the doorway to open again."

"That could take years down here," Lucas pointed out. He tried to mask the panic in his tone, but I still picked up on it. "We're out of food. We don't have the luxury of waiting. I say we try the spell anyway. If it doesn't work, we'll find another way."

"Your friend is right," Cooper said. "You never know when the doorway will open. A day up there could be anywhere from hours to *months* down here. You're running out of time. You should at least try your spell."

I was skeptical, but without the help of the Wand, we were out of options. "Okay, let's try it. Everyone, grab hands."

As we all joined hands, I felt the collective buzz of my friends' magic surrounding me. "Lend me your magic, and I'll do the rest, all right?"

They all nodded, and their magic began sweeping through me, traveling around our circle chaotically. We were powerful, but not nearly as powerful as when I performed spells with the priestesses. The power of all five Casts was unmatched… I hoped four Casts was enough.

I closed my eyes and focused on the magic surrounding me, stabilizing it until it flowed smoothly through our circle. Once I was confident our power was in sync, I began citing the incantation I'd learned for space-bending spells. As soon as the spell took hold, I'd be able to manipulate the stairwell to my will and stabilize its energy.

"*Da mihi potestatem spatio,*" I concluded in Latin, the language of our ancient spells.

I waited for the magic of the stairwell to connect with me... but nothing happened. "Let's keep trying—"

Talia's scream tore through the forest. She yanked her hand out of Grant's hold and pointed deep into the forest. "*Something's* happening! And it's not good!"

My stomach dropped out of my abdomen when I saw that the *forest was shrinking.* The ground seemed to disappear as trees inched closer to one another. Fortune Fairies fled their roost in the treetops, and their beautiful lights instantly dimmed. A gust of wind swept through the forest, kicking up dying embers that lay scattered on the ground. Dead leaves ignited, and flames began to spread across the forest, creeping quickly toward the dead log we'd been sitting on earlier.

"We fucked it up!" Grant cried. "The pocket universe is collapsing!"

"Everybody back to the stairwell!" Lucas screamed.

Talia clutched the Seer Wand tightly, and the five of us took off running, Cooper following close behind. Our path ahead narrowed, and branches snapped overhead as trees collided with one another. We raced past the large boulder where we'd buried Cooper's bones. The boulder connected with a nearby tree, and a huge *snap* sounded.

"Look out!" Cooper yelled.

Lucas grabbed me and yanked me out of the way of the falling tree. All around us, trees began to groan and topple over.

"Faster!" Miles screamed. "The whole forest is going to come down on us!"

I ignored the ache in my joints and pumped my arms faster. Relief overcame me when I saw the archway to the stairwell up ahead. But my relief quickly turned to panic when I noticed that the archway was shrinking, too. Within moments, it went from a tall, open doorway to barely taller than I was. We had to get there *fast,* or we wouldn't make it through.

"Quick!" Lucas shouted to the others. "The doorway is closing."

I'd never seen my friends move any faster. We dodged around trees and falling branches. The door grew inches smaller with each passing second, and I feared we wouldn't make it.

We'd made a horrible mistake…

I had one last chance to save my friends. I drew my wand out of my pocket while I ran and aimed the end toward the shrinking archway. With every ounce of magic I had in me, I thrust my power toward the doorway. Blue magic shot out of the end of my wand and collided with the stone arch. The shrinking stopped for a mere second, but we still had twenty yards to cross until we made it there. I gathered as much energy as I could from my surroundings—from my friends, from Cooper, from the magical plants and the Fortune Fairies. It wasn't a feat I could normally pull off. I had to overpower each and every one of them. But I was desperate, and nothing could stop me when the fate of my loved ones was at stake.

I screamed as the magic surged through me. It felt as if the power was going to rip me apart, and I wasn't sure I could contain it. My ears rang, and the edges of my vision blurred.

That's all I processed before the ground fell out beneath my feet.

I grabbed Nadine around the waist and tossed her over my shoulder.

"GO!" I roared. My friends scrambled through the shrinking passageway.

The ground swayed beneath us. I tossed Nadine through the opening, then dove in behind her. The stones scratched my back as I squeezed through. The opening closed around my ankle, but I yanked it free at the last moment. I landed on the cold stone. The stairwell was dark, but someone cast a witch light and hovered it overhead. A single Fortune Fairy fluttered into the stairwell behind me before the archway closed completely. The sounds of the quaking forest vanished, and silence filled the stairwell.

The forest was gone.

The Fortune Fairy fluttered over to Nadine and landed on her shoulder. I got to my knees and shook her until her eyes focused. I helped her sit up, but she must've been in pain, because she could barely lift her head. "Tell me we all made it," she begged.

I looked around to see Miles and Grant getting to their feet. Cooper appeared nearby, looking horrified.

"We're all safe," I told her.

"Where did the forest go?" Grant asked. "If it's part of the same pocket universe as the stairwell, why haven't we been crushed?"

"Nadine must've stabilized the stairwell with her last spell," Talia theorized. "How did you *do* that?"

"I don't know," she admitted. "I just *had* to, you know? I don't know if it's something I could do again."

"You saved us all, so thanks," Miles said.

I helped Nadine to her feet, and she sagged against me. I practically had to carry her up the stairs; she was so exhausted. No one else moved much faster than us, though. We were all so tired and hungry.

As we rounded the staircase toward the top, despair settled in my gut. The archway I was expecting to see wasn't there. At the top of the landing was nothing but a flush wall. We may have escaped the collapsing forest, but we were still stuck in this stairwell.

Nadine stopped dead. "I thought I stabilized the spell."

"It must've just been enough to reverse our screw-up, but not enough to stabilize it completely," I theorized. "Come on, Nad. You need to sit down."

She was trying to hide it, but I knew damn well when she wasn't feeling well. She'd missed dialysis and hadn't had a proper meal in days. Right now, she couldn't hide a thing. I helped her up the last few steps and lowered her to the floor. I sat beside her, and she put her head in my lap. Our friends gathered around, but everyone remained silent. There wasn't much more to say.

"I'm sorry," Cooper said kindly. "I really hoped you'd make it. If those Fortune Fairies are as lucky as they say, perhaps it will grant you the luck for the doorway to open."

The Fortune Fairy fluttered its wings from Nadine's shoulder.

"You guys should sleep," Cooper encouraged. "I'll wake you if the doorway opens."

It must've been mere moments before I fell asleep, because the next thing I knew, my eyes fluttered open, and I had no idea how much time had passed. Nadine's head was still in my lap. A dim witch light hovered overhead, and I looked around to see Grant and Miles sleeping, but Talia was gone.

I turned to look up at Cooper. "Where's Talia?"

"I don't think she's feeling well," he said. "She keeps doing downstairs. Stomachache, I think."

That meant four of us were sick, and I wasn't doing much better. We'd been saving the last of our food for Grant, and I hadn't eaten in twenty-four hours. Miles was having an arthritis flare-up he wouldn't admit to, and though Grant had been regulating his blood sugar the best he could, I didn't think it was going well.

"How long was I asleep?" I asked Cooper.

He shrugged. "Ten hours?"

That made it Sunday morning.

Nadine stirred, and my stomach knotted. "How are you doing?" I asked as I stroked her hair.

"Weak and nauseous," she said in a strained voice. She was getting worse.

She tried to sit up, but I guided her back into my lap. She was too weak.

"You're breathing heavily," I pointed out. "It's worse than you're saying."

She sighed. We'd agreed to open up to each other more and to let each other help. "I feel like every breath isn't enough. Something's *off* in my body—like my blood pressure isn't quite right. My feet are sore, which means I'm retaining water. There's nothing you can do."

"I can make you comfortable." I gently laid her head on the ground, then knelt at her feet and stripped her shoes off. Her feet were really swollen, which worried me. I began massaging them, and Nadine closed her eyes like it felt good.

The stairs creaked, and I looked over to see Talia climbing the steps. She was carrying the Seer Wand, like she was afraid to let it out of her sight.

"Let me help," she offered. She sat next to Nadine, then scooted over so that Nadine could lay her head in her lap. Nadine relaxed into her best friend, and the girls chatted to pass the time. Soon, Grant and Miles woke. Grant got to work checking his blood sugar immediately, then scarfed down a few bites of what we had left for food.

"When we get out of here, I'm getting a big, juicy burger," Grant said.

"Steak for me," Miles added. "On second thought, I think I'll order a whole cow."

"You guys need to eat something," Grant insisted, shoving the last of the trail mix at us.

"We're not eating," I protested. "You need it more than the rest of us."

"I'm not the only sick one here," he pointed out. "And even then, you're all going to starve if you don't eat."

Grant wouldn't stop insisting, and he made us eat a few handfuls of trail mix. By the time we finished, it was almost gone. We made sure to save the last of it for him, though there were only a few bites left.

Hours passed. We were all too tired to say much of anything, but Cooper kept us entertained with stories.

I was certain we were going to die down here. As morbid as it was, I couldn't help but think about our deaths. Grant would be the first to go, because his blood sugar would drop to deadly levels. Nadine would be next, because her kidneys couldn't filter out the toxins in her body. The rest of us wouldn't last much longer. We'd starve, like Cooper had. I wondered if anyone would stick around in the stairwell, or if we'd all go with our reapers…

I tried to put the thoughts out of my head, but my hope was near nonexistent by now. We said we'd risk it all for the Seer Wand, and we had.

No one had spoken in over an hour. Even Cooper had stopped telling stories. I think he could sense that we'd given up hope. I'd put Nadine's shoes back on and watched her drift in and out of consciousness. The Fortune Fairy fluttered above her, and she opened her eyes to admire it. The insect glowed a pretty blue, then landed in her hair. Talia reached for him and pulled him off her. She placed him on her shoulder, then started smoothing Nadine's hair down. In her other hand, she still clutched the Seer Wand tightly.

"There's an old Miriamic lullaby about Fortune Fairies," Talia said. "Do you want to hear it?"

I thought she was trying to distract us from the hopelessness that had taken over the stairwell. I wanted nothing more than to hear her voice.

"I do," Nadine told her.

Talia began singing, still stroking Nadine's hair as her soothing melody echoed off the stone.

"Deep in the forest
They flutter by
Like magic lights
Twinkling in the sky

> *All you must do*
> *Is walk on by*
> *You'll have luck*
> *When Fortune Fairies fly."*

A light began to glow within the stairwell, brighter than the orb above us. It startled me, and I sat up straighter. I gasped when I saw that it was the Seer Wand. Everyone became immediately alert. Talia's jaw dropped as pink magic swirled around the Wand and up her arm.

"It's working!" I cried. "Talia, what did you do?"

"I don't know," she said, still amazed at the tendrils of magic surrounding her.

"Was it luck from the Fortune Fairy?" Miles asked.

"Talia must've connected with the Wand," I realized. "When Grant got the Alchemy Wand, he had to *prove* to the cauldron that he would use its treasure for good, but he was proving himself to the Wand, too! Talia's song must've convinced it."

"Seers have a unique belief about how to contribute to the coven," Miles said. "We believe that we best serve the coven by becoming our best selves and using our hobbies and passions to empower others. Talia used her song to help us feel better and lift our spirits. The Wand must've resonated with that!"

Nadine pushed herself to a sitting position. "This is great! We have enough power to cast the spell now. We can get out of here. Everyone grab hands."

Nadine looked tired and weak, but she was determined. She stood on shaky feet, then took my hand on one side, and Grant took my other. His hands were sweaty, and his whole body seemed to quiver. He swayed a little on his feet, and I knew we had to get him something to eat right away.

This damn well better work.

Talia swished the Wand through the air. The end glowed white, like the Alchemy Wand had when Grant used it. A melodic chord rang through the stairwell, similar to the Alchemy Wand's song, but different too. Tendrils of magic filled the stairway, so much Seer magic that it could easily rival the magic of all five Casts.

It should be enough... it *had* to be.

Magic left my body as I offered my power to Nadine. The Seer magic swirled up Talia's wand, across her arm, and into Nadine. She began to speak the incantation while she manipulated our magic to her will.

"I can feel the space-bending spell," Nadine announced. "The magic's chaotic. I can see why the stairwell blinks in and out of existence. It's like the magic doesn't know which way to flow."

I felt the magic in my chest shift. Nadine was taking all the magic she could from each Cast and combining it into a single spell.

The magic began to spin out of control. Around us, the staircase began to grow stories taller, and stairs appeared out of nowhere. The ground shook beneath us, and the sound of stone grinding on stone filled the air.

"Nadine!" Miles cried.

"I know!" she shouted back. "Hang on."

I squeezed her hand, and she drew a deep breath. "I *will* get us out of here," Nadine affirmed under her breath.

The trembling came to a sudden halt, and the magic seemed to settle. The stairs began to shrink back to normal. The outline of an archway appeared before us.

"It's working!" I exclaimed. Relief overcame me when I spotted Chloe and our cats on the other side. The long, empty hall beyond her felt so much like home. Chloe stood with her hands pressed to the wall, like she was trying to push through to the other side.

Tendrils of magic floated out of Nadine's chest, then settled into the walls. The magic stabilized, and Nadine's whole body sagged in relief. I caught her and pulled her into the hallway as quickly as possible.

"Thank the Goddess!" Chloe cried as the five of us came flooding out of the stairwell. Our cats meowed loudly.

Miles ran up to her. "You're still here!"

"Of course I am," Chloe said. "It's only been a few minutes. I was worried sick! I was trying to send my magic through the wall so you could do the spell, but… you guys don't look well."

"Believe me, we've felt better," Miles said.

Right now, I'd never felt more relieved.

Talia threw her arms around Grant, and Nadine and I embraced tightly.

"I can't believe you did it!" Cooper said. "The spell really worked. The stairwell is safe again."

I turned to him. "Which means your job is done. You can finally move on."

I'd never seen a ghost cry. I didn't even know they *could*. But the tears of relief on Cooper's face were genuine.

A bright light shone through the hall, and I turned to see a portal blooming behind me. I reached out toward Cooper. "Are you ready?"

He nodded. I didn't think he could find the words. I guided him down the hall, but Cooper paused. "Thank you. All of you. Use that Wand well, okay?"

"We will," Talia said, looping her arm around Grant's waist.

"I hope to see you all again," Cooper said. "But not too soon, all right?"

"Let's hope not," I replied with a laugh. I guided Cooper the last few steps, and his ghost disappeared into the light.

"Wow, you guys must've gone through a lot down there," Chloe said. "But you got the Wand?"

Talia held it up. "We got it."

"We tell you all 'bout it after we eat," Grant slurred.

Everyone stilled in unison. This was *bad*.

"We've got to get him something to eat *now!*" Miles barked. "His blood sugar's dangerously low!"

"I'll be fine—" Grant started, but he never got a chance to finish. Talia screamed as she tried to catch him, but Grant was practically twice her size. Miles and I ran forward at the same time, but it was already too late. His eyes rolled back the same time his knees buckled. He crashed to the floor, unconscious.

I'd never felt my relief turn to horror so quickly. "Chloe, call the infirmary!"

Chloe scrambled for her phone, while I rolled Grant over to get him in a comfortable, safe position so he could breathe properly. Talia subconjured the Wand and choked back a sob.

Nadine went to her side to console her. "We're getting help."

Miles dropped to his knees beside me. "Check if he's responsive!"

Miles shone the flashlight from his phone into Grant's eyes, and I snapped my fingers near his ears.

Nothing.

"He's non-responsive," Chloe told the person on the other end of the phone. She remained surprisingly calm and diplomatic.

Less than a minute passed, though it felt like a lifetime, before we heard the nurses racing down the hall with a gurney.

"Everyone stand back," one of the nurses instructed. She knelt at Grant's side and began assessing him, while another nurse began asking a series of questions. *When was the last time he ate? What was his last insulin dose? Did he have any other known medical conditions?*

Some of it we could answer; some we couldn't.

The nurse assessing him took his blood sugar. She looked really worried at the results, though she kept her voice calm. "Diabetic coma. He needs a glucagon shot now."

The second nurse reached into their medical bag and helped ready the treatment. They administered the shot, then hoisted Grant onto the gurney.

"We're transporting him to the infirmary," the second nurse said. "With treatment, he'll make a full recovery quite quickly. We'll take good care of him."

"I'm coming with," Miles insisted. "I'm family."

"Me, too," Talia said, wiping away her tears.

I wasn't interested in letting Grant get carted off to the hospital without me, but he wasn't the only one who needed medical attention. Nadine had dark bags under her eyes, and she moved slowly and deliberately, as if every motion was calculated to not waste energy.

I was acutely aware of how much time had passed. It was technically Thursday evening, but we'd been inside the stairwell for three nights. Nadine had dialysis Wednesday night, which meant it'd been four days since her last treatment. She usually went two days without it over the weekend, but she couldn't handle much longer than that.

"I'm taking Nadine to the dialysis center," I told our friends.

She didn't protest, which meant it was worse than I imagined. Nadine always tried to stay strong for everyone else. She was the kind of person who would try to figure things out on her own. She didn't like asking for help, especially when it came to her health. To even accept my help driving her to the dialysis center meant she knew she'd never make it on her own.

I knelt next to Isa and Oliver, who were rubbing against my leg. "Go back to the room. We'll meet you there later."

Oliver understood, and he headed down the hall with Isa. Kiki and

Gus shared a loud meow and ran alongside Miles and Talia. Chloe followed them to the infirmary.

I more or less carried Nadine to the car.

"Nadine?" The receptionist sounded confused when we entered the dialysis center. She knew her by name, because Nadine came in so often. "You must have your days mixed up. You were just in for dialysis yesterday. You're not scheduled for another treatment until tomorrow."

"I know, but I really need to fit in another treatment," Nadine said.

"That would mess up your whole schedule," the receptionist replied. "I'm sure you can hold out one more day until your scheduled treatment."

My hands curled into fists. "Nadine knows her body better than any damn doctor in this place. She needs her treatment, and you're going to give it to her."

The receptionist looked a bit taken aback, but she remained calm. "Let me call a nurse."

We were forced to sit in the waiting room. Twenty minutes must've passed before I got sick of it and went to the cafeteria to pick us up some food. The Goddess knew we needed some right now. I dug into a burger and chugged water. I felt much better once my belly was full. Nadine ate slower, as if savoring every bite. Usually when she ate like that, it meant she wasn't feeling well. She knew she had to eat something, but she wasn't sure she could stomach it.

We must've been waiting more than half an hour before someone finally arrived to speak with us.

"I hear you're having some scheduling conflicts," the nurse said.

Nadine sighed. "We've already been over this with the receptionist. I need an additional treatment."

"You were just in yesterday," the nurse pointed out.

"Look, she's not dumb. She knows her own body," I snapped.

"Here's the deal," Nadine stated. "I need my treatment, and I'm not leaving here until I get it. Find me a doctor. Run some tests. Do whatever you need to get me my dialysis."

The nurse looked skeptical, but she finally said, "I'll get a doctor, and we'll see what we can do."

Three hours passed. I counted. Not a single doctor showed up in the waiting room to talk to Nadine. I pressed the receptionist over and over again, but she kept saying the doctors were very busy and would get to

Nadine when they could. Apparently, because she wasn't passed out or convulsing on the floor, it wasn't an emergency worth their time.

Those fuckers.

It was well past dark when a doctor finally showed up. I was half convinced they'd only sent him because we hadn't left yet. His ID badge read *Dr. Smith*.

"The center is closing soon," Smith said. "There's no time for a four-hour treatment tonight, but tell you what. We'll run some tests to ease some of your worries."

"Fine," Nadine said. Though she was clearly exhausted, she managed to sound confident. She was planning to give the doctors a middle finger with her test results. Good for her.

Dr. Smith led her to a private room, and I followed. He took her blood pressure and drew some blood, then took a urine sample. "We'll have your test results expedited. Hopefully we'll have you out of here soon. There's nothing to worry about."

He was smug about it, as if he was about to prove her wrong.

I didn't know how long we'd sat there, but it had to be past closing before Dr. Smith returned. He wore a fallen expression, and I knew the results weren't good. He sat down at the computer and pulled up her test results.

"Your results are a bit unusual for what we'd expect," the doctor said. I nearly fell out of my chair, because I couldn't believe he'd admit it. "Your calcium levels are a bit outside the normal range, and you're testing anemic. Your Urea Reduction Ratio is much lower than we like to see. Usually we want it above sixty-five percent. Potassium levels... we definitely want to get that back into normal range."

"So can I get hooked up already?" Nadine asked, rather harshly. I didn't blame her. We were both quite pissed at the hospital staff.

"I'll schedule you first thing for tomorrow morning," Dr. Smith said. "We'll put you down for six a.m., and you'll be the first patient we see. How does that sound?"

Like shit, I wanted to say, but Nadine spoke first.

"I don't have any other options, do I?" Nadine practically sneered.

"It's the best we can do with our resources," Dr. Smith said. "Rest assured, you'll be back to normal in the morning. Have a good night, Miss Evers."

I was pissed when he left the room. It was like the doctors had deliberately waited to test her until the center closed to teach her a lesson.

"This is bullshit," I complained.

"I know," Nadine sighed. "But what else are we going to do? I can't exactly sneak in and hook myself up to the machines. I'm just ready to get some sleep so I can get up before six a.m. Let's go. I don't want to spend another second here than I have to."

My blood boiled, but Nadine somehow managed to stay calm. I didn't think she had the energy to fight it. I took her back to the school and led her back to my dorm room, where Oliver and Isa had been waiting for us. Grant was still in the infirmary, so we had the room to ourselves. I helped her shower and wash three days of forest grime out of her hair, then helped her into bed. She held Isa tight to her chest as she drifted off.

We woke to my alarm early the next morning, and I drove her to dialysis. After seeing her test results from the night before, the nurse apologized profusely. She kept talking like they were doing her a huge favor by scheduling her a few hours early.

This lady could go fuck herself.

Nadine remained quiet most of the morning, but I stayed with her. I noticed her wincing every now and then.

"Do you need anything?" I asked.

She shook her head. "Remind me never to miss a dialysis session again. The machine has to remove all this extra fluid that built up, and it's making me feel awful."

I got really worried and started to stand. "I'll call in a nurse."

Nadine shook her head. "No, it's just nausea and a headache. Some cramping. But I'll be all right."

I didn't believe her, so I didn't take my eyes off her for the next few hours. She seemed to be doing better by the time she finished, though she still wasn't one hundred percent.

"I want to visit Grant," Nadine said.

I thought she should go back to her dorm room and rest, but I wasn't going to argue with her. I really wanted to see how he was doing, too.

Grant was still in the infirmary, being held for observation. When we arrived in his room, Talia, Miles, and Chloe were already there.

Grant looked to be doing much better. He was sitting up in bed, nibbling on pancakes from the school cafeteria. A tiny orange kitten that couldn't be more than eight weeks old slept in his lap.

From what I knew, people could recover from a diabetic coma fairly quickly if treated immediately. We were lucky we got out of the stairwell when we did.

"How are you doing?" I asked.

Grant plastered on a big, silly smile. "Never better."

"Yeah, because that's the appropriate response after a diabetic coma," I said with an eye roll.

He shrugged. "I like to keep things interesting."

"Where'd the cat come from?" Nadine asked, gesturing to the orange kitten. She took a seat at the foot of Grant's bed since all the other chairs in the room were taken.

"She found her way in last night," Grant said, stroking the kitten's head. "I woke up to her licking my nose."

"Finally, thank the Goddess," Miles said. "I was wondering when your cat would finally show up."

"She was holding out for the proper incarnation, weren't you, Smelly Belly?" Grant scratched behind the cat's ears.

"You're naming her Smelly Belly?" I asked, cringing a little.

"It's short for Bella," Grant said.

Miles laughed. "Short for?"

"She likes it, okay!" Grant insisted.

"Do you have any idea who she's reincarnated from?" Chloe asked. Marley sat on her lap, purring.

"I'm not sure," Grant said. "No one close to me has died. I think she's an ancestor from a few generations back. I get the sense she's my great-great grandpa. A psychic once told me he was one of my spirit guides, and Bella gives off the same energy."

"She must've sensed that you needed her after you got stuck in the stairwell and passed out," Chloe said.

"Yeah, but it was worth it," Grant replied.

"Worth it?" I balked. "Grant, you went into a diabetic coma!"

"I got better! And we got the Wand," he pointed out.

Talia conjured the Seer Wand and twisted it around in her hands. "I'm really going to miss this Wand."

"What do you mean?" Nadine asked.

Talia shot her an incredulous look. "You're giving it to the Imperium Council, of course."

"No!" Nadine protested. "They already have one Wand. I'm not handing them another."

"But you *have* to!" Talia argued. "You need your transplant."

"That is the only way the priestesses will allow it to happen," Chloe added in agreement.

"I handed over the Alchemy Wand to pardon all of you," Nadine reminded them. "We've already failed to obtain one Wand. I'm not giving this one up."

"We'll find a way to get it back," Chloe insisted.

"Unless they continue to manipulate me," Nadine said. "They already know I'll hand over a Wand for my friends. If I give them this, they can use anything against me. This Wand belongs to the coven, and it's selfish to use it for my own gain."

"It's selfish of the priestesses to use it against you to get what they want," Chloe protested. "You need a kidney, and we're not settling for anything less."

"Chloe's right," I stated.

I wouldn't admit it out loud, but I was being selfish. I couldn't watch Nadine struggle for her dialysis again. Witnessing Nadine deteriorate after missing only one treatment was enough to convince me to trade in the Wand—regardless of the consequences.

"The way the doctors treated you last night is unacceptable," I stated. "The doctors are in control of your health, and I don't trust them one bit. What's worse, the priestesses could influence your doctors. They've already done it once by delaying your transplant. They could withhold dialysis again at any point, and you know the priestesses will make them if they're desperate enough. You might only survive a week without treatment. The priestesses can take the Seer Wand, but without all five, they have nothing. This transplant would buy us time to get them back."

Nadine chewed at her lower lip. She knew I was right, but she didn't want to admit it.

"We decided this when you handed over the Alchemy Wand," I reminded her. "You were supposed to use it to get your transplant. You've already made the noble decision once by giving up that bargain in exchange for your friends. Please, Nad. Do this for yourself this time."

"I'll get the transplant after we find the other Wands," Nadine suggested. "We'll restore the coven's magic, and the priestesses won't be able to control me anymore."

"We may not have time for that," I insisted. "The priestesses have already shown us what kind of power and influence they have over the healthcare system. If they decide to withhold your dialysis, it's over. This is the right choice."

"It's *my* Wand," Talia cut in. "It chose me. Which means I can do whatever I want with it. I want you to use it to get your transplant. If you don't turn it in to the priestesses, I will."

"All right," Nadine said, though she didn't sound too happy about it. She wanted to make the noble decision. I understood that. But she *needed* this transplant. We had no other options.

Talia placed the Seer Wand in Nadine's hand. "Go get your kidney."

"But the demon—" Nadine started.

"We'll figure out the rest once you've recovered," Talia pressed.

Nadine hesitated. "Lucas, will you come with me?"

She didn't have to ask me twice. Nadine didn't say much as we left the school and drove to the Imperium headquarters. I could tell she was still contemplating the implications of handing over the Seer Wand.

I hoped she'd go through with it.

We entered the building, and Nadine slowed halfway up the stairs, until she came to a complete stop on the landing. She fidgeted, and I could tell she was nervous.

I placed a gentle hand on her shoulder. "Take all the time you need."

Nadine pulled the Seer Wand from her cloak. She spun it around in her hands, never taking her eyes off it. "Are you sure this is the right thing to do?"

"Absolutely," I stated. There wasn't a future I'd accept where Nadine didn't get her transplant. We could keep fighting, wait out the priestesses, or find another doctor, but that would take time we didn't have. "I know you want to do what you think is right, but please consider that this *is* the right thing to do."

"I know it probably is," she said. "After all, how many times have people told me that you can't pour from an empty cup? I know I'll be able to serve the coven better if I gain control over my health and my life again

—to get rid of this threat the priestesses have over my head. But I just can't help but worry that it won't fix everything."

"Of course it won't," I said. "But I know you'll keep fighting. This is just one battle of many, but it's a battle we're going to win."

A hint of a smile touched her lips. "Thank you for being here, Lucas."

"Always," I promised, before pulling her into a hug.

We heard the door to the Imperium headquarters open. Nadine quickly shoved the Seer Wand back into her cloak.

"You're taking too long," Lilian sneered, her voice carrying down the stairwell. "I'm getting impatient, and rest assured, I *won't* make the same mistake twice."

A man chuckled, and my blood ran cold at the sound. *Professor Leto.*

"No, my dear *priestess*. I wouldn't expect you to," he said coolly. "You will have your precious Wands. Trust me."

Lilian laughed. "If you think for a moment that I trust you, you're sorely mistaken. Now, do the job we hired you for, or you can go straight back to hell."

"Very well, Priestess," Professor Leto said, before I heard his footsteps on the stairs.

There was nowhere for us to go. Leto stopped on the landing moments later, and an amused expression crossed his features as his eyes roamed over us. A shiver traveled down my spine.

"You best hope you have good news," he said with a light chuckle. "The priestesses are a bit… moody today."

"We'll take our chances," Nadine said stoically, not giving anything away.

Leto shrugged. "Very well. Don't say I didn't warn you."

Professor Leto continued down the staircase. I waited until his footsteps disappeared before I turned back to Nadine. "Sounds like he's not making any progress. Perhaps the priestesses will get sick of him and banish him themselves."

"I wouldn't count on it," she said. "They're desperate."

"Let's hope so, because we're going to need them to cooperate."

I took Nadine's hand and led her up the stairs. The door to the Imperium headquarters was open, and all conversation died when we stepped into the room. The three priestesses weren't alone, though.

Claudia Sinclair sat at the table with them, and she blew an exasperated breath when she saw Nadine.

"Dear Goddess," she mumbled.

Lilian looked annoyed. "If you're here to argue, save your breath. We're working very diligently on actually accomplishing change."

Nadine reached into her cloak. She stomped straight up to the priestesses and slammed the Seer Wand onto the table. "I'm here to fulfill our deal."

The priestesses' jaws dropped in unison, and the room went dead silent. They couldn't believe Nadine had found it.

Claudia scoffed. "And what is this? Some sort of *peace offering*?"

"Forgive me, but this doesn't concern you," Nadine stated firmly.

"I believe it does," Margaret countered. "Claudia is an interim priestess. She is privy to any and all information the Imperium Council has access to."

"Like Nadine was before she was inducted?" I blurted. It was clear the priestesses would manipulate the rules at any time to suit their favor.

"She is a student," Margaret sneered.

"And a priestess, nonetheless," I said.

"Never mind that," Nadine cut in. "The three of you agreed to expedite my kidney transplant, should I find another Oaken Wand. Surely as a new priestess, Claudia will honor the terms of that agreement. The Seer Wand, as promised."

Lilian gaped, and the other priestesses seemed equally speechless. I didn't think they expected Nadine to find another Wand so quickly. They were using her transplant as a threat, never realizing they might have to follow through on it.

Claudia reached across the table and picked up the Wand. I didn't know what I expected to happen, but she was a Seer. Perhaps she'd have some sort of influence over it.

But nothing happened. The Wand had rejected Claudia.

"How do we know it's real?" Claudia asked.

"It's real," Lilian said breathlessly. Claudia handed the Wand to her, and Lilian turned it over in her hands. "I've witnessed the Wands before, when I was first inducted to the council. This *is* the Seer Wand."

"Where did you find it?" Margaret demanded. "Knowing where your grandfather stashed this one may lead us to the others."

"He split them up; I'm sure of it," Nadine said. "But you're welcome to go looking for more. We found it inside the Vanishing Stairwell."

Charlotte shivered, like the very thought of going down there freaked her out. It wasn't like they would find anything else there, though—not since we stabilized the spell.

"Very well," Lilian said as she stood. "You've upheld your end of the bargain, and we shall fulfill ours. We will put forth our best effort to get you your transplant—"

"The agreement wasn't for your best effort," I snapped. "You promised Nadine results."

Lilian scoffed. "What do you expect me to do, *force* the doctors to comply? You've already been denied your psych evaluation once. I can't *make* your psychiatrist approve."

My hands curled into fists. "I'm sure you can *persuade* her. You promised Nadine the best doctors, the best Alchemists healing potions—all of it. Nadine's done everything you've asked. She's found two Wands in a short amount of time, which no one else has been able to do. If she dies, the chances of you getting another Wand go out the window. If you want Nadine to continue hunting these Wands, you need her to be healthy enough to do so."

Margaret pursed her lips and stood beside Lilian. "Nadine found the Seer Wand as agreed upon. She *will* get her transplant."

Lilian went quiet, but she seemed to back down. Finally, she cleared her throat. "We will speak with your doctors. We'll get your tests scheduled as soon as possible. Expect a call from your doctors soon."

I could hardly contain my excitement as we left the Imperium headquarters. I waited until we were at the bottom of the stairs and alone before I exclaimed, "We did it! We actually did it. Nadine, you're going to get your kidney! You'll go into remission!"

She beamed, and tears beaded in her eyes. "Oh my Goddess, I could!"

I grabbed her around the waist in a tight hug and spun her around. She laughed, sounding so relieved. I set her down, and she stilled. "There's still a chance my lupus could return."

"What did Dr. Yonker say? A three- to five-percent chance?" I asked. "I'm liking those odds."

Nadine smiled, then pulled me into a tight hug again. "I can't believe you're doing this for me."

I pressed a kiss to the top of her head. "Of course. You're my best friend, Nadine. I'd do anything for you."

If that meant giving her a piece of me, I'd gladly do it.

☾

A WEEK WAS ALL it took for us to get scheduled for surgery. I didn't know what the priestesses had said to Dr. Mack, but they'd convinced her to recommend me for the transplant. She wasn't *technically* my therapist anymore, but no one seemed to care. We were getting the transplant, and that was all that mattered.

We spent the following week preparing for surgery. We gathered our homework early so we could make it up while in recovery. The doctors did all kinds of blood tests, scans, and x-rays, and Nadine went to her last dialysis appointment the day before the surgery. I was required to take a course to ensure I understood the implications of donating my kidney, and they made us both write out a will in case we didn't make it. That made me a bit nervous, but the surgeon assured us it was merely a precaution.

"Living donor transplants have a high success rate," the doctor had told us. "Compared to a deceased donor kidney, risk of complications is much lower, and recovery time is quicker. You have nothing to worry about."

We sat on the floor in Nadine's dorm room the night before the surgery. Grant, Talia, and Mandy had joined us for a game of Clue. The last thing I wanted was for Nadine to feel worried or scared about the procedure, so I figured we could make it into a celebration. I was elated this was finally happening.

We couldn't stop laughing at Grant. He kept tossing popcorn in the air and trying to catch it in his mouth. Most kernels ended up across the room.

"I've got it this time," Grant insisted. "Check this out!"

He tossed another kernel, and it bounced off his cheek and flew across the game board. It landed down Mandy's dress. We all bust a gut laughing. I hadn't felt this at ease in a long time.

"Wow! Nice shot!" Mandy said, reaching into her dress and popping the kernel into her mouth.

283

"You guys are making a mess!" Talia was on her knees behind Nadine, braiding her hair. I thought it was a nice gesture, so Nadine wouldn't have to worry about it in the morning before surgery.

I reached into a bag of chips and shoved a handful in my mouth. Crumbs fell onto the floor.

"Me?" Grant balked. "Lucas is being a slob."

"I *have* to stuff my face," I teased. "Doc says I can't eat after midnight."

"He's right," Nadine said with a full mouth. She was eating some of the Pad Thai I'd brought over, and she had noodles hanging out of her mouth. "Doctor's orders. Your turn, Lucas."

I rolled the dice and moved across the game board.

"I can't believe this is happening!" Mandy exclaimed. "I mean, part of Lucas is going to be *inside* Nadine. It's crazy, isn't it?"

I shrugged. "I've been inside her before. Never this deep, though."

I'll never know how I managed to keep a straight face when I said it, but my friends roared in laughter.

"Hey, no one will ever beat your record for how deep you've been inside a girl," Nadine cracked.

"And you'll never beat your own record again," Talia laughed.

"*Deeper, Lucas,*" Grant mocked in a high-pitched voice. He could barely get it out between his deep-belly laughs. "It holds a whole new meaning."

"Was that supposed to be me?" Nadine asked with a smirk. "It's more like this: *Deeper, Lucas, you fucking animal!*"

Mandy howled, and tears started leaking out of my eyes from laughter.

"I'm gentle with her, I promise!" I insisted.

"Sometimes," Nadine added.

We couldn't stop laughing, and the sex jokes lasted another hour. It was midnight by the time we decided to call it a night.

"We can't eat anymore, so what's the point?" Nadine joked.

"I'm not ready for bed," Grant complained.

"Maybe we can move this party into another room," Talia said lowly, with a wiggle of her eyebrows.

"We all heard that!" Mandy shouted from near the door as she gathered her things.

"I don't care!" Talia laughed.

"If you guys want to go back to our room, I'll stay here with Nadine," I offered. The truth was, there was no place I'd rather be. Our twin-sized beds weren't really big enough for two people, but I sort of preferred it that way. I loved sleeping close to Nadine.

"Keep us updated," Talia said. "Let us know when you're both out of surgery."

"We will," Nadine promised.

Our friends left us alone in Nadine's room, and we got changed and ready for bed. We snuggled in close to one another, and Oliver and Isa curled up at our feet.

"Thank you for this wonderful night, Lucas," Nadine whispered blissfully.

I curled my arms even tighter around her. "Of course. I just want to make you happy."

"I hope that's not why you're giving me your kidney. You know I've always been happy with you, right? Even when I was sick. The transplant isn't going to change that. It's only going to change my body."

"I know that," I said, but I wasn't sure I *did* know until she said it. I knew she loved me, but it was a whole other feeling knowing she was *happy* with me. It made my heart sing, and I fell into a deep, peaceful slumber.

I woke up the next morning feeling incredible. I must've stirred a little, because Nadine stiffened in my arms.

"Everything all right?" she asked.

"It's great," I told her. "There's no better feeling than waking up next to you in the morning. I want to do it every morning, to be with you all the time."

"That'd be great, wouldn't it?"

"Hey, after today, a piece of me *will* be with you all the time," I teased.

She gave a light chuckle. "It will, won't it? I really am the luckiest girl in the world."

Nadine propped herself upright and planted a kiss on my lips. It was light at first, but neither of us wanted it to stop. I wrapped a hand around her neck and drew her closer. She pressed her lips against mine harder, and I pulled her on top of me. Nadine's tongue slid inside my mouth, while my hands roamed over her perfect ass—

I forced myself to draw away. "This isn't great for my blood pressure."

Nadine snickered. "No, the doctors wouldn't be too pleased about that, would they?"

"We should probably stop before things get too out of hand," I suggested. I didn't know how I managed, because all I wanted was to take her right here, right now.

"Technically the doctor didn't say anything about this kind of activity," Nadine pointed out. "But you're probably right. Just to be safe."

I rolled Nadine over again and got out of bed. My whole body seemed to buzz with energy, and I couldn't tell if I was excited or nervous. It had to be a bit of both. Call me crazy, because I was *thrilled* to be giving up one of my kidneys for her. Maybe it was selfish, because it made me feel like the hero, but I wanted nothing more than to help her.

We got ready and headed to the hospital together. They led us into a room with two beds, and the doctors came in and went over the procedure one more time.

"We'll take Lucas into surgery first. We'll make two holes in your abdomen, which we'll insert cameras into to inspect the kidney. If all looks well, we'll make another incision for the surgical probe to cut out the donor kidney. We'll isolate it and cut the blood vessels, and we'll take the kidney out of an incision in your belly button. This procedure will take about forty minutes. By then, Nadine will be prepped for surgery, and we'll place the new kidney into her body through the abdomen. It will sit lower than your other kidneys and attach to blood vessels near your leg. Your old kidneys will remain in the body, but the new kidney will take over function. Are you absolutely certain you want to go through with this? Once the procedure begins, there's no turning back."

I reached over my bedside and took Nadine's hand. Tears brimmed in her eyes when she looked at me, but she wore a big smile that made my heart flip in my chest. I smiled back and said, "I've never been more sure of anything. She'll get my kidney in this surgery, but this girl already has my heart."

"Aw." Nadine sighed, and she wiped a tear from her eyes.

It wasn't just some sappy poetry. It was true.

"Let's get started, then," the doctor said.

We had to sign a few more papers, then we changed into our hospital gowns. The doctors wheeled me down the hall and had me lay on a surgical table. They hooked me up to an IV, and the anesthesiologist squirted meds into my IV line.

It seemed like moments later, I was waking up in the recovery room. I had no concept that any time had passed at all. My head swam as I came out of the anesthesia, and I was vaguely aware of medical personnel moving around the room. I was hooked up to all kinds of tubes, including an IV for administering fluids, as well as a catheter for monitoring my urine output. Slowly, I became more aware of my surroundings, and the pain in my abdomen intensified as the anesthesia wore off. I ran my fingers over the bandages on my stomach, unable to believe I was one kidney short. They gave me painkillers, which made me really tired.

Only four hours had passed from the start of surgery to when they wheeled Nadine back into our room. I couldn't sit up, but I tilted my head to watch her sleep, knowing her body was already working on healing. The doctors said my kidney would start working for her quickly. I hoped it was already filtering her blood.

Nadine woke two hours after me. She stirred a little, before turning her head to look at me. When her eyes met mine, a light smile touched her lips.

"It's done?" she asked, sounding relieved.

I nodded. "We're out of surgery. You've got a new kidney."

Tears filled her eyes. It wasn't a brim of tears she could hold back, either. These were huge, grateful tears that splashed down her cheeks and onto her pillow.

"I don't know how I'll ever thank you, Lucas," she said, her voice breaking.

"You don't have to," I told her gently. "I don't want you feeling like you have to do anything to make it up to me, Nad. It's yours now."

As was I. Perhaps I was still high on drugs, or maybe I was overwhelmed with emotion, but when I looked at her lying in that hospital bed, I knew for certain I had never loved her more.

At that moment, one thing became crystal clear to me. I'd given her a piece of me, but I was ready to give her all of me.

When the time was right, I was going to ask Nadine to marry me.

nadine

SIXTEEN

Recovering from the kidney transplant was difficult, yet one of the most hopeful times of my life. Lucas and I were put on bedrest for a few days, with instructions to walk no more than an hour a day, and to avoid the stairs. The nurses helped us shower and dress, and within three days, Lucas had already gone home. I was out of the hospital the next week.

I came back often for follow-up appointments, blood tests, and prescription refills. The doctors said my blood pressure was getting better and that my blood tests looked good. They were confident that everything was healing well and that my body had accepted Lucas's kidney. After a few weeks, my check-ups became less frequent, and my arthritis caused by my lupus had gone into remission.

It was like I'd been given a new body, and with it, a new lease on life. I wasn't sure I ever believed it was possible. It was so strange, because I'd been fighting for my life for years, and now, all of a sudden, my body had nothing left to battle against. Everything felt completely new, and soon, I was doing tasks easily my body had struggled to perform before. Errands that would've taken me hours before took minutes. The medicine I had to take consistently was no longer a worry.

I wasn't sure how I felt about it all. I was thrilled to be better—sure. And I couldn't be more thankful that I had come out alive at the end of all this. But now that I'd gone into remission, it felt like I was missing a part of who I was. The only thing I could do was use my newfound health to help other sick people as much as possible.

The *Miriamic Messenger* had requested an interview about the transplant. Lucas and I had agreed only because we knew they'd write about us regardless. They made the whole thing into a piece about the priestesses and how noble they were for advocating for my health. At least they'd painted Lucas in a good light, which was more than I'd hoped for.

The snow had begun to melt as we entered the first week in April. Our friends had continued investigating the Wands and vanquishing demons, but the transplant had delayed our research by weeks. Professor Leto hadn't killed again, thankfully, but that didn't mean he wasn't going to soon. The Coven's Shield hadn't met since the transplant. I didn't think anyone wanted to bother Lucas and me while we were recovering.

I was finally able to sleep through the night—until I was roused from my sleep by the sound of my phone. Isa stirred as I rolled over and checked my screen. My stomach instantly dropped. It was the council.

I answered, and Priestess Margaret spoke hastily. "Nadine, we have business to attend to. You're to come to the Imperium headquarters immediately."

"It's the middle of the night," I groaned.

"This is urgent," she pressed.

Talia stirred from across the room. "Is everything all right?"

"It's the council," I told her.

"If that's your boyfriend, tell him to stay home," Margaret said. "This is an Imperium Council matter alone. We will discuss it when you arrive."

Margaret didn't let me get a word in before she hung up on me. My heart hammered as I got out of bed and threw some clothes on. Whatever this was must be super important if they wanted *my* help with it. Priestess Margaret had almost sounded… scared. Were people revolting?

I wouldn't put it past them. The priestesses had been downright evil with the changes they'd been implementing, all in the name of *improving* the coven. They'd shut down two nursing homes, insisting there was enough room at the others. It was an attempt to save money, but really, all it had done was forced our elderly to live in closer quarters. They caught illnesses quicker than ever before, and for many of them, their last days were spent in bed trying to get over a cold.

The priestesses had shut down all funding for public parks and had cut funds to the utilities and water departments. They'd approved the funds to build a new community center, but they were sourcing all their lumber from out of state because it was *cheaper*, instead of hiring the main lumber company in the Miriamic Coven. I argued that would take money out of the coven, and they'd actually lose money through taxes. The priestesses didn't see it that way and just kept arguing about how much money they'd save doing it *their* way.

I pulled my cloak tightly around me and hurried to my car. Isa followed closely. The other priestesses were already at the Imperium headquarters when I arrived, but they weren't seated at their meeting table like normal. Instead, they were all standing. Margaret paced around the room, looking frantic.

"This has to work. It's our only option!" Margaret insisted. "The fae must know they can't get away with this."

I felt all the blood drain from my face. "What's going on?"

Lilian pursed her lips. She wore a permanent expression of dissatisfaction, but this was worse. Claudia had her hands on her hips, and Charlotte crossed her arms. They tried to hide it, but everyone looked very scared. I could tell something was seriously wrong.

"Take a seat," Margaret said. "We have much to discuss."

My guts twisted as I sat around the table with them. What could possibly make them so scared?

Was it possible the fae had launched some sort of attack? Had the priestesses discovered information that pointed to the fae as the culprits of the Waning? There were so many possibilities. I tried to calm myself until I knew what was truly going on.

Margaret's voice shook as she spoke. "Here's what we know. A Miriamic family visited Paris this week for a baking competition their daughter had entered. As you know, France is not far from Malovia. The family went missing yesterday, and our spies were unable to locate them until it was too late. Several hours ago, the fae king Elijah Zlodia hung the family in the main square of the capital city in a very public execution."

My whole body froze. "Kenna Farlane's dead?"

I could see her sweet face in my mind. I'd only met her a few times. She worked at the Cat-fé on campus and made the most beautiful cupcakes. I remembered her talking about how excited she was for the baking competition. I didn't understand how the fae could do this. I'd met a group of fae outside the boundaries of Octavia Falls last semester. They'd been kind to us, and we helped them. How could their society be so ruthless?

Margaret nodded, and her voice filled with anger. "Kenna, as well as her parents Alden and Rumina Farlane were kidnapped and hanged by the fae. Their crime? Belonging to the Miriamic Coven."

She pointed a remote at the TV above the fireplace, and a recording played across the screen. A large crowd gathered in a town square much bigger than ours. In the center of the square stood a gallows, and three people were already standing there with nooses around their necks. They were surrounded by dozens of guards, as if these witches were dangerous criminals. I knew Kenna! She wouldn't hurt a fly. My stomach hollowed as I witnessed tears stream down Kenna's face.

A man stepped in front of them and began reading off a scroll. "Alden, Rumina, and Kenna Farlane, you have been judged. By order of the king, you have been sentenced to death, for the crime of having witch blood. Your sentence will be carried out immediately."

Kenna's whole body shook. "We were just taking a vacation to Paris! We weren't anywhere near Malovia!"

"Silence!" the fae man screamed. "There is nothing that can save you now, abomination."

Rumina somehow remained calm for her daughter, despite the noose around her neck. "It's all right, Kenna. We'll be in Alora soon enough."

"Mother Miriam! Goddess!" Kenna sobbed. "Help u—"

I flinched away from the screen, but it was too late. The fae pulled a lever, and Kenna's voice was silenced by the noose. Their necks snapped all at once, and their feet dangled above the ground.

This had happened hours ago, but it felt like I was witnessing it in real-time. A gaping hole opened in my chest, and I felt the loss permeate my body. Isa curled into my arms, like she couldn't watch it, either.

Claudia slammed her fist down on the table. "This is an act of war! We must retaliate immediately."

"With what troops?" Lilian demanded. "Please, Claudia. Use your head."

"We have the magic to beat them," Claudia argued.

"Without the Oaken Wands or more Curse Breakers, we cannot stand up to the fae," Charlotte cut in.

"I'm afraid I agree," Margaret said. "The power of their monarchy has recently shifted, and we've already lost our opportunity to form alliances with the winners of the King's Contest."

"What's the King's Contest?" I asked.

"It's a fae tradition," Margaret explained. "When it is time to pass the monarchy down, the fae hold a deadly competition in which eligible couples battle for the crown. The winners this time are young and impulsive. Elijah Zlodia, and his mate Gabriella Ciar, are ruthless leaders with no experience or understanding on how to run a nation. Coven spies report they are growing an army, despite political upheaval in their own nation. Their numbers are greater than ours. There are enough fae to cover an entire European nation. Our town may be large, but we're no country. If we retaliate, we will surely doom our people."

"We can't sit around and do nothing!" Claudia protested.

"We won't!" Margaret insisted. "The fae fear us because we have slaughtered them in the past. Where they perform simple illusions, we perform *real* magic that can poison their blood and turn their dead against them. But our magic is growing weaker. They are a war nation, with armor and weapons we do not have. They train to kill from a young age, and we are not equipped to go against their military. Until we can bring an end to the Waning, we cannot fight the fae. *But* they know nothing of the Waning, and we must keep it that way. We must let them believe we have the power and the means to annihilate them at any moment. If we don't draw a line in the sand now, the fae will find any opportunity to attack. Their fear is our greatest weapon."

"And how *exactly* do we convince them of this?" Claudia asked.

"We will send them a message," Margaret stated confidently, like she'd already thought this through. She conjured a spellbook, though it was unlike the ancient spellbooks I'd seen before. This one was modern and looked more like a college textbook. "There's a spell we can perform that will allow us to hack into the fae's broadcasting system. The spell requires a member from all five Casts, and I'm confident we can do it."

"What will we say?" Charlotte asked.

"Leave that to me," Margaret said. "We must perform the spell immediately to show the fae we will not stand for this. Charlotte, get the camera."

Charlotte hurried to set up a camera on a tripod, and we all surrounded it in a circle. Margaret was the only one in the frame, but off camera, we all held hands. We began reciting the spell from the book, and I stabilized our energies like I'd done so many times before.

Once our magic flowed in sync, it began to swell. I could feel it growing, traveling over all of the Miriamic coven, then wider, until it reached across the Atlantic ocean. Visions passed behind my lids, like flashes of movies playing on a screen. I realized it *was* television. Claudia was a Seer, and her powers allowed me to see where our magic had connected. We were tapped into a system—broadcasts across the world, I was sure. I guided our magic through channel after channel, searching for the fae network.

Somehow, I just *knew* when I had it. It must've been part of the spell. At our will, the fae's news broadcast stopped, and we began broadcasting our own message.

"My name is Priestess Margaret," Margaret stated to the camera. I could see the broadcast behind my eyes—see her features from the angle of the camera—and I knew the fae in Malovia must be seeing the same thing.

"I am a member of the Imperium Council, the Miriamic Coven's highest order," Margaret continued. "I am here to deliver a message to every fae—shifter, sorceress, and child. The Imperium has witnessed what you have done to members of our coven, and the despicable acts you put them through last night before their disgraceful execution. The Miriamic Coven would like to say that this heinous crime will not go ignored. Our witches and warlocks are ready to fight, and our magic is strong. Each of our kind is ready to die defending our coven's right to survival. Should the fae move in on our coven again, we will retaliate. From henceforth, if a fae should take another witch life, we will consider it an act of war."

Margaret narrowed her eyes at the camera, looking deadly. "King Elijah, I speak directly to you. You are a young king—don't be getting yourself involved in a battle that you cannot handle. We have beaten you once, and if necessary, we will rally the other supernatural races against you so that we may win again, and this time, we will be sure to wipe the fae off the face of the Earth. If you wish for the vulgar stain of your race to remain on this planet, you will immediately cease all further acts of violence against our coven. You have been warned."

Margaret dropped her hands, and the spell ended. The vision behind my lids vanished, and I felt our magic recede.

Margaret stood. "The fae will hesitate to attack. It is of the utmost importance now more than ever to bring an end to the Waning. We cannot fight the fae without magic."

Lilian scoffed. "That'd be much easier if we had any answers."

"Then we will just have to find the Oaken Wands faster. We will have to *motivate* people." Margaret shot a quick glance at me, like she'd forgotten for a second I was in the room.

She was talking about Professor Leto. I'd delivered them two Wands, and it sounded like he had yet to deliver one. The priestesses still thought I was ignorant to their plan.

Margaret calmed her tone. "It's a feat in itself that we managed to send that broadcast. We must fix this before the fae force us to send another. I trust no one will speak of the incident outside these quarters."

"The coven has a right to know," I argued. "Kenna and her parents deserve a memorial, and people need to know if they're in danger."

"What good will it do?" Margaret snapped. "We don't have the means to fight a war. Telling them the truth will only incite a panic."

"If it comes down to a war between us and the fae like you fear, our people will be unprepared to defend themselves if we lie," I said.

"And what shall you have us do?" Margaret demanded. "Admit we can't defend them? We are the Imperium Council. We are supposed to be as powerful as witches come, and we can't even fight off the king of the fae. I refuse to admit our weakness!"

For the first time, the woman actually sent chills down my spine. She was scared of the fae, and that made her even more dangerous than she already was.

"If I may," Priestess Lilian cut in. "Perhaps Nadine is right."

Had hell frozen over? Priestess Lilian had *never* agreed with me.

"The coven *should* know what we're up against," Lilian stated. "We must gather support and build our own army. In the meantime, we will hold off the fae until we are strong enough to fulfill our threats."

Hours passed as we discussed our options, but it all came down to finding the Oaken Wands and restoring our power. I left the Imperium headquarters at sunrise, still trying to wrap my head around the fact that Kenna was gone. I didn't know her well, but she'd gone to school with us.

I couldn't get the image of her body dangling from the gallows out of my head. It was devastating that she'd never return.

I turned down the road to the school, and the scene ahead of me stole my attention. A group had gathered near the main gate's entrance, and I heard people screaming. Storm clouds had rolled in overhead, and in the dimming light, I could just barely make out something hanging from the archway above the main gate.

I slammed on the brakes, and my whole body became a statue. I had to be seeing things. It looked like Kenna, hanging from the gallows all over again. This didn't feel real. Kenna had been hanged in Malovia. It couldn't be happening here, too.

Isa meowed loudly. My whole body shook as I pulled off to the side of the road and parked my car. I climbed out of the vehicle to hear cries echoing through the forest. My blood turned to ice, and I began racing toward the front gate. When I got close, I could finally see that it wasn't Kenna.

It was Lena.

She hung from a noose, her body swaying in the wind. First Kenna, and now Lena? How did this happen?

Mortana girls who'd been friends with Lena sobbed loudly. People whispered, but it was like their voices didn't exist. All I could do was stare as horror rocked my body.

"Nadine!" I heard my name and managed to tear my gaze off Lena's body to see Lucas, Talia, and Grant racing toward me. They pushed through the crowd, and Lucas came to a dead stop when he saw Lena. I witnessed the moment the shocked pain entered his eyes. He and Lena didn't speak anymore, but she *was* his ex-girlfriend. He'd loved her once... and now she was gone.

Lucas didn't take his eyes off Lena as he wrapped me tightly in his arms. All three of my friends looked like they'd been in the middle of something when they heard the news. Talia wore a nice top, but was still in her pajama pants, and Lucas's hair was still wet from his shower. Grant clutched the music box tightly in his hands, like he'd been in the middle of tinkering with it.

"We just heard what happened," Lucas said in a strained voice. "Did you see anything?"

I shook my head. "I just got here. I don't know—"

"Move aside!" someone shouted. Professor Hernandez pushed through the crowd, followed by Professor Warbright. They took one look at Lena's body and looked like they were about to hurl. Professor Hernandez kept it together better than Warbright, who had gone pale.

"Everyone back to your dorms," Hernandez barked. "This woman deserves some respect!"

Nobody moved. We couldn't take our eyes off the horrifying scene as our professors cut Lena down from the rope. More people emerged from the school, until the crowd was five times bigger than when I arrived.

A car pulled up, and the priestesses emerged. "Everybody stand back!" Priestess Lilian barked. She threw her hands upward, and the crowd was forced apart by her telekinetic abilities. Bodies pressed against me on all sides.

The priestesses stopped beneath the iron archway and looked up at the piece of rope still tied there. They took one look at the bruises on Lena's neck before whirling toward the crowd.

"This is a despicable act, and those responsible will surely meet the noose as well!" Lilian spat. "Last night, the fae kidnapped and hanged three of our people in the Dolinska town square. Alden, Rumina, and Kenna Farlane are dead. And now another life has been taken."

Gasps traveled around the crowd, and Lucas pulled me even tighter to his chest.

"The fae have breached our protection spell!" Gwen panicked.

"That's not possible," Gregory insisted.

"Our magic is weaker than ever!" Ryan retorted. He stood on the opposite side of the crowd, shaking. It looked like he was ready to chop a fae's head off. "Our protection spell is failing, and the fae got in!"

"This is indeed the work of the fae," Margaret said. "We are a strong people, and we will not let them get away with this. I want every Executor to search the town. Find the fae!"

My heart turned to stone in my chest. The crowd began to disperse, and I turned to my friends. "The priestesses are lying. Even with the Waning, our protection spell is strong. I can feel it."

"Why lie about this?" Talia asked.

"To cause a panic," I said. "Kenna and her parents *were* hanged. That's why the council called me last night. Margaret didn't want to tell the coven about the fae, but Lilian insisted. She must've seen this as an opportunity to scare people into compliance. No one's going to question their authority if it's all in the name of defeating the fae. They're using the situation to their advantage. I *knew* Lilian would never agree with me. This is twisted."

"Do you think they hung Lena to scare people?" Grant wondered.

I shook my head. "They have a recording of Kenna and her parents' death. That should be enough to scare people. But you're right. Lena's death is too convenient…"

I began scanning the crowd, and my gaze fell upon Professor Leto. While everyone else was leaving the scene, Leto leaned against the brick wall near the entry gate, watching on with a satisfied smirk.

I grabbed Lucas's arm. "It was Leto! It's traumatic enough that Kenna died, but the knife cuts deeper if we all see it first-hand. He's feeding off the trauma. The priestesses *know* he did this, and they're using the fae to cover it up."

I let go of Lucas's hand and pushed my way through the moving crowd toward Professor Leto.

"Nadine." Lucas rushed behind me and stopped me before I could get to the demon. I paused when I saw Gregory approach Professor Leto. He said a few words I didn't hear, until the crowd dispersed enough that I caught the last words he uttered.

"I'll get right on it," Gregory said. "It's been nice working with you, Professor."

Lucas and I exchanged a horrified glance. When I looked back toward Leto, Gregory had already taken off.

"Gregory's working with him!" I realized, my stomach sinking. "It all fits. Gregory was at the scene of the first crime. And he's a necromancer, which means he could've caused The Hearse accident by planting that skeleton in the road. And now he's here. Leto must've offered him something as payment, and you *know* Gregory would take it."

"This wasn't a demon deal, remember?" Talia said. "My crystal ball showed some other sort of spell."

"If his spell marks people for death, Gregory could be the one carrying it out," I theorized.

Lucas's face paled. He knew I was on to something. "Let's go find out."

We followed the crowd of students back inside the school, never once taking our eyes off Gregory. A bunch of people crowded around the windows in the Main Foyer to watch what was going on outside, but most of the crowd dispersed. Gregory turned down the hall, and we followed. We kept close, but far enough away that he wouldn't notice us.

"Where's he going?" Lucas whispered after we turned several hallways. It didn't seem Gregory was going in any particular direction.

Gregory turned down another hall, and we hurried behind him. My heart jumped as we turned the corner and nearly ran straight into him. Gregory stood there glaring at us, though his confident expression faltered.

"Why are you following me—?" he demanded, but Lucas grabbed him by the collar to cut him off.

He shoved him against the wall. "You're working for Professor Leto, aren't you?"

Gregory flinched away. "Y—yes."

I was surprised he admitted it so easily. "You're working for him *willingly?*"

"What's it to you?" Gregory snapped.

"People are *dying,*" Lucas sneered, slamming him against the wall again. "You're going to tell us *everything.*"

"Everything?" Gregory squeaked.

"If you don't want to be the next one hanging from a noose, you'll talk," Lucas threatened. He conjured a high-powered battle orb and held it close to Gregory's face. Gregory trembled, looking like he was about to piss his pants. "How are you involved in the deaths?"

"I'm sorry!" Gregory cried. "I never meant for anyone to die. First, it was my nan when I was six. I didn't mean to leave those toy cars at the top of the stairs. I never told anyone that's why she tripped and broke her neck. It screwed me up, and I've spent every day of my life regretting it. Then I was in the hospital for my heart condition, and the boy next me went into surgery and never came out. I think I cursed him or something. I didn't mean to. And when I went in for my asthma meds, the doctor just keeled over right there. They said it was a heart attack, but I think death follows me wherever I go. It's gotta be why I'm Mortana. Maybe I'm a necromancer, because all my life, I've been desperate to raise the dead. I didn't think anyone would die when I started dealing nightshade, but they did, and I'm sorry!"

"Why'd you start working for Professor Leto?" Lucas demanded. "What did he offer you?"

"A recommendation letter. That's all!" Gregory insisted.

"You're killing people for a *fucking recommendation letter*!?" Lucas erupted.

"Killing people?" Gregory asked. "No, of course not! You think these deaths have something to do with my internship with Professor Leto?"

My friends and I exchanged a quick glance. "Your internship?" I asked.

"All I do is paperwork. Goddess, I'm not killing anyone!" Gregory shoved Lucas off of him. "Maybe I *am* cursed; death follows me wherever I go. But I'm no murderer."

"Prove it," Grant sneered. He got up in Gregory's face and pointed a finger at him. "You were there when Professor Perez died."

"So were a lot of people!" Gregory spat.

"Someone planted a fake reaper in front of The Hearse when it crashed. You're a necromancer!" Grant accused.

"So is half my Cast—will you get that thing away from me!?" Gregory shrank back as Grant got even closer. He trembled at the sight of the music box in Grant's hands.

Grant hesitated. "What, this?"

He held up the music box, and Gregory winced. "That thing is cursed!"

I furrowed my brow. I'd touched the music box before. It wasn't cursed. "What are you talking about?"

Gregory swallowed. "Professor Leto keeps records, okay? I wasn't supposed to be snooping around, but well…"

It was Gregory. Of *course* he was getting himself into trouble.

"Most of it didn't make sense," he said in a rush. "I don't know what his notes meant. What I *do* know is I found a description of a music box just like that, and it said the box was cursed!"

"What kind of curse?" I demanded.

"I—I don't know," he stammered. "It didn't say."

Grant handed me the box, and I looked it over. I didn't feel anything at first, then I sensed a faint bit of magic I hadn't felt before. "There may be something here…"

Grant's features dropped. "What kind of curse? I've been touching that thing all semester!"

"It's not very strong," I remarked. "I don't even know if it's enough to hurt you. But this could be why you haven't been able to fix it. Gregory's telling the truth."

Lucas relaxed his grip on Gregory's shirt, then raked his hands through his hair. "For Alora's sake, Gregory, get some help."

"What, like a shrink?" Gregory spat, sounding offended.

"Yes," Lucas answered seriously. "It sounds like you really need one. I know a great therapist when you're ready to talk to someone."

Gregory crossed his arms. "I'm doing fine on my own, thanks."

He wasn't interested in our help. We let him go, and the four of us turned our attention to the music box. I felt the smallest hints of a curse rattling around inside of it, so I drew it out and transformed the spell. It was so small that only a few sparks flew from my fingers.

"We can fix it now!" Grant exclaimed. "I've got the parts in my room."

"If there's a spirit inside, we'll need Miles to draw him out and interpret for us," I said. I pulled out my phone and began typing a message. "Grant, you go get the parts. I'll get everyone together, and we'll meet at the Gravestone ASAP."

Within ten minutes, a group had gathered in our secret room. Not everyone had gotten my message, but Miles, Chloe, and Mandy had shown up.

I stood at the head of our meeting table. "By now, I'm sure you've all heard what happened to Lena. The priestesses claimed it was the fae, but we believe Leto did this. We're still not sure exactly how his spell works or how to stop it. Based on what we learned from Angelica, it's possible Adrik Harvey banished Leto when he was in Octavia Falls forty years ago. Up until now, Adrik's spirit has been stuck inside Talia's music box. Grant fixed the box, and we're here to get answers."

Talia stood with the music box in her hands. "This is a vengeful spirit, and he may be confused. Are you all ready for this?"

"Ready as I'll ever be," Miles said.

"Let's see what's inside that box," Mandy agreed.

Talia took a deep breath and opened the box—and my heart stalled in horror. I didn't know what I expected to happen, but it certainly wasn't *this*. Spirits came flooding out of the box, swirling around the room in their spectral form. There had to be dozens of them, screeching as if they were being chased by an axe murderer. The lights overhead flickered, then went out. The ghostly voices overlapped one another, and I couldn't quite make out what they were saying.

A woman's spirit slowed in front of me, glowing slightly so that I could make out her features. *"It was him!"* she screamed. *"He did this to us!"*

She was there for a mere second before she lurched away, pulled by an invisible force with the others as they swirled around the room like a cloud of smoke.

Another man flung himself at me. *"Leave, demon scum. Or die!"*

It had to be Adrik. The man flicked his wrist, and an invisible blow landed against my chest. Lucas and I were both blasted off our feet, and we slammed against the wall. The air knocked out of my lungs, and I gasped as I hurried to right myself. Lucas was at my side in an instant, helping me up. It all happened so fast.

Miles threw his hands over his ears and shouted, "Talia, close the box!"

But Talia couldn't hear us. Though she stood firmly in place, her eyes had rolled back into her skull, and her eyelids fluttered rapidly. She must've been having intense visions.

"The demon did this!" one of the ghosts screamed.

Chloe and Grant rushed forward at the same time. Chloe grabbed the box and slammed it shut. In the same moment the screaming vanished, Talia collapsed. Grant reached her just in time to catch her, and he gently lowered her to the ground.

"Tal!" Grant cried. Talia blinked a few times at the sound of her name, and she gave a shudder.

I stripped off my cloak. "Let's get her comfortable."

Grant propped Talia up in his lap, and I draped my cloak over her. Her shivers didn't seem so intense anymore.

"What *was* that?" Mandy asked.

"It was all of them," Talia whispered. "All the souls trapped inside."

"Adrik wasn't the first, then," Miles said.

Horror filled Talia's eyes. "They showed me visions that were so different from the box's own memories. These memories were… bloody and horrible."

"Who *were* these people?" Chloe wondered. "They said the demon did this. Could the box be trapping all the demon's victims?"

"If it was, why isn't the Lady of the Tower trapped?" Miles pointed out.

Talia shuddered. "They were victims of the Pinewood Manor Massacre."

The room went dead silent as we took it all in. We'd been to Pinewood Manor before, the night we fought the witches who'd killed two young boys. That place was creepy as hell, on account of the mass murder that took place there years ago. The owner, Leroy Pinewood, had gone insane and murdered all the guests at his dinner party. No witch or warlock wanted anything to do with that haunting.

"Monica mentioned the box came from Pinewood Manor when I bought it," Talia said. "I thought it was just an antique, you know? I never thought there were other spirits trapped inside."

"Does anyone know exactly when the Pinewood Manor Massacre took place?" Lucas asked.

Grant's features paled. "Around forty years ago... the same time Angelica and Adrik died. The same time the demon was here..."

Mandy bit her lower lip. "Grant and I passed it in our research, but we never thought it was connected. The reports said he was a troubled man; the police didn't even *suspect* demon activity. I just don't get what would possess Leroy to work with the demon."

It hit me like a battle orb to the chest. "A literal *possession!*" I realized. We'd been looking at this all wrong. "The demon's spell doesn't mark you for death. The demon is possessing people! Leroy must've been one of his victims. He was under the influence of the demon's spell. Angelica said the demon used a spell to poison her. He could've possessed an Alchemist to do his dirty work. And Adrik must've been possessed when he killed himself."

"Leto has an alibi for every murder that happened this semester," Chloe said. "How does this possession work?"

"I'm not sure," I said. "But figuring it out might help us stop it."

"What if it wasn't Adrik who banished the demon like we assumed, but Leroy Pinewood?" Lucas wondered.

"You think he sent a demon to the Abyss after he killed twenty-six dinner guests and then himself?" Miles sounded skeptical.

"Maybe he won in the end," I pointed out. "We have to at least investigate. If we know how the demon was banished before, we can banish him again."

"You're suggesting we go to Pinewood Manor?" Grant asked, his voice squeaking a little.

I didn't blame him for being nervous. It was the most haunted place in all the coven. We were lucky we hadn't seen a ghost the night we were there, but we'd been in the east wing, and the murders had happened in the west wing. I shuddered to think what we might find there.

"Where else are we going to find answers?" I asked.

Talia pushed herself upright. Color had returned to her face, and she was looking much better. "The spirits in my music box are too traumatized to talk. I say we go to Pinewood Manor and see if we can figure out what happened that night."

We all agreed, and soon we were pulling up in front of Pinewood Manor. A shiver ran down my spine as the dilapidated mansion came into view. Half the mansion had collapsed the night we'd faced the three evil witches and confronted Professor Carlisle about the missing kids. A spell had exploded half the mansion, and we'd barely gotten out in time. The remaining half looked like it might blow over once the storm rolled in.

I slowed my car behind Talia's. We climbed out of our vehicles and approached the front doors. My hands curled tighter around the drawstring bag I held, which contained salt to ward off ghosts. Lucas lifted one of the iron fireplace pokers we'd borrowed from a Seer classroom. Iron was another weapon we could use against evil spirits. We weren't the only ones armed with weapons, either. All the girls carried salt bags, and the guys had iron. No one made a move to open the doors first. We all hesitated, waiting for someone else to go first. Talia shivered, and Grant wrapped an arm around her.

"I can hear their screams," Talia said. "The memories are very intense, very brutal."

"Should we open the music box?" Miles wondered. "Maybe the ghosts will remember something."

"And traumatize them more?" Grant asked skeptically. "That's dangerous. They could attack."

"There have to be other clues here," I said. "Let's see what we can find inside before we unleash two dozen vengeful spirits on ourselves."

I turned toward the double doors. When I touched the handle, a feeling of horror grew in my veins. Although the victims were trapped inside

Talia's music box, the terror from that night had permeated these walls. My heart hammered, and my knees trembled. Every instinct told me to turn back—to run as far away from this property as I possibly could.

But the thought of Leto taking any more victims scared me even more. So I twisted the handle and stepped inside. I entered a large foyer, which was cast in dark shadows as the storm clouds darkened overhead. Wind howled from somewhere upstairs—at least, I *thought* it was the wind. It almost sounded like screaming. A shiver traveled down my spine, and my breath turned to vapor in the air. Lucas followed me inside and wrapped a warm arm around me.

"It's just part of the haunting," he reassured me. "It can't hurt us."

I wasn't sure I believed him. I turned back to our friends and gestured for them to follow. "Come on. Let's look for clues."

Chloe wrapped her arms around herself, and her eyes wandered the foyer. "Very creepy. I like it."

Mandy took careful steps. "It's a bit much for me. If people weren't dying, my ass would be hightailing it in another direction."

"You and me both, sister," Miles agreed.

We took another timid step inside—

Bang!

I nearly jumped out of my skin. We whirled around in unison to see that the front doors had slammed shut. The click of a lock met my ears.

"I take it that wasn't the storm," Grant said in a shaky tone.

Miles yanked on the doors, but they didn't budge. "Um, doesn't the legend say no one gets out of here alive?"

"Someone had to," Mandy pointed out. "They've salvaged antiques from this place."

"But they apparently left the bodies," Chloe said in a hollow tone. She peeked down a hallway, and I followed to get a good look. My stomach twisted when I saw a skeleton lying against the wall. The body had decomposed, but I could still make out the decaying fabric of the woman's dress.

"Of course they left them," Miles said sadly. "You can sell the antiques for a pretty penny. All you're going to get from taking these bones is a vengeful spirit."

"The spirits are trapped in the music box, so we should be safe," Lucas said. "We've been here before and got out then. We can do it again. Once we find out how to banish the demon, we'll find another exit and help the spirits cross over. Let's get moving."

We passed by endless doorways. Some were closed, and others hung off their hinges. Various windows had been smashed, and debris lay everywhere. The further we walked, the more chilling the air became. Lightning flashed from outside, followed by a roll of thunder.

"Wait," Talia said, stopping dead in her tracks. She was still wrapped in Grant's arms, but she had a confident look on her face. She pointed down a nearby hall. "There's something down there. I can't make out the memories, but it's strong."

Lucas stepped in front of everyone else. "Let's check it out."

I followed behind him, and the floorboards creaked under my weight. We passed by a few empty rooms before Talia pointed to the door at the end of the hall.

"Something happened in there," she stated.

We approached the room slowly. I held my breath as Lucas reached for the door. In one swift motion, he flung it open.

I didn't know what I expected to find—maybe ghosts—but the room was empty. We stepped into a huge bedroom with a ceiling that stretched up two stories. A big four-poster bed sat along one wall, surrounded by a bunch of other furniture. The whole room was in disarray. One of the posts had been ripped off the bed, and the blankets lay in a heap on the ground. Glass littered the floor beneath a frame that used to be a mirror.

"Can you tell what happened here, Tal?" Grant asked.

Talia began walking around the room, running her fingers along the furniture. "There are a lot of memories here," she said. "It's hard to separate them."

Miles looked under an old lamp shade. "What exactly is it we're looking for?"

I touched the windowsill. "It could be anything—"

A scream cut me off. Everyone froze in place as the sound of footsteps came sprinting down the hall. The door slammed into the wall and shuttered as two ghostly forms raced into the room. My friends scattered as they ran to hide from the vengeful spirits. As the ghosts entered the room, the scene around us changed. The mirror that had been shattered was whole again, and the post on the bed that had been broken stood upright.

An older woman, who had to be around seventy years old, ran into the room. She stumbled against a dresser, and several items scattered onto the floor. A music box like Talia's rattled across the top of the dresser. The woman kept running, heading straight toward me. I grabbed a handful of salt from my bag and threw it at her, but nothing happened.

Lucas grabbed me and yanked me out of the way. She kept running like she never saw me. The woman threw open the window, and the strong breeze from the incoming storm swept through the room.

A man followed her. He was around the same age, and he wore a suit and carried a knife. He didn't run after her, but walked briskly with confidence, like he knew she'd never escape.

"I thought the spirits were trapped in the music box!" Grant cried.

"Why isn't the salt working?" Mandy demanded.

"These aren't spirits." Miles had ducked behind the bed, but he looked a little relieved as he slowly stood. He waved his hand, like he was trying to work his Seer magic on the ghosts, but they didn't so much as look at him.

"It must be a residual haunting," Talia said. "The events of that night imprinted through time. We're witnessing what happened."

The woman put one leg through the window in an attempt to escape, but the man grabbed her by the hair and yanked her back into the room. She stumbled to the side, and glass shattered as her hands went through the mirror. Blood trickled down her ghostly arms. She trembled and backed away from the man.

"Please, Leroy honey," she begged. "Don't do this."

Leroy said nothing. He grabbed her by the hair again and shoved her toward the bed. She caught herself on the bedpost, and wood cracked as her weight snapped it in two. She stumbled, and Leroy yanked her onto the bed. The springs groaned as she landed. He jumped on top of her, moving faster than any old man should. He pinned her hips down with his body and lifted the knife above her head.

Mandy threw her hands over her eyes. "I can't watch."

Leroy lifted the knife above her. "No!" the woman screamed. Her voice seemed to shake the entire room, and a chill settled deep in my bones.

The window slammed shut, and the ghostly figures vanished in a wisp, like smoke disappearing in the wind. We all jumped, and for a moment, nobody said anything as we processed what we'd seen. The room returned to its disheveled state, and the items that had fallen from the dresser were gone.

Lucas broke the silence. "That must've been his wife."

"That can't be it!" Chloe insisted. "How did they banish the demon?"

Lucas didn't have an answer. "If we can find more of these residual hauntings, we might learn—"

A scream sounded down the hall again, and we all turned to look as the door shuddered against the wall. Mrs. Pinewood came tearing through the room, heading straight toward the window. The haunting played out exactly as it had the last time, concluding with the window slamming shut and the ghosts vanishing.

Lucas shivered. "Legend says Leroy Pinewood killed his house guests with a steak knife during a dinner party. The murders must've started in the dining room. Let's go back to where it all started."

We left the bedroom and started down the hall, weaving our way through the mansion. Screams echoed from rooms all around us as residual hauntings replayed over and over.

When we reached the dining room, it was empty of a haunting, though the chill in the air made us all shiver. There were two entrances to the room—the one we'd come through, and another set of sliding double doors on the other side. A long table stretched from one end of the room to another, covered in a thick layer of dust. A skeleton sat slumped in an empty chair next to the head of the table, but there were no other bodies to be found. The table was still set from that night, but there was no evidence of food having been set out. Whatever had happened occurred before dinner started.

"It looks like we're the first people who've been here in the last forty years," Chloe said. I didn't think anyone had dared enter this room to salvage the fine silver.

Mandy wrapped her arms around herself and shot a nervous glance around the room. "There's no haunting here."

My eyes roamed over the table, observing clues. Lightning flashed through the room, and thunder rumbled from outside.

"Maybe we don't need a haunting to figure out what happened." I pointed to a chair that had been knocked over. "Lucas, can you put that chair upright and sit in it?"

"Um, sure," he said. He looked confused, but did as I asked.

"Chloe, can you sit in that spot next to him at the end of the table?" I instructed. "Talia and Grant, sit across from Chloe, and Miles and Mandy, I need you over here by this skeleton."

I arranged my friends into various spots, then stood at the head of the table, running my finger over an empty spot at the place setting. "There's a steak knife at each place setting, except for this one. This must've been Leroy's spot. He must've taken his knife and stabbed this guest first."

I turned to the skeleton that sat forgotten beside me. I made the motion of stabbing the man with an invisible knife. "The other guests witnessed what he'd done, and they fled. Lucas, stand up like you're fleeing a murder."

"Uh, okay." Lucas shot out of his chair, and it fell backward, landing in the same spot it'd been when we arrived.

I pointed to him. "The guest in your spot took off running, but he knocked into the person in Chloe's spot."

Chloe got up to reenact what I was envisioning.

"Chloe's character tripped and caught herself on the tablecloth," I said. "That's why the tablecloth is uneven and Chloe's plate is shattered on the floor. One of the guests behind her must've tripped over her, and that's why the rug is turned up. Miles, your character got up to run…"

Miles stood to play out the scene, and I rounded the table toward him. "But Leroy got to him before he could get away. He stabbed him…" I pretended to stab Miles and shove him up against the wall. "That's where the blood stain on the wall came from. But Miles' character must've taken off with the wound, because there's a trail that leads to the end of the carpet."

"You're getting all this without being a Seer?" Miles asked.

I shrug. "It's the kind of stuff I pay attention to."

"What happened to my character?" Mandy asked, sounding intrigued.

I observed her spot for clues and noticed her wine glass missing. As my gaze roamed over the room, I saw shards of glass near the wall. "Your character threw her glass at Leroy to try to slow him down, but she missed, and it shattered. Grant, your place setting is all messed up. I think your character jumped onto the table to make a break for it. He's probably the reason that chair at the end is knocked over. And Talia's character…?"

I paused for a few beats as I walked over to observe where she sat. I didn't see anything out of the ordinary, and I thought maybe she made it out of the room. Then I saw an unusual fold in the tablecloth, and I bent down to look under the table. My heart dropped when I saw the skeleton.

I sighed as I stood and flipped the tablecloth up for my friends to see. "Talia's character hid under the table. She didn't make it."

Talia's hand shot over her mouth. "Poor woman. I feel awful for her."

"So we know what happened," Lucas said. "But the details don't tell us what prompted him. Was he possessed before he invited his guests over? Was it premeditated? Or did something change that night?"

I walked around the table, looking for any more clues. "We might have to observe the past to get those answers."

Talia wrapped her arms around herself. "I'm trying, but all I can pick up on is the screams."

I noticed the sliding double doors near Leroy's place setting weren't completely open. I stood in the doorway. "Leroy must've come through here…" I stretched my arms out, like I was pushing the doors open. The instant my fingers touched both doors, a chilling sensation passed through my chest, like someone had placed a block of ice where my heart should be. Thunder cracked from overhead, and the room before us shifted. I must've activated another haunting, like I had when I touched the window in the bedroom.

The chandelier above the table lit up, and all the dust around the room vanished. All around us, ghostly figures formed. Chatter filled the room as guests clinked their glasses and laughed with one another. It was strange how happy they all sounded. My friends backed to the corners of the room to observe.

A ghost appeared right in front of me, his back toward me. I realized with horror that the chill I'd felt was the ghost passing through me. I recognized the gray hair and dark suit from the back. It was Leroy Pinewood. He held hands with his wife, and I was shocked to see her smiling expression when he pulled her chair out and helped her sit. This must've happened before the scene we witnessed in the bedroom.

Leroy stood at the head of the table, and his guests all quieted as he addressed the room. "Welcome. My wife and I are so happy you've accepted our invitation tonight. As a priestess, my wife's main priority is the coven."

Mrs. Pinewood had been a priestess? I had no idea.

Leroy continued. "But tonight, we honor her and the life we've shared together for fifty years. The moment I met Cynthia, I knew she was destined for great things. Had I known then that she would say yes to my proposal, I'd have asked her to marry me sooner."

The guests laughed, like they were all having a good time.

Leroy lifted his glass. "So here's to Cynthia and the last fifty years we've shared together. Happy anniversary, dear."

Cynthia smiled. "Happy anniversary."

The guests echoed the congratulations, and Leroy took a sip of his wine.

At that moment, the atmosphere in the room shifted. Thunder boomed overhead when Leroy grabbed for the knife. His entire demeanor changed as he turned to the guest beside him and stabbed him through the heart. We witnessed the blood gargling from the man's mouth. For a moment, the guests just froze.

"He took a sip from his wine glass. It must've had a potion in it to possess him," Lucas said thoughtfully, but his words didn't interrupt the haunting.

"What in the name of the Goddess—?" Cynthia started, but she cut off when he turned to her. A darkness I couldn't explain had entered his eyes, and he set his sights on her.

He lunged for his wife, but she jumped out of the way and yelled, "Run!"

Screams tore through the room as guests leapt from the chairs. People clamored toward the doors to flee, and the scene played out just as I had predicted. Leroy went for another man and stabbed him in the gut. Someone threw a wine glass at Leroy, and it shattered against the wall. Chairs toppled over, and people tripped and scrambled over one another to get through the doors. Within moments, the guests had fled the dining room, the injured man limping behind the others. Cynthia whirled around in the doorway, giving one last hopeful glance at her husband like she thought he might stop. He ducked under the table and stabbed the guest that had hidden there. I saw the hope drain from Cynthia's eyes, and she took off running.

Leroy stood, looking confident. "The doors are locked! It is his will that you all perish!"

He started following his wife out the doors, but he paused and turned back toward the empty dining room. A smirk crossed his features, and I swore his eyes locked directly on mine. A low chuckle escaped his throat. "You have nowhere to run, but I suggest you try."

The ghost lunged toward Chloe. She yelped and threw her arm up to protect herself. Leroy brought his knife down, and it sliced across her arm. Blood sprang from the wound.

"He's not a memory!" Chloe screamed as she scrambled backward. "He's a real ghost!"

He was a fucking strong one! He'd materialized into a solid figure… one that could hurt us.

Chloe threw a handful of salt at the ghost. He flickered out for a moment before reappearing beside her.

"Run!" Miles yelled as he launched himself at the ghost. His arms curled around Leroy's neck, and he yanked the ghost backward, away from Chloe. Leroy spun around, aiming his knife at Miles's chest. My friends and I shot off defensive spells all at once, but they sailed straight through the ghost.

"Our magic is useless!" Grant yelled.

Miles swung his iron rod at Leroy, and it went straight through him. The ghost vanished in a wisp of smoke. Miles quickly scrambled toward the exit where I was standing. My friends and I gathered in a tight group.

"There's got to be a banishing spell we can do together," I said.

Leroy reappeared at the end of the table. He set his gaze on us and started toward us in a confident stride, passing straight through the table. The ghost might be solid when he attacked, but he definitely had the advantage here. Lucas threw up a shield to stop Leroy, but his shield didn't work. Leroy stepped straight through it.

Lucas grabbed my shoulder and shoved me out of the room. My heart raced as my friends and I ran for our life down the hall. Although Leroy's ghost pursued *us*, we could still hear the haunting screams of the other ghosts as they relived their last moments over and over.

"Leroy's still possessed!" Grant cried as we turned the hall.

"How's that possible? He's dead!" I yelled.

Miles scrambled around the corner. "He's reliving his last trauma. Ghosts do that to make sense of it so they can move on, but sometimes they get stuck!"

We entered a sitting room. I rushed over to the windows and tried prying one open, but it wouldn't budge. My friends gathered around and tried to help, but it was like it'd been sealed with magic.

"Stand back!" Lucas ordered. We scattered, and Lucas shot a battle orb at the window. Normally, such a high-powered spell would shatter it, but it just fizzled out.

"There's some kind of shield around the mansion!" Lucas cried.

Laughter came from down the hall. The ghost was coming closer.

"Go!" Lucas barked, pushing us down another maze of hallways.

"We've got to break him out of the loop!" Miles cried.

"How do you suggest we do that?" Mandy demanded.

"There's an intercast ward that keeps away vengeful spirits," Chloe said breathlessly as she ran. "Let's cast that and come up with the rest later."

I kept running, leading my friends down the hall as fast as I could. We had to get far enough away from Leroy to buy us time to cast the ward. I spotted an open doorway at the end of the hall.

"Everyone in there!" I pointed. "We'll cast the ward around the room."

I sprinted toward the room and caught myself on the doorframe as I slowed. I stumbled inside and whirled around, expecting my friends to enter behind me. Instead, what I saw was Leroy closing in on my friends, a steak knife held above his head. I witnessed Lucas's terrified expression a moment before the door slammed shut behind me.

Terror lurched in my gut, and I grabbed the doorknob and yanked as hard as I could. It wouldn't budge. I hammered my fists on the door. "Lucas!"

I could barely make out my friends' voices over the thunder rumbling outside. The rain had started, and it pounded heavily against the windows, drowning their voices even further.

"Cast the ward!" Miles screamed at the others.

I heard Chloe and Lucas speaking an incantation in unison, while Grant screamed Talia's name and Mandy cried out in pain. Goddess, what was happening to my friends?

"You must tell me what's going on," a voice said from behind me. I whirled around to see that the room had transformed, looking cleaner and brighter. It was another residual haunting.

I stood in a small home library. Bookcases lined the walls, and two huge windows looked out over Lake Santos. The room buzzed with an energy I could only attribute to the haunting, because the rain pounding against the windows seemed quieter than before. Leroy Pinewood leaned against a desk in the middle of the room, and his wife sat in a chair nearby.

"Can't this wait, dear?" Cynthia said. "Our guests are expecting us."

Leroy's eyes looked so kind, unlike they'd been when he stabbed those people in the dining room. This must've happened before he was possessed. I realized the night was playing out in reverse through the hauntings.

Leroy sighed. "Cynthia, the coven is scared. A woman was poisoned, and a man was hanged. A priest was murdered in broad daylight! This kind of thing shouldn't happen here. The town can tell the Imperium Council is on edge. Please tell me what's going on."

Cynthia pursed her lips. "I've told you before, it's Imperium Council business. I don't want to worry you."

"What worries me is that you won't tell me," Leroy said, sounding sad. "Cynth, we've been married for fifty years. I realize there's much you can't say as a priestess, but you've always confided in me when times get tough. Why must you go silent now?"

Cynthia hesitated, but she spoke in an even, confident tone that the priestesses were so good at using. "Nicholas's death was a tragedy, and Jebediah is being put on trial for his crimes. The other incidents were… unfortunate accidents."

"There's contention within the council," Leroy insisted. "I can see it in your eyes."

"What do you want me to say?" Cynthia asked. "We inducted two young council members this past year. There are bound to be some growing pains. Lilian shows promise, but Nicholas was never fit to serve on the council. A priest, for Alora's sake! What were we thinking?"

"Nicholas made a mistake?" Leroy wondered. "Is that why he was killed?"

Cynthia stood, looking angry. "*We* made a mistake by inducting him onto the council in the first place. He was our only option, but we were wrong to take it. Nicholas betrayed us, and everything that has happened since was *his* fault."

I was starting to get angry. "My grandfather was trying to protect the Wands from *you*!" I yelled, even though she couldn't hear me.

"So these deaths..." Leroy prodded. "They're a result of a curse Nicholas couldn't break?"

Cynthia's hands curled into fists. "Nicholas himself was a curse upon the coven. He brought this on himself."

"She's lying!" I insisted. My grandfather had tried to protect the coven from the priestesses who wanted to take their power!

Leroy's lips pursed. "I see that you're not going to be honest with me. But at least give me *something* to tell our guests—to ease their worry."

Cynthia stepped in front of her husband and ran her hands down his arms. "Let's focus on *us* tonight and leave the worries of the coven behind. It's our fiftieth wedding anniversary. There is nothing to fear."

Leroy hesitated before finally saying, "Very well. I will shut down any conversation that arises regarding these deaths. We'll allow our friends to forget their troubles for one night."

Cynthia straightened her dress, looking pleased. "Shall we make our debut?"

"Yes, but first, you should open this." Leroy picked up a parcel from the desk and handed it to her. It was a small, narrow box, something you might put a necklace in.

Cynthia furrowed her brow. "There's no return address. What is this?"

"An anniversary gift, I assume," Leroy said. "It came in the mail today, addressed to you."

Cynthia picked up a letter opener from the desk and used it to remove the wrapping. She opened the box, but her breath caught when she saw what was inside. The box fell from her fingers. I witnessed a wand roll across the floor, but I didn't get a good look at it before it disappeared behind the desk.

"Is this some sort of joke?" Cynthia shook as she backed away from the wand.

"I don't know what you mean," Leroy said.

Cynthia quickly pulled a handkerchief from her pocket and wrapped the wand inside, then handed it to Leroy. "We must lock it in the safe immediately."

She rushed around the room, looking out the windows like she expected someone to be watching. Leroy noticed his wife's strange behavior, but he didn't say anything. He went over to a picture frame on the wall and pulled on it. It swung open like a door, revealing a metal safe behind it. I watched Leroy input the combination. He opened the safe door and set the wand inside, on top of other valuables.

As he was closing the door, the wand rolled and slipped. Leroy caught it, then wrapped it in the fabric again. He placed it neatly inside the safe, before sealing it tight. Cynthia kept her eyes on the lake outside the window. Once she heard the safe click shut, she breathed a sigh of relief and turned back to her husband.

"Are you going to explain why you're so afraid of a simple wand?" Leroy asked.

"I will tell you everything once the night is over," she promised. "But our guests are waiting. Right now, we must act as if everything is normal."

Leroy hesitated, but he finally put his arm out to his wife. "Let's see to our guests."

Lightning flashed, and a huge crack of thunder sounded. The next instant, the scene had vanished, and I could hear the rain pounding hard against the windows again. This must've happened moments before they'd arrived in the dining room, where Leroy gave his speech and became possessed.

I couldn't take my eyes off the picture frame that housed the safe behind it. Cynthia had been so wary of that wand, like she expected someone to come and take it from her at any second. Could it be an Oaken Wand?

It *had* to be, and that's why she was so protective of it. My heart hammered at the possibility of finding another Wand. We were so close…

I approached the picture frame, which depicted a vase of flowers. I held my breath and tugged on it. It swung on hinges, and my pulse quickened when I entered the combination I'd seen Leroy use. My breath wavered when I saw the Wand sitting on top, just where Leroy had left it. Another Oaken Wand! We'd found it—

My thoughts halted in their tracks when I unwrapped the wand and saw no Cast markings. The other Oaken Wands all had a symbol of their Cast on the handle. This one was beautiful, etched with a very intricate swirling design, but there was no Cast symbol. Whatever Cynthia thought this was, it wasn't an Oaken Wand.

But it was powerful; that much I could tell. My magic sensed something inside unlike I'd ever felt before. Some wands had magical properties, like those made with unicorn hair or dragon scales, but most were mere tools to focus our magic. This was entirely different, easily as strong as one of the objects we'd worked with in my Enchanting class. There was some sort of spell attached to this wand. If I could figure it out—

A scream tore down the hall, and I jumped. My friends!

I whirled toward the door, and the handkerchief slipped. I felt a surge of magic the moment my skin touched the wand. Magic twisted up my arm and tightened around me. I didn't even have a moment to push against it. In the blink of an eye, the magic had encompassed me. Internally, I panicked, but when I tried to open my mouth and scream, nothing came out.

I was trapped.

Horror flooded my veins when the door slammed behind Nadine. I yanked on the handle, but the door didn't budge. My friends and I huddled in the corner, as there was nowhere else for us to run.

"Cast the ward!" Miles screamed.

Chloe grabbed my shoulder and pulled me away from the door. "We'll get to her!" she shouted. "Follow my lead to cast the spell!"

I had to do *something*, damn it. Chloe and I joined hands, and she began reciting a spell in Latin. I spoke the words along with her, as clearly as I could follow. I stumbled a few times, and I hoped to the Goddess it was a good enough spell.

Talia steadied herself against the wall, and I witnessed her eyes roll back in her skull as another vision overcame her senses. She collapsed, and Grant screamed her name.

Leroy reached us, and he swung his knife down at Mandy. Miles lunged at the ghost at the same time, swinging his iron rod like a baseball bat. The ghost vanished, but not before Mandy got nicked by the knife. She screamed as the ghost reappeared, aiming his knife at Miles.

"Miles!" Chloe yelled as the knife aimed to slice his guts open.

But the knife never got him. Leroy disappeared into a puff of smoke as our spell activated throughout the hallway. Talia's visions cleared, and she blinked as she came back to the present. Grant helped her stand.

Mandy placed her hand over her racing heart. "What just happened?"

"Our spell warded him off," Chloe said. "But it won't hold for long. Let's get Nadine and find a way out of here!"

I jimmied on the door handle again, but it wouldn't budge. I spoke an incantation to unlock the door, but nothing changed. This wasn't an ordinary lock—it'd been sealed by magic.

"Everyone stand back," I ordered.

My friends backed away. I shot battle orbs at the door, but the lock didn't break. Fuck, Nadine was in there all alone! Leroy could return at any moment and go after her! I kicked the door as hard as I could, but it barely shook. Desperate, I backed up and tried again, aiming my shoulder at the door. I thought maybe I could break through it like in the movies, but damn, it did nothing but give me a sore shoulder.

"Everyone conjure a battle orb," I barked. "We're going to break our way through this thing! On three! One… Two…"

The door swung open, and relief flooded through me when I saw Nadine standing there. Her chin was tilted downward, and her hair concealed most of her face. I couldn't read the cold expression she wore. It was like she'd just witnessed something she couldn't explain and she was still trying to process it.

I rushed forward, but her eyes connected with mine and gave me pause. Something in her eyes wasn't quite right. All the warmth I usually saw in them had vanished, replaced by a chilling darkness. It was like some monster had taken on Nadine's features, because they weren't quite right.

"Nadine!" Talia opened her arms to embrace her friend.

I didn't let her get that far, though. I grabbed her by the arm and began backing up. "Nobody touch her! Whatever this is, it's not Nadine!"

Nadine smirked, then pulled something out from the fabric of her dress. Lightning flashed against the edge of a blade—a letter opener, by the looks of it. She lunged toward Talia, but I threw up a shield at the last second.

Nadine wasn't a ghost like Leroy—she was still very much alive and solid, so she slammed straight into my shield. But it barely fazed her. She bounced off it, then waved her hand. My shield vanished, and I felt my magic drain away. Nadine must've been using her Curse Breaking powers to redirect my spell. If her Curse Breaker powers were still working, that meant Nadine was still in there somewhere.

I threw myself in front of my friends. "Nad, please! It's me, Lucas. Don't do this—"

Nadine drew her fist back and wacked me across the face so hard I stumbled to the side. I landed against the wall and tasted blood in my mouth. Whatever spell Nadine was under, it made her fucking strong. I looked at her, begging her to see through the spell, but my Nadine was nowhere to be seen behind those dark, murderous eyes. She aimed her letter opener at me, but I reacted fast with a stunning spell. I didn't want to hurt her—just slow her down.

My spell should've knocked her off her feet, but it did no such thing. It landed on her gut, and she looked down as it fizzled out, like the spell merely tickled.

"What's happening to her!?" Mandy shouted.

I shoved at my friends. "Nadine's been possessed! Everybody run!"

My friends and I took off running down the hall. Nadine followed in that confident way Leroy walked—like she knew we couldn't outrun her. A spell whizzed down the hall, and we ducked to avoid it.

"How do we stop it?" Talia cried.

I sprinted around the corner. "We have to get Nadine to break through it somchow."

"We can immobilize her—" Chloe started, but I shoved her into an open doorway, cutting her off.

"Everyone in here!" I barked.

My friends didn't question me. They trusted me... even though they shouldn't. Once they were all inside, I ducked back into the hall and slammed the door behind them. I spoke a quick incantation to lock the door, then cast a shield around it for good measure. The last thing I wanted was for any of them to get hurt. Nadine would listen to me. She *had* to. I wasn't going to let any of my friends stop me from trying.

My friends pounded on the door, but they couldn't escape. "Open this door *right now*!" Chloe screamed.

I ignored her and turned toward Nadine, who was approaching me. "I'm not scared of you. You may be possessed, but my Nadine is still in there somewhere."

Nadine stopped, and for a second, I thought she would drop the letter opener. Instead, a smirk crossed her face. "You may want to rethink your strategy. I'm going to have fun killing you."

A battle spell erupted from her palms, and I threw up a shield a split-second before it hit me. The spell rocked against my shield so hard, I couldn't keep it up. My shield fell as Nadine advanced.

"This isn't you!" I cried. Nadine loved me, and she would remember that before she ever hurt me. I created a shield around her to hold her in, but she just looked around at my shimmering spell and laughed.

"Is this a joke?" she asked, sounding amused. "You're a very funny boy."

Nadine pressed her hand against the side of my shield, and her powers turned the spell back on me. My magic ricocheted like a rubber band, slamming into my chest so hard it knocked me off my feet. I went flying down the hall and crashed through the door at the end. The door swung open so fast that it knocked off one of its hinges and hung there. I landed flat on my back and gasped for breath. I noticed a bed beside me. We must've entered a guest bedroom.

Nadine's footsteps approached, and I jumped to my feet. "Who are you?" I demanded breathlessly. "Is that Leto in there?"

Nadine let out a chilling laugh as she circled me. "You think *Professor Leto* is capable of everything I am? I'm a Curse Breaker—a *priestess*! Your magic is no match for mine."

"You're not Nadine," I accused.

"Oh, I'm Nadine," she practically sang. "I'm the part of her that wants you dead. And you *will* die tonight, Lucas."

Nadine threw herself at me, the letter opener aimed toward my gut. I caught her wrist and spun her around, pinning her body to my chest. My arm wrapped around her neck. I took no pleasure in this position, but I had to do something to stop her. I squeezed her wrist so tightly that she dropped the letter opener. I winced, because I didn't want to hurt her.

"You're wrong," I growled. "There's no part of Nadine that wants to kill me. Whatever you are, you're no part of her."

Nadine laughed. "You think I *like* listening to you *whine*? Oh, poor Lucas. So depressed and helpless. It'd be easier if you just hanged yourself like your brother."

She might as well have plunged the letter opener into my gut and twisted it around. I'd never heard anyone say anything so hurtful.

But this wasn't Nadine. I refused to believe there was any part of her that ever let that thought cross her mind.

"We're past that," I insisted.

"You may be, but I'm not," she said.

"Whatever you are, you'll let Nadine go," I demanded, pulling my arm tighter around her neck.

"Not before you suffer a painful death," she sneered.

I didn't have a chance to react before she formed a battle orb in her hand and slammed it against my leg. I cried out as electricity rippled downward from my hip. I lost control of my muscles and collapsed onto my knees. Nadine leapt away from me and readied for another spell, but I threw one back just as quickly. Our battle magic collided in mid-air, and a *boom* sounded throughout the room—louder than the thunder outside.

Nadine gave up on the magic, because she could see we were obviously getting nowhere with it. She threw herself at me, knocking us both flat on the floor. Her hands curled around my neck, but I grabbed her and flipped her over.

"I don't want to hurt you—" I started to say, but Nadine grabbed tight to my wrists and created a battle spell that burned me. I leapt away from her on instinct.

"You *should* want to hurt me," she snarled. "I've taken everything from you—even your kidney."

"You're wrong!" I shouted. I jumped on top of her again, pinning her hands above her head so she couldn't burn me again.

Nadine smirked, and her gaze filled with desire. "I'm up for a little S&M before your reaper comes for you. On second thought, maybe he can join us."

"Whatever you are, you're sick," I snapped. "Nadine would never believe she's taken anything from me. She saved me. I'm nothing without her."

"You *need* me!" she shouted. "You rely on me so damn much to give you purpose. What about my purpose? How can I be my own person when you're holding me back?"

"I don't know where you're getting these ideas, but Nadine would never say something like that," I said.

"Doesn't mean I'm not thinking them," she replied curtly.

My guts twisted into an impossible knot. She *had* said things like that before, but she'd said those things to help me, not hurt us. Could she really still feel this way?

"Nadine, please stop this," I begged. "Break through the spell. You can do it. It's me, Lucas. I'm here for you."

"That's the problem," she said. "You shouldn't be here at all."

Nadine twisted her hand, and a spell shot out at me. I didn't think she'd been aiming, just trying to catch me off guard. The spell slammed against my nose, knocking me backward like I'd just been kicked in the face. I landed on my back and felt blood trickle down my face. For a moment, the whole room spun. I couldn't get upright before Nadine was over top of me. She slammed her palm into my chest, and every muscle in my body seized. I couldn't move—couldn't breathe. Magic drained from my chest, and her arm lit up with purple magic as she used her Curse Breaker powers to draw my magic out of me. A look of satisfaction filled her features. She was going to drain me of every bit of energy I had left. There was no spell I could cast and nothing I could do to get out of this.

"N—Nad," I rasped past the sharp pain in my chest.

She didn't seem to hear me, just stared down at the magic with wide, satisfied eyes. Nadine was still in there somewhere. If this was the end, I had to tell her how I truly felt.

"You're right," I forced out. "I needed you to pull me out of the dark place I was in. I relied on you because I didn't know how to function otherwise. It's not fair to let you keep carrying my burden, so if you want me to go, I'll go. But know this. You took nothing from me. All I want is for you to be happy. If you can't be happy with me, then leave me. I'll learn to be happy on my own. I don't need you to save me anymore, but I still love you, and that's enough for me."

Nadine's gaze flickered to mine, then back to the magic, and the satisfaction disappeared off her face, replaced by confusion. Then came a look of determination.

"I. Love. You. Too," she strained.

Nadine ripped her arm away from me. Magic came flooding back into my chest, and I finally gained control of my limbs. Nadine collapsed onto the floor, and her eyes rolled back into her skull as she convulsed.

"Nad!" I cried as I pulled her shaking body into my lap. I was vaguely aware of the sound of a door slamming from down the hall, then footsteps racing toward me. The spell I'd cast to keep my friends safe must've broken when Nadine took my magic.

My friends rushed into the room, but they came to an abrupt halt when they saw Nadine seizing in my arms. My voice broke when I spoke. "She tried to resist the spell, and it backfired on her! There has to be some sort of counter-spell!"

"We have to exorcize her," Grant said.

"We don't have the supplies to pull it off!" Talia cried.

Nadine went limp in my arms.

Pain rippled through my gut, and I quickly checked if she was breathing. Thank the Goddess. "She's still breathing, but she may not be for long."

"I know someone who can help," Mandy said. "We have to get Nadine to her as quickly as possible. Come on, we found a broken window we can get out of. As long as our ward holds against Leroy, we can escape."

Mandy gestured us toward the hall. I cradled Nadine in my arms and followed behind my friends. Mandy turned the corner and stopped dead in her tracks. A scream tore from her lungs the same time I spotted Leroy's ghost materialize in front of her. My stomach plummeted from my abdomen. I couldn't even blink before Leroy's ghost swept forward and plunged his knife into Mandy's stomach.

"No!" I screamed as Mandy's cries turned into whimpers. She stumbled backward, and Miles and Grant caught her, lowering her to the floor. Blood oozed from an open wound, and tears streaked her cheeks. I feared she wasn't going to make it. We just might lose two people we loved tonight...

Chloe began shouting the warding spell, hoping we'd all join in, but she wasn't fast enough. Leroy lifted his knife the same time Talia shoved her way to the front of the group. She grabbed the end of her drawstring bag filled with salt and swung it at him as hard as she could. Leroy's ghost vanished in a wisp of air.

"He won't be gone long!" Talia cried. "We have to get out. Now!"

Mandy reached upward, and Miles took her hand. "Hattie," she rasped. "Take Nadine to Hattie. She can help."

"I'll take Nadine," I said firmly. "You guys take Mandy to the hospital. Now!"

We cast the ward one last time, giving us a few minutes of reprieve from the haunting. We escaped through an open window, and I cradled Nadine in my arms as I raced toward her car. Rain poured down on us, and we were soaked. I set Nadine gently in the passenger seat, then tore out of the long driveway, wheels spinning on the gravel.

Nadine seized in the front seat as I sped down the road, and foam oozed out of her mouth. I pressed the pedal to the floor. We didn't make it far before Nadine began ramming her head into the passenger-side window. The spell was making her hurt herself.

The tires squealed as I pulled up in front of The Jolly Pumpkin. Nadine went limp, and I dragged her out of the passenger seat. I raced inside the shop, and my heart sank when I saw it was empty.

"Hattie!" I screamed. Nadine didn't even stir in my arms, and I feared it might be too late.

I heard the sound of a dog's paws on the hardwood. A large canine emerged from the back hall—a wolf. It was Hattie's Familiar, a creature bonded to her, as was custom in her elemental culture.

The wolf took one look at Nadine in my arms before barking loudly. I thought he was barking at me, warning me to leave. Then I saw Hattie hobbling on her cane behind the dog, a horrified look on her face. The dog was communicating with her.

Hattie's features paled. "She's been possessed. My Familiar can sense it."

"Tell me you can reverse it," I begged.

"I will do my best," Hattie said. "Upstairs. Now."

I followed her and her Familiar upstairs into a small apartment. Hattie guided me through a quaint kitchen to a small room that looked like a closet. There were no windows, and the walls were black. Thunder rumbled overhead, but even the lightning from the next room barely lit the space. Shelves lined the walls, and a cauldron sat in the middle of the room.

Hattie went over to one of the shelves and picked up a container of salt. She poured a large salt circle around the room and instructed me to lay Nadine inside of it, next to the cauldron. I gently set her on the floor and forced myself to take a step back. My guts twisted as I stared down at her unmoving form.

"Now what?" I asked.

Hattie hesitated as her Familiar sniffed Nadine's body. She looked up to me with a confused expression on her face. "This is not a normal possession. Possessions often have an entity attached to them, but this energy inside of her is not conscious."

She hovered her hands over Nadine, like she was reading her energy. "She's been possessed by another's *will*."

"Like a curse?" I asked.

"It's very similar," Hattie explained. "But to be possessed by another's will gives the spellcaster control, even when they are not physically living inside of the victim's body. Curses require no contract, but they also can't be controlled once they are cast. This is different."

That matched what Talia had seen in her crystal ball. And it explained how Leto had killed people even when he had a rock-solid alibi. He didn't need to be at the scene of the crime—he just had to curse people and get them to do his bidding for him.

Hattie tilted her head as she continued reading Nadine's energy. "This is a dangerous spell that seeks to kill by any means necessary. It even makes her stronger."

"That sounds accurate," I said desperately.

Hattie looked thoughtful. "A witch can overpower a demon possession if their willpower is strong enough. But something is amiss..."

"Nadine's a Curse Breaker," I said. "Maybe there's a way we can turn her magic inward and break the spell."

Hattie shook her head. "I suspect her powers are what caused this in the first place. That must be what I'm sensing. If she tried to break the spell, rather than release it, then she would have tangled her magic within it. The spell latched on tighter, like a parasite. It will feed on her until there is nothing left."

"You can still save her, can't you?" I pleaded.

Hattie picked up a velvet bag from one of the shelves, along with several other ingredients. "This will not be like my normal exorcisms. It will require more than a prayer to break this spell. But there is something that may work."

"What do we have to do?" I asked. "I'll do anything."

"Sit," Hattie instructed. "We must summon a god."

I gaped. I couldn't have heard her right. "A god? That's next to impossible."

"*Next to* impossible," Hattie emphasized. "But it can be done if you possess the proper ingredients. Help me, please."

Hattie set her cane aside, and I helped her sit on a cushion beside the cauldron. I sat across from her. She placed several crystals around the cauldron, then began adding ingredients. She wasn't an Alchemist, but any witch could perform a summoning spell.

Hattie poured a vial of liquid into the cauldron, then opened the velvet bag and sprinkled a gray powder on top. It looked like ashes. "Tears shed out of love, mixed with these leshane ashes should do the trick."

I furrowed my brow. "Leshane... that's a monster, isn't it? A forest demon from fae lore? Where did you get its ashes?"

Leshane ashes had to be insanely rare. The only portals monsters could slip through to Earth were located in Malovia, and the fae hunted monsters before they could escape beyond their borders. I didn't even know how a witch could get their hands on such a thing. The fae certainly weren't trading something as valuable as forest demon ashes with a witch—

The fae. It hit me then that Hattie *had* dealt with the fae before. Last semester, when Nadine and I were at Perry's Point, we ran into a group of fae our age. They'd been dragging a man into town, claiming he was possessed by a forest demon. They'd come to Octavia Falls to perform an exorcism. We'd told them where to find Hattie, and we let them through the protection spell.

"Those fae we helped last year..." I realized before she could answer. "You exorcized their demon and kept the ashes."

Hattie had to be the only person in the world in possession of leshane ashes. That meant this spell was extremely advanced.

Hattie smirked. "As you helped the fae sorceress save her mate, now she is helping you to save yours. The leshane was a much older, much stronger demon than the one you currently face. The dark magic within these ashes will help to push out the spirit that has overcome your love. Now, come. Let us pray."

Hattie reached over the cauldron, and I took her hands. "Deities of the Miriamic Coven, we ask for your help. One of your children is sick, afflicted with magic we cannot conquer. We pray that should it be your will, you heal her. So shall it be."

For a moment, nothing happened.

Please, I begged the Goddess. *Please help her.*

The ingredients in the potion began to swirl together, and the liquid rose upward like a tornado. The leshane ashes shimmered all different colors, so brightly they reflected off the walls. I watched on in wonder as the magic swirled upward, forming into the shape of a person.

A flash of lightning lit up the adjoining room the same moment a crack of thunder sounded so loud my ears rang. I jumped, and my eyes landed on a terrifying creature standing over Nadine. He had to be over eight feet tall, because he hunched over so his head didn't hit the ceiling. He had the body of a human and the head of a ram, with curved horns larger than any demon's I'd ever seen. Hair covered his entire body, and long, sharp claws grew out of the ends of his fingers.

We hadn't summoned a god. We'd summoned a demon!

I leapt to my feet, magic ready in my hand. "Where's Mother Miriam?"

"Keep calm, Lucas," the demon said gently. It was very strange.

"We summoned Mother Miriam," I growled. "Who are you to show your face?"

"Perhaps you will feel more confident in my human form," the demon said. He shifted, becoming a man with dark hair and symmetrical features. He wore a long black robe, and I noticed a tattoo circling his wrist. All the Miriamic Cast symbols wove together and disappeared beneath the sleeve of his robe. I should've been terrified of him like I was scared of Professor Leto, but something about this man seemed familiar in a reassuring way. I was certain I'd never seen him before in my life, though.

I wasn't convinced. Magic crackled in my palm. "Give me one good reason I shouldn't fry your demon ass."

"I am no longer a demon," he told me. "Forgive me for my initial appearance. All natural-born gods have an animal form. The demons you speak of were created by damned souls in my image, to mimic the appearance of a god. I assure you I am here to help."

"You can't be a god," I accused. It had to be some sort of manipulation tactic. Demons were known for their sleazy tricks, which was why we no longer associated with them.

Hattie tugged on my hand. "Lucas, I summoned a *god* of the Miriamic coven. There is more than one."

My jaw dropped as I took in the man, and it hit me. "Santos?"

He nodded kindly. "You've summoned me to break the spell inside of

Nadine. This, I can do. However, possessions are a type of contract, and all demon contracts include a consent withdrawal clause."

"This is true," Hattie said. "Even in a normal exorcism, the possessed must cast the demon out themselves. The exorcism spell just helps the process along."

"You have our consent," I said desperately. "Do whatever you have to do."

"I need *her* consent," Santos clarified. He knelt beside Nadine and checked her pulse. His features fell, and I knew something must be terribly wrong. "I fear she may be too far gone to give it."

"She would give it if she could!" I cried. "Take my word. I know her better than anyone."

"I'm afraid even a god's magic can't override this spell without her word," Santos said.

"Then what are you doing here!?" I raged. "You're a god. You must be able to help her. Consider me her power of attorney. We've been through everything together—nearly to hell and back. I know she wouldn't want to die like this. Hell, she just got her kidney. She just got her chance at—"

I cut off when it hit me. Nadine had my kidney... which meant the spell in her body was infecting my body, too.

"Her kidney," I realized. "It's mine... *ours*. The spell that's infecting her is inside that kidney. You have my consent to work your magic on it. Once your magic is inside of her, you can work the rest. You *have* to save her! Her prophecy still needs to be fulfilled."

"Nadine has chosen a path with many possible outcomes," Santo said gently. "Her destiny is not yet determined. I can cast this demon out, but if she survives, she'll continue down a path lined with far worse fates than the one she faces tonight. If she lives, you must allow her to continue down that path and experience that pain."

I hesitated. I didn't want Nadine to suffer, but I didn't want her to die, either. It should be *her* choice, and it wasn't fair that I was asked to make it for her. I tried to think of what Nadine would want... and I knew the answer immediately. She'd choose to suffer to save the coven.

Santos could be wrong about her suffering, though. He said her destiny was not yet determined. If she lived, she could choose any path before her. She didn't have to suffer.

"Bring her back," I stated.

"Are you sure you're willing to do this?" Santos asked. "You cannot shield her from what will come, for it is along this path that she will face her greatest joy, and her greatest pain."

I nodded firmly. "I'm certain."

Santos knelt beside Nadine and placed his hand on her stomach. Black magic emitted from his palm. It shimmered around the edges and grew brighter with each passing second. I had to shield my eyes as the light encompassed Nadine's entire form.

Red magic blasted out of Nadine's chest, flashing like it was fighting to leave her. Her back arched, and a high-pitched note filled the room. I threw my hands over my ears, but it didn't stop the ringing. Glass shattered on Hattie's shelves, and her Familiar began barking loudly. It was the sound of evil, the remnants of the dark spell screaming as it withered away.

Then all at once, it stopped. I dropped my hands, and the room was dark and silent once more. Santos knelt above Nadine and brushed her hair back, as a father would do when their child was sick.

"Did it work?" Hattie asked.

Santos didn't answer. I dropped to my knees beside Nadine and took her hand in mine.

"Nad," I said gently, shaking her a little.

She didn't move, and I thought for certain the spell had failed. I shook her again, and when nothing happened, the last shreds of hope I held on to vanished. I lowered my head to her chest. To anyone else it would look like I was checking her breath and heartbeat, but to me, it was nothing more than comfort to be close to her one last time.

A single tear streaked my cheek and landed upon her chest. She stirred from beneath me, and I gasped as I sat upright. Nadine's eyes fluttered, and relief flooded through me when her gaze landed upon me.

"Is it over?" she rasped.

Happy tears leaked from my eyes. "Yes, it's over."

Nadine flung her arms around my neck, and I wrapped her tight in my arms. I buried my nose in her hair and inhaled her sweet scent.

"I'm so sorry, Lucas," she sobbed. "I never should've said those horrible things!"

"It's all right," I assured her. "It wasn't you. You were possessed with

Professor Leto's will. You were bound to kill me in the most vicious way possible. The spell was just feeding off my insecurities."

"No, Lucas," she wept. "It was feeding off *mine*. I never wanted you to die—*ever*. But the spell was in my head. It knew that deep down, part of me resents the way you feel about me."

My heart shattered. To think I'd ever hurt her was worse than anything she'd said to me in the mansion. I drew her closer in my arms, holding her as tight to my chest as I could. "I don't feel that way anymore. I don't want to be just some guy who follows you around worshiping the ground you walk on. I want to be a team. So we'll get through this together."

Nadine sniffled. "How can you say that after all the horrible things I said? You must think I hate you."

"I don't," I said simply. "Because if you really believed everything you said, you wouldn't have resisted the spell. You were right, and it was never fair of me to put my self-worth in your hands. But if you believed we were still in that place, you never would've trusted I was telling the truth. And I was, Nad. I don't *need* you to give me purpose anymore. With or without you, I am a complete and whole human being. But if it were up to me, I'd choose a life with my best friend every single time. I may not *need* you to live, but I didn't *want* to live without you."

Nadine began sobbing harder, and I pulled her close to my chest. To hold her again was a great blessing, because I had almost lost her tonight. Whatever she had said to me in the manor didn't matter, because we were a team, and as long as we both chose to stay, we'd work through it. Tears welled in my eyes. I was just happy she was alive.

When I drew away to look at her, her hair stuck to the side of my wet face. "Hattie!" I turned to her and held my hand out urgently. "Your vial."

Hattie handed me the vial she'd poured the tears of love from. I put it up to my face and captured the tears leaking from my eyes, then handed it back to her.

"Payment for helping us," I told her as I handed the vial back. "If it's not enough—"

"It is plenty," Hattie said kindly.

Nadine turned toward Santos and tilted her head. "I don't believe we've met."

"This is Santos," I told her. "He saved you."

Nadine gaped. "You're... Mother Miriam's husband? How are you here?"

"Rare magic, harnessed by the leshane ashes," Santos said. "You can thank Hattie and Lucas. They are the ones who truly saved you."

"This is perfect. Now that you're here, you can banish the demon forever," Nadine said.

Santos frowned. "I'm afraid I cannot."

"But you're a god!" Nadine cried. "You broke the spell on me—you can do it again!"

"The demon's spells are a contract," Santos said. "I can't break contracts once consent is given, unless it is withdrawn."

"I never gave him my consent," Nadine insisted.

"Demons work in mischievous ways to obtain consent," Santos said. "But contracts can be broken by either of the consenting parties. Your case was unique, because you share a piece of yourself with Lucas. He was able to break the contract you entered enough to let me in. To banish the demon from your town, you must find a way to void his contract."

"We would if we could," I said. "But it's not our contract."

"Contracts can be broken in other ways," Santos said mysteriously.

Nadine grabbed my arm. "Of course! If Leto can trick me into giving consent, then we can trick him into breaking his contract. Then there's nothing that can hold him here!"

She turned back to Santos. "Thank you for your help."

Santos stood. "It has been a pleasure, but the magic keeping me here will not last."

Nadine and I stood beside him. "Before you go, can I ask how you knew my name?" I wondered. "It's like we've met before."

Santos smiled. "You are my children. Of course I know you by name. You came here for a purpose, Lucas, and shall you fulfill your destiny, we will meet again. Until next time. Farewell."

We bowed to our god, then he vanished.

All I could do was stare at the spot he'd been standing. Everyone in the coven got to meet Mother Miriam at least once, but I'd never known anyone to meet Santos. For him to show himself to us was incredible.

I helped Hattie to her feet. "We can't thank you enough."

"It is my pleasure. I am here to help," Hattie said. "I'll walk you to the door."

She led us downstairs, and we started out of the shop. Hattie stopped me before I could leave, and Nadine went on ahead.

"What you and Nadine have is very special," Hattie said in a low voice. "I can feel with my powers how much you love her, and she loves you deeply, too. You better marry that girl."

I smiled. "I plan on it."

I left the shop, and we drove to the hospital to meet up with our friends. They sat in the waiting room, chatting lowly and looking worried. Their chatter died abruptly, and relief fell over their faces when they saw us.

"Nadine!" Talia rushed over to give Nadine a hug.

Nadine grunted as she squeezed her tightly. "How's Mandy?"

"In surgery," Talia said. "The doctors say she'll make it. What about you?"

Nadine drew away from her. "I'm all better now."

"Thank the Goddess," Miles said.

"Actually, we have Santos to thank," I said. "His magic saved her."

"You summoned Santos?" Chloe balked.

I glanced around the waiting room. "We should talk in private."

My friends and I ducked down the hall and into an empty patient room.

"Let's start with the basics," Grant suggested. "How did any of this happen in the first place?"

I turned toward Nadine. "Yeah. How *did* you enter a possession contract?"

"There was a wand," Nadine explained. "I saw a residual haunting of Leroy from that night. His wife received a wand in the mail, and I thought it could be an Oaken Wand. Leroy locked it in his safe, so when the haunting was over, I opened it to investigate. I accidentally touched it, just like Leroy had. It was an enchanted object that somehow tricked me into a contract."

Chloe crossed her arms. "If there was an inscription somewhere on the wand, it could include a clause that said touching the object equated to informed consent. Nobody ever reads the terms and services, and demons rely on that."

"That has to be it," Nadine said. "There was a very intricate swirling design up and down the wand. It could've been letters."

Talia furrowed her brow, looking thoughtful. "A wand is an everyday object. No one would think twice about touching it. Leave the contract laying around, anyone could pick it up."

"We need to destroy that wand, before it can possess anyone else," Nadine said.

"And go back to that haunted dump?" Miles practically squeaked. "No, thank you."

"I'll take care of it," I offered. I'd handle it later. No one dared enter Pinewood Manor these days, so the wand would be fine to sit there until we could go back.

Nadine pressed her lips together. "The wand has been locked in Leroy's safe for over forty years. How's Leto possessing people now?"

"A new contract, a new object, perhaps?" Chloe suggested.

"It must be," Nadine agreed. "Something else happened. Cynthia seemed very wary of the wand, like she knew what it was. Lucas, do you remember when we heard Lilian tell Leto that she wouldn't make the same mistake twice?"

I nodded. "We know he was here before, but we don't know who summoned him last time. You're thinking the council summoned him then, just as they summoned him now?"

"Absolutely," she said. "The demon was here the same time my grandfather took and hid the Oaken Wands. They must've hired him to find them, but he was banished before they could. Lilian summoned him again when the council got desperate."

"We still don't know how he was banished, or how to replicate it," Talia said.

"We don't want to replicate it," I countered. "Leto may have been banished before, but that wand still worked to possess Nadine. Whatever happened last time wasn't enough. We have to do it right this time. Sending him back to hell isn't enough. We have to shred the whole damn contract."

"We would need to get a priestess to do that," Chloe pointed out. "They're the ones who signed it."

Grant's features fell. "We'll never convince them. If the priestesses didn't banish him after The Hearse Tragedy, there's nothing they won't tolerate."

"Then we'll break it ourselves," Nadine stated confidently. "There has to be something in the fine print that will void the contract and send him back to the Abyss. We can trick them into breaking it."

"We'd have to find the contract," Chloe pointed out.

"It's got to be in the Imperium headquarters," Miles said. "We could astral travel in, or send in a ghost."

Nadine shook her head. "I've already tested that theory. It has too many wards. I'd have to go in person, and I could get caught snooping around. We should do a tracking spell."

"Contracts are bound by magic," Talia said. "A spell strong enough to track it down would require something belonging to the demon or one of the priestesses."

"I've got something." Chloe reached up to unclasp the necklace she wore. "It's a family heirloom my grandmother gave me when I was little. It should work."

Miles eyed her. "I thought you were disowning your family."

Chloe scoffed. "That doesn't mean I'm going to throw out a genuine ruby."

We all joined hands, and we spoke the incantation I'd learned in my intercast magic class. With all five Casts, it was a powerful spell that should produce visions and show us where to find the contract. I felt the magic surging through me... but all I saw was black behind my lids.

Air whipped through the room, and the six of us were blasted backward as the spell backfired. I fell flat on my ass, and Nadine landed beside me.

"What happened?" Miles groaned as he sat up.

"I felt resistance," Nadine said as she stood. "It was like our spell touched some other type of magic."

Chloe put her necklace back on. "The contract must be protected. If we want to find it, we're going to have to find a stronger spell."

I drew myself upright. "Then let's get to work."

EIGHTEEN

We were determined as ever to break the demon's contract, but as the snow melted and April turned into May, we were no closer to finding the contract than before. Our research confirmed that we'd used the strongest tracking spell available. If we couldn't overpower the magic hiding the contract from us, we had no hope of finding it.

The Waning was only getting worse. Even if we *found* a better tracking spell, getting all five Casts together to perform it was next to impossible. On a *good* day, only half of my friends had access to their magic. Even the crystal arsenal we were building wasn't enough to track down the contract.

Worse, the cursed wand was still out there. Lucas had returned to Pinewood Manor with the intent to destroy it, but he couldn't get inside without the ghost of Leroy Pinewood chasing him off. After Mandy was stabbed, we weren't keen on going back and risking our lives.

Several weeks had passed, and Lucas and I figured Mandy should be up for visitors by now. We hadn't seen her much since she'd been in the hospital, as she was taking it easy during recovery. Mandy answered her door wearing pajamas, even though it was afternoon.

"Is everything all right?" she asked.

"Everything's fine," I told her. "We came by to see how you were doing."

"Oh." Mandy opened the door wider to welcome us inside. Isa and Oliver followed behind us. "I'm fine."

"How are you healing?" Lucas asked as he took a seat on the couch. I sat beside him, and Isa jumped into my lap.

Mandy grabbed a container of beads she'd been sorting through and moved it onto her nightstand. She crossed her legs on her bed. "I'm healing well. I'm still not allowed to lift too much weight."

"We brought you a present." I held out a gift bag.

Mandy raised her eyebrows. "You shouldn't have."

"It's not a big deal," I said. "We just thought it might help keep you busy until you're feeling better."

Mandy moved the tissue paper aside and pulled out a jewelry-making kit. She glanced between it and the beads on her nightstand. "I'm all set on my jewelry-making for the next few weeks, but thank you. It really means a lot. I thought you guys had come because The Coven's Shield had learned more about the contract."

"Not yet," Lucas said. "But we were wondering if you could help us."

Mandy set the jewelry kit aside. "I'm not sure I'll be much help."

"What do you mean?" I asked. "You found the information on Adrik Harvey. That helped us nail down the time period we were looking at. It led us to the Seer Wand."

Mandy frowned. "And to Pinewood Manor, where you were possessed and I got stabbed. So please tell me how I'm supposed to help, because it seems like no matter what I do, people get hurt."

"We want to prevent that," Lucas said. "You have the power to enter people's dreams. We were wondering if it was possible for you to enter a demon's dream. Professor Leto has to sleep, right? If you can get in his head, maybe you'll find a clue in his subconscious that will lead us to the contract."

Mandy shot him an incredulous look. "You can't be serious."

Lucas's brow furrowed. "I am… You *can* do it, can't you?"

"I don't know," Mandy said. "This is a *demon* you're talking about. I've never entered a demon's mind before. Who knows what could be in there? If I can enter his subconscious, who's to say he can't enter mine? Do you have any idea of the risk you're asking me to take?"

"We don't really know until we try, right?" Lucas asked. "We all agreed to take risks when we joined The Coven's Shield."

"No," Mandy said firmly. "This isn't what I signed up for. I didn't want people getting hurt. Amy's dead. I got stabbed. You guys are protesting against the priestesses, and people are getting *killed*. Hector and William are both dead because they joined your cause. Have you ever stopped to consider you're pushing things too far?"

My stomach sank. I never intended for any of my friends to get hurt like this.

"I know it's tough," I said gently. "We should've done better, and you never should've gotten stabbed. But we started a revolution. We can't protest for change without taking risks."

Mandy pursed her lips. "Do you know what it feels like to be stabbed in the gut by a ghost, Nadine?"

I understood that Mandy was mad, and I wanted to be there for her. I opened my mouth to respond, but Lucas beat me to it.

"Are you seriously going to ask *Nadine* that?" Lucas fumed. "She just recovered from a kidney transplant. Hell, we both did. We know what it's like to recover from your insides being sliced open. And we've given you the space *to* recover, but it's time to get back to work, just like Nadine and I did."

I placed a hand on his to calm him down, but he didn't stop. Oliver's fur bristled as Lucas continued.

"We know what it's like to go through tough shit, Mandy. Nadine's been sick for years, and no matter how sick she got, she's out there doing what she has to do. You're choosing to sit here and give up, when we're out there doing the work despite everything that's happened."

"I'm not giving up!" Mandy insisted.

I sighed. "Of course not. We know how hard this must be for you, Mandy."

"Hard for me?" she balked. "Nadine, this is taking a toll on *everyone*. The fact is that if you keep pushing this, more people like Amy are going to die."

"We knew that going into this," Lucas said harshly. "We're doing what's necessary to save our magic and save our people. So what are you going to do, Mandy? Go back on your vow?"

"I will *never* side with the priestesses," Mandy promised. "If you want my help, go to the Protection Tree. Don't expect me to help any more after that."

"Mandy—" I started.

"Please, Nadine," she snapped. "Just go."

I could see that Mandy was in a lot of pain, and I didn't want to make it any worse. She'd been through a lot, but she was still on our side. She'd come around eventually.

I took Lucas's hand, and we left her room with our cats following. I stopped in the hallway and turned toward Lucas. "You were a jerk to Mandy, you know that?"

"I was defending you. She was being insensitive. You're the *last* person she should have said those things to. Yeah, of course Nadine doesn't know what it's like to be in recovery," he said sarcastically.

"Mandy's hurting," I reminded him. "She needs us to be there for her right now."

He crossed his arms. "She doesn't want us around."

"Maybe because we waltzed in there with an agenda," I shot back. "Mandy needs her friends right now, not The Coven's Shield."

Lucas frowned. "What do you want me to do? Because the only thing I can do right now is give her space. She's clearly pissed at us."

"We'll give her space for a while," I offered. "But when she's ready to let us back in, we'll be there for her, all right?"

He sighed. "All right. We need to do *something*, though. Let's check out her lead with the Protection Tree."

As Lucas and I left the school, I worried what Mandy might've found at the Protection Tree. Had someone vandalized it? Carved nasty words into the trunk? Broken branches off? Burned the tree to the ground?

When we emerged from the path into the park, the tree looked perfectly fine. There were no marks, and all the branches seemed to be intact.

"I don't get it," Lucas said. "Was this Mandy's way of saying *fuck you*?"

I furrowed my brow as I took in our surroundings. Something wasn't quite right about the Protection Tree. All around us, spring was in full bloom, filling the forest with beautiful shades of green. The Protection Tree had barely started budding.

"No, look," I said, reaching for one of the low-hanging branches. "It's weeks behind the other trees. It's *dying*."

Lucas's features paled. "Our magic supports the Protection Tree. With the Waning, the magic's not getting replenished fast enough."

My stomach dropped. "The Protection Tree fuels the spell that's keeping Octavia Falls safe. The priestesses reinforce it, but that only does so much. The real source of the protection spell comes from inside the tree—and that magic originates from us."

"If the Waning continues, the protection spell will fail." Lucas sounded horrified. "We'll be completely exposed, and the fae won't hesitate to slaughter us."

It hit me like a spell to the chest. "I don't think the Waning is causing the tree to die. I think the *tree* is causing the Waning."

Lucas gasped. "Of course. The coven's dividing, which means our magic is no longer working together to support the spell. The tree has to siphon more magic to keep up, but it's draining us. That's why the Waning is getting worse. The more we divide, the worse it gets."

"This must be why the Waning is centered around the school," I realized. "Because the students are the closest source of magic to the tree. I need to tell the priestesses! I need to get them to listen and to see we're on the same side. Maybe Mandy was right that we can do this peacefully. We all want to end the Waning. There has to be a way to reach a compromise."

"I'll come with you," Lucas offered.

"No," I told him. "I'm a priestess. I have to negotiate with them alone. I've got this."

He hesitated for a moment, but I saw the trust in his eyes. "Be careful."

"I will." I practically ran to my car, and Isa followed. I tore out of the parking lot toward the Imperium headquarters. I didn't know if the priestesses would be there, so I called Priestess Margaret on my way.

"I know what's causing the Waning," I told her.

Margaret didn't say anything for several moments, but I heard a distant conversation on the other end.

"Did you hear me?" I demanded. "We have to talk about this!"

"Meet us at the Imperium headquarters as soon as possible," Margaret said diplomatically. I thought she was trying to sound indifferent, but I sensed worry in her tone.

When I reached the Imperium headquarters, the priestesses were already there. Concern marred their features.

"It's the Protection Tree!" I blurted as I burst through the door. Isa meowed loudly as she followed me in. "The tree is siphoning our magic to maintain the protection spell around Octavia Falls! The buds aren't blooming. The tree is dying."

Claudia leaned back in her chair. "The spell has kept us safe for centuries. How could it possibly be failing now?"

"Because we're dividing," I pressed. "Our magic doesn't work together unless *we* work together."

Margaret sat straighter in her chair. "It's a fine theory, but you're forgetting the spell we cast last year, indicating the Waning was caused by demon magic."

"*We* have demonic origins," I reminded her. "Perhaps the spell was picking up on that."

Lilian wore a worried look. "It's certainly something we should look into. Thank you for the heads-up, Nadine. You are dismissed."

"No!" I slammed my fist down on the table. "I will not be blown off as if I'm not a part of this council. If you don't let me work with you, you only perpetuate the divide. The Waning will only get worse. We all want to protect the coven, but we must—"

"How *dare* you try to tell us what to do!" Margaret exploded, shooting out of her chair. "You are nothing but a broken little child who wants to play the hero. All you're doing is getting in our way. You wouldn't be on this council if we had any other choice. You're here for nothing more than appearances. We *will* have solutions, and we *will* unite, but it will be on *our* terms."

"Then let's talk about the solution," I begged. "I am a priestess, too. Let me join the conversation."

"Join the conversation?" Lilian laughed. "You're lucky we've let you live this long, considering your list of crimes."

"What crimes?" I crossed my arms.

Lilian narrowed her eyes. "You and your friends have been nothing but trouble since the day you arrived in Octavia Falls. You have voted against us at every turn."

"That's not a crime," I argued. "I'm simply doing my duty as a priestess."

"Priestesses uphold the law, which you and your friends do not!" Lilian snarled. "I know Chloe's been getting prescription medication for other students. I know you're in cohorts with Everly Hall, who's been spreading anti-Miriamic propaganda. Don't think I don't know about your other violations."

She didn't know a damn thing, or she'd be accusing me of it right now.

"You have no idea what you're dealing with," Lilian spat. "You will do as you are told, or you will get us all killed."

"You want to control your people," I shot back. "How does that *save* anyone?"

"Because it's the only way to stop what's coming!" Lilian shouted. "On the morning of May fifteenth, King Elijah Zlodia was slaughtered by his own people, and his queen fled the fae's capital. If the fae are ruthless enough to kill their own king, then they're capable of putting someone *worse* than Elijah Zlodia on the throne. If you think it was terrible that they hung witches on their own soil, you have no idea what they have in store for us next. The fae are in the middle of a power shift, and if our people come together, we can overthrow the fae while they're vulnerable. You have no idea of the powerful resources that would become available to us. We could bring an end to the fae once and for all!"

"You want to slaughter an entire people!?" I balked. "There are innocent fae in Malovia."

"No fae is innocent," Margaret growled. "You never saw the aftermath eighty years ago when the fae attacked. My parents lived through the Great Supernatural War. We must take every precaution to ensure that never happens again."

"Attacking the fae will *start* a war," I pressed. "Do you truly think the coven will support this? Tell them the truth, and see what side they stand on."

Margaret stood and held her shoulders back. "By the end of this, there will only be one side, and we will end our war with the fae before it begins. One way or another, the Miriamic Coven will unite. Consider us compassionate for giving you one last chance to decide what side you're on. Join us or not, Nadine, but choose your side wisely."

She sat down calmly, putting her back to me. It was a rude indication that I was no longer welcome. I left the Imperium headquarters fuming. Isa jumped on my lap when I got into the car. She rubbed her head against my chin, trying to soothe me.

It didn't work, though.

I returned to the school and met my friends in the Gravestone. I told them about what had happened with the priestesses.

"We should leave town," Miles suggested. "We can split off, create a new coven."

"That's not what Mother Miriam would want," I said. "Wherever we stand on our issues, the coven belongs together. If our magic is dying now, imagine what it would do if we severed ties with one another."

"We'll create new ties," Miles said. "The coven has survived with fewer people before."

"But it's never disavowed its own," I reminded him. "Even in times when witches lived in smaller communities, they cooperated and supported one another."

"You can't argue with these people, though," Miles insisted.

"We've spent all semester gathering supporters," I said. "The priestesses can't hang us all at once."

"You're willing to become a martyr, then," Grant said.

"If it brings change to the coven, then I suppose I am," I replied. "When we started The Coven's Shield, we agreed that we were all in—that we were willing to die for our cause. I would sooner die than watch my fellow coven members be stripped of their basic human rights. The priestesses have already taken their bodily autonomy by failing to provide healthcare. If the priestesses win, they'll control their magic, too. I'd die for each of these items alone. Together, it's not even a question."

I wasn't sure my friends were buying what I was saying. Part of me wanted to leave town like Miles suggested, to just stop fighting and let the coven figure it out on their own.

But I knew what the priestesses would do to the coven if that happened. People who had helped us before would be hurt in unimaginable ways. I couldn't abandon them.

"Nadine, you have to be absolutely sure that this is what you want," Miles said firmly. "Because as it stands, we're the only ones fighting for the coven anymore, and if we're gone, there's no one left to save it. You have to consider if sacrificing your life is good for the coven long-term. It might feel like the right thing to do, but it could be a selfish choice."

"Nadine's offering to sacrifice her life for other people! How is that selfish?" Lucas asked.

"Because if Nadine dies, all she becomes is a symbol, and that's not enough to change things here," Miles growled. "If this is the way things are going to be, we stand a better chance of creating a new coven elsewhere. Or at least continuing the fight from higher ground, where we can stay alive long enough to end this. What do you want, Nadine? Do you want to win, or do you want to become some sort of marble statue that people worship, but that fails to move people's hearts toward making any sort of change?"

I turned away and muttered, "I don't know."

"I hate to say it, but I'm with Miles on this one," Talia said. "If we perish, our cause dies with us, and then there will be no one left to oppose the priestesses."

"People will always rise up against tyrants," Lucas said.

"Yeah, but how many bodies do you want to throw at their feet before something gets done?" Miles challenged.

Grant looked between us, unsure of who to side with. Lucas gave me a look that told me he'd die wherever I asked him to—either by my side here, or on the road, running away from it all.

I didn't like making that kind of decision, not for Lucas, or my friends. I didn't even want to make that decision for myself. There was no way I could face it. At least, not yet.

"Maybe we need to run away." I shrugged. "But I'm not going to make that kind of call on a whim."

"We don't have time to waste," Miles insisted.

"Just give us a couple of days," Lucas promised. "We'll come to an agreement."

Miles scoffed. "If we all aren't dead by then."

By morning, we still hadn't made up our minds. I'd tossed and turned all night, trying to separate my intuition from my ego. It didn't matter which decision we made; both options terrified me to my very core.

I sat on Lucas's bed that morning, stroking Isa's fur.

Talia sat next to Grant across the room. "I want you all to know I'm going to go wherever you go," she said. "Have you guys made a decision?"

I shook my head. I truthfully didn't know where to go from here.

"Let's forget about the coven for a second," Lucas suggested. "What do *you* want, Nadine?"

"I honestly don't know," I told him. It was an impossible decision. "Right now, I'd really like a warm bath and some sushi."

"I can help with the sushi," he offered. "Maybe getting out and doing something normal will clear our heads. Why don't we all go have lunch at Wasabi Lounge?"

I sighed. "If you think it will help."

We left our cats in the room and drove into town. Wasabi Lounge was located in the town square. The shopping area was lined with boutique shops and specialty cafés, with a fountain in the center where people liked to toss in coins to make wishes.

I was looking forward to a quiet day with my friends, but we were two blocks away from the square when we started to notice a large crowd. Finding a free parking space was difficult, but we eventually parked the car and walked to the square. I could hear a voice through loud speakers, but I couldn't make out what they were saying.

When we reached the square, I saw a stage set up near the fountain, where a large crowd had gathered. As I glanced around, I noticed Executors all over the town square, passing out thick pamphlets and proclaiming to be *witnesses of the truth…* whatever that meant. Mira was aggressive, slapping pamphlets into people's hands when they walked by. That girl didn't take no for an answer.

Someone barked into a microphone, and my stomach hollowed when I saw Cody White standing at the center of the stage. Talia's expression fell, and I could tell the sight of him made her sick.

Cody waved his pamphlet over the crowd. "Mother Miriam is taking our magic because of the non-believers. If we bring an end to the non-believers, the coven shall unite once more!"

"*Hang the non-believers!*" a man in the crowd shouted.

There had to be at least a hundred people listening to Cody's fierce words. Some were students, like Gregory and Brayden watching on from a coffee shop nearby. Others were our parents' age, and some of them were young parents with their children along. Several police officers watched on, not making a move to stop a single thing.

Lucas whirled toward one of the guys passing out pamphlets. "What the hell is this!?"

The guy handed him a pamphlet. "Join Miriam's Chosen, and stand with us as witnesses of the truth!"

It was Finn, one of the Treacherous Tarantulas.

Lucas eyed the pamphlet skeptically. "I thought you were Executors. Now you're the Chosen?"

Finn looked down his nose at Lucas. "I'm both. As an Executor, I've already been chosen to restore the balance."

"What's that supposed to mean?" Lucas demanded.

"The priestesses have received a vision," Finn said snidely, like Lucas was stupid. "Mother Miriam has declared a reform to the coven. Follow her will, and the Waning will come to an end. Deny her, and our magic will be stripped forever."

"Hold on," I said. "You think *Mother Miriam* is causing the Waning and holding our magic hostage? She would never do that."

"It's people like you who have caused this in the first place by questioning her orders," Finn spat. "Being a member of this coven is simple. Follow Mother Miriam, and protect the coven. Mother Miriam has given us instruction, and if you can't obey her, you don't belong in the coven at all."

As my eyes roamed over the pamphlet, my stomach sank. *The Chosen are those who are deemed worthy in Mother Miriam's eyes... Mother Miriam has decreed a separation of Casts, to preserve our bloodlines and magic...* The priestesses wanted to tear families apart!

"Mother Miriam would never demand these things," Grant argued.

"Mother Miriam gave us this revelation," Finn insisted. "If you don't join, you're going against her."

"You can't seriously be buying into this," Lucas said.

Finn scoffed. "Forget it. You're a lost cause anyway. I know how you have a habit of turning against your own."

Lucas curled his hands into fists, but I grabbed his wrist. Finn turned away and started passing out pamphlets to other passersby.

"We'll fight this," I promised Lucas. "But let's figure out what we're up against first. Listen to this. *Miriam's Chosen are an elite group of witches and warlocks hand-picked by Mother Miriam with one common goal: to restore the coven's magic. Through total cooperation, we can bring an end to the Waning.*"

Talia looked skeptical. "They're not exactly wrong. We *should* be cooperating. What's the catch?"

"Forcing families apart," I said. "But it doesn't make any sense. Cast magic is chosen, not inherited. Mother Miriam doesn't decide who goes to Alora or the Abyss—you choose that for yourself. She told me. Not even Mother Miriam gatekeeps your worthiness."

Grant's eyes widened as he scanned the page. "They're calling to ban intercast magic and intercast relationships. You're not even allowed to live with anyone outside of your Cast if you join!"

"It's a ploy to weaken our people so they'll do anything the priestesses say," I insisted as heat flared through my veins.

"Talk about false prophets," Lucas said bitterly.

I only got angrier the more I read. To become a member of Miriam's Chosen, you had to undergo a ceremony to confess your sins and pledge yourself to Mother Miriam. "They want you to get a tattoo of a five-pointed star on your wrist, symbolizing the five Casts. It seems a little hypocritical, considering they want the Casts separated. *Through this ceremony, you will be purified.*"

Horror crossed Lucas's features. "Look what it says here if you don't join. *Those who deny Mother Miriam will remain subject to the Waning. A ten-percent income tax will be imposed for non-magical members of the community.*"

I gaped. "They're branding this as a cure. They're saying that if you don't join, your magic will disappear."

"You can stay in Octavia Falls, but you'll be ostracized for it," Lucas sneered. "No wonder people are so eager to join. Keep your magic, save some money. Pretty attractive deal, huh?"

A voice from behind me caught my attention. "The first ceremony is tonight. We have to go."

I turned to see Gregory. He walked behind us, his head ducked as he read over another pamphlet. It was a different color than the one I held.

"Of course we do," Brayden agreed.

"What's happening tonight?" Lucas demanded.

Gregory came to a stop and pushed his glasses up his nose. "There's a Chosen ceremony tonight in the ballroom at school. Anyone can come. I figure we might as well be the first to join."

My eyebrows shot up. "You can't seriously be considering this."

Gregory narrowed his eyes. "And why not?"

"Intercast relationships are banned within Miriam's Chosen," I pointed out.

Brayden blushed a bright pink, and Gregory shot a look around. "Who are you to lecture me on intercast relationships?"

"I'm someone who's in one," I reminded him. "*And* I'm a priestess. This *revelation* isn't real."

Gregory turned up his nose at me. "Perhaps if the other priestesses are keeping you in the dark, there's a reason. I'm not sure I trust you."

"Nothing's *really* going to change if we join Miriam's Chosen," Brayden added. "It's just a precaution. We'll bring an end to the Waning."

"That's a lie," I insisted.

"Things are different now that the priestesses received the vision," Gregory said. "I, for one, choose to be on the right side of history. The only way to keep our relationship a secret is to blend in. Come on, Brayden. These apostates don't know what they're talking about."

Gregory and Brayden walked off, and my jaw dropped. "Apostates?"

"This is bad." Grant's voice shook. "This morning, I overheard Professor Clarke threatening to drop Alchemists from his classes. He must've already seen the pamphlets if he thought he could get away with that."

"He's my Criminal Justice professor!" I cried. "He should know how wrong this is."

"Why would he think that as long as Mother Miriam sanctioned it?" Grant said sarcastically. "Sheriff Baker agreed with him, too. He was headed to try to convince Verla, last I saw him."

"Verla won't let that happen," Talia insisted.

"There's a school board who will argue otherwise," Lucas pointed out. "Most of them side with the priestesses. They'll do anything to keep the coven in line."

"And they're getting better at it," I pointed out. "Everly's been gathering support, and the priestesses have realized the threat of an execution isn't enough. People like us—like Everly—are a threat because we can't be controlled. Miriam's Chosen is designed to separate us and eliminate the threat. Creating a common enemy is the most effective way to control the masses."

"Then why don't they just blame the fae?" Grant asked. "They're an enemy we can fight against. We've united against them before."

"Because they don't *want* to unite with us, as long as we think differently from them," I said. "They already have a use for the fae, and that's to scare people into turning against each other. If they turn this into an *us versus them* scenario, they eliminate compassion for anyone who doesn't join their movement. The burnings and hangings will only get worse, and people will allow our suffering, because they'll learn to hate us. If you thought the priestesses were using executions as a threat before, this is worse. These people will be *calling* for them now."

My attention was stolen by a group of people in black cloaks leading a woman on stage. They weren't like the cloaks the priestesses wore. These ones had long sleeves and pointed hoods. Though the hoods were meant to hide their faces, I could easily make out the features of their jawlines. Ryan and James held the woman by the arms, and Mira pointed a wand at her back threateningly. Except it wasn't a threat at all, because Mira didn't even have magic yet.

The woman's hands were bound in front of her by metal cuffs, and she wore a bag over her head, so I couldn't tell who it was. Around her neck hung a noose on a short rope that acted as a sort of symbolism. She walked alongside the others with a steady step, like she had gone willingly —like she was confident in the midst of her demise.

People booed as they passed, and a man threw his coffee at her. It had to be hot, but she didn't miss a beat in her step.

Beside him, a woman sneered, "She's a non-believer! Expel her from the coven!"

I realized in horror that it was Lucas's mother. Lucas gaped, but his shock only lasted a split second. The next moment, he was crossing the square toward them.

"Lucas," Grant hissed.

I ran behind Lucas. Grant and Talia followed, but they stayed a few feet behind us, ready to back Lucas up at any moment. By the time we reached his parents, Ryan and James were already past with the woman, parading her around as others yelled obscenities at her.

"Dad, what the hell?" Lucas demanded.

His dad crossed his arms. "Rich of you to show your face around here."

"I'm trying to help the coven," Lucas insisted.

"You think we're not doing the same?" his dad snarled.

"We're not the ones putting nooses around people's necks," Lucas snapped. "Goddess, why don't you people just *listen*?"

His mother gasped. "Have some respect for your father! Jay—"

His dad held up a hand to his mom, silencing her. "No, Margo. Let him talk. Perhaps his big mouth will earn him the noose next."

Lucas's nostrils flared, and I thought he might punch his father out right then and there. For him to say that, after the way Eric died, was the lowest blow possible.

"Why should any of us meet the noose, Dad?" Lucas raged. "Don't you get how wrong this is?"

"It's necessary," his father said, before turning to watch the Executors' display. He looked pleased as Ryan and James pulled the woman on stage and forced her to stand in the center.

Cody pointed a finger at her, and his voice rang out over the square. "You think the fae are our enemies? Our true enemies have been lying in wait, awaiting the opportunity to tear our coven apart from the inside out. *This* is what an apostate looks like!"

Ryan yanked the bag off the woman's head, and I gasped when I saw it was Everly. Not a beat passed before Lucas and I were rushing toward the stage. Cody barked into the microphone, but I didn't hear his voice as four figures stepped in front of us, blocking us from reaching the stage.

"Where are you going, Nadine?" Priestess Margaret asked innocently.

My teeth gritted at the sight of the priestesses. Claudia wore a dark cloak like theirs, as if she belonged, though she hadn't been inducted yet.

"You're just going to let this happen?" I demanded.

"You want us to silence our own people?" Lilian asked. She was mocking me.

"You were right," Margaret said, a hint of a smile twitching at her lips. "We must let the public decide."

They were *pleased* to see this play out, because they knew now that the coven would believe their lies and deception. Nothing we said mattered, because people would believe whatever they wanted to believe.

"You cannot unite our people forcefully! We are here to serve our people, not control them," I said. "You're asking people to give up their friends and their families to pledge themselves to your cult."

Claudia gasped. "Miriam's Chosen is not a *cult*! This is our culture, our way of life."

"We already have a coven," I shot back. "You're trying to form a new one."

"That's exactly what we need," Lilian spat. "All those who want to restore order will join the Chosen. By the time this is over, we will know who stands with Mother Miriam and who doesn't."

"So why don't you just arrest me already?" I asked. "Better yet, why not kill me?"

"And make you a martyr?" Lilian scoffed. "Your hanging would not satisfy the coven. You won't die until every last member of the coven has turned against you. Don't you see what you've done, Nadine? You're the enemy now, and it is our duty to *protect the coven.*"

Shadows fell over Lucas and me, and hands landed upon us. Men in dark cloaks had approached us from behind—more Executors, I was certain. I didn't get a chance to defend myself before someone slapped noxite cuffs onto my wrists. I felt my energy drain, and no matter how much I struggled to regain control of my magic, I couldn't break through the magic cuffs.

"Get off of them!" Grant cried. He reached for one of the Executors, but he got an elbow to the nose and landed on his back. Talia rushed to his side.

I screamed and tried to break free of the men, but they were too strong. Lucas struggled from beside me, but three guys just as big as he was held him still. The Executors dragged us on stage, and they forced Lucas and me to stand beside Everly.

"More apostates!" Cody spat. "These people are young and poisoned by the ways of the world!"

"You're, like, two years older than me," Lucas said flatly.

Cody swatted him upside the head. It looked like it had really hurt. Cody smirked as he circled the three of us. "Tell me, Priestess Nadine," he said into the microphone. "Do you believe in Miriam's Chosen? Will you follow the Goddess in this new revelation?"

I gritted my teeth. I could lie, get us all off this stage, play my part —survive.

But they would find someone to take my place, another innocent to hang or burn. What was survival if I was living a lie? Lucas and Everly thought it, too. I could tell in the firm expressions they gave, telling me to stand firm in my truth.

Cody shoved the microphone into my face, and I answered calmly, "I do not believe this is the way. The priestesses wish for you to give up your rights so they can use your magic to annihilate the fae. The fae could be our allies. There is no need for this war!"

Cody pointed a finger at me, and his words echoed across the square. "She defies the revelation! She defies Mother Miriam!"

"Nadine's right!" Lucas shouted. "I used to be prejudiced against the fae, too, but then we met them. They're not all bad."

"Not bad!?" Cody barked. "If we do not unite as Miriam's Chosen, the fae will kill us! Anyone who sides with the fae is a traitor to our people. Give yourself up to Mother Miriam. Surrender to her will."

"We saved a fae's life, and they saved ours in return," Lucas said.

"You are allies with the fae!" Cody accused. "It was *you* who let the fae in to hang Lena!"

"No, we didn't," I insisted.

"Burn them!" someone shouted.

Grant and Talia pushed their way through the crowd. Grant jumped on stage and yanked the microphone out of Cody's hands. "Witch hunts are not the answer! We must come together and—"

"Don't listen to him!" someone in the crowd yelled. "He's only half-witch, just like that fraud priestess!"

I couldn't place who had said it, but the voice sounded young. It had to be someone from school.

"They're a burden to the coven," someone else added. "Half-witches are sick because they're cursed. They don't belong."

They were talking about our chronic illnesses, which were common among witches with non-Miriamic parents. Our human genes didn't play well with our magic, but that didn't make us any less Miriamic. Our magic was just as strong as theirs. Stronger, even, and I had proved that time and again.

"We shouldn't be paying for your medical care," a woman piped up. "You drive up the prices for everybody. If you're only half-witch, you should only get half the support."

"They should get nothing!" Ryan added. "They weren't born here! They aren't one of us."

"I *was* born here," Grant spat into the microphone. "I *do* belong."

"You're not Miriamic," Ryan accused. "You're a mutt."

Grant was getting visibly angry, and the crowd seemed to be having fun taunting him. Grant spoke up. "Being mixed race doesn't invalidate my heritage. All my life, I've struggled to find the box I fit in, but I've realized one side of my heritage doesn't invalidate the other."

Grant gestured around the crowd. "Look around you. The coven has been racially diverse since it was formed, because our ancestors came from many places. If you think *all* your ancestors were Miriam's descendants, you're wrong. Witches married outside the coven for hundreds of years before coming together to form Octavia Falls. We're a colorful society, and we must see the strength in our diversity—from race to sexuality to disability—just as we are stronger with diverse magic. Race is nothing more than a concept created by people to control others. We can find strength in our differences, just as we find strength in our Cast marks."

His voice grew stronger as he spoke. "Our coven is our family, no matter how distantly related—by blood or by marriage. My mother wasn't born here, yet she stood as a member of this coven for a decade, because Mother Miriam accepted her as family. Our Goddess knows family isn't just about blood—it's about connection, and we can heal that connection."

"Then why'd your mom leave?" Ryan spat. "She didn't belong!"

Grant got visibly flustered. His parents had divorced years ago, but it was over personal matters, not coven issues. Grant ignored Ryan and continued. "There is much we can learn from each other. The answer isn't in shunning people who are different from you. Our uniqueness should unite us."

"He's right!" Someone pushed through the crowd. When he made it to the front, I saw that it was Quentin. "I was born in the Miriamic Coven. My family has lived here for generations, and no matter how different all of us are, we're all still witches and warlocks. We need to work together, not fight amongst ourselves. That's what Mother Miriam would want."

Their speech should have given people pause. It was everything The Coven's Shield stood for and more. But the tense silence following Quentin's words was more horrifying than hopeful.

Cody broke the silence by shouting, "They're distracting us from the truth! Their deception will not be tolerated!"

The crowd broke out into cheers of agreement, and people began sprinting forward to get to Grant and Quentin.

"Run!" I cried.

Grant, Quentin, and Talia could still get away. They weren't bound by noxite and being held by Executors like Lucas and I were. Grant dropped the microphone and jumped off the stage. He grabbed Talia's hand, and they took off running beside Quentin. One of them cast a shield, protecting them from the crowd as spells whizzed over their heads. At the back of the crowd, the priestesses watched on, looking pleased.

My heart lurched as someone came up behind me and slipped something over my head. I gasped, but my air was immediately cut off as someone tightened a rope around my throat. *A noose*, I realized. I was certain this was the end. I would finally hang. My only hope was that it was all worth it in the end.

Someone leaned into me and whispered in my ear. "I told you I'd take pleasure putting a noose around your neck."

James. That fucker!

I couldn't protest. I couldn't even scream. James yanked on the rope, and several hands were suddenly dragging me off stage. Lucas screamed protests and tried to yank free of his cuffs as he was dragged behind me, along with Everly. The Executors uncuffed one of my wrists, then yanked my arms behind my back. The cuffs clanged against something metal, and I felt a post in my back. I realized they were chaining me to a lamp post. They forced Lucas's arm through mine on one side, and Everly's on the other, then cuffed the two of them together. As they both struggled, my arms were pulled in opposite directions, and I cried out in pain. The noose loosened on my neck, though it was still hard to breathe.

Lucas and Everly stopped struggling. They backed against the lamp post as the crowd closed in on us.

"We'll get out of this," Everly said, but her hope was futile. We didn't stand a chance against this mob. Not only were we hopelessly outnumbered, but we had no magic as long as these noxite cuffs were on.

Mira stood at the front of the crowd, her smirk visible beneath the shadow of her hood. She bent down to pick up a rock in the road. She drew her arm back and flung the rock straight at me. It hit my cheek, and I felt blood spring from a fresh wound. The crowd followed her lead, gathering rocks and throwing them at us. Stones large and small landed against my skin, and I screamed as I felt bruises break out all across my stomach and legs. Lucas grunted and cursed. Everly tried not to show her pain, but I could hear her drawing in sharp breaths. A spell sped through the air, and I heard a *snap* as it connected with Everly's leg. Her scream echoed off the surrounding buildings.

The crowd descended upon us. Fists sank into my abdomen, and pain radiated across my skull as knuckles pounded into me. Something hard slammed into my knee, and I could no longer keep myself upright. I sank to the ground, dragging Lucas and Everly with me. The three of us crouched there, trying to block the blows, but it didn't matter. There were too many feet, fists, and stones landing upon us. My vision blurred, and through the crowd I spotted the priestesses smiling.

A foot smacked into my head, and in the fleeting moment before I lost consciousness, I had one single thought. If Lucas was going to hear me die, I had to make my last thought a good one.

I'll be with you soon, I thought before everything went black.

LUCAS

NINETEEN

I didn't know at which point I lost consciousness. I found my mind swimming in a blackened nothingness while my thoughts tumbled around without direction. I thought for certain this was the end, and it surprised me how much I *didn't want to die.*

There'd been so many times that I had wished for death, moments I would never admit to, even to myself. I only ever went that far because I had lost hope. Accepting death felt like giving up. Maybe at one time, that seemed appropriate, when there was no one left to care about—no one to miss me. But that wasn't the case anymore.

It made no sense. Life went on for the coven after we died, so why couldn't I accept it?

It hit me like battle magic surging at me from all angles. *I feared death.*

It never occurred to me until then. There was a reason I'd never attempted to take my own life. No matter how many intrusive thoughts I'd had that made me want to do it, no matter how many times I'd gotten close, it was never something I'd actually tried to go through with. At times, I'd had the thought that I was a coward, that I should just get it over with. But something had always kept me holding on. It wasn't because I was weak, or because my mental illness wasn't severe.

Depression hit everyone differently, and for me, wallowing in my pain was more comfortable than the thought of dying. Perhaps it was the fact that life *did* go on after death that scared me the most—that even if I died, it wouldn't fix anything… that I could make it *worse*. I wasn't ready to find out.

It's why I'd had such a hard time accepting my gift, because the thought of dying terrified me to the very core.

Or, it had… I thought of Nora, the girl from the hospital. I thought about how I'd felt so hopeful after meeting her, how death didn't have to be a sad thing. We could live full lives no matter how long we had, and reaching an end only made every moment that came before more precious.

My heart warred with itself, one piece knowing this truth deep to my core, and the other terrified to accept it because staying within my comfort zone was easier than accepting a better alternative.

If this was truly the end, I didn't have a choice. I couldn't delay the inevitable because I didn't want to face it. Death would claim me, whether I was ready or not.

But that's all belief was… a *choice*.

I could choose to believe something differently. Maybe dying next to the woman I loved wasn't so bad.

I heard something, like the shuffling of footsteps. My thoughts stabilized, and the world slowly came back into focus. When I came to, darkness had enveloped the town square. I must've been knocked out for hours. I sat slumped against the lamp post like a ragdoll. Chilly night air swept across my skin, making me shiver. I ached as I shifted, but I could barely lift my head. My skull felt like it weighed a thousand pounds, and it fell back against the post.

A shadow approached. The person leaned down toward me, and I thought for certain we were being attacked again.

"No, please," I rasped. I hadn't drank anything all day, and I was parched.

"I'm here to help," a woman said.

She reached for my cuffs, and I heard a *click* as she freed me. I sat up and looked toward Nadine. She sagged against the lamp post, tangled against Everly. Her lips were dry and cracked, and bruises marred her skin. The woman moved to help Nadine out of her cuffs.

I finally got a look at her face in the light of the streetlamp. "Headmistress Verla?"

"Shh…" she whispered. "We don't know who might be watching."

I looked around, but I saw no silhouettes through the darkness. "Where is everyone?"

She frowned. "They left you for dead."

"Why weren't we slaughtered?" I wondered.

Verla hastily worked on Nadine's cuffs. "They certainly intended to. When I got to the square, the mob was already beating you. By the time I realized what was happening, you'd already lost consciousness. I cast a shield around the three of you to protect you—close to your bodies, so they wouldn't notice. Shortly after, the priestesses ordered the crowd to stand down, but many of them stayed like it was something to celebrate. I've been here all day, waiting for the last of them to leave."

"The priestesses wouldn't have left us unattended," I pointed out. "They'd have let us rot here until they confirmed we were dead. Where are the police? The Executors?"

Verla shot a glance around the square. "I knocked them out with a powerful spell. I broke through their alarm that would alert the priestesses, then cast a ward of my own. I don't know how long it will be until the police wake, so we must hurry."

Nadine groaned as the cuffs came off, and I caught her in my arms before she could slump onto the sidewalk. I quickly pulled the noose from her head and tossed it aside.

"Lucas?" Nadine slurred.

"It's all right, baby," I told her gently, wrapping her tight in my arms. "I'm here."

Nadine cleared her throat. She placed her hand to her neck, like it pained her to speak. "Why would the priestesses tell them to stand down?"

Verla quickly worked on Everly's cuffs. "The longer you're alive, the more the coven will tolerate in the name of defeating you, until everyone complies with the priestesses. They don't want to eliminate you until they've turned everyone against you."

Everly came to and winced as Verla undid her cuffs.

"We must get you someplace safe where you can recover," Verla said.

"What about our friends?" Nadine asked. "They were chased off."

"Quentin left town with Lydia. He wants to get her far away from here. The others are safe," Verla assured us. "We must get moving. Everly, can you walk?"

She shook her head. "I don't think so."

My tender muscles ached as I moved. For the first time, I saw that Everly's pants were covered in blood.

Verla gently pulled back Everly's pant leg, and my stomach dropped. Bone had pierced the skin, and the wound was swollen and purple.

"My car's just down there." Verla pointed to a nearby alley. "We can't stay a moment longer. You'll have to lean on your good leg, and I'll help you walk."

Everly nodded, but she winced as Verla helped her stand. Nadine was worse for wear than I was. I put an arm around her and helped her up. We hobbled behind Verla to her car. The four of us climbed in, and Nadine sagged against me in the back seat as Verla drove us to her house.

The thick trees shielded us from the road, and we emerged from the car unseen. The front door burst open, and a woman raced outside. A black cat hurried behind her.

"Nadine!" Helena cried. Verla must've told her what happened. Tears rose to Helena's eyes as she took in Nadine's bruises under the porch light. Cornelius meowed at her feet. "I'll get the tea on. I know a potent healing brew."

I'd never been inside Verla's house before, but it reminded me a lot of the school, with red carpet and black furniture. Relief flooded through me when I saw Grant and Talia curled under a blanket on the couch, asleep.

Grant stirred. When he saw us, he sat straight upright, waking Talia. "Goddess, you're alive!"

Talia scrambled to her feet. "We had no idea what happened to you! Miles and Mandy, Chloe and Onyx—*everyone*—they're on lockdown at the school. The Executors won't let them leave. We weren't sure you'd made it!"

"Lucas and I will be fine," Nadine said gently. "It's Everly who needs help."

All eyes turned to Everly's bloody leg.

"How can I help?" Talia asked immediately.

"Help me get Everly to the bedroom," Verla said. "It's just down here."

Grant hurried to help support Everly. "I take it we have no allies at the hospital?"

Verla shook her head. "After what happened tonight, I'm not risking it. I can set the bone, but I'll need help."

Verla stripped off her coat and hung her purse on a hook next to the door. The three of them helped Everly to the bedroom. Helena came back with our tea and a few ice packs, then rushed to help brew a potent painkiller for Everly.

Nadine and I were in no condition to help. I led her over to the sofa in front of the fireplace. She snuggled into me to warm up. I pressed my ice pack to my shoulder, but Nadine just hugged her ice pack to her chest with one hand and held her teacup in the other. She stared into the flickering flames, like she was some other place entirely.

"Where does it hurt the most?" I asked her.

"My knee," she said, without taking her eyes off the fire.

I took the ice pack off her chest and pressed it to her knee. She offered a kind smile, but it didn't meet her eyes.

"Drink your tea," I encouraged. "It will help."

Neither of us said anything as we sipped our tea and watched the fire. We could hear voices coming from down the hall, but I never once heard Everly scream. Whatever Helena had brewed for her must've knocked her out. I kept throwing glances out the window, expecting to see flaming torches through the trees as the mob returned to finish us off. I saw nothing but darkness.

The more tea I drank, the more my heartbeat began to slow. I set my cup and saucer aside when I'd finished, and at some point, I must've drifted off.

It couldn't have been more than twenty minutes before I awoke again. I sat slumped on the sofa with a blanket over me. My cup and saucer were gone, and so was Nadine. Grant and Talia were curled up together in a big chair and were asleep again. I heard voices coming from the kitchen.

Curiously, I stood and followed the sound. I stopped in the doorway when I saw that Nadine was all right. She sat at the table as Verla cleaned up the herbs and medical supplies. Her cat, Odin, followed her around the kitchen. Helena must've been down the hall tending to Everly.

"For the first time, I don't know what to do," Nadine admitted.

"We keep fighting," Verla said simply.

Nadine dropped her head. "What if that's not the answer? I'm afraid we're too angry to see the solution."

Verla paused and turned to Nadine. "Anger is not a weakness. Your strength lies in what you do with it. Anger has its place. It will drive you to ignite change."

"What if we've ignited a fire we can no longer put out?" Nadine asked.

Verla drew a deep breath. "So we adapt. We must leave town and head to the safe house tonight."

"The safe house?" Nadine asked. "But William—"

"Left it to us," Verla finished for her. "Despite William's death, the house is still available to The Coven's Shield. You can't still be against using it."

"I just don't see how we can fight if we leave," Nadine said. "I won't give up."

Verla wore an incredulous look. "Sometimes you need to come up for air, Nadine. Staying here is going to get you killed!"

"Verla's right," I said, stepping into the kitchen.

Nadine's gaze darted toward me. It was the first time she noticed me. My stomach twisted at the sight of bruises all over her face. Helena's healing teas were good, but not *that* good. It'd take a few days for her to heal.

"The coven is ready to hang us," I said. "We have to make adjustments."

Nadine hesitated, but I could see the defeat written all over her face. "Everly's in no condition to travel."

"We'll leave in the morning, when she wakes," I suggested.

"We need to leave as soon as possible," Verla argued.

"We need more than an hour to recover," I said. "We're not leaving without everyone. We still need to go back to school for our friends, as well as our cats. I'm not leaving Oliver and Isa behind."

Verla sighed. She could clearly see I wasn't going to budge on the matter. "Fine. We'll leave in the morning. In the meantime, I have a guest room that your friends refused. You're both welcome to it."

Nadine stood. "Thank you. For everything."

Verla smiled kindly. "You're welcome."

She led us to the guest bedroom, and we both collapsed onto the bed. I curled Nadine in my arms and pressed my nose into her hair. Inhaling her scent calmed me more than a magical potion ever could. We fell asleep soundlessly.

When I woke the next morning, I was feeling a little better, but I wasn't a hundred percent. The potion Helena had brewed into the tea helped speed up healing, but witch magic could only do so much. I was still sore and tender everywhere, but my headache had gone away.

Nadine stirred from beside me, and she winced when she rolled over. I drew away from her quickly, afraid I'd hurt her.

"You're fine," she told me, pulling me closer. "It's just my knee. It twinges when I move."

I hated seeing Nadine in pain. "If I knew who messed up your knee, I'd pound his face in."

Nadine sighed. "There was no knowing who's responsible. There were too many people."

"And I blame each and every one of them."

"Karma will deal with them." Nadine winced as she sat up.

"You should rest," I protested.

"I want to check on everyone." Nadine wasn't taking no for an answer.

I helped her downstairs, and we heard voices coming from the bedroom. I followed the sound and found that Everly was awake. Everyone was gathered around her bedside.

Helena peeled back the dressing on Everly's leg. "The wound is infected."

"We need to get her to a doctor," Talia demanded.

Everly shook her head weakly. A fever had spread over her, making her face sheen with sweat. "The doctors aren't going to help me."

"We'll take you out of town," Grant suggested. "There are other hospitals."

"I was hit by a spell—some sort of curse," Everly said. "There's magic inside my system infecting the bone. Human doctors can't fix this."

"I can." Nadine hobbled into the room, and everyone moved aside to let Nadine through. She knelt at the bedside and placed her hand in Everly's. I watched on curiously, waiting for her magic to work… but nothing happened.

Nadine furrowed her brow. "It's not working. I can't feel anything."

"It must be the Waning," Helena said. "My powers were gone when I woke up."

"Mine, too," Grant added.

I tried to cast a simple orb, but my magic was gone. It made sense that the Waning was taking a toll on all of us; the coven was more divided than ever before.

Nadine's features paled. "What are we going to do? Without my powers, Everly's life is in danger! I can't break this curse!"

Verla drew her shoulders back. "My magic is still working. I know a powerful brew that can counteract magical infections. I'll get to work on it immediately."

She left the room, and everything fell silent as Helena worked on redressing the wound. I wanted to hurl when I saw the black lines spiderwebbing down Everly's leg. We were so far out of our league here; it wasn't even funny. We needed to get Everly to a doctor, but the coven's doctors would sooner hang us than help us.

Nadine squeezed Everly's hand. "We're going to fix this. I promise."

I heard whispers coming from the kitchen, and I followed the sound. I realized the voice was coming from Verla, even though she was alone.

"Everything all right in here?" I asked. "I thought I heard you talking to someone."

Verla's features fell. The cupboard she'd been looking through hung open. "I—I'm out of scaleweed. It's the main ingredient in the brew."

"So we'll get some more," I offered. "Helena's got a garden full of herbs."

Verla shook her head. "It's a rare magical herb that doesn't grow in Octavia Falls. It comes from merfolk societies and grows underwater. It's a type of seaweed with healing properties that combat magical injuries."

"Where can we find this herb?" I asked.

"Avery's Apothecary was the only place that sold it, but the shop owner… he died a few weeks ago, and the place shut down. Everything's shutting down."

"Maybe there's still stock left in the building," I suggested.

"And what exactly do you plan to do?" Verla demanded. "Steal it?"

"If that's what we have to do," I stated.

Verla pursed her lips. "That's out of the question. If you're caught, you'll be arrested or hanged. If I go and *I'm* caught, the police will be here to search my place within minutes. You won't have time to escape. We should have left last night."

"We didn't, so what are we going to do? Let the infection spread? Everly could die." It was cruel. We couldn't let that happen.

Verla lowered her voice, so no one down the hall could hear. "There are two lives here that matter above anyone else's, and that is yours and Nadine's. You are the ones the prophecy speaks of. I will not do anything to put either of you in danger."

My blood chilled. I couldn't believe she would suggest such a thing. "I don't accept that. I won't let Everly die just to protect myself. It's not what The Coven's Shield stands for."

"The Coven's Shield needs to get comfortable making tough decisions," Verla insisted. "We can't save everyone, Lucas. So please, let me save who I can. Right now, I can save you and your friends. We're gathering our things, and we're leaving. Now."

Verla didn't give me a chance to argue. She breezed out of the room. End of discussion.

But I couldn't do it. I couldn't walk out of here knowing Everly's infection could spread before we recovered from the Waning. Everly could die as soon as we made it to the safe house. Verla thought she was saving me, but maybe I didn't want to be saved at the expense of someone else's life.

I snuck down the hall, to where I'd seen Verla hang her purse last night. No one heard me reach into her purse for the keys or sneak out the front door. I sped out of the driveway before anyone noticed me missing.

The streets were deserted when I made it into town. After what happened yesterday, I didn't blame people for staying inside. I slowed the car as I neared Avery's Apothecary. A group of guys gathered in front of the jewelry shop next door. The front window was shattered, and they grabbed expensive jewelry off the displays. The sign out front read *All Casts Welcome*.

They weren't shy about exactly what they thought of the situation. One of the guys—a Mentalist, by the looks of it—moved his hands through the air and used telekinesis to carve obscene words into the shop door. Two others threw a rope over the sign above the door and yanked on it. A skeleton tied to a noose rose into the air, and my stomach clenched.

The last thing I wanted was to run into these guys. I circled around to the back and parked on a secluded street. I had no plan but to get in and out as fast as possible. As long as I was gone before the cops showed up, it didn't matter. I was already a dead man walking the moment I set foot in town.

I kept my hood up as I crossed the parking lot. The back door to Avery's Apothecary was made of glass, and I could see that the lights inside were turned off. The shop was completely deserted like the others surrounding it. This place was a complete ghost town.

I had no magic to speak of, so that wasn't going to help me get inside. I was going to have to do this the old-fashioned way. I went over to a nearby rock bed and grabbed the biggest rock I could find. I aimed it at the door and threw it as hard as I could. The glass shattered, and I winced as the sound echoed off the buildings around me.

The owner had left this place completely defenseless—no wards, no alarms, nothing. I worried that I wouldn't find what I needed.

I was already this far. I wasn't turning back now. I kicked glass aside as I entered the shop. The shelves were bare, except for a few supplies piled in boxes behind the counter. I hurried over to them and flipped them over, looking for labels, but there weren't any.

"Fuck," I growled under my breath.

I placed the first box on the counter and quickly tore it open. There were all kinds of herbs packed in here, along with other medical devices. I found nothing labeled scaleweed, but I found a knee brace. I tucked it into my back pocket; I was definitely taking that for Nadine. I tossed the box aside and moved on to the next one. It was nothing but junk, but I found a puzzle box I thought Nadine would like, so I shoved that in my pocket, too.

I tore open several more, until I reached the last box. *This shit better be in here.*

I tossed herb packets aside, until I reached the bottom. My heart leapt when I saw a single pouch labeled *scaleweed.*

Thank the Goddess! This better be enough for the brew.

I shoved the packet in my pocket, but a voice out front made me jump. I ducked behind the counter. "Hey!" someone shouted.

Fuck, they'd found me!

Wait, no... I'd come in through the back.

I peeked over the counter, and I saw several police officers run by the window. "You vandals better stop, or I'll shoot!" an officer yelled.

The guys hanging the skeleton must've gotten themselves into trouble. I had to get out of here *now*.

I turned to slip out the back—and my heart stalled in my chest. A ghostly figure hovered in front of me. He was a middle-aged man dressed in modern clothing. His dark eyes were sunken in, and there was a big bloody wound out one side of his head. It looked like he'd been hit with an intense spell. I wasn't the kind of warlock to see ghosts, which mean this one had to be fucking strong.

"You dare steal from me!?" he screamed.

Aw, fuck. This guy didn't even know he was dead.

I held up my hands in surrender. "Please, I came to save my friend— Everly Hall. You might know her. She's a Seer with a shop just a few doors down. She's been infected by a—"

The ghost let out a high-pitched scream unlike anything a living being could produce. I threw my hands over my ears, and the front windows shattered.

"Over here!" the police shouted.

Fuck.

I took off sprinting toward the back door. I caught my pant leg on a glass fragment as I jumped through the broken frame, and my jeans tore. I tripped and rolled across the pavement. When I looked back, I saw two officers racing through the shop toward me. One raised a gun to me, and another pointed a wand in my direction. I knew that if I ran across the parking lot to the car, they'd shoot me before I made it.

I scrambled to my feet and made a break for the first escape I could find. I yanked on the door to a nearby shop, and it swung open, to my relief. I quickly pulled it shut and turned the lock, then ducked around the corner.

"Where'd he go?" one of the officers yelled. I peeked around the corner to see the officer glancing around like I'd just vanished into thin air. *Idiots.*

"There's the vandals!" the other officer shouted. They took off running in the other direction.

I sank to the ground and breathed a sigh of relief. When I looked around the shop, I realized I'd ducked into the jewelry shop. The looters had knocked over the displays, and glass lay shattered everywhere. All the jewels were gone, and the lights above my head flickered.

A whimper came from across the room. I curiously got to my feet and followed the sound. An old man crouched behind the counter. He held his hands up and shied away from me. "P—please, don't hurt me!"

"I'm not going to hurt you," I told him.

He lowered his hands. "You're not?"

I helped him to his feet. "You were in here this whole time?"

He nodded, and his whole body shook. "They took everything… everything but this."

He pulled a box from his pocket and opened it. I could hardly believe my eyes. Inside sat the teal ring I'd spotted months ago. Sparkling teal stones swirled with clear diamonds and hugged a shimmering diamond in the center.

"We should get you out of here before the vandals come back," I said.

But he didn't move. He just stood there, eyeing me curiously. "You're Lucas Taylor, aren't you? The Reaper's Apprentice?"

My mouth went dry. He probably wanted to hang me, too. "I am. What's your name?"

"Theodore Knox," he introduced himself. Then he took the ring out of the box and held it up to me. "Paraiba tourmaline and diamonds. This ring will calm the mind, promote wisdom in the wearer, and help the wearer make good choices about their future."

I took a step back. "That's great and all, but we should really go."

"I'll find my own way out," he said, before placing the ring back in the box. Then he took my hand and curled my fingers around it. "I believe in you and the priestess. I want you to have this."

I shoved the box back at him. "You were just *robbed*. I can't take this. You need to sell it, in order to survive."

"What I *need* is for you and Priestess Nadine to save our people," he insisted.

I thought of the sign he had out front. *All Casts Welcome*. This man had been willing to risk his business—risk his *life*—for our cause.

"You don't have to give this to me," I insisted.

"This ring is all I have left. Take it as a reminder that there are people in the coven who stand by you. Don't let them break you, Lucas. We need you."

My heart swelled as I looked down at the ring. I'd been thinking about this ring for months, but never in my wildest dreams did I think I'd ever own it. I thought about slipping it on Nadine's finger, and nothing had ever felt so *right*. It was like no conflict existed at all, because all I could think was that I was going to ask Nadine to marry me. I didn't know how, and I didn't know when the wedding would happen, but even in the midst of all this, I wanted to be her husband, for however long we had left.

He placed the box in my hands again and pushed me. "Go, before they find you."

"What about you—?"

"I'm not the one they want to hang. Leave, hurry!" He shoved me.

I hurried out of the shop and glanced around. I didn't see the police, so I made a break for Verla's car. I tucked everything I'd found into the glove compartment, then reached for the ignition.

Before I could turn the car on, someone yanked the door open. I didn't see who it was before I was dragged to the ground. They must've been waiting for me.

I tried to create a shield, until I realized I was still affected by the Waning. Someone smashed my face against the asphalt, and I felt the cool metal of noxite cuffs being slapped onto my wrists.

"Lucas Taylor," a deep voice barked. *Sheriff Baker.*

"I'm not stealing the car. I swear!" I cried.

"You are under arrest by order of the Imperium Council."

I gritted my teeth. "Yesterday wasn't enough for you people?"

"This is another matter entirely," Baker said. I heard footsteps and knew he wasn't alone. "You're under arrest for conspiracy to overthrow the Imperium Council. You have the right to remain silent—"

"Overthrow? I never intended "

"Anything you say or do can and will be used against you in a court of law," Baker said. Something hard pressed into my back, and I stilled. "Come willingly, or you'll be shot with noxite darts. They'll knock you out, so I don't suggest fighting back if you want a chance to plead your case."

Baker yanked me to my feet and shoved me into the back of a squad car. I turned the best I could to look out the back window. As I rode away, I saw the other officers pulling things out of the car. An officer dug into the glove compartment and opened the jewelry box. Horror tangled in my gut when he saw it was of no interest and tossed the box into the street.

Of all the things the Miriamic Coven had done to us, that was one of the most heartbreaking. I'd only had the ring for five minutes, but I'd already decided I was going to use it to propose. It was a promise I'd already made to myself and to Nadine. No matter what happened, I was here to stay. Now it felt as if that choice was being stripped from me, too.

The officers were not kind when they dragged me into the station. Sheriff Baker followed behind, as if I was such a threat I needed a whole battalion to keep me in line. I kept my head down and didn't say a word, until I heard the sound of Nadine's voice. "Ow, that hurts!"

I must've been hearing things, because Nadine was back at Verla's. How could they have found her?

I looked up to see two officers dragging her across the station ahead of me. If I thought the officers weren't kind to me, it was nothing like how they treated Nadine. One of them had her by the hair, and the other held tight to her arm, where one of her bruises was clearly visible.

"Get off of her!" I shouted. I started struggling, though I knew I'd never make it out of the cuffs.

Someone smacked me in the back with something hard. I wasn't sure if it was a baton or a spell or what the hell it was. It hurt so bad that I stumbled to my knees. *Fuck!*

When I looked up, Nadine was gone. *No, no, no, no!*

"On your feet!" one of the officers bellowed. The two officers yanked me upright and dragged me down the hall.

They led me through a guarded doorway into a room lined with three jail cells. The door on the end squeaked open as the officers tossed Nadine inside, shoving her so hard she landed on her knees. I witnessed her wince, but she didn't let the officers see. Her hair concealed her face, and she sat there for several moments without protesting.

"That's right, little bitch," one of the officers sneered. "It's time to give up. When you walk out of here, you'll be headed to the gallows."

"Stand down, Davenport," Sheriff Baker commanded. "We have strict orders from the priestesses. They're not to be harmed while awaiting trial."

Like he gave a fuck. He didn't have anything to say about the way they dragged her in here.

The officers undid my cuffs, then opened the closest door and shoved me inside. It left a cell between Nadine and me so we couldn't reach each other. Our cells were small, barely five feet wide, with nothing but a metal bench attached to the wall for us to sit on.

The door clanged behind me, and I turned to curl my hands around the bars. "What trial, exactly?" I demanded. "What's our crime?"

Sheriff Baker began reciting our charges like he had them memorized. "One felony count of attempting to overthrow the Imperium Council, two misdemeanor counts of unauthorized intercast spellwork, multiple felony charges of black magic use with intent to do harm, and seven charges of first-degree murder. Need I go on?"

The blood in my veins turned to ice. How could they possibly have that much on us? They had to be fabricating evidence, because it wasn't true. But if the people believed it, we didn't even stand a chance.

"If they think we've done all that, why are they giving us a trial at all?" I asked. "Why not just burn us at the stake? It'll save you time and resources."

"This is what you wanted, isn't it? A chance for your voices to be heard?" Sheriff Baker smirked, and I knew it was far more than that. It was the Imperium Council's way of making a show out of our execution. They had no intention of giving us a fair trial… only creating a spectacle to convert people to Miriam's Chosen.

"The Imperium Council has no evidence to back up any of this," I argued.

Sheriff Baker stepped inches away from my cell. He smirked and lowered his voice. "Believe me, boy. We've got all the evidence we need. Once your trial is over, you're headed straight for the Abyss."

Sheriff Baker turned from my cell, and he walked out of the room laughing as the other officers followed.

The second they were out of the room, I whirled toward Nadine's cell. She was still on the ground, hair concealing her face. "Nad!" I cried. "Are you hurt?"

She pushed her hair behind her ear and sat upright, though her whole body shook. "I'm fine. How are you?"

My back was still sore from being beat, but I could handle it. "I'll be all right. How did they find you?"

Nadine winced as she pulled herself onto the bench in the corner. "I came after you once we realized you were missing."

"Verla *let* you come into town?" I balked.

"Goddess, no," Nadine said. "I snuck out, same as you. I turned a corner, and the officers jumped me."

"We'll get out of this," I promised. We *had* to.

Nadine dropped her gaze. "I don't know if we can, Lucas."

"We've defied the odds before. We'll do it again." I eyed the metal bars and tried to conjure a battle orb, but my magic was completely drained. "There's got to be a way out of here."

Nadine lifted her hand, but she could only manage a few sparks.

"How come your magic is working more than mine?" I asked. "It wasn't working this morning."

She furrowed her brow. "Maybe Curse Breakers recover from the Waning faster. Either way, my magic won't be strong enough when it returns, not locked behind noxite bars. Our magic can't help us."

A lump rose to my throat. "You can't give up. I'm the one who gives up, and you're always there to lift me back up again."

"I'm not giving up," she promised. "We can win the trial, but we have to decide for ourselves where we stand on our wrongdoings. If we don't, we put all our hope in the priestesses' hands."

Nadine glanced around the room, and her eyes stopped dead when she looked in the corner. I followed her gaze and realized there was a security camera mounted on the ceiling. The officers could certainly hear everything we were saying.

"We have each other. That's all that matters," I said, but my words felt hollow.

Nadine and I didn't say much else, because we knew the officers were watching. Hours passed, but there were no windows in the holding room to indicate the time of day. I racked my brain for hours, trying to find a way out of this, but I came up empty each time.

It had to be past nightfall when the door opened. It was the first time anyone had been in here since they'd shoved us in these cells. They hadn't even had the courtesy to provide us a meal. Sheriff Baker entered the room, followed by none other than Headmistress Clarice Verla.

I scrambled off my bench. "What's going on?"

"Your lawyer's here." Baker didn't sound too happy about it.

I remembered that Headmistress Verla had said she had a law degree. She'd helped Chloe when she'd been arrested earlier this semester. She must've convinced the priestesses to let her take our case, too.

Baker approached my cell, and his keys clanged as he unlocked the door.

"We're getting out?" I asked.

"Your bail's been posted," Baker sneered.

I hesitated as I stepped out of my cell. "Aren't we supposed to have a bail hearing?"

Baker barely acknowledged me as he moved on to unlock Nadine's cell. "Be grateful you're getting out at all."

The priestesses didn't care about procedure, apparently. Was this another ploy to parade us around town again?

The moment Nadine's cell opened, she rushed toward me, and I scooped her into my arms. For the first time since we'd been arrested, my heart finally began to settle. They could beat us, hang us, send us straight to the Abyss. As long as Nadine was by my side, it didn't matter. I smoothed her hair down, and I didn't want to let her go.

But I also didn't want to spend one more moment in this hell hole.

Baker cleared his throat. "You're free for tonight, but your trial begins in the morning. Don't think we won't be watching."

It was a threat if I ever heard one.

"Come. We have much to discuss," Verla said curtly. She was trying to appear indifferent. The coven still didn't know she was on our side.

Sheriff Baker didn't look pleased as Verla led us out of the station. Twilight had already fallen by the time we stepped outside. In the night air, I finally felt like I could breathe.

"Do you have any idea the trouble you've gotten yourselves into?" Verla hissed as she led us toward her car. Looks like the police gave it back to her.

I frowned. "Yes, we know. We never should've snuck out. Did Everly at least get the scaleweed?"

Verla stopped at her car. "Yes. That's one good thing that came from this. Now get in."

She opened the back door for us, and Nadine climbed into the back seat.

I slid in next to her. "I don't get it. Why would the priestesses set bail? Considering our charges, you'd think they'd want us locked up for good."

"I'm sure they have their reasons," Verla said as she slid into the driver's seat.

Nadine crossed her arms. "Knowing Claudia, I wouldn't put it past them to be using this as a money grab."

I leaned forward. "Who posted our bail?"

Verla pulled the car onto the street. "It was a combined effort from The Coven's Shield. We couldn't leave you in the holding cell. We need to talk to prepare your defense."

"How did the priestesses agree to letting you be our lawyer?" Nadine asked.

Verla sucked a breath. "Being that you're students and I'm your head-mistress, I legally have to represent you. Plus, once I told them Lucas stole my car, they were more than willing to assign me the case. The priestesses think I want revenge on you, but I believe we can get you off your charges without implicating all of us. The Coven's Shield has already begun preparing your defense… but the priestesses have substantial evidence against you."

"It has to be fabricated or…" It hit me, and my heart spiraled out of my chest. "Someone turned us in. If the priestesses found the Gravestone, that means someone betrayed us. But we trusted everyone who knew about it. Unless… *Chloe.*"

Nadine shook her head. "Chloe will do anything to get her way, but she wanted to go against the priestesses with us."

"Unless she was a spy the whole time!" I said. "I know she helped us during the Burning, but her grandmother could be manipulating her. We've done spells with Chloe that didn't work."

The tracking spell we'd done to locate the demon contract had resisted our power. Could Chloe have influenced it to throw us off track?

"Chloe took the witch's vow with us," Nadine reminded me.

"Then it's got to be someone who didn't take the vow," I realized. "Onyx?"

Nadine didn't look convinced. "I trust Onyx."

I frowned. "Perhaps you trust too easily. Whatever evidence they *think* they have on us is bullshit. We never tried to overthrow the council. We never used black magic to harm anyone. And *seven* murders? Where would they even get an idea like that?"

Nadine shot me a pointed expression. "Lucas…"

I started counting in my head. Professor Carlisle, along with Agnes, Betty, and Sandy, all died last year at Pinewood Manor. But Nadine had killed the three witches to save everyone. They had kidnapped and killed two boys, and they intended to do the same to Nadine and Chloe. If Nadine hadn't killed them, we'd *all* be dead.

Professor Carlisle's death, on the other hand, wasn't our fault. He was alive when we walked out of Pinewood Manor. Then the explosion happened. We still didn't know what had caused it, but it sure as hell wasn't one of us. The coven would never believe that, though.

Then there was Priestess Stella. She'd died at Wicked Alchemy when we'd gone into the basement to retrieve the Crock of Death and the Alchemy Wand. I'd knocked her off her broom, and she'd fallen into the twisted vine.

Finally, Grant had killed two officers the night of the Burning. Miles, Talia, and I had been captured, and he'd come to save us.

Everything we'd done had been to save each other from certain death. We hadn't any other choice. We would never kill in cold blood. There had to be laws protecting us in cases of self-defense… right?

"Dear Goddess," I muttered, sagging down in my chair. "We really are going to hell."

"No," Nadine said firmly. "You know that's not how this works."

I sighed. "I want to believe that. I really do."

"Maybe we have to start thinking differently about all this," Nadine suggested. "There are moments when we have to decide which side we stand on, and forgive ourselves if we end up on the wrong side. We have to prepare for anything."

Even death.

I heard it in her voice. She wasn't sure we were going to survive this.

"So, what?" I asked. "We're just *okay* with letting them hang us?"

"That's not what I'm saying," Nadine insisted. "I'm saying that we can't let them break us, because they will *try*, Lucas. They'll put everything we've ever said or done on display. They will make us out to be villains."

"We *did* kill seven people," I pointed out flatly. "Maybe we've always done it for the right reasons, or maybe we've made mistakes, but the fact still stands. We can't undo what we've done, and that already gives the priestesses the upper hand."

"But we know everything we've done has been in the name of saving innocent lives," Nadine said desperately. "Yes, we've made mistakes. Bad ones, I know that. But we are *not* heartless. Every day, we can do better.

We have to be more confident in our story than in theirs, because if they convince us that we can't be redeemed, they've won. The coven is already hanging on by a thread. This is our last chance to show what we stand for. If we crumble, the coven will forever live by the precedent that mistakes cannot be forgiven, and *that* is going to be the final breaking point for us all."

Silence stretched through the car, and a shiver traveled down my spine. Nadine was right. We had one last chance to prove to the coven that we were here to save our people, protect their rights, and restore their magic.

I hoped to the Goddess this didn't end with both of us hanging on the end of a noose.

nadine

TWENTY

We had a single night to prepare for our trial. It wasn't enough time. I was sure the priestesses were cackling away in the Imperium headquarters right now, laughing about how they finally *got us* and everything was playing out according to their plan. They were probably already popping champagne, knowing that they'd convert thousands more to Miriam's Chosen before the trial ended.

I refused to believe this was over just yet.

We got take-out because we didn't think it was safe to be seen, and we didn't have time to waste. I scarfed down a chicken sandwich in the car; I was ravenous. Verla drove us back to school.

"What are we doing here?" I asked. "The school is the worst place for us right now."

"The priestesses are watching," Verla reminded me. "They've entrusted me with keeping a close eye on you, and if I take you back to my house, I'll appear as an ally. We must let them believe otherwise until your trial. You'll stay here tonight."

We followed Verla inside the school. The halls were silent, and the place seemed deserted. The students obviously felt the weight of this conflict, and they were all hiding in their rooms.

Verla led us to her office, and she sat behind her desk. Odin lazed on the cat tower, purring. Verla handed me a folder. "Here's everything I know about the case."

We spent the next several hours discussing our case. It quickly became clear that the priestesses had found the Gravestone. We were right to think there was a traitor inside The Coven's Shield. Verla went over everything she knew from the court files, but they'd been slapped together in a matter of hours. We were certain she was missing details. We discussed what evidence the priestesses might present to the court, and how we could counter it with our own—what little we had. Verla coached us on how to answer questions in the courtroom, but I wasn't entirely convinced it would be enough.

"Most of these charges are bogus, but what about the murders?" Lucas asked. "Whether they were accidents or not, we *did* kill people."

Verla drew a deep breath. "That's going to be the hardest part of the trial. Your only hope is to say as few incriminating things as possible to make it look like the priestesses' evidence is faulty. That's the only way the coven will side with you."

"Or we tell the truth," I suggested.

"The truth will get you hanged!" Verla insisted.

"The truth is that we killed in self-defense," I said. "That means we're innocent of the charges they've brought against us. More so, we didn't kill Professor Carlisle. He was alive when we left Pinewood Manor. The explosion that followed killed him. And Stella's death was an accident. So if we prove the priestesses are wrong on these points, they're going to look wrong about everything else."

Verla shook her head firmly. "You've never been in a courtroom. If you tell the truth, the priestesses will use your word against you."

"To be charged with first-degree murder, the priestesses have to prove that we had premeditated intent to kill," I pressed. "We didn't."

"Forget everything you think you know about the legal system, because this trial will operate under Miriamic law," Verla replied. "To the priestesses, this isn't a real court case. It's a performance. We have to prepare for that. You will tell me everything you know. We will prepare a response, and you will speak *only* these responses in the courtroom. Do you understand?"

I sank a little in my chair. "Yes."

Verla coached us until after midnight. The words on the court documents were no longer making any sense.

Verla stood. "You two should get some rest before the trial. Let's call it a night."

"But we only have a few hours—" Lucas started.

"A few hours to get some rest," Verla said gently. "You need to clear your heads and be ready for anything. Let me walk you to your rooms."

"You don't have to do that. We can find our own way back," I assured her.

Verla sighed. "Very well. I have to arrange some things before the trial begins. Do your best to get some sleep, both of you. Lucas, can I have a word?"

Lucas furrowed his brow, but he stayed in the room while I headed out into the hall. I saw her hand him a bag, along with something else, though I couldn't be sure what it was. He left her office with a hint of a smile on his face.

"What was that about?" I asked as we started toward his dorm.

Lucas wouldn't stop smiling. "The police gave Verla her stuff back that was in her car. She managed to get this back for you."

He reached into the bag and pulled out a knee brace. The swelling had gone down thanks to Grammy's potion, but it still twinged when I moved.

"Lucas, thank you so much," I told him. "You shouldn't have."

"It was no problem."

"No, I mean, you really shouldn't have. The police wouldn't have found us if you hadn't gone into town."

"I had to get Everly's herbs. I found this while I was searching for them. Do you want to wear it?"

"Sure…" I said in uncertainty. Lucas was acting weird.

"Here, let me help." Lucas bent to one knee, and I steadied myself against the wall as he helped me slip into the brace. I giggled, because it tickled when he touched the back of my leg. He must've liked getting a reaction out of me, because he purposely tickled me harder. Heat pooled between my thighs, and I suddenly wasn't tired anymore.

It should feel weird to laugh at a time like this, but we had one last night together before our verdict was read. It seemed appropriate to make the most of every moment we had left. Some people might be turned off at the threat of death, but I was a witch. We kind of had a thing for death. If anything, it only made every touch hotter and made me desire him more. If we were going to die, I would make the most of our last night together.

The brace fit snugly around my knee, and the pressure helped dull the ache. Lucas paused for a long moment. He had this deeply contemplative look on his face, and his hand shook as he reached for his pocket. Definitely weird. I hoped he hadn't gotten hexed or something.

"Everything okay?"

His gaze snapped up to mine. "Just tired."

He leaned forward and placed a gentle kiss on my knee, then stood. "Let's get somewhere—"

The sound of footsteps cut him off. We both went rigid. Usually, no one was out of their dorms this time of night. We thought it was safe to walk back to our rooms alone, but if we ran into the wrong person, we were in trouble.

Lucas grabbed my hand and pulled me down the hall. He opened the first door we found—a red door I hadn't ever noticed before. It must've been a supply closet or something, because it certainly didn't lead to any classrooms I'd been in. We slipped inside the dark room, and Lucas quickly shut the door behind us. After a few beats, it became obvious no one was following us. He opened the door a crack to peek down the hall, and he breathed a heavy sigh.

"It was just Verla. She's probably headed to the library to prepare for our trial. We can..." He trailed off when he turned to me. Lucas dropped the door handle, and the door swung shut, clicking behind him. Darkness enveloped us from all angles.

"What is it?" I asked.

"Do you have any idea where we are?"

"Um, no. It's pretty dark," I said flatly.

Lucas searched for the light switch on the wall, and a few moments later, the lights clicked on. The room filled with a soft, orange glow. Quiet music began to play on speakers overhead, and twinkling lights reflected off the walls. I turned around and gasped at what I saw.

This room didn't look like it belonged inside the school. It was so unlike our dorm rooms, more like an executive suite in a five-star resort.

The room was huge, with a large heart-shaped bed in the center and twinkling lights strung above it. Nearby, a whirlpool tub sat filled to the top with steaming water, looking warm and welcoming. Rose petals floated on the surface. A faint floral scent filled my nose, relaxing me instantly.

"This room definitely wasn't here before. What is this place?" I couldn't help but walk across the room and run my fingers over the red silk sheets on the bed. This had to be a fae illusion or something. It was too perfect. I mean, I'd just been thinking about giving Lucas the night of his life, and then this room appeared?

"It's the Presidential Suite," Lucas said. "It's an enchanted room that moves around the school and appears when you need some… alone time. Students enchanted it ages ago, to hide it from the staff."

I sat down on the bed, continuing to run my fingers over the soft silk. It was definitely real. "So this is all for us?"

"That's how the enchantment works," he said.

"That's awfully convenient, considering the things I was just thinking about you."

Lucas smirked. "And here I thought I was the one who conjured this room."

"Perhaps we both did," I said. "I know it's weird considering the circumstances, but with everything going on, I don't want to waste a moment with you."

"I feel the same way," Lucas said as he sat beside me.

He took my hands in his, and I swore looking into his green eyes had never felt so good. Maybe it was this room, or maybe it was the desperate times we were living in, but my whole body shivered at his proximity. It honestly didn't matter if we made love tonight. All I wanted to do was fall asleep in his arms, because being close to him was the best part of this human experience.

Lucas reached up and pushed a strand of hair behind my ear. "There's so much I want to say to you, and so much I don't know *how* to say. If we don't make it—"

"If we don't make it, we'll be together again," I interrupted. "If we go down, we go down together."

Lucas gave a light smile. "That's a good way to look at our impending doom."

"I have a gift for staying positive in the worst of circumstances," I teased. Didn't mean I wasn't scared, though.

Lucas's gaze roamed my face, looking deeply contemplative. "I don't know how you do it—how you manage to stay positive. It's something I really love and admire about you."

"This isn't the first time I've been faced with the threat of death," I reminded him. "When I was in the hospital before my diagnosis, I wasn't sure I'd live. And when I did… I learned pretty quickly that giving up just wasn't an option."

"Aren't you scared?" he wondered.

"Of course I am. Lucas, I'm terrified. But I have to believe there's still a chance."

He ran a hand up and down my thigh, eyes roaming by body. "Say you knew we wouldn't win our trial. What would you do with our last night?"

I took his face in my hands and kissed him gently. "I'd kiss you a million times."

I kissed him again, and a third time. He leaned in even closer, and we tumbled onto the bed together. He propped himself up over me, kissing my lips while he ran his hands down my sides. My heart beat wildly at every gentle caress.

I drew away from him to add, "I'd run away with you and just talk until it was all over."

"Then why don't we?" he asked.

I sighed. "Because there are people relying on us. What would you do?"

His eyebrows pinched together. "I don't know. One night… it's not enough. We have whole lives we've never lived, things I wanted to do with you that would take years."

"Like what?" I wondered.

He ran a finger across my cheek. "I want to build a life with you, Nadine. I want to buy a house together and have kids. I want to invite our friends over for barbecues and séances. I want to skinny dip in Lake Santos with you—fully nude this time. I want to travel with you to other magical communities and ride dragons. I want to take you rock climbing and kayaking. I want to investigate hauntings and mysteries with you. And when we grow old, I want to sit on our front porch holding hands saying, *we did it*. We did everything we said we were going to do, and it was great. And when we die, I want to be the reaper leading you to the other side."

I sighed happily. "That sounds perfect."

"It terrifies me that the priestesses can take that away from us." Lucas stopped dead and inhaled a sharp breath.

I stilled beneath him. "What is it?"

His jaw dropped. "I just realized something… When we were tied to that lamp post, I didn't want to die, and I thought it was because I was scared of death, but I'm not. I'm scared of *not living*."

He drew away from me and placed his hand over his mouth, like the realization was more profound than anything he'd discovered before. I sat up beside him. Of all the emotional talks Lucas and I had shared, nothing could compare to the deep emotions I witnessed flitting through him at that moment. It was like everything in his life finally made sense.

"Nadine, I want to live, so badly," he said. "And I *wasn't* living for so long. Now that I have something to live for, something to fight for—hell, something to *die* for—I'm terrified of losing it."

"Then you won't," I told him firmly. I wasn't sure where the words came from, because a moment ago, it would've felt like a lie. Now it felt like a promise. "Everything you said you wanted, we'll have. I don't care if it's in this life or the next. I'll be there with you."

That was something I was absolutely certain of.

"I don't want to wait any longer," Lucas said. "I don't care if we only have one night left. I'm going to start living now."

He stood and drew something out of his pocket and handed it to me. I eyed the tiny wooden box curiously. It was a cube with lines carved into it in a pretty design and two pegs on top that slid panels both ways.

I got excited and bounced on the bed a little. "Oh, a puzzle box! What's inside?"

He smirked. "That's the surprise."

I flipped the box around in my hands, and I didn't see any obvious place to open it. It had to have something to do with the sliding panels, unless that was just to trick me. I wiggled the pegs and slid the panels around, but nothing happened. I poked a fingernail into the carvings, trying to see if any of them hid an opening. Lucas looked proud that I couldn't figure it out right away, until I wiggled one of the side panels and it popped out. Once that was free, it made room for the top panel to slide off.

"Damn, I knew you'd figure it out, but that was fast," Lucas said.

I laughed as I slid the top panel off. "You'll have to give me a better challenge next time—"

My words came to a screeching halt when I looked inside the box and saw a diamond ring with teal stones. Time seemed to freeze—I couldn't even think. For a moment, I had no idea what I was looking at. Lucas pulled the ring out of the box, then knelt to one knee.

"Nadine Evers, I don't care how much time we have left. I want to spend every moment of it with you. Will you marry me?"

Tears welled in my eyes, and I forgot how to speak.

"Yes!" I cried. "Yes, I will marry you!"

I tossed the puzzle box aside and threw my arms around him. My lips connected with his in a passionate kiss, and the ground fell out from beneath us. It felt as if a spell had swept us upward, spinning us toward the stars.

"I love you," I whispered.

"I love you, too," he said passionately. Lucas drew away from me, and my heart settled again, like I'd been placed upon a cloud. His arms wrapped around me, and he lifted me back onto the bed. He set me down gently, trailing kissed down my neck. I was so entranced by his touch that I closed my eyes and tilted my head back.

We were engaged. *Engaged!* I couldn't believe it.

"Do you want to wear it?" he asked.

My eyes sprang open to see him holding the ring above me. "Yes!" I cried, giving him my left hand. Lucas slipped the ring on my finger, sealing our promise to one another. I held the ring up to admire it. It was so beautiful, so perfect. I melted into the bed as complete bliss overcame me.

He kissed my neck again, then whispered, "You look surprised."

"I am," I said. "I had no idea you were even thinking about proposing."

"Really?" he asked, sounding shocked. "So I surprised you?"

"A hundred percent."

"Surprises are good, then?" he teased.

I smirked. "This surprise was the best one yet."

He pressed his nose into my hair. "Tell me what you want. I'll do anything."

"You don't want to surprise me?" I teased.

He ran his fingers up my shirt, making my heart hammer. "I like it when you take the lead. It turns me on. It pleases me to see you get everything you desire."

"Lucas, you just proposed. As long as I have you, I *have* everything I desire."

He smiled playfully as he slipped his fingers down my pants. My breath quivered, and I involuntarily lifted my hips toward him.

"Not everything," he whispered. "I can feel you want more."

Fuck, he was right.

"What are you going to do about it?" I begged breathlessly.

"You're not the one asking the questions, dear," he whispered. "How would you like me to pleasure you?"

Oh, fuck. If I thought he was the man of my dreams when he put that ring on my finger, he was something otherworldly now.

"I want you to make love to me," I whispered.

Lucas was gentle with me in every sense of the word. He carefully took off my shoes and knee brace and set them aside. Then in a sensual motion, he pulled my pants down my legs and tossed my panties aside. Starting at my ankles, he trailed kisses up my body, teasing me with his hot breath as it warmed my skin. His kiss lingered at my knee.

I lifted my head off the bed to look at him. "What are you doing?"

He dropped his gaze. "Your bruises make me sad."

"I don't want you to be sad," I whispered. "If it helps, your kisses make me feel better."

He pressed his lips against my skin again, then continued upward, pushing the fabric of my shirt away so he could kiss my belly. He moved higher, until he stripped my shirt off completely. I closed my eyes and soaked in every blissful moment, every touch of his warm lips on my skin. He hugged me close to him, then undid the clasp on my bra in one motion. I shivered as cool air rushed across my exposed skin.

He drew away. "Are you cold?"

"A bit—" I moved to readjust myself on the bed, but I winced as my knee twinged.

Lucas got a concerned look on his face. Before I could tell him I was fine, he'd scooped me up into his arms. I got a thrill throughout my entire body as he carried me across the room to the tub. He gently sent me down in the warm rose-scented water, and my whole body felt like it was melting into the bath.

Lucas began stripping down. In the dim lighting, I could make out the deep shadows on his chest and the toned muscles in his arms. His body was splayed with bruises, and I knew how he felt when he said he was sad.

It must've shown on my face. He caught me watching him undress, and a moment of self-conscious shock quickly turned to a beaming smile. His green eyes sparkled down at me, and I swore I'd never seen anything more beautiful in my entire life. "Don't worry about me. Your kisses make it all better, too."

His dick was hard and ready for me. He climbed into the bath and lowered himself across from me. The tub was huge, and his legs fit effortlessly around me. He took my legs into his lap and began massaging my knee under the warmth of the water.

"Does this help?" he asked.

I swore in that moment, all the pain in my body melted away. Every tender bruise and every aching muscle seemed nonexistent, all because he cared.

"It feels amazing," I told him. I reached for his feet to begin massaging him back.

He drew away and clicked his tongue. "I told you, I'm here to pleasure you. I need to focus. Would that be all right?"

He was really serious about asking the questions.

"Yes, but promise me one thing," I said.

"Anything."

"When we get our house, we have to get ourselves one of these tubs."

Lucas beamed. "Absolutely."

We both relaxed into the peaceful water and listened to the soft music play as he continued massaging me. My knee really was starting to feel better, and he continued massaging up my thighs, never once touching my sensual areas. He was teasing me, and though I wanted him inside me right now, I didn't want this to end.

"Do you want your shoulders rubbed?" he asked.

That sounded amazing. "Sure," I told him as I pulled my hair over one shoulder to expose my skin.

"Can you turn around for me?"

I curled my legs to my chest and spun through the water, practically floating because the tub was so huge. I cuddled close against Lucas, our naked bodies melding together as he ran his hands over my shoulders and down my arms. I closed my eyes and took in every motion of his body, the feel of his hands on my skin, the motion of his muscles in his chest.

He leaned back against the side of the tub, and I followed, pressing my back against him. I could feel his rock-hard erection against my back, and I fucking loved it. Lucas reached for a soap dispenser on the edge of the tub and pumped it a few times, then began rubbing soap across my chest.

"Mm…" I breathed a sigh as he squeezed my breasts. He continued rubbing soap up and down my body, until finally dipping his clean hands between my legs. I couldn't take it any longer. "Take me to the bed," I begged.

Lucas gladly complied. He climbed out of the tub and grabbed a towel. He quickly dried off, then helped me out and wrapped the towel around me to keep me warm. He swept me into his arms, and I yelped a little in surprise.

"Do you want me to make love to you, *fiancé*?" he asked.

Holy fuck. He was my fiancé. I'd never heard a sexier word in my life. I was definitely going to need another towel, because I was *wet*.

"Yes, please!" I said.

Lucas led me over to the bed and set me down, before taking my towel away. He reached for his jeans and pulled a condom out of his wallet, then rolled it on. I shivered as he crawled on top of me, his naked skin touching my own.

"Are you still cold?" he asked.

"No," I told him. Quite the opposite, actually.

Lucas began kissing me all over again, and I gasped as he pulled my nipple into his mouth and bit it gently.

"I want more of that," I begged. I loved it when he played with my nipples. It sent a wild sensation straight between my legs that drove me crazy.

"Like this?" he asked, nipping playfully at me.

I gasped again, louder this time. "More."

"Oh, like this?" he teased. He pulled my nipple deeper into his mouth, sucking hard and intensifying the wanting sensation. Fuck it all if I wasn't in heaven right now.

I buried my fingers in his hair and tugged on the strands. I got lost in my desire for him and could no longer find the words. All I could do was beg him for more with my hands. I liked when it hurt just a little, when he was just a little rough and oh so gentle at the same time.

Lucas trailed kisses down my body, until he placed one last kiss below my belly button. I lay naked on the bed, more turned on than ever before, and wanting nothing more than his cock deep inside me.

I didn't say anything, though. I was curious what he might come up with himself. He spread my legs apart and knelt between them. My heart hammered even harder in this position. I was open and ready for him—*so, so ready.*

Lucas didn't move to position himself right away. Instead, he ran his fingers between my legs, teasing me before drawing circles around my clit. I relaxed even deeper into the bed.

"You like that?" he asked.

"It feels amazing," I said breathlessly.

"I think it's hot," he admitted. "What could possibly be better?"

"Mm…" I pretended to think about it. "A really good mystery novel?"

Lucas nearly choked on his laughter. "It's kind of like a mystery novel. It's mysterious, and I can spread the pages."

He slid his fingers downward, spreading my legs further apart like he was opening a book. I laughed so hard that not a single sound came out. I threw my hands over my face, and my whole body shook in giggles as he continued playing with me. He apparently liked the reaction he got out of me, because he started tickling my thighs, until I couldn't take it any longer.

"Lucas!" I laughed, swatting at him playfully. "I am *not* a mystery novel!"

He smirked. "I know. You can't do *this* with a book."

He ducked his head, and all my laughter died in a single moment, replaced with a pure sense of bliss as he ran his tongue over my most sensitive areas.

"No, you *can't* do that with a book," I teased. "You'd get in trouble."

"Am I in trouble?" he joked, lifting his head.

"You're going to be in trouble if you stop," I told him.

Desire flared in his eyes, and he ducked his head again. I moaned and wrapped my legs around his neck. I sank deeper and deeper into the bed, until I thought I couldn't relax any more. Lucas slipped two fingers inside of me, and that's when I lost it completely. The most amazing sensation came over me, sending tingles all throughout my body as I reached a glorious peak. All the magic in the school couldn't compare to the magical sensation pulsing through my entire body. The orgasm continued longer than I thought possible as Lucas continued circling his tongue around my clit. I rode the high so long, I wasn't sure I'd ever come down. When the tingles finally subsided, there was nothing I wanted more but to feel his passion inside of me.

"Please," I begged.

Lucas positioned himself over me, and he slid into me effortlessly. I gasped as he filled me up, satisfying my sexual desire. I curled my legs around him, holding him so tight to me that it felt as if we'd become one. He pounded into me, deeper than he'd ever gone before. I wanted him *that* badly. With every thrust, another wave of passion surged through me, and I felt myself climbing the peak of orgasm all over again.

"Yes," I begged, the same time Lucas moaned in my ear. Fuck, the sound of his pleasure drove me wild.

He curled an arm under my leg, pulling one knee toward my chest. Hell, he went even *deeper*, and that was my undoing. I tipped the peak again, contracting around him the same time he sank deep into me, filling me completely. We tumbled into a mind-blowing orgasm together, and for the briefest of moments, it felt as if our souls left our bodies and entwined into one complete being. It was unlike astral traveling, in which we could see and hear everything around us. This was like existing on a whole other plane, a level of consciousness we'd never encountered before. The room around us ceased to exist, and the only real thing in that moment was our love and passion melding together.

Our spirits settled back into our bodies, and Lucas rolled over, pulling me on top of him. For the longest moment, we lay there, our naked bodies pressed firmly against one another. I nearly forgot how to breathe as I snuggled my head against his chest.

Finally, Lucas moved his hands, running them down my back and across my ass. "That was amazing."

"Better than amazing," I told him. "There are… no words."

"Did you feel that, at the end?" he asked.

I drew away to look him in the eyes. Goddess, he looked so at peace. "That feeling like you left your body?"

He nodded. "Yeah, what was that?"

I shook my head. "I don't know, but we can do that again anytime."

He smiled, then drew me close to him again to kiss my forehead. "We absolutely will."

We crawled beneath the sheets, and Lucas curled an arm around me to spoon me. I had never felt so at ease, so in love.

"I can't wait to marry you," I whispered.

He kissed me behind the ear. "Darling, I promise it will be worth the wait."

☾

THE BEAUTY of our moment together in that enchanted room didn't last long. By the next morning, we were faced with reality all over again.

I didn't feel ready for our trial, but we'd given Verla everything we had. We'd gone over everything the priestesses might throw at us and prepared our answers.

We woke early to get to our dorm rooms before anyone spotted us. When we walked into my room, I was surprised to see Grant and Talia lying on the floor surrounded by piles of open books. Talia was curled up in Grant's arms—she looked so tiny next to him—and they both slept soundlessly. It looked like they'd fallen asleep studying.

Isa meowed loudly and bounded over to me, jumping over my friends. It felt like ages since I'd seen her last, and I quickly swooped her into my arms, burying my nose into her fur. Isa was so excited to see me, pawing at my face and licking me.

"It's okay, girl," I told her, while scratching her head. Isa began purring loudly.

Talia stirred, and she startled when she saw me. She nudged Grant, and he yawned as he woke up. Gus and Bella perked up from where they lay on the couch.

"What are you guys doing here?" I demanded. "You'd be safer at Verla's."

"We're going to take the witness stand," Talia blurted. "We've been researching Miriamic law all night."

"Verla won't let you take the stand," Lucas argued. "If Nadine and I are found guilty, you'll be hanged, too."

Grant took a step forward. "I'm the one who killed those officers during the Burning. It'll prove you're both innocent on that account."

"No," I objected. "You'll be arrested."

"But it's the truth," Grant said. "I made a decision that night—"

"We all did," I protested. The night of the Burning, Lucas, Talia, and Miles had been taken hostage with Darcy, Samantha, and Felicia. The priestesses had intended to burn them at the stake like they'd done to Amy and the others. Killing those officers was the only way to free our friends. We'd *all* decided that night to do whatever was necessary to save their lives.

"I'm the one who pulled the trigger, and I won't let you take the fall for that," Grant insisted.

Lucas pressed his fingers to his eyes. "Grant, you can't say that on the stand. Besides, Verla's already got her witness list—"

"And we're on it," Grant said. "We've already talked to her. We've got it sorted it."

Lucas's eyebrows shot up. "And you know what she said about keeping your mouth shut. She knows more about this stuff than we do. We agreed to let her do the talking, and you have to do the same."

Grant crossed his arms. "Fine, but I'm proving you innocent."

I sat on the bed, continuing to scratch Isa behind the ears. "What are you looking for in the textbooks?"

"Anything that will help," Talia said. "We're hoping for a loophole that will get your case thrown out."

"Don't you think Verla would've brought that up?" I asked.

"We might have found *something*, though." Talia reached for one of the open textbooks. "Witches deal with death differently than most other magical races. Because Lucas is Mortana and has power over death, we might be able to claim that the deaths you're charged with were predestined—and therefore not your fault."

"But Lucas doesn't have the power to see fate," I pointed out. "It won't work."

"We have to do *something*," Talia insisted.

"I appreciate the help, Tal, but I don't know what more we can do," I told her. "We're going to sit on that stand and follow Verla's lead, and things will turn out how they're meant to."

"That's not good enough!" Talia insisted. "Everything you're charged with was done to save us!"

"Maybe this is how I save us, too," I told her.

"So you're just going to let them hang you at the gallows!?" she shouted, sounding deeply hurt.

"I don't know what's going to happen, but I have to believe that whatever *does* happen is part of my prophecy, because I can't handle accepting the alternative," I said.

"How about leaving town?" Talia demanded. "Let's just all go before the trial. We can run away."

"They'll hunt us down," I pointed out. "Do you really think the priestesses would just let us get away?"

Grant's features darkened. He didn't like my answer. "We'll give you a potion like the one you gave Monica. We'll fake your deaths."

"We don't have time to replicate the brew," Lucas said. "We can't run from this, you guys. The only way we're getting out of here is if we win our trial."

"This isn't a fair trial!" Talia cried. "You're naive to think you can win. If you don't leave now, I'll hit you with a stunning spell and throw you in my trunk! I'm not kidding."

I sighed. "Tal, yesterday you had no magic because of the Waning. Can you even *cast* a stunning spell? If you two want to go, please do. Go, be *safe*. But if Lucas and I leave now, we'll be putting you in danger. We're going through with this."

Tears welled in Talia's eyes. "I refuse to accept this is the only way, Nadine. I'm not letting another one of my best friends hang. If you're not going to save yourselves, then I will!"

Talia pushed past me and stormed out of the room.

"Tal!" I ran to follow her, but Grant stopped me.

"You have to get ready for the trial," he said. "I'll go after her."

I didn't have a choice; the trial was going to start soon. I knew she'd be safe with Grant.

I dressed in my nicest slacks and a black blazer, and I slipped my wand into the inner pocket—just in case. I left my cloak behind, because Verla said the jurors would sympathize with us more if we dressed like them.

We went back to Lucas's dorm so he could borrow a suit from Grant's closet, because he didn't have one of his own. I piled the cats' bowls full of food, then stroked Isa's fur and gave her kisses. She yowled loudly, like she knew something wasn't quite right.

"You can't come with," I told her. "We'll be back soon, all right?"

I had to believe that.

Verla drove us to the courthouse, and Lucas held my hand the entire way. I noticed more people crowding the streets the closer we got to the courthouse. They'd all come to watch. It made me sick knowing the priestesses were using me as a puppet in their twisted theater.

We drove over a bridge, and the river below looked so calm and peaceful. It seemed so strange to see on a day like today. How could the river not feel the torrent of this conflict sweeping through the coven?

The courthouse stood next to the river, and a crowd so large had gathered out front that I couldn't even see the steps. They yelled over one another, and I couldn't tell what they were saying. Nothing kind, I was sure.

Verla drove around to the back of the courthouse, away from the crowd. We were greeted by several police officers, who promptly slapped metal bracelets on our wrists and ushered us inside. My energy drained the moment the metal touched my skin. They were noxite, surely made so we didn't cast spells in the courtroom.

The officers didn't say a thing as they led us into a private room. I stopped in the doorway when I saw Mandy sitting there. Had she been called as a witness? I didn't want our friends being put on the stand like this.

"What are you doing here?" I asked.

Mandy stood, but it was Verla who spoke first. "Mandy asked me to arrange a meeting before the trial. I'll give you three a minute, but be quick. The trial starts soon."

She shut the door, leaving Lucas, Mandy, and me in private. I rushed to speak. "If they called you to the stand, I'm sorry. We didn't know you'd get involved, and I know you didn't want to be a part of this anymore."

Mandy sniffled. "That's not why I came. I came to say goodbye."

"We're not headed to the gallows yet," Lucas said sadly. "We still have a chance to turn this around."

"I don't know that you do." Tears beaded in Mandy's eyes. There was so much sadness, but behind that, I saw guilt.

My blood turned to ice. "You're the one who turned everything over to the priestesses."

Mandy timidly nodded.

Lucas's hands curled into fists. "You said you'd *never* side with the priestesses!"

Tears spilled over her lids. "I didn't mean for this to happen! They said they'd grant you immunity if I told them everything!"

"You took an oath—*a witch's vow*!" Lucas fumed. "You should be dead right now. Or did you fake the vow, too?"

"I *kept* my vow!" Mandy cried. "I did what I thought was best for the coven—for *you*. I wanted to stop this. You and Nadine were getting out of control. I thought stopping you guys was the only way to save more lives and bring the coven together. I didn't want anyone else to die, but the priestesses lied to me!"

Lucas blew a breath. "This is the problem with witch vows. If the wording is too specific, it can kill you for no reason. If it's just a little off, your friends can *betray* you!"

Mandy began to sob. "Please believe me when I say that I never intended to betray you. I came here to tell you that I'm sorry."

"How could you do this?" I demanded. "After losing Amy to *them*?"

"I did this *because* of Amy, for *her*," Mandy said tearfully. "I'll never forget the way she screamed that night when those bitches burned her at the pyre. And I'll be damned if I let that happen to anyone else."

"That's what we were trying to prevent!" I screamed.

"Really?" Mandy challenged. "Because Hector and William are dead all thanks to your *cause*. Things are worse than ever."

"It's not our fault," Lucas seethed.

"Isn't it? Isn't it yours, and mine?" Mandy challenged. "Things would've been better if we had stayed out of it and let the priestesses do as they pleased. We should've done nothing at all! Because if Amy had, she'd still be alive. And so would everyone who's died for us."

Mandy shook her head. "But that wasn't good enough for you, was it? You had to win, Nadine, and you would've killed everyone in the coven for the virtue of *saving it*. And as much as I regret turning you in, I can't help but admit I'll get some sort of satisfaction that you're going to face some consequences for putting everyone's life in danger. Don't worry about me. I'm sure I'll receive my penance soon."

I didn't even know what to say to her. People often said betrayal felt like a knife to the back, but this was far, *far* worse. It was more like being impaled by a hundred swords, cutting you into a million pieces all at once. My eyes stung as if they were filled with shards of glass. I honestly wanted nothing to do with Mandy right now.

The door opened, and Verla entered. I was surprised to see Grammy following behind her. Verla crossed her hands in front of herself. "It's almost time."

I cleared my throat, ignoring Mandy as I turned to my grandmother. "Thank you for coming, Grammy."

"Of course, Nadine," she said softly. "I wouldn't miss it for the world."

Grammy opened her mouth to say more, but three officers burst into the room then.

"Your time is up," one of them growled. He grabbed Grammy by the shoulder and started dragging her out of the room. "You're not supposed to be here."

My stomach hollowed. "Leave her alone!"

"My granddaughter—ow!" Grammy cried.

I started forward, but one of the officers grabbed me. The other put his hands on Lucas, and they shoved us out of the room. With the noxite bracelet on my wrist, I wasn't strong enough to fight back.

"It's time to go," the officer barked. "Your trial begins now."

I shot one last look behind me, and I saw Mandy standing in the doorway, her eyes sparkling. "Goodbye," she said, like it was the last goodbye we'd ever have… and it just might be.

We entered a large, crowded room that felt dark and foreboding. There were no windows, merely dark mahogany walls on all sides that seemed to block us in. Mahogany was meant to represent strength, but if anything, I felt like a frayed piece of firewood about to be reduced to ash. The room was lit by sconces. I thought they were meant to look comforting, but they reminded me more of torches.

Loud protests from outside filtered into the room, but the crowd inside remained quiet. Familiar faces stared back at me—some supportive, like Chloe and Onyx in the front row. The officer who'd snatched Grammy shoved her into a seat beside Professor Warren. Her eyes narrowed on the priestesses across the room, like she was trying to set them on fire with her mind.

I didn't see Grant and Talia anywhere, which was unnerving because they'd agreed to testify. Miles was noticeably missing, too. They must be held back by the crowd.

Other faces didn't appear so friendly. The priestesses sat in the front row behind the prosecutor. They wouldn't be the ones to judge the trial, but they sure as hell looked proud, like they already knew they had this in the bag. They knew exactly what they were doing, parading us in front of the coven.

Claudia didn't even look at me. She held her nose high, and I overheard her whisper to Margaret. "I hope this ends quickly, because I have dinner reservations."

Professor Leto sat in the front row, grinning smugly. He certainly looked hungry for an execution.

Behind them, Mira and Avery laughed. James and Ryan had shown up in their Executor uniforms like they were ready to deliver our execution themselves. There were so many faces I didn't recognize—people who had never even met us, but prayed for our downfall nonetheless. A jury sat in two rows next to the judge's stand. I didn't know any of them, and I couldn't place if they were allies or not. Knowing the priestesses, I wasn't counting on it.

"All rise for the Honorable Judge Patricia Calloway," the bailiff said.

Everyone in the courtroom rose, and a woman in a black robe entered the room. I hadn't met her before. She had to be in her fifties, with tight red curls piled atop her head. Her expression remained stoic, and it was impossible to read her. She definitely walked with the confidence of a priestess, though there was something that set her apart from them. I couldn't place it at first.

When she turned to the crowd, I saw it. Her eyes were kinder. Not totally unforgiving, but it didn't appear she'd made a decision about this case just yet. We might still have a chance, if the jury was as open-minded as her.

"Court is now in session," the judge said with a smack of her gavel. "You may be seated."

Everyone took their seat, but nobody spoke.

"We are here today to begin proceedings in the trial of the Miriamic Coven versus Priestess Nadine Evers and Lucas Taylor," the judge announced. "Will the defendants please rise?"

We stood to face the judge.

"On one felony count of attempting to overthrow the Imperium Council, how do the defendants plead?" the judge asked.

"Not guilty, your honor," Verla said.

The judge continued through our list of charges: two misdemeanor counts of unauthorized intercast spellwork, twelve felony charges of black magic use with intent to do harm, and seven charges of first-degree murder. We plead not guilty to all.

"You may be seated," the judge announced. I squeezed Lucas's hand underneath the table. "The prosecution may begin with its opening statement."

The lawyer across from us stood. She was a tall woman, with dark hair and a smug look that rivaled Lilian's harsh features. She reminded me of Claudia, though she was much younger. Her heels clicked against the floor as she stood in front of the jury.

"Members of the jury, you have heard the charges brought forth against these criminals," she began. "In today's proceedings, I will prove to you that Nadine Evers and Lucas Taylor are in fact guilty of the crimes they have been accused of. You will see photographs of their secret society headquarters, and secret files they kept hidden from the Imperium Council. I shall prove without a shadow of a doubt that Nadine Evers and Lucas Taylor have conspired against the Imperium Council, with intent to destroy the coven. I will present to you audio recordings and testimony detailing the murders these two have committed in the name of their secret society. By the end of the day, these two criminals will be walking to the gallows, because the coven will know the truth about what they've done. You shall be the ones to deliver justice."

She returned to her seat, and Verla stood to pace in front of the jury.

"Members of the jury, I am here today to prove that the charges brought against my clients are nothing more than false claims," Verla said. "We are here to tell the truth, and you will find by the end of these proceedings that the evidence Miss Olivia Sinclair claims to have paints a very different picture when put into context."

Sinclair? I mouthed to Lucas. No wonder the prosecutor reminded me so much of Claudia. She was her daughter! She had everything to gain by winning this trial—namely, securing her mother's position on the council and bolstering their family business.

"I will present you with witness testimony that will prove my clients had the best interest of the coven at heart, and that my clients are in fact innocent," Verla concluded.

Dear Goddess. All we had was witness testimony. The prosecutors had photographs and recordings, and who knew what else. We were totally fucked.

"The prosecution may call its first witness," the judge announced.

Olivia Sinclair stood. "The prosecution calls Priestess Margaret Weber to the witness stand."

I watched curiously as Margaret stood and approached the stand. Never once did she look my way. The bailiff held out an old leather-bound book, and she placed her hand atop it. "Do you swear on Mother Miriam's holy grimoire to tell the truth, the whole truth, and nothing but the truth, so help you Goddess?"

"Yes," Margaret said firmly.

She sat, and Olivia began pacing in front of her. "Priestess Margaret, can you state for the jury what your role is among the Imperium Council?"

Margaret turned to the jury and spoke softly. She sounded so much like when I first met her, before she'd shown her true nature. "I'm the Alchemy Priestess. It is my job to represent my Cast and make laws that will benefit the entire coven. As a priestess, I help facilitate strong rela-tionships with other magical races, as well as speak for the coven in times of controversy."

"You are the oldest member of the council, correct?" Olivia asked.

"Yes, the oldest in age," Margaret said. "Priestess Lilian has been sitting on the council longer."

"Thank you," Olivia said. "Being the oldest on the council, the other council members look up to you, correct?"

Margaret nodded. "Yes, I would say that's accurate, although none of us are above each other in rank."

"When the council requires a single spokesperson, that responsibility typically falls on you, correct?"

"Yes," Margaret said.

"So you are somewhat of the leader of the Imperium Council?"

"You could say that, yes."

"And you are present at every meeting?"

"Every single one, yes."

"You were present when the Imperium Council met with Nadine to discuss inducting her onto the council?"

"Yes."

"Priestess, did any of the council members take issue with placing Nadine on the council?"

"At the time, we were all in agreement that we needed a Curse Breaker on the council," Margaret answered. "We had reservations, considering her grandfather's downfall on the council many years ago, but we thought Nadine would be different."

"Can you clarify for the jury what you mean?"

"Nadine's grandfather, Nicholas Tucker, served on the Imperium Council for a short time four decades ago," Margaret said. "He was caught stealing from the council, and was executed for it."

Behind me, Grammy huffed. Margaret was already lying. She spoke as if he'd had a fair trial—like his murder had been sanctioned by the Imperium Council. He'd been murdered without a chance to plead his case.

"We had faith that Nadine's intentions were genuine, as her grandfather had died long before she was born, and she had no personal connections to him," Margaret said. "She was the only Curse Breaker alive, so the job defaulted to her. It was our belief that we should induct her as soon as possible, to restore the five-Cast system on the council."

"And how does the council feel about that decision now?"

"Objection, your honor!" Verla said. "Hearsay."

"Sustained," the judge said. "The priestess can only speak for herself, Attorney Sinclair."

Olivia cleared her throat. "Priestess Margaret, how do *you* feel about the decision to place Nadine Evers on the council?"

For the first time, Priestess Margaret looked at me, and her stare turned my blood to ice. "I believe it was the greatest mistake the council has ever made."

Olivia tried to hide her proud smirk, but she wasn't very good at masking it. "Priestess, can you tell the jury what made you change your mind?"

Margaret turned to the jury again, avoiding my gaze entirely. "When we first met Nadine, she appeared very kind and willing to do anything to help the coven. We were blinded by our enthusiasm to call a Curse Breaker onto the council after so many years. We held several meetings prior to her induction, and she seemed enthusiastic and a great fit. We worked well together—until she was inducted."

"What happened then?" Olivia asked.

"Nadine changed her tune," Margaret said simply. "She began objecting in council meetings and protesting our ideas. When we were presented opportunities to investigate the Waning, she would refuse to work the spells with us. On several occasions, she claimed that her chronic illness was too severe to perform the spell, and she used it as a weapon against the council to delay our investigation."

"Objection!" Verla said calmly.

The judge frowned. "Overruled."

Margaret continued. "She often brought her boyfriend Lucas to meetings without prior approval, and on several occasions, she threatened to expose sensitive coven information if we did not help cure her disease through a kidney transplant."

My blood began to boil. Margaret was telling half-truths, not even remotely representing the story accurately. *They* had threatened *me*, and I'd been on the coven's side every step of the way.

Olivia checked her notes. "Can we bring up evidence file number one-one-two?"

A picture popped up on a large TV on the courtroom wall. It was a photograph of the Gravestone.

"Priestess Margaret, can you describe for the jury what we are looking at here?" Olivia asked.

Margaret shifted in her chair. "This is a photograph of Nadine's secret headquarters. A few nights ago, we were alerted by an anonymous source that Nadine Evers and Lucas Taylor had formed a group they call The Coven's Shield. They were headquartered inside Miriam College of Witchcraft, in an old storage room. With the help of the Miriamic Police Department, we were able to break through an unauthorized ward and find this secret room, which contained articles written in secret code with messages detailing how The Coven's Shield planned to infiltrate and destroy the Imperium Council from within."

More lies.

"Objection!" Verla yelled. "Where is the evidence?"

Olivia smirked proudly. "Please bring up evidence number two-six-two."

A new image came on the screen. It showed a photocopy of our first article written in *The Shield*. Words had been circled, and there were scribbles all over the page, showing our message decoded. I got a nervous twinge in my belly, but I realized there was nothing damning here. The message simply encouraged a meet-up. It said nothing about standing against the priestesses.

"Can you describe what we're looking at?" Olivia asked Margaret.

The priestess sat up proudly. "This is one of the articles the Miriamic Police Department was able to decode."

More lies. I recognized Onyx's handwriting. It was her copy she'd left in the Gravestone.

"The Coven's Shield is the same organization that released anonymous articles under the name Caesar Peppertrine and distributed them around town, correct?" Olivia asked.

Margaret nodded firmly. "The very one."

"Objection!" Verla insisted.

"Overruled," the judge said.

"No further questions, your honor," Olivia said, before sitting down.

Verla stood with her notepad to begin her cross-examination. She paced confidently in front of the witness stand. "Priestess Margaret, you mentioned that you were present at every council meeting, is that correct?"

"Yes," Margaret said.

"Who else was present at these meetings?"

"A council meeting includes a priestess from each Cast, so there were five of us at each meeting," she answered. "That would include myself, Priestess Lilian, Priestess Charlotte, Priestess Stella—Miriam rest her soul —and Priestess Nadine. Upon Priestess Stella's death, Claudia Sinclair began attending our meetings as an interim priestess until her induction next Halloween."

"Were there any meetings that took place without all five Imperium members present?" Verla asked.

Margaret nodded. "Yes. Being a priestess is a full-time job, and there were times when Nadine's class schedule interfered with our meetings and coven events. We did our best to work around her busy class schedule."

She was trying to look like a *hero*. They purposely scheduled meetings at times I couldn't come—or blatantly omitted the invite altogether.

"Is it possible, then, that when you claim Priestess Nadine objected to certain council measures, it was due to the fact that she was not given complete information on the subject matter, due to not being present at previous meetings?"

Margaret tilted her head, like she didn't understand the question. It was all for show. "We briefed Priestess Nadine on all council matters and made every effort to keep her in the loop. Her protests were merely—"

"A simple yes or no would suffice," Verla interrupted.

"No," Margaret answered.

Verla pursed her lips, but quickly moved on. "Priestess Margaret, you mentioned that Priestess Nadine often refused to perform spells with you, due to her chronic illness, and that she would make demands to obtain a cure through a kidney transplant. Is that correct?"

"Yes," Margaret answered, leaning closer to the microphone to drive her point home.

"Are you aware of Priestess Nadine's diagnosis?" Verla asked.

"Yes."

"Can you state her diagnosis for the jury?"

"To the best of my understanding, she has a condition called lupus." She spoke in a way that made it sound dirty, or like I was lying.

"Are you aware that there is no cure for lupus, as you have claimed in your testimony?" Verla asked.

Margaret furrowed her brow. "I don't believe I said that."

Verla checked her notes. "You said, and I quote: *she threatened to expose sensitive coven information if we did not help her cure her disease through a kidney transplant.* End quote."

The smallest bit of color drained from Priestess Margaret's face, but she leaned toward the microphone to say, "I misspoke when I said *cure*. I meant to say *treatment*."

Verla looked pleased by her answer. She was trying to discredit her as a witness, though I wasn't sure yet if it was working. The jury was difficult to read.

Verla continued. "Priestess Margaret, you mentioned that the police found evidence of secretly coded messages in The Coven's Shield headquarters, which detailed plans to infiltrate the Imperium Council. Can we please bring up evidence file two-six-two?"

The coded article shone on the screen again.

"Can you please read out loud the decoded message that the Miriamic Police Department claims is contained within this article?" Verla asked.

"The message reads: *Meet at The Epitaph on Saturday if you wish to save the coven.*"

"Where, in this message, does it state that Nadine and Lucas planned to overthrow the Imperium Council, as you stated in your testimony?" Verla asked.

"It's right there," Margaret insisted. "*If you wish to save the coven.* It's a threat."

"Is it possible this message held another meaning—that students were simply gathering to help each other with their magic amidst the Waning?" Verla asked.

Margaret pursed her lips. She'd entered this courtroom thinking Verla was on her side. Surely, she was getting fed up with her by now. "Considering the other evidence we found, it's unlikely."

"But possible?" Verla pressed.

Margaret wore a confident look, not giving anything away. "I suppose."

"Please answer the question with a simple yes or no," Verla insisted. "Is it possible this message held another meaning?"

Margaret took a breath. "Yes."

Verla moved on. "You mentioned that Nadine's grandfather was executed for stealing from the coven four decades ago, implying that Nadine's connection to him may have caused controversy on the council. Nicholas Tucker was executed by the use of battle magic, correct?"

"Yes," Margaret said.

"Jebediah Olson was the executioner?" Verla asked.

"Objection!" Olivia cried. "Relevance?"

"Overruled," the judge said.

Margaret sat straighter in her chair. "Yes."

"Let the record show that Priestess Margaret has identified the late husband of Priestess Lilian Olson as Nicholas Tucker's executioner," Verla said, before continuing. "Was this execution sanctioned by the Imperium Council?"

"Yes, due to his crimes against the coven," Margaret answered.

"This execution was sanctioned before or after his death?" Verla asked.

Margaret hesitated. "I'm not sure I understand the question."

"You just testified that the execution was sanctioned by the Imperium Council," Verla said in a firm tone. "If his murder was, in fact, sanctioned by the Imperium Council, why did Jebediah Olson serve a life in prison for first-degree murder?"

All the color drained from Priestess Margaret's face. She sat on the stand looking dumbstruck. Finally, she leaned forward and said, "I don't believe I'm qualified to answer that question. I was not on the Imperium Council at the time."

"I make a motion to strike Priestess Margaret Weber's testimony regarding Nicholas Tucker's execution from the record," Verla said.

The judge nodded. "Sustained."

It seemed the judge was playing fair, which was a relief. Verla was making a risky move, but she'd already done the damage she intended. She'd planted a seed of doubt in the jury's mind.

"No further questions, your honor." Verla sat back down. Her expression gave nothing away. She'd had a few good questions, but I didn't think it was enough to convince the jury.

Olivia called her next witness—Sheriff Baker. Oh, this would be a joy. Baker wore a smug expression as he approached the witness stand. I knew it in my gut he would say whatever he had to in order to please the priestesses. This man was like a child seeking validation.

Olivia began pacing in front of him. "Sheriff Mitchel Baker, can you state for the jury your occupation?"

He straightened in his chair, looking proud. "I am the sheriff at the Miriamic Police Department."

"Sheriff Baker, where were you the night of May twenty-first, during the raid of The Coven's Shield headquarters?"

"I was at Miriam College, heading the raid," he answered.

"And it was there that you found evidence of The Coven's Shield's conspiracy to overthrow the Imperium Council?" Olivia asked.

"Objection!" Verla cried.

"Sustained. Attorney Sinclair, please reword the question," the judge said.

"Sheriff Baker, can you describe the evidence the Miriamic Police Department gathered that night?" Olivia asked.

He turned toward the jury. "You have already seen evidence of secretly coded messages. We also found evidence of unauthorized intercast spellwork."

"Please bring up evidence file number two-one-seven," Olivia said.

A side-by-side photo came on the screen. The first photo showed a black and white image of the storage room before we'd performed the space-bending spell on it. It looked like it'd been scanned from an old newspaper. The photo beside it showed the room as it was today.

"Can you describe what we're looking at here?" Olivia asked.

"We are looking at the same room," Sheriff Baker explained. "The photo on the left shows the room ten years ago, and the picture on the right shows the room yesterday."

"Can you explain to the jury what this evidence suggests?" Olivia asked.

"This photo comparison proves that a space-bending spell was performed on the storage room, of which no records of authorization exist," Baker said.

"And how does one perform a space-bending spell?" Olivia asked.

"Space-bending spells can only be performed by a member of all five Casts. Since there were no Curse Breakers ten years ago, the evidence shows that the space-bending spell must have been performed within the last year, after Nadine Evers obtained her powers."

Olivia looked pleased. "No further questions, your honor."

She sat back down, and Verla stood to cross-examine Sheriff Baker. "Sheriff Baker, you testified that Nadine Evers performed an unauthorized space-bending spell. Is that correct?"

"Yes," Baker said confidently.

Verla held up a thick book. "Sheriff Baker, can you tell the jury what I'm holding here?"

He narrowed his eyes on the book, then answered, "That is the Miriamic Law Code, third edition."

"Can you state for the jury where you have seen this book before?"

"Every officer is required to read this book and take a written test on it before being placed on the police force. As part of our ongoing training, we review the book frequently in order to uphold Miriamic law."

Verla flipped the book open to a page she'd bookmarked. "Sheriff Baker, are you familiar with section twenty-nine, subsection three?"

Baker looked confused for a moment, then said, "The specific wording eludes me, but I do know this section bans unauthorized intercast magic use."

"Can you please read the highlighted paragraph out loud?" Verla handed him the book.

Baker shot a glance at the judge. "I need my reading glasses."

He was stalling, for whatever reason. It seemed strange to me that he'd come to court knowing he'd be presented with documents and evidence and didn't come prepared. I wondered if he needed the reading glasses at all.

It must've taken ten minutes before the court managed to find him a pair of reading glasses. He put them on and cleared his throat. "Section twenty-nine, subsection three?"

Goddess, he was playing an idiot. I didn't get it.

"Yes," Verla said. "Please read the highlighted section to the jury."

"Section twenty-nine, subsection three reads: *Under Miriamic law, unauthorized intercast magic use will be defined as any spell performed by two or more witches or warlocks of different Casts, with the intent to do harm—*"

Verla yanked the book out of Baker's hands, and the sheriff cut off. "*With the intent to do harm,*" she emphasized. "No further questions, your honor."

The prosecution continued calling witnesses to the stand. It took hours for the court to interview other officers and supposed witnesses I didn't even know. Each one of them backed up Priestess Margaret's claims that we'd intended to overthrow the council. Each one of them supported her lies.

The prosecution hadn't once brought up our murder charges, and that worried me. I didn't know what they might possibly have in store. When Olivia called Priestess Lilian to the stand, all the blood in my body drained to my toes. I'd wondered why Lilian hadn't testified yet, and now I knew. They were saving the worst for last.

I held my breath as Lilian swore upon Mother Miriam's holy grimoire and took the stand.

"Priestess Lilian Olson," Olivia said. "You are a member of the Imperium Council, correct?"

Lilian sat straight up, lifting her nose slightly to the jury as she answered, "Yes."

"Can you state your role among the Imperium Council?" Olivia asked.

"I am a high priestess of the Mentalist Cast," Lilian stated. "I have served on the Imperium Council for over forty years. As a priestess, it is my job to serve the coven as both a lawmaker and a law enforcer."

"What level of authority does your position provide you with?" Olivia asked.

"As the highest governing power, the priestesses have the authority to implement new laws, as well as enforce the laws as they are already written," Lilian answered. "New laws require a majority vote by council members, as does dealing out punishments. It is most common for the Miriamic Police Department to handle arrests, and it's the job of the judge to sentence criminals. However, in severe criminal cases that require a timely response, the Imperium Council will step in to ensure the coven is as safe as possible."

That's how they got away with calling for executions without a trial.

"So not only do you work closely with law enforcement personnel, but you yourself are an enforcer of the law in the Miriamic Coven?" Olivia asked.

Lilian nodded. "Yes, of the highest rank."

"Priestess Lilian, you worked a case last year investigating an explosion at Pinewood Manor, correct?" Olivia checked her notes and quickly verified the case number.

"Yes," Lilian said. "Due to the intensity of the case, the priestesses headed the operation."

"Can you describe the nature of the case to us?"

"One year ago on the night of May eighth, the Imperium Council received a call that led us to Pinewood Manor. When we arrived, we found that the east wing had completely collapsed and was on fire. Nadine and Lucas were among five survivors at the scene. At the time, we believed them to be the only ones in the building, but after months of clean-up, we uncovered four bodies."

"Please bring up evidence file one-eight-two," Olivia said.

The entire courtroom gasped. My stomach lurched when photographs of burnt, charred bodies appeared on the screen. I couldn't make out the faces of who they once were, though I could easily guess.

"Can you describe the evidence shown here?" Olivia asked Priestess Lilian.

Lilian looked like she was going to be sick, though I was certain it was all for show. These wouldn't be the first burnt bodies she'd seen. "With the help of the Miriamic Police Department, we were able to identify these remains as Emmett Carlisle, Agnes Britches, Sandy Summers, and Betty Smith. Upon further investigation, we were able to determine the cause of death to be magical. Trace magic left at the scene showed the *potens crepitus* spell was used, which is an ancient spell that can be only performed by multiple Cast members, as it's too powerful to be performed by a single witch or warlock."

I gritted my teeth. That may be the case, but she had no proof that we'd been the ones to cause the explosion. It'd been some sort of fail-safe the kidnappers had created to hide what they were doing at Pinewood Manor. We had no idea that a blast was coming—and we'd gotten out just in time.

Olivia continued putting evidence from that night on the screen, painting us to be heartless murderers. They'd neglected to mention the connection to the missing boys we'd attempted to save. They wanted to make us out as monsters.

By the time she finished questioning Lilian about the Pinewood Manor deaths, the jury *had* to believe we were guilty of premeditated murder. The priestesses made it out like we'd gone there that night with the intent to kill.

But Olivia Sinclair didn't stop there. She brought up photo after photo, evidence file after evidence file, showing our connection to these murders.

Shock riveted through me when Olivia called up evidence file number one-seven-one. An image of the Alchemy Wand appeared on the screen.

"Priestess Lilian, can you state for the jury what we're looking at?" she asked.

"This is an Oaken Wand—an Alchemy Wand," Lilian said.

A gasp traveled around the courtroom. The stories of the Oaken Wands were old. Some people hadn't even heard of them, and anyone who *had* heard of them believed them to be nothing more than urban legends.

"The Oaken Wands exist?" Olivia asked.

"Yes," Lilian stated. "We provided photo evidence for the safety of the coven, because these artifacts are too valuable to be presented in court today."

I never thought I'd live to see the day when the priestesses admitted they had their hands on an Oaken Wand. They wouldn't want the coven to know, because they didn't know who might try to take it from them. This was risky.

"Can you describe for the jury what exactly an Oaken Wand is?" Olivia asked.

Lilian turned toward the jury and told the story of the Oaken Wands—how they were carved from the Protection Tree and had the power to attract the magic of a Cast. "With all five Wands, we will be able to redistribute magic and end the Waning," Lilian told them.

I witnessed the jury's eyes light up. They looked at her like she was the Goddess herself come to save them.

"The Oaken Wands were stolen from the Imperium Council forty years ago, correct?" Olivia asked.

"Yes," Lilian said. "By Nicholas Tucker, in fact. It is why he was executed."

Lilian's husband had spent a life in jail, and she was still sticking to her story that he'd *executed* my grandfather? She was trying to get the jury to believe I'd had the Alchemy Wand all along, that I'd infiltrated the Imperium Council to continue my grandfather's work—all without stating it explicitly. Still, the coven would believe it.

These women were spinning a web of lies, and the only hope I had is that they would trap themselves in it. Problem was, webs were built to catch prey—and I was the greatest prey they'd ever hunted.

"How did the council come into possession of the Alchemy Wand again after all this time?" Olivia asked.

"We confiscated it from Nadine Evers the night of the Burning," Lilian said.

I was shocked to hear her refer to that night as the Burning. The priestesses had never acknowledged it as such before. When I saw the expressions on the jury's faces, I realized she was playing them—telling them what they wanted to hear. She wanted to invoke horrible emotions, all tied back to us.

"With the power of this Wand, could the owner, say… poison the blood of their enemies?" Olivia asked.

"Absolutely," Lilian said.

Olivia brought up more photographs on the screen, and several jury members gaged at the sight of corpses. The images showed the two dead officers Grant had killed using the Alchemy Wand. Their bodies lay on morgue tables, and their faces were purple and swollen, so much that they barely looked human anymore. It looked like they'd been beaten to death from the inside out. The prosecution knew exactly what they were doing bringing up the Alchemy Wand. I'd never looked so guilty.

They went on to present more photos and evidence from that night. The prosecution neglected to mention the lives we'd saved in the process. Darcy, Samantha, and Felicia were alive because of us. Lucas, Talia, and Miles, too.

The jury looked to be eating this up.

"Priestess Lilian," Olivia continued. "Is it true that Nadine Evers used the Alchemy Wand that night to poison these two officers?"

"That is what the evidence suggests," Lilian said proudly.

"How is that possible if Nadine is a Curse Breaker?" Olivia asked.

I didn't like where this was going. She wouldn't ask the question unless they'd already prepared a damning answer.

"Curse Breakers are capable of manipulating Alchemy magic," Lilian stated. "Nadine proved this when she posed as an Alchemist for a full semester following her Evoking Ceremony. She brewed many potions by stealing Alchemy magic from other students. She's fully capable of wielding the Alchemy Wand."

Olivia looked pleased but continued on. "These two officers were not the only individuals to die that night at the hand of Lucas Taylor or Nadine Evers. Is that correct?"

"That is correct," Lilian said. "They murdered Priestess Stella."

A murmur traveled around the courtroom. This had been a point of contention throughout the entire coven for months. We'd tried to tell the truth the night of the Burning—how Stella had been behind nightshade production—but we'd been forced into silence. The priestesses had made us lie and change our story. At this point, I wasn't sure the coven knew what to believe.

"Please bring up evidence file one-six-six," Olivia said.

This time, it wasn't an image that appeared on the screen, but an audio recording. It was the first bit of evidence they'd provided that wasn't a photograph.

The sound of Stella's voice blasted out of the speakers. *"I don't answer to you."*

"You're not going anywhere!" Lucas shouted in the recording.

We heard the sound of scrambling feet, then the blast of a spell, followed immediately by Stella's dying screams. They echoed throughout the courtroom, sending a chilling sensation down my spine.

I was certain we all felt it… the horror of death permeating through the speakers. For a moment, the entire courtroom went silent. Then, all at once, the room exploded in an uproar.

"Burn them at the stake!"

"Send them to the gallows!"

"Rot in the Abyss!"

I knew that last voice. It was Professor Leto. He was *loving* the chaos.

The judge smacked her gavel against the tabletop, though we could hardly hear it over the sound of the screams.

"What are you waiting for? They killed a priestess!" someone shouted.

Olivia smirked proudly. "I rest my case, your honor."

I felt like the walls were closing in on me. Of all the evidence shown, any of it could be doctored. Any of it could be lies. But Lucas's voice in this recording was damning.

The priestesses knew it, and they wore smug expressions as the courtroom exploded in rage. It was odd how comfortable they seemed in the midst of the coven calling for a witch hunt. This is exactly what they wanted… why they gave us a trial at all. They wanted to leave no single soul who doubted our guilt. They wanted to unite the coven in rage.

It was over. We'd lost.

Horror permeated my bones. The recording was real, and the jury knew it. But the prosecution had cut out all the rest. They didn't show how Stella's death had been an accident, or how we'd tried to *save* Stella. The clip they chose told a very damning story, one that didn't remotely reflect the truth.

But the coven didn't care. They wanted our heads on a stake.

"The court will take an hour recess!" the judge yelled, smacking her gavel.

People got out of their chairs and started pushing through the crowd, trying to get to us.

"Get them out of here!" the judge yelled at the bailiff.

Verla whirled toward Professor Warren in the front row. She quickly gestured to him, and he leaned over the barrier separating us. She said something in his ear, but I couldn't hear what it was over the sound of protests.

We were escorted out of the courtroom through a private door, to a small room away from the crowd. I curled Nadine in my arms as she shook in fright.

"The coven's not going to believe anything we say after that." Nadine's voice trembled.

"We can work with this," Verla said. "We've known all along they had that recording."

"But we didn't know they'd twist it like that!" Nadine began pacing. "If they played just five more seconds, they'd hear that we tried to save Stella from the twisted vine she fell into. This recording makes it sound like Lucas cast a killing spell!"

My stomach twisted. I regretted that the recording ever existed in the first place. I'd been the one to record the whole encounter. We thought it would prove our side of the story. But the priestesses had forced us to hand over the recording device in return for saving our friends.

"You still get a chance to tell your side of the story," Verla said calmly.

My tone came out sounding flat. "The coven's already made up their minds. Hell, the priestesses pulled everything they've got. They even exposed the Oaken Wands."

"They did that because if we brought it up first, they'd look like villains," Verla said. "Being the first to expose the Wands paints them as the good guys. It makes them look honest. We can change the coven's mind. Trust me, this happens all the time in the courtroom. We've prepared our defense—"

"Our defense isn't here!" Nadine cried. "Grant was supposed to testify. Where is he? Where's Talia? I'm worried about them."

"I've sent Jonathan to find them," Verla reassured her.

Goddess, I hoped Professor Warren knew where to look. I wanted to hurl. For all we knew, Grant and Talia had been dragged out of the school and beaten by an angry mob for defending us. Problem was, we couldn't get out of the courtroom to look for them.

"We can't draw any conclusions yet," Verla stated. "If we get to the end of the trial and things are still looking bad, I'm fully prepared to advocate that you be sent to the Darke Institute for Supernatural Offenders. You're both considered supernatural minors, so you're eligible to attend the reform school on Darke Island."

"The Darke Institute is a prison for college kids!" I cried. "We can't save the coven if we're locked up on some remote island."

Verla sighed. "I'm merely stating there are alternatives. Be that as it may, we still have a chance to win our case. Let's look at the facts. We'll go over everything one more time."

We reviewed everything the priestesses had presented and how we might counter their claims. At one point, an officer brought us lunch, and Verla used her Alchemy powers to make sure it wasn't poisoned. It sucked that we even had to consider that, but I wouldn't put it past the coven.

It felt like mere minutes before our hour was up, and we hadn't had a chance to discuss everything we'd wanted to. When we returned to the courtroom, it was only half full. We could still hear shouts coming from the hallway. I assumed the officers had cleared the room of anyone who seemed threatening. It didn't stop most of the courtroom from giving us evil glares. I could see it in their eyes that they wished for our death. Professor Warren was noticeably missing, but Chloe, Onyx, and Helena sat behind us in the front row.

"Court is now in session," the judge announced with a smack of her gavel. "The defense may call their first witness."

Verla stood. "The defense calls Chloe Olson to the stand."

Chloe stood from where she sat in the crowd and approached the witness stand. She held her chin high and didn't even look at her grandmother as she passed. Lilian narrowed her eyes on her. Chloe swore upon Mother Miriam's holy grimoire, then took her seat.

"Please state your full name for the jury," Verla said.

"Chloe Jane Olson."

"Can you state your relationship with the accused?"

"We go to school together," Chloe said.

"Where were you the night the east wing of Pinewood Manor collapsed?" Verla asked.

"I was there, at Pinewood Manor."

"Do you remember how you got there?"

"No."

"What *do* you remember from that night?"

"I remember being in the woods with Nadine, and we were both hit by a stunning spell," Chloe said. "When we woke, we were tied up in Pinewood Manor. Agnes Britches, Sandy Summers, and Betty Smith came into the room and told us they wanted to kill us for a resurrection spell."

"So you were kidnapped?" Verla asked.

Chloe leaned toward the microphone. "That is correct."

"Did you witness anyone else there that night?"

"Yes," Chloe answered. "Professor Carlisle was there. He entered the room shortly after the other witches. Lucas and his friends Talia and Grant discovered we were missing, and they were able to find us using Seer magic. They came to save us, so they were there as well."

"Chloe, you testified that your kidnappers admitted their intent to kill you in a black magic ritual," Verla said, driving the point home for the jury. "Did your kidnappers tell you anything else that night?"

"Yes," Chloe said confidently. "They said we were not the first people they'd taken for the resurrection spell. They told us they had also killed Caleb Thomas and Isaac Miller in an attempt to raise the dead."

A gasp traveled around the room, but no one spoke, for fear of being thrown out.

Verla took a moment for the information to sink in, then continued. "Where were you when the explosion occurred and the east wing collapsed?"

"I was outside with Nadine, Lucas, Talia, and Grant. We got out of the building right before the blast."

"Can you describe what Lucas and Nadine were doing at this time?"

"They were helping us out of the building," Chloe said. "Lucas was carrying me, because the witches had attacked us, and I'd sustained several injuries."

"Can you describe your injuries to the jury?"

"Nadine and Lucas had some cuts and bruises. Grant had a broken arm. Talia and I both had to get stitches," Chloe said.

"While Nadine was helping you escape your attackers, did she have time to cast the *potens crepitus* spell?"

"No, she didn't," Chloe said. "Besides, it's not a spell we cover in our classes, so none of us would even know how to do it."

"What did you and your friends believe had happened?"

"We assumed the witches had implemented a fail-safe spell to cover their tracks in case they were discovered," Chloe said.

"Where were the four kidnappers when the blast happened?" Verla questioned.

"Inside the building."

"So they got caught in their own spell?"

"Yes."

"Objection!" Olivia shouted. "She can't know that for certain!"

"Sustained," the judge said.

"No further questions, your honor," Verla said confidently before she sat.

Olivia stood to begin her cross examination. "Miss Olson, you testified that you and Nadine Evers were kidnapped, and that Lucas Taylor and his friends came to save you. Is that correct?"

"Yes, that is correct," Chloe replied dryly.

"If you were truly kidnapped, why did Lucas not go to the police?"

Chloe kept eye contact with the prosecutor. "If he'd gone to the police, we would have been dead by the time they arrived."

"How could Lucas and his friends possibly know that?" Olivia cocked an eyebrow.

Chloe held her head high. "It's my understanding that the Imperium Council had already been informed. Lucas and his friends got us out of the building before the blast. The Imperium Council showed up after. If he hadn't been there, we'd be dead."

Olivia's features faltered, but she kept her voice strong. "Lucas purposely put people in danger and took risks without regard to anyone's safety. Isn't that right, Miss Olson?"

"Like I said, they used Seer magic to find us," Chloe said. "They knew we were in grave danger."

Olivia could see Chloe wasn't going to crack, so she shifted her tactics. "Lucas Taylor was writing an article for the school paper about the two missing boys, isn't that correct, Miss Olson?"

"Yes, that's correct."

"He had information about these missing boys. He knew what the kidnappers were capable of, and he still went to Pinewood Manor *on his own*," Olivia told the jury. "Miss Olson, isn't it possible that Lucas Taylor went to Pinewood Manor to get revenge on the kidnappers he'd been researching all semester? Isn't it possible that he intended to harm these women all along?"

"No. That's not what happened," Chloe said in an even tone.

"But you weren't there when he made the decision to come after you," Olivia alleged. "So you could not be certain of his motives. Isn't that right?"

"It is correct that I was not there when he made the decision. Like I said, I was tied up in Pinewood Manor. He saved me."

"You say that your friends pursued you because they didn't believe the police would get there in time. Are you shining doubt on the Miriamic Police Department's finest? You want to defund the police department, just as Lucas Taylor and Nadine Evers do! Isn't that right, Miss Olson?"

"Objection!" Verla shouted. "Lucas and Nadine have never advocated for defunding the police department. The defense requests that the prosecution submit evidence of this claim, and if they cannot provide it, we make a motion to remove the claim from the court records."

The judge nodded. "Sustained. Attorney Sinclair, please provide the court with evidence, or you will have to rescind your statement."

"I rescind my former statement," Olivia said. "No further questions, your honor."

Olivia smirked. It didn't matter. She'd already made the jury believe we were against the police.

Verla called Nadine to the stand.

I squeezed her hand and whispered, "I'm right here. I'm not going anywhere."

Nadine nodded. She took a deep breath and approached the witness stand.

"Priestess Nadine Evers," Verla said, deliberately using her title as a sign of respect. "You have testified upon Mother Miriam's holy grimoire to tell the truth, so help you Goddess. Is it true that you had intentions to overthrow the Imperium Council?"

Nadine's tone was even as she answered. "No."

"What were your intentions, Priestess?"

"My only intention has always been to protect the coven, as I swore to do during my Induction Ceremony."

"Priestess Margaret testified that you objected during council meetings," Verla said. "Is this correct?"

"Yes," Nadine answered.

"What exactly were you objecting, Priestess?"

"There were several matters which I did not agree upon, that I felt would hurt the coven rather than help them. Most notably, the priestesses voted to revoke school-sponsored healthcare for all students, even though it is paid for through our tuition plan."

"Priestess, when did this new policy go into effect?" Verla asked.

"This past January. The priestesses didn't even notify the students."

"Objection!" Olivia yelled. "That was not the question."

"Sustained," the judge said.

Verla flipped through her notes. "Priestess, what did you witness as a result of this policy change?"

Nadine dropped her gaze. "I witnessed my peers lose access to vital health-care resources. I watched diabetics ration the last of their insulin shots, until they could no longer afford the life-saving treatment. I watched my friend go into several thousand dollars of debt due to an overnight hospital stay that was required after he went into a diabetic coma. This was not a choice he made—he would have died without treatment. I witnessed people I love lose access to mental health resources and therapy. I watched as they were refused birth control, simply for having no health-care plan; and I saw them ride out chronic pain flare-ups without intervention because the treatments are too expensive for students to afford."

Nadine teared up the more she spoke. "And I watched the priestesses walk by a woman in the infirmary who had been paralyzed from the waist down during The Hearse Tragedy. She was a student, and they didn't care that she couldn't afford to ever walk again. They did nothing to help her. In fact, Priestess Margaret looked me in the eye and said— and I quote—*We'll save the ones who can pay.*"

Several jury members gasped, but Priestess Margaret leapt out of her chair and shouted, "Objection! She's lying."

The judge frowned. "Priestess, this is a court hearing. Please consult your council if you wish to object."

"We object," Olivia stated.

The judge nodded. "Sustained. Attorney Verla, please stick to the evidence."

"Certainly," Verla replied curtly. "Please bring up evidence file number two-two-five."

Medical records appeared on the screen. With my friends' consent, Verla had gotten her hands on dozens of medical bills that showed the crushing weight of the priestesses' new policy. The jury members' faces fell as they took in the numbers. There were thousands of dollars in medical bills here.

Verla held up an empty insulin bottle she'd gotten from Grant. "Members of the jury, this is a single vial of insulin, a life-saving drug that several students at Miriam College *require* for survival. This small vial costs close to two-hundred-and-fifty dollars apiece. This vial will not last a patient a *week*. Think of that. Over a thousand dollars per month, just to survive. This is something that *used* to be covered in our student-wide healthcare plan, funded by tuition. These students' healthcare is no longer supported because *four women* voted to shift the funds elsewhere. One of these women, I might add, is not even a priestess. These women voted to end the health insurance of children. They voted to end their lives."

"OBJECTION!" Margaret yelled. "What is the relevance? She's on trial for murder!"

The judge didn't wait for Olivia to speak for the priestesses. "Sustained. Attorney Verla, we are here to address Nadine Evers's charges. The other priestesses are not on trial."

"Yes, of course," Verla said. "Please bring up evidence file number one-seven-one."

An image of the Alchemy Wand appeared again.

"Priestess Nadine, have you seen this wand before?" Verla asked.

Nadine nodded. "Yes. It's the Alchemy Wand."

"Priestess Lilian testified that the Imperium Council confiscated the Alchemy Wand from you the night of the Burning," Verla said. "Is that correct?"

Nadine shook her head. "No."

"Is it true that you had the Wand in your possession?" Verla asked.

"Yes, but I gave it over willingly."

"Why would you do that?" Verla questioned.

Nadine leaned toward the microphone and spoke clearly. "Because the priestesses asked me to find it."

Verla spoke sympathetically. "How did you come into possession of the Alchemy Wand?"

"I tracked down clues that my grandfather had left behind," Nadine said. "Being the granddaughter of Nicholas Tucker, the priestesses believed that I had knowledge to where he'd hid the Oaken Wands. I did not, but I agreed to work with the priestesses, because uniting the Oaken Wands could end the Waning. We learned that the Alchemy Wand was hidden inside a magic cauldron, which we found at Wicked Alchemy."

Nadine's voice cracked. "We returned from the alchemy shop to find that the priestesses were burning four women alive on school grounds. Riots broke out, and I was able to escape the school grounds with my friends. Once everything settled, I returned to the Imperium Council headquarters and gave them the Alchemy Wand, as promised."

"She's lying!" Margaret accused. "She made threats—"

The judge smacked her gavel. "Order in the court! Priestess Margaret, you are no longer on the witness stand. I'm going to have to ask you to remain silent, or I'll have the bailiff escort you out."

"I am a priestess of the Miriamic Coven!" Margaret argued, as if that meant she could do whatever she wanted.

"And you're in *my* courtroom," Judge Calloway shot back. "The defense may proceed."

Verla stepped closer to the witness stand. "Priestess Nadine, are you aware that you are being charged with murdering two police officers that night, and that the spell used to kill them could only be performed using an object as powerful as the Alchemy Wand?"

"Yes, I'm aware," Nadine said.

"Have you ever used the Alchemy Wand to perform magic?"

"No. It would be impossible, because I'm not an Alchemist," Nadine said.

"Priestess Nadine, would you describe yourself as a criminal?"

Nadine shook her head. "I would not. If I have committed any crimes, they were sanctioned by the Imperium Council. The priestesses told me to do whatever it took to find the Oaken Wands so that we could stop the Waning. All I've ever done was my best to restore the coven's magic."

"Priestess, you are on trial today for murder. The coven needs the truth. Are you guilty of murder?"

Nadine leaned toward the microphone and said with firm conviction, "The only thing I am guilty of is protecting my coven."

Verla let the statement sink in for a moment then said, "No further questions, your honor."

Olivia stood to begin her cross examination. "Nadine, you testified that you are not able to use the Alchemy Wand, because you yourself are not an Alchemist."

"That is correct," Nadine said.

"Please bring up evidence file one-three-four," Olivia said.

An image of Nadine sitting near the fireplace in the Main Foyer at school appeared on the screen. I didn't know when it'd been taken, but it was clearly without her consent. In it, she was reading a textbook, oblivious that the photo was being taken at all. She was reaching up to push a strand of hair behind her ear. The image clearly showed the cauldron tattoo on her forearm.

"Miss Evers, you have the mark of an Alchemist, do you not?" Olivia questioned.

"It's a non-magical tattoo I had done at a tattoo parlor," Nadine said.

"These marks are sacred to our Casts," Olivia stated. "Why would you falsely mark yourself with the Alchemy symbol?"

"When I discovered I was a Curse Breaker, I feared what the coven might want from me," Nadine admitted. "I posed as an Alchemist the following semester, so that the coven wouldn't abuse me for my magic—which they've done since the moment they found out."

"Objection," Olivia stated.

"Sustained," the judge said. "Please strike Nadine's last statement from the record."

Olivia looked proud as she continued. "In order to convince the coven you were an Alchemist, you needed to be able to *use* Alchemy magic. Is that correct?"

"Yes," Nadine said.

"So you *can* use Alchemy magic?"

"I can transfer magic from one place to another, so I can pull Alchemy magic from a crystal and put it into a potion. I cannot cast Alchemy magic myself—"

"Have the record show that Nadine Evers testified that she can, in fact, use Alchemy magic."

"That's not really how it works—" Nadine started, but Olivia cut her off.

"You'll answer my questions and nothing further."

Nadine went silent, and Olivia smirked. The jury would believe Nadine could use the Alchemy Wand. They'd believe she poisoned the officers.

Olivia flipped through her notes. "Nadine, you testified that you objected to the council's policy change regarding school-sponsored health insurance, correct?"

"Yes."

"Isn't it true that as a patient on dialysis, you were benefiting from this school-sponsored health insurance program?" Olivia asked.

"Yes, but I was also paying for it," Nadine said curtly.

Olivia's tone turned condescending. "You were paying over seventy-five-thousand dollars per year for your healthcare?"

Nadine furrowed her brow. "No, I'm not sure where you're getting that number."

Olivia checked her notes. "That is how much dialysis costs, correct?"

"Roughly," Nadine agreed. "However, my insurance was paying for it."

"So you paid a relatively low insurance premium, and got tens of thousands of dollars in benefits, *funded by* your fellow students," Olivia sneered.

"Yes, that is how health insurance works," Nadine stated simply.

Olivia pursed her lips. "Isn't it true then that you objected to the policy change because you were directly benefiting from it?"

"I objected because it affected *all* the students."

"But not the ones who didn't need it," Olivia retorted. "There are healthy students who never used their health plan, yet they were paying premiums to support your treatments. Isn't that correct, Miss Evers?"

"I wouldn't say they didn't use it," Nadine countered. "Emergencies happen all the time. Lydia Larson, for example, was a perfectly healthy student who was *paralyzed* in The Hearse Tragedy. She lost all financial support when her health plan was defunded."

"Lydia is a young student," Olivia stated. "She could easily be on her parents' insurance."

"Not everyone has their parents' support," Nadine replied. "Lydia's parents were laid off. They had no insurance at the time of her injury."

"It *is* true that not all students are supported by their parents," Olivia agreed. "Which is why you objected to this policy change. Because your parents are dead, aren't they, Nadine?"

My hands curled into fists. How dare they speak of Nadine's parents like that!

Nadine shifted in her chair, and she visibly swallowed. "Yes, my parents are dead."

"So you had selfish intentions when you objected to the Imperium Council's rulings?" Olivia pressed. "You stated that you had the coven's best interests at heart, but you only had your own. Isn't that right, Nadine?"

"No," Nadine stated firmly, but I could see Olivia was getting to her.

"And isn't it right that you and Lucas Taylor murdered seven people who got in your way?" Olivia demanded.

"No!" Nadine's voice cracked this time. Fuck, this wasn't looking good.

"You were *there* that night four members of the coven were killed at Pinewood Manor. You were *there* the night Priestess Stella died. You were in possession of the Alchemy Wand the night two esteemed officers of the Miriamic Police Department were murdered in cold blood. You were at the school when Professor Zachary Perez was killed. You were riding in The Hearse the night it crashed. Your car was parked beside the front gate the morning Lena Hahn was hanged. You killed them all, and you should be charged with far more than seven murders!"

"I didn't kill all those people!" Nadine cried.

Murmurs spread throughout the courtroom, and Judge Calloway smacked her gavel. "Attorney Sinclair, please stick to presenting the evidence regarding the current charges."

The courtroom quieted, though the tension in the air was palpable.

Olivia straightened her blazer. "No further questions, your honor."

Verla stood. "The defense calls Lucas Taylor to the witness stand."

Nadine squeezed my hand as she sat back down, and Verla whispered to her, "You did great."

I admired Nadine for the grace she showed on the stand, but I could tell she was shaken by it all. My knees quaked as I stood. I swore on Mother Miriam's grimoire before taking the stand. I drew a deep breath and tried to relax as the examination began.

Verla approached the witness stand. "Lucas Taylor, you were present the night Pinewood Manor collapsed, correct?"

"Yes."

"And what drew you to Pinewood Manor that night?"

"Nadine's roommate woke to find Nadine missing, so she called me. Through her visions, we were able to find out that Nadine had been kidnapped and taken to Pinewood Manor."

"Did you enter the building right away?" Verla asked.

"No. We weren't sure where Nadine had been taken, so we searched the grounds first."

"Did you find anything there?"

"Yes. We found the bodies of two dead boys."

"Please bring up evidence file number three-one-one," Verla said.

Crime scene images appeared on the screen, showing the children's bodies in shallow graves.

"Lucas, do you recognize these photographs?"

"Objection!" Olivia cried. "How can we be sure these images are authentic?"

"Counselors, please approach the bench," the judge announced.

Verla and Olivia went up to the judge's stand. They spoke in low whispers, so I couldn't hear what they were saying. Eventually, Olivia frowned and went back to her seat with a sour look on her face.

"Let the record show that these case files were supplied by the Miriamic Police Department," Judge Calloway said.

Verla turned back to me and continued. "Lucas, where have you seen these bodies before?"

I looked at the jury, but they were hard to read. "We found them in the Pinewood graveyard, the night Nadine and Chloe were kidnapped."

"Thank you," Verla said, before moving on.

She brought up evidence file one-six-six, which was the voice recording of Stella's death. I winced as I listened to her dying screams all over again.

"Lucas, is that you in the recording?" Verla asked.

I nodded. "Yes."

"And what is happening here?"

"We were looking for the Alchemy Wand, which we found in the basement of Wicked Alchemy. It was protected by a magical plant called twisted vine. Priestess Stella followed us and admitted to brewing nightshade in an attempt to find the Wand herself. The Wand was hidden inside a magical cauldron, and you had to brew a specific potion to retrieve it. Nightshade was the product of the potions she'd hired Magnus Knight to brew for her."

"Objection!" Olivia protested. "Where is the evidence?"

"Sustained," Judge Calloway said. "The defense may proceed."

Verla stood tall as she asked, "In this recording, it sounds as if you hit Priestess Stella with a killing spell. Is that what happened?"

"No," I stated. "The recording is missing pieces. What you're not hearing is Priestess Stella's confession and how we wanted her to be given a fair trial. You don't hear that the spell I cast was a stunning spell—not a killing spell. You don't hear that the twisted vine grabbed her and crushed her to death, and you don't hear us scrambling to save her. Priestess Stella's death was an accident."

"Lucas, you tried to tell this truth the night of the Burning, isn't that correct?" Verla asked.

"Yes," I answered. "Four innocent women were accused of producing nightshade that night. We had the recording of Stella's confession, and we tried to tell the coven the truth, but the priestesses wouldn't let us."

"Objection, your honor!" Olivia demanded. "The priestesses are not on trial here. We don't know that these women were innocent like he claims."

"Sustained," the judge said, but her tone was difficult to read. I couldn't tell where she stood on this whole trial.

Verla turned back to me. "Lucas, if you had the recording that night, how did the priestesses get their hands on it?"

"We made a deal," I admitted. "Nadine went to the Imperium headquarters that night to meet with the priestesses. They threatened to have us arrested, along with our friends. In exchange for our lives, we were forced to hand over the Alchemy Wand, the magic cauldron, and the recording. The priestesses forced us to release a statement in the *Miriamic Messenger* saying we'd lied about Priestess Stella's involvement with nightshade."

"You were hesitant to hand over these artifacts?" Verla asked.

I drew a deep breath and answered the way we rehearsed. "Yes. We believe the Oaken Wands are dangerous in the hands of the presiding priestesses, but we were given no choice. We made the difficult decision to hand them over, in order to live long enough to protect the coven from further threats."

The priestesses looked angry, but they didn't outright protest. They still appeared confident that the jury was on their side. I shot a glance at the jury, and I was certain the priestesses were right. After everything Nadine and I had said, the jury wasn't swayed. They thought we'd made it all up.

"Did anything else happen that night?" Verla asked.

"Yes. I had followed Nadine to the Imperium headquarters, because I worried she was in danger. After she left and told me what happened, I turned back to confront the priestesses about their threats. That's when I saw the portal."

The priestesses went pale simultaneously. It was the first they'd ever heard that we knew anything about the demon. Leto narrowed his gaze at me, like he could force me to take back the confession. I kept my eyes on him, never once backing down.

"A portal to where?" Verla questioned.

"A portal to the Abyss," I said. "The priestesses summoned a demon and made a deal to find the rest of the Oaken Wands. They knowingly allowed the demon to kill Professor Perez, Lena Hahn, and several others in The Hearse Tragedy."

"Objection!" Olivia shouted.

"He's lying!" Priestess Lilian shot out of her chair and pointed an ugly finger at me.

The courtroom burst into protests, louder than before. My ears rang, and the jury shot nervous glances at one another.

"Where's the evidence!?" Margaret shouted. "They're liars!"

The judge smacked her gavel, and this time, no one quieted at all.

"We want to see the evidence!"

"Burn them for their lies!"

"Lucas, can you identify the demon?" Verla asked, but she couldn't be heard over the uproar. I never would've known what she was saying if we hadn't rehearsed the questions.

"This charade has gone on long enough!" Priestess Lilian shouted. "It's time to read their sentence."

"Tell us the truth!" someone shouted. "Have you unleashed a demon upon the coven?"

People started moving forward, demanding answers. Priestess Lilian took a step back, fear in her eyes. I'd never seen her look so scared. Everyone shouted over one another, some of them searching for my blood, and others demanding the priestesses tell the truth.

Bang!

The doors to the courtroom burst open. At first, I thought it was the mob from outside finally breaking through. I never would've predicted what happened next.

"I have the evidence you're looking for!" Talia yelled above the protests.

The courtroom quieted, and all eyes turned to her. Slowly, three figures entered the room behind her—Grant, Miles, and Professor

Warren. He'd found them in one piece, thank the Goddess. Miles turned back and gestured someone forward.

"It's okay. They're waiting for you," he said. He held out his hand, and to the astonishment of everyone in the room, a ghostly figure appeared. She wore a long black cloak and had dark curls framing her young features.

Priestess Stella.

The room fell dead silent. It was eerie, because even the protests outside could no longer be heard. Every member of the coven had been struck silent by the dead priestess's appearance.

"I am here to testify the truth," Stella announced in her ghostly form.

Nobody moved. We all watched as Priestess Stella floated down the aisle and turned to the crowd in front of the judge's table. Lilian's jaw dropped, and she watched on incredulously. Claudia kept throwing glances around the room, like she couldn't believe this was happening.

"I am Priestess Stella Jones, witness to my own death," she announced. "I am here to tell you that Lucas Taylor did not kill me. My death was an accident. There is corruption among the Imperium Council. This corruption existed when I served as priestess, and it persists now. I was the one manufacturing nightshade, and I framed others for my crimes. I'm telling you this because I see more clearly now where this corruption is headed, and I know now that the coven will fall if it continues."

She turned to the jury. "The priestesses forced Nadine and Lucas to lie about my involvement with nightshade in order to protect themselves, but I was guilty all along. And I'm guilty of one other thing… The priestesses have every intention of obtaining the Oaken Wands to control your magic. They will claim they want to restore your magic, but they are lying. Nadine and Lucas have been trying to prevent these dark dealings—"

"They weren't trying to save the coven!" Priestess Lilian barked, finally recovering from her initial shock. "They're trying to destroy it! This is a deception! Ghosts can't legally testify. They're confused. She doesn't understand what she's saying!"

Margaret was quick to agree, pointing a finger at Talia. "*You* put these ideas in her head. You manipulated her. Stella is stuck here. You promised her that the Reaper's Apprentice would help her cross over if she said what you wanted."

Olivia shot out of her chair. "I make a motion to remove this testimony from the record and to hold these four in contempt of court!"

She pointed to our friends and Professor Warren.

"I'm telling the truth!" Stella insisted. "I came here to set things right—"

Stella's words were cut off as she let out a guttural cry of pain. I shot out of my chair and glanced around the courtroom. What the hell was happening? Ghosts weren't supposed to be able to feel pain.

The screaming continued, echoing off the walls. Stella's back arched, and she wore an agonizing expression.

"Somebody help her!" the judge cried.

Nobody could do anything, because we didn't know what had happened.

My eyes landed on Professor Leto. He was smirking, like the sight of someone in pain gave him pleasure. I knew demons could influence spirits if they were strong enough. This was *his* doing.

Before I could act, the screams came to an abrupt halt, and Stella vanished in the blink of an eye.

The courtroom shared a collective gasp. Judge Calloway's features paled as she stared at the place Stella had been floating. It was at that moment that I saw the decision solidify in Judge Calloway's eyes. She may have walked into the courtroom impartial to the case, but the moment Stella vanished, rage marred her features.

Judge Calloway pointed a finger at my friends. "You have tortured a priestess's soul! You manipulated the dead and forced her to testify. You have defiled my courtroom with your lies. Officers, arrest them!"

"We didn't! You have to believe us!" Talia screamed, but several officers were already crossing the room.

"These students are telling the truth!" Professor Warren protested as an officer slapped cuffs on his wrists.

"The only truth *you* should be concerned with is the jury's guilty verdict," Priestess Margaret sneered. "If Lucas and Nadine are found guilty, then *you're* guilty as well for fabricating evidence, and you will burn with them."

All the air sucked out of my lungs, and horror crossed Nadine's face.

"You can't do that!" I yelled. "This isn't their trial!"

"Order! Order in the court!" The judge smacked her gavel over and over again, but one side of the courtroom continued to scream at the other. If the coven wasn't divided before, they sure as hell were now.

A group of officers dragged our friends out of the courtroom, while we screamed protests. I didn't know where they were taking them—probably to holding cells somewhere. I shuddered to think what they might do to them.

"I said ORDER IN THE COURT!" Judge Calloway screamed.

All at once, the room went silent. People clutched at their throats, like they couldn't figure out where their voices went. My gaze darted to the judge, and she was holding up a wand, controlling the crowd with magic. I spotted the gnarly tree tattoo on her wrist. She was a Mentalist, messing with people's heads to get them to quiet down.

"Attorney Verla, please proceed," Judge Calloway said calmly.

Verla glanced around the room. How the hell was she supposed to follow up to that? "No further questions, your honor."

Olivia shook as she stood and announced, "No further questions."

"The court will enter jury deliberation," the judge announced with a smack of her gavel.

Nadine and I were once again ushered into a private room. We weren't even given a chance to give our closing statement. At this point, I didn't think it'd be enough to convince the jury anyway. Thanks to whatever spell Professor Leto had cast on Stella, it looked like we'd fabricated everything.

"Goddess!" Nadine cried the second we were alone. "We can't be found guilty! Our friends will be executed with us!"

"Nad, we did all we could." I drew her into a tight hug, but my words tasted stale in my mouth. Even my hug didn't quite feel like it belonged. We were fucked.

I didn't know how long we waited, but it had to be past dark before we were ushered back into the courtroom. There were more people here than ever before. They filled every seat and stood against the wall, crammed together to hear the verdict.

"Will the defendants please rise for the verdict reading?" the judge said.

Nadine and I stood nervously beside each other. I took her hand in mine. If we were sent to the gallows, then at least I had one dream of mine fulfilled—I'd get to help her cross over.

"In the case of the Miriamic Coven versus Priestess Nadine Evers and Lucas Taylor, on two misdemeanor counts of unauthorized intercast spellwork, how does the jury find the defendant?"

A jury member rose with a piece of paper in their hand. "We the jury find the defendants not guilty."

It was a small victory, but I wasn't celebrating just yet.

"On twelve felony counts of black magic use with the intent to do harm, how does the jury find the defendants?"

"Not guilty."

Nadine squeezed my hand harder. Here came the worst of it—the charges that could get us executed.

"On seven charges of first-degree murder, how does the jury find the defendants?"

Silence hung in the air for a beat, and I swore the entire room held their breath.

"Not guilty," the juror read.

Relief flooded my entire body.

"On one felony count of attempting to overthrow the Imperium Council, how does the jury find the defendants?"

The juror hesitated, and not a single soul in the room moved. My heart hammered, and Nadine's hand shook in mine.

"We the jury have determined the charge..." The juror took a deep breath, then spat out, "Inconclusive."

The courtroom broke out into chatter.

"They can't do that!" Lilian barked, pointing a finger at the jury.

Verla shot out of his chair. "Your honor, I make a motion to sentence these students to four years at the Darke Institute for Supernatural Offenders—"

Judge Calloway smacked her gavel. "Order! Order in the court!"

"This can't happen," Priestess Margaret insisted. "The coven prides itself in conducting accurate trials. We've never had an inconclusive case before. We must have a conclusive verdict!"

Judge Calloway smacked her gavel again to bring the court to order. "I'm aware of the legal proceedings, Priestess. You are correct—the coven *always* reaches a verdict, and we will not be ending that tradition today."

She narrowed her eyes at Nadine and me. She had death in her eyes, and it became very clear that she wanted to see us hang. She lifted her nose, looking down at us like we were nothing more than dirt on the bottom of her heels. "If the jury can't offer an official ruling, we will have to *force* a confession out of them. The modern way didn't work, so we'll have to resort to the old way."

She smacked her gavel, ruling her word official.

Nadine's eyes widened as she turned to me. "What does that mean!? The old way? They can't—"

Nadine never got a chance to finish, because several officers lunged for us and grabbed us both.

"Nadine!" I shouted as they yanked us apart. The noxite bracelet they'd slapped on me before the trial drained all my power, and I couldn't fight back.

"You can't do this to them!" Verla protested. "Under Miriamic law—"

Several officers grabbed her, and they slapped noxite cuffs onto her wrists. They dragged her away from us, but stopped when Margaret stepped in front of them.

"What game do you think you're playing, *headmistress?*" Margaret sneered. "You were supposed to incriminate them."

I didn't hear anything else they said, because more people came forward. The officers didn't care—they let them right through. Executors grabbed for Nadine and began dragging her out of the courtroom. Chloe and Onyx shouted protests, and Helena screamed Nadine's name. Someone grabbed me by the hair, and they yanked me out of the court-room behind Nadine.

"Get the devices from storage. We're going to need them all!" Judge Calloway shouted. I shuddered to think what *devices* she was talking about.

The mob pulled us outside into the darkness of night. They dragged us down the stairs at the front of the courthouse and threw us to the ground. I was shoved so hard that I landed face-first onto the concrete. Blood trickled down the side of my face, and my skin stung. Several people grabbed my arms and yanked them behind my back so I couldn't get to Nadine.

"Stop! We mustn't torture them!" someone shouted. I looked up to see it was Professor Loren, my Astrology professor.

"We want a confession!" Corbin shouted. He was one of the Tarantulas, and I saw that he was backed up by his entire gang.

The coven was divided, but the ones who wanted our heads were more ruthless. Someone yanked me upright, and I felt cool metal touch my skin, restraining me. I didn't realize what it was until I saw them fit the same device onto Nadine's face. It was a metal restraint that fitted around a prisoner's head so they didn't bite their torturers, much like a muzzle on a dog. We had a name for it—a witch's bridle.

"You've brought shame upon your coven!" Leroy Benson spat in my face.

"Shame is a kind word," Avery sneered, and the whole coven turned to listen to her. She pointed a finger at Nadine. "Nadine Evers is possessed by evil! She cursed me, and if she lives, she'll curse us all!"

"That's not true!" I tried to shout, but it came out muffled against the witch's bridle.

Mira stepped forward. "They're both possessed! I was there the night of The Hearse Tragedy. I saw them cast the spell that killed all those people!"

What a fucking liar. She'd lied about Monica, and now she was going to use her lies to get us killed, too.

"Nadine infiltrated the Alchemy Cast and tried to kill us all!" Gwen claimed. "She brewed potions meant to kill. They were so powerful her cauldron exploded!"

"You're lying!" Onyx insisted.

Chloe tried to rush forward, but Gwen and Camille grabbed her and held her back. These three girls used to be best friends, and now they were fighting over whether we should live or die. Chloe conjured battle magic, but Camille was faster than her, and she slammed a stunning spell into the side of her head. Helena wailed as people yanked her backward, keeping her from getting to her granddaughter.

A blood-curdling scream tore through the night, and all protests ceased as everyone turned to look. Stacey lay on the ground at Nadine's feet, convulsing like she was having a seizure. Valerie stood above her, her hands thrown over her mouth as she backed away in horror.

Valerie pointed a finger at Nadine. "See!? It's true! All of it! Nadine has cast a curse!"

Two guys managed to push their way to the front of the crowd. It was Talia's brother Tyler, along with a guy named Alex from school.

"You have to stop this!" Tyler shouted.

"Stacey's putting on an act!" Alex insisted. The coven wasn't interested in listening. Hands landed on both of them, and the crowd dragged them backward.

Two members of the Tarantulas walked up behind Nadine—Declan and Nolan. Horror filled her eyes as they forced her to her knees in front of Stacey.

"Touch her again!" Nolan demanded. "Heal her!"

Nadine trembled.

James stepped up to Nadine and grabbed her by the hair. "Break the curse!" he roared, before throwing Nadine to the ground beside Stacey. I winced, but no amount of struggling against my captors would allow me to break free and get to her. Nadine landed close enough to Stacey that their shoulders touched. Stacey immediately stilled, and she sat up and shook her head, like she'd just come to. She looked over at Nadine, like she was noticing her for the first time. She quickly scrambled away, like she was terrified of her.

"She cursed me!" Stacey insisted in a trembling voice.

I had to hand it to her, that girl put on one hell of a show.

James yanked Nadine upward and spat, "One way or another, we'll get an answer out of you!"

The crowd began cheering, and I realized they were looking at something behind me. I turned my head as far as I could to see a group of men carrying a heavy chair down the stairs. My stomach hollowed at the sight of hundreds of iron spikes protruding from all over it. It also came with shackles to restrain the torture subject.

The chair went by many names. Some called it the Iron Chair, others the Iron Maiden. The coven knew it as a witch's chair. A heavy *thud* sounded as the men dropped the chair beside me.

"No!" Nadine screamed. Her voice cut through all the others, slicing straight through my heart. I struggled against the men dragging me toward the chair, but there were so many of them. I tried to find Nadine in the crowd, but I couldn't see her.

Complete terror rocked my body as the men shoved me into the witch's chair. Hundreds of spikes connected with my skin, and when I struggled, the spikes stabbed in even harder. Several broke the skin, and I was forced to stop struggling as the men shackled my hands and legs to the chair. If I sat still, the spikes didn't hurt as much. Any slight movement, though—any misdirection of my weight—would send the spikes straight through my skin.

I couldn't understand why the coven would have these torture devices. These were items used on *us* hundreds of years ago by humans who feared our magic. The coven must've kept them as historical relics. That they couldn't see the irony in the witch hunt was beyond me.

People surrounded me, closing in so tightly that I couldn't even see the stars above me. "Confess!" Finn spat, and spittle flew into my face. Protests grew around me, until my ears began to ring.

"Nadine!" I screamed, but I couldn't hear her protests any longer. I didn't know what they'd done with her.

The crowd parted, and my heart hammered even harder when I saw Cody coming forward with several logs in his arms, followed by Ryan, who carried a lighted torch. Cody laughed maniacally as he arranged the logs beneath my chair. "You're going to burn until you confess."

Ryan joined in on the laughter. "Burn, baby, burn!"

The warmth of the fire touched my legs as Ryan lit the logs.

"You're a liar!"

"He's deceived the coven!"

"He's defiled Mother Miriam's good name!"

"We're telling the truth!" I insisted.

"You're lying!" Cody accused, before grabbing me by the hair and forcing me to look straight forward. "You'll admit what you've done, or your girlfriend will die."

Every spike on the chair might as well have impaled me right then, because the crowd parted, and I finally saw Nadine again. They held her down as she screamed and struggled against them. Several people brought forth large rocks and placed them across her limbs to hold her down. Nadine cried out as the heavy rocks pressed down on her.

It was an old torture technique sometimes used in the execution of witches. We'd learned about it in Miriamic History—a technique known as *pressing*. With enough weight, Nadine would die a slow, painful death.

I'd never known the coven to use it against their own. It was a horrible, excruciating way to go, and it was meant to be Nadine's torture as much as mine. More painful than a thousand spikes, and more deeply aching than a searing fire, was to watch the woman I loved slowly perish. I shifted in the chair, as if I could break out of the shackles by pure will and run to her—but the spikes only pierced harder. They were heating up quickly, and the metal burned my skin.

"Confess to your lies!" people shouted.

"We can't do this to our own people!" someone yelled. I was surprised to see it was Samantha Stone. She'd always seemed so terrified to stand up to anybody. Now she was demanding the crowd stand down.

She wasn't the only one who opposed the torture. Coven members looked on in uncertainty, discomfort clear on their faces.

But I also saw fear, and though they didn't want this to happen, they didn't step in to stop it, either. They knew if they tried, they'd be next.

I spotted Gregory nearby. He tugged the end of his sleeve over the star marked on his wrist. It was the sign of Miriam's Chosen. I thought I witnessed regret in his eyes underneath the indecision.

The fire beneath me grew hotter, and the heat permeated my clothing and seared my skin. My body moved involuntarily as the heat became too much to bear. The small movements forced the spikes deeper into my flesh.

The mob placed more and more rocks onto Nadine's limbs, until she couldn't struggle anymore. James placed a heavy rock on her chest, and I swore all the air left my own lungs as I was forced to watch Nadine struggle for breath.

"Confess, Curse Maker," he growled.

Tears leaked from Nadine's eyes as she tried to fight against the pain. She rasped, "I won't."

James's nostrils flared, and murderous intent entered his eyes. He grabbed one of the rocks and lifted it above his head.

"No!" I screamed. The shackles pinched against my limbs as I leaned forward, and the searing spikes pierced deeper, but the physical pain was nothing compared to the horrifying scene before me. James was going to smash her face in.

Someone caught his wrist, and for a moment I was relieved, until I realized it was Cody. "I want to hear her say it," he demanded.

"*Yeah!*" Several others agreed, cheering for Nadine's confession. The priestesses stood nearby, watching on, but not intervening. Lilian and Margaret looked pleased, like they were happy to let the coven do the dirty work for them.

James hesitated. He looked down at Nadine, then growled, "Then we will. Get them to the river!"

The mob surrounded Nadine and me again, until I couldn't see her anymore. They released me from the shackles around my wrists and ankles. My skin was raw with burns and bled from endless wounds, but I felt a sense of reprieve as several people yanked me out of the hot iron chair.

The coven dragged Nadine and me around the side of the courthouse and down a hill. I could barely make sense of what was going on, because there were so many people surrounding me.

I didn't see the water until I was already in it. The icy chill of the river felt good on my burns, but it was anything but soothing. I heard Nadine scream, and then all sound was gone as someone shoved me downward.

I inhaled a breath, but water burned my nostrils. I tried to stand upright, but someone held my head under water.

I couldn't breathe. I couldn't fight back.

Someone grabbed my hair and yanked my head out of the water. I gulped a greedy breath and caught sight of Nadine gasping from several feet away. She was drenched from head to toe, and her skin was mottled with bruises. She looked like she was in so much pain.

"Confess!" someone screamed from above me. I recognized the voice and realized it was Leroy who had me by the hair.

Someone else grabbed my jaw and forced my head backward. He leaned down to snarl, "Tell us the truth, or I'll drown you myself."

It was Ryan.

James smacked Nadine on the side of the head, while Cody threatened to dunk her under again. She winced, but she didn't speak.

For a brief moment, I thought about confessing, just to make them stop hurting Nadine—just to take her pain away. Then her eyes connected with mine, and between the straps of her witch's bridle, I could see the pleading expression on her face. *Don't do it, Lucas.*

"I will not confess," Nadine said in the strongest tone she could muster.

I knew at that moment, we were in this together, until the very end. We would die to keep the others fighting.

"Nor will I," I stated confidently.

I barely finished speaking before Leroy shoved my head underwater again. I held my breath and kicked against the river bottom, trying to save my life by sheer instinct. I knew how this went. It was another torture technique we'd learned about in Miriamic History, one that had been performed during the witch hunts hundreds of years ago. It was called dunking, and it only ended one of two ways. Either the accused confessed to the crimes, whether they were truly guilty or not... or they drowned.

It was sick and twisted, but all I could think was that if I had to go out by one means of a witch hunt, at least it was this. It was far less painful than being burned on a pyre, and perhaps less shameful than walking to the gallows. If they killed us before they reached a verdict, then perhaps they'd spare Talia, Grant, and Miles. Professor Warren and Headmistress Verla would go free. The coven would have reason to continue fighting.

It was odd how calm the river was in the midst of what was happening. I barely felt the current. It was like the river didn't care either way if it took a life.

This was our prophecy. Nadine and I were meant to unite the coven. Nowhere in our prophecy did it state that we would survive to see it through. If our death motivated the coven to heal after this, as stated in our prophecy, then it was worth it. I didn't wish to live long enough to witness the alternative.

Nadine and I were good people. We had followed Mother Miriam's teachings to *protect the coven*. Every day, we fought tooth and nail to do just that. This was our final chance to show that everything we'd done had a purpose. That purpose would live on in our people.

Leroy yanked my head out of the water, and I inhaled a deep breath. The world spun around me, and I could barely make out the screams from shore as my head spun. It was like my head was still underwater.

"Are you ready to confess now!?" Leroy screamed in my ear. He yanked on my hair, forcing me to look at Nadine. James held her head underwater, and she thrashed as she fought against him. It wouldn't be long until she drowned. All I wanted was to save her life.

Fuck the coven. Fuck them all.

I had to confess, or she would die. I opened my mouth the best I could with the witch's bridle on, but before I could say anything, splashes sounded all around me. I looked up to see a group had formed on the bridge. They were tossing stones at our assailants. It was hard to make out who it was in the darkness, but I noticed Chloe and Onyx among the silhouettes.

"Stop!" Chloe shouted. "You're going to kill them. Is this what we want? More bloodshed?"

My eyes scanned the shore. So many coven members had backed away. Their uncertainty had turned to horror. Half of the coven wanted our torture to continue. The other half couldn't stomach it.

Someone threw a rock at the back of James's head. He cursed loudly and dropped Nadine. She finally came up for air, gasping loudly. She tried to stand, but she was so deprived of oxygen that she was ready to pass out. She stumbled and fell to her knees. Ryan went to dunk me under again.

"Stop!" Priestess Margaret shouted.

All eyes turned to the priestesses. The crowd parted as the priestesses came down the hill, their heads held high like this was nothing more than a minor spat.

Leroy and Ryan dragged me through the water and tossed me into the mud along the shore. I landed on my face, gasping for breath. Nadine landed beside me, and she sputtered water out of her mouth. She must've been moments away from drowning before James dropped her. Weakly, she turned her face toward mine, and I saw the heartache in her eyes, mixed with something I couldn't quite put my finger on—courage or determination, perhaps. I didn't think I had any of that left. Every inch of my body ached, and I didn't have the strength to move anymore. I just lay there, awaiting my reaper.

The priestesses reached us. I felt one of them digging in my pocket. It took me a moment to realize they'd taken my wand. Nadine's, too, by the looks of it. They held both wands up to the coven.

"This matter is in the hands of the Goddess now," Priestess Lilian said. "It is *she* who will determine their verdict, for no member of the coven can defy the Goddess. It is a tradition of old. We will place their wands in the river. If their wands sink, the Goddess has determined them innocent. If they float, they are undoubtedly guilty."

It was a modified version of the swimming test used during the witch trials. Accused witches were brought to the nearest body of water and thrown in. People believed that witches had rejected the sacrament of baptism, and so the water would reject them, too. According to lore, a witch would float, while an innocent would sink. But we were all witches here, and the original test didn't work on us. The priestesses had to modify it for their own gain.

I wasn't fooled. We all knew a wooden wand would float. Nadine and I would be deemed guilty for sure. It's why the coven hadn't used the test in so long—because it wasn't a *real* determination of guilt. It was just a story the priestesses told when they had no other options.

The coven didn't seem to care. They believed the Goddess would intervene. People on both sides began cheering.

"Yes, leave it up to the Goddess!"

"No one is above the Goddess. She will reveal the truth!"

The priestesses approached the water. I barely had the strength to lift my head, but I managed to roll myself onto my side to watch. The priestesses carefully set our wands in the river. It was no surprise that they floated, yet my stomach seemed to shrivel into a stone that somehow weighed six tons.

"Mother Miriam deems them both guilty!" Priestess Margaret announced, turning back toward the coven. "Nadine Evers and Lucas Taylor have been sentenced to—"

"Wait!" Chloe shouted.

The whole world seemed to tilt as every coven member in attendance watched the river. A white, magical glow shimmered beneath the surface of the water. Magical tendrils drifted upward and curled around our wands. Slowly, the magic dragged the wands beneath the surface, sinking them to the bottom of the river.

Silence permeated the night. Not a single soul spoke, because we were all stunned by what had just happened. I'd seen that white light before, when Mother Miriam had appeared to me in her energetic form. I wasn't the only one who knew what it meant, either. Everyone knew the stories of Mother Miriam, and how she was the only witch to possess white magic.

This wasn't something that could be faked. Mother Miriam *had* intervened, and she'd determined us both innocent.

The relief that flooded through me was unmatched. I reached out for Nadine, and her fingers curled around mine as she began to cry.

"They're innocent!" Professor Loren shouted. "Look what you've done to them!"

The coven broke out into protests once more.

"How many other innocents has the coven killed?" someone I didn't know demanded.

"This torture has to end! We must stop hurting our own people!" another insisted.

They weren't the only ones with opinions. Other people stood up for the priestesses. They couldn't see the truth right in front of them, and they were in denial.

"The priestesses wouldn't execute anyone without proof!" Leroy insisted.

"They gave Nadine and Lucas a fair trial," Olivia added.

We were a rare exception. So many others had been burned or hanged without a trial... Professor Daniels, Professor Ward, Amy, Christine, Ashley, and so many others. The priestesses had never intended for our trial to go this far. They'd had every intention of executing us at the end of it.

But now? Now they couldn't hang us unless they wanted the coven calling for their own heads, because to do so would go against the will of Mother Miriam. The shock on their faces was unmistakable, but in the darkness of night, most of the coven couldn't see it.

Priestess Margaret quickly collected herself. "Mother Miriam deems Nadine Evers and Lucas Taylor innocent. They are free to go."

I couldn't believe it. I *literally* couldn't believe they would just let us go like that, after everything they'd done to us.

It took all my strength to crawl closer to Nadine and help her sit up. Several people came forward to remove the witch's bridles and noxite bracelets. I wasn't sure I'd ever felt more relieved in my life. I pulled Nadine close to me, and she sagged into my arms as she hugged me with all the strength she could muster. I didn't even care about the burns and shit right now. I got to hold her again, and that was everything.

"*However*," Priestess Lilian added, halting my relief in its tracks. "Priestess Nadine is no longer the only Curse Breaker in the coven, and if her Cast rejects her, it is grounds for removal from the Imperium Council."

Nadine's form went rigid, and she sat up straighter. "What are you talking about?"

"Mira, dear," Margaret said kindly. "Come forward. Show the coven what you showed us."

I watched incredulously as Mira Benson stepped forward, looking timid. Priestess Margaret conjured a witch light to illuminate Mira's features. The young Executor lifted her arm and pulled back her sleeve.

A collective gasp traveled around the crowd. I couldn't believe my eyes. On Mira's wrist sat a crescent moon tattoo. Mira Benson bore the mark of a Curse Breaker.

I didn't even know she'd turned nineteen yet. She must've gone through her Evoking Ceremony recently, because the mark was unmistakable.

Nadine was no longer the sole Curse Breaker in the coven.

TWENTY-TWO

I couldn't be sure of what I was seeing. Mira, a Curse Breaker?

My throat ached as I rasped, "You can't take me off the council."

Priestess Lilian smirked as she looked down at me. "I think you'll learn that we *can*."

Mira turned toward the crowd and raised her voice. "I am a Curse Breaker of the Miriamic Coven! I hereby oppose Nadine Evers's spot on the council, and I call to have her removed."

Lilian looked over the crowd. "Any objections from the Curse Breaker Cast?"

Of course, there was no one *to* object. Mira and I were the only Curse Breakers alive.

"*I* object," I said.

Margaret pursed her lips. "An even fifty-fifty split. I believe a motion like this requires a majority vote, and as it's split down the middle, the vote goes to the one who made the motion."

I didn't know if that was a real law, or if they were making it up on the spot. It didn't matter. Half the coven was just glad to see the torture end. The other still wanted me to pay, and this was the most shameful sentence the priestesses could deliver, next to execution.

"The Imperium Council hereby removes Nadine Evers from her position as a high priestess of the Miriamic Coven," Lilian announced. I didn't think such a thing had ever happened before, but the coven didn't protest.

"Seeing as there is now a vacant seat on the Imperium Council, would the Curse Breaker Cast like to nominate a Curse Breaker for the position?" Claudia asked.

"I nominate myself," Mira said.

"Do any Curse Breakers oppose this nomination?" Priestess Lilian asked, glaring at me. She was *daring* me to oppose them. She was *begging* for more controversy, but if I defied the priestesses now, it gave the priestesses cause to hang me—to hang us all.

I itched to protest and squirmed in Lucas's arms. But I didn't have a choice anymore. "No objections."

Margaret smirked and spoke just low enough for Lucas and me to hear. "You may have won your trial, Nadine. You will live, but you are off the Imperium Council. I hope you learn that that's a hell far worse than the Abyss."

The priestesses turned away, their cloaks billowing in the wind as they headed back up the hill, leaving us sitting in the mud completely forgotten. They seemed far more interested in Mira as they escorted her away. Priestess Charlotte remained for a brief moment. I raised my head to snap at her and ask what she was still doing there, but she turned away before I got the chance.

The priestesses didn't offer us any help. It didn't matter to them that we were hurt. For all they cared, we could crawl back into the river and never return.

Slowly, the crowd began to disperse. Several people approached us, and I looked up to see Chloe soaking wet, holding our wands out to us. She must've retrieved them from the river.

"Thanks," I said as I took them.

"You were both very brave," Onyx said kindly. "The coven has been inspired by you."

Lucas snorted. "Half of them still want to see us hang."

"And the other half will defend you," Chloe insisted.

"Nadine!" Grammy cried as she pushed through the departing crowd to get to us. She dropped to her knees in the mud beside us and drew me into her arms.

"I'm all right, Grammy," I said breathlessly.

Grammy looked me over. "But you're hurt."

"I'm *alive*," I said. "My body will heal."

"I know just the herbs," Grammy said. "Let's get you two someplace safe."

Lucas reached for me, but he winced in pain. Grammy insisted on helping me hobble up the hill, and Onyx and Chloe helped Lucas.

By the time we reached the top, most of the crowd was gone. A group of Executors stood across the street, glaring at us. Mira was noticeably missing; she was probably headed back to the Imperium headquarters with the priestesses.

The crowd parted, and I was shocked to see Lucas's parents standing there. Jay had his arm around Margo, and they both looked really broken up. They stared at Lucas, as if waiting for him to say something first. I took Lucas's hand.

"Mom, Dad," he said curtly. He obviously didn't want to talk to them. "I didn't know you'd come."

"Of course. We were here to support you," Margo said, but her tone sounded disingenuous.

Lucas cleared his throat. "I appreciate that."

"Turns out you were innocent," Jay said with a stilted laugh. What the hell was he laughing about? This wasn't funny. "Who would've thought?"

"Mm… I don't know. I was pretty sure about it the whole time I was on trial," Lucas stated flatly.

Jay's features turned sour. "Come on, Lucas. I was trying to lighten the mood."

"I'm not really in that place right now, Dad," he insisted. "Give me a couple of days to process, all right?"

Lucas winced as he shifted his weight. Jay looked down and seemed to notice his condition for the first time. Of course, because all he ever thought about was himself. Why should I be surprised?

"Maybe we can celebrate," Margo suggested, like they were one big happy family.

"Mom, I'm not—" Lucas started

"That's a great idea," Jay interrupted. "Why don't you come by for dinner tomorrow night? Bring your girlfriend. Your mother can make that famous clam chowder she's so well known for."

It baffled me why he would suggest such a thing. A few days ago, it sounded like he was ready to disown Lucas. But that was before our verdict was read.

Lucas looked at me, and I saw sadness in his eyes. It seemed that all he wanted was approval from his parents. I squeezed his hand tightly and told him, "I'll go wherever you go. It's up to you."

Lucas turned back to them. "All right. I'll see you tomorrow."

Jay looked pleased as he walked away with his wife. Lucas turned to me and wrapped an arm around my waist. He kissed my forehead and closed his eyes as he pulled me close.

"I wasn't sure you'd tell them yes," I said. "Why did you?"

Lucas looked thoughtful, like he wasn't really sure. "I guess I figure my parents must feel remorse for how they treated me. Now that they have a clear answer from Mother Miriam, it seems they want to make amends. I just wished they would've believed me sooner. Part of me wanted to tell them to fuck off, but the child inside of me still wants their approval. I want to hear an apology."

"Will that really make you feel any better?" I wondered. "It won't change the past."

"No, but… maybe that's not the point," Lucas said. "I can't explain it, but I *need* to do this. I'm ready to move on, and if I'm going to do that, I have to say goodbye."

"Thank the Goddess! I thought you were dead!" a voice came from nearby. I looked up to see Verla rushing down the courthouse stairs.

She was followed by the others—Talia, Grant, Miles, and Professor Warren. They'd all been set free.

"You're alive!" Talia cried.

Grant took in our sopping wet forms. "What *happened* to you?"

"Let's get them someplace dry and warm, then we'll talk about it," Verla suggested.

We took separate cars and drove to Verla's, where we'd be safe for the night. Lucas and I rode with the headmistress. She kept a blanket in her car, and Lucas wrapped it around the both of us. He kept his arms around me as we climbed the front steps. I couldn't stop shivering.

The three of us entered the door, and my stomach dropped out of my abdomen. Everly lay on the ground in the front hall, gasping for air. The veins in her neck had turned black, and it looked as if the magic was choking her.

"Dear Goddess!" Verla rushed to her side. Everly began to thrash, like she was having a seizure.

"What's going on?" I demanded. "You gave her the antidote, didn't you!?"

"Of course I did!" Verla cried. She checked Everly's airways, and when she didn't find anything blocking them, she ripped open Everly's shirt to inspect the magic. My guts clenched when I saw the black lines all over her chest.

I quickly knelt beside her and placed my hand on her chest. My magic wasn't a hundred percent yet, but I could feel bits and pieces of the curse working its way through her system.

"The scaleweed must've been fake!" Verla panicked. She rushed to a hutch in the hall filled with alchemy ingredients. She frantically searched for something to help, tossing boxes and canisters to the floor. Potion ingredients and bottles rolled across the hardwood where Everly lay.

Everly grabbed my wrists and yanked me toward her. She gasped in my ear, but I couldn't tell what she was trying to say. "D—do…"

Her voice faded, and her hands went limp. Her head tilted to the side, and her eyes stared ahead lifelessly.

"Everly!" I screamed. I shook her to get her to wake, but she didn't move.

Lucas knelt beside me and curled me in his arms. "It's too late," he whispered.

I curled into him. How could this happen? After everything Lucas had risked to get her treatment, how could it fail?

"Did she say anything?" Verla asked urgently.

I shook my head. "I couldn't understand her."

Lucas swallowed audibly, and I realized he must've heard her last thought. I drew away from him to ask, "Did she say anything to you?"

Lucas shivered. "All I heard was… *Don't trust anyone.*"

"*Obviously* we can't trust the coven," Verla said, throwing her hands up. "Didn't she have anything more helpful to say?"

"Verla!" I shouted, more out of shock than anything. "Everly *died.* Whatever she was trying to say, she was using her last breath to try and help us!"

Verla bowed her head. "Yes, I… I'm sorry. It's just… after everything, even more loss…"

A few tears slipped out of Verla's eyes, and she turned away.

We heard footsteps, then several gasps as the others arrived. Our friends stood on the porch, along with Grammy and Professor Warren, staring down at Everly's lifeless form.

My voice cracked. "The antidote didn't work."

Lucas stood and gently explained, "We can't even trust the coven's own herbs. Everly must've been unable to conjure her phone, so she got out of bed to try getting help. We got here too late."

Grammy was the first to step forward. "If the coven finds out about this, they'll blame you, and they won't give you the courtesy of another trial. This time, they won't hesitate to hang you. We'll give Everly a proper burial."

Lucas started for the door. "I'll find a shovel and start digging."

He was delusional if he thought he could dig a grave in his condition.

Professor Warren placed a hand on his shoulder to stop him. "You and Nadine need to rest. We'll handle this."

Lucas scowled. He didn't like that he couldn't help, but both of us could hardly stay on our feet right now. Lucas knew it, too, and he was in no position to argue. I took his hand and led him to the bathroom, where we stripped down to get out of our wet clothes.

All I could do was wrap my arms around him and hold his body close to mine. We'd won our trial. We were alive and free to go. We should be celebrating.

But we weren't.

I could feel the pain of death permeating the house—the melancholy creak of slow footsteps as people passed in the hall, the quiet whispers coming from the other room. I couldn't help but feel that this was somehow our fault. It was a miracle that we'd been found innocent. It felt like something bad had to happen to even out the balance of the universe, and somehow, Everly had been our sacrifice. It wasn't fair.

Sobs rocked my body, but Lucas didn't move. I didn't know how long I stood there before I drew away from Lucas and wiped the tears from my eyes. "What is it?"

He shook his head. "It's nothing."

"It's *something*," I insisted. "Let me help you."

He sighed. "I must be broken or something. Everything we'd gone through tonight should elicit *some* reaction from me. I should be crying from sheer trauma or from utter relief, but I'm just... numb."

"You're not broken," I assured him.

"I've heard you say that a million times, and sometimes I believe it. Right now, it doesn't make any sense."

"You and I handle things differently, and that's okay," I told him.

He turned to look in the mirror, looking contemplative. I ran my fingers over his back. My stomach twisted at the sight of bruises and sores all over his body.

"Maybe you're right," he said. "I handle trauma by turning inward, by going numb and just shutting it all off. Maybe that isn't bad or wrong. Maybe it's just how I process it, and maybe I *can't* fully process it until I accept that's how I work."

"We'll learn how to handle it together," I promised, eyeing his wounds.

Lucas watched me in the mirror, and his features got even sadder. "I never wanted you to suffer."

My throat closed up. "You couldn't have saved me from this."

"I don't like that I can't save you," he whispered.

My fingers grazed a blistered welt on the back of his leg, where the burns were the worst. He winced.

I pulled away instantly. "I'm sorry. I don't want you to hurt, either."

He turned and took my hands in his, then kissed them. "I don't mind how it feels. All I want is to hold you close."

I tilted my head up and kissed him. "We can do that."

Neither of us said anything as we climbed into the shower together to wash the mud and blood off our bodies. We didn't have the energy left to speak. I gently rubbed soap over Lucas's bloody wounds. He closed his eyes, like the cold water felt good against his burns. Lucas helped me wash the mud from my hair. He ran the suds down my arms, and he stilled when he felt the ring on my finger.

"I keep forgetting you agreed to marry me," he whispered.

I tilted my head up to look into his green eyes. "I'd have married you at the gallows."

We finished cleaning up, and I rubbed ointment over Lucas's wounds and bandaged the ones that were still bleeding. We dressed in bath robes we found in the closet, then tossed our wet clothes into the washing machine down the hall.

Something clinked in the kitchen, and we followed the sound to find Chloe, Onyx, and Talia sitting at the table sipping on tea. Grammy stood at the stove, brewing a fresh batch. The others must've been outside, digging Everly's grave. I choked up all over again.

"Here, have some tea," Grammy said. Even though her voice came out soft, it still felt too loud. She handed Lucas and me each a teacup. We sat at the table and began sipping on the healing herbs.

Nobody spoke for a long time. Eventually, the others came in from outside.

"Is it done?" Grammy asked Verla softly.

Verla spoke in a sad whisper. "Yes."

I saw the dirt on her hands and looked away. I couldn't believe that Everly was gone. I didn't *want* to believe it.

Once they finished cleaning up, we all gathered in the kitchen.

I cleared my throat. "Thank you all for being there for us today. You stood up to the priestesses for us. This night would've turned out differently without you."

Talia gazed into her teacup. "I'm afraid we made things worse by involving Stella."

"No," I argued. "There were a lot of people who weren't convinced until Stella spoke up. You helped convince them."

"But it was *because* of her that the judge ordered your torture," Talia said.

Lucas shook his head. "That wasn't your fault. I saw Leto cast some sort of spell. Stella vanished because of *him*. He's the one who made us look bad."

Miles wore a thoughtful expression. "That must be why I can't see her anymore. When she vanished in the courtroom, I completely lost contact with her."

Professor Warren furrowed his brow. "A demon would have to be very powerful to influence spirits. He must be more powerful than we thought."

"Which is another reason to get out of town as soon as possible," Verla said. "You won your trial. You'll live for now, but the coven won't let you stay. It won't be long before they find a reason to hold another execution."

"We'll give ourselves twenty-four hours," Lucas suggested.

Verla glared at him. "That is the exact suggestion that got us into trouble the last time. We should leave now."

"You can't expect us to leave without making preparations," Lucas argued. "We don't know how long we'll be gone. If we're leaving for good, everyone deserves a chance to say goodbye to their families. We're not leaving our cats behind, either. That's non-negotiable."

Verla sighed. "You better hope that your verdict protects you for that long. We'll meet back here in twenty-four hours. Don't be late."

Verla offered us her guest room, because Lucas and I were in no shape to go anywhere.

"We'll check on the cats and bring you clean clothes in the morning," Talia offered.

"Be careful," I told her.

I didn't sleep well that night. I should've felt safe now that we'd won our trial, but I didn't. If anything, I felt more in danger than I ever had before.

I dreamed Lucas and I were being marched to the gallows. When we reached the hilltop in my dream, half a dozen people swayed lifelessly from the trees. In the distance, a scream tore through the night. The bodies spun in the wind all at once, until each of their faces came into view.

My friends.

My heart leapt, and I startled awake. My whole body was covered in a sheen of sweat, and I forgot where I was.

"Nadine." Lucas placed a gentle hand on me. I calmed as I snuggled closer to him.

I could barely move, and I didn't feel like getting out of bed. I was really fucking sore. Grammy's potions helped speed up healing, but we weren't like other supernatural races that could use magic to heal instantly.

We must've lain there for hours after sunrise, but I didn't know how much time had passed as I dipped in and out of consciousness. Grammy came in to check on us a few times. She made us sit up in bed and eat soup, then forced us to drink a few more cups of healing tea. She turned on the TV, and the meteorologist spoke of a huge storm traveling across the country. No one bothered changing the channel. Grammy gave us a homemade salve that I rubbed on Lucas's open sores. It was a good thing that we'd waited another day, because without the healing herbs, I didn't think Lucas nor I could've gotten out of bed.

It was late afternoon before either of us felt well enough to get up. We dressed in the clothes Talia had left us, then drove Grammy to her house so she could pack the last of her things. We borrowed her car to say our final goodbyes.

Lucas's parents lived in a small apartment complex. They'd been living there ever since their house burned down last semester. His mom greeted us at the door wearing an apron. It didn't quite suit her.

"Lucas, Nadine," Margo said brightly. "It's so great to see you. Come in."

Lucas shoved his hands into his pockets as he looked around the apartment. "Where's Dad?"

"He's setting the table. Please, have a seat. It'll only be a few more minutes." She quickly returned to the kitchen.

Lucas turned to me and lowered his voice. "Dad never helps my mom cook or clean."

"Maybe he's mellowed since you moved out," I suggested. I *hoped*. I knew it wasn't true. They were putting on a charade and trying to look good for once.

"What is this?" we heard his dad say from the kitchen.

Margo cleared her throat. "It's clam chowder."

"Why's it so thick? It needs more cream."

"No, Jay—" Margo started to protest, but I heard the sigh in her voice saying it was already too late.

"You don't think I know how to cook in my own house?" Jay demanded harshly.

"I wasn't implying that," Margo said gently.

My eyes widened, but Lucas looked oddly at ease. He noticed my expression and said lowly, "This is why my dad doesn't help cook. He always takes over and ruins it. And yet he still somehow thinks he's better at it than my mom."

"Your dad is an ass," I whispered.

Lucas shrugged, like it was normal. I didn't think he had any concept of how *not normal* his parents were. Not all parents beat the shit out of you.

Jay entered the living room and opened his arms out wide. "Lucas, my boy! You wanna give me a hug?"

His question sat wrong with me. On the surface, it seemed like an innocent question, but he wasn't asking for consent. He was making it

Lucas's responsibility to show *him* affection, rather than giving it to his son freely. I could see why Lucas despised the guy.

Lucas hesitated, like his dad had never once hugged him in his life. Finally, he leaned into his father. I'd never seen him look so uncomfortable.

"Hi, Dad," Lucas said, in a voice that wasn't quite his own. "It's, uh, good to see you."

Jay clapped him on the back, and Lucas winced. "Come, have a seat before the food gets cold."

His father was acting strange, and that was saying a lot considering I'd only met him twice. Jay definitely seemed different than the time we'd seen him leaving the liquor store, or the other day in the town square. Perhaps he was sober.

We stepped into a tiny kitchen with a table set for four. Lucas pulled out a chair for me, and I sat. The food smelled delicious, and it looked like Margo had spent a lot of time on it. The table was set out with clam chowder, roasted veggies, and homemade dinner rolls. I noticed a pumpkin pie on the counter for dessert.

"And who's this?" Jay asked, looking at me like he was confused.

"Uh, this is Nadine," Lucas said, eyeing his father like he was worried he might be ill.

"Right, right. The ex-priestess," Jay said.

I was certain he was trying to make a joke out of it, but it fell flat. I shifted uncomfortably in my chair.

"Dad, can we not do this?" Lucas begged. "We haven't even started eating yet."

Margo quickly scrambled to grab a few dinner rolls and distributed them around the table. "There's two for everybody. They're fresh this morning."

Margo was obviously used to keeping the peace, because she knew exactly how to keep everyone quiet. I bit into my dinner roll, and nobody said anything as Margo scooped each of us a bowl of clam chowder.

The chowder wasn't very good—*at all*. It was too thin, and it tasted like someone had dumped an entire saltshaker in it. Lucas and I were both supposed to be careful with our salt intake after the kidney transplant.

Lucas spooned the chowder into his mouth. He was surprisingly good at masking his disgust, because there was no way in *hell* he was enjoying this. I pulled my dinner roll apart and dipped it into my bowl.

The silence was odd, and I shot a glance around the table, waiting for someone to speak. Everyone kept their eyes on their own meals. Jay looked up, and his eyes connected with mine. I quickly looked away and placed another piece of salty bread in my mouth.

"You don't like it?" Jay asked. His gaze narrowed on my spoon, which I'd left lying beside my bowl.

"No, it's good," I lied.

"Margo spent all day on this." Jay didn't say it out loud, but I heard the message in his voice. *Don't you dare come into my home and disrespect my wife.*

"I have to be careful with my diet," I explained.

"That's right. You have that *condition*," Jay said. "What is it? *Lupine?* Sounds like werewolf disease. I didn't know you couldn't *eat*. Lucas should've said something to us. Margo could've made something you weren't allergic to."

"She's not allergic, Dad," Lucas said through clenched teeth. He sounded really fucking annoyed, but he didn't look up from his food.

Jay cleared his throat before changing the subject. "You're a Curse Breaker. Aren't you, Nadine?"

I didn't miss how he pronounced my name using a soft *a* instead of a long *a*. I wasn't dumb. I knew what he was doing. He was acting as if he didn't know anything about me in order to belittle me. He acted like my presence in the coven wasn't *that* significant. I wasn't going to play his stupid games.

"Yes, sir, I am," I stated confidently.

"And how does that work exactly?" he asked, sounding genuinely interested. I certainly wasn't expecting that. "How would a Curse Breaker identify a curse?"

Lucas nervously reached for my hand under the table and squeezed it.

"I read the energy signatures of magic," I told him. "Magical energies feel different to me. Like now, I can feel your Mentalist magic coming off of you in this constant electric pulse. Lucas's Mortana magic has less of a pattern. A curse feels... chaotic and dark."

"So if you walked by someone on the street who was cursed, would you be able to tell?" Jay wondered.

"I'd have to stop and study them," I told him. "Depending on the strength of the curse, it might lay further beneath the surface, so I'd have to spend some time identifying the different magic sources I felt."

Jay stretched his hand across the table. "Can you show me?"

I eyed his outstretched hand, but I didn't reach for it right away. Lucas sighed and set his spoon down.

"Is that what this is?" Lucas asked calmly, though his eyebrows knitted in anger. "Did you invite us here so Nadine could work her powers on you?"

Jay frowned and pulled his hand back. "Why shouldn't I take advantage?"

"Because a few days ago, you wanted Nadine to hang," Lucas snarled.

"And she didn't! That's a good thing, isn't it?" Jay demanded.

"You're trying to take advantage of my fiancé!" Lucas snapped.

Margo gasped, but Jay's expression remained impassive. He went completely silent, and I couldn't read him at all.

After a few beats, Jay leaned forward and said, "Excuse me. *What?*"

"Honey, they said they're *engaged*—" Margo started, but Jay cut her off.

"I heard them," he growled. "What I don't understand is *why.*"

Lucas leaned away from his father, his spine pressed against the back of the chair. He didn't seem bothered by his wounds. I was almost certain he'd consider the pain a distraction from his dad.

"I love her. That's why," he stated simply.

Jay scowled. "Boy, what happened to you? You used to *respect* the coven. Now you're screwing a half-witch who got kicked off the Imperium Council. Did you knock her up, too? Do you have any idea how much shame this brings upon our family?"

"You think I *care* about our family!?" Lucas shouted so loud I was certain the neighbors could hear. He shot to his feet, and his face became red with rage. "You might be blood, but you're *not* my family. All you ever did was tell me and Eric how useless we were. You think a father does that?"

"It's how my father did it, and I turned out just fine," Jay sneered as he stood beside Lucas.

Jay was tall, but Lucas was at least two inches taller. His nostrils flared as he stared down at his father. "You think beating your wife and kids is *fine*? You've fucking lost it, Dad. I came here because I thought you actually felt sorry! Instead, you insult my fiancé and try to use her. I should've known, because you've always been a selfish, abusive pig. I stood by for years and let you get away with it, but not anymore. Not with Nadine. I don't know what curse you think you have or who did it, but I'm sure you deserve it."

Jay began shaking in rage. He was losing control of his Mentalist powers. Dishes rattled across the table, and the cupboard doors began opening and slamming by themselves.

"Don't you *dare* speak to me that way!" Jay roared. "Who the hell do you think you are?"

Lucas leaned toward his father, until he was right up in his face. "I'm the guy who's fucking done with you. I came to say goodbye, and guess what? It's the last goodbye you'll ever get. You can be sure as hell that I won't return. Ever."

Lucas turned to me. "Come on, Nadine."

I scrambled out of my seat and hurried toward the front door. We didn't even make it out of the kitchen before Jay screamed—just straight up screamed. There were no words, just pure rage. I shot a glance back at him, and my heart leapt as I saw the pot of clam chowder flip over, dumping hot liquid all over Margo's lap. She screamed and leapt to her feet, but the pot didn't slow. Jay's telekinesis sent it spinning through the air, straight toward my face.

Lucas jumped in front of me and caught the handle of the pot mid-air. He didn't hesitate for even a second. Lucas crossed the kitchen in two strides and swung the pot as hard as he could at his father's face.

Jay went down *hard*. All at once, the rattling in the room stopped. The cupboards swung shut as Jay lay unconscious on the kitchen floor.

Lucas and I both froze, but Margo began wailing. She fell to her knees beside Jay. After quickly checking that he was still breathing, she narrowed her eyes on Lucas. "What have you done!?"

"What have I—?" Lucas gaped. "Mom, are *you* all right? Are you hurt?"

Lucas went to comfort her, but she pushed him away. "Of course I'm hurt!"

"Then come with us," Lucas begged. "Mom, this is your chance to get away from him. You'll be gone before he wakes up."

Margo's lips trembled, and tears streamed down her cheeks. She didn't even contemplate Lucas's invitation. All I saw was rage. "How could you even *suggest* that, after what you just did?"

"You saw what he did! He was trying to attack Nadine! He hurt you in the process!"

"You started it!" she screamed. "You know how your father gets when he's upset!"

"That's not my fault!" Lucas yelled. "The way Dad chooses to deal with his emotions is not your fault, either. You're only staying because you think it's your responsibility to clean up his messes. It's not, Mom. You can be free of him. Please, come with us."

Lucas reached for her again, but Margo threw her hand outward. Lucas's shoes squeaked across the floor as she forced him back with her telekinesis.

"Don't come near me," she threatened. "Don't come near me or your father ever again. I hope you meant it when you said this is your last goodbye, because if you ever *think* about coming around here again, I'll turn you in to the priestesses myself."

My jaw dropped. I truly didn't understand how anyone could stay with a man like Jay, let alone defend him. Lucas was her *child*. She was supposed to protect him.

That's when I realized how deeply wounded this woman was… deeper than anything I had the capacity to understand. We wanted to help her, but there was nothing we could do if she wouldn't accept our help.

Slowly, Lucas backed away. I grabbed his hand, and it was like he suddenly remembered I was there. He obviously didn't want to spend another second with his parents, because we darted into the hall as fast as we could.

Lucas sat in the driver's seat of Grammy's car, but he didn't start it right away.

"Fuck!" he growled, slamming his palms against the steering wheel. "We should go back."

I grabbed his arm before he could get out of the car. "No, Lucas. Your dad will—"

"My mom's hurt!"

"And she made her decision," I reminded him. "I don't like it, either. I wish there was a way to help her, but it's *her* choice. We can't force her to leave with us. If you go back in there and your dad comes to, it's going to be hell for both of you."

"I can't just leave her in there with him! He's going to blame her. She'll have to clean up another one of his messes, and it was my fault to begin with."

"It wasn't your fault, and you need to realize that right now," I stated firmly. "You said so yourself. Your dad is responsible for his own emotions. Anything that tells you otherwise is an old wound, an old thought pattern. You don't think that way anymore."

Lucas drew a deep breath. He kept his eyes on the apartment complex, as if praying his mother would come running out to join us.

But she never did.

Lucas punched the shifter into reverse and tore out of the parking lot. He didn't say anything until we were a few blocks away from Grammy's. "Fuck this. Let's just leave now. There's nothing worth staying behind for. We'll get your grandma, then go back to school, gather the essentials from our dorms, and get our friends out of town..."

Lucas trailed off when we caught sight of smoke billowing into the sky.

"That's coming from Grammy's neighborhood!" I cried.

He stepped on the gas and passed a few cars. The tires squealed as we turned onto Grammy's dead-end street. Flames engulfed her house, and I spotted Grammy racing outside with Cornelius in her arms.

Lucas stopped the car, and I kicked the door open. "Grammy!" I screamed.

"I'm all right," Grammy insisted, but she choked up. "Cornelius and I are fine."

"You don't look fine," I said. Her eyes were puffy and red, and there were welts on her hands, like she'd tried to put out the fire herself.

"Tell me this was an accident," I begged.

Tears began streaming down Grammy's cheeks, and I knew without being told that this was intentional.

My hands curled into fists. "How'd they get into the house? Who did this?"

Grammy shook her head. "It started in the garden..."

Grammy choked up again, and my stomach plummeted. I abandoned

Grammy and raced across the lawn, until I reached the side of the house. My breath caught when I saw it.

Grammy's garden was completely destroyed. Flames licked into the sky so high, they nearly reached the second-story window. All of Grammy's rare magical herbs… her life's work and her passion… had been reduced to ash.

My hands shook as I backed away. This was worse than someone targeting her house. Homes could be rebuilt. A magical garden like this didn't sprout up overnight. Grammy had spent her *life* building this garden, tending the soil, and maintaining her rare herbs. The fact that someone could do this was downright cruel.

I whirled toward Grammy and Lucas. "You were targeted because you mean something to me. This is nothing compared to what they have planned for us, I'm sure. I'm not interested in sticking around to see what they'll do next. We're going to pick everyone up at the school and get out of here. Okay?"

Grammy nodded, knowing there wasn't any other option. "Let's go get your friends."

I watched the house fade away in the rear-view mirror. My stomach felt like it'd been replaced by rocks. The last thing I wanted was for Grammy to get hurt because of me… and now she'd lost everything.

The sun had set by the time we made it to the school. Grammy shook as she stroked Cornelius's fur. "I'll wait out here so we can leave as soon as possible."

"We'll only be a few minutes," I told her.

Lucas and I hurried to my dorm room, but I stopped dead in my tracks when I opened the door. Lucas came to a halt behind me.

"What are *you* doing here?" Lucas demanded of the red-headed figure standing in front of my window. The skull tattoo on her wrist was unmistakable.

Priestess Charlotte turned, her black cloak billowing around her. "I'm here to help you."

LUCAS
TWENTY-THREE

"Help us!?" Nadine spat, stepping further into the room.

Priestess Charlotte nodded calmly. "Yes. I've come in peace."

"You've come on assignment from the council," Nadine accused. "How could we possibly trust you?"

I followed behind Nadine, and for the first time, I got a good look at the room. Priestess Charlotte stood in front of the window, directly across from the door, but she wasn't alone. Talia and Grant sat on the couch, and Miles sat beside Chloe on Talia's bed. Our cats gathered around them. They all looked completely at ease.

I didn't understand. They should be on full alert, ready to blast battle magic at this bitch.

Talia stood and spoke gently. "Please, Nadine. Just hear her out."

"I renounced my priesthood," Charlotte said, before Nadine nor I could get in another word.

We both stopped dead. We couldn't have heard her right.

"You did... what?" Nadine asked carefully.

"I've always gone along with the other priestesses, because I thought it was my duty," Charlotte said. "I never questioned Margaret and Lilian, because I didn't think a priestess could lie to each other. I trusted them and believed that everything we were doing had a divine purpose from

Mother Miriam. Then you were declared innocent, and I realized the priestesses are imperfect. I thought for certain you were trying to tear the coven apart from the inside. I realize now that I was deceived."

Charlotte had always been the quiet one anytime we confronted the priestesses. I never thought much of it, but I realized she looked to Margaret and Lilian for guidance.

"You believed Stella's confession, then?" I asked. "The judge thought we coerced her."

"I happen to know a certain demon had something to do with what happened in that courtroom," Charlotte said. "The Imperium Council allows the coven to believe many lies, but I am done with the lies. The other priestesses wish to place a false Curse Breaker on the council, and that is not what Mother Miriam would want."

Nadine gasped. "Mira's not a Curse Breaker?"

Charlotte shook her head. "Mira approached us after The Hearse Tragedy. She offered to do anything for us. Lilian came up with the idea to have her pose as Curse Breaker after her Evoking Ceremony, in order to throw Nadine off the council. Mira's Mortana, like me. Lilian figured that if Nadine could pose as an Alchemist, we could fake our own Curse Breaker."

Nadine looked to be contemplating this information. "How can we trust you're telling the truth?"

"Margaret and Lilian have already made the announcement of my resignation public," Charlotte said. "Ask around. People are already inciting riots."

Nadine gasped. "Grammy's garden."

"What happened to Helena's garden?" Talia demanded, her gaze darting between the two of us.

"Someone burned it to the ground, and the fire spread to the house," Nadine said. "I thought it was because of my verdict, but people must be mad Charlotte left the council."

"Without a doubt," Charlotte said in a serious tone.

"People must see the council is in the wrong if priestesses are leaving," I insisted.

"I thought they would, too," Charlotte said. "Perhaps some coven members *are* swayed, but others are not convinced. I never intended to divide us even further."

"How can you help us?" Nadine still didn't sound convinced.

"We can start by banishing the demon," Charlotte suggested.

"He's been banished before, but it didn't break his contract," Nadine said. "He was still able to possess me under the old contract. If we're going to do this, we're going to do it right. How do we get rid of him for good?"

"By withdrawing my consent, the contract is broken," Charlotte said. "All we have to do then is find Leto and perform a banishing spell."

Nadine and I exchanged a wary glance. We still weren't sure if we could trust her. We didn't exactly have the best track record when it came to priestesses.

I leaned toward Nadine and whispered. "Charlotte could be trying to infiltrate our side to get information."

"They could've sent someone else," Nadine whispered back.

I was fully aware all eyes were on us, but we couldn't make a decision without thinking this through.

Except… what benefit would the priestesses have for faking this? Sure, they could keep an eye on us if we chose to trust Charlotte, but leaving the council would only turn more people away from Miriam's Chosen. The council wanted to convert as many as possible. It'd do more harm than good. It was a huge risk for her to leave the Imperium Council, because it would divide the coven more than ever before. Anyone on the fence would be forced to take sides. It didn't make sense for Charlotte to lie about this.

"If we want people to side with us, we have to be willing to believe they can switch sides," Nadine whispered.

"What does your intuition tell you?" I asked.

Nadine paused and looked around the room. She contemplated Charlotte for a few moments, then raised her voice. "I believe in uniting the coven, and that starts with us. We don't stop being priestesses because the others told us we were no longer worthy. I still feel my priestess duty in my blood, and if Charlotte is willing to join us, then I believe we are stronger together."

"Then I trust her, too," I announced.

The others joined in agreement.

"We've made plans to leave town tonight," Nadine told Charlotte.

The priestess shook her head. "We can't leave a demon roaming free among our people. We must banish him before—"

Boom!

The entire room shook as a clap like thunder exploded around us, louder than any thunder I'd heard in my life. Nadine clung to me as we both tried to stay upright. Lightning flashed outside, and thunder rumbled above our heads.

"What the hell!?" Miles demanded.

"The storm must be rolling in," Talia said in a shaky tone.

"Storm, my ass," Chloe replied. "I've never heard thunder like that before."

Isa jumped onto Talia's piano and peered out the window. She gave a loud *meow*, and we all rushed to look outside. Below us, shadows moved through the night. Torch lights flickered as hundreds of people descended upon the school. Storm clouds brewed overhead, but the explosion that shook the school was a far cry from thunder.

"Again!" someone shouted.

The mob joined hands, and I watched in horror as magic of all colors swirled together above their heads. An enormous spell formed. It looked like lightning bolts sizzling together in an orb larger than the school.

Charlotte's features paled. "They must've found out I came here. They've come to execute us! The priestesses won't stop them this time."

Below us, the leader of the mob began shouting. "Mother Miriam has spoken! The outcast priestesses shall be cast to the Abyss!"

It was *Cody*.

The spell above their heads shrank into a tight battle orb. Another explosion sounded, and the spell blasted forward and connected with the school. I grabbed Nadine on instinct. Talia's antique collection toppled over and fell onto the ground, and dust rained down on us from a crack that had formed in the ceiling. Our cats yowled loudly, and we heard people screaming from out in the hallway.

"They're trying to get through the school's wards!" Chloe shouted. "Once they do, they can take the whole school down in one blow!"

"They can't kill everyone inside to get to just two people!" Talia insisted.

"Watch them try," Chloe said.

Nadine started for the door. "We have to get out of here and stop this!"

I grabbed her wrist to stop her. "What are you going to do? Turn yourself in?"

"I have to distract them, at least!" Nadine cried. "I can't let everyone inside the school die for me—"

Another spell blasted into the school, and the window shattered, spraying glass all over the room. I pulled Nadine into my chest and curled my arms around her so she wouldn't get hurt. The mob was closer to breaking through the wards, and the school could come down on us at any moment.

Nadine pulled away from me. "If they want me, they can come and get me!"

She turned toward the window. She was going to show her face and make them stop to save us all… but she stopped dead in her tracks. The window was gone.

The frame was still there, but behind it, the night sky had vanished, and the mob had disappeared. In its place was nothing but a brick wall. Nadine placed her palm on the brick and pushed hard, as if to test if it was real.

"What the hell's going on?" Grant asked.

Isa sniffed the brick wall, then pawed at it like it was a doorway she wanted to be on the other side of it.

Nadine whirled back toward us. "Their spell trapped us in."

Charlotte wore an incredulous look. She'd obviously never seen anything like this. "That's not possible."

"It's got to be Mentalists, messing with our heads," Chloe theorized. "Or Fae illusion artifacts someone got their hands on."

"Does it matter what's causing it?" Grant demanded. "I say we find a way out of here!"

Grant darted for the door and opened it. What we saw made my stomach drop. Instead of opening the door to the hallway, we looked straight into a classroom.

"There's supposed to be a hallway there!" Grant panicked.

Before anyone could respond, another crash sounded overhead, and the room shook so hard that the door slammed shut. Once the room steadied, Grant swung open the door again, but the classroom was gone. Instead, we looked out into the Main Foyer. Screams echoed throughout the school, and heavy footsteps sounded down the hall. Doors slammed, and students sprinted past the grand staircase.

"Get to the main doors!" Nadine instructed, pointing to the large double doors on the other side of the Main Foyer.

I scooped up Oliver at my feet, and we all took off running toward the main doors. We had to get the mob to stand down, or the whole school would be destroyed.

The seven of us sprinted out of the room, our cats following closely behind us. I reached the main doors first, and I yanked them open. I expected to walk straight into the mob, but instead, I found myself staring into one of the school's meditation rooms. Across the room were two windows, and outside of them stood the forest behind the school. I rushed over to the nearest window and threw it open.

"Everyone outside!" I barked.

The others followed me. I took Nadine's hand and helped her through the window. Isa followed closely behind. As I turned to help Talia through, my heart leapt. Nadine stood in front of the second window, glancing around like she didn't know where she was at.

"I don't know what happened!" she cried.

What the hell? I ducked my head through the window, and instead of seeing the forest outside, I saw the same room we were standing in, only from a different angle.

Grant threw his hand over his mouth. "Your head's there, but your ass is over there!"

He pointed to my face, then toward the other window. I craned my neck, and sure as hell, I could see myself leaning through the window.

My heart raced. This was freaking me the hell out.

I quickly ducked my head back into the room. "We have to gather as many people as we can. If we're stronger than the mob, we can overpower whatever spell they're using to fuck with our heads."

Nadine shook her head. "This isn't a Mentalist spell. I can feel the magic in the walls of the school. Their attack is literally hurting the school. The space-bending spells can't hold."

"Can't hold—?" I nearly choked. We had to get out of here.

"Lucas, tell me you can portal us out!" Grant begged.

I hesitated. Last time Grant touched one of my portals, he'd been blasted backward. My portals were impassable. "I haven't perfected my portal magic yet. Someone could get hurt."

"We'll get hurt if we stay!" Chloe insisted. "We should at least try."

I raised my hands. I pictured the first thing that came to mind—the abandoned mansion. It was protected, so the mob wouldn't be able to find us there.

But nothing happened.

Desperately, I turned my focus inward, but I couldn't feel my magic. "Fuck!" I growled. "The Waning!"

I'd only just started getting my magic back since the last time I was affected, and now this? This was the worst fucking time.

Chloe lifted her hands, but I didn't see even a spark of magic. "I'm out, too."

Miles started to panic. "We all are!"

"If the whole coven's affected, how did they create that spell out there!?" Grant demanded.

"It makes sense that this would happen under attack," Charlotte said. "The coven is attacking its own people, so it's hurting our magic even more, and dividing us further."

She lifted her hands. Wisps of silver magic swirled from her fingers. "My magic is still working."

Everyone tried, but only Charlotte and Nadine could get their magic to work.

"Why us and no one else?" Nadine wondered, like it was a puzzle she was trying to solve that might help us escape.

"There are talented supernaturals among us," Charlotte explained. "That's why I was called onto the Imperium Council. Even though you were the only Curse Breaker, we've suspected for some time you may be a talented supernatural. The Waning will still affect you, but not as intense as it will your friends."

That's why Nadine's magic returned sooner than mine when we were tossed in the jail cells. She was only becoming stronger every day.

Nadine looked down at her hands. "If I'm strong enough to maintain my magic during the Waning, then maybe I can stabilize the space-bending spell and get us out of here."

Nadine walked up to the wall and splayed her palms over it. She closed her eyes, and her brow knitted together in concentration. Nadine's hands lit up with her signature deep blue magic, and the confusion on her face settled into an expression of confidence. She might actually be able to do this…

Another blast rocked the school. Nadine was thrown off her feet and slammed hard against my chest. I caught her as we both crashed to the ground. Our friends all lost their footing, and *thuds* sounded around us as they were thrown to the ground. Talia screamed, and Oliver screeched as I landed on his tail. My head spun—wait, no. It was the *room.*

Gravity shifted, and my friends and I began sliding across the floor. Our cats yowled and clawed at the hardwood. Objects fell off shelves and spun around us. We landed against the wall, which had become the floor now. The room kept spinning, until we were on the ceiling. Finally, gravity settled, but the room was upside down.

Talia rubbed her head and groaned. She'd hit it against one of the supply shelves, and blood matted in her hair.

Grant immediately scrambled to her aid and checked her wound. He grabbed a towel that had fallen off the shelf and pressed it to the back of her head. "They must've broken through the ward."

Nadine winced as she sat upright. "That wasn't the mob. It was me. There's too much magic in these walls for me to stabilize it on my own. The magic backfired. Tal, I'm so sorry."

"I'll be fine," Talia said, but she flinched as Grant shifted the towel slightly.

"Guys!" Chloe yelled. She pointed to the walls, and my stomach plummeted to my toes. The room was shrinking as we spoke. We'd be squished if we stayed much longer.

"Let's get out of here!" Miles cried. He grabbed Chloe's hand, and they led the way as we all scrambled to our feet and sprinted through the upside-down doorway. I nearly tripped over Marley and Bella as the cats scurried along at our feet.

We entered a long, dark hallway with stone walls. The hallway narrowed with each passing second as the walls inched closer together. It had to be one of the halls in the basement of the school, but there were no doorways like there should have been.

Miles skidded to a halt, and we all stopped behind him. We glanced around, looking for a way out. I whirled around, but the doorway we'd come through had vanished. The hall seemed to elongate and go on forever.

"There's no way out!" Miles yelled.

"There has to be," I barked. I wasn't letting my friends die here—not like this. "Come on!"

Nadine and I locked hands as we sprinted down the hall, but no matter how far we ran, it seemed we got nowhere. We were literally stuck in a living nightmare. The coven had fucked up their own space-bending spell, and now the school was folding in on itself.

Oliver raced by my side, meowing loudly. There had to be a doorway up ahead, because if there wasn't, we'd all be crushed. The walls were so close together now, Nadine and I could hardly hold hands.

Fuck!

"This is getting us nowhere!" Chloe shouted.

I stopped dead in my tracks and whirled around. "What else do you suggest!?"

Unless she had any better ideas, I wasn't interested. By now, I could reach my hands out and press both of my palms to either wall. The school was shrinking quickly, and soon it wouldn't be able to hold us any longer. Once the hall vanished, we'd either be crushed, or we'd be stuck in a pocket universe and starve to death like Cooper had.

Chloe remained silent. She was a smart, cunning witch, but she had no better insights than the rest of us.

Oliver yowled loudly at my feet again. We didn't have the fucking time. "Oliver!" I growled. "I'm not—"

I looked down at him, and I realized he wasn't meowing at me at all. He sat at my feet, looking straight upward. I followed his gaze, and my heart lifted. Above us was a door set straight into the ceiling—a wooden door, like the ones in our dorm hall.

"Of course!" Nadine cried. "The rules of spatial reality as we know it are no longer relevant. We have to think outside of the box."

"Let's get moving then," I said quickly, lacing my fingers together to help boost Nadine up. She put her foot into my hand, and I hoisted her upward. Nadine grabbed the door handle above our heads. I expected her to have to heave the door upward, like a trap door, but it swung open effortlessly. Gravity had no rules here, either, apparently.

I hoisted Nadine up further, and she pulled herself through the doorway. She barely needed my help, and I realized it was because her center of gravity had shifted. Nadine crawled across the floor of the next room to scramble inside, but she was perpendicular to the rest of us. She should have fallen straight back through the doorway, but she didn't. She looked relieved. It seemed like the room was a safe escape for now.

"Quickly!" I shouted, ushering the others through. Talia went next, clutching both Gus and Isa to her chest. I hoisted Chloe and Charlotte through next, along with our other cats. By the time they were through, the hall had shrunk to one person wide.

"You're next!" I barked at Miles. Grant and I hoisted him through. My heart hammered as my shoulders touched both walls. Grant and I were the last ones standing there, and he hesitated.

"You first," Grant offered through heavy breaths.

"There's no time," I demanded. I laced my fingers together firmly and bent down, showing him I wasn't fucking around. Grant knew we didn't have time to argue, and he reluctantly stepped into my hands. He kicked off the ground, and I used his momentum to toss him upward. Miles dangled his hand out of the doorway and helped Grant through. I could feel the resistance of his shoulders against the shrinking walls.

Oh, fuck!

The walls touched me on both sides, and my heart lurched. I spun to the side, giving myself a few extra inches of space, but there wasn't any room to jump.

"Lucas, I've got you!" Grant screamed, holding his hand out toward me. The ceiling was too high to reach him.

I didn't have time to think this through. I pressed my back against the wall on one side and my feet and palms against the other, wedging myself between the walls to push myself upward. My heart slammed against my rib cage. I wasn't sure I was going to make it.

I tried not to look upward, because I knew if I did, I'd see the doorway disappearing above me. The walls were narrower now than the doorway was. This was bad.

I pushed my feet against the wall once more, but as the walls closed in on one another, my balance faltered, and one of my feet slipped. I was nearly straight upright now, unable to wedge myself between the walls for much longer.

"Lucas, now!" Grant cried.

I threw my hand upward, and by some miracle, my hand connected with his wrist. Grant curled his fingers around my arm, locking our hands tightly together as he pulled me upward. My feet grazed the walls on both sides. The world seemed to tumble around me, and I got dizzy as gravity shifted. I landed hard on top of several other people. I heard the slam of the doorway as the hall behind us disappeared for good.

We were all alive, thank the Goddess!

As my heart settled, I managed to sit upright. I realized I'd landed on top of Grant and Miles. Grant must've leaned into the hallway to grab me, and Miles had made sure he hadn't fallen through the doorway. That's why I'd been able to reach his hand at the last second.

"Thank you guys," I said breathlessly.

"No one's getting left behind, all right?" Grant said.

I nodded. "Not a chance."

Nadine helped me to my feet, and I finally got a look at the room we were in. It was one of the Seer classrooms, with several fireplaces along the walls and crystal balls on the mantles. The walls seemed steady here, so that was a relief.

"There's got to be a way out," Nadine theorized. "It's like a puzzle—a Rubik's cube being twisted and mixed up."

"Then one of these doors has to lead outside," Talia suggested.

"Or maybe it's just an endless loop," Chloe added.

Miles began pacing. "Let's think logically."

"I don't think logic is going to get us far in this situation," Charlotte said. "Magic got us into this mess, and it's going to be the key out of it. The school is full of magic, and we just have to find the right tools to get us out."

"Crystals could do it," Nadine theorized. "We spent all semester building an arsenal to combat the Waning. If you all get your powers back, we could stabilize the spell!"

"The priestesses confiscated our crystals," Miles pointed out.

"Those weren't the only ones in the school," Nadine reminded him. "The school has their own crystal storage. We just have to find a way to the Crystallary."

A high-pitched scream met our ears. It was the sound of bloody murder, of a woman in desperate need of help.

"Please, Avery. Don't!" a woman cried.

I felt all the blood in my body drain to my toes. "That's Felicia!"

"Your friends caused this!" Avery yelled. "You must bear the mark of Miriam's Chosen if you wish to be saved!"

The cats scrambled toward the door ahead of me. I hurried behind them, and I flung the door open, but the screaming abruptly stopped.

I stared into an empty hallway. My guts sank, and I felt like crumbling into a ball in the doorway. Felicia had desperately needed our help, and we hadn't been there.

I didn't think it'd end this way.

Agony slammed into my gut as Felicia's last thought flitted through my mind. It had happened so fast, and there was nothing we could've done.

The room fell dead silent. Everyone must've noticed the horror in my stance and knew what had happened.

I didn't have the luxury of freezing up right now. I forced down the lump in my throat. The only sound that could be heard was the rustle of my shoes on the carpet as I turned back toward my friends.

"We're not the only ones who have to get out of here," I said in a hollow tone. "We'll find those crystals, and we'll get everyone out."

"Then let's get moving," Nadine said. "We're not going to find the Crystallary by sitting here."

I could hear the hopelessness in her tone. She knew as well as I did what Avery had done to Felicia. We couldn't save her, but we still had a chance to get everyone else out.

A dark hall loomed ahead. Nadine took my hand and spoke in a shaky tone. "Stay with me."

She didn't have to ask twice. I wasn't letting this girl go for anything.

We started down the hall cautiously, but it was unlike the school halls we normally walked. It was the same... but different. The ceiling was higher than it should be, and the walls were stretched out and distorted. Portrait paintings that had been mounted long before I was even born were suddenly jumbled up, and faces of old coven officials had been twisted like Picasso paintings. Their frames were no longer square, but had been stretched into odd shapes. Cauldrons were embedded in the walls, as if the space-bending spell didn't know what else to do with them.

Disembodied screams echoed down the hall, sounding like they were coming from behind doorways, but when we opened them, there was nothing but empty classrooms. The doors were all different sizes now, some of them too small to fit through and others twice as large as they should be.

We passed by a long mirror, and Nadine and I both stopped dead. Our friends gathered around curiously, but the effect was the same.

There was no reflection.

Grant waved his hand in front of the mirror. "This *definitely* defies logic."

I looked behind us, and all the paintings on the wall opposite the mirror were depicted accurately—but it was like we didn't exist at all. "Spatially, we're here, but we're also not…"

Even my voice didn't sound quite right, like the sound waves were having trouble traveling through the distorted reality.

A door burst open from the way we came. Everyone whirled around to look, and a girl ran through the doorway so fast that she slammed straight into the wall. She spun around and cowered against it.

"Please, spare me!" she whimpered. I realized it was Stacey, an Alchemist who hung out with Gwen.

"You made your choice," a man sneered from behind the doorway.

"I was going to get the mark of Miriam's Chosen," Stacey insisted in a shaky tone. "I didn't get the chance—"

"You had your chance!" he roared as he stepped through the doorway. The heavy boots of an Executor landed, and I saw that it was Leroy Benson. "This curse has been brought upon the school by all those who do not bear the mark of Miriam's Chosen. The only way to free ourselves is to rid the school of this plague!"

"Leroy, *stop!*" I screamed, but it was too late. Black magic swirled out of Leroy's fingers and curled around Stacey's throat.

"Valerie, help me—!" Stacey screamed, but her pleas died the moment Leroy's death magic touched her. Life drained from her eyes, and her body collapsed. Her skin turned gray and shriveled around her bones. Her eye sockets hollowed out as Leroy sucked the life straight out of her.

I never believed the coven could turn on me.

Stacey's last thought echoed in my mind. My stomach clenched all over again as the coven lost another witch.

Leroy had dark Mortana magic, but he wasn't an exceptional super-natural. He'd gotten lucky that the Waning had spared him his powers for the time-being. Something told me he'd find a way to execute anyone he wanted, whether he had magic or not. The Executors had decided to kill anyone who hadn't joined their movement, thinking it would save them from this mess.

It didn't matter that Stacey was on their side—that she'd *intended* to join Miriam's Chosen. She was considered an enemy as much as the rest of us.

Anger billowed in my chest. It didn't matter that I didn't have magic right now. I was going to choke this motherfucker out myself.

"You fucker!" I screamed. There wasn't a word to describe the deep, dark, horrible being this guy was. I started toward him, and Leroy looked up with a smile on his face, like he was pleased with his handiwork. He noticed me for the first time, and his features turned into a sneer.

There was something dark in his eyes... darker than I'd ever seen before. Leroy was an ass, that was for sure, but the strange look in his eyes hinted at something more sinister.

"You want to be next?" he taunted. "I can arrange that!"

He threw a battle orb, and I instinctively tossed up my hands to create a shield, but my magic never came. Nadine sprinted forward and grabbed my arm, yanking me backward.

Leroy's orb flew past me the same time a second battle orb whizzed over my head. It sizzled with energy unlike I'd ever seen before. It flew down the hall toward Leroy with the intent to kill, but he ducked out of the way, and it missed him entirely.

I whirled around, and I realized Charlotte had been the one to come to my defense. But she wouldn't be throwing many battle orbs any time soon. Leroy's orb might have missed me, but it'd connected with Charlotte's chest. She gasped for breath as Miles and Chloe tried to hold her upright. It wasn't a killing orb—Leroy apparently intended to have fun with me first. But I could tell it hurt like a son-of-a-bitch.

Leroy's laughter echoed down the hall. "The disgraced priestesses themselves. Killing you should solve all our problems."

Dark magic billowed from his fingertips as he walked toward us. Nadine shoved me. "Run!"

We didn't have the magic to fight Leroy, and he could literally take us all out in one go. We had no choice but to flee. We ran down the hall, Leroy's laughter echoing behind us. A battle orb whizzed by our heads just as we turned the corner. I heard it explode, but we were already winding down a second hallway, getting lost in a labyrinth of twisting corridors I no longer recognized.

"Where'd you go, pretty priestesses?" Leroy's voice sounded around the corner. "I know you couldn't have gone far."

The hall broke off in so many directions, and we passed by long corridors and turned down others. Students and professors ran through doorways and passed through hallways ahead of us. I saw a large group with a bunch of cats, and my heart gave a start when I spotted Nadine running alongside them.

But she was right next to me! One of the guys wore the same shocked expression as I did.

Of course he had, because he *was* me.

"Did you guys just see—?" Grant started.

"The rules of spatial reality don't apply, remember?" Nadine said as we kept moving.

That was *freaky*, but we didn't have the time to stand around contemplating it.

Screams echoed off the walls, but they died abruptly. Several thoughts entered my mind, each one overlapping the others so I couldn't make them out. My skull pounded as I tried making sense of them, and my vision blurred.

"Lucas!" Nadine cried as I steadied myself against the wall.

I gulped. "The Executors are killing people."

I barely got the words out before more screams came. Ahead of us, students raced across the hallway, running from one open doorway to another. Professor Warbright scrambled out of the doorway behind them, looking like he was running from something. His hair was disheveled, and his pocket watch dangled out of his coat. They looked to be running from someone.

"We have to stop the Executors," I said, racing forward.

What I found wasn't Executors at all. I gazed through double doors into the cafeteria, where Professor Leto stood in the center of the room, laughing maniacally while he raised his hands into the air. He was *loving* this—all this death, all this trauma. It was a demon's playground here.

"This is all *your* doing!" I accused.

Leto's laughter died, and his amused gaze roamed over me. "I appreciate the faith you have in me, but I'm merely taking advantage of the situation. You'd do the same."

"Go to hell," Priestess Charlotte sneered, pushing past me and into the room. She clutched her injured chest, but she found the strength to conjure magic in her hand and aim it at him.

Leto noticed her, and his laughter died abruptly. "Priestess, we had a deal," he said coolly.

"Not anymore," Charlotte sneered. "I withdraw my consent, and I banish you to the Abyss!"

She flung her spell at him, and it hit Leto square in the chest. Magic sizzled across his form, but he just laughed, like it merely tickled. Charlotte's spell hadn't worked. He quickly blasted his own spell back at her.

"Priestess!" Chloe screamed. She and Miles ran into the room and caught Charlotte just in time to dodge the attack. Their cats screeched as they narrowly missed the spell. The spell hit the wall, and Leto ducked through the doors near the kitchen.

"I'm not strong enough. We have to banish him together!" Charlotte cried.

Nadine and I ran forward. The moment we passed through the doorway, Chloe and Miles disappeared, along with Charlotte. Instead of stepping into the cafeteria, we'd entered another hallway. The space-bending spell must've shifted the same time we walked through the door.

Talia and Grant had followed us, and they glanced around the hall in confusion. Cats screeched, but when I looked down at the four of ours, they were perfectly fine.

We whirled around to see cats flooding out of the door we'd come through. Beyond the doorway sat the Cat-fé, but the walls were shrinking again—the doors, too! Dozens of cats scurried out of the room to find safety, until the doorway shrank so small they couldn't fit through anymore. Two cats ended up side-by-side, struggling to get through. Nadine and I rushed to help them, and we yanked the cats out of the tiny doorway.

My heart leapt, and I scrambled backward. Nadine screamed. There'd been a gray cat and an orange cat, but they'd melded into one. The front half was two cats—two heads, two sets of front paws. They were connected at the middle, leaving only one set of back legs and a single tail. The back half was mottled with gray and orange fur.

The poor cats yowled, like they were in pain. All the cats from the Cat-fé had fled, but our four cats approached the orange and gray ones and lay next to them, licking their fur and offering comfort.

My heart shattered into a million pieces. Even our cats knew these two wouldn't make it. It defied all logic and reality—their bodies couldn't occupy the same space at once. The cats let out one final, collective yowl, then went silent as they collapsed. Nadine shook as she backed away from them.

"What just happened?" Grant asked carefully.

Nadine swallowed. "The spell's chaotic. It's like it's trying to correct itself, but it doesn't know where each room belongs. It's shifting at random."

"And… that could happen to us?" Talia questioned.

Nadine nodded solemnly.

"What about my brother!?" Grant demanded. "Chloe? Charlotte?"

"If the rooms are shifting, then we entered the room at the wrong time. They're still out there," I said.

"Then we have to keep moving and find them," Grant demanded. "There's only four of us, so even if we found the Crystallary, we're still fucked. We need to find them."

"We will," Nadine promised. She had a way of assuring people even when she wasn't sure herself. "Mother Miriam didn't save Lucas and me from execution for nothing. Let's see if any of these rooms lead us back to the cafeteria."

We started down the hall again, and I felt relief when I saw Head-mistress Verla walking toward us, her cat following close at her heels. She wore a look of determination, like she was going to help us all out of here. She had to know more about this space-bending spell that we did. We could work together to correct it.

We raced toward Headmistress Verla, and another group of students ran up behind her. We met up with Verla at the same time… but something was off. The students behind her slowed at the same time, in the same rhythm.

It was us again, but this time, it wasn't a spatial anomaly. It was our reflection; we were looking into a mirror.

Nadine drew a sharp breath. "She's trapped."

Slowly, Nadine approached the mirror, her reflection mirroring her movements perfectly. She placed her hand to the glass, as if to test if it was solid. I half expected her hand to go through it, like she could just walk straight through the mirror and join Verla on the other side. But the glass was solid.

Nadine began pounding on the mirror. "Verla!"

The headmistress approached her curiously, like she couldn't believe what she was seeing. "Nadine?"

"How did you get here?" Nadine panicked.

Verla must've misunderstood the question. "I came to the school when I heard about Priestess Charlotte. I needed to get you all out of town immediately."

"But how did you get inside the mirror?" Nadine asked.

Verla furrowed her brow. "You four are the ones inside the mirror."

"We have reflections," Talia said. "If magic could trap us inside a mirror, we wouldn't have reflections... right?"

Verla eyed the mirror curiously. "I have a reflection, too. The mirror itself may not even exist. We're simply communicating from two spaces at the same time."

"Two spaces... that occupy the same space?" Grant wondered.

"Verla, how do we fix it?" Nadine begged. If anyone had the answer, it had to be her mentor.

Verla's entire form went rigid. "Nadine, I beg of you. Don't try to fix this. Fixing it will only make it worse!"

"Then what do we do!?" Nadine cried.

"Get to a stable room and stay there. I'm working on finding us a way out—"

Nadine and Talia both screamed as the mirror shattered. Verla's instructions were cut off as glass rained down over us.

Talia trembled. "Verla must have some sort of theory that will save us."

"A stable room..." Nadine said thoughtfully. "There must be rooms that are unaffected by the space-bending spell! If we find one, it can't hurt us."

"An original room," I realized. "From before any space-bending spells were put on the school. If the spell collapses, those rooms will remain intact."

"What kind of room would that be?" Grant asked.

"The dorm rooms were all expanded on—same with the classrooms," Talia said.

"Anything that's not duplicated is a safe bet," Nadine said. "The library or the ballroom would be my guess. But we have to get to one before we end up like those cats."

We started down the hall again, opening doorways that led only to longer hallways. Screams continued to permeate the halls, and I winced each time a new thought entered my mind. This nightmare wasn't going to end until the spell was either fixed or destroyed completely.

Around us, the hall began to shift again. Doorways grew or shrank at random, and the floor twisted at odd angles, creating a swirling labyrinth ahead of us.

"I found the library!" Talia exclaimed, pointing toward an open doorway. Bookshelves lined the walls, and relief washed over me.

We ran inside, but my stomach dropped at what appeared before us. We thought the library was a safe place, but if anything, it was more fucked up than the rest of the school. Bookshelves encompassed the entirety of the room, closing us into a circle instead of its usual four walls. The ceiling stretched so high, there had to be a hundred levels to the library now, all filled with endless bookcases. The bookshelves rotated around the room, creating a nausea-inducing kaleidoscope of colors.

The staircase leading to the second level stood in front of us, but there were so many other staircases that it didn't make sense. Some of them were upside down or sideways, creating impossible pathways and endless staircases that you could never escape. Above us, a group of students raced up one staircase—or down? I couldn't tell. They appeared to be stuck to the ceiling. As soon as they reached the top of one staircase, they appeared at the bottom of another far across the room.

"Uh… that's a no-go on the library!" Grant cried.

"Yeah, I can see that," Nadine said through gritted teeth. "The problem is getting out—*there!*"

Nadine pointed to a doorway that appeared between the shifting bookcases, and we took off running with our cats at our heels. We burst out of the library and into the grand ballroom.

The walls here seemed stable, thank the Goddess, but there was nothing but blackness beyond the big arching windows.

We weren't the only ones here. Students flooded through doorways all around the room. Some people looked hurt, while others trembled in fear. Gregory and Brayden raced into the room. They glanced around in confusion, like they'd been expecting to enter a different room. Samantha and Darcy stumbled through the door next to us. I saw that Darcy had a long, bloody gash across her cheek. I rushed over to them as Darcy nearly collapsed against Samantha.

"What happened?" I demanded as I ripped a piece of fabric off my t-shirt.

"The Tarantulas," Samantha sneered. "They didn't have any magic, but they came after us. They said we caused this, and that we'd suffer for it. They can't be far behind!"

I pressed the fabric to Darcy's wound, and she winced. "Let me guess," I said. "Avery was with them?"

Darcy sobbed. "Sh—she went after F—Felicia."

My stomach dropped to think of Felicia and Stacey—of all the lives we lost tonight. All because our people had turned against one another, all because they were afraid.

A pair of double doors across the room blasted open. Students screamed and scattered as something heavy flew through the doorway and skidded across the floor. A woman whimpered, and I realized it had been *a person.*

I shot to my feet, and as the crowd parted, I realized the person who had been thrown was Rosemary, the librarian. She cowered as a group of Executors followed her into the room.

"Apostates like you will pay!" James sneered as he marched into the room.

He was closely followed by all five members of the Treacherous Tarantulas. They each carried some sort of makeshift weapon. Ryan held a candlestick, and Nolan carried a statuette. Finn had a thick tome in his hands he must've grabbed from the library. Funny, since I hadn't seen that kid read a book a day in his life. Declan and Corbin both carried rope, which they'd fashioned into nooses.

None of them had magic right now. We could defeat them.

"Leave her alone!" I shouted.

James and the Tarantulas paid me no attention. James looked to the crowd of terrified students and shouted, "All you apostates will pay for what you've done! This is *your* fault!"

He locked eyes with a group of girls near him—Gwen, Camille, and Valerie. The girls cowered together, then quickly raised their wrists to show they bore the mark of Miriam's Chosen. James smirked, then turned away from them.

He pointed to Rosemary, who was scrambling backward while the Executors approached her. "This one's going to suffer first."

Professor Blackbird threw himself between Rosemary and the Executors. "You'll do no such thing!"

"Out of my way, old man," James snarled, shoving the professor aside.

I sprinted across the room, but James pulled a knife out of his pocket. He drew his arm back as he knelt to Rosemary's level, then shoved the blade toward her stomach. I reached him a split second before the blade touched her, and I tackled him to the ground. The knife clattered across the floor. The crowd gasped as I slammed my fist into James's face over and over again.

The Tarantulas surrounded me, and one of them smashed a weapon into the back of my head. My head spun, and I landed on the ground beside James. I didn't get a chance to steady myself before someone wrapped a noose around my neck and yanked backward, cutting off my airways. People began shouting protests, and others egged them on.

"Hey!" someone shouted. It sounded like Gregory. "He was trying to save her! Let him go or I'll—I'll—"

Behind me, Corbin gasped, and the pressure on my throat loosened as he dropped the noose. I yanked it off my head and scrambled to my feet. Nadine reached me then, and I grabbed her to pull her back from the others. When I turned to look at what happened, my heart lurched.

James's knife stuck out of Corbin's back, and blood oozed onto the carpet below him. Gregory took a few cautious steps backward, like he couldn't believe what he'd done. Brayden looked horrified, but he approached Gregory and gently took his hand—showing he was by his side no matter what.

"I—I was trying to save..." Gregory stammered.

"Save the apostates!?" Ryan roared. "You may bear the mark of Miriam's Chosen, but you are an apostate as well! Get 'em!"

The room erupted into chaos. Magic whizzed overhead from students and professors who had been spared from the Waning. People found whatever objects they could and used them as weapons or shields. It didn't seem to matter what side people were on—everyone was a target. Students fled out one set of doors, only to appear back inside the room through another entrance.

Nadine threw her hands up to create a shield around us, but a rogue spell hit her in the side before she could cast the spell. I caught her before she crashed to the ground, but the sound of voices in my head brought me to my knees.

Shadows surrounded us, and people began attacking us from all angles. I threw myself over top of Nadine, taking the blows for myself. It was like the night in the town square all over again—fists, magic, and weapons pounding down upon us. We'd been beat down so much over the past week, I didn't know how much fight we had left in us.

"Lucas!" Nadine protested. She tried to push me off of her. She knew I'd be beaten to death if I took it all for her, but I wasn't going to let her get hurt.

Over the sound of the whispering voices in my mind, cats screeched so loud, my ears rang. I heard Grant and Talia screaming. I wanted to get to them, to save them, but I couldn't move. There was no one coming to our rescue.

Nadine tried to create a shield, but the Executors and other members of Miriam's Chosen stomped her hands down, preventing her from casting. Each time she shot off a defensive spell, someone else would come in to hurt her again. She couldn't cast fast enough.

I heard the chilling sound of Avery Mitchel's laugh. "Let's see how well you cast magic without fingers!"

Horror permeated every inch of my body. I opened my eyes to see the light glisten off a knife in Avery's hand. It had to be the same one Gregory used to stab Corbin, because it was already covered in blood. Avery knelt on Nadine's wrist and pressed the tip of the blade to the base of her pointer finger.

"No!" I screamed as I reached out, as if I could stop it.

Someone grabbed my arm and twisted it behind my back so hard I felt it pop. Laughter came from above me, and I realized it was Declan, one of the Treacherous Tarantulas.

"Kill them already!" Finn shouted.

Pain radiated through my shoulder, and the breath left my lungs as I was met with blow after blow. Nadine screeched from beneath me, shattering my heart. I couldn't save her.

"Fuck, it's time to go," I heard James snarl.

"I order you to *stop!*" Charlotte's voice rang across the ballroom.

She was off the Imperium Council now. Miriam's Chosen wouldn't listen to her. But they did. By some miracle, they did.

The blows came to an immediate halt, and I experienced a moment of reprieve from the attack.

And then the voices came.

There had to be two dozen voices, at least. Angry voices shouted awful things in my head all at once. I couldn't make out what they were saying, but the rage made my skull feel as if it was splitting in two. I cried out in agony and clutched my skull as I rolled over and curled into a ball.

So many deaths all at once…

"Lucas!" Nadine shouted. Her voice sounded like it was coming from miles away. I thought she shook me, but I couldn't be sure I felt *anything* past the pounding in my head. I wanted to hurl, but nothing came up. Voices filled the room, but I couldn't be sure what any of them were saying.

"Lucas, it's all right," Nadine's soft voice came in my ear. "They're gone."

Gone. She said it like it should reassure me, but I heard the hollowness in her tone. They were *gone*—dead. How was that possible?

Soon, the pounding in my head eased enough that I opened my eyes to see Nadine kneeling above me. Nearby, Grant curled Talia in his arms. Oliver ran over and licked my face. Nadine trembled as she gazed around us, and I finally lifted my head to see bodies strewn everywhere. Their lifeless eyes stared toward the ceiling, but I didn't see any wounds.

Declan lay with his arm twisted beneath him. Three of the other Tarantulas sprawled out beside him. Finn, Corbin, and Nolan shared the same empty stare. Avery Mitchel's blonde curls splayed around her in all directions, her jaw hung open. The knife she'd been using to carve Nadine's flesh lay beside her.

I gasped and looked down at Nadine's hand, expecting to find a finger missing. Her hand was covered in blood, and there was a deep gash at the base of her finger. It was still attached, thank the Goddess!

"You're hurt." I tore off another piece of my shirt and wrapped it tightly around her finger. I could barely get it on, because my arm didn't want to move.

Nadine helped with the makeshift bandage, then said, "Hold still."

She grabbed my arm and twisted, and I screamed as my shoulder popped back into socket. Son of a bitch, that hurt.

The whole ballroom went silent as people took in the carnage. The only sound was the pad of feet across the carpet. Charlotte walked across the room. The sleeve of her dress pulled back just enough that I caught sight of the skull tattooed on her wrist. She was one of the most powerful Mortana in the coven. Her power was a lot like Leroy's, but more extreme. She could kill hordes of people in an instant. I don't know if she'd ever done it before, but the masses of bodies lying on the floor was a testament to her power.

"I didn't want to hurt anyone," Charlotte said in a broken voice.

Chloe and Miles followed behind her, along with their cats. It was a relief to see they were okay.

Samantha stood on shaky knees and regarded Charlotte. "You saved us all. You are a *true* priestess."

"It wasn't enough," Charlotte said. "I didn't get them all. Several of them fled, but they could be back at any moment."

I glanced around the room, and I noticed Ryan and James were missing. Leroy was still out there with Death magic, too.

I looked down at the bodies, and I realized something I hadn't noticed before. Each of the Executors wore a badge, and the badges had inscriptions that weren't there at the beginning of the semester. "Leto's possessing Executors through inscriptions on their badges!"

He must've been planning this for a while—creating contracts so that he could strike at an opportune time.

"If he's created this many contracts, it's made him stronger," Charlotte said.

"The only way to banish him then is to break these contracts or use a bigger spell," I theorized.

A *boom* overhead shook the entire ballroom. People cowered together. A crack formed across the ceiling, and plaster rained down on us. It was another attack on the school.

I curled Nadine in my arms and dragged her backward as huge chunks of the ceiling broke off and crashed to the ground. Several people screamed as they were injured. All around the room, the ballroom doors slammed shut.

Nadine and I scrambled backward, until we were in the corner of the room. I nearly squashed someone, and I looked back to see Professor Warbright standing in the corner. He looked frozen in fear, his back pressed against the wall like he couldn't move even if he tried. His hair stuck straight upright, and he clutched his pocket watch, as if it was a token of good luck.

"Students," he said breathlessly. "I—I don't know what's happening."

"We're going to get out of here, Professor," Nadine promised him. She turned back toward our friends, who were running toward us, trying to dodge the raining plaster. "Hurry!"

Grant and Talia reached us first, followed by Chloe, Miles, and Charlotte. They'd nearly reached us when the room shook even more violently, and a huge chunk of building materials fell from the ceiling. I screamed a warning the same time Nadine tried to create a shield, but it was already too late. A huge chunk landed on Charlotte's head, knocking her out.

Nadine's shield bloomed around us, encompassing Charlotte and the others. We all squished into the corner, our cats squeezing in close to us. Talia dragged Charlotte's head into her lap and tried to get her to wake up, but she didn't move.

"Priestess!" Talia cried.

"Expand your shield!" I instructed.

"I can't!" Nadine cried. She winced as she lifted her hands to steady her shield.

Nadine sagged against me. It didn't matter how good her powers were. Right now, her body was ready to give out. She'd been beat down so much these last few days, I was surprised she was still going. But that was my Nadine—a fighter until the very end.

Screams continued to fill the air, and loud cracks sounded above our heads. Windows shattered, and though we could see nothing beyond the empty frames, violent winds and heavy rains swept inside the room.

All I could do was hold Nadine close. The room shook violently around us. Deafening screams and the haunting whistle of the wind pierced the air, but it all seemed distant. All that mattered was that I was here with my friends; I was here with *Nadine.* However this ended, we were here together.

"I'm sorry," I whispered in her ear. "I'm sorry I couldn't save us."

"That was never your responsibility," Nadine said in a broken tone. "Don't talk like this is the end. It isn't."

"How can you be so certain?" I pulled her even closer to my chest.

Nadine paused. All semester, she'd been asking herself this question. I hadn't thought about what I'd said, and I realized now that it was a cruel question. She shouldn't be contemplating such a thing in a dire time.

But Nadine didn't seem bothered by the question at all. In fact, her tone sounded confident. "I just have to believe it. Certainty is not knowing the outcome, but knowing *ourselves* and believing in our power."

Nadine gasped. "Lucas, that's it! We're going to get out of here for certain, because we *decided* to. We can make it happen, and it doesn't matter how uncertain the possibilities are. We'll always find a way, because we always have. It's not about accepting any outcome—the power is in deciding that one outcome is the only reality. *How* we get there is the uncertain part. That's not up to us. We can't control it. But we have tools to get there."

"It's like creating portals," I realized. "You can choose your destination, but you can't control the pathway there."

That's why my portals failed. I'd been trying to control the pathway, imagining it like a wormhole connecting two points in space. In reality, all I had to do was trust my magic to get me to the destination.

"What does your intuition say?" I asked.

"Find your strengths," Nadine said.

I always thought my strength lied in what I was able to endure. The more burden I could carry for others, the stronger I was. If I broke, I was weak.

As I held Nadine close in my arms, I realized something profound. I found strength through Nadine. Not because she validated something inside of me or gave me purpose I didn't already have within myself—but because she inspired me to see the good already inside of myself.

The *power* inside of me.

Each of us was strong on our own, but together, we were stronger. Nadine's space-bending spell had failed earlier because she tried to do it alone, and I would fail too unless I accepted help. I used to think asking for help was admitting defeat, but it took strength to recognize when you needed help and when you were ready to receive it.

"Nadine, will you help me?" I asked.

"Yes."

"I need Mortana magic."

Nadine nodded like she understood. She splayed one hand on the ground, then placed the other on my chest. Charlotte had been right about the magic within the school. Magic from all Casts permeated these walls. It's what kept the space-bending spell stable all this time.

Wisps of magic traveled up Nadine's arms. My chest glowed as she channeled Mortana magic into me. We'd been so focused on our individual powers before that we'd forgotten what we could do together.

I felt a surge of power as the magic filled me up from head to toe. Lifting my hands, I aimed them toward the other students scrambling around the ballroom. Magic swelled in my chest.

Whoosh!

A portal bigger than anything I'd conjured before swept through the ballroom. An image of the abandoned mansion appeared like a hole had been punched through space. Rain pounded down on its rooftop, and trees nearly cracked as they bowed over in the wind. With a flash of lighting, I saw the welcoming front doors of the safe haven.

Students screamed as they were sucked into the portal, then appeared on the other side. I saw them racing into the safety of the mansion, before the portal reached the other side of the room and fizzled out completely.

The ballroom continued shaking, and debris came down in huge chunks from above us. The screams, however, had stopped. My friends and I were the last ones here.

"That was amazing!" Grant cried.

"Amazing, but can you do it again?" Miles asked.

I had to, whatever it took. I tried to create another portal, but only sparks appeared before us. I'd used up all the magic Nadine had given me.

"It's not working!" I yelled over the groan of the building.

"I'm trying to give you more, but—" Nadine cut off.

"Try my magic," Professor Warbright offered. He was behind us and hadn't been swept up in my portal. "I'm Mortana. Whatever you're doing will work—won't it?"

Nadine reached for his outstretched hand, and I felt Mortana magic surge through me once again. I scrambled to make the magic work and quickly instructed the portal to take us to the mansion.

A portal bloomed beneath our feet, and my stomach flew to my throat as a falling sensation overcame me. We all went tumbling through the portal, our cats yowling as we came spiraling out on the other side.

I landed on a hardwood floor. Outside, lightning flashed and thunder crashed, but I was relieved to feel the ground was stable beneath me. Groaning, I lifted my head to see we'd all made it. Nadine lay beside me, with Oliver and Isa licking her face. Chloe and Miles were nearby, as well as Grant and Talia. Charlotte came to, and she pressed her palm to her head.

Professor Warbright trembled as he got to his feet. "Wh—where are we?"

"An abandoned mansion behind the school…" I trailed off, because when I looked around, it was all wrong. There was a big four-poster bed and broken furniture everywhere. The hardwood floor was heaved up in spots. A chill traveled down my spine, which had never happened in our mansion before. Our mansion lay forgotten, but it was a happy place—not a haunted one.

I'd meant to take us to the mansion, but I'd brought us to the wrong one.

I'd portaled us to Pinewood Manor.

TWENTY-FOUR

Wind howled from outside, and thunder cracked. Rain pounded down so hard; I couldn't even see outside. I'd never seen a storm this bad before.

Every inch of my body ached, but I managed to sit upright and look around. Pinewood Manor. Why had Lucas brought us here?

I got to my feet and steadied myself on the bedpost. As my eyes adjusted, I realized I recognized the room we were in. It was the bedroom where we'd witnessed the residual haunting—where Leroy chased down his wife.

Ghostly howls permeated the walls, and Grant shot a nervous glance around the room. "Guys, this isn't good. We don't have the magic to fight off ghosts."

Lucas let out a pained groan, and I turned to see him clutching his head. I knew that look. Lucas winced as he lifted his head. "The Executors are still out there killing people. We have to break the demon's spell controlling them, or more people will die."

A scream tore down the hall, and we all jumped as the door burst open. Our cats scattered and ducked under furniture to hide. Two ghostly figures ran into the room. The haunting played out as it had before, with Cynthia throwing open the window, then Leroy grabbing her and pinning her to the bed.

"No!" Cynthia screamed.

This time, I noticed something I hadn't before. Complete terror entered Cynthia's eyes, but it was darker than death—like her demise would bring about something far more sinister. Cynthia knew something we didn't. I could feel it in my bones.

I whirled toward Talia. "Tal, do you still have that music box?"

She trembled. "It's in my stash. I can't get to it."

"Let me help." I walked over to her and took her hands in mine. I didn't know if my idea would work, but I had to try. I poured my own magic into Talia's hands, and the music box appeared between our palms.

Talia's eyebrows knit together. "What are you doing?"

"Getting answers," I said.

I opened the music box, and ghostly figures wailed as they broke out of the box. Professor Warbright gasped and backed against the wall. The ghosts swirled around the room, until a woman floated down in front of me. She gave a kind nod, like she knew I meant well.

It was Cynthia—her real spirit. The one in the haunting was merely an imprint of her memory.

"Priestess Cynthia," I said. "I'm Nadine, a high priestess of the Miriamic Coven. The demon you summoned over forty years ago is back, and he's killing our people. You banished him once, but you made a mistake, didn't you?"

She nodded, then turned to gesture around the room, like she wanted to show me something. The door burst open once more, and the room transformed around us as the haunting played out. This time it was different; everything was solid. Cynthia's memories must've made the vision clearer. She threw open the window, and Leroy tossed her onto the bed. He lifted the knife above his head.

This was where the vision usually ended, but this time it continued. Leroy plunged the knife straight downward, piercing her heart. Cynthia gasped as blood pooled over her chest.

"The coven shall suffer the demon's spell," she rasped as she clutched her chest. She took a few more ragged breaths, before her entire body went limp.

Leroy yanked the knife from her chest, then backed away. He stumbled into the dresser, and a music box clattered to the floor. I realized it was Talia's music box—the very one I held in my hands. The top popped open, and we all watched as the vision showed Cynthia's ghost rising out of her body and spiraling into the music box. The ghostly screams became deafening, and we all covered our ears. Spirits from all over the house swept through the walls, being sucked into the music box that existed only in the vision. It was how it happened that night—how they'd become trapped.

The music box snapped shut. Leroy lifted the knife in both hands… then plunged it downward into his own stomach.

The scene fast-forwarded through time, showing people who had come and gone to move their bodies and salvage the antiques. It was only after they disturbed the bodies that we saw people screaming as they were chased out of the house by the hauntings. They must've left the other victims behind because they feared disturbing more spirits.

The visions washed away, and we were left again in the decrepit mansion with the thunderstorm raging outside. The ghosts swirling out of the music box settled, and dozens of spirits surrounded us. They weren't vengeful, and they didn't look confused anymore. They looked like they were exactly where they needed to be.

"Your death banished the demon without breaking the contract," I realized. "But you knew if he was in the Abyss, there was no way to kill him. That's what you meant by *the coven shall suffer the demon's spell.*"

The ghost nodded. "There was a clause in the contract. If the demon caused a priestess's death, he would be banished from the coven. It was meant to protect us. When I died by his spell, he was cast to the Abyss. But banishment and contract dissolution are not one in the same. Our contract stated only one way out, and it required one of the priestesses to sacrifice herself for the coven. I feared death more than anything, and I was unable to make the decision to save us all. Leroy kept our memories alive, to scare people away from the contract he was tricked into."

"The cursed wand?" I asked. "That's what kept him here all this time?"

"It's why my husband couldn't move on," Cynthia told us. "But he couldn't control his memories. Adrik faced the same issue in his wand shop."

A man stepped forward—Adrik Harvey, the man who had been hung in his wand shop many years ago. "It's become clear to me now. My spirit couldn't let go, because I was trying to keep people from suffering my same fate."

"You're free from the music box now," Lucas said. "You can all move on."

Cynthia shook her head. "Not until that demon is gone and his contracts destroyed. I had a hand in creating this mess, and I won't leave until the coven is free from him."

"My contract stated nothing about a priestess sacrifice," Charlotte said. "All demon contracts can be broken by conscious choice."

"It is not enough," Cynthia said. "Demons can manipulate contracts to require specific decisions to be made, as he did with mine. Even if you broke yours, he'd still have control over the coven through the original contract. By holding two contracts with different priestesses, he's secured his reign."

"That must be why the spell didn't work in the cafeteria," Chloe said. "Charlotte withdrew her consent, but Leto's still protected by Cynthia's contract."

Charlotte's features paled. "Lilian is the only one who was part of them both. We'd need her help, and she'd sooner die."

"There is another way," Cynthia said. "If he dies, his power dies with him, and all contracts will be void."

"That's impossible," I told her. "Demons are immortal."

"You must find a way to kill him!" Cynthia insisted. "Demon contracts give them power, and if they are broken, he will be weakened."

"But there are… how many contracts now?" I wondered. "The wand, all the Executor badges, and whatever he used to possess someone earlier this semester. We may have to destroy them all to weaken him, and we don't even know what they all are."

Professor Warbright shrank into a corner of the room, clutching his pocket watch and looking around nervously. I eyed him curiously, and all the pieces began coming together in my head.

"Or… maybe we do?" I realized.

Professor Warbright's gaze darted toward me, and he trembled. "I—I don't know what you're talking about."

I took a cautious step toward him. "I think you do. You said in the ballroom you didn't know what was happening. You'd blacked out, hadn't you? In fact… you've been blacking out all semester."

"I—I've been having health issues," he stammered.

Goddess, Professor Warbright had no idea.

"You were at the scene of the first crime," I pointed out. "You were supposed to meet up with Professor Perez, but you found him dead."

"*It wasn't him,*" Lucas said in realization. "That's what Perez said when he died. He knew you'd been possessed. He meant to tell me it wasn't you who killed him, even though it appeared that way."

"You're a necromancer," I added. "Leto used you to plant that skeleton to run The Hearse off the road. You were at the school the day Lena was hanged. Leto must've targeted you because no one would suspect you. You're too kind."

Grant gasped, like he'd just realized something. "I brought you the music box because you're the music teacher. I thought you could help us, but *you* cursed it so we couldn't fix it."

Professor Warbright shied deeper into the corner. "I don't remember a music box."

I glanced down at the watch he fiddled with. The inscription was unmistakable if you knew what you were looking for. "Your pocket watch..."

"I bought it at an antique shop over winter break," Warbright said in a trembling tone.

"Right when your blackouts started?" Talia asked.

Warbright's jaw hung open in disbelief. He couldn't believe what he'd done—but it hadn't been him. Dark magic had taken over him and made him do these terrible things.

"Professor, it's not your fault," I assured him. "We can end this, if you just give me the watch."

Professor Warbright's features changed in an instant, and he lunged at me. I landed hard on my back on the floor, and Warbright pinned me down. His hands curled around my throat, and I gasped for breath.

Several hands landed on him all at once, and my friends pulled him off of me. I gulped a greedy breath of air, but my throat felt like it was on fire. Warbright fought against my friends.

"Don't touch his watch!" Chloe shouted.

Warbright yanked free and pinned Lucas against the wall by his throat. He was several inches shorter than Lucas, but he was strong. Warbright pulled his wand from his pocket and pointed it between Lucas's eyes.

A blast sounded throughout the room, and a ball of light smashed against Warbright's back. His eyes rolled back in his skull, and he crumbled to the ground.

My gaze darted toward Charlotte, who was pointing her wand at Warbright. Lucas stepped away from the professor's limp body, breathing heavily.

"Is he dead?" Miles asked.

"No." Charlotte dropped her wand to her side. "It was merely a stunning spell."

"And a potent one at that," a sinister voice came from across the room. We all turned to see Professor Leto stepping forward. He must've followed us here. Demons could teleport if they were strong enough.

Charlotte threw herself in front of us, aiming her wand at Professor Leto. "You will control him no more!"

Leto held a wand in his hand, and with the simple flick of his wrist, we were all tossed upward. His magic pinned us to the wall, all lined up in a neat row with our toes dangling inches off the ground. It was like we were life-sized dolls placed on a shelf for display. Lucas's fingers touched mine, and he strained to move, but there was no breaking through this spell. Energy poured off of Leto, so much that it made my whole body buzz. There'd been so much death tonight, so much trauma for him to feed off of. He was more powerful than ever.

So why did he need a wand?

"Demon scum!" Adrik's ghost shouted. All around the room, spirits lunged for Leto. They were dead set on revenge.

He flicked his wrist, and the ghosts all came to a complete halt. The anger melted off their faces. Their features turned blank, and not a single ghost moved. Leto was strong enough to control them all.

"I must say, I'm impressed with your magic, Priestess," Leto practically sang to Charlotte. "My spells tend to make my puppets a bit stronger than average. It takes an impressive spell to take them down."

"I won't let you keep doing this," Charlotte said in a strained voice.

Leto laughed. "Break your contract all you want. I have others in place that will ensure I can continue my work here."

"You told Lilian the old contract was void," Charlotte accused. "You tricked us into a new contract, so that if one was broken, the other remained."

"I'm a man of my word," Leto said. "I believe I mentioned there were certain *aspects* that had been voided. Jebediah, for instance… well, that man unlocked a lot of potential for me. When Lilian found out the Oaken Wands were missing all those years ago, she summoned me to track them down. I found the Mentalist Wand and a man to wield its power."

I eyed the wand he held, and I noticed a familiar symbol on the handle —the twisted tree of a Mentalist. He'd had an Oaken Wand all this time!

"When he killed that priest, I was golden," Leto continued. "The contract stated I was free to do as the coven would do against its own. If they were capable of murder, well… so was I."

"That's how Jeb got his hands on the Mentalist Wand that killed my grandfather," I accused. "You gave it to him."

"Of course I did." Leto laughed. "He was intent on killing the man, and I was hungry for death."

"You've had it all along," Chloe said in a strained voice as she fought against the spell. "Everyone thought my family kept the Wand after the murder, but you took it! That's why the Olsons never knew what happened to it."

Leto smiled proudly. "Yes. This Wand and I have been working together for quite some time."

"Your contract requires you to hand that over to the priestesses," Charlotte said.

Leto smirked. "I was contracted to unite the Oaken Wands. I didn't have to hand over anything until all five Wands were found. And of course, I was going to hold on to this one for as long as I could. This wand is mine. It chose me."

"Oaken Wands can't choose demons!" Grant spat. "You're not a Mentalist. You can't use it!"

"What do you know of Oaken Wands?" Leto demanded. "You forget that your power originated from demons themselves. My magic is compatible as long as the Wand wants to work with me."

"You talk as if the Wands are sentient," Chloe said. "How could they choose someone who would hurt the coven the way you have?"

"You think they owe allegiance to you just because you created them?" Leto laughed. "This Wand knew I was of exceptional power. It wanted to be used. And used her, I did."

The Alchemy Wand and the Seer Wand may have only chosen those with good intentions—those who'd proven themselves—but if the Wands were sentient, it meant they had different motives.

"The Mentalist Wand messes with the mind," Leto continued. "She *likes* getting into the heads of my little puppets. She wanted me to influence them. And the way she did it was so… powerful. Your professor here had no idea what he was doing. The only one who really caught on was that student years ago… what was his name? Walsh?"

"Clyde Walsh?" Lucas asked through gritted teeth. I recognized the name. He'd been driving The Hearse the night it crashed.

"Yes," Leto said brightly. He was enjoying parading his pride. "After Jeb murdered that priest, it unlocked a few things in my contract. I was able to kill as I pleased. Clyde was merely an innocent student who needed materials for his wand class. I gave him the wand with the inscription on it, and he carried out my will to perfection. He killed that awful female professor, who'd been working with the priest to hide the Oaken Wands. She wouldn't tell me where he'd hidden them, so of course she had to go. Poisoned, by the student's own brew! He must've realized something was wrong, because he pawned the wand to that shop owner."

"And you killed Adrik for kicks!" Talia shouted.

Leto flicked his Wand again, forcing Talia's jaw shut. "I took advantage of an opportunity! Walsh figured out the wand was cursed and that the priestesses were involved, so he stole it from the shop and mailed it to the priestess to send a message. It's his fault I was ever banished, so I had to deal with him when I returned."

"You killed all those people in The Hearse Tragedy to get to one man," Lucas spat.

Leto laughed. "I killed those people because it was *fun!*"

"You never should've been able to kill so many people," Charlotte growled.

"I knew what I was doing when we struck a deal," Leto said proudly. "Lilian summoned me because she knew I'd found the Mentalist Wand before, and she knew I could do it again. You priestesses were so desperate for the Wands that you'd risk any number of lives. And you *could*, because you preside over the coven and could make a deal for them all. You had the power to trade for the coven's souls, and you just gave them up freely."

Leto approached Lucas and ran the tip of the Wand over his jawline. It was a threat that he could end him at any second. "I've had so much fun playing with the coven—and you especially, Lucas. Watching you scramble to find clues was entertaining. I watched you struggle to fix that music box of yours, which I'd cast a curse on—thank you again, Professor Warbright. I especially loved when you tried tracking down my contract. What a pathetic little spell that was. But I'm bored now, and I'm ready to ascend to my full power. The entire coven shall die at my hand, and I will possess all five Oaken Wands. All the power of the Miriamic Coven will be mine. The gods will welcome me into their ranks, and Octavia Falls will be nothing more than a forgotten ghost town."

Leto took a step back and pointed the Mentalist Wand at Lucas's chest.

"No!" I screamed as protection magic welled inside of me.

I never got a chance to cast it. Leto was knocked to his feet, and Professor Warbright landed on top of him. He'd regained consciousness and tackled Leto to the ground.

The spell that had been pinning us to the wall let up, and we all collapsed to the ground. Leto used his magic to toss Professor Warbright off of him. Warbright flew across the room and smashed into the dresser so hard it crumbled to pieces. Lucas jumped on top of Professor Leto before he could get upright, and the Mentalist Wand flew out of his hand. It rolled across the ground and stopped at Chloe's feet.

Lucas must've thought the Wand was the source of his power, but Leto didn't need it. A single flick of his wrist swept us all off our feet. My friends and I screamed as his magic pinned us to the ground so hard I could barely breathe.

Leto focused his attention on Lucas and used his powers to dangle him in the air. "You want to fight a demon? Fine. I'll give you *a demon.*"

His voice took on a deep, hellish growl as he shifted before us. Leto's attractive features morphed to become animalistic. His entire body grew to at least eight feet tall, and he towered above us as his curved horns grazed the ceiling. His face became that of a ram's, and his eye sockets glowed bright red. His nails elongated into sharp claws, and massive fur-covered feet burst from his shoes.

He laughed a deep, guttural laugh that sounded anything but human. Dark magic swirled out of the tips of his fingers and entered Lucas's body through his nostrils.

It had to be some sort of torture magic demons learned in hell, because Lucas's whole body convulsed as he screamed out in pain. I'd never heard such a hollowing cry before. It was the sound I imagined a person might make if they were being skinned alive and their flesh was on fire. I couldn't move my head, but Leto had positioned me in a way that forced me to watch.

Lucas's body trembling from head to toe. Rage flared in my bones, and I threw up a shield between them. Leto's demon magic was strong, though. He broke straight through my shield like it was a thin sheet of ice. We'd sorely underestimated this demon. He'd been gaining power for months, and he was capable of more than we could ever imagine.

He paused for a beat and turned to me. He looked amused that I would even *try* to defend Lucas. *"You wait your turn, little priestess. I'm going to torture each of you one by one, until your frail little bodies give out."*

He flicked his wrist, and the ghosts began swirling around us to his command. The air chilled around us, and I began to shiver. Leto was using the ghosts' energy to drop the temperature. A ghost floated over me, then plunged its hands into my chest. I screamed as the ghostly hand swept through my insides, chilling my body from the inside out. It was as if someone had sliced my chest open and placed a block of ice where my heart should be.

Instinct kicked in, and I tried to create a shield. Over and over again, shields bloomed out of my chest, but it did nothing to deter the ghosts. Spirits surrounded us at all angles. Leto had grown strong enough that their hands turned solid, and the ghosts began striking me, leaving large welts all over my body. I tried to fight it, but I barely had the mental capabilities to find my magic, let alone control it.

Echoing screams pierced the night. My eyes watered, and through the tears I saw the hungry look in Leto's eyes. He thrived off trauma. It gave him power. The ghostly hand inside of me drew away, moments before I thought my heart might give out.

Killing us wouldn't satiate the demon. He had to make sure we suffered.

I gasped for breath as warm blood filled my heart again. It was a pain I never thought I'd feel—like the sting of running your ice-cold fingers under warm water, except *everywhere*, inside and out. The moment I felt the air enter my lungs, it left again. Solid, cold hands curled around my throat.

"You're no god," Lucas strained to say. "You never will be."

"You wouldn't believe my power," Leto said. *"I have your coven to thank for that. I used to be just a lowly demon, but all your trauma has made me strong. I am a powerful Mentalist now, and I can make you do whatever I want—no contract required. These are spells you cannot break."*

My head spun as we were all whipped upright with the force of his magic. I landed on my feet, but not to my own free will. Before my eyes, Lucas's flesh began to peel off his body. I saw the bone and muscle beneath his skin.

"Lucas!" I screamed, the same time I heard him cry out for me. All around me, my friends screamed each other's names.

Abruptly, Lucas's flesh appeared back on his body. He continued dangling in the air where the demon left him, but he was in one piece.

"I can play with your minds," Leto said. *"I can make you see whatever I want you to see."*

The scene around us shifted, until we weren't in Pinewood Manor anymore. My friends and I stood on a large rock overlooking a lava pit. Steam rose around us, and it looked a lot like what I'd picture hell to be like. Sweat broke out on my brow, and I felt close to passing out from the heat.

"I can make you feel what I want you to feel," Leto said.

The false lava began to rise, and boiling bubbles popped, sending hot lava splattering over our skin. I screamed, but I barely heard my own voice over the sound of my friends crying out in pain. The lava may only be in our heads, but the pain was real.

Leto laughed. *"I can make you do whatever I want you to do."*

The lava disappeared in an instant, and we stood in the bedroom at Pinewood Manor again. I spotted the Mentalist Wand at Chloe's feet, but none of us could move.

"Stop it!" Talia begged.

My head snapped in her direction, but not of my own free will. I began moving across the room toward her. I couldn't stop it.

"Shut your mouth, you bitch," I heard myself say, before I cracked my palm against the side of Talia's face. It'd been so hard that Talia landed on the ground, and a welt formed on her cheek.

I hadn't wanted to do it. Leto had become so powerful; he didn't need to trick me into a contract to become his puppet. I imagined Talia had no intention of punching me in the stomach either, but her fist sank into my gut. I dropped to my knees as my breath ceased.

Talia brought her knee up into my jaw, and my whole body lurched backward as I was thrown to the ground. I lay flat on my back, staring up at my best friend who wanted nothing more than to kill me.

It was the worst torture of all. Leto knew that we were stronger together, and that the way to break us was to turn us against one another. I knew Talia would never hurt me, but seeing her face above me as she beat on me was horrifying.

I tried breaking the spell by connecting to Leto's power and siphoning it away from him. The physical beatings made my own power unreachable.

Leto pitted each of us against one another. He forced Miles to slam Chloe's head into the wall, and he made Charlotte whack Professor Warbright with the broken bed post. Grant pinned Lucas against the wall by his throat, until Lucas's face turned purple.

I couldn't move. I was one of Leto's puppets now. I may be a talented supernatural, but he'd become a demigod, and I wasn't strong enough to overpower him.

Leto threw his head back, and the room filled with his amused laughter. He was certainly enjoying the show. He flicked his wrists again, and half of us went flying to one side of the room, and half to the other. He pitted Charlotte against Chloe and Miles against Talia.

I was forced to stand in front of Lucas and punch myself in the jaw over and over again. Pain radiated through my knuckles and across my face. Tears welled in Lucas's eyes, knowing there was nothing he could do to stop it.

Leto circled us, and hunger grew in his eyes. *"I warned you not to make an enemy out of me."*

Lucas let out a scream through gritted teeth. "Go. To. Hell."

Leto laughed in that chilling, animalistic way. *"Gladly."*

The ground beneath us started to shake, and Leto begin to grow again. The ceiling groaned as he went from eight feet to twelve. He continued growing until the ceiling gave out completely. Debris rained down on us as he burst through the roof, becoming a giant demon that could squash us with a single step. He had to be twenty feet tall now.

He lifted his arms, and we all levitated in the air. The mansion crumbled to bits. Shards of glass, broken doors, and dismembered furniture swirled around us like a tornado, and we were in the eye of the storm. Leto brought his arms down in one swift motion, and everything went crashing to the ground.

My friends and I lay flat on our backs in the middle of the raging storm. Ghosts hovered above us. Heavy water droplets passed through their ethereal forms and turned to ice that pummeled us.

Lightning flashed, illuminating the demon's terrifying silhouette. His voice boomed over us. *I'm going to hell, and I'm taking you all with me!*

The most deafening sound came—louder than him, louder than the thunder. It sounded as if the whole earth was breaking in two. The earth rumbled, and I felt the ground snap beneath me. Straining against his spell, I turned my head to see a huge cavern open mere feet from me. A terrifying red glow emitted from the break in the earth. The four-poster bed shuddered across the ground, then toppled into the cavern.

My blood turned ice cold. That red glow was unlike anything I'd seen on Earth before. Leto had opened a passage to hell!

My friends and I were separated. Lucas, Chloe, Charlotte, and I were stuck on one side of the cavern, while the others trembled from twenty yards away.

"You will all be tortured properly in hell," Leto said. *"You will serve me."*

"Never!" I screamed.

Leto bent down and grabbed me by the back of the shirt. He lifted me off the ground. *"I see we have a volunteer. How'd you like to go first, little priestess?"*

He tossed my body into the air, and I screamed as I flew toward the pit. I thought I heard my friends screaming, too, but I couldn't be sure. My legs failed, and my hands clawed at the empty air, desperate to catch anything.

By some miracle, my hands clamped around something, and I caught myself before plummeting to the bottom of the pit completely. I gasped as my legs dangled below me, and I realized I'd caught myself on a rock protruding from the side of the pit. Rain poured down around me, soaking me from head to toe and making the rocks slippery. I didn't think

I had the energy left to hold on, but if I didn't, I'd die. I mustered up all the strength I could and clung on for dear life.

Lucas screamed, and I gazed up into the rain to see a shadow falling. He caught himself on the edge of the pit, dangling several feet above me. I scrambled to find my footing.

"Lucas!" I screamed.

He clung on to the side of the pit and held a hand down toward me. "Climb to me!" he shouted.

My whole body ached. I put every ounce of energy I had into pulling myself up, until something grabbed me from below. I screamed as I was yanked downward, my fingers barely gripping to the rocks.

I looked down to see *demons* crawling from the red pit. They were unlike Leto—less human-like and more like monsters. They were bipedal, with long limbs and red skin flecked with black spots. They looked more like shadows than solid beings. I couldn't make out their faces, only the blazing red of their eyes. They let out horrible cries, like they were being tortured themselves. One of them grabbed me and yanked me down, tearing my pant leg.

I slammed my foot into its face, and its head snapped backward. It let out an angry cry and swiped its long, twisted fingers at me. Sharp claws dug into my skin and tore at the flesh. I felt blood spring out of the wound on my leg. With as much force as I could muster, I smashed the heel of my foot into its face again, and the creature went spiraling down in the glowing red pit below us.

Others were coming in fast. I scrambled to grip onto the rocks above me, but my feet slipped against the wet cliff.

"Hang on!" Lucas screamed from above me.

I was so weak and tired. All I wanted to do was cling to the side of the cliff and never let go. I didn't think I could move. As I held my body close to the rocks, I felt the demon's magic pulsing through the earth. I could barely conjure magic in my weakened state. I was ready to let go and fall into the pit.

Hordes of monsters reached me. Their spindly fingers curled around my legs, and the flashing lightning above our heads seemed to disappear as monsters closed in on us from all angles. They grabbed Lucas, and my heart stuttered. Lucas screamed my name. It seemed far off, like I was already falling.

I wasn't willing to let things end this way. These monsters couldn't have us.

Gathering all the will I had left, I siphoned what magic I could from the earth—and let it go. Defensive magic blasted outward, and monsters went flying in all directions. They hissed and screamed as they spiraled down into the pit. Gathering my strength, I created a shield below me, providing me a solid foundation to set my feet so I could climb to Lucas. He grabbed my hand and yanked me upward.

We crawled out of the pit, but my legs gave out when I tried to stand. I landed face-first in a puddle of water, which was only growing larger by the second. The rain was coming down so hard. Lucas lay beside me, like he too had lost all the fight left within him. Bruises mottled his entire body, and he looked at me like he was trying to find me but couldn't see straight.

Above us, Chloe screamed.

"You're a pretty one," Leto said in his deep demon voice. *"I know how you'll serve me."*

Weakly, I lifted my head to see Leto had picked Chloe up. He clutched her in his massive demon hands and pushed her dark hair out of her face.

"Let me go, you filthy pig!" Chloe screamed, trying to struggle out of his grasp.

Leto laughed. *"As you wish."*

He lumbered over the pit and held Chloe over top of it. He was going to drop her in!

"No," I rasped as I tried to push myself upright. No one heard me over the roar of the wind. I began crawling toward Chloe, as if there was something I could do to help. There was nothing, not anymore—but I'd be damned if I didn't fight until the very end.

My hand landed on something hard, and I looked down to see the Mentalist Wand lying beneath my palm. My heart lurched.

Chloe was a Mentalist. If the Wand would have her, she could use it!

"Chloe!" I screamed. I could barely see her through the rain, but the quick flashes of lightning lit up her silhouette. Grasping the Mentalist Wand, I drew my arm back and threw it as hard as I could.

The Wand soared through the air... and disappeared. I had no idea where it'd gone. It had vanished into the night.

The demon opened his fingers, and Chloe screeched as she went tumbling downward. My stomach twisted into tight knots as Chloe fell to her death—straight into the Abyss.

Across the cavern, Miles let out the most excruciating wail. Lightning flashed, showing him on his knees, cursing the skies as Chloe met her bitter end.

The demon whirled around, red eyes narrowed toward me. *"You're going to learn the consequences of defying me, little priestess."*

He reached down to grab me, but a voice came from behind him. "You're not going to touch her."

I gasped when lightning lit up the sky and I saw Chloe's silhouette rising from the pit. It was like she was flying, using telekinetic power to move herself around. I don't know how she'd done it. She'd lost all her magic to the Waning.

Then I noticed the glow swirling around her form. In her hand, she held the Mentalist Wand, and I realized she'd caught it as she fell. It glowed brighter as she drew Mentalist powers from the coven to the Wand.

The Wand wanted to be used; it didn't seem to matter by whom. Chloe would use it well, and it accepted her.

Chloe landed firmly on her feet at the edge of the cavern. She pointed the Mentalist Wand at the demon and flicked her wrist. His arm jerked away from me, and I saw the horrified look on his face when he realized what had happened.

"I don't need the Mentalist Wand to be stronger than you," Leto sneered.

"Oh? Let's test that theory," Chloe shouted.

She swished the Wand, and Leto landed flat on his back. His massive form shook the ground. I scrambled backward so I wouldn't get hit. Lucas grabbed me and curled me into his arms.

Leto aimed his gaze on Chloe, and without even moving, he flung her into the air. She caught herself using the Wand, but the ghosts Leto had been controlling surrounded her. They clawed at her, leaving long, bloody gashes all over her skin. Chloe didn't have power over the ghosts, but she used her telekinesis to fly away from them. She landed on the ground facing the demon, then readied her Wand again.

Leto let out an angry roar. He lifted a heavy fist, then slammed it straight into the ground. The ground shook so violently, Lucas and I were tossed into the air. Lucas held me tight, and we landed in a pile of debris. I heard something snap beneath us, and Lucas cried out in pain. I looked down in horror to see Lucas's leg was trapped in the debris. The snap I heard has been his bone!

I grabbed at broken building materials as quickly as I could to free his leg. My heart stuttered when I removed a piece of wood and found the cursed wand beneath it—the one that had possessed me. We'd left it in the study weeks ago, but Leto had blasted the mansion apart and swirled its contents around.

"Lucas! It's one of his contracts!" I cried. "If we destroy it, it will weaken him."

Lucas winced, then shouted over the raging storm. "How are we going to destroy it? It's too powerful."

"We have an Oaken Wand!" I reminded him.

Lucas looked around, and his eyes landed on an old, tattered curtain beside him. He tore the fabric, then curled it around the wand so he wouldn't touch the contract.

"Chloe!" Lucas screamed, waving the wand above his head. Her eyes darted in our direction. "Destroy the contract. Now!"

Lucas threw the cursed wand into the air as high as he possibly could. Chloe aimed the Mentalist Wand at it, making it levitate above our heads. Magic shot out of the end of the Wand, and the contract glowed a bright red, before shattering into millions of pieces.

Leto cried out, and he appeared to shrink by a foot. *"What have you done!?"*

He threw his hands upward, and debris swirled overhead to mimic his rage.

"Chloe, destroy the pocket watch!" Lucas yelled.

Chloe used her telekinesis to dodge around Leto and the flying debris. Professor Warbright had seen what we'd done. He stood on the other side of the cavern, holding his pocket watch above his head. Chloe aimed her Wand, and the watch shot into the air. It glowed bright red, then shattered.

Leto roared, his anger rippling through the skies louder than the thunder. He shrank again, but he still towered at least eighteen feet above us.

Chloe whirled toward him, but he was already coming for her. At the last second, magic erupted from the Wand and assaulted Leto. His back arched, and his head lifted to the skies like he was in pain. It barely lasted a moment before his screams turned to dark laughter. He was still too strong for her spell.

"Your magic is no match for me!" He pushed through the spell and snatched Chloe out of the air. He tried to yank the Wand out of her grasp, but she must've been making him see things, because he stumbled from side to side as he tried to grab it.

"You bitch!" he growled.

"Finally, a compliment," Chloe said.

Leto dropped her, and she rolled across the ground as she landed. He stumbled around blindly.

"You can blind me, but you don't know how to use the power of the Wand!" Leto shouted.

He swiped his hands outward, and I gasped as I was swept off my feet. Lucas screamed my name, but with a broken leg, he couldn't move.

Leto dangled me upside down. *"I can't wait to torture you, pretty one."*

He thought I was Chloe.

"Let her go!" Chloe screamed.

I thought she blasted off another spell, but my vision blurred as all the blood in my body rushed to my head. The flashes of lightning seemed merely like flashlights blinking from miles away as everything faded out of focus. All I could make sense of was the glowing red pit below me as the demon dangled me above it.

"We have to work together to kill him like Cynthia said!" Lucas shouted. "Kill him, and all his contracts are voided!"

Please, Mother Miriam, I prayed. I was in so much pain, I just wanted to be done with it, but my soul wasn't ready for this to end. *Please save me.*

I didn't know what happened, but the demon took a step back. I witnessed a bright light swirling from below me, near the demon's feet. Could it be Mother Miriam?

The light wasn't quite right. It wasn't the bright white glow of Mother Miriam's magic. It had a silvery hue to it.

I realized it was *Charlotte's* magic. Through the dark of the night, the magical glow lit up her form. I saw she was standing at the demon's feet, her hand pressed against his leg as she aimed all the Death magic she could muster into his form.

He dropped me, and I landed with a hard *thud* on the ground.

The demon looked rather annoyed as he growled, *"I am immortal. You cannot kill me. Your Death magic merely tickles."*

"I don't have to kill you!" Charlotte yelled. "I only have to distract you!"

The demon whirled around to face Chloe. She stood in the pouring rain, aiming the Mentalist Wand straight at the demon's chest. The end of the Wand glowed white as she attracted the magic of her Cast. Charlotte had bought her enough time to charge the Wand with her Cast power.

Chloe's red magic swirled up and down her entire form, sparking with electricity like the lightning bolts overhead. It was powerful battle magic —a spell designed to kill. Charlotte's magic may not be enough to kill Leto, but Chloe had the Mentalist Wand. That made her power stronger than ever. Leto lunged for the Wand.

Boom!

Magic exploded out of the end of Chloe's Wand, blasting toward the demon. His claws swiped at the Mentalist Wand and knocked it out of Chloe's hand. The Wand went spiraling through the air and straight into the pit.

It happened in the blink of an eye, but the spell had already been cast. Telekinetic magic strong enough to move mountains slammed into the demon's chest. He was blasted backward—straight into Priestess Charlotte.

Charlotte tumbled over the side of the pit, her screams echoing as she plummeted to her death. The demon clawed at the empty air, like he may be able to climb the rain drops. He fell backward, straight toward the pit.

He never made it. Chloe's killing spell enveloped his entire form. The demon's skin glowed a bright red, then he exploded into ash.

Around us, the ghosts broke free of the hold he had on them. They were swept back up into the music box, which sat in the rubble mere yards from me. The top slammed shut, trapping the ghosts inside once again.

Everything seemed so silent, even though the storm raged around us. It was nothing compared to the calm that overcame me knowing the demon was gone.

The red of the pit faded, and the ground shook as the cavern closed, leaving only a gap a few feet wide.

Cautiously, I crawled through the sopping rain to the edge of the cavern. There was nothing but blackness below me. The monsters were gone. The demon was gone…

Charlotte and the Mentalist Wand were gone. The portal the demon had opened in the earth had sucked them all to the Abyss.

Except the demon. He had exploded into ash.

As the dust settled, our cats came out of hiding. Isa meowed as she rubbed up against me. I stroked her wet fur.

"You did it, Chloe!" Miles exclaimed as he jumped over the narrow cavern. He was joined by Grant, Talia, and Professor Warbright. "Your spell was powerful enough to kill him."

Chloe breathed heavily. "I'm not sure I could've done it alone. You heard what Cynthia said about her contract. The only way out was if a priestess sacrificed herself for the coven. Charlotte may not have signed that contract, but she was a priestess. She put herself into the line of fire and died for it. She broke the contract, which made Leto weak enough for that last spell to kill him."

I got to my feet and limped over to Lucas. Blood trailed down my leg from where the monsters sliced my skin. I helped Lucas break free of the debris, and we sagged against each other. I couldn't believe it was over. With Leto dead, all his contracts were void. He could never possess another coven member to kill for him again.

"The demon is gone, but the priestesses are still going to use the Executors to hunt us down," I said. "We need to leave. Now."

Lucas winced. "I don't think I have another portal left in me."

"We have to get out of this storm," Chloe said.

Rain continued to pour down on us, and lightning flashed overhead. We were a long walk from shelter. The rest of the town was on the other side of Lake Santos. Neither Lucas nor I would make it far on two legs.

I spotted headlights through the rain, coming down the driveway that led to the manor. It wasn't a manor anymore, though. It'd been completely demolished.

Someone got out of the car, and I heard a voice screaming into the night. "Nadine!?"

My heart leapt with joy. "It's Grammy! We're over here!"

Our friends came to help us stand, and we started making our way through the rubble. Grammy ran to me when she saw our shadows moving through the night. I fell into her arms.

"Thank the Goddess I found you!" she cried. "I've looked everywhere. Quickly, everyone get into the car. I'm taking you to the safe house."

Grammy's hatchback didn't have enough seats for us all, but Miles, Lucas, and I sat in the cargo area behind the back bench. I was just grateful to be alive and out of the storm.

Lucas wrapped an arm around me as Grammy drove us out of town. "We're safe now," he whispered.

I should have felt safe. The demon was gone, and we were finally escaping the priestesses. But as I watched the lights of Octavia Falls fade into the distance, all I felt was dread.

I didn't know if I'd ever see my home ever again. I'd failed to stop the priestesses from tearing Octavia Falls in two, and now, I was running away from everything that had made me the witch I was today.

I vowed that I wouldn't return until I was certain we'd reunite our coven, for good this time. That, or we'd die trying, because this could *not* happen again.

"No, Lucas. We're not safe," I said darkly. "We'll never be safe. Not until this is done."

And I intended to finish this. Once and for all, the Imperium Council was going straight to the Abyss, where they belonged.

Even if I had to take them down to hell with me.

TWENTY-FIVE

I woke to the sun shining through the floor-to-ceiling windows. Nadine lay curled in my arms on the bed, and she hadn't woken yet.

A week had passed since we'd fled town. Helena had brought us to a big house a few miles outside of Octavia Falls. It was tucked deep in the forest and built into the side of the mountain. The house was all clean lines and big windows, which made me feel exposed, but the wards surrounding the safe house concealed us well.

The house was huge, with enough beds for all of us. William used to rent it out as a mountain retreat. That was obvious by the smell of fae still lingering on the sofa. We noticed it as soon as we walked in.

We searched the lodge high and low for fae intruders. We came to the conclusion that the fae hadn't been there in quite some time, back before William had made this our safe house. The fae we'd helped last semester must've stayed here after they'd gotten what they needed from Hattie.

Headmistress Verla had arrived later that night, along with Professor Warren and Onyx. Verla had made it out of the school alive, and she'd found the other two nervously awaiting our arrival at her house, like we'd planned. Things had completely gone off the rails that night.

Settling into the safe house gave us time to recover, but it couldn't cure the trauma we'd endured. I'd dreamt of that night again—the pain that had permeated my bones when the demon used his spells on me, the horrors of watching him beat Nadine to near death. I knew the dreams weren't real, and yet they still felt like they were still happening. When I closed my eyes, I could still see his burning red eyes behind my lids. Often, I replayed how I could've killed the bastard myself and saved my friends from the pain.

But there wasn't anything I could've done. He was gone, and I had to accept what had happened as reality. There was no going back and changing it. It was in the past, and I didn't live there anymore.

Still, I got physically ill as my eyes roamed Nadine's body. She wore a thin nightgown, which showed off the purple and yellow bruises all over her body. Her finger was in a splint, since it'd been stitched up after Avery's attack. Onyx had done a really good job on the stitches, and she'd put my leg in a cast using the medical supplies William had left us. She'd learned a lot working at the hospital, and we were lucky to have her here.

Nadine would be able to take the stitches out tomorrow. The ones on her leg had to stay a few more days. Those cuts from the monsters had been deeper, and I was surprised she could move at all after what they'd done to her.

I ran my fingers lightly down her arm, over the mottled bruises. Every inch of her seemed to be covered with them. I had my fair share of bruises and fractures, and that made it all the worse—because I knew exactly what it felt like to move wrong and feel the pain of the attacks all over again.

Nadine stirred. Her ribs had been fractured in several places, and she hadn't gotten out of bed much since we got here. Nadine winced as she rolled onto her back.

I startled. "Did I hurt you?"

Her eyes fluttered open, and she got a light smile on her face when she saw me. "No. You could never."

"Well, technically—"

"Technically, you worry too much," she teased.

The fight was over, and it was her light mood that reminded me of that daily. Without it, it was easy to slip into survival mode. To be honest, I wasn't sure I'd ever come out of it, but we were safe here at William's lodge. The Waning had passed after a few days, and we were able to cast wards and protection spells that even the priestesses couldn't penetrate.

This wasn't exactly the ski resort weekend we'd talked about weeks ago, but we *were* staying at a mountain retreat, and we *had* escaped the priestesses.

From the foot of the bed, Isa stretched, and Oliver stirred awake beside her. He placed his paw over her and started licking her ears.

"It's my job to worry," I told Nadine. "How are you feeling today?"

"Well enough to go for a walk," she said. "I want to try, at least."

The gashes on her leg were tender and made it hard for her to get around, but if she was ready to try, I was ready to help. It was like recovering from the kidney transplant all over again. One step at a time.

I helped Nadine sit up in bed, and I checked her wounds. "Everything seems to be healing well. No infections."

"I'm getting some range of motion back in my finger," Nadine said. She reached for the salve Helena had given her that sat on the nightstand.

I took it and began rubbing the herbal mixture over her leg, before bandaging it all back up. I took her hand in mine and gently removed the splint from her finger. As I rubbed the salve over her skin, my fingers grazed her engagement ring. A thrill traveled through my stomach. I was still getting used to it.

I flipped her hand over to look at the diamond. "After everything we went through, this ring survived."

"Of course it did," she said. "It symbolizes our love, and that's not going anywhere."

I needed that reassurance sometimes, and my heart filled with joy when she reminded me that no matter what, we would always be together. I leaned toward her, and Nadine closed the gap between us. My whole body got hot when she kissed me. It was a sweet, tender kiss, and yet I wanted to throw her down onto this bed and never come up for air.

But I didn't, because I didn't want to hurt her. Or myself, for that matter.

I swung my legs off the side of the bed and grabbed the crutches there. William had only left one pair with our medical supplies, so I took one and gave the other to Nadine. We each leaned on a crutch, and I took her fingers in my opposite hand.

"Can you do stairs?" I asked.

"I think so."

We limped out of the bedroom and down the hall. The lodge was oddly quiet, which made me more alert than ever. Usually, we could hear

Grant and Talia playing video games downstairs, or Miles and Chloe chatting over a game of chess. Helena was usually in the kitchen cooking, and Onyx often joined her. I didn't know what Headmistress Verla and Professor Warren had been up to. I assumed they were making plans and didn't want to bother us with them until we recovered. We hadn't seen them much since we arrived.

I used the railing to steady myself as I slowly descended the stairs. We entered the living room and heard laughter coming from the patio out back. We followed the sound of voices and found everyone sitting outside. It was the first day of June, and there was still a morning chill in the air, but the sun warmed my skin. A light breeze rustled the trees. The cats ran around in the yard, chasing a dead chipmunk up a tree that Professor Warbright had reanimated for them.

If I could forget that night, I could believe we'd stepped into a pleasant slice of paradise.

Our friends' bruises and bandages were a cruel reminder of what happened. Chloe had a string of stitches on the side of her face from when Miles had been forced to smash her head into the wall. Grant had a black eye that was still healing, and Talia still had bruises on her neck from where she'd been choked. Miles was covered in bruises from head to toe, as were the rest of us.

Our friends gathered around a patio table. Onyx placed a fresh pan of cookies in front of them, and they all grabbed some. Spread across the table was a large map that featured the locations of every supernatural city in the world, and the coordinates of where they could be found.

Talia held the music box in her lap. It was open, and dozens of ghosts surrounded my friends—some of them floating above our heads, and others chilling on the patio blocks. Adrik hovered at the center of the patio, making big hand gestures as he told a story. Helena threw her head back in laughter, and our friends giggled as Adrik did different voices. He was really funny and so full of life. It was sad that it'd been cut so short.

"You're so funny!" Onyx told him.

Adrik shrugged. "I'm a ghost. The afterlife isn't much fun unless you make it so."

"Speaking of ghosts…" Miles turned to his brother with a full mouth. "I heard some strange noises coming from your room last night. Sounded like moaning. You don't happen to have a ghost problem, do you?"

Grant leaned back in his chair and smirked. "Aw, man. I feel so bad for you. You don't know what it sounds like to make a girl moan, do you?"

Talia laughed so hard she nearly choked on her cookie.

Miles clicked his tongue. "You think I'm not getting any? Poor, naive brother."

Chloe elbowed Miles lightly. Nobody missed the glance she shot him.

"Wait." Grant's eyes darted between Miles and Chloe. "Are you two dating?"

"Not officially! Well, I don't know. Maybe?" Chloe pushed a strand of dark hair behind her ear and looked at Miles.

He raised his eyebrows. "Maybe. Yeah? I mean, if you want to."

Grant's jaw dropped, and Talia shot him an incredulous look. "Grant, you can't have *missed* their flirting all semester."

Grant crossed his arms. "I think I would know if my brother was flirting."

Onyx scrunched up her face. "Would you, though?"

"We were not flirting!" Chloe cried.

"Eh, you kind of were," Talia said.

Helena gave them a pointed look. "Even *I* can sense the hormones rolling off you two."

"All right, so we flirted," Miles admitted. "Sue us."

Nadine chuckled, and all eyes turned to look at us in the doorway.

"Nadine! Lucas!" Talia shoved the music box into Grant's hands and leapt from her chair. "It's so great to see you up and about!"

She threw her arms around Nadine, and they both winced. "Sorry," Talia said as she drew away.

"It's fine," Nadine assured her. "I need all the hugs I can get."

"In that case, come here," Helena said. She wrapped Nadine in a gentle hug, and I thought Nadine looked like she was about to cry. I didn't think she was sad, or even in pain. She looked happy to see all her friends laughing after everything we'd been through.

"Where's Headmistress Verla and Professor Warren?" Nadine asked as she drew away.

"They're on a call with one of our contacts inside the coven," Helena said. "They should be out soon with an update. Why don't you two have a seat? There's still some breakfast."

She gestured to the patio table, where there was still a pile of pancakes, along with freshly baked cookies beside the map.

"Thank you," I said, but I didn't move to grab food right away. Instead, I turned to Adrik and the other ghosts. "Why are you all still here? The demon's dead. You can all move on. I thought your reapers would've come for you by now."

Cynthia stepped forward, and Leroy joined her. "Our reaper is right here," she said gently.

A tingle of magic spread through my form, and I realized she meant *me*. "I can't help all of you at once," I said. There were so many of them. "I've never done it."

"Then you don't know it's impossible," she pointed out. "Miles had enough power to pull us all onto this plane. Perhaps you can lead us to the next."

I took a deep, calming breath, and magic surged through me. A portal bloomed at the end of the patio, shining a beautiful white light down upon us brighter than the sun. All the ghosts turned to look. They were the only ones that could see it besides me.

Cynthia drew a sharp breath and clutched her husband tighter. "Oh, Leroy! We've been waiting for this for so long."

Leroy smiled. It was so strange to see on a man who was supposed to be a killer. He turned to me. "Thank you all for freeing us. If there's anything we can do…"

"You can move on," I said. "We'll rest easier knowing you made it to the other side."

"And put in a good word with Mother Miriam for us!" Miles piped up.

Chloe nudged his shoulder playfully, but then added, "Actually, it couldn't hurt."

I hobbled to the edge of the portal and reached out for the ghosts. "Come. It's time to go home."

The ghosts took my hand one by one, then stepped through the portal into Alora. A weight seemed to lift off my shoulders with each one, like reaping their souls somehow freed my own.

The last ghost passed through, and a gust of wind swept across the patio as the portal closed. Talia's music box began playing a lovely tune, and Grant sat up straighter. "Hey! It's working again."

The patio doors opened, and Headmistress Verla and Professor Warren stepped outside to join us.

Chloe sat up straighter in her chair. "Professor, Headmistress, what did you learn?"

"You can call us by our first names, seeing as neither of us will be returning to the school," Verla suggested.

Miles scrunched up his nose. "Jonathan and Clarice? That's too formal. I think I'll stick with calling you by your last names."

Verla nodded. "All right. Verla and Warren it is."

We all gathered around the table again. Nadine kept close to my side.

"We were able to get in touch with Hattie, who has agreed to keep us informed on developments within the coven," Verla told us. "What we know is that a coven-wide memorial took place this morning, and the school's been shut down for repairs. The school board isn't sure they're going to use spellwork again to expand. It's too dangerous. As for the priestesses, they are working to find a new Mortana priestess as soon as possible, and it sounds like they may be moving up the induction ceremonies, in order to restore a five-Cast Imperium Council."

"They can't do that," Nadine said. "Mira's not even a real Curse Breaker."

"The coven doesn't know that, though," Professor Warren reminded her.

"Will the Induction Ceremony even work before Halloween?" Talia asked. "It's traditionally done on Halloween because our spells are stronger then."

"Stronger, yes," Verla stated. "But the Induction Ceremony can still be performed. The Imperium Council will soon have five members again. We can safely assume that their priority will lie in finding the Oaken Wands. We all know how catastrophic it will be if the Imperium Council possesses them all. We must find the remaining Wands before the priestesses do."

"How are we going to get back inside Octavia Falls to go looking for them?" Grant wondered.

"We don't have to," Nadine replied. "I've done everything I can to figure out where my grandfather hid them, and I'm not sure the others are *in* Octavia Falls. It's time we start looking elsewhere."

"We already know where to find one of the Wands," I said. "The

Mentalist Wand fell into the demon's pit, which was a portal to the Abyss. The Oaken Wands can't be destroyed. That means the Wand is still out there."

Miles frowned. "All right. Let's just *waltz into hell*."

"Why not?" I asked. "If I can open a portal to Alora, I should be able to open one to hell."

"You can't be serious," Helena protested.

"I am serious," I stated. "The coven's magic is everything. It's what makes us the Miriamic Coven. We need to unite the Wands to end the Waning, and we know where one is."

Grant stood. "How about before we go jumping into the Abyss, we think of some better options? You're still learning your reaper powers. You've never opened a portal to hell."

"The least I can do is try." I lifted my palm. I knew how to cast portals now, so maybe I could do it. Sparks flew through the air… but the portal never opened. A mere moment passed, and my head was already spinning.

Grant grabbed my arm to stop me. "I know you want to get the Mentalist Wand, but we don't know what the Abyss is really like! This isn't the same as opening a portal somewhere on Earth. You're trying to access an entirely new realm, and you're either going to hurt yourself trying, or you could unleash something dangerous."

Chloe was quick to take charge. "We all need time to recover. We're not diving head-first into hell without a plan. I say we take the summer to rest and figure this out."

"The whole summer?" I balked.

Helena gestured to Nadine and me leaning on our crutches. "If you think you're going to fight monsters with those injuries, you're sorely mistaken. You're going to need all summer to get your strength back! I can't believe you're even suggesting going to the Abyss."

"I agree," Verla stated. "We know the Mentalist Wand is in hell, but the priestesses don't. They're not going to go after it, so we should put all our effort into finding the Mortana Wand and the Curse Breaker Wand before the council gets to them first."

"We're going to have to go to hell at some point, though," Nadine said. "It's risky, but we need to unite the Wands. We said when we started that we'd walk through hell and back to restore the coven's magic. Well, the time's come to do just that. *But* Chloe's right. We need to be prepared."

"What are you suggesting?" Talia asked.

"For one, we need a way to get into the Abyss," Nadine pointed out. "As of right now, Lucas's powers aren't strong enough to portal us there—though they might be strong enough to get us out. We also need a safeguard against the Waning, in case we get stuck there. We're not going without backup plans."

"That's a tall order to fill," Miles said skeptically.

"So we split up," Nadine suggested.

"We can go in groups," I added. I set my crutch aside and leaned over the map. "I can portal us to different magical locations. We can gather information about the Wands from other races."

"*You're* staying here," Helena demanded, pointing a finger at Nadine and me.

Nadine's jaw dropped. "If we're going to research the Wands and how to get through hell alive, Lucas and I—"

"Are *staying here*," Helena repeated firmly. "Neither of you are in any condition to leave. Besides, if you are all going to go off on your adventures, you need a central point of contact. This is your one safe house. If the priestesses get word that you're roaming other magical cities, there will be nowhere left for you to hide. You know as well as I do the priestesses have contacts and spies all over the supernatural world. The rest of you might be able to blend in, but spies will recognize Nadine in an instant. Besides, she needs to be here to maintain the wards and protection spells. The spells we're using are too strong for any one Cast to maintain them alone, but a Curse Breaker can stabilize the magic so we aren't caught. And Lucas needs to remain behind, so he can portal everyone in and out."

I didn't know if Helena was saying it because it made logical sense, or because she didn't want to see her granddaughter dive head-first into danger. I was almost certain it was the latter.

"If we want to learn anything about hell, our best bet is Malovia," Talia said. "Monsters are flooding into Malovia all the time. The fae are literally sitting on gateways to hell. If anyone knows anything about getting there and back, it's them."

"I guess that means Grant and Talia are going to Malovia for summer break," Miles said.

Grant scowled. "Yeah, what a *vacation*. If you think this is going to be easy, I suggest you back out now. I, however, am up for the challenge."

Miles drew himself upright. He wasn't scared of shit. "Chloe and I will go to *Hok'evale*. It's neutral territory, full of supernaturals outcast from their societies. If you want rumors, you start there. There have to be whispers of the Oaken Wands. If we don't find anything there, we'll see what we can learn from the Elementai. Their tribe isn't far from *Hok'evale*."

"I can travel to Atlantis and see what the merfolk know," Onyx offered. "If the Wands ended up with other magical societies, we have to cover them all."

Verla nodded in agreement. "Then I'll see what I can learn from the vampires."

"I'll go to Celestial City," Professor Warren suggested. "The angels know a lot about historical relics. They may know something about the Oaken Wands."

Nadine bit her lower lip. "Are you guys sure you should be going off alone?"

"Merfolk are allies to the Miriamic Coven," Onyx said. "I'll be all right."

"Jonathan and I can handle ourselves," Verla added.

Helena was obviously staying. She'd been over the top with Nadine's recovery lately. I could tell she was really worried. She wasn't letting her granddaughter out of her sight anytime soon.

That only left one person. I turned to Professor Warbright. "You can join us, if you'd like."

Warbright nearly trembled at the suggestion. He reached for his pocket watch, but it wasn't there anymore. I noticed he did that a lot, like he was searching for comfort.

"I would love to help, but I… I can't," Warbright admitted. "After everything I've done, I owe it to the coven to leave."

"Professor, it wasn't your fault," I told him.

"I wish I could agree with you," he said sadly. "After what I've done, the coven will never take me back. It doesn't matter that I was possessed. The priestesses will convince everyone that I killed those people, and I'll hang. I must seek asylum and never return to Octavia Falls. There's an island in the Pacific Ocean owned by the United Supernatural Union. It's neutral territory, and there's an opening for a Miriamic teacher at the Darke Institute for Supernatural Offenders. That's where I'll be going for… a while."

The way he said *a while* told me he was more or less planning to stay there forever. He was wrecked by guilt, and no matter how much we told him he wasn't responsible, he didn't believe us.

I'd heard of the Darke Institute, and to put it shortly, it wasn't a nice place. It was more or less a prison school where the supernatural world sent all the kids they wanted nothing to do with. I couldn't help but think Warbright was choosing to go to this island as a way to punish himself, teaching magical delinquents how to use their magic. I didn't think he'd be able to survive a place where the very students he was supposed to be teaching were dangerous inmates.

Either way, the man had a lot to work through. I wasn't sure how much of the last few months he remembered. It was clear he needed help, and I hoped he found that someday.

I turned toward the map of the supernatural world and surveyed it, spreading my hands across its span. Everything was on the line. If we didn't find the rest of the Oaken Wands, there was no point in continuing to fight any longer, because we couldn't unite the coven without them.

We had one job, and no more distractions. Find the Oaken Wands. Save the coven. There simply was no other option. No matter what we had to go through to face it.

"So… to the Abyss we go?" Grant asked.

Chloe gave a dramatic sigh. "I'm not sure we'll ever be ready for it."

I gave a dark laugh. "We might not be ready to face hell. But I know one thing."

"What's that?" Nadine tilted her head to the side.

I grasped her hand, then ran my thumb over her engagement ring and smirked. "It damn sure isn't ready for us."

END OF BOOK FOUR

Flip the page to read a special excerpt from book five: *The Warlock's Trial!*

Hidden Legends

Read more from the Hidden Legends universe! Each Hidden Legends series takes place within the same world, but in separate and unique societies. Every series stands on its own, and they can be read in any order.

☾

ELEMENTALS, DRAGONS, & MORE

Academy of Magical Creatures by Megan Linski & Alicia Rades

☾

SHIFTERS, FAE, & SORCERESSES

University of Sorcery by Megan Linski

☾

SUPERNATURAL PRISON

Prison for Supernatural Offenders by Megan Linski & Alicia Rades

☾

Never miss a new release! Join our newsletter at www.hiddenlegendsbooks.com/fanclub

THE WARLOCK'S TRIAL
CHAPTER ONE

I'd rather be in hell right now than stare at this damn whiteboard any longer.

My eyes roamed over the information I'd been compiling for three months. All kinds of clues had been tacked up and connected by strings. The longer I looked at it, the less it made any sense.

I eyed the drawings of the Oaken Wands, along with other clues we'd replicated from memory. Journal entries from Helena's diaries had been ripped out and tacked alongside the photos. We thought we'd find clues that her late husband had left behind, but Nicholas hadn't told her where he'd hidden the Wands. His journal was long gone, so we had nothing to go off of.

My vision blurred the longer I stared. I couldn't remember the last time I slept.

"It was the butler," Nadine muttered. "It's always the butler."

"Huh?" I whirled toward her. She'd been quiet for so long, I'd forgotten she was there.

Nadine sat at a table in the sunroom we'd commandeered for our research purposes. A thick layer of clouds blanketed the September sky, and raindrops trickled down the windows around us. She set aside the thick binder she'd been flipping through, then hit *pause* on the phone in front of her.

"I said the butler did it," she repeated. "Are you listening to the podcast?"

I'd totally forgotten it'd been playing. Nadine had started listening to true crime podcasts a week after our friends left to investigate the Oaken Wands. I'd portaled them to different supernatural societies in order to help us gather clues. They reported back twice a month, but so far, no one had learned anything useful. Even though Helena and our cats stayed at the safe house with us, it could get boring and lonely sometimes. There was only so much Oaken Wand research we could do when we were stuck here. Nadine thought true crime podcasts would help us pass the time, and we'd both gotten really into it. We tried to solve the mysteries together, and it was a lot of fun.

Today, though, I couldn't focus on any mystery that wasn't our own.

"Sorry, I wasn't listening," I said. "I'm trying to find answers before everyone else shows up. I'm portaling them for check-in today. We've got to give them *something*."

Nadine sighed. "I know this is hard, Lucas, but we can tell them the truth."

"The truth is that we're no closer to finding the Oaken Wands than we were three months ago."

"We're *getting* closer," she insisted. "Grant and Talia have made allies in Malovia. They're meeting with their contact as we speak. This contact might know a way inside the Abyss. We're so close to finding an entrance, so that we can find the Mentalist Wand that we lost through the demon's portal."

Hence my point—I'd rather be in hell right now. At least then we'd be closer to the Mentalist Wand. We'd decided three months ago that we'd walk through hell for that Wand. Without it, the other four were useless to us. We needed all five Oaken Wands to end the Waning and win our fight against the priestesses' tyrannical rule.

"*I'm* not any closer to making Abyss portals, though," I pointed out. "If I could make portals to the Abyss like I *should*, we wouldn't have to send Grant and Talia to a warring fae nation who places every witch they come across at the end of a noose. Malovia is in the middle of a civil war. They've got two monarchs competing for the throne. It's dangerous enough as it is for their own people, let alone witches and warlocks. Don't forget what they did to Kenna and her family a few months ago."

Kenna and her parents hadn't even *been* in Malovia when they were captured and hanged. They'd been visiting Paris, and the fae took it as a threat because they were too close to the country's border. I didn't want to think about what would happen to Grant and Talia if the fae found them *inside* their borders. Their sentence would be far worse than hanging, for sure.

"Grant and Talia know the risks," Nadine reminded me, though she sounded worried.

I raked my fingers through my hair. It felt pretty grimy, and I realized I couldn't remember the last time I showered, either. This research had practically consumed me. "I just thought we'd have answers by now."

"You should sit down," Nadine suggested. "The last time you were standing this long, your leg started giving you trouble."

My broken leg had healed, but it still twinged painfully if I was on my feet forever. Still, I couldn't sit down right now, even if I wanted to. I was too on edge.

I began pacing instead. "I don't want to sit down, Nad. I want answers."

"Have you ever considered that maybe that's not your job?" she asked calmly. "Our friends are out there getting answers. Our job is to be a safe place for them to come back to."

I gritted my teeth and pointed to the stacks of textbooks on the table in front of her. "Our *job* is to do our research and draw connections. And I feel like a fucking idiot because I can't see how it all connects!"

"It may be simpler than we think," Nadine pointed out. "Perhaps it isn't this big puzzle that needs solving but just breadcrumbs to follow."

I turned back to the whiteboard and tapped my chin as I surveyed the information we had. "All right... breadcrumbs. Where do we go from here?"

The room went silent, and I was starting to get really freaking pissed. What did I expect? For the whiteboard to answer back?

"Maybe a new perspective will help..." I mused. The whiteboard hung off a frame on wheels, so I spun it ninety degrees. It probably looked like I was crazy, but it was the only thing I hadn't tried yet.

My gaze darted from one string to the next. My eyes began to cross, and it felt like I was looking at the board from under water. Even the sound of raindrops on the window became distant. My hands curled into fists, and my whole body shook in frustration. I shoved my hands into my hair and yanked on the strands. This was fucking pointless. I'd been studying this board for months, and none of it made a damn bit of sense. Three months caught up to me in a single moment, and I snapped.

"These breadcrumbs are useless!" I screamed as I grabbed the strings and yanked them off the board. Papers went flying across the room, and one of the strings tangled around my finger. I grabbed the corners of the whiteboard and threw it at the wall, which was a feat in itself, because the thing was huge. Pain sliced across my hand. The whiteboard hit the wall, then bounced back toward me. It landed on my head pretty dang hard, and I collapsed onto the ground, pinned beneath the massive whiteboard. A piece of paper landed in my mouth, and I sputtered, but it went nowhere.

Nadine rushed to my side and helped lift the whiteboard back onto its wheels. "Lucas, are you okay?"

Truth was, I'd hurt my pride more than anything. I huffed as I got to my feet and spat the paper out of my mouth. "I'm fine," I grumbled.

Nadine placed her hands on her hips. "That was a bit dramatic."

I crossed my arms but didn't meet her gaze as I mumbled, "These breadcrumbs are dry and stale anyway. They taste awful."

Nadine stared at me for a few seconds, before a smile crept across her face. She burst into laughter. I froze, until I looked down at the papers at my feet and began laughing along with her.

It wasn't funny. Not in the slightest. But it was better than the alternative—and that involved wallowing in my own self-pity because I'd somehow tied my worth to solving this mystery. I'd get an earful from Nadine and Helena both, because neither of them were going to stand for my bullshit anymore. They heard enough of it last June. I tried my best to find the joy where I could, and that was pretty damn difficult today. So when Nadine laughed, I allowed myself to laugh along with her.

"Come sit down," she said between laughs. She led me over to a chair, then leaned down to inspect the cut on my hand. It throbbed, but I didn't really give a fuck. Nadine gasped.

"What?" I asked, sitting up straighter.

"You broke a nail!" she said dramatically. She was trying to lighten the mood.

I scowled. "What a tragedy—oh, wow. That's not good."

Nadine stretched my skin a little, and I saw that the cut was deeper than I thought. The corner of the whiteboard had sliced across my whole palm. Blood began pooling in my hand.

Her voice turned serious. "Stay here. I'll get a first-aid kit."

She left me in silence, and I glanced around the room. Papers were scattered everywhere, and the string lay in a tangled mess on the floor. This was going to be a bitch to put back in order.

I got up and knelt beside the closest pile of papers, trying hard not to drip blood everywhere. I started gathering our clues and stacking them together with my good hand.

"Lucas." Nadine stopped me when she returned. "Your clues aren't going anywhere."

She was clearly annoyed by how consumed I'd become with this. I sighed and sat down again. She took my hand and gently wiped the blood away, inspecting it closely. "You're not going to need stitches, but I need to get it cleaned up. Hold still."

Nadine positioned a towel on the table, then placed my hand palm-up on top of it. She poured hydrogen peroxide over the cut, and damn, that stung like a son of a bitch.

She cleaned out the wound, then gently wrapped gauze around my hand. I couldn't help but let my eyes roam over her as her fingers moved over mine softly.

She caught me staring and turned a deep shade of pink. "What is it?"

"You," I said simply. "You're so nice to me."

"That could be because I'm madly in love with you," she teased. She taped the gauze, then placed a gentle kiss on my hand. "All better."

"Thanks," I told her, before drawing her in for a kiss.

After she cleaned up, Nadine plopped herself in front of her thick binder again. "Do you prefer pumpkin spice or apple cider?"

That was an odd question, but I thought she was trying to distract me. "Um… apple cider, I guess."

She scrunched up her nose. "You *guess*? Are you sure?"

I shrugged. "If I was given the choice, I'd choose apple cider. Pumpkin spice isn't a real thing."

Nadine gasped dramatically, like I'd thoroughly offended her. "It is! How can you not love the impeccable blend of cinnamon and nutmeg and ginger and cloves!?"

"Is that all?" I teased flatly.

"And sometimes allspice," she added proudly.

"It's fine, but have you ever had fresh apple cider straight from the orchard?" I asked.

"Yes. You took me last fall."

"Right, and it was fantastic, wasn't it?"

"Yeah, it was good, but…"

"But you want me to say pumpkin spice," I finished for her.

"No," she answered quickly. "I want your *honest* opinion."

"My honest opinion is apple cider. What's this about?"

Nadine propped up the binder for me to see. She'd pasted all kinds of photos of various cakes and recipes inside. She wore a goofy grin and exclaimed, "It's for our wedding cake!"

I furrowed my brow. "How'd we get from apple cider and pumpkin spice to cake?"

"I'm trying to decide our flavor."

"Apple cider isn't a flavor," I said. "It's its own thing. It's a drink."

"No, but like… you make an apple cake with cream cheese and cinnamon frosting. It's a whole thing. But then there's the pumpkin one, and I was leaning toward that."

"Then go with pumpkin," I offered.

Her shoulders sagged. "But it's *your* wedding, too. I want to make these decisions together."

I reached across the table and took her hand in mind. My fingers trailed over her engagement ring. "As long as I'm married to you by the end of it, I don't care about the details."

I tugged on her arm, and she came around the table to sit on my lap. I curled my arms around her middle and pulled her close to me. I inhaled the rose scent of her hair, which always made my head spin. My fingers trailed down her body.

Nadine wiggled her hips. "Mm… right here?"

I kissed the back of her neck. "I get excited when I think about marrying you. In just a few short weeks, you'll be my wife."

Nadine turned around, until she was straddling me. "October thirty-first can't come soon enough," she whispered, before pressing her lips to mine.

I leaned back in my chair and ran my hands over her backside as she began kissing me. The stress of the whiteboard completely fell from my mind as desire for my fiancé consumed me. Nadine reached down for the button on my jeans…

"*Eh hem.*" Someone cleared their throat in the doorway, and Nadine jumped.

My shoulders slumped. Not again.

I loved Helena as if she was my own grandmother, but god damn it. This woman was always *right there* whenever Nadine and I were about to get it on. Hell, Nadine and I were about to fool around in the master bath the other night. As soon as we filled the jet tub, Helena knocked and wanted to *clean*. Nadine had gotten rid of her, thank the goddess, but it'd really put a damper on the mood.

"I made tea!" Helena said brightly as she came into the room carrying a tray. Isa, Oliver, and Cornelius followed along at her feet, meowing like they were waiting for treats. Helena stopped in her tracks and eyed the mess. "Oh, my."

She set down her tray, then went to start cleaning up the papers.

"That's not necessary," I told her quickly. "I'll get it."

Helena hesitated, like it physically pained her to witness a mess without cleaning it up. I swear, all she'd done in the last three months was clean and cook. She wasn't faring well with the cabin fever any better than we were.

Helena cleared her throat. "You should have some applesauce. It turned out perfect."

Nadine and I had gotten really bored here at the safe house, so we gardened over the summer, then canned fruits and vegetables with Helena whenever we needed a break. Helena had found stacks of empty jars in the basement our first week here and suggested we use them, and we just… never stopped. She'd planted all kinds of vegetables around the property, and we'd found a handful of apple and pear trees near the house we'd been harvesting. I didn't know how many batches of applesauce we'd made, but we'd started storing food in the basement because the pantry was too full. We certainly weren't going hungry anytime soon.

Nadine climbed off of me and returned to her seat. "Thanks, Grammy."

I tried the applesauce, and all kinds of flavors burst in my mouth. "This is our best batch yet. What'd we do differently?"

Nadine snickered. "I snuck in a pumpkin spice blend."

I frowned. "You're trying to convert me."

"I am not!" she insisted with a giggle.

At Helena's feet, the cats continued to yowl.

"All right, all right," she said impatiently. "But only one for each of you."

Helena reached into the pocket of her apron and tossed three cat treats on the ground. Isa gobbled hers gone, then shoved Oliver out of the way and ate his, too. Oliver just licked her ears, like he didn't care. What a doormat.

Helena turned back to us. "I brought something for you two as well. Picked it up on my last supply run."

She reached into her apron and set several large boxes on the table. All I saw was the big bold letters reading *Value Pack!* Then I realized in horror what it was.

"Condoms!" Nadine gasped. "Grammy, what makes you think we need that many? Wait... how much sex were you having when you were our age?"

Helena scowled. All it took was one sharp look to know she wasn't about to answer that question. For someone who walked in on us every freaking time we tried to get it on, she seemed pretty encouraging of our physical relationship. I must've turned the brightest shade of red.

"They're not just for you," Helena said. "Your friends are coming back today. We all know Chloe and Miles will need a whole pack to themselves. I want *everyone* to be safe."

I laughed. "You're not wrong."

"Now finish up," Helena pressed. "You're scheduled to portal everyone in soon."

Helena left the room, and Nadine and I quickly finished our tea before heading out into the living room. The room was large, with a ceiling that reached two stories and a balcony from the second level. A sectional sofa faced the fireplace, along with a large TV mounted above the mantle.

Helena was already sitting on the couch, and the cats surrounded her, purring in her lap.

"Are we ready?" Helena asked.

I checked the clock on the wall, then nodded. "Ready."

I lifted my hands, and magic surged down my arms as a portal bloomed in front of me. It was like a hole had been punched straight through reality. The fireplace was replaced with the image of a forest lit by the rising sun. A warm breeze rustled my hair, and it smelled like pine trees. A couple holding hands stepped through the portal. Their cats followed, and they hopped onto the couch beside the others, looking excited to see them. I closed the portal behind them.

"Chloe. Miles," I said, nodding to them. "How's life in *Hok'evale?*"

"It's a lovely town," Miles said. "Last week, we rode a dragon!"

My face fell. His enthusiasm really rubbed me the wrong way. "This isn't a theme park, Miles. You're supposed to be out there hunting down clues for the Oaken Wands, or did you forget about that while you were on *vacation?*"

Chloe's jaw dropped. "Whoa! *Someone's* in a mood. It's better to be on vacation than to hang out here, where you're either moping around or hounding us for answers."

"That's not all I do," I shot back. "We canned a batch of pears yesterday."

Chloe scoffed. "Forgive me if I'd rather be sipping mimosas on the beach."

"*Mimosas on the beach—*" I nearly choked on the words. "Dear Goddess, we're never going to find answers."

"Actually, the mimosas paid off," Chloe said proudly.

"Yeah, I'm sure the afterparty was a blast," I replied flatly. "Hopefully someone else found something."

I turned, then lifted my hands again, forming another portal. The air was cold, and I smelled a fresh sea breeze. A girl with purple hair stepped through the portal, along with her cat.

"Welcome back, Onyx," I said. "Learn anything from the merfolk?"

"Let's bring everyone back before we start sharing our discoveries," Miles pressed, sounding annoyed. Clearly, I was a bit too harsh.

A light dusting of snow had covered the ground when I portaled Verla through from the Midnighter's society. The vampires were spread all over the world, but Verla had been trying to get information from a group in Canada. The headmistress shivered when she stepped through the portal.

"Come," Helena said quickly. "I made tea."

"That's so kind of you," Verla said as Helena ushered her to the kitchen.

I couldn't see what Celestial City looked like when I portaled Professor Warren back to the safe house. He was holed up in a nice hotel room, with white sheets and a golden bed frame. He seemed the coziest out of everyone. The angels weren't the nicest supernatural race on the planet, but they'd pretty much do anything for you as long as they thought they could convert you to their religion, and Professor Warren was good at placating people.

"Good to see you, Lucas," he said kindly.

I nodded back, then turned to Nadine. "Nad, I'll need your help with this one."

She stood at my side, and we combined our powers together to create a portal. It wasn't easy, because we were fighting against wards to get inside the fae's borders, but we managed. A forest appeared in front of us, but it was different from the last. The coniferous trees were smaller here, and it smelled of damp mountain air. The sky was overcast, and the ground was wet, as if it had just rained. Wind whistled through the portal, but everything else was silent. I didn't see Grant or Talia anywhere.

I hesitated. "They're supposed to be at the meeting point."

"Give it a minute." Nadine's voice trembled. "They should be on their way."

I held my breath, waiting to hear the sound of their footsteps through the mud. But there was nothing.

"Something's wrong!" I insisted. "Grant and Talia have never missed a portal."

"Are we sure about the coordinates?" Chloe asked. "This doesn't look like where we've picked them up before."

"I'm certain," I stated. "Grant and Talia were meeting with a contact inside Malovia's borders earlier today. We moved the meeting point so they didn't have as far to travel."

"Maybe they got lost?" Onyx suggested.

Miles crossed his arms. "Or they were betrayed. We shouldn't have trusted the fae!"

The portal faltered around the edges, and my hands shook as I tried to steady it. "I can't hold it much longer."

"We have to go after them!" Nadine decided immediately. She ran toward the front door and grabbed our shoes and coats. She tossed mine at my feet, then slid hers on.

"You can't go alone," Professor Warren protested.

"The fewer witches we bring to Malovia, the better," Nadine said. "We don't want to draw attention, and Lucas and I can get in and out using portals. We'll be back soon. I promise."

Helena and Verla heard the commotion, and they raced into the living room. "What do you think you're—?" Helena started, but I didn't hear the end of it. I grabbed Nadine's hand, and we leapt through the portal together.

My stomach dropped from my abdomen, and my body seemed to stretch and distort as we tumbled through the portal. We landed firmly on our feet on the other side, still holding hands. The air was chill and damp, and a shiver traveled down my spine as I glanced around. We stood on the side of a mountain, but we couldn't see much through the pine forest except the darkened clouds covering the afternoon sky.

"We've got to find a vantage point," Nadine said, tugging on my arm.

We traipsed through the forest, our feet squishing through the mud. The trees broke ahead, and when we stepped out of them, my stomach turned to a rock in my belly. Nadine drew a sharp gasp.

We stood on the highest point of a hill, looking out over a large battlefield. The battle had already been lost, judging by the bodies strewn across the muddy landscape. There had to be at least a hundred fae shifters and sorceresses lying down there. Fresh blood seeped into the ground as wolf, dragon, alicorn, and griffin shifters lay still beside their mates, who'd perished trying to save them.

Below us, a makeshift camp had been set up with large tents. Someone cried out in agony, their voice carrying up the hillside. On the other side of the battlefield, far out in the distance, we could make out the shadows of a small town.

Nadine covered her mouth. "What happened here? You don't think Grant and Talia got caught up in it? The fae are known for taking hostages!"

I shook my head. I refused to believe that unless I saw it with my own eyes. "No. They wouldn't involve themselves in fae affairs. Though this could certainly be why they were held up."

Nadine's eyes glistened. "So how do we find them?"

"We're here!" a ragged voice came from behind us.

We turned to see two figures climbing the hill. They wore large back-packs and were covered in mud from head to toe.

"Talia! Grant!" Nadine cried. She rushed over to them and threw her arms around them, not caring about the mud. "Thank the Goddess you're okay."

Grant blew a breath. "No kidding. We were nearly ambushed, but we managed to slip into the trees until the battle was over. The fae king attempted to take the city of Pruska, which you can see over there, because the rival queen captured it for herself. He ended up losing, though, and it's pretty clear his forces were demolished."

He sounded really winded, and Talia hadn't said a thing. They were both in pretty rough shape. They must've been on their feet for days.

"Are you alone?" I asked. "Where's your contact? Don't tell me he led you into this battle on purpose!"

"No," Talia promised. "Oakley never showed up. He was a member of the king's army, and…"

Grant dropped his gaze. "He fought in the battle. He didn't make it."

My stomach clenched. "He was supposed to show us the way into the Abyss! We don't have time to scour Malovia for entrances. We'll never find an opening on our own."

Grant scowled. "I'm sorry our friend was too preoccupied with *dying* to show us the way to hell!"

My shoulders fell. "I'm sorry, Grant. I didn't mean it like that."

"We've been gone for three months," Grant reminded me. "Forgive us for making friends while we were away. *You* might not trust the fae, but Oakley was one of the good ones. He was fighting with the king's army to end persecution of dark magic wielders in Malovia. He sympathized with us and really wanted to help. I just… can't believe he's gone."

The hill went quiet for a few beats, before Nadine broke the silence. "If the king's army is sympathetic to dark magic users, then maybe we can go straight to the king himself."

Talia scoffed. "There's the kicker. You'll never believe who's on the throne. Remember those fae you helped last year, the one who needed

Hattie to help them out with a demon problem? You said their names were Ethan and Emma."

I nodded. "Yeah, that's them."

"Ethan's the king now," Talia said. "Emma's his queen."

Excitement rushed through me. "This is great!" I cried. "They owe us a debt for helping them. We can go to them and—"

Grant held up a hand. "Not so fast. We've tried to get in contact with the king and queen, but we can't touch them. Even Oakley couldn't get a message. They're guarded more than ever, with the state of the Malovian Revolution. And I don't blame them."

Grant gestured out over the remnants of the battlefield.

Movement caught my eye in the camp below. A man and a woman stepped out of a tent, surrounded by uniformed men. Whoever they were, they looked important. The woman turned, and her red hair flowed around her. It hit me then that I recognized her.

"That's Ethan and Emma!" I realized. "We can talk to them!"

I was already on the move, but Grant grabbed my arm. "Lucas, we can't. Look at their security detail."

"Emma will recognize us," I insisted. "We helped save her mate."

"Emma and Ethan will want to help us, but the rest of those soldiers will kill us on sight for being witches," Grant pointed out. "You can't just waltz up to royalty and expect a meeting. We'll never get close enough before their guards kill us first. They just lost a battle. They're not going to ask questions."

Fuck, he was right. We were so close, but they were untouchable.

"All right," I said reluctantly. "Let's get moving."

My friends and I hurried into the trees, where we couldn't be seen, and Nadine helped me form a portal strong enough to hold against Malovia's wards. Shouts came through the portal, and we hurried through as quickly as we could.

The shouting stopped abruptly as the portal slammed shut behind us. "Thank the goddess!" Helena cried.

"We're fine," Nadine assured her. "Grant and Talia... are alive."

Talia shivered a little. "We're just glad to be back."

"What *happened* to you?" Verla demanded, eyeing their dirty clothes.

"We, um, got a front row seat to the Malovian Revolution," Grant admitted.

"You're not going back," Verla insisted. "This is too dangerous!"

Grant sighed. "Well, our luck has run out anyway. Our fae contact is dead. We're not finding a portal to the Abyss anytime soon."

"Good," Helena said firmly. She'd never been a big fan of us walking through hell to retrieve an Oaken Wand, but it wasn't like we had any choice. We couldn't exactly send someone else after it. All eyes turned to her, and she quickly added, "I mean, it's good that you're alive. You're safe now. Let's get you a warm bath and a hot meal."

Helena took their backpacks and helped them to their rooms.

"What are we going to do now?" Onyx asked. "Malovia is the only place we know of with portals to the Abyss. It's our only way to get to the Mentalist Wand."

"Technically, not the *only* way," Nadine pointed out.

I scowled. "You're *not* talking about making a demon deal. That's worse than going in alone."

There were all kinds of reasons that was true. Demons could turn on you or trick you into faulty contracts. For a task this big, they'd want something major in return, something none of us were willing to give up. The last demon we'd dealt with had killed dozens of people before we were able to kill him, and it hadn't been easy. I wasn't putting my friends in danger by entering into a demon deal.

"If we can't find another way in, we may have to consider it as a last resort," Nadine said.

"You have no idea the cost you'd have to pay!" Verla protested. "You can't, Nadine."

"I don't *want* to," Nadine replied. "I'm only saying it's an option, even if it's a bad one."

"It's off the table," I stated. "If I have to kill myself making Abyss portals, that's better than working with a demon."

"There has to be a way to get the Wands without people dying," Professor Warren demanded. "No one's making deals with demons."

"Perhaps we should focus more on the other two Wands," Verla suggested. "Let's take some time to think about pursuing the Mentalist Wand. We can't afford any mistakes."

"We may be closer than you think," Chloe stated.

Everyone turned to look at her. She stood with her arms crossed and lips pursed.

"What do you mean?" Nadine asked.

Chloe drew herself upright. "As I was *trying* to say before, our mimosas paid off. Miles and I had a drink with someone we deem to be a credible source… and we learned something big."

My heart leapt. "How big?"

Miles hesitated, like he wasn't sure where to start. Finally, he sighed and said, "You need to come with us. This could change everything."

Continue The Warlock's Trial to find the Oaken Wands!

BONUS OFFERS

Find coloring pages, games, quizzes, and bonus content at
hiddenlegendsbooks.com.

Join the *Orenda Academy: Hidden Legends Fan Group* on Facebook for all things
Hidden Legends!

Check out the *College of Witchcraft Official Playlist* on Spotify!

Never miss a new release! Join Alicia's email list at aliciaradesauthor.com/
newsletter.

About the Author

Alicia Rades is a USA Today bestselling author of young adult and new adult paranormal fiction. When she's not dreaming up magical stories, she's either binge-watching Netflix, meditating, or spending time with her family. She has an unhealthy obsession with psychic characters and writes with a deck of tarot cards next to her computer.